ALSO BY JENNIFER CHIAVERINI

The Aloha Quilt

A Quilter's Holiday

The Lost Quilter

The Quilter's Kitchen

The Winding Ways Quilt

The New Year's Quilt

The Quilter's Homecoming

Circle of Quilters

The Christmas Quilt

The Sugar Camp Quilt

The Master Quilter

The Quilter's Legacy

The Runaway Quilt

The Cross-Country Quilters

Round Robin

The Quilter's Apprentice

Elm Creek Quilts: Quilt Projects Inspired by the Elm Creek Quilts Novels

Return to Elm Creek: More Quilt Projects Inspired by the
Elm Creek Quilts Novels

More Elm Creek Quilts: Inspired by the Elm Creek Quilts Novels

Sylvia's Bridal Sampler from Elm Creek Quilts:
The True Story Behind the Quilt

An Elm Creek Quilts Collection

Three Novels in the *New York Times*
Bestselling Series

JENNIFER CHIAVERINI

SIMON & SCHUSTER
New York · London · Toronto · Sydney

Simon & Schuster
1230 Avenue of the Americas
New York, NY 10020

This book is a work of fiction. Names, characters, places, and incidents either are products of the author's imagination or are used fictitiously. Any resemblance to actual events or locales or persons, living or dead, is entirely coincidental.

The Sugar Camp Quilt Copyright © 2005 by Jennifer Chiaverini
Circle of Quilters Copyright © 2006 by Jennifer Chiaverini
The Quilter's Homecoming Copyright © 2007 by Jennifer Chiaverini

All rights reserved, including the right to reproduce this book or portions thereof in any form whatsoever. For information address Simon & Schuster Subsidiary Rights Department, 1230 Avenue of the Americas, New York, NY 10020.

This Simon & Schuster hardcover October 2010

SIMON & SCHUSTER and colophon are registered trademarks of Simon & Schuster, Inc.

For information about special discounts for bulk purchases, please contact Simon & Schuster Special Sales at 1-866-506-1949 or business@simonandschuster.com.

The Simon & Schuster Speakers Bureau can bring authors to your live event. For more information or to book an event contact the Simon & Schuster Speakers Bureau at 1-866-248-3049 or visit our website at www.simonspeakers.com.

Manufactured in the United States of America

10   9   8   7   6   5   4   3   2   1

Library of Congress Cataloging-in-Publication Data
Chiaverini, Jennifer.
An Elm Creek quilts collection : three novels in the *New York Times* bestselling series / Jennifer Chiaverini.
p. cm.
1. Quilting—Fiction. 2. Quiltmakers—Fiction. 3. Women pioneers—Fiction.
4. Domestic fiction. I. Chiaverini, Jennifer. Sugar camp quilt. II. Chiaverini, Jennifer. Circle of quilters. III. Chiaverini, Jennifer. Quilter's homecoming. IV. Title.
PS3553.H473E48 2010
813'.54—dc22

ISBN 978-1-4391-9779-0

These titles were originally published individually by Simon & Schuster.

Contents

A Bergstrom Family Time Line

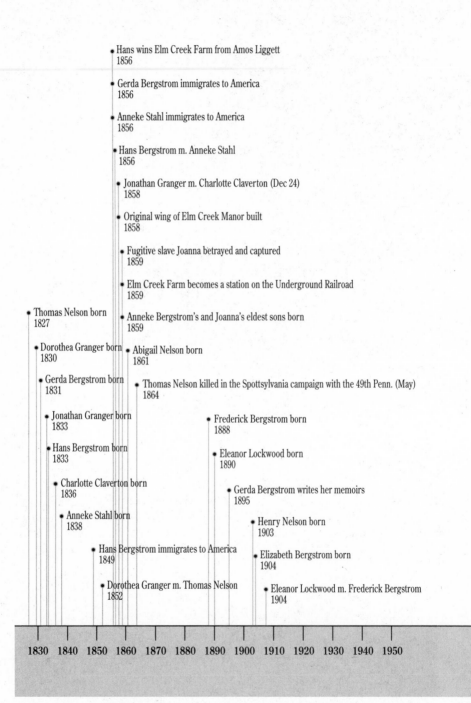

Hans wins Elm Creek Farm from Amos Liggett
1856

Gerda Bergstrom immigrates to America
1856

Anneke Stahl immigrates to America
1856

Hans Bergstrom m. Anneke Stahl
1856

Jonathan Granger m. Charlotte Claverton (Dec 24)
1858

Original wing of Elm Creek Manor built
1858

Fugitive slave Joanna betrayed and captured
1859

Elm Creek Farm becomes a station on the Underground Railroad
1859

Thomas Nelson born
1827

Anneke Bergstrom's and Joanna's eldest sons born
1859

Dorothea Granger born
1830

Abigail Nelson born
1861

Gerda Bergstrom born
1831

Thomas Nelson killed in the Spottsylvania campaign with the 49th Penn. (May)
1864

Jonathan Granger born
1833

Frederick Bergstrom born
1888

Hans Bergstrom born
1833

Eleanor Lockwood born
1890

Charlotte Claverton born
1836

Gerda Bergstrom writes her memoirs
1895

Anneke Stahl born
1838

Henry Nelson born
1903

Hans Bergstrom immigrates to America
1849

Elizabeth Bergstrom born
1904

Dorothea Granger m. Thomas Nelson
1852

Eleanor Lockwood m. Frederick Bergstrom
1904

1830   1840   1850   1860   1870   1880   1890   1900   1910   1920   1930   1940   1950

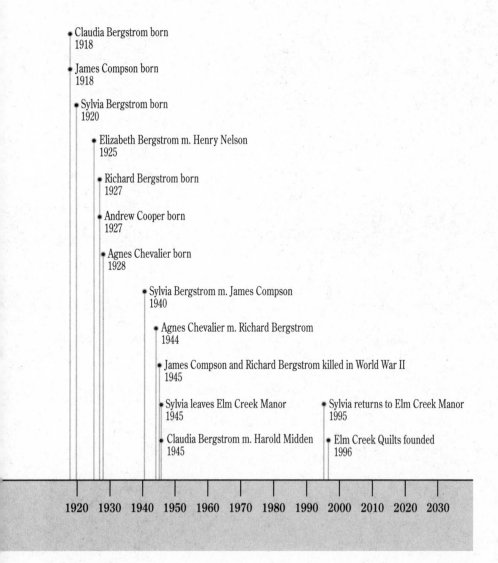

Claudia Bergstrom born
1918

James Compson born
1918

Sylvia Bergstrom born
1920

Elizabeth Bergstrom m. Henry Nelson
1925

Richard Bergstrom born
1927

Andrew Cooper born
1927

Agnes Chevalier born
1928

Sylvia Bergstrom m. James Compson
1940

Agnes Chevalier m. Richard Bergstrom
1944

James Compson and Richard Bergstrom killed in World War II
1945

Sylvia leaves Elm Creek Manor
1945

Sylvia returns to Elm Creek Manor
1995

Claudia Bergstrom m. Harold Midden
1945

Elm Creek Quilts founded
1996

1920 1930 1940 1950 1960 1970 1980 1990 2000 2010 2020 2030

Introduction

When *The Quilter's Apprentice* was published in 1999, I never imagined that it would become the first in a series, or that my novels would be translated into other languages and inspire pattern books, websites, and fabric lines. Yet year after year, the number of Elm Creek Readers has steadily increased as fans have spread the word about these heartwarming, thought-provoking stories that capture the spirit of quilting, past and present. Quilters enjoy seeing the art they love portrayed with accuracy and affection, while history buffs appreciate the respect shown to quilting's rich traditions and folklore. From the very beginning, readers have wanted to return again and again to Elm Creek Manor to spend time with the characters they have come to think of as friends, and I have been very happy to offer more stories about the Elm Creek Quilters and the beautiful manor in rural Pennsylvania where they reside. My readers know that each new Elm Creek Quilts novel will be filled with quilts and history, and the three books offered in this collection are no exception.

The first, *The Sugar Camp Quilt,* is set in Creek's Crossing, Pennsylvania, in the years leading up to the Civil War. Friends and neighbors take sides in the national debate over abolition, and, as events unfold, an extraordinary young woman named Dorothea Granger becomes aware of the division in her community after she and several other ladies sew an opportunity quilt to raise money to build a library. The members of the library board choose the Album block, a traditional "friendship quilt" pattern, but instead of the customary signatures of friends, they obtain scraps of muslin autographed by renowned writers. When library board president Violet Pearson Engle rejects several of Dorothea's favorite authors because of their abolitionist writings, Dorothea is dismayed to find herself set against some of the most prominent ladies in town.

The "Sugar Camp Quilt" itself is the most significant and mysterious quilt in the novel—and the most reluctantly made. When Dorothea's stern Uncle

Jacob inexplicably asks her to sew a Delectable Mountains variation with several unusual blocks of his own design, she complies, but she angers him when she "corrects" several odd features in his sketches. Bewildered and fuming, she nonetheless obeys his orders to rip out the stitches and start over. Only after Uncle Jacob unexpectedly dies does she discover why he had insisted she follow his drawings to the last, exacting detail—and why he had kept his righteous, courageous actions a secret from his own family.

Circle of Quilters, the second novel in this collection, returns to the contemporary Elm Creek Quilters at a time when they face significant changes in their business and challenges that test the bonds of their friendship. Two founding Elm Creek Quilters have decided to pursue other professional interests, and aspiring teachers vie to win a prestigious spot on the quilt camp faculty. *Circle of Quilters* was an especially enjoyable story to tell because it allowed me to explore the lives of five new characters while still portraying the Elm Creek Quilters in important roles. I thrived on delving into these new characters' pasts, discovering their unique interests and the twists and turns in their lives that inspired their love for the art of quilting. The most difficult part of the writing process was deciding who would be offered the jobs, since I had come to care about each character and didn't want to reject any of them. In fact, I didn't know who would be chosen to join the circle of quilters until I began writing the last chapter!

The Quilter's Homecoming, the third book in this collection, again beckons readers into the past, but it also takes them far from Elm Creek Manor in a Roaring Twenties adventure featuring Sylvia's favorite cousin, Elizabeth. In 1925, as Elizabeth Bergstrom Nelson leaves Elm Creek Manor with her new husband, Henry, the couple's trunks are packed with bridal quilts and wedding gifts—and they also hold the deed to Triumph Ranch, one hundred twenty rich, fertile acres in the Arboles Valley north of Los Angeles. The newlyweds' future looks bright, but in a cruel reversal of fortune, they reach California only to discover that they've been swindled and left penniless. After selling their precious wedding trousseau and hiring on as hands at the farm they thought they owned, Henry struggles with his pride, but clever, feisty Elizabeth draws on the Bergstrom women's inherent resourcefulness and resilience and vows to overcome this unexpected adversity.

The "Chimneys and Cornerstones" quilt that Elizabeth receives as a wedding gift made its first appearance in *The Quilter's Apprentice,* and the scene in which Great Aunt Lucinda explains the symbolism of the red squares and the dark and light rectangles to a young Sylvia is one of my favorites. Antique quilts I discovered at the Stagecoach Inn Museum in Newbury Park, California, while researching *The Quilter's Homecoming* inspired two other quilts featured in the novel: the octagonal "Road to Triumph Ranch" quilt and the intricate "Arboles Valley Star," which Elizabeth discovers in the ramshackle cabin that has become the Nelsons' home. I thoroughly enjoyed writing *The Quilter's Homecoming,* not only because my research led me to such lovely antique treasures, but also because the Arboles Valley is based upon the Conejo Valley, where I once lived, and where my mother, brother, and sister still reside.

"Apparently quilting makes the world a better place," *Kirkus Reviews* remarked about *Circle of Quilters.* I think that's close but not quite right; I'd say instead that *quilters* and *quilt lovers* make the world a better place. As my longtime readers have discovered, quilting is a wonderful form of artistic expression that beckons one into a community of talented, supportive women and men who teach and encourage one another. Novices find themselves warmly embraced by experienced quilters eager to pass along their traditions, and quilters of all ages form enduring bonds of friendship that time, distance, and hardship cannot overcome.

Quilters and the quilts they create inspired me to write *The Quilter's Apprentice,* the first of what grew into an enduring, beloved series. But I am only one of countless many to find inspiration, comfort, enchantment, and intrigue in the beauty, history, and folklore of quilts. Whether you are a longtime quilter, a novice, or simply a quilt aficionado, I invite you to enjoy *An Elm Creek Quilts Collection* and be inspired yourselves.

Jennifer Chiaverini
June 2010
Madison, Wisconsin

The Sugar Camp Quilt

Acknowledgments

I am deeply grateful to Simon & Schuster and Witherspoon Associates for their ongoing support and for their tireless efforts on my behalf. I especially wish to thank Denise Roy, Maria Massie, and Rebecca Davis for their countless contributions to the Elm Creek Quilts novels through the years.

Many thanks to Lisa Cass and Jody Gomez, for caring for my boys so I could write, and to my dear friend Anne Spurgeon, for her careful reading of the manuscript, insightful suggestions, and historian's eye for detail.

I also wish to thank Tom McCrumm, Executive Director of the Massachusetts Maple Producers Association, for his gracious and informed responses to my questions about maple sugaring in the early 1800s.

Thank you to the friends and family who continue to support and encourage me, especially Geraldine Neidenbach, Heather Neidenbach, Nic Neidenbach, Virginia and Edward Riechman, and Leonard and Marlene Chiaverini.

Most of all, I am grateful to my husband, Marty, and my sons, Nicholas and Michael—and they know why.

In memory of my father,
Nicholas Robert Neidenbach,
who left us too soon to read any of my books
but knew I would write them someday.

Chapter One

1849

"A bel Wright intends to purchase his wife's freedom before the month is out," Dorothea's father said to Uncle Jacob.

"At long last," Dorothea's mother declared. "If Abel has raised the money he must do it quickly, before her owner can change his mind again. You will go with him, of course?"

Robert Granger nodded. They had spoken of this occasion often and had agreed that Robert ought to accompany Mr. Wright south to Virginia, both to share the work of driving the horses and to discourage unscrupulous interlopers. The abolitionist newspapers told of proslavery men who became so incensed at the sight of a newly freed slave that they would seize him and sell him back into slavery. Not even Mr. Wright was safe from their ilk, for all that he had never been a slave. If anything, enslaving him would bring them even greater pleasure.

Uncle Jacob's face bore the grim expression that Dorothea likened to a block of limestone. "You can't think of leaving in the middle of harvest."

"Abel needs to leave at sunup," Robert explained apologetically, as if humility would protect him from Uncle Jacob's wrath.

"Surely he can wait a few weeks until the crops are in."

"He said he can't. He'll go alone rather than wait for me."

"Then let him go alone," glowered Uncle Jacob. "Hasn't he done so often enough to sell that cheese of his?"

"This time is different," said Robert. "He will be exchanging a considerable amount of money for the person of his wife."

"Wright raises goats. He likely has more goats than corn on his place. He can afford to leave his farm during the harvest. We can't."

Dorothea waited for her uncle to announce yet another visit to his lawyer. The implication was, of course, that he intended to change his will, and not in favor of his only living relatives. Dorothea waited, but Uncle Jacob said nothing more until mealtime gave way to evening chores. As they cleared the table, Dorothea's mother remarked that Uncle Jacob had not expressly forbidden Robert to go, which in his case was almost the same as giving his blessing.

"According to that logic," Dorothea replied, "if I tell my pupils not to put a bent pin on my chair, what I really mean is that I would prefer a nail."

"Your pupils have far too much affection for you to do either," said Lorena, deliberately missing the point. They both knew she was putting her brother's obvious disapproval in a better light than it deserved. Dorothea knew her uncle would have expressly forbidden the journey for anyone but Abel Wright. Uncle Jacob had no friends, but he respected Mr. Wright for his independence, thrift, and industriousness, qualities he would have admired in himself if doing so would not have occasioned the sin of vanity.

Uncle Jacob had never declared whether he was for or against slavery, at least not in Dorothea's presence. According to Lorena, Uncle Jacob's long-deceased wife had been a Quaker and a passionate abolitionist, but he never spoke of her and Dorothea had no idea whether he shared her views. Still, she suspected her uncle's objections to the journey had nothing to do with his moral position on the subject of slavery and everything to do with the pragmatics of farming. Despite Mr. Wright's reasonable urgency to free his wife from bondage, Uncle Jacob likely could not comprehend how a sensible farmer could take off on any errand when the most important work of the year needed to be done. Of course, Uncle Jacob knew all too well that his sister's husband was *not* a sensible farmer. If he had been, Uncle Jacob would not have been obligated by the ties of family and Christian charity to take in his sister's family after they lost their own farm.

Later that night, Dorothea asked her father if she might accompany them, but her father said this particular errand was too dangerous for a girl of nineteen.

"But Mr. Wright has made the trip so many times," protested Dorothea.

"You are needed at home," said Uncle Jacob. "Already I will have to hire hands to make up for your father's absence. I will not hire kitchen help, too."

Even without Lorena's look of warning, Dorothea knew better than to protest. Her uncle had not even looked up from his Bible as he spoke, but any interruption of his nightly devotion was unusual enough to reveal the strength of his feeling on the subject.

Robert left for the Wright farm as soon as the sky had lightened enough for safe travel. Though the sun had not yet risen, Uncle Jacob was already at work in the barn, but he did not break away from his chores to wish his brother-in-law a safe journey. Lorena had packed the horse's rucksacks with so much food that they strained at the seams, and Robert thanked his wife for providing enough to eat for a month of sightseeing. Mother and daughter smiled at his joke, for they knew he intended to make the journey as swiftly as possible. They kissed him and made him promise to take care, then followed him down to the Creek's Crossing road, where they stood and watched until horse and rider disappeared into the cool, graying mists that clung to the hills south of the farm.

When they could no longer see him, Lorena glared at the barn and said, "See how little he cares for us. He might never see my husband again, and yet he cannot even stir from the barn to bid him farewell."

Dorothea's heart quaked at her mother's ominous words, but she said, "Likely Uncle Jacob knows how little we care for him and feels no need to make any pretense of fondness. Likely, too, he knows Father will certainly return."

Immediately Lorena was all reassurance. "Of course, my dear. Of course your father will return. Perhaps earlier than we expect him. Mr. Wright will not want to linger in the hostile South." She frowned at the barn. "If I would not miss him so, I would ask your father to take his time just to spite your uncle."

Dorothea smiled, knowing her mother would never wish for anything that would part her from her husband. Dorothea knew, too, that her mother often spoke wistfully of small acts of disobedience none of them dared commit. They were beholden to Uncle Jacob and must not commit any transgression that might tempt him to send them away. Uncle Jacob had no wife and no children, and therefore, no heir save his nephew, Dorothea's younger brother. If they served Uncle Jacob well and bided their time, one day Uncle Jacob's 120 acres, house, and worldly goods would belong to Jonathan.

For five years her parents had clung to these hopes with almost as much fervor as they pursued the abolition of slavery. They rarely seemed troubled by the doubts that plagued Dorothea. Uncle Jacob might marry again. He was older than her mother but even older men had taken young brides, although Dorothea could name no young woman of Creek's Crossing whose prospects were so poor she should settle on a stern, gray-haired, humorless man who had ample property but eschewed anything that hinted of romance. If he had once had a heart, he had buried it in the maple grove with his young bride and twin sons long before Dorothea was born.

Sometimes Dorothea suspected her parents were not entirely certain Jonathan would succeed in inheriting his uncle's farm. From an early age they had fostered his interest in medicine, and for the past two years he had served as an apprentice to an old family friend, a physician in far-off Baltimore. Jonathan had learned enough about farming to earn Uncle Jacob's grudging acceptance during his infrequent visits home, but he made no overt attempts to win his potential benefactor's affection. Dorothea wondered if his assured success in the vocation of his choosing had made him indifferent to the inheritance the rest of his family relied upon.

Either way, Jonathan surely would have been permitted to accompany their father and Mr. Wright south to Virginia. Though he was three years younger than Dorothea, he was a boy. Dorothea felt herself restricted and confined every minute she spent beneath Uncle Jacob's roof, even when he himself was not in the house. Her only moments of ease came as she walked to and from the schoolhouse on Third Street where she taught twenty youngsters reading, arithmetic, natural sciences, and history. When she felt the wind against her face as she crossed Elm Creek on the ferry, she feared that this was as close as she would ever come to knowing the freedom Jonathan took for granted.

At noon, Uncle Jacob and the hired hands came inside to eat. There was little conversation as Dorothea and her mother served; the men, whom Dorothea knew to be lively enough in other company, were uncomfortably subdued under Uncle Jacob's critical eye. It was well known in Creek's Crossing that he had once fired a man for taking the Lord's name in vain when a horse kicked him, breaking his jaw. Dorothea did not care for rough language, either, but even she could concede the injured man had had cause.

The men had seconds and thirds, clearing the platters of corn, baked squash, and shoofly pie as quickly as Dorothea and her mother could place them on the table. The other men quietly praised Lorena's cooking, but Uncle Jacob did not address her until after he finished his meal, and only to state that Robert's absence had hurt them badly. As they did every year, the Creek's Crossing Agricultural Society had arranged for a team from Harrisburg to bring a horse-powered thresher into the Elm Creek Valley. Every farmer of sufficient means paid for a share of days with the machine, and Uncle Jacob's turn was fast approaching. Robert had left before the oats and wheat could be cut and stacked, and if Uncle Jacob did not finish in time, the threshers could not wait for him. He had no choice but to go into Creek's Crossing and hire more men.

Dorothea and her mother exchanged a hopeful look. "May we accompany you?" Lorena asked. "Dorothea and I have many errands we were saving for a ride into town."

"I have no time to waste on your errands," said Uncle Jacob, pushing back his chair, "and your time is better spent on your chores."

The hired men recognized the signal to leave and bolted the rest of their food. One man quickly pocketed the heel of the bread loaf, while another hastily downed a generous slice of pie in two bites.

"What errands?" asked Dorothea as the men returned to the fields.

"I would have invented some for the chance to go into Creek's Crossing." Lorena sighed and began fixing a plate for herself, motioning for her daughter to do the same. "It has been three weeks. We might as well live a hundred miles from the nearest village."

"If Uncle Jacob goes on horseback, we could take the wagon."

Lorena shook her head. "Chances are we would run into him in town if not on the ferry. Even if we managed to avoid him, he would discover our incomplete chores upon his return."

"No two mere mortal women could finish all he has assigned us." Briskly Dorothea scraped the remnants of her uncle's meal into the slop bucket for the pigs. "He cannot be satisfied. He knows you and Father are merely waiting for him to die so that Jonathan may have the farm, and he is determined to thwart our every attempt at happiness until then."

"Dorothea." Lorena laid her hand on her daughter's arm. "Clearing can wait. Eat something. We have a long day yet ahead of us."

Rather than argue, Dorothea complied, although the ravenous men had left little for the women to share. She resented her uncle for his power over them, but her parents' morbid anticipation shamed her. She remembered a time when they would not have been content to live at the whim of another. Perhaps they had been too idealistic in those days, but at least they had insisted upon setting the course of their own lives.

※

Dorothea and her mother could not have stolen into town in the wagon after all, because Uncle Jacob took it. Three hours after his departure, Dorothea heard the wagon coming up the road. She stopped scattering chicken feed and straightened, shading her eyes with one hand. What she saw made her want to duck behind the hen house and hide.

Her mother had also paused at the sound of the wagon. "It couldn't be," said her mother, with a soft moan of dismay. "Not Amos Liggett."

"I wish it were anyone else." Dorothea watched as the wagon brought the gangly, round-shouldered man closer. His red face was beaming with jovial pride behind greasy, unkempt whiskers. Uncle Jacob drove the horses stoically, apparently oblivious to his companion's chatter. "I can almost smell the liquor on him from here."

"Dorothea," her mother said reprovingly.

"You don't like him any more than I do." For that matter, Uncle Jacob despised him. Every winter Mr. Liggett asked Uncle Jacob to exchange work with him at sugaring time, a request Uncle Jacob always refused. "I don't want that blasted fool to set one foot inside my sugar camp," he had grumbled the previous winter, after Mr. Liggett had cornered him in church before Christmas services to plead his case yet again. "He's more likely to overturn the kettle and tap an oak than to give me a penny's worth of real help." There must have been no one else in all of Creek's Crossing to hire, or her uncle never would have brought Amos Liggett home.

Mr. Liggett offered the women a gap-toothed grin as the wagon rumbled past. Dorothea and her mother nodded politely, but quickly averted their eyes. "Stay clear of him," her mother cautioned, as if Dorothea needed the warning.

Mr. Liggett had brought his own scythe, an implement Dorothea surmised must be as sharp as the day he purchased it, given his inattention to his own fields. Uncle Jacob put him to work cutting oats with the others. Throughout the afternoon, as Dorothea passed from the garden to the kitchen where she and her mother were pickling cabbage and beets, she glimpsed him at work, swinging his blade with awkward eagerness, with none of the practiced, muscular grace of the other men. More often than not, he was at rest, his scythe nowhere to be seen, probably lying on the ground. The blade would not keep its shine for long.

At sundown, the men washed at the pump and trooped wearily inside for supper, smelling of sweat and grass and fatigue. Uncle Jacob offered Mr. Liggett the loan of a horse so that he might return to his own home for the night—an uncharacteristic display of trust and generosity that astonished the women—but Mr. Liggett declined, saying he would spend the night in the hayloft quarters with the others. Then he said, "Before we retire, I surely would like to get a look at that sugar camp of yours."

Uncle Jacob frowned. "For what reason?"

"Because everyone knows you make the best maple sugar in the county." Mr. Liggett let out a cackle. "And you never let anyone near your sugar camp. I know folks who'd pay good money to know your secret."

"I have no sugar-making secrets to share," replied Uncle Jacob.

Mr. Liggett chuckled and waited for him to continue, but when Uncle Jacob said nothing, his grin faded. He had thought Uncle Jacob spoke in jest, which, of course, he never did. Dorothea doubted Mr. Liggett had noted her uncle's careful choice of words. He did indeed have sugar-making secrets, but he had no intention of sharing them with Mr. Liggett.

"Perhaps you burn the syrup," suggested Lorena as she offered Mr. Liggett more mashed turnips. "It must be watched and stirred constantly or it will be ruined."

"I can't stand in front of a kettle all day," said Mr. Liggett, scowling. Then he brightened. "Say, Jacob, how about we trade work this winter? I'll help you with your sugaring, and you can help me."

"Thank you, but my family will provide all the help I need."

With that, Uncle Jacob excused himself and retired to the parlor. Mr. Liggett resumed eating, glancing hopefully at the doorway now and again as if expecting Uncle Jacob to appear and beckon him within. But Dorothea knew her uncle was by now well engrossed in his Bible, and he would not have invited Mr. Liggett to join him in the house's best room in any event.

❧

At breakfast, Mr. Liggett spoke to the merits of various woods for producing steady flame, as well as the skill of local blacksmiths in producing cast-iron kettles of size and durability. When his hints about visiting the sugar camp became too obvious to ignore, Uncle Jacob said that too much work remained for them to consider indulging in idleness.

Dorothea was relieved when the men left the breakfast table for the fields, and in the two days that followed, she learned to dread mealtimes. When Mr. Liggett was not querying her uncle he was grinning at her, casting his gaze up and down her person with shameless appreciation, as if his sour smell alone were not enough to turn her stomach. Lorena kept her out of his sight as much as she could and never left them alone together, but once he came upon her unaccompanied in the washhouse. He complimented her dress and had just asked if she might like to go riding some Sunday after he had his horse breeding business going when Uncle Jacob rounded the corner and fixed them with an icy glare. Mr. Liggett muttered excuses and slunk away, while Dorothea stood rooted to the spot until her uncle ordered her back to the house. She left the laundry in the washtub and obeyed, shaking with anger, her cheeks ablaze as if she had earned the accusation in her uncle's eyes. She wished her father would hurry home so that Mr. Liggett would no longer be needed.

Her father had been gone one week on the morning Mr. Liggett did not come to breakfast. Uncle Jacob ordered one of the hired hands back to the barn to rouse him from his sleep, only to learn that Mr. Liggett had been gone all night. "He left right after sundown," the hired man said. "He told us he desired to slake his thirst."

"Perhaps he fell into the well," said Lorena. Uncle Jacob sent a man to check, but when he found no sign of any mishap, Uncle Jacob told Lorena to serve the meal. His expression grew more stern as they ate in silence, listening for Mr. Liggett's approach.

He did not come. The other men went to the fields to cut the last two acres of wheat, looking to the sky as a low rumble of thunder sounded in the far distance. There were few clouds overhead, but the air was heavy and damp, and Dorothea knew they must hasten before rain pelted the heavy shafts of ripe wheat, dashing the grains to the earth, ruining the crop.

She was gathering carrots in the garden when Mr. Liggett returned, shuffling his feet in the dirt on his way to the barn. "Pray tell, Miss," he addressed her, with slurred, exaggerated formality. "Where might I find the master of this establishment?"

"My uncle is cutting wheat with the others."

He made a mocking bow and headed for the fields. Dorothea watched him as she worked. When Mr. Liggett reached the men, Uncle Jacob rested on his scythe, mopped his brow, and said something low and abrupt to the latecomer before raising his scythe again. Mr. Liggett took his hat from his head and fidgeted as he tried to explain, but Uncle Jacob did not appear to respond. After a moment, Mr. Liggett slammed his hat back on his head and hurried to the barn for his scythe, muttering angrily to himself. Dorothea had never seen him move so quickly, though he stumbled and once nearly fell sprawling to the ground.

At midday, through the kitchen window, Dorothea overheard the hired hands talking as they washed up at the pump. "Have to run home to care for your livestock, Liggett?"

Dorothea recognized the teasing drawl of the youngest of the men, a former classmate named Charley Stokey.

"Never you mind," snapped Mr. Liggett as the other men guffawed. It was well known that Mr. Liggett owned only one scrawny mare and a few chickens, for all that he boasted of one day raising prize racehorses.

"No, he was tending to his vast acreage," said another, evoking more laughter. Mr. Liggett was forever bragging about the improvements he planned for his farm, though he rarely would lay hand to plow or hammer. Though he owned forty of the valley's finest acres, he had let all but a few run wild.

"I know more about running a farm than you fools ever will," said Mr. Liggett. "My people own one of the richest plantations in Georgia."

"Then why aren't you down there helping them tend it?" Charley inquired.

Another man answered before Mr. Liggett could. "His people don't care for him any more than anyone else."

Over the laughter, Mr. Liggett said, "I'm telling you, it's one of the richest and the biggest. When I was a boy I could climb on my horse at sunup at the eastern edge of the plantation, ride west all day, and still be on my grandfather's property at sundown."

"I had a horse like that once," remarked Charley. "We named him Snail."

The men burst out laughing, and a moment later, Mr. Liggett swung open the kitchen door with a bang and stormed over to the table. "Are you going to feed us or let us starve?" he barked at Lorena.

She regarded him evenly. "We're waiting for my brother. He will be in shortly."

Uncle Jacob had come in from the fields ahead of the others in order to work on his ledgers. He entered the kitchen just as Lorena finished speaking and took his seat at the head of the table with a stern look for Mr. Liggett. Mr. Liggett dropped his gaze and tore a chunk from the loaf of bread.

The men ate swiftly, mindful of the threatening rain. The wind had picked up; the low growls of thunder in the distance had grown louder and more frequent. Dorothea wondered where her father was and hoped he was well out of the storm's path.

Not long after Uncle Jacob and the men returned outside, Dorothea heard a furious shout from the direction of the wheat field, followed by a string of curses.

"What on earth?" gasped Lorena as she and Dorothea hurried outside. Two of the hired men were heading for the house supporting Charley between them, his face covered in blood. Behind them, Uncle Jacob stood before Mr. Liggett, palms raised in a calming gesture. Mr. Liggett quivered and tightened his grip on his scythe. The blade was stained red.

"Put it down, Liggett," commanded Uncle Jacob.

"I didn't mean to," shrilled Mr. Liggett as the women ran to help Charley. "He got in the way. He came up behind me."

Uncle Jacob again ordered him to put down his scythe, but whether he obeyed, Dorothea could no longer watch to see. Charley was moaning and scrubbing blood from his eyes as Lorena and Dorothea lowered him to the ground. Lorena tore off her apron and sopped up the blood. "I cannot tell where he was struck," she murmured to her daughter. "There is too much blood."

Dorothea, Charley's head resting on her lap, snatched off her own apron and dabbed at his face. Distantly, she heard the voices of Uncle Jacob and Mr. Liggett coming nearer. "Here," she said, pointing, as blood seeped from a long gash along Charley's hairline.

"Is it bad?" one of the men asked.

"It is not as bad as it could have been," said Lorena, a tremble in her voice as she pressed the cloth to the wound. Charley flinched, but Dorothea held him firmly. "Nor as bad as it seems. It is not deep, but cuts on the scalp bleed profusely. Dorothea, run inside and fetch my herbs and plasters."

Charley let out a yelp, and as Dorothea set him down gently and ran for the house, she heard one of the hired hands ask Lorena if they ought to give Charley a strong drink to ease the shock and the pain. He might not know that Uncle Jacob permitted no liquor on his farm.

"Squeeze Liggett, and you'll get a pint," the other hired man said darkly.

Dorothea returned minutes later in time to see Uncle Jacob, the bloody scythe in his hand, order Mr. Liggett off his property. "It's bad enough that you were too drunk to find your way back last night," said Uncle Jacob. "It's far worse that your drunkenness could have killed a man today."

He waved Mr. Liggett off, gesturing toward the road. When Mr. Liggett realized that Uncle Jacob meant for him to walk home, he said, "What about my scythe? And my pay?"

"I'll deliver your scythe to you tomorrow. As for your pay, consider it forfeit."

Mr. Liggett flushed. "But I worked six full days for you. You owe me for six days."

"You worked five and a half days. Bearing in mind what has happened here today, considering that the work is not finished, and that you have cost me Mr. Stokey's labor as well as your own, you are fortunate I am willing to let you go without calling in the law."

"I want what's owed me."

"I'll give him what's owed him," said Charley weakly, lying on the ground as Lorena threaded a needle beside him.

"You," jeered Mr. Liggett, but he took a step backward, then turned and broke into a trot.

"It was only a glancing blow," said Lorena when Mr. Liggett was out of earshot, with an inscrutable look for her brother, which turned into a glance to the sky as thunder pealed overhead. "Help me get him up. This is better finished inside."

The cloudburst soaked them before they could reach shelter indoors. As the furious rain battered the ground, Uncle Jacob glowered out the window in the direction of the wheat fields.

The threshers would not arrive for two more days, but they had done all they could. They had lost the last acre of wheat to the storm.

❧

The next morning, Uncle Jacob paid the hired hands and agreed that Lorena could drive them back into town, and that Dorothea could assist her with her errands. When Lorena suggested they deliver Mr. Liggett's scythe to him, Uncle Jacob snorted and told them to spare the horse a few miles and leave it at the tavern. Dorothea had her doubts, but when Mr. Schultz readily agreed to hold the scythe for Mr. Liggett, she acknowledged that perhaps Mr. Liggett did indeed spend more time at the tavern than within the crude log walls of his cabin home.

Afterward, Lorena stopped the wagon in front of the general store, and as she shopped for coffee and sugar, Dorothea fingered the yard goods and thought wistfully of the dressmaker's shop across the street.

"Dorothea," a woman called from behind her. "Dorothea, dear, did you hear the news?"

Dorothea turned to her greeter, the mistress of the farm directly to the north of Uncle Jacob's property. One stout arm was linked with that of her young daughter, a beautiful dark-haired girl not yet fourteen years old. Their simple calico dresses belied the prosperity of their farm.

"Good afternoon, Mrs. Claverton," said Dorothea, and smiled at the girl. "Hello, Charlotte."

Charlotte returned her greeting softly, smiling but with eyes cast down shyly.

"Did you hear the news, dear?" repeated Mrs. Claverton eagerly. "Creek's Crossing has acquired a prominent new resident."

"Yes, I know," said Dorothea. "My father is traveling with Mr. Wright to bring her home."

"What?" For a moment confusion clouded Mrs. Claverton's face. "No, no, dear. Good heavens. Not the Wright girl. Mr. Nelson. The young Mr. Nelson is coming to take possession of Two Bears Farm."

"I had no idea the Carters intended to leave." They had been the Nelson family's tenants so long that few people in town remembered the farm's true owners. Dorothea herself had never met them.

"As I hear it, they had no such intentions." Mrs. Claverton lowered her voice in confidence. "The young Mr. Nelson forced them out."

"Forced them?" Dorothea echoed. "He sounds very unlike his father. The Carters always referred to him as a generous man."

"He was. And still would be, I suspect, if his son had not driven him to such ends."

Intrigued, Dorothea glanced at her mother, safely out of earshot on the other side of the store. Lorena disapproved of gossip. "What ends? This sounds dire."

"By all accounts Thomas Nelson did not inherit his father's strength of character. I have it on very good authority that he comes to Creek's Crossing almost directly by way of prison."

"Prison," exclaimed Dorothea.

Mrs. Claverton shushed her and lowered her voice to a whisper. "He says that he has been suffering ill health, and that his father sent him out here to manage Two Bears Farm while regaining his strength in our milder climate. What he does not say is that the depravities of prison caused his illness, and that his father banished him here, where his shame is unknown."

"It will not be unknown for long," said Dorothea, amused.

"I don't doubt it, although if he wanted to avoid being the subject of gossip, he should have lived more virtuously. Unfortunately, many members of society will welcome him for his father's sake, regardless of his past, and we can hardly shun him after that." She shook her head. "I confess I have some misgivings about exposing my daughter to such an influence, but as he will be charged with the education of our youth—"

"What?"

"Mama," warned Charlotte, too late.

"Oh, my dear," said Mrs. Claverton, dismayed. "I certainly did not mean for you to find out this way. The school board has written you a letter."

"Mr. Nelson is to be the new schoolmaster?"

Mrs. Claverton nodded. "After all, his father did donate the land and the funds to build the school. When he wrote to request a position for his son, well, the school board couldn't refuse him, could they?"

"Apparently they could not, since it would seem the decision has already been made."

"Now, Dorothea." Mrs. Claverton patted her hand. "Don't be angry. You do remember you were hired as the interim schoolteacher only. You may have been the brightest pupil in the Creek's Crossing school, but before his more recent troubles, Mr. Nelson attended university."

"Did he? Then if he is a felon, at least he is an educated felon."

"Mr. Nelson's minister assures us he has repented his crimes and that he has been entirely rehabilitated," said Mrs. Claverton. "If we withhold from him the opportunity to contribute to society, he may never be able to atone for his misdeeds. You are a properly brought-up girl; you shouldn't need me to remind you of these things. You must drive your poor mother to distraction. You should look beyond your own apparent misfortune and find the opportunity."

"I completed the Creek's Crossing school years ago," Dorothea reminded her. "Even if Mr. Nelson were qualified to teach at a secondary academy, I cannot imagine what education I should care to receive from him."

"I was not speaking of your education. Did I mention that Mr. Nelson is unmarried?"

Dorothea could not help laughing. "Mrs. Claverton, did you not just inform me that Mr. Nelson is a former convict?"

"But a repentant one from a good family," she retorted. "And, I might remind you, he is an educated man with a prosperous farm. Why, if my Charlotte was not already promised to your brother, I might consider Mr. Nelson for her."

The girl started, setting her two ribbon-tied braids swinging down her back.

"She didn't mean it," Dorothea assured Charlotte.

"No, indeed, I did not." Mrs. Claverton gave her daughter a quick hug. "Well. It is plain to see young Mr. Nelson has already upset us. I cannot imagine what will happen when we are finally forced to meet him."

❧

On the way home, Dorothea told her mother about the arrival of Mr. Nelson only to discover that she already knew. She had learned from the shopkeeper, who was also the mayor, that there would be a party in Mr. Nelson's honor on Sunday afternoon at the home of the school board president.

Dorothea wondered if the shopkeeper had mentioned the rumors circling the guest of honor. "I would rather not attend."

Mother regarded her, eyebrows raised. "You would prefer to stay home with your Uncle Jacob?"

Dorothea said nothing.

"It is a pity you lost your position so close to the start of the new term, and after you spent all summer preparing your lessons," said her mother. "But you mustn't sulk. You did a fine job and will receive a good reference from the school board. You will find something else."

"Perhaps it is Mr. Nelson who ought to find something else."

Her mother said nothing, the silence broken only by the sound of the horse's hooves striking the hard-packed dirt road. "Your father and I wish we could afford to further your education, but since we cannot, you must make the best of it. You need not set your heart on the women's academy in Philadelphia when you have a library full of books at home. Look to books and nature for your teachers. You shall learn more from them than in any classroom."

Dorothea nodded, although she did not entirely agree. She had read all of the books in her parents' modest library at least twice, even the dullest collection of essays. As for learning from nature, for most of her first twelve years she had explored the forest and fields of the Elm Creek Valley until she had learned them by heart. She knew every bend of Elm Creek, every type of tree that grew along its banks. A woman of Shawnee heritage who had lived at Thrift Farm for a time had taught her the lore of local herbs and roots. She knew which leaves to brew into a tea to ease the pain of toothache and where to scrape the bark of a tree for a poultice to reduce the inflammation of wounds. Jonathan had abandoned this knowledge as soon as he left to study real medicine, but it was all Dorothea had and she cherished it.

When Uncle Jacob declared that it was unseemly for a girl her age to wander about in the wilderness without an escort, her heart constricted in grief, but she resolved to learn as much as she could within the confines of her uncle's farm. Indeed, she did learn much from her uncle about the raising of crops and the husbandry of animals, but she mourned the loss of everything she would never learn. She tried not to envy her brother and told herself the people of Creek's Crossing were fortunate that books and nature alone were not considered adequate teachers for a future physician.

When she was the schoolteacher, Uncle Jacob had claimed half her wages, but Dorothea had saved every penny of what remained. Even that was not enough for one semester's tuition at the women's academy. Dorothea shook her head and told her mother, "If I do not have enough education to teach the pupils of Creek's Crossing, where people know me and have confidence in me, I cannot see how any other school would have me."

"Then you cannot see far enough."

Dorothea frowned at her quizzically, but her mother looked beyond her. "Look," she said, nodding to the pasture. "Father is home."

Dorothea heard the clanging of a cowbell and quickly spotted her father driving in the two Guernseys and the calf. He waved his hat and shouted something, but the breeze carried his voice away.

"He's home a day early," exclaimed Dorothea.

"Yes, and already your uncle has him working. We lingered in town longer than we should have if he has had time to begin your chores as well as his own." Dorothea's mother chirruped to the horse and shook the reins to quicken his pace. "Your uncle will be stomping around the fields like an old bear, wondering why I have not started his supper."

"If we hurry, perhaps he won't see us. He won't know when we arrived."

"Deception by an omission of the truth is as bad as a lie," her mother chided, but mildly. Dorothea was expected to speak respectfully of her elders, but her parents often made an exception for Uncle Jacob if no one but themselves were around to hear.

It was not for Uncle Jacob that her mother hurried to the barn, Dorothea knew. Her father met them there, and her parents greeted each other with a warm embrace and a discreet kiss Dorothea pretended not to observe. When her father removed his hat, she saw he was sunburned beneath his thinning blond hair. He was slender, although years of farm labor had added muscle to his frame, and he was scarcely as tall as his wife.

"Tell us about your trip, Father. Please," she remembered to add, hungry for news of the world beyond the valley. "Did Constance's master change his mind again? Did you have to elude slavecatchers?"

Father smiled, but his eyes showed the strain of hard travel and little sleep. "No, Dorothea. You would have found our journey dull. We reached Virginia, paid the plantation owner the ransom he demanded, and were on our way. It was all very civilized, like any business transaction." His voice was so mild no one but Dorothea and her mother would have detected his disgust. "Mrs. Wright carried all she possessed wrapped in one small quilt, so it took us only minutes to load the wagon. We left as soon as the horses were rested and stayed one night at the home of a sympathetic friend an hour's ride north."

"How is Mrs. Wright settling in?" asked Mother. "What a poor wedding party awaited the bride and groom. I wish we could have prepared a meal for them, but I was not certain when you would return."

"They're happy just to be north and home. They weren't expecting a party. On our way south, we pushed the horses as hard as we could without ruining them." He glanced at Mother and unhitched the horse. "We arrived a day earlier, but none too soon. A few days more . . ." He shrugged and led the horse away.

Mother turned toward the house and Dorothea fell in step beside her. "What did he mean, a few days more?" she asked.

Mother was silent for a moment, as if considering how much to say. "The last time Mr. Wright visited Constance, other slaves warned him of rumors that Constance's master wished to increase his number of slaves."

"He intends to buy more?"

"No," said her mother carefully as they entered the house through the kitchen door. "He does not mean to buy them."

A moment passed before Dorothea understood. "I see."

"The indignity of having his wife taken by another man—that, Mr. Wright could bear. If Constance could endure it, he certainly could, and they have had to throughout the two years of their marriage. Her owner is a greedy, spiteful man. He only turned his attentions to Constance after she married Mr. Wright, to punish her for marrying and, I suppose, to punish Mr. Wright for being born free in the north. Mr. Wright had to obtain Constance's freedom before she became pregnant. Her owner would not have allowed her to leave until after her child was born and weaned, if he did not change his mind entirely. There was also no guarantee he would have parted with the child, or sold him to the Wrights rather than another slave owner."

"Even if the child had been Mr. Wright's?"

"Even then. And I'm sure I don't need to remind you never to mention this to the Wrights, or anyone else, for that matter. They have enough to bear without adding the embarrassment of gossip regarding how Mrs. Wright has been violated."

Dorothea nodded, her heart going out to the Wrights as she imagined what they had suffered, and the certain anguish they had narrowly escaped.

With Dorothea's help, her mother finished cooking supper with moments to spare. Dorothea was setting the table when they heard Uncle Jacob working the pump handle outside as he washed up for the meal. Dorothea did not look up at the sound of two heavy footsteps on the wooden floor, the sound of the kitchen door closing behind him, and a pause while he removed his boots. She greeted him in a murmur as he pulled back his chair and seated himself; he replied with a nod. Like his sister, Uncle Jacob was thin and tall, but where Lorena was dark he was gray-haired, down to the scruff of beard he shaved off every Saturday night. The hollows in his cheeks were a darker gray; they might have been dimples except he never smiled.

He had not always been so grim, Lorena had confided to Dorothea not long after they came to live with him. As a boy he had been proud and pious, but lighthearted. He had won the affection of the most beautiful girl in the valley and had been the envy of all his friends. His farm had prospered; his wife bore him two fine, strong sons. Then scarlet fever swept through Creek's Crossing. Uncle Jacob thought they would be safe, isolated on their farm, away from the contagion of the town, but his wife insisted on returning to nurse her stricken parents. She fell ill soon after her parents died, and against his better judgment, Uncle Jacob brought her home to care for her. Lorena offered to take the children to Thrift Farm, but Uncle Jacob thought the sight of her children would encourage his wife to fight off the illness.

Uncle Jacob did not tell his wife when her precious babies died, and to the end, he soothed her with lies about how they grew stronger every day, how they were playing outside or sleeping when she begged to see them. When she died, Uncle Jacob nearly went mad with grief. He would let no one into the house to attend to the bodies. He chased the minister off with his rifle. Only Lorena was permitted to enter, and he sat in his chair by the window, face buried in his hands, responding numbly when Lorena asked him what his wife and children should wear, where he would like them to be laid to rest. He picked a clearing in the maple grove and dug the graves alone, rebuffing Robert's offers of help.

After a time he regained himself and resumed the work of the farm. He rid the house of all relics of the woman and children he had loved. At first Lorena assumed he would marry again, but his heart had scarred over and would permit no more joy within it. He never again smiled, or laughed, or showed any sign that life was anything more than a burden to be endured. His Bible was his only consolation. The two decisions he had made with his heart rather than his head had cost him all that he held dear in this life, and he would not make that mistake again.

Outside the pump clanged and gushed as Dorothea's father raced through his washing. He joined them, breathless, just as Lorena began to place serving dishes on the table—boiled turnips, sweet corn, stewed greens, bread from the previous day's baking. Uncle Jacob waited for them to be seated before leading them in prayer. Wordlessly, he served himself a heaping spoonful of turnips and passed the dish to Robert on his left, repeating with each of Lorena's dishes in turn. He spoke only to ask for butter for his bread; at a glance from her mother, Dorothea hurried to fetch it from the cool of the cellar.

By the time she returned, Uncle Jacob had sated his hunger enough to engage her father in a discussion about the crops. The threshers had sent a man over early that day to report that they would arrive the next morning, as scheduled. "We lost an acre of wheat because of you," said Uncle Jacob. "Why you could not have waited another week for your trip down South is beyond me. We'll need to work day and night to make up for the time you wasted."

"Except for Sunday afternoon," said Dorothea's mother. "There is a social in town to welcome Mr. Thomas Nelson, and we are expected."

"A social?" Uncle Jacob shook his head. "What fool planned a social for the middle of harvest?"

"The mayor, I believe. And the school board."

"What nonsense. No one will attend, not at this time of year. Likely not even Thomas Nelson would care to interrupt his harvest chores for a silly party. If we want to be good neighbors, we should leave him in peace to finish his work."

"We must have some representative of the family present," said Robert. "Dorothea, at least, ought to meet with Mr. Nelson, as he is to take over as schoolmaster."

Uncle Jacob looked Dorothea squarely in the eye. "You said nothing of being replaced."

"I learned of it only today."

"Your wages will be sorely missed." Uncle Jacob took a bite of greens and chewed slowly, thinking. "Very well. Dorothea must go, and since she cannot go unescorted, you two must accompany her. Fortunately, I see nothing requiring my presence." He regarded Dorothea again. "Do you think you can be gracious to this man who is taking your situation when he likely has no real need of it?"

Surprised, Dorothea said, "I believe I can manage to be civil."

"Then it's settled. I'm sure you won't do anything to shame this family." Uncle Jacob wiped his lips, set his fork and knife neatly on the edge of his plate, and pushed back his chair. "You worked hard as you always do, Dorothea, but they made their choice and it can't be helped. Robert, join me in the barn when you're through."

With that, he left.

As soon as the kitchen door swung shut behind him, Robert quietly said, "If I didn't know better, I'd say that was an expression of sympathy."

"He regrets only the loss of her wages." Lorena began clearing the table. Dorothea quickly shook off her astonishment and rose to help.

Two days later, Dorothea put on her best dress and rode with her parents to the home of Mr. and Mrs. Hiram Engle. None of the Grangers had called upon the couple since their marriage six months before, a slight somewhat excused by the fact that they had not been invited. Mr. Engle owned the livery stable and the only hotel in town. Until the former Mrs. Violet Pearson had ensnared his affection a year after her first husband died, Mr. Engle's prosperity had rendered him a highly desirable bachelor despite his facial tic and ample waistline. Uncle Jacob spoke approvingly of Mr. Engle's business acumen, but Dorothea's parents did not care for his politics and avoided spending too much time in his company.

Mr. Engle had offered his livery stable for guests traveling from outlying farms, and from there it was a short walk from the riverfront to the more fashionable street in the center of town. It was not the oldest block; the more modest, wood-frame buildings along Elm Creek were the first to be built when the village that became Creek's Crossing was settled, but as their own-ers prospered, they moved their families to more spacious limestone dwell-ings farther away.

The Engles had hired several servants and a quartet of musicians for the occasion, and as one servant took their wraps, Dorothea glanced through an open doorway and saw that what was presumably the parlor had been all but emptied of furniture to make room for dancing. Several couples danced merrily to a popular schottische, but when Dorothea's father headed in that direction, her mother took his elbow and steered him toward the publisher of the local newspaper, no doubt to prevail upon him to write another editorial denouncing slavery or supporting woman's suffrage. On her own, Dorothea decided to stroll through the house in search of her friends before seeking out the hostess and an introduction to the guest of honor.

She found a small group of young men and women laughing and chatting near the punch bowl, friends since her first days as a student at the Creek's Crossing school. The young men were tanned from long hours in the fields, but the women had endeavored, as Dorothea herself did, to protect their skin from the harsh sun. The condition of their hands revealed their sta-tion in life; town girls had smooth, pale hands, while the hands of farm girls were as sun-browned as the men's faces. Since Uncle Jacob did not permit trips into town for mere social calls, Dorothea had not seen them all together in months, and she eagerly caught up on their news. Apparently her own news had not circulated as rapidly as she had expected; one young man, who had always teased Dorothea for knowing all the answers in class, grinned as he asked her if she planned to send her pupils crawling along the creek banks looking for curious rocks as she had the previous year, or if she had moved on to studying pictures in the clouds. Dorothea strained to betray no emotion as another young woman murmured in his ear, and struggled to smile graciously as he apologized. "Nelson might be a good teacher but he can't be as clever as you," he said, and as the others added their assent, Dorothea's smile threatened to collapse, forcing her to pretend to look around for her parents rather than let them see how much the loss of her position grieved her.

As some of her friends left to join the dancing, Dorothea heard a polite cough and turned around. "Why, Miss Granger," said Cyrus Pearson, giving her a slight bow and a mischievous grin. "I'm honored by your presence at my party. If I had known your uncle would allow you to have a bit of fun on a Sunday, I would have delivered your invitation myself."

Dorothea smiled back. "It's your mother's party and her invitation to give, but thank you just the same."

"Quite right," replied Cyrus, rueful. "It's not even truly my home, however welcome my stepfather has made me feel beneath his roof."

"So welcome that you have spent most of the past six months abroad."

He raised a finger in playful warning. "No more questions, Miss Granger. I am not a plant or insect for you to study." He offered her his arm. "I see I must ask you to dance before you have me entirely figured out."

Uncle Jacob would have been offended to see his niece dancing on a Sabbath afternoon, but despite this—or perhaps because of it—Dorothea accepted. It was, as Cyrus had promised, difficult to talk during the lively country dance, and whenever they did have an opportunity, Cyrus kept her laughing with amusing observations about the party. She learned nothing more about his stepfather. If only she could dispense with her obligation to the guest of honor as easily.

After a second dance, Cyrus escorted her from the floor, explaining that his mother had made him promise to see to it that no young lady was allowed to remain a wallflower at one of her parties.

Dorothea regarded him, eyebrows raised. "Is that why you danced with me?"

"Miss Granger, I believe you know the answer to that." He gave her a wicked grin as he bowed over her hand, then he moved off into the crowd.

"He is full of fancy manners, that one," said Dorothea's best friend, Mary, appearing at her side, her light brown hair braided into a knot at the nape of her slender neck. "I suppose he thinks he's charming."

Dorothea watched him depart, his golden curls visible above most of the other men in the crowd. "I'm sure he is not alone in that opinion."

Mary sniffed. "I hope you do not share it."

Dorothea hid a smile. From the time they were children, Mary had secretly admired Cyrus—so secretly that no one else but Dorothea knew of it—but Cyrus had never noticed her. Mary had never spared a kind word for any girl who did attract his attention, and after she fell in love with a more receptive young man, she had nothing good to say about Cyrus, either.

"Cyrus is neither as fine as you once thought nor as terrible as you think now," teased Dorothea.

"I do not believe your parents would approve," warned Mary. "It is no secret where his mother stands on the slavery issue. I confess I do not always share your parents' fervor, but unlike Violet Pearson Engle, at least my heart is in the right place."

"Cyrus Pearson is not his mother," said Dorothea. "I would no more condemn him for his mother's sins than I would have anyone condemn me for the wrongs my parents have committed."

She smiled to soften her words, but slipped away before Mary asked her which wrongs she meant.

By that time the newlyweds' home had filled almost to bursting with what appeared to be nearly every resident of Creek's Crossing within the range of Mrs. Engle's condescension. Dorothea found her father engrossed in conversation with the mayor, but merely waved to him on her way to the kitchen, where she found her mother chatting with the colored cook about abolition and woman's suffrage. The cook regarded Dorothea's mother curiously and with some wariness, as if she did not know what to make of this white woman who spoke so passionately about impossibilities in the heat of the kitchen, rather than enjoy the laughter and music of the party. Dorothea was so accustomed to her mother that she sometimes forgot that others often found her inscrutable.

Dorothea's mother greeted her affectionately and introduced her to the cook, who nodded a greeting as she removed a pan from the oven and looked Dorothea over with renewed cautious curiosity.

"So, Dorothea," her mother said. "How was your conversation with Mr. Nelson?"

"I have not met him yet. I had hoped someone would offer a toast to him so that I might be able to pick him out of the crowd."

"You must have gone out of your way to avoid him." Mother described him—a bespectacled, brown-haired man, slender, somewhat pale—and pointed out that he would be one of the very few people in the familiar crowd Dorothea did not already know. "Swallow your pride and meet him soon," she added. "We must leave before long or all the evening chores will be left to your uncle."

With a sigh of resignation, Dorothea left the kitchen and made her way to the parlor, where she spied a man who fit her mother's description chatting with Cyrus Pearson. He was not quite as tall as Cyrus, but he wore a finer suit with an overlarge but not unattractive boutonniere on his lapel. Dorothea made her way to an unoccupied spot nearby, where she could await a suitable moment to introduce herself, if Cyrus did not see her there first and take care of the formalities.

She fixed a pleasant smile in place and observed the dancing. Abner whirled Mary about; Mrs. Claverton waggled her fingers and called out a greeting as she and her husband passed. Dorothea returned the greeting with a smile and looked around the room for Charlotte, hoping for the girl's sake that her parents had possessed the sense to allow her to remain home, as befitting her age.

"You have not danced one single set all afternoon," Dorothea overheard Cyrus chide the young Mr. Nelson, if that was, in fact, who he was. "Surely your health cannot be as bad as all that."

"It is not for my health that I refrain," came the reply, in a voice both deeper and more disdainful than Dorothea expected.

"What is it, then? Come, now, my mother made me promise that there would be no young ladies unattended at her party, and I insist you help me."

"While I regret disappointing the woman who so kindly organized this gathering for me," said Mr. Nelson, "you will have to satisfy your obligations to your mother yourself. I dance when I am inclined to do so, and at this moment, I am not so inclined."

"Why not? Look—there are three, four, no, five ladies not engaged at present. Your legs are obviously not broken whatever else might ail you. You will not do yourself an injury if you take one turn about the floor."

"Nevertheless, I decline." He paused and gave Cyrus a slight bow. "With my apologies."

"I cannot understand you, Nelson. You are newly arrived in Creek's Crossing, and apparently you mean to stay. Surely you wish to make the acquaintance of our charming local beauties."

Mr. Nelson frowned and indicated his boutonniere. "If their taste in conversation resembles their taste in flowers, we will have very little to say to each other."

Cyrus laughed, incredulous. "You cannot mean it. I am as well traveled as you, sir, and I defy you to say the ladies of Creek's Crossing are not as pretty or as charming as those of New York, Paris, or London, without all their artificial graces."

"Pretty?" Mr. Nelson paused. "Yes, perhaps one or two of them are somewhat pretty, but I do not find ignorant country girls amusing. It is far better for me to avoid them than to subject us both to an excruciating attempt at conversation."

"I cannot believe you seriously mean this. What about her?"

Dorothea closed her eyes, hoping fervently that Cyrus was directing Mr. Nelson's attention toward the other side of the room.

"That young lady is Dorothea Granger," said Cyrus, with a suggestion of pride. "Surely you can see how lovely she is. She is not yet twenty, and yet she is so clever she was appointed interim schoolteacher after your predecessor stepped down."

"That says more about your school board's standards than her cleverness. In any event, the manner in which she gazes so longingly at the dance floor suggests that she has not set foot on one in quite some time. I assure you, I have no intention of directing my attention to any woman ignored by other men, especially those here, who know her character."

"Don't be ridiculous," said Cyrus. "Some may say she is too clever for her own good, but no one would ever question her strength of character. Let me introduce you. Miss Granger?"

When he called to her, Dorothea took a quick, steadying breath before turning around to face them. "Yes, Mr. Pearson?"

"Allow me to introduce you to Mr. Thomas Nelson, our guest of honor. He just finished telling me how very much he wishes to make your acquaintance."

Mr. Nelson masked his annoyance poorly as he bowed to her.

"Welcome to Creek's Crossing," said Dorothea. "I regret that so far you have found very little to like about it."

Mr. Nelson gave not a flicker of acknowledgment, but Cyrus had the decency to appear mortified. "Miss Granger, please accept my apologies for my companion's boorish remarks. You were not meant to overhear them."

"You are not the one who should apologize."

Mr. Nelson gestured impatiently to his boutonniere. "If you refer to my criticism of this collection of twigs and vegetable matter—"

"I do not refer to it, but since you mention it, I must speak in its defense." Dorothea gave the boutonniere a quick survey. "It is an unusual arrangement, but its maker's intention is evident. Those twigs, as you call them, are maple seeds, and maple sugar is a significant part of our local economy. These are the leaves of the elm, which grow in abundance throughout the valley and whose beauty is a particular source of pride for us. The leaves of the rose, here and here, represent hope, while the water lily symbolizes purity of heart. The ribbon I recognize—the mayor's wife wears a similar trim on her spring bonnet. To speak plainly, this nosegay that you disparage welcomes you to enjoy the beauty and prosperity of the Elm Creek Valley, with hopes that you will remain honest and true to your calling as the educator of our youth."

"You could hardly ask for a better welcome than that," remarked Cyrus.

"What I would ask for," said Mr. Nelson, "is to be permitted to wear the flower of my choosing."

Dorothea glanced at his hands. "Would that have been a blossom plucked from a round cluster of small white flowers growing on a rather tall stem?"

He almost managed to hide his surprise. "Yes, that's right. Queen Anne's lace. You must have seen me discard it."

Dorothea let out a small laugh. "No, I assure you, I was not paying you that much attention. Nor was your flower Queen Anne's lace. We call it cow parsnip, although it is actually a member of the carrot family. Curiously enough, while it is edible, it is a particularly noxious weed to the touch. The rash on the back of your hands will pass in two or three weeks, longer if you scratch it. I would offer you a healing salve, but as I am merely an ignorant country girl, I am sure my humble medicines are beneath your regard. Next time, if you wish to choose an appropriate flower, I would recommend a narcissus." She turned a blistering smile on Cyrus and ignored his companion. "Good afternoon, Mr. Pearson."

She quickly departed, nearly bumping into Mary as she and Abner left the dance floor. "Goodness, Dorothea, what's wrong?" asked Mary. "Your face is so flushed! Are you ill?"

"I am not ill." Dorothea refused to allow Mr. Nelson and Cyrus to see how angry she was. "Abner, will you excuse us, please?" She linked her arm through Mary's and drew her toward the far end of the room, where she asked, "Have you had an opportunity to meet our new schoolmaster?"

Mary nodded. "Mrs. Engle introduced us. He's handsome in a bookish way, but I suppose that suits his profession. He certainly doesn't look much like a farmer. Would you like to meet him?"

"No! No, thank you. I know him as well as I care to." She told Mary about the encounter.

Mary glanced at the ill-humored schoolmaster and turned away quickly, unable to contain her amusement. "Honestly, Dorothea! Mrs. Deakins may have little talent for flowers, but she meant well, and he had no call to be so unkind. In your place, I would have been tempted to slap him."

"I did not say I wasn't tempted."

"I considered him somewhat aloof when we were introduced, but I had no idea he was so rude." Mary's eyes widened and she grasped Dorothea's arm. "Oh, he's looking this way. He surely knows we're talking about him. But I suppose he doesn't care about the opinion of a couple of ignorant country girls."

"I suppose not," said Dorothea, laughing. "Ignore him. We cannot let him think he is important enough to be the subject of our conversation."

At that moment, she felt a hand on her elbow. "I'm afraid you must bid your friend good-bye," said her father, her mother at his side. "We have chores to attend to at home."

Dorothea let out an exaggerated sigh. "That's fine, Father. I was merely gazing longingly at the dance floor, wondering if I shall ever set foot on one again."

Mary giggled as Dorothea's parents exchanged a puzzled look. Then Dorothea's mother said, "You did find an opportunity to speak to Mr. Nelson?"

"Yes, I spoke to him, the odious man."

Lorena's eyebrows shot up, but before she could inquire, Dorothea hugged Mary good-bye and promised to call on her soon. After giving their regards to the hostess, the Grangers left the party.

"I gather," said Robert carefully as they walked to the livery stable, "that Mr. Nelson did not make a favorable impression upon you?"

"Entirely the opposite," said Dorothea, and she told them what had happened.

"What a rude young man," said Lorena, but she smiled. "Of course, he assumed he was speaking in confidence, unaware of your eavesdropping."

"I was not eavesdropping. I was merely waiting for an appropriate moment to introduce myself," said Dorothea. "Besides, you have often told me one should not do in secret what one would be unwilling to have known in public."

"Not all deeds fall into that neat category, dear. Nor all words."

Her father shook his head. "Are you sure you did not misunderstand him, Dorothea? His father is such a reasonable, just man. I considered him a friend and was disappointed when he returned to the East. It is difficult to believe his son could be so unlike him."

"I understood every word with perfect clarity." Dorothea threw up her hands and quickened her step. "I cannot bear for you two to defend him! Whatever fine qualities his father may possess, Mr. Nelson the younger does not share them."

"Still, it was a fine party," offered her father.

"He seemed as oblivious to its charms as to those of everything else in Creek's Crossing," retorted Dorothea, quickly outpacing her parents.

"Cheer up," called her mother. "He has only just met us. Perhaps once he knows us better, he will decide to move on to some other town, where the women have greater skill with flowers."

Dorothea tried to stay angry, but she could not help it; she burst out laughing. "One can hope," she said. She paused and allowed her parents to catch up to her. She thought, but did not say aloud, that if Mr. Nelson did leave, Creek's Crossing would need another schoolteacher.

Her father was right. It had been a fine party, but it was wasted on Mr. Nelson. Dorothea's thoughts went to the small farmhouse to the southwest where Abel and Constance Wright were finally enjoying the comforts of freedom. No wedding supper, no bridal quilt, no wedding party had marked their homecoming. How much more appropriate it would have been for the people of Creek's Crossing to welcome Constance with music and celebration, and to allow Mr. Nelson, the convict-turned-schoolmaster, to eat a cold supper alone.

Chapter Two

Dorothea's father and uncle finished the harvest, aided by the threshers and a spell of temperate weather that made Dorothea wistful for the long-ago days that she and Jonathan spent exploring the shores of Elm Creek barefoot and happy. Once they wandered so far they scaled the peak of Dutch Mountain, unaware of the distance they had conquered until the entire Elm Creek Valley lay spread out before them. They returned home to Thrift Farm late for their chores, but it never would have occurred to their parents or the other adults who occupied the cabins scattered about the main residence to scold. They were a community of Christians with strong Transcendentalist inclinations, and they believed children had to be allowed to pursue their own hearts' desires without adult interference. If they had not also believed human beings were obligated to treat the animals in their care with respect and kindness, the Granger children might never have learned any part of what it meant to run a farm.

Dorothea wondered what had become of those optimistic men and women who had tried to build a utopia in the Pennsylvania wilderness. None had perished in the flood, but after Thrift Farm lay underwater, the group was forced to disperse. There was some talk, at first, of moving out west to start again, but the money for the journey and the perfect plot of land could never be found. Singly or in pairs, the former residents of Thrift Farm drifted away from the Elm Creek Valley like cottonwood seeds on the wind. Dorothea's parents occasionally received letters from friends who had gone to Kansas or California; Lorena would linger over them, caressing the precious words with her fingertips.

Uncle Jacob had taught the Granger children how to run a farm properly and a child's proper place within the household. Their education was swift and jarring, but they learned. Dorothea's parents caught on more slowly, but Uncle Jacob eventually made able farmers out of them. Dorothea learned, too, that as hard as Uncle Jacob worked them, there were advantages to his methods: Her days were no longer hers to fill as she chose, but the forest did not reclaim the fields and the crops did not fail. Jonathan no longer complained of hunger in the middle of the night and his persistent headaches disappeared. Dorothea grew three inches the first summer after Uncle Jacob took them in, after which he ordered Dorothea's mother to put her in long skirts rather than dungarees and forbade her to wander the valley as if she were, as he put it, a wild Indian or Irish.

If nothing else, Uncle Jacob's restrictions on the children's carefree wanderings allowed them more time for books. Jonathan's aptitude for the scholarly life was apparent even to his uncle, who generally mistrusted such inclinations. It was Uncle Jacob who first introduced his nephew to the local physician, who, after a year as his tutor, recommended that the boy broaden his experience in a larger city. For two years Jonathan had lived in Baltimore, and as proud as Dorothea was of his accomplishments, she could not deny feeling an occasional stab of envy.

In the past Jonathan had returned for at least part of the harvest, but that year he did not, citing important ongoing cases that his mentor insisted he observe to the end. Uncle Jacob grumbled but did not order him home, and instead kept on the hired hands and agreed to exchange work with Abel Wright. He had done so every year as far back as Dorothea could remember, even though the Wright farm was nearly eight miles away, southwest of Creek's Crossing.

This season Abel Wright came to their farm first, but despite Lorena's repeated entreaties, he did not bring his wife with him, saying that she sent her apologies but had so much work to do in her new home that she could not spare even a day away. The next week, when Uncle Jacob and Robert were to help at the Wright farm, Dorothea was pleased when Uncle Jacob told her she and Lorena must come, too, to assist Mrs. Wright however she needed.

"At last we can give her a proper welcome," said Lorena. "We should take a gift. Something useful for the home."

"And something to eat," said Dorothea. "A wedding cake."

"Yes. That's a fine idea." Lorena instructed her to begin beating eggs for the cake while she searched the house for an appropriate gift.

Dorothea went to the hen house, gathered eggs in her apron, and hurried back to mix the cake batter. She cracked the eggs in her mother's large mixing bowl and beat them until her arm ached, pausing only to build a fire in the oven. The eggs were stiff and the oven hot by the time her mother returned, hesitating in the doorway, hands behind her back.

"Did you find something?" asked Dorothea, mixing sugar into the bowl.

Lorena nodded and revealed what she carried.

Dorothea recognized the quilt top before her mother unfolded it. The appliqué sampler quilt top was the first she had begun after coming to live with Uncle Jacob, and it had taken her nearly two years to complete. At that time she had still believed she might complete the customary thirteen tops for her hope chest, but was practical enough to realize that just in case she could not, she ought to make at least one very fine top that could serve as her bridal quilt. Knowing she was hungry for details of city life, Jonathan had written of a new style of appliqué quilt the fashionable ladies of Baltimore were making. Their intricate designs created still life portraits in fabric—floral bouquets, nestling birds, wreaths, beribboned baskets, urns of greenery. Inspired by her brother's descriptions, Dorothea sketched images from her own life, capturing her memories of Thrift Farm and the Elm Creek Valley with every stitch into the fourteen-inch squares. She had drawn each appliqué template by hand on old newspapers and had spent a good portion of her modest savings on the soft muslin background, bleached to a snowy white by the sun, to which she had sewn the calico flowers, leaves, and figures. She arranged the sixteen blocks in four rows of four, then fashioned an appliqué border of elegant swags gathered by roses. Once she had succumbed to a local superstition and had slept beneath the unquilted top so that she might dream of her future husband. She woke the next morning with no memory of her dreams, a worrisome omen that now made perfect sense.

"You want to give this to the Wrights?" she managed to say. "But—but it is not finished yet. It is not quilted."

"Yes, and the fact that you never bothered to do so tells me it is not very close to your heart. Not so dear that you cannot bear to part with it. Mrs. Wright can quilt it herself, or she can leave it as it is for a summer quilt."

Dorothea thought quickly. "A quilt is a fine idea, but perhaps Mr. Wright would prefer a Rail Fence quilt. I have enough blocks finished. Do you remember how he admired them?"

"We don't have time to stitch your blocks together. Besides, this is a gift for the bride. The flowers will suit the occasion."

Dorothea said nothing.

"Constance Wright came north with little more than the clothes on her back," said Lorena. "Wouldn't she treasure this beautiful quilt? Wouldn't it be a wonderful expression of the friendship we hope will grow between us?"

"It would," said Dorothea. Her mother watched her so expectantly that Dorothea could not bring herself to explain that she had not quilted the top because she was saving it for her engagement party. Everyone in the Elm Creek Valley expected the bride-to-be's best friend or sister to host a special quilting bee where the bride's thirteen tops would be unveiled and all the women would help quilt them. Telling her mother this would be no use. Lorena did not believe that people should allow custom to dictate their behavior, especially if it steered them away from finer impulses such as kindness and generosity.

Dorothea was not betrothed. Even if she became engaged that afternoon, a highly unlikely occurrence, she might still have time to make another bridal quilt before the wedding. She had saved her sketches and most of her templates. She could make another.

"I suppose it would make a fine gift," she said. Her mother smiled and hurried off to find some clean muslin to wrap it in. Dorothea turned her attention to the cake, a hollow sensation growing in her heart. Back at Thrift Farm, she had been taught not to value earthly possessions. She felt ashamed that her instinct was to snatch the quilt top from her mother's arms, race off to the attic, and stash it away in some secret place.

She tried to think only of Constance Wright's happiness as the cake baked and she and her mother packed a basket with jars of preserves, a new ball of butter, and other things Mrs. Wright might need. As Dorothea's father helped them into the wagon, her mother told her that, as the maker, she ought to be the one to present the quilt to the bride.

"What quilt?" said Uncle Jacob as he shook the reins to get the horses underway. When Dorothea's mother explained about the gift, Uncle Jacob said, "Whose idea was this?"

"I suppose it was my idea," said Lorena. "But it is Dorothea's generosity that makes it possible."

Uncle Jacob shook his head. "Lorena, let the girl keep her quilt. Look at her. She's holding it so tight she might squeeze it in two. Mrs. Wright doesn't expect any fool wedding present from people she doesn't even know."

"It's fine, Uncle," said Dorothea. "I can make another."

"It took you all winter to make that one."

Longer, actually, Dorothea was tempted to reply, but instead she said, "It's just as well. I will need something to keep myself occupied in the evenings, since I will no longer have lessons to prepare."

Uncle Jacob snorted. "If you need something to do, I will find work for you."

Dorothea glanced at her mother, who shot her a look of warning. "Thank you, Uncle," she said. "Anything to be useful."

He peered over his shoulder at her, perhaps sensing something less than sincere in her tone, but she looked away, gazing at the passing scenery as if she had not seen those hills and trees a hundred times before.

They followed the road south for a mile, past lakes and marshland until they reached the ford over Elm Creek. They climbed down from the wagon as they crossed the waterway on the ferry, Uncle Jacob and Dorothea's father holding tightly to the reins of the horses. Dorothea withdrew to the railing and watched the town on the distant riverbank. At the ford, the creek was merely an eighth of a mile across, the waters calm unless a storm stirred them. Among the young men of the valley, it was considered a test of courage to swim across Elm Creek three miles upstream at a point called Widow's Pining, where it was nearly twice as wide and far more treacherous, with dangerous currents, sharp rocks, and unexpected undertows. Dorothea considered it a test of great foolishness. It was difficult enough for someone who knew Elm Creek well to manage a boat that far east of the ford, much less swim.

She and her brother had discovered that for themselves not long after the waters had claimed Thrift Farm. It had been Dorothea's idea to take the rowboat to see if they could find the place where their house had once stood. They thought they spied the foundation through the cloudy waters, but the swift current overturned their boat. They clung to it as they were swept downstream, and only providence in the form of a log that snagged the boat before they lost their grasp spared their lives. Uncle Jacob had wanted to switch them when they returned home, exhausted, cold, and bedraggled, but their mother had intervened. She said they had learned their lesson and that the river had already beaten them harder than any man could. Lorena was right. Jonathan had feared the water ever since that day, and he would only wade in the creek up to his ankles. If obliged to cross on the ferry, he lay down in the back of the wagon, feigning lazy indifference as he fixed his gaze on the sky rather than look at the water, clinging to a book or his hat with white-knuckled hands.

Dorothea, who had not acquired his wariness, never shamed her brother by trying to cajole him out of his fears. She had decided, after their adventure was over, that the river had twice endangered them and had twice left them unscathed. If Elm Creek intended to claim their lives, it would have done so already. Knowing her conclusion was irrational, she confided it to no one, but wished her brother shared her quiet certainty that the creek would not harm them.

The ferry reached the opposite bank, and before long the travelers were back on dry land aboard the wagon. Dorothea hoped Uncle Jacob would drive through town on the chance she might encounter some of her friends, but as she expected he took the longer route south past the wood and limestone buildings, then turned west to rejoin the road along Elm Creek. Uncle Jacob usually preferred direct routes, but he would go out of his way to avoid unwanted conversation.

Not far south of town, Elm Creek diverted from the roadside as it curved around an oxbow to the west, and the road continued past several well-tended farms. Dorothea knew the families—the Shropshires, the Craigmiles—and waved to acquaintances as they rode past. The third and largest farm was Two Bears Farm, which until recently Dorothea had always thought of as the Carter farm. She recalled the two youngest children, girls she had taught at the Creek's Crossing school, and wondered how the family had received the news that they were to be evicted. It was not uncommon for an eastern family to own land in the region and to allow others to live upon it in exchange for improving the land and raising crops, but in the Elm Creek Valley, most tenants eventually bought out their distant landlords. The Carters probably had assumed they would one day, too. Perhaps, with that possibility in mind, they had saved enough money to give them a good start somewhere else. Dorothea hoped so.

She saw several figures working in the fields with horse and plow, but did not wave in case Mr. Nelson was among them. Far likelier he was sitting inside an oak-paneled study in the white house on the hill, reading a book or writing a letter home, begging to be released from his exile to the hinterlands.

"Mr. Nelson has one hundred sixty acres," remarked Lorena. "He does not look to have even half of them harvested yet. Does he expect the oats and rye to wait until he has time to attend to them?"

"He started late," said Uncle Jacob. "A better question would be why the Carters did not finish the harvest before he arrived. *If* one felt obliged to ask such questions, and stick his nose into his neighbors' business."

Lorena said no more, but Dorothea wondered. Perhaps the Carters had known or suspected that they would soon be evicted and decided not to complete the harvest any more swiftly than necessary. She could not blame them for begrudging Mr. Nelson the benefit of their labor under such circumstances. At any rate, Mr. Nelson would not have to complete the work himself, or even share in it. According to Mary, who lived in town and heard every rumor, he had advertised in the *Creek's Crossing Informer* looking for hired hands. Many had responded, some from as far east as Grangerville, the town of Dorothea's birth, the town founded by her grandparents.

They passed the well-tended fields of Two Bears Farm and approached a thickening forest, where a rough dirt road barely wide enough for a wagon disappeared into the trees. Dorothea had never had occasion to venture down it, but she knew it led to the small clearing Mr. Liggett called Elm Creek Farm. She and Jonathan had explored his land as children—uninvited—as they followed the creek through the valley and discovered the places where local legend claimed the waters were narrow enough to be crossed by a bridge. When Dorothea asked her parents why the region's first residents had not built a bridge there instead of the ferry north of town, her mother had suggested that perhaps no one had known of the easier crossing because of the thick trees, or that perhaps once the narrows had been discovered, the owners of the ferry and the town founders had not wanted another ford built lest they lose the prestige and commerce their passage over the waters brought. Dorothea's father had chuckled and remarked that it was fortunate the narrower places had not been discovered earlier, or Creek's Crossing would have been built on Elm Creek Farm, and Mr. Liggett would own most of the town. Then both parents warned the children to avoid Mr. Liggett and his land, because he was reputed to be a drunkard and violent.

Dorothea and Jonathan would have stayed away, except the creek was so pleasant there, and it would have been a shame to waste so many wild blueberries on the birds, especially since they were the sweetest either child had ever tasted and Mr. Liggett apparently never picked them. It was not only the blueberries he ignored. He had built only one bridge that the Granger children could find, and they had never seen more than a tiny patch of tilled land and one rough log cabin on his forty acres.

Uncle Jacob despised drunkenness, and he held little regard for Mr. Liggett after learning that soon after buying his land, Mr. Liggett felled and burned a half-acre of maple to plant corn. A half-acre of corn would be barely enough to support one man and his livestock, so Mr. Liggett would find no profit in it. In Uncle Jacob's opinion, Mr. Liggett should have cut an acre or two of oak instead, sold the wood to the new lumber mill in Grangerville, and saved the maple from the flames. More recently he had embarked upon a harebrained scheme to raise racehorses—racehorses, when draft animals and the occasional fancy mare to pull a lady's carriage were all anyone ever saw need for in the Elm Creek Valley. Uncle Jacob could not abide the man.

As only infrequently happened, Dorothea's parents shared his opinion, though for Mr. Liggett's poor moral character rather than his questionable business acumen. Seven years earlier, when Thrift Farm still stood above water, Mr. Liggett had secretly purchased a slave woman in Virginia and set her to work in his fields and his grim little cabin. After too many drunken confidences in the tavern, his secret became widely known, and a committee of citizens of the Elm Creek Valley, led by the residents of Thrift Farm, called the law upon him. They demanded that he release the woman, since by law, once in the North, she was immediately free. Mr. Liggett then insisted that the unfortunate woman was not his prisoner but his bride, a claim that outraged an entirely different segment of the local citizenry and one that the woman vehemently denied.

With the entire valley against him, Mr. Liggett had no choice but to acquiesce. When the sheriff visited to be sure he had complied, the woman was gone. Mr. Liggett claimed to have freed her, but months later other rumors surfaced: He had not, in fact, given her the necessary papers, fifty dollars, and passage to Canada as he had claimed, but had taken her south and sold her. Outraged, Abel Wright and others sent word to an organization for freedmen in the city to which Mr. Liggett said she had gone, but as best they could determine, she never arrived.

This alone was not sufficient evidence to convict Mr. Liggett of any crime, and the local law enforcement seemed reluctant to pursue the matter after so much time had passed. Still, it was enough to condemn him in the opinion of many residents of Creek's Crossing. Isolated and shunned, he became even more of a recluse than Uncle Jacob, which was perhaps why Mr. Liggett had thought he spied a kindred spirit in him and had persisted in the misunderstanding that they were friends. Dorothea surmised that recent events had disabused him of that notion.

Not long after they passed the road to Elm Creek Farm, Dorothea heard horse's hooves on the road behind them. Uncle Jacob stiffened, but he did not turn. Expecting to find Mr. Liggett, Dorothea peered over her shoulder to see who followed them and was surprised to discover Cyrus Pearson urging his horse into a trot.

As he caught up to them, Cyrus slowed to match their pace. He greeted Uncle Jacob and Dorothea's parents before turning his smile to Dorothea alone. "Good morning, Miss Granger," he said. "It's a pleasant day for an outing in the countryside, wouldn't you agree?"

"We are farmers," said Uncle Jacob without looking at him. "We don't take outings in the countryside. We live in it."

"Quite right, sir," said Cyrus genially. He glanced at Dorothea; she gave him an apologetic shrug. "Those of us who live in town are not so fortunate."

Uncle Jacob snorted, but before he could say anything more, Dorothea quickly asked, "What brings you this way, Cyrus? Surely you didn't come so far just to bid us good morning."

"I wish I could flatter you by saying I had, but as you surmised, I am out on a matter of business."

His gaze shifted away from hers before he finished speaking, which told her he did not wish to elaborate. At once she suspected he had been to see Mr. Nelson, as his stepfather was on the school board.

"We're on our way to the Wright farm," she told him, ignoring the urge to press him about the visit. She did wish to know what Mr. Nelson had thought of her pupils, but suspected he was unlikely to have said anything favorable about them or Dorothea's teaching.

His eyebrows rose. "Are you?"

"There's plenty of work if you want to help," said Uncle Jacob.

"I wish I could, but I'm afraid I have obligations elsewhere." Cyrus returned his attention to Dorothea. "I see you are too busy for me at the moment. I had hoped to speak with you about the upcoming benefit for the library."

"I was not aware of any benefit," said Lorena. "You're welcome to call on us at home to discuss it. I'm sure we would all be glad to assist such a worthy cause."

Dorothea's father glanced dubiously at Uncle Jacob, who hunched his shoulders but otherwise ignored them. Since he voiced no objection aloud, Dorothea said, "Please do call on us."

"Is Sunday too soon?"

"Not at all," said Lorena, and it was quickly agreed that Cyrus would come out the next Sunday afternoon. Then he bade them good-bye, turned his horse around, and headed back toward Creek's Crossing.

Shaking his head, Dorothea's father murmured something to Lorena, who let out a laugh and murmured something back. "What are you whispering about?" said Dorothea, amused.

Lorena shrugged. "We were merely agreeing that it is good to see a young man so committed to improving our city's access to fine literature."

"I quite agree," said Dorothea. "And naturally, as the former schoolteacher, I ought to be involved."

"I wonder if the new schoolmaster will want to be involved as well," said Robert.

Dorothea frowned. "Surely Cyrus would know better than to invite us both after—" She broke off when she realized her father was teasing her. "I for one would welcome Mr. Nelson's advice. No doubt he has seen the country's finest libraries and would be delighted to tell us exactly how and to what degree our plans fall short."

Not long after that, the Wright farm came into view. From a distance Dorothea spied Mr. Wright already at work in the fields; closer to the house, a tall woman in a head scarf worked in the kitchen garden. A dog barked, another answered, and suddenly the pair burst from a nearby field and raced down the road to the wagon. The dogs escorted them to the house, tails wagging in a frenzy of welcome.

Mr. Wright greeted them outside the barn with a courteous nod and handshake for Uncle Jacob and warmer smiles for Dorothea's parents. Constance Wright hung back, unsmiling, even as Mr. Wright proudly introduced her to the visitors. When he spoke Dorothea's name, Constance's gaze fixed on hers in a silent, bold challenge, and Dorothea looked away first. She had not expected Mrs. Wright to be a girl close to her own age, as Mr. Wright was nearly as old as her parents. Nor had she expected such a cold welcome.

"Congratulations on your marriage," said Lorena, clasping one of Constance's hands in hers. "And on your emancipation."

Constance allowed a small nod. "Thank you."

"We hope you'll not think us too forward, but we hoped you would indulge us in a belated wedding celebration. We brought a cake, if that will tempt you to say yes."

Lorena handed over the covered cake plate, which Constance accepted with some surprise. "We jumped the broom two years ago," she said, peeking under the cover. "Seems a little late to celebrate."

"Does that mean you don't want the cake?" teased Lorena, reaching for it.

At this, Constance gave a tentative smile. "I didn't say that," she said, holding it out of reach. "I suppose a little party won't hurt none."

"Our daughter has a gift for the bride," said Robert. "Dorothea?"

With a start, Dorothea remembered and returned to the wagon for the quilt. Constance wiped her hands carefully on her apron before accepting the bundle, then slowly unwrapped the muslin dust cover. She said not a word as she held it up, arms outstretched, face expressionless.

"My," said Mr. Wright. "That sure is a pretty quilt."

"It's a new style fashionable in Baltimore, or so my brother tells me," said Dorothea as Constance studied the quilt, and, in an echo of her mother, added, "You can quilt it if you like, or leave it as it is for a summer quilt."

"Thank you." Constance carefully folded the quilt top and wrapped the muslin around it. "I'll quilt it and keep it nice for company."

It was soon agreed that Dorothea would assist Constance in the garden while Lorena prepared a meal and the men worked in the fields. "We'll take these inside first," said Lorena, indicating the cake and baskets of food, still in the wagon.

"This should go in, too," said Constance, handing the quilt to Dorothea as the men left for the fields. Caught off guard, Dorothea almost dropped it. Without another word for her guests, Constance headed for the garden.

"I rather hoped she would show us where she would like us to put things," murmured Lorena as they carried the baskets and bundles inside.

Dorothea had rather hoped she would have shown a trifle more appreciation for her quilt top. "Where shall I put this?" she asked as they entered the house. It was small and tidy. Mr. Wright had managed well for a bachelor, but as far as Dorothea could discern, Constance had made few changes since her arrival. A vase of flowers stood on a corner shelf in the house's front room, but Mr. Wright could have arranged the decoration for his bride. A sewing basket sat on the floor beside a chair loaded with a pile of clothes, likely for mending.

"Leave it in the bedroom, I suppose."

As her mother went to the kitchen, Dorothea found the bedroom but lingered in the doorway, studying the quilt already spread upon the bed. It was an unusual string-pieced star pattern, one Dorothea had never seen before, probably stitched from the leftover scraps or even remnants of older quilts.

"Dorothea?" Lorena joined her in the doorway and spotted the quilt that had captured Dorothea's attention. "Perhaps you should place the appliqué sampler over it."

"Why?" The fabric in the quilt did not appear to be new, but the colors had held fast, the stitches were small and even, and the binding was not worn. Perhaps the quilt had been made more recently than it appeared. "I think it's rather striking."

"Yes, but it is not quite the thing for a bridal chamber."

Dorothea thought of the elaborately pieced, appliquéd, and stuffed creations some of her friends had made as their own nuptials approached—beautiful, decorative, and often too fine for daily use. Her best friend and her husband, married only seven months, had last slept beneath their quilt on their wedding night, although Mary was considering releasing it from the hope chest for their first anniversary. In comparison, Abel Wright's quilt was less lovely and impressive, but far more comfortable and enduring. She wondered how he had come to own it. He did not piece quilts himself, as far as she knew.

"Perhaps it is not a proper bridal quilt," said Dorothea. "But it is a perfect marriage quilt."

"I suppose so." Dorothea's mother put her arm around her daughter's shoulders as she regarded Abel Wright's quilt. "A summer quilt is not enough for these cool autumn evenings, anyway. Since Mr. Wright is not a quilter himself, he is not likely to have anything more suitable, and Constance was unlikely to bring a wedding quilt with her, much less the thirteen pieced tops required of a bride of fashion in this county. It is a pity we no longer have yours. All those tops would have made a fine wedding gift, quilted or not."

"They would have, indeed," said Dorothea, managing a tight smile. "The appliqué sampler top will have to do."

She saw no reason to tell her mother she never would have agreed to give away all her quilt tops. Why confess her selfishness when such a sacrifice was impossible, as the seven quilt tops she had pieced, appliquéd, and tucked away in her hope chest had been lost in the flood that had taken their farm? Dorothea had intended to re-create them and complete the thirteen that, according to local custom, would have shown she was properly trained and prepared for marriage. Lorena had her own ideas of proper training, however, and with so many more important items to replace, a new hope chest remained a luxury they could not afford. With home, land, and livestock lost, thirteen unquilted tops for Dorothea's own use in some distant and uncertain future were a secondary, even frivolous concern. What no one in the family had yet admitted aloud was that Dorothea, with no wealth of her own, was unlikely to need even one wedding quilt.

Her throat constricting, she set the muslin-wrapped bundle on a pine bureau. "I should help Constance in the garden," she said, and left the house.

Constance did not look up as Dorothea approached, nor did she respond when Dorothea asked where Constance would prefer for her to begin. "I suppose I'll start over here, then," said Dorothea brightly. Constance made a noise of assent, so she set herself to work. On her hands and knees, she dug onions, brushed the dirt from them, and stacked them in the grass beside the garden.

After a few minutes of silence, Dorothea said, "How was your journey north?"

"You can see for yourself we made it safe."

"Have you had an opportunity to go into Creek's Crossing? It's not a large town, but it has some fine shops and friendly people."

"I saw enough."

"We also have a lending library, although it's not much at the moment—two dozen books on a shelf in the post office. As long as I've lived in Creek's Crossing, there have been plans to enlarge the collection, and possibly even build a room onto the school to hold it. Perhaps now it will finally happen. I understand a benefit is being organized."

"I don't care about no library. I don't read."

"Oh. I see." Dorothea hesitated. "I could teach you. I used to be a school-teacher—only for six months, but—"

"Maybe you don't understand." Constance stuck her trowel into the ground. "I don't need your charity. Not your teaching, not your help in the garden, not your mama's food, not your fancy quilt. You're here because my husband invited your people. I don't want to be your friend."

"I see." Dorothea sat back on her heels, brushed the dirt from her palms, and shaded her eyes with her hand as she looked up at Constance. "I suppose we needn't fear that happening."

Constance frowned before taking up her trowel again. "There are plenty of colored families around here. I don't see why we need to ask white people for help."

"My uncle and your husband have been exchanging work for years. It's the neighborly thing to do."

Constance barked out a laugh. "You aren't our neighbors. Abel says you live clear on the other side of Creek's Crossing." She chopped at a weed, hard. "I met our neighbor, and he ain't nobody I want to speak to again."

"Whom did you meet? Was it a thin man, loud and unkempt?" Constance's silence confirmed Dorothea's guess. "I know that man, and I can tell you he is a drunkard and a fool. It is uncharitable to say so, but it's the truth. Whatever he said or did, you must not assume all people in Creek's Crossing are like him."

Constance worked on as if Dorothea had not spoken.

"I'm afraid you're wrong about something else, too. There are not plenty of colored families in Creek's Crossing. There are only a handful in the entire Elm Creek Valley, and none of those nearby. I'm afraid you'll have to settle for some white friends unless you're determined to be stubborn and lonely."

Cross, Dorothea pushed herself to her feet, took up the spade, and began overturning earth along the edge of the garden. At first Constance ignored her, but before long, she stopped working to watch.

"What are you doing?"

"I'm adding another row to your garden."

"I can see that. Why? We won't be planting until spring."

"Because every spring for the past three years, my mother has traded some of her seedlings for some of your husband's cheese. Last year it was pumpkins. This year I believe it will be sweet potatoes."

"I didn't know about no sweet potatoes."

Dorothea was tempted to retort that there seemed to be a good deal that Constance did not know, but instead she said, "If I overturn the earth and mix in some manure with the grasses, in the spring, the soil will be richer for my efforts."

Constance watched her work for a while, then picked up the hoe and began to help. When the new row was nearly complete, Dorothea left Constance to finish and went to the barn for a wheelbarrow half-full with manure.

Facing each other on opposite sides of the new row, they mixed the manure into the freshly overturned earth.

"A man came to the farm my second night here, so drunk he could barely sit his horse," said Constance eventually. "He had a torch and said he was going to set fire to the barn, and if we didn't clear off after that warning, he'd set fire to the house. He slid off his horse and made like he was going to fling that torch into the hayloft, but all he did was scare his horse so it lit off down the road the way he came. He stumbled around and swore, all red in the face, and went into the barn saying we owed him one of our horses for the one that ran away. When he came out with a horse but left the torch behind, Abel ran to the door, but I wouldn't let him leave the house. So Abel set the dogs on the man. They just nipped him a bit to make him let go the horse. They chased him away and came right back to the house once he was off our land, but from the way he was screaming, you'd have thought they'd taken his legs off. Abel and I both ran out to the barn, but the torch had just fell on a bare spot of ground. But not two feet away was a bale of hay. If he'd dropped the torch there instead—" Constance shrugged, studiously overturning soil. "I guess Abel would have asked you all to come help with a barn raising today instead of harvesting."

"You must have been terrified."

"The man didn't have no gun. It could have been worse." Constance looked away, her eyes sweeping from the barn to the place where the road from Abel's barn met the main road. "He stood right there hollering that he'll be back with friends to finish the job."

"He wouldn't dare. You must inform the authorities at once."

"Why? They wouldn't do nothing. They can't lock up every drunk who swears at colored folks, not even here in the North."

"He did much more than swear at you."

"I'm not afraid of him." Constance stuck her hoe firmly into the ground. "If he comes back, Abel's going to shoot him."

Dorothea felt a sickening shiver of dread. "If he should kill him—"

"Then he's as good as dead himself. I know. You white folks don't take kindly to having a colored man kill a white man, even a white man you don't like."

"Constance—" Dorothea did not know what to say. "If you go to the authorities, they will warn Mr. Liggett to leave you alone."

"Liggett. So that's his name." Constance nodded, satisfied. "Abel wouldn't tell me. I figured he didn't want me to find out how close he lives. He lives close?"

Dorothea nodded reluctantly. "His farm lies no more than a mile away, in the direction of town."

"Too close." Constance gazed off to the northeast, to the thick mass of elms and oaks that hid Elm Creek from view.

"It may be some small consolation to know that one part of his threat rings hollow," said Dorothea. "Mr. Liggett does not have any friends, so if he does return, there will be no one to help him, as he put it, finish the job."

"I guess that's something." Constance took up the hoe again and resumed her work. "I knew we'd have trouble with white folks up here. Abel didn't tell me what it would be like, but I knew."

"But you came anyway."

"Of course. What choice did we have? He couldn't live with me on the plantation, him being free and me not. He wouldn't have wanted to leave this farm anyhow, nor all his goats." She snorted and shook her head, but she could not conceal a smile, or the affection in her voice. "He could have saved himself a lot of work and trouble by marrying some free girl up here instead of me."

"But he chose you."

"Lord knows why. Maybe he knew I'd say yes if he promised to buy my freedom."

Dorothea regarded her with surprise. "Is that how it happened?"

"No, no. He always said he'd get me free, even before he ever said he loved me. I just thought he was the crazy cheese man, trying to fill my head with notions just like folks had warned me he would." Constance stuck the hoe into the earth again and rested her chin upon it. "Every few months he would come by with that wagon selling his cheese. My master's wife loved it and always bought some. Of course I noticed Abel, being as he was the only free colored man I had ever seen, but I didn't know he had taken any notice of me until one day he gave me a big wheel of cheese and said he had brought it all the way from Pennsylvania especially for me."

Dorothea smiled. "He wooed you with cheese."

Constance grinned and nodded. "He brought me other presents, too. I liked his stories about the North best, about how he could go where he wanted, when he wanted. About how he had his own house and farm and didn't answer to no one. Then he started talking about me running away—" Abruptly Constance fell silent.

"Running away, or running away with him?" prompted Dorothea.

Constance shrugged. "Both, I reckon. I wouldn't do it, though. I didn't know him all that well, for all his stories and gifts." She looked abashed. "I was too scared."

"You had every reason to be."

"I don't know about that. Others have done it. Abel thought I didn't want to go because it wasn't proper, us not being married." Constance shook her head. "That wasn't it at all, and I told him so. Once we jumped the broom and I still wouldn't run off, well, then he believed me."

"You must have been so lonely when he left."

She considered. "I was, but I always knew he would come back for me. The mistress liked me and she liked Abel, so she thought it was real sweet. My master hated us being married, though. He only had ten slaves and didn't want any of us to think about being free."

"How could he expect you not to think about it?"

Constance shrugged. "Lord knows. My master was real sorry he ever said we could get married, so when Abel finally understood that I wasn't going to run away, he asked about buying my freedom. He told Abel to pay two thousand dollars."

"Two thousand?" Dorothea echoed, aghast. It was an enormous sum and yet shamefully little for a human life. "How did he expect Abel to raise so much?"

"Well, he didn't. We figured he expected Abel to tire of visiting me only now and again and either leave me, and stop being a nuisance, or settle down there. My master thought he would get another slave out of the bargain, but he didn't know my Abel. Or his own wife. She made him lower the fee to one thousand, and a few months later, Abel paid it."

Dorothea smiled. "And here you are."

"And here I am." Constance waved a hand toward the house, the barn, the fields, the goat pens, shaking her head in disbelief. "Never thought I'd be working in my own garden on my own piece of land. Abel's a good man, too. I don't suppose I'll ever know why he fell in love with me, but I thank the good Lord he did."

"He must love you a great deal to have fought for you so determinedly."

"Most days I think so." Constance grinned. "Some days I think he just didn't want to lose to my master. Abel's quiet, but he's like an old dog that's got hold of a bone. Try to take it from him, and you might never hear him growl before he bites you." She glanced toward Mr. Liggett's farm. "Some folks around here haven't yet learned that, but they will."

Dorothea, too, looked off to the northeast in silence. She could not imagine what had possessed Mr. Liggett to try to frighten off the Wrights. She hoped it was nothing more than the drunken notions of a lazy man who would abandon his hateful promises once he sobered up.

Just then Dorothea's mother emerged from the house and called them to dinner. Dorothea and Constance gathered their tools and returned them to the barn before going to summon the men.

As they strode out into the fields, Constance said, "I still don't need no reading lessons."

"And no friends, either, I assume."

Constance gave her a sidelong look. "I guess I don't mind that part so much. I don't need no reading lessons because Abel is teaching me."

"That's good. Where reading lessons are concerned, I'm sure a devoted husband would be more agreeable company than an old schoolteacher."

"And I already have a wedding quilt."

Dorothea thought of the string-pieced star quilt in the bedroom. "I know. I saw it."

"It ain't as fancy as yours, but I'm sure I can sew as fine a seam as you." Constance kept her eyes fixed on the men in the fields as they walked. "I saved scraps from what the mistress threw out ever since I was a little girl, ever since I was old enough to understand that every nice thing on that place belonged to the white family and not me, and that none of those pretty things could ever be mine. I saved all those scraps and kept them clean, and when Abel asked me to be his wife I started the quilt. I gave it to him when he came to bring me home. He said it was the prettiest patchwork ever made, and until today I'm sure he truly thought it was."

Dorothea was ashamed. "I'm sorry. I had no intention of insulting you with my gift. If I had known—"

"I know. Now I know. And that's why I suppose I'll keep it." Suddenly Constance grinned at her. "I'm not contrary or foolish enough to give it back. I did say I like pretty things."

❧❧

After dinner, the Grangers and the Wrights worked on until nearly dusk, when they hastily ate a cold supper so the Grangers could leave while there was still enough light to travel by. On the return journey, Uncle Jacob did not circumvent the town of Creek's Crossing but passed along its main streets, knowing they would be quiet at that hour. Dorothea looked for, but neither saw nor expected to see, any of her friends. She did glimpse a slender man in spectacles—who might have been Mr. Nelson—entering a tavern, but she could have been mistaken.

They were the only travelers on the ferry, so Dorothea stretched out in the back of the wagon, determined to rest as long as she could until Uncle Jacob ordered her to sit up and act like a lady. She watched the stars appear in the darkening sky, and the next thing she knew, the wagon jerked as the horses pulled the wagon from the ferry to the landing. She sat up properly again, returned a smile from her mother, and absently picked dried mud from the hem of her skirts.

"Niece," said Uncle Jacob suddenly. "If you truly need work to occupy your idle hands, and since you are so inclined to give away your quilts, maybe you would make one for me."

Dorothea and her mother exchanged a look of surprise. "Of course," said Dorothea. "Did you have a certain pattern in mind?"

She expected him to say no, since few men admitted to being able to distinguish one quilt pattern from another, but instead he nodded. "A scrap quilt like one my mother once made," he said. "I will draw it for you. And I will need it by winter."

Chapter Three

The next evening after the chores were done, Dorothea was making the most of the fading daylight by reading the last chapter of a borrowed book when Uncle Jacob interrupted to show her a sketch of a block he wanted in his quilt. Dorothea had not thought he would expect her to begin the quilt so soon, but she hid her reluctance and set the book aside. He lit the lamp and gestured with his pen as he explained the various features of his small, neat drawing.

"It resembles the Delectable Mountains pattern," remarked Dorothea, studying the arrangement of large right triangles set at right angles to each other, with smaller right triangles lining their shorter sides. Uncle Jacob nodded brusquely, frowned at the interruption, and directed her to make the blocks exactly as he had drawn them, with clear and distinct points.

Dorothea declined to assure him that she was not known for sloppy piecing. "I assume you mean for me to fill in these blank places with light-colored fabric?" she inquired, indicating a diagonal row of squares from the upper left corner to the center of the quilt. In an ordinary Delectable Mountains quilt, those squares would have been part of larger triangles of background fabric.

"Do no more and no less than you are told," said Uncle Jacob. "I'll need more time to sketch those squares. Make the part of the quilt I have drawn first and do the rest later."

Delicately, because her uncle had clearly given his design a great deal of thought, she said, "It will be difficult to assemble the rest of the quilt with these important blocks missing, especially the center. Perhaps I should wait until you have completed your drawing."

"I've watched you sew," her uncle retorted. "I've seen how long it takes you to stitch two little triangles together. If you wait until my drawing is done, you'll never finish the quilt in time."

Dorothea managed to keep from sighing. "Very well," she said. "What colors would you like?"

"Serviceable colors. Whatever scraps you have in your sewing basket will be fine."

"You have said nothing about how large you would like your quilt to be."

"The usual size will do."

Abruptly as that, he departed for the barn, calling over his shoulder for Dorothea's father. Dorothea watched the men go, mystified. A quiltmaker would never spend so much time on the design for a quilt only to dismiss qualities as important as color and size. Of course, Uncle Jacob was no quilt-maker, despite the care he had lavished on his drawing, or he would have known it was no simple matter to leave empty spaces in a quilt top to fill in later. Perhaps he did know, but did not mind the extra work and difficulty it created, since he was not the one to sew it.

Since her uncle had neglected to douse the lamp, Dorothea got to work, beginning by calculating how large one Delectable Mountains block should be in order to make a finished quilt suitable for Uncle Jacob's bed. Then she made templates out of stiff paper, trimming the edges carefully, since even an error the width of a pencil mark, when multiplied over the many pieces that made up a quilt top, could alter a quilt's size considerably.

"I hardly know what colors to select for such a quilt," said Dorothea to her mother as she set the completed templates aside.

"I believe some bright pinks and blues and cheerful butter yellows will suit your uncle nicely," advised Lorena, looking up from her darning to grin at her daughter.

Dorothea laughed and opened the scrap bag. She searched through the pieces of cloth and retrieved scraps of brown, tan, Turkey red, and somber blue, as well as lighter shirting fabrics for the background; Uncle Jacob typi-cally wore such colors, so she supposed they could be considered his favor-ites. The fabrics were serviceable, just as he had requested, since they were the leftover scraps from the household sewing.

Every evening thereafter Dorothea took up her needle and triangu-lar scraps and worked on the quilt. If she happened to take up mending instead, she felt the weight of her uncle's disapproving glare until she switched to his quilt. She forced herself to think of it as a gift, since the task was more tolerable if she pretended he had not all but commanded her to make it.

Within three days she had completed two blocks and Uncle Jacob had brought her another sketch, a lopsided, four-pointed star. One point was longer than the others, reaching from the center of the star all the way to the upper left corner. Uncle Jacob asked for the original drawing and indicated that the new block was to be inserted in the very center of the quilt. When she asked if the other blank spaces in the design were to be filled with similar stars, he said, "You have plenty of work to do now without worrying about the work that will come later."

"It would be easier—and faster—to make your quilt if I knew the entire design," she told him.

"You've made more difficult quilts than this one," he said shortly. "But if you can't manage on your own, get your mother to help you."

It was her uncle's cooperation, not her mother's help, that Dorothea needed, but of course she could not say so. After he left, Dorothea studied both drawings and realized that her uncle's design was not as well crafted as she had first thought. While the lines were straight and precise, she detected some accidental variation among the Delectable Mountains blocks. Most of the larger triangles had four smaller triangles along each side, but a very few had only three, and some five. Dorothea was tempted to point out his error to him, since he took so much grim pleasure in finding the faults of others, but such impertinence would alarm her parents, who were sure that one single offense would be enough to compel Uncle Jacob to strike the Grangers from his will. Instead Dorothea decided to spare his pride and correct his mistake without drawing attention to it.

Sunday came, bringing with it the promised diversion of Cyrus Pearson's visit. He arrived promptly at two, and at the sound of his horse's hooves on the road, Uncle Jacob broke his customary rule about keeping the Sabbath as a day of rest and made excuses about harnesses that needed mending. He withdrew to the barn, but it was Dorothea's father who met Cyrus and helped him tend to his horse.

Dorothea and Lorena sewed in the parlor while they waited for Dorothea's father to bring in Cyrus. When she heard their boots on the floor, Dorothea wondered fleetingly what Cyrus would think of Uncle Jacob's austere furnishings compared to the grandeur of his stepfather's home, but when he entered

wearing the same cheerful grin with which he greeted her in brighter surroundings, she forgot her worries.

Lorena invited him to sit, and Dorothea went to the kitchen for tea. "Tell
us, Mr. Pearson," said Lorena as Dorothea poured. "What do you have in
mind for the library?"

"Yes, do tell us we are finally going to expand beyond a single shelf of
books," said Dorothea, taking the chair beside her mother. "I believe I could
recite all sixteen verbatim."

"You needn't boast of your cleverness," said Cyrus, a naughty twinkle in
his eye. "You are famous in Creek's Crossing for your prodigious memory."

"I was not boasting," protested Dorothea. "I merely meant because I have
read them so often, lacking other choices."

"Mr. Pearson, please do not tease my daughter or I shall have to ask you
to leave," said Lorena, smiling. "I would hate to do that, because you've
piqued our curiosity. What is this grand scheme of yours?"

"I cannot take all the credit for it," said Cyrus, accepting the cup Dorothea
handed him. "My mother is the catalyst that motivates me. Her new husband
is so occupied with matters of business that my mother needs other diver-
sions. She insists that a few volumes of poetry and novels would not sustain
her for long, but her new husband has neither the funds nor the space in his
home for the number of books that would suffice. Therefore, expanding the
town library seems the best solution."

"Agreed," said Dorothea. "Unfortunately, the good people of Creek's
Crossing seem far abler at settling upon a solution than implementing
one."

"Dorothea," said her mother, gently chiding. To Cyrus, she added, "Perhaps we could look to local benefactors to donate funds."

"My stepfather has already agreed to a substantial gift," he replied. "More
to appease my mother than out of any literary interest of his own. Other
prominent families have also promised donations, although not enough for a
separate building. In fact, we will need quite a bit more if we are to afford an
addition to the school and new books to fill it."

"It is perhaps too much to hope that one wealthy patron would contribute
enough for an entire building," said Dorothea. "Even for the privilege of having his name over the door."

"Have you asked Mr. Nelson?" Lorena asked Cyrus. "After all, his father
did pay to have the school built."

"Ah." Cyrus allowed a polite cough. "I believe—well, I did approach Thomas Nelson and was rebuffed."

"But he's the schoolmaster," said Dorothea. "He has a decided interest in the establishment of a proper library in Creek's Crossing. Think of the benefit to his pupils."

"I did remind him, but he was unmoved." Cyrus shrugged apologetically and looked almost as embarrassed as he had the night of his mother's party. "I do not think we can rely on his support."

"How disappointing," said Lorena. "When I think of how his father supported intellectual pursuits in the Elm Creek Valley, I confess I am surprised by his son's disinterest."

"We do not need the younger Mr. Nelson's support," said Dorothea determinedly. "Perhaps no one person can afford to donate an entire building, or even an addition to the school, but many could surely donate something a trifle smaller but no less essential. Those who contribute three dollars, for example, could have their names engraved on a plate affixed to a bookshelf."

When Lorena and Cyrus nodded their approval, Dorothea continued. "We could ask those less able to donate the gift of their labor. We will need people to build the addition."

"Of course," said Lorena. "Mr. Pearson, you should consult Mr. Wright. His carpentry skills are unparalleled in the valley and I'm quite certain he would design your addition free of charge. He would be an excellent choice for construction foreman."

"Mr. Wright?" said Cyrus, puzzled. "Do you mean Abel Wright?"

"The same. He's a good friend of ours. Use my name when you call on him and I'm sure he'll agree to help."

Cyrus looked dubious. "I cannot imagine he would be interested." He shrugged, his smile returning. "I think that we should impose only upon members of the community, people who would be likely to use the library."

"The Wright farm is not that far away," said Lorena, regarding Cyrus curiously. "I'm sure the Wrights will use the library as much as anyone else."

Dorothea thought of Constance Wright, how she was only just learning to read, and how she had declared she had seen as much of Creek's Crossing as she cared to see. She wondered if Cyrus had already met Constance or if he was simply more insightful than he appeared.

"These are all excellent ideas," said Cyrus. "I knew you would come through for me, Miss Granger. This is precisely why I told my mother you should be named secretary of fund-raising on the new library board."

"Secretary of fund-raising?" asked Dorothea. Lorena beamed at her.

"Of course. You would be ideal. My mother insisted on assuming that role herself, naturally, but she would very much appreciate your assistance."

"While I would like to help—" Dorothea shook her head, uncertain. "I was not expecting to play such a prominent role. I have my obligations to my uncle—"

"Surely he would release you from your chores occasionally so you might assist in such an important community effort."

"Mr. Pearson," said Lorena dryly, "have you met my brother?"

"I suppose it was too much to expect that you could be spared. I continue to underestimate the amount of work required by every member of a farmer's family, including the ladies." Cyrus looked endearingly disappointed. "I had so hoped you would be able to assist us. Your status as the schoolteacher lends credibility to a cause that has often floundered, and I had looked forward to seeing you more often in town."

"I am only the former schoolteacher," Dorothea reminded him. "Considering how briefly I held that position, I suspect I have little credibility to lend."

"You underestimate the esteem this town holds for you." The familiar mischievous light returned to his green eyes. "And my esteem, too. But very well. If the thought of a well-functioning lending library does not tempt you, if the prospect of escaping the drudgery of farm chores for what I hope you would consider pleasant company does not move you, if my personal appeals to your generous nature do not persuade you—" He rose. "I confess the latter wounds me the most, but—"

"Mr. Pearson," said Dorothea, laughing. "You have persuaded me. I want a library as much as your mother does, and I will assist in the effort as much as I am able."

"I cannot tell you how much this pleases me. My mother would like you to call on her at three o'clock Thursday afternoon for the first meeting of the library board. May I tell her you will be there?"

Dorothea nodded. She would obtain her uncle's approval somehow.

"Perhaps I might also escort you to the meeting?"

"Thank you," said Dorothea, "but I do not believe that will be necessary."

"I think that is a fine idea," said Lorena. "It is possible you will not be able to take our wagon. Your uncle may need the horses."

Dorothea reconsidered. Her mother was wise to anticipate an objection that might prevent her from attending. They agreed that Cyrus would come for her a half-hour before the meeting and bring her home afterward.

Cyrus lingered long enough to finish his tea, but left soon thereafter, citing other necessary errands. Dorothea changed out of her Sunday dress and met her mother in the kitchen garden. That morning at breakfast, Uncle Jacob had announced that he did not want any preening young peacock of a man to interfere with the gathering of the potatoes. Dorothea was determined to show her uncle she could have callers and still complete her chores.

"What are you thinking, Mother?" Dorothea asked when her mother worked a long while in silence.

"I'm thinking that it seems as if the new library may at last become more than a fond wish," she said, brushing clumps of soil from a potato. "I also think it is very fine that you are wanted so badly on the library board. However . . ."

"Yes?" prompted Dorothea.

Her mother hesitated a moment longer before saying, "Nothing. I suppose it is good that Cyrus is so devoted to his mother."

Dorothea laughed. "You would fault him for being attentive to his mother's needs?"

"Only if it means he neglects the needs of others. Of course, there is no reason to assume he will." Lorena smiled ruefully. "I suppose if I did not dislike his mother so, his attentiveness would not bother me in the least."

Dorothea's mirth dimmed. She had not considered that joining the library board would mean more time in the presence of Cyrus's formidable mother.

Dorothea and Lorena hurried, but they did not finish in the garden by the time they needed to begin making supper. Since only the potato rows were left, Lorena suggested they finish in the morning, since Uncle Jacob would likely not notice the neglected garden but would certainly notice a late meal. They washed quickly at the pump and ran to the kitchen, but although they raced through supper preparations, Uncle Jacob still sat at the table a full five minutes before his plate was set before him. They learned soon enough a further reason for his displeasure: As he cut into his bread, he announced that Lorena would return to the garden after her regular chores were through and remain there until the last potato was collected.

Lorena nodded without a word; Dorothea took a drink of water and tried to maintain the appearance of calm. Later, when her mother went to the back door, Dorothea followed.

"Where are you going?" said Uncle Jacob, reading his Bible in the fading daylight.

"To the garden with Mother."

"You have other work to do." He gestured to her sewing basket on the floor behind her usual chair.

"It's my fault we didn't finish the potatoes. I should help her."

"You should attend to your own business." He returned his attention to the page, holding the book close.

"It will be dark before she finishes."

"Dorothea." Lorena shook her head and reached for the lantern hanging on the peg beside the door.

"Leave it," said Uncle Jacob.

"It will take her twice as long in the dark as in the light," said Dorothea.

"Dorothea," said her father. "Mind your uncle."

"It's all right," murmured her mother. "I won't be long."

Lorena threw a shawl over her shoulders and slipped out the door. Simmering with anger, Dorothea stormed across the kitchen to her seat by the fireplace, unlit now though the early autumn evening was cool. She sat, fuming, hands clasped in her lap.

Uncle Jacob closed his Bible and put away his reading glasses. "You ought to get to work on that quilt."

"I ought to be helping my mother," said Dorothea. "Better yet, she ought to come inside. The garden can wait until morning."

"And fall behind on every chore entrusted to her tomorrow?" Uncle Jacob countered. "That is no way to run a farm, niece. I should think your father's failure would have taught you that."

Her father never looked up; Uncle Jacob might have been speaking of a stranger for all he seemed to care. "Thrift Farm was lost to a flood," said Dorothea tightly.

"Thrift Farm was in serious decline long before the waters claimed it. Elm Creek merely put it out of its misery."

"I have the milking," said Dorothea's father suddenly. He touched Dorothea's shoulder in passing and left out the back door, taking the lantern. Dorothea yearned to follow, but she understood her father's unspoken request and grudgingly opened her sewing basket. She sewed the pieces of her quilt block in silence, glancing at the door at the slightest noise for her parents' return. Her father entered first, without the lantern; she guessed where he had left it and, unfortunately, so did Uncle Jacob. He ordered her father to go and fetch it, but Dorothea announced that she would do it and left her sewing behind on her empty chair.

She found her mother on her hands and knees in the potato plot, working by lantern light. Dorothea swiftly knelt to help her.

"You should get back inside," said Lorena. "Your uncle will be furious."

"I don't care."

"You will care well enough if he should see fit to switch you."

At her words Dorothea could almost feel the sting of the hickory branch. "He hasn't switched me since I began wearing corsets and long skirts. I don't believe he will do so now."

Lorena sighed, pulling furiously at the weeds. "The older you get, the more you provoke him."

"Someone ought to stand up to him."

"Dorothea—" Lorena sat back on her heels. "You don't understand."

"I do understand. How long must we endure this? We don't need Uncle Jacob or his farm. We can go out west, to Kansas, to California. We can stake a claim and make our own farm." She was almost in tears. "We can summon Jonathan. He will come. Surely they need doctors in the west."

"That's a very romantic notion, but your brother is only sixteen. We cannot interrupt his training now, and he is unlikely to receive a proper education in unsettled country." Lorena picked up the spade and stabbed at the earth. "Your uncle is right in one respect: Your father and I were very poor farmers. We would have no chance of establishing a farm in unfamiliar climate, on ground that has never felt a plow."

"We have learned a great deal in eight years."

"Not enough to risk our lives when we stand to inherit a well-tended farm right here."

Dorothea knew the argument was useless. She yanked on a fistful of weeds and said, "Uncle Jacob is likely to leave the farm to someone else just to spite us."

"To whom would he leave it? He has no friends and no other relations."

"Then he will probably live forever." Her anger spent, Dorothea listlessly brushed soil from a potato, shadowed and strange in the flickering light. "He sent me to fetch the lantern."

"Then you should take it to him." When Dorothea hesitated, Lorena smiled. "Go ahead. I'm almost finished."

"Very well," said Dorothea, but she stayed with her mother until the last potato was harvested.

❧

Dorothea waited until Thursday morning at breakfast to tell Uncle Jacob she had been specifically requested as the former schoolteacher to assist with the creation of a new library.

"Why don't they ask the new schoolmaster?" asked Uncle Jacob.

"They did. Mr. Nelson refused."

"So once again you are their second choice."

Dorothea refused to be baited. "I suppose I am. Nevertheless, the request is a great honor, and I am obliged to assist them."

Uncle Jacob shook his head. "I cannot spare the horses to take you into town."

"That is your only objection?" asked Lorena, piling more flapjacks on her brother's plate.

"It is." Uncle Jacob waved her away before she buried his plate entirely. "But it is reason enough."

"Then you will be pleased to know Dorothea does not require the horses," said Lorena brightly. "Mr. Pearson has offered to escort her."

Uncle Jacob's jaw tightened. "I see." He knew he had been tricked, but he could not retract his words. "See that you return home promptly afterward. Your chores will be finished before you go to bed if you must stay up all night."

"Thank you, Uncle," said Dorothea, but he spared her only an irritated glare as he pushed back his chair and rose from the table.

"Never mind him," said Lorena as they cleared the table. "I will finish your work as well as my own. You are a young girl and you deserve a pleasant outing."

Riding into Creek's Crossing to attend a board meeting at the home of Mrs. Violet Pearson Engle was hardly Dorothea's idea of a pleasant outing, but she was interested in the library, and Cyrus never failed to be an engaging companion. For all the friendliness between them when they met in town, they did not truly know each other well. They had attended school together only one year, a brief interval immediately following the Granger family's arrival in Creek's Crossing and preceding Cyrus's departure for a boys' academy in Philadelphia. When they were in school together, Cyrus had sat in the back row with the other older boys who thought themselves too old for school, laughing in whispers and genially ignoring the teacher, the sweetly befuddled Miss Gunther. Dorothea did not care for such disrespect and laziness, and she had ignored Cyrus and his friends except when her best friend Mary's lovesick admiration forced her to notice him. While Mary mourned when Cyrus left Creek's Crossing, Dorothea never missed him. To her pleasant surprise, however, when she encountered him during his rare visits home for holidays and summers, it was evident that his time back east and abroad had greatly improved him. He behaved in a far more gentlemanly fashion than he had as a boy, and if he did tend to tease, a manner Mary now derided, Dorothea found it a welcome and refreshing departure from Uncle Jacob's mercurial tempers.

Cyrus arrived, not in a wagon as she had expected, but driving a gleaming black carriage pulled by two lively Morgans. Uncle Jacob glared balefully from the barn door as Cyrus helped her inside, neither bidding them good-bye nor forbidding her to go. "He's not an easy fellow to live with, I presume," Cyrus said as they rode away.

"He has given us a home," said Dorothea, reluctant to appear ungrateful. "But he can be . . . difficult."

Cyrus grinned. "I'm sure you're being kinder than he deserves."

They chatted easily as they rode, and when they crossed on the ferry, Cyrus placed a hand on her elbow to steady her—unnecessarily, for she was quite comfortable on the river—and alternately alarmed and amused her with stories of his boyhood exploits on the riverfront. "It's a wonder your mother survived such a mischievous son," she remarked as they climbed back aboard the carriage and left the ferry.

"It is indeed, but my mother is a wonder herself." Cyrus's grin turned rueful. "I suppose I should be grateful that Mr. Engle recognized that as well."

Dorothea regarded him curiously. "You objected to the marriage?"

"I did not. Mr. Engle is a decent sort, and my mother cares for him. Still . . ." He shrugged. "She did not need to marry again. I was rather surprised she did not realize that."

"Perhaps she did not marry for need, but for love."

Cyrus looked as if the thought had not occurred to him. "I suppose it's possible. I also suppose that if I had been engaged, the promise of my upcoming wedding would have been inducement enough to encourage her to remain unmarried."

Dorothea laughed. "Now you say she married because she longed for the gaiety of a party! Goodness, Cyrus, can you not admit it is possible she loves your stepfather?"

Cyrus frowned thoughtfully at the horses. "When you put it that way, I suppose she must adore him. I feel quite foolish for not noticing before."

"Now you're teasing me."

"Not merely now, Dorothea. I tease you every chance I get."

They had left the older section of town behind and were just about to turn on to the Engles' street when a man seated unsteadily on horseback rounded the corner at a canter. His clothes were dusty as if he had taken a hard fall or two on the road into town, his filthy hat pulled down low over unkempt hair. In the moment it took Cyrus to avoid a collision, Dorothea recognized the rider as Amos Liggett.

His bloodshot eyes widened at the sight of them. "Pearson," he rasped, wheeling his horse around. Tobacco juice dribbled into the dark stubble of his beard. "I was just coming to talk to you."

Cyrus straightened. "To me?"

"Yes, yes. That matter we talked about. I took care of it. I mean, I *will* take care of it. But I need a little money first. Just a bit more, like last time."

Cyrus's brow furrowed, but his voice was polite when he replied, "I'm afraid I don't understand."

The man sawed at the horse's reins. "You remember. At the tavern. You asked me—" Suddenly his eyes narrowed as his gaze shifted to Dorothea. "Say. Ain't you the Granger girl? When's your uncle gonna pay me what he owes?"

At once, Cyrus chirruped to the horses and the carriage pulled away. "Call on me at my office if you have business to discuss," he called over his shoulder as they continued around the corner. To Dorothea, he said, "Please accept my apologies. I never should have paused long enough for him to address you."

"What business would you have with Amos Liggett?" said Dorothea, shaken.

"No business at all. I have no idea what he is talking about. However, sometimes it is expedient to humor men in his condition." He shook his head, frowning. "I don't know what Creek's Crossing is coming to when drunkards can accost young ladies in the street."

Dorothea managed a smile. "I hardly feel as if I had been accosted." She did not care for Mr. Liggett, especially after what he had done to Charley Stokey, but she had to admit he was right: Her uncle ought to pay him something for the days he had worked. She turned around to see what Mr. Liggett would do next, but he was nowhere to be seen. "He seemed convinced you had hired him for some chore."

"Either the liquor has confused him or he has pride enough to disguise the request for a handout. Or . . ."

"Yes?" prompted Dorothea.

"I should not bring it up. I would hate to be accused of spreading tales. But perhaps he has mistaken me for someone else. After all, he could not have been on his way to call on me. He already passed my house."

"Who, then?"

He leaned closer and grinned. "If I tell you, will you think me a vile gossip?"

"If you do not tell me, I will be quite furious with you."

"I could not bear that. Very well. Thomas Nelson."

"Mr. Nelson? Why?"

"Some people claim we bear some resemblance to each other."

Dorothea had to laugh. "I do not see it."

"Really?" Cyrus pretended to be wounded. "But most women of my acquaintance say Mr. Nelson is a handsome man. Do you mean to say I am not?"

"I mean to say nothing on that subject at all. You will not trick me into flattering your vanity."

"And yet you have done so, by revealing it would be flattery." Cyrus stopped the carriage in front of his stepfather's house and smiled wickedly at her. "Perhaps you are not as clever as your reputation would have us believe."

Dorothea opened her mouth to protest and felt heat rise in her cheeks as she realized he was right. His grin broadened at her speechlessness, and he jumped down from the carriage. "I have heard that Mr. Nelson has recently been hiring farmhands," she said as Cyrus assisted her down from the carriage. "But why would he hire a man of Mr. Liggett's reputation?"

Cyrus shrugged and offered her his arm. "A man hires another man to do what he cannot do, or what he will not do. But he usually hires a man of like mind."

Not in Uncle Jacob's case, Dorothea thought. "If you are right, I fear for the pupils of Creek's Crossing."

Cyrus laughed, but Dorothea's misgivings ran deep. Mr. Liggett was bad enough. It was unsettling to think of what a like-minded man in a position of influence and authority might do.

❧

To her disappointment, Cyrus departed shortly after seeing her inside, promising to deliver her home once the meeting concluded. She had assumed he would be on the library board as well.

Five women had already gathered in the parlor, which with its furniture and rugs restored looked much different than it had on the night of Mr. Nelson's welcoming party. Mrs. Engle sat on the overstuffed sofa by the front window with the others seated in pairs on her right and left hand, giving her the air of a queen presiding at court. The others glanced up as Dorothea entered: Mrs. Deakins, the mayor's wife; Mrs. Collins, married to the banker; Miss Nadelfrau, the timid dressmaker; and Mrs. Claverton, who smiled a welcome and beckoned Dorothea to come and sit beside her. Dorothea murmured an apology and seated herself; she had not realized she was late.

"Before you entered, Miss Granger," said Mrs. Engle, "we had just decided that your suggestion about selling nameplates for bookshelves was inspired."

"Thank you," replied Dorothea. Cyrus must have told his mother, for Dorothea had not.

Mrs. Engle smiled graciously. Her glossy black hair was piled in formal curls on top of her head and tied with a white velvet ribbon. Her skin was very fair, and her slight plumpness gave her an appearance of softness despite her sharp green eyes, which were as haughty as her son's were mischievous.

"Still," piped up Miss Nadelfrau, the dressmaker, who was known to be good with figures of all sorts, "it will not be enough."

"So, assistant to the secretary of fund-raising," said Mrs. Claverton, nudging her. "What ideas have you brought us?"

"I think we would be wise to consider a social event," said Dorothea as they watched her expectantly. "Something so splendid no one would dream of missing it."

"And no one would mind spending their money to attend," added Mrs. Claverton.

"I know the very thing," declared Mrs. Engle. "An evening of musical celebration. My cousin is a former soloist with the Philadelphia Opera. I'm sure I could persuade her to donate her services."

The other women murmured their agreement. "That does sound wonderful," agreed Dorothea, thinking of how much her mother would enjoy it. Unfortunately, they had no suitable auditorium large enough to suit a soloist and still accommodate the crowds Dorothea hoped to draw. "But I thought perhaps a celebration with dancing and a covered-dish supper."

Mrs. Collins tittered. "One does not dance to opera."

"I also would not expect my guests to bring covered dishes," said Mrs. Engle. "My cook is capable of a truly remarkable feast."

As the others discussed a possible menu, Dorothea gradually understood. "You mean to hold the event here?"

"Of course." Mrs. Engle waved a plump hand gracefully. "Unless one of you would prefer to offer your home."

Miss Nadelfrau, Mrs. Collins, and Mrs. Deakins hastened to assure Mrs. Engle that no one would prefer their homes to hers, while Mrs. Claverton watched Dorothea with a tolerant smile, waiting to see what she would say.

"As lovely as your home is, Mrs. Engle," said Dorothea, "and it is, truly, the loveliest in Creek's Crossing, it would not accommodate the entire town."

The other women exchanged glances. "You mean to invite everyone?" asked Mrs. Collins.

"Yes," said Dorothea. "After all, it is a fund-raiser. The greater the attendance, the more money we shall raise."

"My dear," said Mrs. Deakins. "We cannot expect common farmers to be interested in a library. It is unkind to take the hard-earned money of people who will never peruse the collection."

"I expect quite the opposite will happen. I am sure many people will make use of the library who were not able to offer a cent at the fund-raiser."

All but Mrs. Claverton, who hid a smile behind her handkerchief, regarded her incredulously. Then a nervous smile flickered on Mrs. Collins's lips. "You must excuse young Miss Granger," she said. "She is an idealist. As a former schoolteacher she has an exceptionally high regard for books and assumes all others feel the same."

"She has a very good point, however," said Mrs. Claverton. "As the wife of a common farmer, I plan to visit the library frequently. Since most of the citizens of Creek's Crossing are farmers, we would be foolish to ignore the potential of their accumulated contributions."

"I suppose it would do no harm to open the event to the whole town," said Miss Nadelfrau. "If they are interested enough in a library and if they can pay the admission charge, I suppose they should be welcome."

"Just as everyone will be welcome at the library," said Dorothea, fervently hoping that she would not have to argue that point, as well. "The more people who are involved in creating the library, the more community support we will have, and the greater our chances for success. Which brings me to my second idea."

The others looked wary. "And what would that be?" asked Mrs. Engle.

"An opportunity quilt."

The others looked so relieved that Dorothea was tempted to ask them what they had expected her to say. "What a charming idea," said Mrs. Engle. "I believe I might have a quilt I could donate."

"I'm sure everyone in the Elm Creek Valley would be thrilled to own a quilt made by your hands," said Mrs. Deakins. "We will sell a thousand tickets, surely!"

Dorothea hid her exasperation. "That is very generous of you, Mrs. Engle, but I believe this occasion calls for something unique. I thought instead we might make a quilt of Album blocks."

Mrs. Claverton and Mrs. Nadelfrau nodded, intrigued, but Mrs. Deakins glanced nervously at Mrs. Engle, who said, "A what? I've never heard of such a thing."

"I'm sure you have," said Mrs. Claverton. "Any variety of patterns might be used, as long as there is a piece of plain muslin at the center, upon which the quilter signs her name, her place of residence, the date, and so forth. A lady might collect a variety of such blocks from the ladies of her circle, then embroider over the ink, sew the blocks together, and quilt a delightful remembrance of her friends."

"Since we are raising funds for a library," said Dorothea, "I thought we might write to our favorite authors and ask them to send us scraps of muslin bearing their signatures. We shall embroider the names and piece the blocks ourselves. Think of the excitement that will grow in town as we announce what illustrious autographs have arrived in the post."

"The social event can be a quilting bee," Mrs. Collins guessed, delighted.

Dorothea nodded. "But we'll make it more than a quilting bee. We will have a dance, a covered-dish supper, and of course, the drawing for the quilt."

"Such a quilt would be quite valuable," mused Mrs. Engle. She glanced upon the sofa, as if imagining the Album quilt draped over the back.

Dorothea cast her final hook. "Quite valuable indeed, especially if we include the autographs of local persons of note, including, of course, the president of the library board and the mayor's wife, if they would condescend to participate."

Mrs. Deakins beamed, and Mrs. Engle smiled indulgently. "Indeed we would. Well, Miss Granger, I must congratulate myself for including you on the library board. You have already been of great service to us."

Dorothea thanked her, but confessed that her motives were completely selfish. She wanted a library and was willing to do almost anything to ensure that one was built as soon as possible.

After some discussion—in which Dorothea repeatedly had to gently remind the others that they could not have the quilting bee within a month and call it a Harvest Dance, charming though the idea was, because they had to allow time for writing to the authors, receiving their replies, and piecing the quilt top—they settled on the end of February. It was a dreary month much in need of brightening with festivity, Mrs. Engle thought, while Dorothea and Mrs. Claverton noted that the weather would be favorable for travel, but not mild enough to interfere with spring planting.

Before they parted, Mrs. Claverton assigned everyone a part of the work of planning the event. Dorothea's task was to compose the letter that would be sent to the authors. Mrs. Engle also instructed each of them to make a list of ten authors who should be contacted. Already Dorothea could think of twice that many, and she was sure her parents would be eager to contribute more names.

On the ride home, she told Cyrus how the meeting had gone and queried him about his favorite authors. "What men and women of letters would you like to see immortalized in our quilt?" she asked. "For whose autograph would you be willing to buy a chance?"

"Shakespeare and Homer."

"That helps me not at all," she scolded him.

"The only person of letters whose autograph I would care to possess is your own. If your name is embroidered on that quilt, I would offer twenty dollars."

"Then you would very likely win the drawing," said Dorothea, trying to hide her astonishment. "Since the chances will likely cost only twenty-five cents."

He shrugged. "If that is what I must do to be assured of winning, then that is what I shall do."

At first, Dorothea could not find the words to reply. She was not certain if he was in earnest, if he only meant to flatter her, if he thought her a silly, giddy girl who would be impressed by such a lavish show. She could not deny being pleased that he would be willing to spend so much money for a quilt with her name on it. "The library board will be very grateful for your contribution," she eventually said, but he merely smiled.

That evening after chores were done, Dorothea drafted a letter to the authors, then set it aside to revise later. She took up the pieces of a quilt block for her uncle's quilt, eager to finish it so that it would not interfere with the Authors' Album once the autographs began to arrive. Lorena worked on her mending on the opposite chair, suggesting writers the library board should contact. "Knowing where to send the letters will be the trick," she mused, threading a needle. "Some writers are reclusive, others are itinerant, and many are both."

Uncle Jacob, mending a boot sole in the light of the fire, snorted. "You could sign the names yourself and no one would know the difference."

"We may resort to that if none of our authors favors us with a reply," said Dorothea seriously, with a wink for her mother.

Uncle Jacob looked up. "If I thought you might engage in such dishonesty—" He peered at the quilt block in her hands. "What's that?"

"This?" Dorothea did not understand. "It's a Delectable Mountains block for your quilt."

"That's not right at all." In two strides Uncle Jacob crossed the room and snatched the quilt block from her hands. Pins scraped her palms. "Why are these triangles pointing this way?" Suddenly he dug into her sewing basket and scattered the completed blocks on the hearth, searching. "All of these squares have four triangles along the side. All of them! Didn't I make a drawing for you? Didn't I tell you to follow it precisely?"

"You did."

"Then why did you deliberately disobey me? Some of the squares were to have three, some five."

"I did not mean to disobey," said Dorothea, astounded by his fury. "I thought those were errors. I meant only to correct—"

"Don't be presumptuous, niece. If I give you a drawing and tell you to reproduce it exactly, it is not your place to add or subtract a single stitch."

"Jacob, it is only a quilt," said Robert. "Dorothea meant no harm."

"I assure you I will fix my mistakes." Dorothea's voice shook with surprise and offense. "Your quilt will be precisely as you have drawn it."

"See that it is," her uncle growled. He retreated to his chair and took up his torn boot again. "And do not think I will allow you to work on this library quilt until you have finished mine."

"Of course, Uncle."

She lowered her gaze so he would not see the anger she could not mask. There was no need; already he had returned his attention to his work, ignoring her. On hands and knees, she gathered the scattered quilt blocks, setting aside those she would have to rip apart to suit her uncle's whims.

Chapter Four

Dorothea ripped out the seams and made over five of the Delectable Mountains blocks according to her uncle's drawing. She had no idea why he insisted on his peculiar design, but in her less charitable moments, she believed his only intention was to be contrary. He provided her with three additional sketches: one with curved pieces like a Fool's Puzzle in disarray; one with narrow, pieced lines like a braid; and one that resembled the Spiderweb block with eight pieced triangles seamed together to make an octagon. When she remarked that such unique blocks would stand out, surrounded as they were by the traditional Delectable Mountains blocks, Uncle Jacob thought for a moment, jabbed a thumb at a piece of light shirting fabric, and said, "Make those blocks from that lighter fabric."

"All of the pieces?" queried Dorothea, who had assumed that he wanted his original designs to attract attention.

"Not the star in the middle. It is fine as it is. The other three blocks."

Dorothea tried to convince him that this was a mistake, since the individual pieces would be indistinguishable from one another, but he refused to listen. "What is the point, then?" she asked her mother after he had left the room. "I might as well use solid fabric if the piecing is going to be all but invisible. He said he wanted a quilt like his mother's, but I cannot imagine Grandmother making any quilt like this."

Lorena admitted that she could not recall such an unusual quilt among her mother's creations.

Dorothea contented herself with using slightly darker tones for some of the pieces so the elements of his designs would not entirely disappear. She also suggested adding a border of blue cotton salvaged from a worn coverlet to frame the quilt. Uncle Jacob considered, and replied, "I guess that wouldn't do any harm." It was a less than enthusiastic response, but she decided to add the border anyway, for her own satisfaction if not his.

Dorothea complied with his wishes as well as she could, and once, when he seemed in an agreeable mood, she asked if she might make one slight change to his design to reduce the number of seams. He objected without explanation, so she resigned herself to repeated tests of her sewing dexterity until his quilt was finished—except on one later occasion, when Dorothea forgot prudence and remarked that a certain new sketch resembled a ladder. Uncle Jacob frowned at the paper, then turned it ninety degrees and added four angled lines. "There," he said, leaving Dorothea with a design that required three additional seams and that still resembled a ladder, albeit a crooked ladder on its side. After that, she learned to keep her artistic commentary to herself.

The first of November came, and the first snowfall. Uncle Jacob grew increasingly impatient for Dorothea to complete the quilt, to her mother's consternation. "He already has three wool blankets for his bed," she reminded Dorothea, as they took advantage of one last sunny day to boil the winter bedding in the washhouse. "He is in no danger of freezing without his precious new quilt."

"I imagine he is eager to see his artistic vision realized," replied Dorothea. "No, I am quite certain he is simply growing more disagreeable with age. I am glad you and Father have managed to keep your senses of humor, although I suppose Uncle could not be expected to keep something he never had."

"I never thought I would say this, but I am determined that you should marry."

"What?"

"You should marry and leave this farm."

Dorothea forced a smile. "Are you that eager to be rid of me?"

"It is my fault you are not married yet." A deep groove of worry appeared between Lorena's brows as she stirred the boiling kettle of laundry with a stick. "Other mothers—and how I disdained them for it—train their daughters from an early age how to attract a suitor and win his undying devotion. In my hubris I thought I should train your mind instead."

"And I am heartily glad you did."

"But if you had married, you would have a home of your own now and be out from beneath your uncle's thumb."

"Firstly, Mother, I am only nineteen and may marry yet. Secondly, it is entirely possible I would have married into a situation less pleasant than this." Dorothea fed one of her father's newly cleaned shirts into the mangle. "Do not despair. I suspect you shall be rid of me eventually."

She did not tell her mother how often she had imagined having a home of her own, with an affectionate husband rather than a sour old uncle as her companion, but she did not blame her lack of suitors on her upbringing. No man she would consider marrying would disdain an educated wife, so the love for learning they had instilled in her would not have kept a prospective husband away. Her lack of any wealth aside from her saved wages, however, did act as a deterrent. Young men in love did not mind if their beloved lacked thirteen quilts, but their mothers did, and mothers and fathers alike cared if a young woman brought nothing to the marriage except herself.

It was little wonder that Lorena and Robert had cast their principles aside when opportunities arose to secure their son's future. Charlotte Claverton was demure, lovely, and the only child of one of the wealthiest farmers in Creek's Crossing. After Jonathan inherited Uncle Jacob's farm and married Charlotte, he would be master of the largest farm in the Elm Creek Valley. If he preferred, he could continue to practice medicine and leave the management of the farm to his family. Either way he would provide for them—as long as everything came to pass as Robert and Lorena hoped. The engagement, if one could call it that, was an agreement between the parents alone, even though Jonathan or Charlotte would likely find it difficult to refuse when both sets of parents were so eager for them to marry. The Clavertons did seem to favor the match as much as the Grangers, although they had hinted that they would withhold their consent if Jonathan and Charlotte did not learn to be fond of each other, or if Jonathan did not inherit his uncle's farm. Still, it was a future, one that left Dorothea alternately appalled and envious.

"I have only myself to blame for your unhappiness," said Lorena.

"Mother, I assure you I am content."

In truth, she was somewhat less than content. She had been more content by far when she was Creek's Crossing's schoolteacher. But she knew marriage was not the only road leading from Uncle Jacob's farm. And, too, there was Cyrus.

He called for her every other Thursday to carry her to his mother's house for meetings of the library board. He came even after Uncle Jacob approached as Cyrus was helping her from the carriage and told him gruffly that he need not call for Dorothea anymore. He would drive her himself, and if he was too busy, she was more than capable of driving herself. To her satisfaction, Cyrus declared that he would not think of inconveniencing Uncle Jacob when escorting Dorothea brought him so much pleasure. "Nevertheless, it is not necessary for you to return," said Uncle Jacob. When Cyrus appeared the following second Thursday as usual, Dorothea enjoyed seeing her uncle thwarted almost as much as she delighted in realizing that Cyrus came for her because he wanted to, not because she had no other way to get to his mother's house. He was becoming a good friend, even if he did tend to tease and joke any time she tried to engage him in more thoughtful discourse.

Still, his merry conversation was a welcome diversion from Uncle Jacob's sour grumblings, and planning the library benefit made her feel useful again, as she had when she was the schoolteacher. She knew little of how the school fared without her. If she encountered a former pupil in Creek's Crossing, she could query him only so much without seeming to be eager for bad news. All she knew was that the students appeared to be progressing in their lessons, their parents seemed satisfied, and, to her chagrin, her darling pupils did not seem to miss her as much as she had secretly hoped.

Dorothea speculated that, since the young people of the town seemed to think well of him, time in Creek's Crossing must have softened the new schoolmaster's heart toward its inhabitants. Her theory was soundly disproven one Sunday when Mr. Nelson walked his bay stallion onto the ferry she and Cyrus had already boarded. They had left the carriage to stand by the rail, and when Cyrus called out a polite greeting, Mr. Nelson gave him a curt nod and offered Dorothea a wordless glance before continuing forward. After securing his horse, he took a position at the far opposite side of the ferry near the pilot, although Dorothea and Cyrus were the only other passengers on board.

"How is that dreadful irritation, Mr. Nelson?" Dorothea called to him brightly. His back was ramrod straight, and she knew that he had heard her, though he did not turn around. "You see how he shuns me," she added in only a slightly lower tone to Cyrus, not caring if Mr. Nelson overheard. "He is so offended by the presence of an ignorant country girl that he must stand at the far side of the ferry."

"Perhaps he wants to avoid the embarrassment of another intellectual thrashing. If the most agreeable woman in Creek's Crossing would trounce him at his own welcome party, what might she do elsewhere?"

Dorothea flushed with pleasure and shame. She was pleased that Cyrus found her so agreeable, but until that moment she had not considered that it might have been inappropriate to point out Mr. Nelson's ignorance of local customs and flora at his first introduction into Creek's Crossing society. Then she remembered how he had provoked her and she hardened her heart. "I wonder if any mortal creature could hope to win his approval."

"A more puzzling question is what occasions his travels today," mused Cyrus. "Do you suppose he is on his way to visit your uncle, or perhaps your parents?"

"I doubt that very much," said Dorothea with a little laugh. "He has never called upon us before, and my uncle's reputation is usually enough to keep away even the most determined uninvited guest."

"If it is any consolation, I strongly suspect he wishes to avoid me, not you."

"I thought you were friends." They had seemed companionable enough at Mrs. Engle's party.

"Merely acquaintances, and recently less than that." Cyrus shifted so that his back was to Mr. Nelson, an unnecessary gesture since Mr. Nelson's attention was studiously fixed on the distant shoreline. "His ungentlemanly behavior at my mother's party concerned me, especially since I know the school board hired him solely on the basis of his father's recommendation. I hope you will not think ill of me that I decided to inquire into his background."

"Not at all." Dorothea could not help feeling wounded that she was so readily replaced by a man about whom the school board had known so little. She hoped for her former pupils' sakes that he at least had earned the university degree credited to him. "What did you discover?"

"While his father's reputation is beyond reproach, I regret that Thomas Nelson's is not. He has some decidedly questionable views on the subject of slavery, opinions that led to certain actions, which, in turn, led to imprisonment."

"You're joking." Astonished, Dorothea stole a look at Mr. Nelson. He chose that moment to look their way, and his gaze locked with Dorothea's. She raised her chin and met his gaze boldly, determined to show him she was unafraid, despite hearing the worst of the rumors about him confirmed.

She had thought from their first encounter that his eyes burned too brightly for the solemn scholar he purported to be, and now she knew why.

"I wish it were not true, but it is." Cyrus frowned and shook his head. "He spent two years in prison but was released before completing his sentence, it is said, because his father exerted his influence upon the local judiciary."

Dorothea knew all too well what influence the elder Mr. Nelson wielded. "I assume you told your stepfather," she said, looking away from Mr. Nelson to Cyrus at a sudden thought. "Surely the school board was not happy to discover he had been falsely represented."

"On the contrary, they had known all along. After the school board agreed to make Thomas Nelson schoolmaster but before he came to Creek's Crossing, his father disclosed his son's incarceration, although he declined to reveal the particulars of the crime. Mr. Nelson the elder assured them that his son had repented entirely and asked only that a compassionate, Christian town allow him the opportunity to redeem himself through useful service."

"So he will stay on as schoolmaster?"

Cyrus shrugged. "My mother says the school board was moved by his father's pleas, and since he has all the other necessary qualifications and no other likely candidate has appeared, he will suffice as long as his criminal activities remain a part of his past."

"I see." No other likely candidate, indeed. Dorothea crossed her arms, drawing her shawl around herself at a sudden chill gust of wind from the creek. How could the school board entrust the impressionable minds and characters of the young people of Creek's Crossing to a man whose objectionable opinions about slavery had driven him to commit criminal acts? For that matter, what had he done? Beaten a fugitive slave in the streets of Philadelphia? Set fire to a school for freedmen? Dorothea could easily imagine a dozen possible offenses, each reason enough to keep Mr. Nelson far from the Creek's Crossing school, despite his respected father's entreaties.

Cyrus eyed her and chuckled. "Now, Dorothea, don't be cross. The school board was pleased with your efforts, but they never expected you to stay on. A young woman with your prospects—well, they had already recently lost one maiden schoolteacher. They did not want to so soon lose another."

Dorothea shrugged and forced a smile as if she understood the school board's judgment, when in truth she found it unfathomable. Then, when she thought of how Miss Gunther had been "lost," the smile came easier, and with it, a blush. She turned so Cyrus would not see the color rising in her cheeks, knowing he enjoyed any opportunity to tease, and her eyes met Mr. Nelson's again. She gave him her brightest, most cheerful smile, as if they were the very best of friends, and was delighted to see him turn away again, frowning in irritated bewilderment.

✾✾

By the end of November, the harvest was complete, Uncle Jacob had drawn the last odd patch for his quilt, and the other members of the library board had debated and revised Dorothea's letter for what felt to her like the hundredth time. Delicately, not wishing to appear overly protective of her prose, she suggested that they allow her to send out the most recent version without further revising, or they would have no time left to complete the quilt.

To Dorothea's enormous relief, they agreed at last. "Now that we have a suitable letter," said Mrs. Engle, "to whom shall we send it? I do hope each of you remembered to make up a list of proper candidates."

"How many authors and personages of note do we require?" asked Mrs. Collins anxiously, clutching a sheet of paper in her lap. Dorothea glimpsed a list of perhaps five names, half the number Mrs. Engle requested from each woman present.

"I think we should send out a great many invitations," said Miss Nadelfrau, glancing to Mrs. Engle for approval. "It will mean more letter-writing and more postage, but not everyone will respond, and the more requests we send out, the more signatures shall be returned."

Mrs. Engle nodded, and Dorothea also agreed, but Mrs. Collins hesitated. "What if we receive too many autographs? We would not want our quilt to be too large and cumbersome or it will seem ridiculous."

"We should be fortunate to have such a problem," said Mrs. Claverton. "If we receive too many signatures, we can stitch the extra blocks to the back of the quilt."

"We shall do no such thing," declared Mrs. Engle. "That is a fine way to insult a renowned author, to tell him his signature is good enough only for the back of the quilt. No, if we receive more than we need, we shall choose those written in the most pleasing hand. The others we shall discard. If a discarded author should ever view the quilt and wonder what became of his signature, we shall feign ignorance and pretend his autograph was lost in the post."

Dorothea was about to object to this plan when Mrs. Deakins said, "A splendid solution. This will give us the opportunity to pick and choose."

"Which brings us again to our proposed authors." Mrs. Engle turned to Mrs. Collins. "Hester, would you be so good as to record the names?" Mrs. Collins nodded and lifted her pen to indicate her readiness. "My list is as follows: President Zachary Taylor, of course; Mrs. Zachary Taylor; Governor William Freame Johnston; Mrs. Johnston; Mr. Charles Dickens; Sir Walter Scott; Miss Catharine Maria Sedgwick; Mrs. Ann Sophia Winterbotham Stephens; Miss Maria Jane McIntosh; and Mrs. Ann Radcliffe."

"I believe Sir Walter Scott is deceased," murmured Miss Nadelfrau. "Mrs. Radcliffe, as well."

"Is that so? Very well, then. Scratch out their names and substitute mine and my husband's. That should make ten."

Mrs. Collins nodded, scribbling.

Next, Mrs. Claverton read her list—which boasted Washington Irving and James Fenimore Cooper as well as the painter Thomas Cole—followed by Mrs. Deakins. "Nearly all of my authors have been named," wailed Mrs. Collins when Mrs. Deakins had finished, and insisted upon reading her own list next, before every person on her list had already been proposed.

Then it was Dorothea's turn. "It was too difficult to choose only ten, so I have twelve," she said, unfolding her paper. "Ralph Waldo Emerson, Henry David Thoreau, Walt Whitman—"

"Goodness gracious, no," said Mrs. Engle.

"Who is Walt Whitman?" asked Mrs. Collins.

"I believe he is the lieutenant governor," replied Mrs. Deakins, looking to Mrs. Engle for confirmation.

"He is without question the most disgraceful poet of our age," declared Mrs. Engle. "My dear Dorothea, I cannot imagine you have read his notorious works or you would have known better than to suggest him."

"I did not know the lieutenant governor wrote poetry," murmured Mrs. Collins to Mrs. Deakins.

Astounded by the objection, Dorothea asked, "Mrs. Engle, have you read his work?"

"I most certainly have not. I would not have any such trash in my house, nor the name of its purveyor in my quilt."

"But if you have not read his work, how do you know it is trash?"

Mrs. Engle tittered, but her mirth carried an edge. "I do not need to be kicked by a horse to know it is not a pleasant experience."

"We can't expect to like all of one another's choices," said Mrs. Claverton, with a look that, while sympathetic, suggested Dorothea forgo further argument. "Besides, controversy may sell tickets. Dorothea, please continue reading your list."

"Margaret Fuller," said Dorothea, pretending not to notice the hard stare Mrs. Engle now leveled at her. "Robert Browning and Elizabeth Barrett Browning. William Cullen Bryant."

"Absolutely not," Mrs. Engle broke in.

Dorothea lowered her paper and suppressed a sigh. "He is a writer, and a personage of note. Why should he not be included?"

"Apparently we must make our criteria more specific," said Mrs. Engle. "Dorothea, dear girl, I do not blame you. I am sure you have no idea what sort of radical diatribes in the guise of literature these so-called authors on your list have shamelessly paraded in front of the public. Your parents likely fed you these names, taking advantage of your innocence to turn our quilt into a political tool."

Dorothea smiled, but regarded Mrs. Engle levelly. "I have read every one of these authors, and I do not understand how including a certain writer is any more political than including a governor or a president."

"Presidents and governors are meant to be political," explained Mrs. Collins. "A writer is supposed to enlighten and amuse."

Dorothea looked around the circle of women, eyebrows raised. "I have found the writers on my list to be quite enlightening."

"Let us agree that we shall include men who practice their politics overtly by running for office, and exclude those who conceal their politics in writing," said Mrs. Engle. "Now go on, Dorothea, and finish up."

Dorothea knew the rest of her list would not make the other women any happier. "Elizabeth Cady Stanton, Lucretia Mott, William Lloyd Garrison, James Russell Lowell, and Frederick Douglass."

The women drew in a collective gasp, all save Mrs. Claverton, who seemed to be struggling to contain her laughter. "You do seem determined to shock us," she said.

"I did not mean to." Dorothea handed her list to Mrs. Collins, who, she had observed, had not added any of her proposed names to the official list. "I confess I do not understand why these men and women would not be worthy additions to our project."

"We will simply have to come up with more names on our own," said Mrs. Engle to the others. "Dorothea has done us more harm than good today."

"She cannot help how she was brought up," said Miss Nadelfrau. "She did write a fine letter, and the quilt was her idea."

As all but Mrs. Claverton nodded and agreed, Dorothea decided she had had quite enough of being discussed as if she were not present. "I beg your pardon," she began, but Mrs. Claverton reached over and clasped her hand. In an undertone she urged Dorothea to allow Mrs. Engle to have the last word in the argument. She would never back down today, not after expressing her opinion so forcefully, but later she might be persuaded to tolerate the signatures of authors she did not necessarily admire, especially if the quilters fell short of their goal of eighty Album blocks. With some regret, Dorothea complied. Life with Uncle Jacob had taught her the unpleasant necessity of occasional outward compliance to conceal inner dissent.

The rest of the afternoon was devoted to cutting pieces of muslin to send with the invitations, because, as Miss Nadelfrau pointed out, the male authors were more likely to respond if they did not have to first obtain the proper fabric from their wives. As they cut, they proposed additional names for the list. Mrs. Collins and Mrs. Deakins noticeably flinched whenever Dorothea spoke. Dorothea was amused but indignant; she would have spoken up more staunchly for her authors if not for Mrs. Claverton's request and for her own reluctance to further offend Cyrus's mother. She held her tongue when, at the conclusion of the meeting, Mrs. Engle assigned each of them a portion of the list, distributed the scraps of muslin, and instructed them to send invitations to the authors. Of Dorothea's candidates, only Emerson, Thoreau, and the Brownings remained.

Cyrus must have sensed a certain tension in the air when he arrived to take her home, for he regarded her quizzically as they left the house. "Mother seems disturbed," he remarked. "Did something upset her?"

"I regret that I was the source of her displeasure," said Dorothea as he helped her into the carriage. As they rode toward the ferry, she gave him a brief, lighthearted account of the afternoon, taking care not to insult his mother's taste or judgment.

"This is most unfortunate." Cyrus's characteristic grin had fled. "Mother's good opinion, once lost, is rarely regained."

"I assure you, I will do such a fine job on this quilt that she will forgive me entirely," said Dorothea, studying him, not certain if he was once again teasing her, and would at any moment laugh with her about his mother's behavior.

"I do hope so." He shook the reins and chirruped to the horses, frowning.

He remained all but silent as they crossed Elm Creek, lost in a brood, but as the carriage brought her closer to home, he assumed a close approximation of his usual joviality. When he assisted her from the carriage and promised to call for her two weeks hence, she nodded, troubled by his obvious displeasure.

That evening after supper, Dorothea recounted the events of the afternoon for her mother as they layered Uncle Jacob's eccentric quilt top with a pieced muslin lining and an inner layer of cotton batting. Lorena listened thoughtfully, but looked surprised when Dorothea told her how much the other women's objections had astounded her. "Are you surprised that they object, or that they object so strenuously, without any appearance of shame for their opinions?"

Dorothea considered. "Both, I suppose." She was not so naïve as not to readily understand the reason for their dismay, but she had not expected these particular women to react in such a manner. If Creek's Crossing were a southern village, she might have expected objections to including abolitionists, advocates of woman's suffrage, and freedmen in the quilt, but not so in the free commonwealth of Pennsylvania. If anyone did harbor secret prejudices, she would have expected them to be too ashamed to allow them to be detected.

"You assumed you were among like-minded women," said Lorena, threading a tapestry needle. She tied a knot on the end of the thread and began basting the three layers of the quilt with large, zigzag stitches.

"I did," admitted Dorothea. She'd had no reason to, but she had also had no reason to do otherwise. She had never talked politics with any of the women but Mrs. Claverton, whom she knew despised slavery. "They seemed sensible enough, so naturally I assumed they would agree with me."

In his usual chair by the fire, Uncle Jacob snorted, but did not look up from his Bible. She thought of the often silly prattle of Mrs. Deakins and Mrs. Collins and silently agreed that perhaps sensible was too generous a term.

"Sometimes it is best to keep your opinions to yourself until you have discovered what those around you believe," said Robert.

Dorothea felt a spark of indignation. Her list had contained several of his favorite authors. "The philosophy of Thrift Farm was to speak one's own truth, whatever the consequences to oneself."

Chagrined, her father shrugged and nodded. Dorothea would have been happier if he had scolded her for showing such disrespect.

"The philosophy of Thrift Farm," muttered Uncle Jacob, shifting in his chair. "Write poetry about the Oversoul, allow your children to run wild, and hope the wheat learns to sow and harvest itself."

Lorena ignored him. "What of Mrs. Engle? Why did you assume she shared our enlightened ideals? You have read what her husband has published in the *Creek's Crossing Informer*."

"Those articles expressed her husband's views, not hers."

"She chose to marry the man who holds those views."

Dorothea hesitated. "I suppose knowing how Cyrus feels, I assumed his mother would be sympathetic to the inclusion of abolitionists, or at worst, indifferent."

"And how does Cyrus feel?"

She was aware of her uncle's sudden keen interest, though he had not moved a muscle. "He jokes and teases so much I do not know how he feels on any serious subject," she admitted. "I do know it distresses him to see his mother offended."

Uncle Jacob radiated animosity. "In my day we had a word for a young man like that. He squires young ladies about in a fancy carriage, but he hasn't worked a day in his life."

"You do not believe any man works if he does not own a farm," said Dorothea.

"Dorothea," warned Lorena.

"It is unfair to condemn Cyrus for the political views of his stepfather, a man who did not raise him, a man who has been married to his mother for less than a year." Dorothea struggled to keep her composure as she worked her needle with broad, furious stitches. "Even if Cyrus's opinions are not widely known, our family's are. Surely he would not seek out my company if he found our views in any way objectionable."

Uncle Jacob slammed his Bible shut. "Maybe he doesn't seek out your company for your conversation, or haven't you thought of that? I should forbid him to set foot on my property for your own sake, since you're apparently determined to be as foolish and as easily deceived as all of your sex."

They stared after him as he stormed from the room.

"Mother, Father." Dorothea took a deep, shaky breath. "I have done nothing to provoke such censure. I assure you Cyrus Pearson has never been anything less than a gentleman in his conduct."

Her mother reached for her hand. "Of course, dear. We know."

Her parents exchanged a worried look, but her father said, "He's in a sour temper today because a calf was stillborn last night. Say nothing more, and he will forget about it by morning."

But if anything, her uncle's temper worsened overnight. At breakfast he chastised Lorena for serving flapjacks instead of eggs, although Dorothea had heard him request flapjacks before heading to the barn to milk the cows. In the days that followed, his demands became more exacting, his sudden bursts of anger more swift and vengeful. He hovered over Dorothea whenever she sat at the quilt frame, glaring as if he suspected her of quilting slowly just to vex him. He left the house mornings and evenings alone, saying only that he would be at his sugar camp. Once Dorothea was sent there to fetch him, but although the scuffled dirt around the fire pit and a newly mended roof on the shack indicated recent activity, he was nowhere to be found. Another time, while gathering hickory nuts, she could have sworn she heard him arguing with someone, but when she ran to see what was the matter, she found him alone, with no reasonable explanation for wandering about the forest on the westernmost edge of the property after he had said he would be working in the barn. When she asked to whom he had been speaking, he first denied that he had spoken at all, then said he had been praying. Dorothea knew of no psalm that encouraged believers to make an angry noise unto the Lord, but she pretended to believe him.

Uncle Jacob's increasingly erratic behavior made her long to unburden herself to Jonathan, the confidant of her childhood. She wrote to him often, but found it difficult to strike the appropriate balance of care and confession, to share her concerns with him without provoking any undue guilt or worry. She knew she had failed when he wrote back to thank her for her cheerful letters and praised her for accepting their uncle's eccentricities with grace and humor. As Christmas approached, she grew ever more anxious for his impending visit. When he came home, he would see for himself how their uncle had worsened with age. Perhaps—she seized upon a wild hope—he might sympathize with her plight and invite her to spend part of the New Year in Baltimore with him.

But when his letter arrived a week before Christmas, she did not have to read it to know that her hopes were in vain. Her mother's expression as she scanned the lines told her that he would not be coming home. One of his mentor's patients, a young boy with unexplained recurring fits, took more comfort from Jonathan than the doctor himself. The boy's parents begged Jonathan to remain in Baltimore so that their son's final days would be eased by the presence of a trusted friend. Jonathan apologized for canceling a second visit and assured them he would find some excuse for the boy's parents should his parents find themselves unable to do without him. Lorena, though obviously disappointed, said that she did not have the heart to deny the grieving parents their one small measure of comfort, and she wrote back to tell him he should remain.

Lorena asked Uncle Jacob's permission first, of course. He told her that Jonathan might as well stay in Baltimore where he might do some good, since he had already missed spring planting and the harvest, when he was needed on the farm the most. Lorena tried unsuccessfully to hide her dismay at his apparent indifference to his nephew and presumptive heir, and both she and Robert were especially attentive to Uncle Jacob for the next few days, a display Dorothea regarded with disgust.

Her disappointment over Jonathan's prolonged absence made her ever more determined to finish Uncle Jacob's quilt so that it would not annoy her any more, and so she fixed herself a deadline of Christmas Eve. That way, she thought somewhat meanly, she would not be obliged to get him any other present, and she could enjoy the holidays without him hovering over her at the quilt frame. Besides, already a few authors had returned autographed pieces of muslin to the library board, and she was eager to join in the work of piecing Album blocks. She had not forgotten her uncle's decree that she sew no other quilt until his own was complete. The more blocks she sewed, the greater her role would be in determining which authors were included—and since she had disregarded Mrs. Engle's instructions and sent invitations to her own authors as well as those assigned to her, she could not afford to be left out of the selection process.

She sewed the last stitch into the binding of Uncle Jacob's quilt on the morning of Christmas Eve. She concealed the finished quilt in her attic bedroom until the next morning, wistfully recalling long-ago Christmases on Thrift Farm, the curious amalgam of tradition and whimsy, solemnity and joy, the fragrance of candles and gingerbread and Yule log, the sound of Bach's Christmas cantatas on dulcimer, fiddle, and organ. One of the founding members of the community would read the story of the Nativity, bringing it to life for Dorothea and Jonathan and the other children so vividly that Dorothea was filled with a rush of awe and reverence and gratitude. They would exchange gifts, but only things they had made or had found in nature. Looking back, Dorothea had to smile recalling how her father had once given her mother the second of the Four Brothers, the mountains framing the north end of the Elm Creek Valley, and how it had seemed a perfectly normal thing to do.

The gift of a handmade quilt would have met with approval on Thrift Farm, but Christmases at Uncle Jacob's were a more subdued affair. He permitted the giving of gifts since the magi had brought gifts to the Christ Child, but there was no music save the hymns at church services, and certainly no parties. Dorothea had been invited to several Christmas Eve gatherings, one at her best friend Mary's new home with her husband Abner, but Uncle Jacob would not allow her to attend. He emphatically forbade her to attend a sleigh riding party with Cyrus; anticipating this, she would not have bothered to ask him except Cyrus repeatedly entreated her, and she had promised she would.

Christmas morning church services were too festive for Uncle Jacob's taste, but he could not very well forbid the family to attend church on Christmas. Dorothea could almost forget her longing for Jonathan in the merriment of the day. The people of Creek's Crossing were cheerful and smiling as they wished one another a Merry Christmas, forgiving disagreements and past quarrels, if only for the day. The Ladies' Auxiliary had arranged for a magnificent Christmas tree to adorn the sanctuary, and when services concluded, all were invited to take ribbon-tied oranges and wrapped parcels of roasted nuts down from the boughs. Most of the congregation lingered in the pews to share fellowship and laughter, but just as he did every year, Uncle Jacob urged his family toward the door as soon as the final hymn was sung. They had nearly reached it when Lorena spotted Abel and Constance Wright amidst the throng and broke away to greet them; as Uncle Jacob scowled after her, Dorothea felt a tap on her shoulder.

She turned to find Cyrus dangling a small parcel by its ribbon, so close it almost brushed her cheek. "There were toys on the tree for the children, too. Dolls for the girls and drums for the boys. Didn't you get yours?"

"I must have forgotten," she said, returning his smile.

"I thought you might, so I took the liberty of fetching yours for you. And now, before the crotchety old geezer turns around, I'll have my Christmas present from you."

Before she knew it, he kissed her swiftly on the cheek and disappeared into the crowd.

Too astonished to worry that Uncle Jacob had seen, she stood rooted in place. A moment later her mother was at her side. "Constance brought chestnuts for the dressing and said she'll make the pudding at our place." Lorena peered at her daughter. "What's that in your hand?"

Dorothea glanced down and saw the ribbon-tied parcel. "A gift. From Cyrus."

She quickly slipped it into her coat pocket, but not before Uncle Jacob turned around and spotted it. He scowled and urged Dorothea and her parents outside.

The parcel seemed heavy for its size as it weighed down Dorothea's pocket on the ride home. The Wrights, having been invited for Christmas dinner, followed in their own wagon. Her parents conversed cheerfully, even laughing aloud as they rode, but Dorothea was as silent as Uncle Jacob. She had not expected that Cyrus would give her a gift. It had not even occurred to her to get him one.

At home, as the men tended to the horses and the women went to the kitchen, Dorothea slipped away to her attic bedroom to unwrap Cyrus's gift. She untied the ribbon, unwrapped the paper, and discovered inside a hand mirror and comb, intricately worked with carvings of vines and roses, gilded in silver.

She had never owned anything so fine.

She sat on the bed with the gifts in her lap, then, hesitantly, lifted the mirror and ran the comb through her hair. Her reflection showed flushed cheeks and startled eyes; with a sudden jolt of embarrassment for her vanity, she quickly wrapped the comb and mirror in the paper and tucked them into the drawer of the pine table that served as her nightstand.

She hurried back to the kitchen and tied on her apron. Her mother and Constance were so engrossed in a discussion of the best way to dress a goose that they did not seem to notice her absence. The men returned from the barn and settled in the parlor, where Uncle Jacob took up his Bible and Dorothea's father and Mr. Wright played draughts. After a game, Mr. Wright came into the kitchen, stole a kiss from his wife, and offered to help the women prepare the meal. At first they refused, but when Robert drawled, "Better let him help, if it will get the meal on the table faster," they laughingly tied an apron on Mr. Wright and threatened to put Robert in one, too. Lorena and Constance teased Mr. Wright as he picked up a paring knife and offered to take care of the vegetables, but he worked diligently if not swiftly. Dorothea surmised he had gained a great deal of practice living as a bachelor. She doubted Cyrus would be so proficient in the kitchen, having first his mother and then a housekeeper to cook for him, but she quickly severed that train of thought.

At Lorena's request, Dorothea set the table with the fine china her grandparents had brought over from England, the plates and bowls and tea service that spent most of the year wrapped in linen and tucked away in a lined chest decorated in golden fleur-de-lis. Translucent white with a border of roses, they were so delicate she was almost afraid to handle them, knowing that a single place setting was worth more than she was likely to earn in her lifetime. She had once asked her mother why people prosperous enough to own such treasures would have left their homeland to immigrate to the New World. Lorena had told her that the china had been the entirety of her grandparents' fortune. Her grandfather, a soldier, had been given the trunk and its contents for saving the life of his commanding officer in battle in France. Upon his discharge, he sold enough pieces to purchase second-class passage to America for himself and his wife, determined to start a new life far from the seemingly endless warfare of Europe.

Plainer fare adorned the table service than its original owners could have imagined, but the food was plentiful and delicious. Even Uncle Jacob's dour blessing seemed heartfelt that night, and although Dorothea ached for her absent brother, she could not dwell on her own misgivings after Constance remarked that she had never sat at a finer table. It suddenly occurred to Dorothea that this was Constance's first Christmas in freedom. Truly it was a blessing, Dorothea reflected, to have Constance among them at Christmas, as a reminder that so many people still waited to be redeemed from their suffering.

After the meal, they exchanged gifts. Her parents had bought Dorothea a fine edition of Henry Wadsworth Longfellow's anthology, *The Poets and Poetry of Europe,* and an autobiography, *Narrative of William W. Brown, an American Slave.* Dorothea wondered how welcome the latter would be on the shelves of the Creek's Crossing library, but Constance took a special interest in it and reflected that one day she might write her own story. Dorothea was pleased to hear this, for her gift to Constance, as yet unwrapped, was a pen with several nibs, a primer, and a copybook.

Uncle Jacob gave his sister and brother-in-law nothing, but he offered the Wrights two large cakes of his best maple sugar; since the Wright farm did not have enough maple trees to support their own sugaring, the gifts were much appreciated. To Dorothea he gave a collection of the Proverbs, with a narrow strip of brocade fabric marking the thirty-first. Since the verses praised the pious, thrifty, industrious wife, Dorothea knew the placement was no accident.

Then Dorothea returned to her attic bedroom for the Delectable Mountains quilt. "For you, Uncle," she said, placing the folded bundle in his arms. "I trust it is exactly as you wished it. I hope it pleases you."

He unfolded the quilt and studied it. "I think it will do. You did justice to my drawings. Thank you, niece."

"It is lovely handiwork," said her mother, since her uncle did not.

Dorothea thanked them both. She had hoped for more pleasure in her uncle's expression, but she should have expected no more than his taciturn approval of her accurate reproduction of his sketches. He took no true delight in anything and was not capable of offering greater appreciation.

The Wrights were examining her quilt—out of politeness, she thought. Mr. Wright looked over each of the blocks in turn, and Dorothea could see him pausing to count the triangle points on the blocks that had three or five when most had four. He looked over the other, odd squares her uncle had drawn, arranged in a diagonal line amidst the Delectable Mountains blocks, looked at Uncle Jacob, then glanced at Dorothea. "Sure looks warm," he said, returning the quilt to its new owner.

"You did not need to make it so fine," murmured Constance to Dorothea, so low no one else knew she had spoken. Dorothea glanced at her in surprise and hid a smile. She used her finest quilting skills out of pride, not because her uncle deserved them.

"It'll do," said Uncle Jacob, folding the quilt and placing it on the back of his chair. There it sat for the rest of the afternoon and into the evening, while they told stories of Christmases past, while the women brought out pie and tea for dessert, when the Wrights bade them good-bye and headed home, and after Uncle Jacob and Robert left to do the chores. It remained there still when Dorothea came down to help her mother prepare breakfast the next morning.

After all of his demands, after all of Dorothea's exacting labor, he had not even put it on his bed. "Perhaps he is saving it for company," suggested Lorena, trying to spare Dorothea's feelings.

"When do we ever have company?" said Dorothea. "Constance was right. Uncle Jacob did not deserve my best handiwork."

She deliberately chose not to resent his indifference. The quilt was finished, she had done her best, and now she could move on to a project much more pleasing to her. Seven autographed pieces of muslin had already arrived at Mrs. Engle's home, and two more belonging to authors that Mrs. Engle had rejected had been sent to Dorothea directly.

At the previous meeting of the library board, Dorothea had been assigned the task of sketching a plan for the quilt, something that would suit the varying skills of the participating quiltmakers and something that could be adapted easily according to the number of Album blocks they made. She and Miss Nadelfrau had joined forces to convince the others to use the traditional Album block, even though Mrs. Engle had balked when Mrs. Deakins remarked that she knew the pattern by another name, Chimney Sweep. Dorothea had needed five minutes of her most tactful persuasion to reassure Mrs. Engle that the block's association to another, less distinguished profession would not offend the authors, should they learn of it. Miss Nadelfrau's point that the block would be easy to assemble since it had no curves or set-in pieces ultimately won the argument. Mrs. Engle was less willing to consider that she might receive fewer than the eighty blocks she wanted, as she was accustomed to receiving everything she desired. She insisted that the eighty blocks would be arranged in ten rows of eight, the most pleasing rectangular ratio, and cut short any "pessimistic" suggestions to the contrary. Dorothea decided not to waste breath on further argument and to plan alternative settings secretly, just in case.

At the same meeting where Dorothea would present her sketch, Miss Nadelfrau would bring swatches for them to consider, and—assuming they could reach a consensus—the meeting would adjourn to the dry-goods store, where they would purchase and divide up the fabric. Board members would piece blocks at home, completing all blocks by the end of January and the entire quilt top by the last week of February in time for the dance. Dorothea was confident she would find some way to sneak her banned authors into the quilt at an intermediate step.

Dorothea and her mother were so busy making up for the usual chores they had neglected the previous day that it was almost suppertime before Dorothea noticed that Uncle Jacob's quilt had been removed from the back of his chair. When she was sure he was out of the house, she passed by his bedroom and peered inside, but she did not see it. She was tempted to ask if he had put it in his chest for safekeeping or passed it on to one of the horses, but knew any reply he gave was unlikely to please her.

That evening, as she worked on the drawing and idly pondered more polite ways to inquire about the whereabouts of the quilt, her mother suddenly said, "Goodness, Dorothea. I had completely forgotten Cyrus's Christmas gift. Have you opened it?"

"Yes," said Dorothea, wishing her mother could have chosen a different time to ask, preferably when Uncle Jacob could not overhear.

"What was it?" asked Robert.

"A silverplated comb and mirror."

Uncle Jacob snorted. "That would be a fine gift for himself. I have never met a young man more likely to enjoy gazing at his own reflection."

"I cannot imagine you know him well enough to determine that."

"Dorothea," said her father mildly.

Dorothea set down her pencils. "I am sorry, Uncle, but I do not care to hear my friend so unfairly maligned, especially when he is given no opportunity to defend himself."

"Then by all means, let us give him opportunity," said Uncle Jacob, a hard glint in his eye. "Tomorrow when he calls for you, let us have him stay for supper. We will have him make both his character and his intentions plain."

"He is not coming to call," said Dorothea. "He is coming to take me to the library board meeting."

"After he brings you home, then," thundered her uncle.

Dorothea could not see any way out of it. "I shall ask him."

"See that you do."

The room was silent for the rest of the evening. The others went to bed—first her uncle, then her parents—but Dorothea remained to finish her sketch by candlelight. She was nearly done when she heard a creak on the floorboards behind her. She turned to find her uncle, still in his nightshirt and cap.

"Niece," he greeted her gruffly.

Dorothea hurriedly drew a last stroke and began clearing the desk. "I am sorry if the light kept you awake."

"I am only looking out for what is best for you." Uncle Jacob crossed the room in long, slow strides. "He is no good for you and I know you do not love him."

So he wanted to speak of Cyrus. She almost smiled. She had never known him to be kept awake, troubled by an argument. Usually his confidence in his own perfect judgment provided him sufficient righteousness to sleep soundly every night.

"I have seen nothing to persuade me he is *not* good," said Dorothea, "and I never claimed to love him. We are friends. Nothing more."

"Don't be coy. A young man does not call on a young lady so many times unless he has intentions."

Dorothea gathered up her papers. "If he has any, time will reveal them."

"By then it might be too late." He clasped her shoulder and spoke earnestly. "Niece, if you must marry, choose a good, God-fearing man. If you can't find one in Creek's Crossing, then go out west, where a woman is valued as much for her strength as for her beauty."

The steadiness in his voice turned to trembling as he spoke; his eyes were strained and pleading as they pooled with tears. A tear slipped from his eye, ran down his cheek, and disappeared into his scruff of beard. Dorothea stared at him in stunned disbelief. Suddenly he seemed to come to his senses; he glanced at his hand resting on her shoulder and snatched it away. Dorothea clutched her papers to her chest, too astonished to speak as her uncle hurried from the room, scrubbing his eyes with the back of his fist. In another moment he had disappeared down the hallway. She heard the door to his bedroom close and the latch fall into place.

Chapter Five

D orothea slept little, but she woke when the first gray light of dawn touched the attic windowpane, worry fluttering in her chest like a trapped bird. She did not know what to do about her uncle's unexpected tears. In all the years she had known him, she had never seen him weep. And he had seemed as shocked by his sudden emotion as she.

Dorothea did not like to keep such a troubling secret from her parents, but she knew she must keep silent. Uncle Jacob had too much pride to endure such shame. Any mention might compel Uncle Jacob to banish them from the farm rather than acknowledge his weakness. She could not cost the family Jonathan's inheritance.

She lingered as long as she dared before going downstairs to help her mother with breakfast, where she learned that her uncle had taken a cold breakfast with him to the sugar camp. "He has gone several times a week since late summer," remarked Lorena. "Perhaps someone should remind him that this is not the time of year to tap the trees."

Dorothea knew he had left early that morning to avoid her. "Let's not tell him, or he might not spend so much time away from the house."

Lorena allowed a small smile, but she looked worried. "I wonder . . ." She hesitated. "I wonder if he is, perhaps, not altogether well."

Dorothea held herself perfectly still. "What do you mean?"

"Have you not noticed he has been even more irascible than usual? He is more forgetful, more snappish. Do not forget he is fourteen years my senior, and he drives himself hard."

"He drives us all hard." Still, her mother's words brought Dorothea a small measure of relief. An illness would pass.

Her uncle did not reappear even for lunch, and while Lorena wondered aloud if someone ought to run to the sugar camp to look for him, Dorothea was glad he remained absent. She spotted him trudging through the old wheat field, now shorn and muddy and dusted with snow, as she went outside to meet Cyrus's carriage. In her eagerness to leave, she climbed inside without waiting for Cyrus to assist her.

She delivered Uncle Jacob's invitation to supper as they crossed Elm Creek on the ferry, the water too turbulent there to freeze over completely during all but the coldest winters. Cyrus seemed pleased to be asked, but he declined, citing the presence of two important out-of-state business associates. When she inquired what business, he grinned and said, "The pursuit of lucre. I regret that I do not engage in the altruistic profession of teaching, such as yourself, or the essential craft of farming, like your uncle."

Dorothea noticed he did not mention her father. Robert might spend the rest of his life working Uncle Jacob's land, but no one who knew him considered him a farmer. Dorothea often thought he would be happier living in a rented room in a city back east, writing philosophical essays at the behest of an indulgent patron.

She brightened considerably as the distance increased between herself and her uncle, now that the unhappy prospect of subjecting Cyrus to his baleful scrutiny had been averted. The library board meeting passed pleasantly, the members settling on a popular green, Turkey red, and Prussian blue color scheme, then leaving for Mrs. Engle's favorite dry-goods store to purchase fabric. Dorothea had brought some of her saved wages, believing that each of them would be responsible for purchasing her share of the fabric, but to her surprise, Mrs. Engle insisted on paying for it all.

"She thinks she's going to win the quilt," said Mrs. Claverton to Dorothea when the others were in another part of the store selecting bolts of calico. "She doesn't mind buying so much fabric for a quilt for herself."

Before Dorothea could reply, a thunder of horses' hooves passed just outside, followed by loud shouting somewhere down the block. Dorothea and Mrs. Claverton were the first to the door. From the front steps they saw three men on horseback leveling their rifles at the door to Schultz's Printers. One man slid down from his horse, pounded on the door, and shouted for Schultz to come out. Dorothea saw the flicker of a curtain in an upstairs window, but no other sign of life within. Then from somewhere unseen came another cry, a furious shout that Schultz had escaped through the back door and was fleeing down Water Street. The man at the door leapt back onto his horse and raced off with the others, vanishing around the corner.

The rest of the women had crowded onto the steps after Dorothea and Mrs. Claverton, but none of them knew what to make of the commotion.

"Isn't the eldest Schultz girl a friend of yours?" Mrs. Claverton asked Dorothea.

Dorothea nodded. "A very dear friend."

"Well, go on, then." Mrs. Deakins nudged her. "Go find out what's the matter."

Dorothea, who had been on the verge of dashing over to the printers to see if she could help, now resolved to stay away. "Mary would not be there. She's married with a home of her own."

Mrs. Deakins sniffed and went back into the store, disappointed that her appetite for gossip would not be satisfied. The rest of the library board followed, Dorothea last of all. For the rest of the shopping trip, the other women speculated on the curious incident, but Dorothea was too worried about Mary's father to participate in the conversation. No one knew who the men were, or what their purpose with Mr. Schultz could have been. Mrs. Collins declared that one of the strangers resembled a cousin's husband, but when she admitted he was a farmer in Maryland, no one was inclined to believe her.

As Cyrus drove Dorothea home a few hours later, she recounted the scene to him and asked him what he made of it. As it happened, he had been on Water Street at the time and had witnessed the three men apprehending Mr. Schultz. He stood accused of assisting a fugitive slave across the Maryland border by concealing him in his wagon. The men claimed to be law officers and announced as a warning to other would-be lawbreakers that they were taking Mr. Schultz to Maryland to stand trial.

"They cannot," gasped Dorothea.

Cyrus shrugged. "They can take him since they have him, but I doubt much will come of any trial. No one has any evidence Schultz aided runaways in the past, and he can always claim that the runaway climbed aboard his wagon and hid amongst his freight when Schultz was not looking. His son-in-law and brother have already headed south to fetch him. On one point, however, the constables are quite correct: Schultz did break the law."

"A law that has existed for more than fifty years without this manner of enforcement. The people of Pennsylvania would never stand for it."

Cyrus grinned. "That is precisely the problem. The southern states have had enough of northerners mocking federal laws that support slavery. Until a stronger law is enacted—and it is coming, mark my words—it's little wonder they believe they must enforce the laws themselves."

Dorothea felt sick at heart thinking of Mr. Schultz's wife, of Mary and her younger sisters. "If they are as adamant as you say, I cannot see how this will end without violence."

"Schultz should have thought of that before choosing a time of heightened animosity to help runaways."

Dorothea could not reply. She never would have imagined the unassuming Mr. Schultz capable of such courage. Likely he had acted on noble instinct, helping the fugitive in an instant of need without thinking of the potential consequences to himself. Circumstances requiring heroism often did not permit contemplation or forethought.

Suddenly she had another thought. "What became of the fugitive slave Mr. Schultz assisted?"

"I gather he escaped, which is unfortunate for Schultz. Perhaps they would have been satisfied with the return of the runaway."

Dorothea shuddered, thinking of the various dreadful punishments captured runaways received at the hands of slavecatchers: beatings, starvation, amputations. "Unfortunate for Mr. Schultz, but fortunate indeed for the runaway. Perhaps Mr. Schultz considered it a worthy sacrifice."

Cyrus chuckled. "That would not surprise me."

Dorothea supposed it was amusing that Mr. Schultz had outsmarted the slavecatchers, but she could not manage even a smile. She marveled at Cyrus, who seemed to have a depthless well of good cheer to draw upon even in the face of horrors.

❧

Lorena was disappointed that Cyrus could not stay for supper, but she seemed to forget the invitation when Dorothea told her about Mr. Schultz. "We must send word to Mrs. Schultz that we will help her however she needs." Lorena wiped her hands on her apron and sent Dorothea for a pen and paper. "She will need a lawyer familiar with Maryland law. Dr. Bronson will surely know someone."

While her mother wrote to Mrs. Schultz and Jonathan's mentor in Baltimore, Dorothea packed a basket of food for the family. Lorena sealed the letters and tucked them into the basket as Dorothea threw on her wraps, instructing her to ask her father or uncle to drive her to the Schultz's if the men were in the barn, and to take a horse and ride alone if they were not.

Dorothea hurried outside, and when she entered the barn, she found her uncle alone, sitting on a bench cleaning mud from his boots. "I'm looking for my father," she said, peering around for him. She was reluctant to ask her uncle to drive her or to try to ride off on horseback against his wishes, because he would surely forbid the errand.

"Last I saw he was bringing in the cows."

"I will meet him." As she turned to go, Dorothea glimpsed a familiar cluster of color amid the folds of the rag her uncle rubbed over his boot. "What's that?" Before the words were past her lips, she knew. "My quilt. That's my quilt."

He glanced up at her, unconcerned. "No, it's my quilt."

She could not comprehend it. "You are using the quilt I gave you for Christmas—the quilt we both put much thought and labor into—to clean mud from your boots?"

He studied her for a moment before saying, "I told you I wanted serviceable fabrics. It can be washed."

"Even the most thorough scrubbing could not remove those stains. Surely you know that." Dorothea could not bear to look upon the ruins of her quilt any longer, and she suddenly no longer cared if Uncle Jacob attempted to stop her. Without a word of explanation, she saddled her mother's horse and rode off down the road to the Elm Creek ferry. Absorbed in his work, Uncle Jacob did not interfere.

Either her uncle was crueler than she had ever supposed, or he was going quite mad.

The Schultzes lived on the upper story above the printers, and Dorothea arrived to find several horses and wagons already tied up outside. She could hear fervent and angry voices on the other side of the door as she knocked. Mary answered, her face ashen and eyes rimmed in red. Dorothea embraced her and offered words of comfort and asked about Abner, but Mary was so upset she could only cling to Dorothea and choke out that she had not heard from any of the men yet.

Mary took Dorothea into the other room, where other neighbors and friends surrounded Mrs. Schultz. Dorothea gave her Lorena's letter and said, "My mother sends you her most sympathetic regards and offers her services in helping you obtain a lawyer."

Mrs. Schultz managed a wan nod. "Thank you, my dear. Your mother is very kind, but we have already made arrangements."

"The Marylanders have sent word already," said another man, whom Dorothea recognized as the editor of the *Creek's Crossing Informer*. "They have levied a fine and will release Mr. Schultz when it is paid."

"How could they have so swiftly determined his guilt?" asked Dorothea. "They apprehended him mere hours ago."

"There was no trial," said Mrs. Schultz. "They are holding him for ransom, pure and simple."

"They will take cash payment or the return of their slave," another man said.

Dorothea shook her head. "This cannot be legal."

"Slavecatchers live by their own laws," said the newspaper editor. "Make no mistake, Schultz is not in the hands of legitimate authorities. It was sensible of Abner to accept Nelson's offer to go along. He will help sort this out."

"Mr. Nelson?" echoed Dorothea. "The younger Mr. Nelson?"

The others nodded and resumed their discussion, oblivious to her astonishment. Then she understood. Of course it made perfect sense to include Mr. Nelson; as a southern sympathizer he would not engender the Marylanders' offense. He could speak to them in a language they understood. And naturally he would have no compunction against the return of the fugitive slave. Dorothea prayed the unfortunate man was far away in some safe haven.

He was, but not in the manner Dorothea had hoped.

The following week, as Dorothea and Cyrus crossed on the ferry, they spotted a knot of men on the opposite shore. As the ferry drew closer, Dorothea recognized the undertaker's black carriage and saw the men reach for something tangled in the weeds on the riverbank.

"Dorothea, avert your eyes," ordered Cyrus, but she did not. Transfixed by horror, she watched as they hauled the corpse from the creek, paused to rest, then loaded it into the undertaker's carriage. The undertaker had driven off by the time Dorothea and Cyrus came ashore, but a few onlookers still lingered, and from their remarks, Dorothea was able to piece together what had happened. The body had been identified as that of the runaway slave. He had tried to cross the creek upstream at Widow's Pining, but the ice had not held, and he had plunged into the frigid waters. Bone-chilling cold and treacherous currents had hastened his drowning.

"He can't be returned to his owner now," remarked Cyrus as they left the scene behind them. "That will be unhappy news for the Schultzes."

Dorothea doubted they had ever had any intention of trading the runaway for Mr. Schultz. "It shall be unhappy news for this unfortunate man's family, as well."

"If they ever learn of it," said Cyrus.

Dorothea did not reply. She could not disagree with him, but something in the lightness of his manner annoyed her. Almost always she enjoyed his perpetual good humor, but sometimes circumstances warranted more gravity. He did not seem to know this, or he was concealing his concern to spare her more worry. Either way, she did not care for it.

Before taking her to his mother's house, Cyrus drove her to the post office so she could mail a letter to Jonathan. She had needed two pages to tell him of recent happenings in their once-quiet town. A letter awaited Dorothea, and when she saw the New York return address, she realized it must have come from one of her banned authors. She slipped it into her pocket to read later. Cyrus was certain to inquire if she opened it in the carriage, and he might feel obliged to inform his mother.

With Mary's father gone, it was difficult to think of anything but his safe return. The library board meeting went on as usual, except that talk of Mr. Schultz's captivity dominated the conversation. Everyone had some bit of news to report, though Dorothea wondered how much truth was in the rumors. Abner and Mr. Schultz's brother had returned from Maryland to report that Mr. Schultz was in good spirits but concerned for his family, and he refused to declare whether he had knowingly helped the runaway or if the runaway had stolen aboard without his knowledge.

"Mr. Schultz's silence is confession enough," said Mrs. Engle with a trace of disapproval in her tone. "He surely helped the runaway." Nevertheless, it was she who suggested they have the tickets for the opportunity quilt printed at Schultz's, to give the family the commission in their hour of need. Dorothea would have been more impressed with her generosity if Mr. Schultz's were not the only printer in town, the nearest rival ten miles away in Grangerville.

The Schultzes would need every penny. According to Mrs. Collins, the fine, or ransom, was five hundred dollars. Dorothea was aghast, knowing Mary's family could never raise such an enormous sum without selling the printing press and sacrificing their livelihood. She suggested to the rest of the library board that they use the proceeds from the opportunity quilt to free Mr. Schultz. Her idea was met with laughter and scorn by all but Mrs. Claverton, who privately told Dorothea that her heart was in the right place, but the quilt was not even finished, would probably not raise five hundred dollars, and would not raise any amount as swiftly as Mr. Schultz needed. "Late is better than never," retorted Dorothea, frustrated by the consensus opposing her. The others seemed to believe that Mary's family should solve their problems unassisted. Mr. Schultz got himself into his present circumstance and ought to get himself out.

Dorothea complained about their lack of compassion to her mother that evening as they cleaned up after supper. "What happened to Mr. Schultz could have happened to any one of us."

"Not to just anyone," said Uncle Jacob, returning from an errand outdoors in time to hear. "Only folks who decide to help runaways."

Dorothea snapped off her apron. "Are you saying Mr. Schultz should have ridden right past that poor man without stopping?"

"Not at all." Uncle Jacob shrugged out of his coat. "I'm saying he should have hid him better."

Dorothea, who had been expecting a different reply, opened her mouth and closed it again without a word.

"Mr. Schultz's act of courage should not be mocked," said Lorena.

"Helping runaways is a dangerous business and those who don't know what they're doing shouldn't meddle in it." Uncle Jacob settled into his usual chair and opened his Bible. "Schultz is a prisoner and the runaway is dead. If Schultz had left well enough alone—"

"The runaway might still be dead, or recaptured, but not likely any closer to freedom." Dorothea gestured to the Bible in his hands. "Look up John 15:13 while you contemplate Mr. Schultz's choices. Aunt Rebecca was a Quaker. What do you think she would have done?"

"Dorothea," her father warned. "That's enough."

Deliberately, Uncle Jacob closed his Bible and set it on the table. "You did not know my wife," said Uncle Jacob, his voice a quiet warning. "You have never risked your life for anyone. Without giving the matter any thought, you praise Schultz for his actions, but would you have done the same?"

Dorothea hesitated. "It is what I would have wanted to do."

"But would you have?"

"I—I don't know. I like to think I would have shown sufficient courage. I suppose I cannot know for certain, having never been confronted with such circumstances."

"Well." Uncle Jacob almost smiled, but no mirth touched his eyes. "An honest answer at last."

"Leave her alone," snapped Lorena. "At least she considers such actions, which is more than you have ever done for the abolitionist cause. Mr. Schultz is a better man than you by far."

Uncle Jacob opened his Bible again. "Then you will be gratified to learn he is coming home."

They all stared at him. "Coming home?" echoed Robert.

"Yes, I heard it from Abel Wright this afternoon. The ransom has been paid and Mr. Schultz was set free. He is on his way home if he is not there already."

Dorothea and her mother exchanged a look of astonishment. "How did Mrs. Schultz obtain the money?" asked Lorena.

Uncle Jacob turned a page and drew the lamp closer. "It did not occur to me to ask such an intrusive question."

Dorothea was too overcome to speak at first, but then she snapped, "You knew he had been released and yet you did not tell us. Instead you prolonged our worry and tormented us with this silly argument."

"Such cruelty is beneath you, brother," said Lorena in a softer tone. "What you did to your niece's quilt was bad enough, and now this—"

"I needed a quilt to keep up at the sugar camp. I did not ask for finery."

"You were very particular about every detail," countered Lorena. "If you had told us your purpose I could have given you any number of suitable quilts. You did not need to mock my daughter's efforts by treating the work of her hands so indifferently."

"Take a lesson from Mr. Schultz," growled Uncle Jacob. "Keep to your own affairs."

Dorothea wanted to declare that the matter of the quilt *was* her affair, but when Lorena pressed her lips together and turned away, she knew the argument was over. She helped her mother finish cleaning the kitchen, then took her sewing basket to a chair by the fire. Only then did she remember the envelope she had received at the post office earlier that day. She retrieved it from her coat pocket and discovered inside a piece of muslin bearing the signature of William Lloyd Garrison. He had also enclosed a brief letter. "What an immense pleasure it is to assist in a benefit for the town that has recently become the home of a longtime acquaintance," he had written. "Please give my regards to Mr. Thomas Nelson if you should meet him."

Dorothea read the letter over, thunderstruck. How could it be that Mr. Nelson was acquainted with Mr. William Lloyd Garrison, newspaper edi-

tor and renowned abolitionist? She read the letter a second time, scrutiniz-
ing each line. Mr. Garrison had called him a "longtime acquaintance," not
a friend. Perhaps Mr. Garrison was a friend of Mr. Nelson's more amiable
father, and knew little of the son's quite different inclinations. Or perhaps Mr.
Garrison had indulged in a bit of sarcasm; after all, he did not say to give
Mr. Nelson his "best regards" or "warmest regards." The greeting could have
been a taunt, mocking Mr. Nelson in his exile.

It did not matter, as Dorothea had no intention of delivering the message,
should she be so unfortunate as to have the opportunity.

❧

An event Dorothea had anticipated with almost as much eagerness as the
quilt raffle fell upon the following Saturday: the Creek's Crossing school
annual exhibition. Last year she had directed the students in their recitations
and various displays of their academic accomplishments, and was pleased
to hear it declared a resounding success. She was determined to attend this
year's program and satisfy her curiosity regarding how her students fared
under Mr. Nelson's tutelage.

Like nearly everyone else in Creek's Crossing, her parents also wanted
to attend, but on the evening of the exhibition, Uncle Jacob found additional
work for them that he insisted must be completed before morning. Robert accepted this without a word of complaint, but Lorena protested on her
daughter's behalf. Dorothea's absence would be conspicuous since she was
the former schoolteacher, and that would reflect badly upon the entire family.
At first Uncle Jacob resisted, saying that even if he did not object to Dorothea
driving into town at night alone, he needed the wagon himself, but Lorena
convinced him to leave Dorothea at the schoolhouse before his errands and
pick her up afterward.

Dorothea was reluctant to ride alone with her uncle, but since the alternative was to remain at home, she accepted the arrangement. They rode in
silence until they had nearly reached the ferry, when her uncle said, "My
sugar camp quilt washed up well."

"Yes, Mother managed to rid it of nearly all the stains." She could not help
emphasizing *nearly all.*

"I told you to use scraps and serviceable colors."

"You have reminded me of that already. You might be surprised to discover what beautiful works may be created from those same materials."

They reached the ferry. Uncle Jacob drove the wagon on board, but Dorothea ignored his hand as he reached to help her down. He scowled at the rebuff, but followed her to the railing. "If I had known you and your mother would be so upset, I would have made my intentions more clear."

Dorothea sighed. "If that is an apology, Uncle, then I accept."

"You're right, too, what you said about your aunt. Rebecca."

He spoke her name carefully, as if it were a word in an unfamiliar language, a taste he had craved and never thought to savor again. Dorothea was so astonished to hear it she could not form a reply, only stare at him as he gazed out upon the creek. She hoped he would say more about the aunt whose passing had left him so crippled with grief that the Grangers understood implicitly they were never to mention his lost family, but if he intended to speak, their arrival at the schoolhouse rendered further confessions unspoken.

He left her at the door with a warning to be ready to leave at half-past eight even if the exhibition was not over. Dorothea went inside and tried to find a seat in the crowded schoolroom. Even the choir loft, included in the design at the senior Mr. Nelson's request so that the building could double as a church on Sundays, was full of eager spectators—and numerous parents giving last-minute instructions to their nervous children. Dorothea spotted Mary waving to her on the main level. Mary had saved her a seat with her and her husband, and as Dorothea sat down, she observed that Mary clutched Abner's arm tightly as if to reassure herself that he had indeed returned from his dangerous journey to Maryland.

"How is your father?" asked Dorothea.

"He is faring well," said Mary, "but my mother will not let him out of her sight."

"You did not have to mortgage the print shop to raise the ransom?"

"Oh, no. Didn't you hear? They released him without receiving a penny from us. I don't know what Mr. Nelson said to them, but it was evidently very persuasive." Mary gave a little shudder and drew her shawl around her shoulders, tightening her grasp on Abner's arm. "One scarcely knows what to think about that man."

"On the contrary, one knows precisely what to think," said Dorothea. "No doubt he threatened violence, and with his prison background, I'm sure he knew how to make the threats convincing."

Abner leaned forward. "I don't care what he said or did. He obtained Mary's father's release, and that is good enough for me."

Mary and Dorothea exchanged a look of knowing exasperation. Men too often confused success with moral worth. They could say no more about it, though, for at that moment, Mr. Nelson stepped up to the front of the school-room and introduced himself, an unnecessary formality given the size of their town and the speed with which news traveled when there were few other novelties to distract its citizens. His spectacles caught the lamplight, empha-sizing his scholarly air, though he was neither as pale nor as slender as he had been upon his arrival in Creek's Crossing. Apparently the climate of their little hamlet agreed with him. If he did not manage to escape, in a few months he might become almost robust.

Mr. Nelson introduced his twenty-two pupils in ascending order accord-ing to age, then led them through an exercise in grammar. Next followed an examination in arithmetic, with the youngest pupils solving simple addition and subtraction problems, and the very eldest presenting geometric proofs. Dorothea was surprised by this; she had not taught them any advanced geometry, but she would have, she told herself, if she had been given the opportunity. The students made so few errors that she whispered to Mary that they had surely been given the problems in advance. Mary giggled and whispered back that they simply remembered all Dorothea had taught them. Someone shushed them, so Dorothea contented herself with silently correct-ing the pupils' errors before Mr. Nelson did, and guiltily wishing there were more of them.

She forgot to criticize when the students began their recitations in history and poetry. The youngest children were so earnest, their voices so sweet as they carefully repeated the pieces they had memorized. The eldest class, nearly all girls, recounted the history of Pennsylvania so well that she found herself regretting the end of the presentation. She applauded as loudly as anyone present, putting aside, for the moment, Mr. Nelson's part in the stu-dents' success.

"They did very well," remarked Abner.

Dorothea had no choice but to agree. Despite his other faults, Mr. Nelson was apparently an adequate teacher. Perhaps better than adequate. Mary must have sensed her ambivalence, for she hastily added that the students would have performed just as well, if not better, had Dorothea been their teacher.

After a few closing remarks, Mr. Nelson dismissed his pupils to another round of applause. Dorothea accompanied Mary to the cloakroom, but when she did not see Uncle Jacob in the vestibule, she gathered her wraps and returned to the warmth of the schoolroom. Others filed past her. Mothers and fathers praised their children; young men met young ladies at the door to see them home. The schoolhouse steadily emptied, but although the clock on Mr. Nelson's desk read a quarter to nine, still Uncle Jacob did not appear.

Dorothea checked the vestibule again, and even peered outside to see if he had decided to wait in the wagon rather than push against the departing throng, but he was nowhere to be seen. She returned to the classroom, but stopped short at the sight of Mr. Nelson, alone, wiping down the blackboard.

She decided she preferred the chilly vestibule, but before she could turn to go, Mr. Nelson looked up. "Is there something you require, Miss Granger?"

"I did not mean to disturb you. My uncle is coming for me, but he has not yet arrived."

His eyebrows rose slightly. "Your uncle, not Cyrus Pearson? I rarely see you in town except upon his arm."

Something in his tone made her bristle. "Yes, my uncle. Mr. Pearson had a pressing business engagement that prevented him from attending your exhibition. You should not consider it a slight."

"On the contrary, I consider it a stroke of good fortune." Mr. Nelson nodded at the coal stove in the corner. "I will keep the fire going until I have finished straightening the classroom. You are welcome to wait in here."

"Thank you," she said, and took a seat at the desk nearest the stove. She sat in silence, staring at the door rather than watch Mr. Nelson dust off the chalk railing and replace books on the shelves. The clock chimed the hour just as she realized Mr. Nelson was straightening the bookcases slowly and methodically, postponing the completion of his tasks rather than put her out of the schoolhouse.

She rose and began putting on her wraps. "It appears my uncle has been delayed. I'm sorry to have kept you. Good evening."

"You can't mean to walk home."

"I have a friend in town. I will leave a note on your door for my uncle and stay with her until he comes for me."

"Nonsense." Mr. Nelson closed the dampers on the stove, dousing the light. "You do not need to impose on your friend. I will take you home."

"So that I might impose on you instead?" Dorothea laughed shortly and wrapped her muffler around her neck. "I think I would prefer Mary."

He followed her into the vestibule, pausing only to snatch his coat from the cloakroom. "I will have to escort you wherever you decide to go. I would prefer to escort you to my horse and carriage, which is just next door, rather than to the edge of town and back on foot."

"My uncle's farm lies to the north. Your farm is to the west."

"If you mean that I will be traveling out of my way, I cannot dispute that." Mr. Nelson reached up to turn down the oil lamp hanging beside the door. "If we are fortunate, we will encounter your uncle along the way, and he can carry you the rest of the way home."

His manner was so abrupt, so completely without courtesy, that she almost told him she would rather spend the night in Mary's rocking chair than indebt herself to him, but she knew her parents' worries would increase the longer she stayed away. "Very well, Mr. Nelson," she said. "You may take me home."

He frowned at the condescension in her tone, but he offered her his arm.

His horses were a perfectly matched team of Arabians; his carriage not new, but well fashioned and comfortable. The wind had picked up, and though it blew from the southwest, it was biting. The ride home would have been much colder in Uncle Jacob's wagon, the company only a trifle more pleasant. She wondered if her uncle had forgotten their arrangements. Perhaps she had not accepted his apology regarding the sugar camp quilt graciously enough, but of course, it had not been graciously given.

When they turned on to Water Street, Dorothea suddenly remembered. "I forgot to leave a note for my uncle."

"I will do so upon my return."

"Thank you." Dorothea felt that she ought to say more. "Your students conducted themselves quite well this evening. You must be proud."

"They performed adequately, but they are no match for their counterparts in the east," said Mr. Nelson. "It is not through any fault of their own. Their intellectual capacity is comparable, but they have lacked the necessary resources and guidance."

"I see."

He glanced at her. "And I see that you have chosen to take offense. Do so, if you insist, but be aware that I do not blame you for their deficiencies. You could hardly be expected to pass on a better education than you received."

She smiled thinly. "That is generous of you."

"Furthermore, you were their teacher for only six months, which is hardly long enough to have much influence upon them."

"It was eight months, actually. Please, Mr. Nelson, do desist. If I hear any more of such praise I shall be compelled to fling myself into the creek."

"It was not my intention to praise you."

"Then you have succeeded," said Dorothea. "Oh, and before I forget, I was asked to pass along a message to you. Mr. William Lloyd Garrison sends his regards."

Mr. Nelson did not so much as flinch. "How did you come to possess a message from Mr. Garrison to me?"

"He was kind enough to respond to my request for an autograph for the library board's opportunity quilt. However did you come to meet Mr. Garrison?"

Mr. Nelson gave the barest of shrugs. "Our acquaintance is long-standing. I do not recall how or when we met."

"Perhaps you met him in prison," exclaimed Dorothea, as if inspired. "I understand Mr. Garrison has quite a reputation for engaging in charitable works. Perhaps he visited you there to offer you words of comfort."

Mr. Nelson kept his gaze fixed on the horses. "You are quite right," he eventually said. "Mr. Garrison was kind enough to visit me in prison. Several times, in fact."

He said nothing more, but it was confession enough. Dorothea was torn between triumph and astonishment. She had not expected him to so readily acknowledge the criminal past he surely had assumed was unknown in Creek's Crossing. Part of her had even disbelieved the rumors as too shocking to be true. Now she had his own admission, but he made no attempt to excuse his crimes or beg her to tell no one. Perhaps at last he regretted his offensive behavior since his arrival in their town. If he had been less insulting, less arrogant, she might have agreed not to reveal what she had discovered, had he asked.

They reached the ferry dock. The pilot had left the craft for the warmth of the boathouse, but he soon emerged and allowed them to drive the carriage aboard. "You got here just in time," he remarked. "I was about to go home for the night."

"Has my uncle crossed recently?" asked Dorothea.

The ferryman shook his head. "Not since earlier this evening when you both came over together."

Troubled, Dorothea asked him to tell her uncle, if he should appear before the ferry ceased operating for the night, that she was already on her way home.

"I gather this is not typical behavior for your uncle," said Mr. Nelson after the ferryman left them to push away from the shore.

"Not at all. Ordinarily he is as conscientious as he expects everyone else to be."

But he had not been his usual self for months. His forgetfulness, his outbursts of anger—perhaps her mother was right and he was not well.

Mr. Nelson seemed unconcerned. "It is likely he has preceded you home."

"Yes." She forced confidence into the words and settled back into her seat. "Very likely."

When they reached the road up the hill to Uncle Jacob's farm, the distant light from the house's windows offered a soft welcome. Mr. Nelson asked if he could water his horses in the barn before departing. Dorothea consented, and as soon as he swung open the doors, she saw that neither Uncle Jacob's wagon nor his horse was inside.

"Thank you for seeing me home," said Dorothea, climbing down from the carriage. "Please take whatever you need for your horses."

She ran toward the house, in her haste forgetting to invite Mr. Nelson to warm himself by the fire before he left. She opened the door with a bang, startling her parents, who looked up from their chairs in alarm, which faded when they saw her. Lorena set down her knitting and smiled. "How was the exhibition? We did not expect it to run so late."

"Is Uncle Jacob here?"

"No," said her father. "Didn't he bring you?"

"He never arrived. Mr. Nelson brought me home instead."

Her parents exchanged a look of puzzlement and joined her in the kitchen. At her father's request, Dorothea repeated what Uncle Jacob had said regarding the time and place he planned to meet her. "It is unlike my brother to be so late," said Lorena, turning quickly at the sound of a knock on the door. She hastened to open it, but it was only Mr. Nelson.

"Is Mr. Kuehner missing?" he asked.

"Missing or delayed," said Robert.

Mr. Nelson addressed Lorena. "You know his habits best. Is it too soon to begin a search?"

"If it were a temperate night, I would say yes, but because it is so cold . . ." Lorena shrugged helplessly.

The men quickly agreed to ride back to Creek's Crossing. Mr. Nelson would search south of town on the route toward his home while Dorothea's father inquired at the houses of Uncle Jacob's few acquaintances. Lorena and Dorothea would search the farm. As the men rode off, Lorena investigated the outbuildings while Dorothea headed for the sugar camp.

The lantern in her fist swung as she ran, casting stark shadows on the ground. Frozen tufts of grass crackled underfoot; her nostrils prickled and lungs burned from the cold. She began calling for her uncle as soon as the lantern light lit up the shelter and the large log tripods that had once suspended an enormous black kettle over the fire at sugaring time. There was no reply. She reached the shelter, but inside she found only the quilt she had made him, draped clumsily over a wooden bench.

She searched the forest next, stumbling over tree roots and windfall hickory nuts the squirrels had abandoned. She called for him, but listened in vain for a reply. She then began to search the fields, following the post-and-rail fence that marked the boundary of Uncle Jacob's property, and met her mother coming from the opposite direction. Her search of the outbuildings had yielded not a single clue as to Uncle Jacob's whereabouts.

Their faces and limbs were numb from the cold, their throats aching and hoarse from shouting. Lorena decided that they should return to the house, await word from Robert, and keep the kettle on the fire in anticipation of the men's return.

Hours passed with no word. Dorothea and Lorena fell asleep in their chairs beside the fire, bundled in quilts. The first pale pink shafts of dawn were appearing on the horizon when Dorothea's father returned, haggard and shaking from fatigue. He had found no sign of Uncle Jacob.

"Perhaps Mr. Nelson—" Dorothea began, but her father interrupted her with a shake of his head. Mr. Nelson, too, had searched all night. They had encountered each other southwest of town; Mr. Nelson suggested they concentrate their search in that region, since the last sighting of Uncle Jacob's wagon located him heading south, following the road along Elm Creek.

None of them could imagine what he might have been doing there at that hour. Robert suggested a second, more thorough search of the farm now that daylight had arrived, but Lorena insisted he rest while she and Dorothea combed the grounds once more. He wearily agreed, but when they returned two hours later, they found him in the barn doing the chores.

"Someone's got to tend to these animals," he said before Lorena could scold him. He was right, of course; together they completed the usual morning chores. They forgot about breakfast until it was nearly lunchtime, but when Lorena prepared a meal, none of them could eat more than a mouthful. Dorothea felt sick and apprehensive. Something dreadful had happened, and now all they could do was wait until they discovered what it was. Suddenly an image flashed before her mind's eye: the fugitive slave, bloated and decaying, being dragged from the reeds along the creek bank.

She jumped up from her chair. "Someone should go in to town to see if there is any word."

Her father nodded, but at that moment, they heard horses coming up the road toward the barn.

Dorothea reached the door first and dashed outside, the cold wind biting her cheeks and whipping her dress against her legs. She hugged herself for warmth and halted in the middle of the road, shivering, as her parents caught up to her. Her mother drew in a sharp breath, her father murmured something, but Dorothea was insensible to everything but the wagon and riders coming slowly toward them.

It was Uncle Jacob's wagon, but an unfamiliar horse pulled it, and the man driving it sat stiffly, shoulders hunched against the wind. Two men on horseback flanked the wagon: Charley Stokey, a scar running the length of his face where Mr. Liggett had cut him with the scythe, and Linus Donne, the county constable. The wagon rolled awkwardly, its front corner smashed, the wheel wobbling uncertainly.

The men would not meet their gaze as they approached. That and the condition of the wagon told Dorothea that Uncle Jacob was dead.

Chapter Six

The wagon had been found overturned in Elm Creek, but since the wounds upon Uncle Jacob's body were merely scratches and bruises, they knew the crash had not killed him. Mr. Donne speculated that Uncle Jacob had been felled by an apoplexy, and, unable to control the horse, he had driven the wagon down the riverbank.

The accident had occurred in the woods belonging to Mr. Liggett, who had chanced upon the scene earlier that morning. According to Mr. Donne, Mr. Liggett insisted that he had not been expecting a visit from anyone, least of all Uncle Jacob. He had not known that Uncle Jacob was missing or that others had been searching for him. Charley Stokey added that he had seemed less concerned with Uncle Jacob's death than with figuring out why Uncle Jacob had been on his land. Dorothea and her parents were equally bewildered. The scythe had been returned long ago, and they could think of nothing that would have compelled Uncle Jacob to seek out Mr. Liggett's company.

When Mr. Donne and Charley offered their condolences, Lorena took a deep breath and said, "Thank you for your kindness. It was a terrible accident, but we will take comfort in knowing my brother is now in a better place."

"An accident." Mr. Donne's brow furrowed. He scratched his head and rolled the brim of his slouch hat. "Only one thing bothers me."

"What's that?" asked Robert.

"Where's his horse?"

Charley looked grim. "We should check Liggett's barn."

Donne shook his head. "Now, Charley, I told you. Just because it happened on Liggett's land don't make him responsible."

Charley absently fingered his scar. "I'm not saying he done it, but maybe he saw a chance to steal a horse whose owner wouldn't miss it."

"This isn't the time or place to talk about this."

"That horse didn't unhitch itself."

Charley's voice rose, but Mr. Donne cut him off with a low word. Dorothea was numb to the exchange. All she could think of was Uncle Jacob, lying dead on his bed, wrapped in a coarse sheet.

Mr. Donne asked Dorothea's father if he could do anything more for the family, but when Robert shook his head, the visitors departed. Alone, the Grangers sat silent and motionless in their chairs.

Lorena broke the silence with a murmur. "The Lord be praised, we are delivered."

"Mother," exclaimed Dorothea.

Lorena shot her a frown. "Don't look at me that way, Dorothea. I do not celebrate your uncle's death, but I cannot help feeling that a great yoke has been lifted from my shoulders."

"We must see to his burial," said Robert, rising woodenly from his chair. "He would want to be buried on his own land, and he would want prayers said."

"Mr. Donne should have taken him to the undertaker's rather than bringing him here," remarked Lorena.

"Perhaps they thought his family would want him," said Robert, a new sharpness in his voice.

"All I mean is that the ground is too frozen for you to dig a grave. He will need to be buried in the town cemetery."

Privately, Dorothea agreed. Each fall, the undertaker had the grim task of estimating how many citizens of Creek's Crossing were likely to perish before the spring thaw. Before the first snow, he would arrange for the corresponding number of graves to be dug, plus a few more in the event of unforeseen dire circumstances. A few years earlier, an outbreak of typhoid fever filled all the prepared graves before January, and the remains of the additional deceased had to be stored in the undertaker's barn until late March.

"He would want to be put to rest on his own land with Rebecca and the children," said Robert more firmly. He took pen and paper from the desk and dashed off a letter, which he handed to Dorothea. "Please take this to the reverend. I'll get to work on a grave."

Dorothea nodded. She was halfway to the barn when the numbness of her hands woke her to the realization that she had left the house without her wraps. She returned inside and threw on her coat and muffler, but as soon as she stepped outside again, she discovered she no longer carried the letter. Her frantic search of the kitchen called her mother to the doorway, but Lorena did not ask what she was doing and it did not occur to Dorothea to explain. She stopped short in the middle of the room, pressed her palms to her head, and squeezed her eyes shut, willing the noise and confusion from her mind. Slipping her hand into her pocket, she grasped the familiar roughness of paper. She withdrew the letter, threw her mother a look of helpless apology, and tucked the page back into her pocket.

"It will be all right," said Lorena. "Everything will be all right."

Dorothea could not find the words to reply.

As she rode to the ferry, she tried not to think of how long her parents had waited for Uncle Jacob to die, how often they had all wished him dead. Now that their wishes had been satisfied, she almost thought she could sense her uncle just beyond the range of sight, scowling at her accusingly, as if their anticipation had brought about his death.

He had probably died from an apoplexy, Mr. Donne had said. He had investigated many scenes of death and understood them more thoroughly than any man should be obliged to. But what, indeed, had happened to the horse?

There was no visitation. Uncle Jacob would not have appreciated such a gathering in life and would not gain anything from one in death. He was buried beside his wife and sons the next day, with only his closest kin and the minister in attendance. With a pickax Dorothea's father had hewn a grave in the icy ground within the maple grove not far from the sugar camp, which they surmised must have been his favorite place on the farm. No one wept. Mired in shock and disbelief, Dorothea could not mourn her uncle because she could not believe him truly gone.

The ceremony was brief, flat and empty despite the minister's words of comfort. Lorena had suggested that Robert play a hymn on the fiddle after the last prayer, but he had refused, flexing his fingers and rubbing his callused palms together as if unaware that he did so. Although Dorothea longed for the solace of music, she was relieved by her father's reply. To play hymns at the grave of a man who considered music a frivolity would be to mock him, powerless as he was now to enforce his wishes.

Dorothea left her parents at the gravesite while Robert covered her uncle's coffin with earth. Listless, she wandered through the maple grove to the sugar camp, to the sturdy, windowless sugarhouse and the outdoor work-space that had preceded it. A heavy chain still hung from the timber Uncle Jacob had secured between two sturdy oaks and the ring of large stones beneath it remained, but the enormous cast-iron kettle that had once been suspended from the chain over the fire had been stored in the barn for years, ever since Uncle Jacob decided that a series of smaller kettles produced a far superior syrup than one large kettle alone. Why he had left the kettle stand and fire circle in place after building the sugarhouse, Dorothea did not know, unless it was to mislead curious rivals.

She crossed the camp to the sugarhouse, passing beneath the suspended timber, her fingers brushing the chain, shoes kicking up black soot from the accumulated cinders of seasons past. Since the sugaring season lasted only a few weeks, other farmers made do with crude log shacks, but Uncle Jacob had built a sugaring house large enough for three or four adults to work in relative comfort, protected from the elements, with a loft for storage.

Each year her father helped Uncle Jacob collect hundreds of gallons of sap, and she and her mother did their part to boil the clear liquid into syrup, but Uncle Jacob alone decided when the work would begin. In mid-February, Uncle Jacob would begin taking careful note of the weather, marking the time of the sunrise, observing if the temperature had risen above freezing during the day before dropping at night, consulting his meticulous notes from previous years. A few days before he thought the sap would begin run-ning, he and Robert would traverse the maple grove, drilling a hole in each trunk, inserting wooden spiles, and hanging buckets beneath the spouts to collect the sap. Uncle Jacob never failed to tap the trees at precisely the right time, though sometimes he chose the last days of February and other years the first weeks of March. He always managed to collect the pure, precious sap in abundance, even in seasons when their neighbors complained of stub-born flows from their trees or woody flavors in the sap.

Each day the men would empty the buckets into barrels loaded on the wagon and haul the sap to the sugarhouse, where Dorothea and her mother boiled it down in three kettles hung in a row over an open fire, which they were careful to keep burning steadily. As the sap boiled and thickened in one kettle, they would ladle it into the next and replenish the first, holding back their skirts from the flames, wincing when an errant splash of bubbling syrup struck their hands or faces. When the syrup in the last kettle had thickened enough, Dorothea or Lorena would stir and stir as the liquid turned into grains of sugar. Together they would pour the maple sugar into the wooden molds Uncle Jacob had fashioned and then set them aside to harden.

Occupied though he was with collecting sap, Uncle Jacob still kept a watchful eye on the women's work, never too busy to remind them to stoke the fire or chide them if their attention seemed to wander from the boiling kettles. And to Dorothea's chagrin, the time-consuming labor required to boil forty gallons of sap down into a single gallon of syrup did not relieve the women of their ordinary chores. They rose early to fix breakfast and tend the livestock; at midday and late afternoon either Dorothea or her mother would race back to the house to prepare another meal. Often, long after the men had returned from the barn and had gone off wearily to bed, Dorothea and Lorena labored over the housekeeping neglected during the day—the baking, the churning, the never-ending laundry and mending.

Dorothea's thoughts went back to the previous year, to a sugaring season when the days dawned sunny and nightfall brought new snow that dusted grassy slopes and underbrush. The lingering pattern of daytime thawing and nighttime freezing had extended the sap run. Uncle Jacob, hardly able to contain his satisfaction, expressed his enthusiasm by working his family harder than ever. Dorothea was alone in the sugarhouse stirring a kettle when her uncle entered, peered at her through the clouds of steam, and inquired as to her mother's whereabouts.

Dorothea brushed damp hair back from her forehead, the sweet scent of maple clinging to her skin, her hair, her clothing, and told him Lorena was back at the house preparing dinner. He nodded, but did not depart as she expected. Instead he took the long-handled spoon from her hand and checked the sap in the center kettle, which had thickened and acquired a rich, amber hue. "Some people think I begin my sugaring earlier than most folks because I'm too impatient to wait when there's work to be done," he said. "That's nonsense. I start as soon as the sap runs because the early run of sap is the sweetest. Better sap means better sugar. This syrup is ready to be moved to the next kettle. Quickly, now."

Dorothea obeyed without a word, and after the task was done, Uncle Jacob began to ladle boiling sap from the first kettle into the second. "You must care for the trees just as you do the fields and livestock," he instructed. "Keep the sugarbush thinned. Don't tap them too young or use more than one spile per tree or tap anything but sugar maple."

"The Craigmiles say they have used red and Norway maple with no discernible difference in taste."

"This is not the Craigmile farm. You are my niece and you will do it my way." He handed her the ladle. "Finish this while I fetch more fresh sap."

Dorothea nodded, taking the spoon, wondering why he had chosen that day to share his sugar-making secrets and make her as his confidante.

Uncle Jacob hefted a barrel of fresh sap and poured some into the first kettle. "Some folks can work the land all their lives and never learn a thing from it. You have to tend the sugarbush as you would any crop. Not like Amos Liggett." He nearly spat the name. "The fool man chops into the tree with an ax to get to the sap instead of drilling a hole. All that does is injure the tree and allow pestilence and infection to ruin the sap in years to come. I've seen trees on his land that had six buckets around them collecting the sap that dripped from those hatchet cuts. Six holes on one tree! It's no wonder his sugar tastes like burnt sand."

He had gone on to instruct her in the proper carving of a spile from a branch of sumac, but Dorothea had not paid as much attention as she would have had she known he would not see another sugaring season. At the time she had wondered, idly, how her uncle had come to discover how Mr. Liggett's sugar tasted, since they never traded work and were definitely not friends. Now, a new realization struck her: Uncle Jacob must have observed Mr. Liggett's trees firsthand in order to know such specific details of his sugaring methods. Evidently the night of his death was not Uncle Jacob's only occasion to visit Elm Creek Farm.

Troubled, Dorothea swung open the door to the sugarhouse and stepped inside. Uncle Jacob's tools lay in their proper places, exactly where he had left them. Dorothea tried to imagine sugaring without him, but her mind's eye refused to form the pictures.

One object out of place caught her eye: The quilt she had painstakingly created from her uncle's drawings lay on the ground beside an old wooden bench. She remembered last seeing it draped across the bench, but she must have jostled it in her haste to search for her uncle. She bent down to pick up the quilt, brushing dirt and stray bits of crumbled maple leaves from the fabric. Her gaze traced the path the triangles made, lingering upon familiar scraps she recognized from sewing her uncle's work shirts and Sunday trousers. Without realizing it, she had made him a memorial quilt.

She folded the quilt and tucked it under her arm.

"We must send for Jonathan," said Lorena as the family walked back to the house from the gravesite. Dorothea felt a stirring of feeling then, a distant gratitude. Jonathan would surely come to hear the will read. If, as they all hoped, he inherited Uncle Jacob's estate, he might even decide to stay and continue his studies with the local physician.

Once Uncle Jacob was safely beneath the ground, Lorena began sorting through his papers. She found his ledger and the will, which she wanted to open but declined to do so without his lawyer present, lest anyone accuse her of tampering with it. Dorothea knew a simple comparison with the copy on file with the county clerk would clear her of any such charges. She suspected her mother hesitated to read the will out of fear that it would not fulfill her hopes.

A steady flow of condolences came once the death notice appeared in the *Creek's Crossing Informer*. Friends visited with gifts of food and words of comfort. All who came agreed that he had been a hard man, but decent and God-fearing, and that surely he would receive his just reward. "The Lord is merciful and I am confident he will reward my brother as he deserves," Lorena always replied.

Dorothea wanted to remind her that it was not always a mercy to receive what one deserved.

❧

A week after Uncle Jacob's death, Abel Wright came to pay his respects. Dorothea took him to the grave and stood some distance away while he bowed his head in silent prayer. Then he looked up and said, "I have something to tell you and your folks."

Dorothea took him back to the house, where her mother had been emptying Uncle Jacob's bedroom of his clothes and books and his few other possessions. She could not dispose of anything until after the will was read in case the worst happened and Jonathan did not inherit, but she wanted to have the room ready for her son should he decide to take it, or for herself and Robert if Jonathan declined.

Lorena put the kettle on and sent Dorothea to the barn for her father while Mr. Wright took a seat in the front room. He shifted uncomfortably in his chair while Dorothea poured, but gave her a kindly smile and thanked her as he took his cup. His expression grew more serious as he returned his attention to her parents.

"There's something about your brother you need to know," he said. "I can tell you why he was on Liggett's land that night."

Startled, Dorothea set the teapot on the table too hard, rattling the china. She murmured an apology, sank into her usual seat by the fire, and picked up the pieces of an Album block with trembling hands. She held her breath and waited for Mr. Wright to confirm Charley's suspicions: Mr. Liggett had been involved in her uncle's death.

Robert began, "How—"

"I remember now," Lorena interrupted. "You saw him that day. He said you had told him of Mr. Schultz's return."

"I saw him later, too." Mr. Wright hesitated. "He was coming from my place. He was going to cross Elm Creek at the place where it narrows in Liggett's woods."

"Why?" asked Robert. "Why not use the ferry?"

"He couldn't be seen crossing so many times in one night. Folks might ask questions."

"Questions? What questions?" asked Dorothea. "Why could he not be seen?"

"He didn't want any of you folks to know." He directed his gaze at Dorothea. "Except you. He was proud of you. He thought maybe you could be told. The older he got, the more he wished he could ask for your help. But he knew it was too dangerous."

Robert's voice was slow and direct. "What was too dangerous?"

"Helping runaways."

The room was silent.

"My brother—" Lorena paused and began again. "My brother was no abolitionist."

"He didn't talk about it, but he was," said Mr. Wright. "Do you really think I saved up enough money to free Constance selling cheese?"

"But he objected to your trip," said Lorena. "If it had been up to him, Constance would have perished enslaved."

"No," said Dorothea, suddenly remembering. "He objected to the timing."

"He objected to putting a single penny into the pockets of slavers, too," said Mr. Wright. "He wanted me to help Constance escape, like we helped the others. That's what I wanted at first, but when Constance wouldn't run, I agreed to do it her way. When we couldn't wait any longer, Jacob gave me the rest of the money I needed."

"You brought escaping slaves north in your wagon after delivering your cheeses in the South," said Robert.

"Sometimes. Other times I just brought them things they needed. Directions, false papers, money, things like that."

"Why did Jacob not tell us?" asked Lorena, bewildered. "He knew we loathe slavery. We would have assisted him."

Mr. Wright almost allowed a smile. "Sure, he knew how you felt. So does everyone else in town. Jacob thought you two were too free with your opinions. You might not have been able to keep quiet."

Insulted, Lorena said, "That is just like my brother. Selfish even in his altruism, not to allow us to share in his mission."

"Well, you can surely share in it now. We need this station. We already lost one on this route when the Carters left—"

"The Carters?" echoed Robert.

"Goodness," gasped Lorena. "Are there any more abolitionists in this town who have not dared to reveal themselves to us?"

"Some serve the cause of abolition by speaking out, and others by operating in secrecy," Dorothea broke in. "Clearly Uncle Jacob was able to assist runaways because no one, not even his family, would have suspected him."

"Be that as it may." Lorena lifted her palms and let them fall to her lap. "I only wish we could have helped him."

Mr. Wright said, "Dorothea already has."

He exacted their solemn vow that they would never reveal the rest of the tale before he agreed to explain.

The escape route through the Elm Creek Valley was relatively new, as the southern pass through the Appalachians was difficult to navigate except by those who knew it well. Most stationmasters knew little about the other stations along the route, a necessary precaution should any one of them be compelled to confess what he knew. The safe havens for runaways ranged from the house proper, in the case of the Wrights, to a secret cellar beneath a stable, to Uncle Jacob's sugar camp. "He wasn't so protective of his sugar-making secrets," said Mr. Wright. "He just pretended to keep folks away. He thought it was right funny anyone believed it."

Mr. Wright knew of at least one station between his farm and the southern pass; there could be more, but he wasn't speculating. It was safer not to know too much about any station but one's own and the next one down the line. Runaways who reached the Wright farm used to travel on foot to Two Bears

Farm two miles to the north, making a risky journey across Mr. Liggett's property in order to ford Elm Creek at its narrowest point.

Two Bears Farm was lost to them after the Carters moved away, since no one knew Mr. Nelson well enough to ask him to continue the dangerous work. Until then, Uncle Jacob had occasionally allowed runaways to spend the night in his barn out of respect for his late wife's beliefs, but with the Carters gone, he had agreed to assume a more significant role and became a stationmaster. Unwilling to risk his family's safety and reluctant for them to discover his clandestine activities, he made his sugar camp the station. Unfortunately, the distance between the Wright farm and Uncle Jacob's was too great to navigate on foot in a single night. For the past eight months, fugitives had been forced to find shelter in corn fields or woods between the Wright farm and Uncle Jacob's sugar camp, unless Mr. Wright could carry them north in his wagon or Uncle Jacob could travel south to fetch them. This was not always possible, as frequent travel between the two farms would draw unwanted attention. To conceal the truth from the Grangers, Uncle Jacob would pretend to have an appointment with his attorney.

"But he made frequent visits to his attorney long before the Carters moved away," interrupted Lorena. "And on occasion I saw him bring back legal papers. Did he forge those, as well, merely to deceive us?"

"No, many of those visits were genuine," said Mr. Wright. He gave a rueful shrug, either to apologize for Uncle Jacob's behavior or for what he intended to say next. "He said you folks were always on your best behavior after he met with his lawyer. That's why he considered it such an advantageous excuse."

"Well," huffed Lorena. "I hardly know what to think."

But Dorothea knew. So much of her uncle's strange behavior now made perfect sense—his self-enforced isolation in the sugar camp, the occasions when he could not be found when needed, the meals he carried with him as he went off to work early, his frequent visits to the attorney. He had not been changing his will at the slightest offense after all, as he had encouraged them to believe. In hindsight Dorothea was certain he had enjoyed deceiving them.

"You said I helped him," said Dorothea, "but I cannot imagine how."

"Do you still have that quilt you made him?"

Dorothea nodded and retrieved the Sugar Camp Quilt from her attic bedroom. Mr. Wright unfolded it and ran his hand across its surface. "Your uncle never knew when runaways would come, and since he couldn't wait around the sugar camp to greet them, he had Dorothea make this quilt. It marked the sugar camp as a safe haven, of course, but it also told runaways where to go next, in case they had to leave before Jacob had a chance to explain."

Robert shook his head. "The *quilt* told them?"

Even as he spoke, Dorothea understood. "Those odd blocks my uncle drew—the varied number of triangle points on the Delectable Mountains blocks. This is a map."

"In a way it is." Mr. Wright held out the quilt to Dorothea. "It's more like a list of directions."

"Where do they lead?" asked Lorena, gazing eagerly at the quilt as Dorothea draped it over her lap.

Even as Mr. Wright confessed that he did not know, Dorothea began to puzzle it out. "These represent the Four Brothers mountains to the north of the Elm Creek Valley," she said, indicating the upper left portion of the quilt where the three- and five-triangle edged blocks stood apart from those that had the traditional four. She wondered how she had not noticed before how the number of triangles in the blocks mirrored the most prominent peaks of the mountain range. "And these . . ." She examined the five blocks Uncle Jacob had so deliberately sketched. "These must be intermediate steps along the safest route north."

"My brother's insistence on accuracy at last becomes clear," said Lorena, a trifle dryly. "He could not leave a map or written directions at the sugar camp where a slavecatcher might discover them."

Nor would written instructions have been useful to fugitive slaves who could not read. Dorothea thought of her uncle's request for scraps of serviceable fabrics, of the mud he had wiped from his boots. He had wanted the quilt to seem old and worn, nothing so precious that it could not have been left behind in a sugarhouse.

Dorothea stroked the quilt and was suddenly struck by a profound sense of loss. Her uncle had concealed his brave secrets, unwilling to incriminate his family but also wary that they might expose him. What an unnecessary effort his secrecy had been. The Grangers were outspoken in their views, but they were not fools. They would have been a great help to him, had they but known. He had underestimated his family, and it may have cost him his life. Dorothea could have assisted him on the night of the school exhibition. She could have helped him think of a plausible excuse for crossing on the ferry. If only Uncle

Jacob had trusted her, he would not have been alone on Mr. Liggett's land when the apoplexy befell him.

But he had not been alone. "What became of the runaway who was with Uncle Jacob on the night he died?"

From Mr. Wright's expression, she knew he had been expecting the question—and dreading it. "I figure he continued on north, on horseback."

"Of course. What other choice had he?" said Lorena briskly. "He could not have done anything for my brother in any event."

"I hope he at least tried," said Robert.

He spoke quietly, but there was an odd note of contempt in his voice that drew Dorothea's attention away from the quilt.

"Robert," said Lorena steadily. "There is no reason to believe that this unfortunate fugitive killed my brother for his horse. He had no need. Jacob was transporting him in greater safety than if he attempted to go alone."

"I'm not saying he killed him," said Robert, "but perhaps he left him to die."

"The runaway didn't know the way to the next station," Mr. Wright reminded him. "He needed Jacob."

"All he needed to know was how to get to the sugar camp. If he gave the horse her lead, she would have taken him right past it on the way to the barn. Once the runaway saw the quilt, he would have known where to go."

Lorena reached out and stroked his arm. "You heard what Mr. Donne said. My brother almost certainly died instantly. There was no sign of any struggle, any suffering. Can you imagine how terrified the runaway must have been? Would you have expected him to stay rather than flee for safety? Why? Out of respect for the deceased, out of concern for our sensibilities?"

"Sam," said Mr. Wright. His face was stone. "His name is Sam. This runaway is a man. He has a name. He is not some killer on the run. He is fleeing *for* justice, not from it."

Robert looked away. "We'll never know that, will we?"

Dorothea studied the quilt. "It may be possible." She addressed Mr. Wright. "You said you do not know where the signs in this quilt are meant to lead?"

He shook his head. "It's better that I don't know."

"One of us must find out." She plunged ahead before her parents could object. "One of us must know where the next station lies if we mean to continue Uncle Jacob's work. We do mean to continue?"

Mr. Wright tensed almost imperceptibly, but only Dorothea saw it. Her parents were looking at each other, debating their decision without saying a word. A moment later they turned back to Dorothea and Mr. Wright and nodded. "Of course," said Lorena. "We would have helped before if your uncle had allowed."

"You should think carefully before you decide," cautioned Mr. Wright, though his relief was evident. "There are laws against helping runaways, and folks like Liggett who would give you up in a heartbeat."

Dorothea thought of how Uncle Jacob had disparaged Mr. Schultz for following his better nature. "I am not afraid," she said, emboldened by her disappointment that Uncle Jacob had not shown more faith in them. "Were we not already exposed to prosecution by virtue of my uncle's actions? Had he been detected, who would have believed that we had not known?"

"No one would have considered a girl your age complicit in any crime, Dorothea," said her father. He nodded to Mr. Wright. "I will figure out the riddle of this quilt tonight. Tomorrow morning, I will follow wherever it leads."

"No, Father," said Dorothea. "I should do it."

They regarded her with surprise. "It is good that you want to help," said her mother, "but you are too young. It is too dangerous."

"I am a grown woman and I know the Elm Creek Valley better than anyone." Only Jonathan knew the forest and fields so well, and if he were there, Dorothea knew he would insist upon going instead of her parents, who never left the well-traveled roads. "It is as Father said: No one would suspect me. That is why, like Uncle Jacob, I should be the one to do this. I know I can."

They looked doubtful, even fearful. She thought they would forbid it outright. Instead they sent her from the room to begin supper while they discussed it. By the time she called them to the table, they had decided.

Dorothea would follow the route depicted in the Sugar Camp Quilt to discover where it lay and to meet the stationmaster there. He and Mr. Wright would advise them how to proceed. The Grangers knew little of the operations of the Underground Railroad, but they would learn. The sugar camp would remain a haven for runaways. There was never really any question of doing otherwise.

Together the Grangers would continue the work Uncle Jacob had begun, the work he had not trusted them to share.

❧

Snow fell overnight, but the next morning dawned clear and brisk. Dorothea set out after completing her chores, bundled warmly against the cold. Her breath ghosted through her muffler in faint white puffs as she broke a trail to the sugar camp, the quilt under one arm. She and her father had begun studying it as soon as Mr. Wright had departed the day before, and they had stayed up late into the evening, uncertain how to decipher the patchwork symbols. Lorena had searched through Uncle Jacob's belongings for a journal, letters, anything that might explain the meaning of the quilt's design. Mr. Wright had warned them this would be a wasted effort, for like any good stationmaster, Uncle Jacob knew better than to put his secrets in writing. Some might consider even the wordless symbols of the Sugar Camp Quilt too great a risk. Sure enough, Lorena's search turned up nothing. Even the sketches Uncle Jacob had made for Dorothea were gone.

Eventually the Grangers concluded that the designs had so many potential meanings the quilt was, perhaps intentionally, incomprehensible to anyone who could not see their actual counterparts. Since Dorothea was fairly confident she understood the first clue, she decided to proceed and hope she recognized the other landmarks when she encountered them.

She committed the patterns to memory and draped the quilt over the bench as she had seen it the night Uncle Jacob went missing. On the day of his burial, she had found it on the ground and had assumed she had knocked it down in her haste, but gazing at it now, she wondered if the runaway named Sam had done so. Perhaps her father was right and he had let the horse lead him there before continuing north. Perhaps her father was right about Sam in other matters.

Dorothea shook off the thought and focused on the five unusual blocks Uncle Jacob had sketched. The star in the center of the quilt, with its longest point directed to the upper left corner, had seemed off-kilter and strange to her before, but now that she understood the quilt's true purpose, the design resembled a compass rose pointing to the northwest. Since the Four Brothers were depicted in the upper left corner of the outermost border of Delectable Mountains blocks, and since the real mountains lay northwest of the farm, Dorothea surmised that the fugitives were supposed to bear in that direction.

She studied the quilt one last time and left it behind in the sugar camp, regretting the necessity. She would have liked to bring it along in case she had neglected an important detail in the patterns, but she could not afford to be seen using the quilt as a map. Uncle Jacob's compass was a reassuring weight in her pocket as she made her way through the maple grove, her footsteps muffled by the thin layer of snow covering the fallen leaves. Her father had insisted she take the compass, though she had argued she probably would not need one, since the fugitives did not and had to be able to follow the quilt regardless. Now she was glad he had insisted.

At the last moment her father had also urged her to travel on horseback rather than walk. Mr. Wright had told them stations were ideally no more than ten miles apart, a long day's walk even in fair weather. Dorothea had been tempted, but Uncle Jacob would have assumed the runaways would travel on foot. The landmarks might be so subtle that she would miss them if she rode. So she packed food and dry stockings in her coat pockets, hoped the stationmaster would allow her to spend the night by his fire, and prayed the journey would not be long.

An old worm fence marked the boundary between Uncle Jacob's land and his neighbor's, zigzagging off in both directions and disappearing into the trees. Dorothea lifted her skirts and climbed over it, glancing up through the bare-limbed trees for the position of the sky to be sure she still headed northwest. She considered checking the compass when, with a sudden flash of insight, she halted and peered over her shoulder at the fence. It resembled a crooked ladder on its side, or the quilt block she had inadvertently encouraged her uncle to redraft.

She hesitated, uncertain. The fence did seem to run almost due north, the logical direction for a runaway slave to go, but if she were mistaken, she could find herself wandering far from the correct route until nightfall with no shelter from the cold. "Any wrong choice will have the same consequences," she said aloud. The air seemed colder when she stood still, so she approached the fence and rested her hand upon it. She had to keep moving; she had to choose.

The crooked ladder block lay in the ring of blocks encircling the central compass rose. If the center indicated the beginning of the route, the crooked ladder clue, which could indeed depict a worm fence, would be the second clue, the first landmark.

Lacking any reason to choose otherwise and unable to conceive of anything that would resemble Uncle Jacob's sketch more than the fence, Dorothea decided to follow it north. She quickly dismissed the troubling thought that the fence snaked off to the south as well as to the north, and that even if she had found the right landmark, she might be traveling in the wrong direction.

Twenty minutes later, she emerged from the maple grove at the bottom of a low slope that rose to the west. She followed the fence to the top, from where she looked out over acres of old cornstalks sticking up through the snow. A house, barn, and three smaller outbuildings sat at the far edge of the fields. Dorothea searched her memory for the name of the family. "Wheeler," she murmured. They had eleven children and had sent only the youngest boys to her school. She was not sure how they would feel about her trespassing on their land, or what excuse she might invent for her presence there.

Walking would be easier on the open ground on the Wheelers' side of the fence, but she quickly climbed back to the eastern side and concealed herself in the woods. She could still glimpse the fence through the tree trunks as she made her way north, but she feared she might miss the next landmark entirely. The next concentric square of Delectable Mountains blocks contained a patch that resembled a narrow braid stretching from left to right on a slight angle. She assumed that was the next block pattern to interpret since it followed the sequence moving outward from the center.

Her dress caught on a tree branch; she tried to pull free but stopped at the sound of fabric tearing. She stopped to untangle herself, wishing Uncle Jacob had been more explicit despite the need for secrecy. It was a wonder Uncle Jacob's runaways had not given up and returned to the sugar camp for better directions.

She continued, stumbling through the underbrush with the worm fence six paces to her left. She passed the Wheelers' house and barn. In the distance, she heard a dog bark, but she did not see it nor any sign of the home's inhabitants, save a thin trace of smoke curling from the chimney.

The corner post of the fence appeared. Dorothea paused to catch her breath, regarding it with misgivings. The fence continued west along the road directly in front of the Wheeler farm. Anyone walking alongside it could easily be spotted from the house or barn.

Uncle Jacob surely would not have sent the runaways so close to an unknown household. She considered, for a moment, that the Wheeler farm might be the next station, but she could not be more than two miles from the sugar camp and had three clues yet to follow. She held perfectly still and listened for the sound of horses on the road, but heard only the wind in the trees. Reassured of her solitude, she made her way stealthily through the woods, drawing closer to the corner fence post. Suddenly she tripped over a low depression in the ground; naked branches scratched at her face as she stumbled and struck her shoulder on the rough trunk of an oak. Instinctively she pressed her lips together to hold back a cry of pain. She quickly regained her footing but had to pause to collect herself. Her shoulder ached. She rubbed it with a mittened hand and searched the ground for the obstruction. It was not a hole, as she had assumed, but a narrow patch where the under-growth had been worn away to bare earth.

With the tip of her boot she cleared away fallen leaves from one end of the patch. When she found more worn ground, she eagerly looked up and detected an indistinct path winding to the northeast for a few yards before it disappeared into the forest. It was an old Indian trail, abandoned for decades—or perhaps not entirely abandoned. The path did lie along the same angle as the next block in the Sugar Camp Quilt, and the braid appearance could be meant to evoke an association with Indians.

Dorothea concealed the part of the path she had uncovered and set off to the northeast. The trail that had seemed all but invisible until she knew what to look for widened slightly a quarter mile east of the Wheeler farm, wide enough for a horse and rider. Years ago, Dorothea and Jonathan had explored old Indian trails that crossed Thrift Farm, and they had followed one all the way from Widow's Pining to the foothills of the Appalachians at the southern end of the Elm Creek Valley. Such trails laced the valley; European settlers had widened some into roads, but most remained overgrown and forgotten. Pennsylvania remained difficult to traverse despite the rise of towns such as Creek's Crossing. Most easterners traveling to points west still preferred the water routes to the south along the Maryland and Virginia border rather than the national roads through Pennsylvania's mountains. Mr. Wright had said that the rugged terrain of the Elm Creek Valley had compelled weary fugitives to find easier routes to the north, but as slavecatchers increased their patrols along the more well-traveled crossings, more runaways would be forced into their valley.

The sun rose higher in the sky as Dorothea followed the Indian trail through the woods. It was past its peak when she finally had to stop to rest and eat. Her shoulder still hurt where she had slammed it against the tree; her hands were cold, but not numb. Her feet were cold inside the work boots she had borrowed from her mother, but they were dry, and the three pairs of socks she wore would hold off frostbite.

Dorothea saved half of the bread, cheese, and meat for later and sated her thirst with a handful of snow. She shivered from the cold but took another mouthful before pulling her muffler over her mouth and nose and continuing on.

Another hour passed, or so Dorothea guessed. She had meant to note how long the journey took, but the passage of time had become a blur of weariness and cold and the glare of sunlight on snow. Her feet ached in the overlarge boots; despite the three pairs of socks, a blister had formed on her left heel, and cold had crept into her bones. Her hand, nose, and feet steadily grew colder until they became numb. She longed to stop somewhere to warm herself, but the woods surrounded her. There was no place to go, and she could not be certain that home was closer than her destination.

Runaways could not turn back. She pressed on.

She should have taken the horse, she thought as she floundered through a thick patch of underbrush. Once she lost the trail, but found it again. The next block in the sequence was the one that resembled the curves of the Fool's Puzzle block. The Indian trail must eventually cross another path, perhaps a circuitous or hilly road. She shook off the anxieties that had been growing ever since she left the familiarity of the worm fence. She told herself she would recognize the next landmark when she saw it.

Another hour passed, or perhaps more. She stopped to rest on a fallen tree, to remove her boots and rub feeling back into her toes. The temperature had steadily dropped as the sun descended in the sky. It could be no more than midafternoon, but she was as fatigued as if she had walked from dawn until sunset. Wave after wave of weariness overcame her as she sat rubbing and pinching her feet. They tingled a bit and she could still move her toes, but she yawned as she tried to work sensation back into them, great, enormous yawns. Her hands moved ever slower.

She woke with a jolt as her hip struck the ground. Dazed, for a moment she did not understand what had happened. When she did she yanked on her stockings and boots and laced them, shivering from fear as much as from cold. She had dozed off and fallen from her seat on the log. If she had not, she might have slept until she froze to death.

Fright sped her footsteps. The trail grew more difficult to discern as the forest thinned and shadows stretched out longer and longer. The trees grew more sparse, the path all but invisible. Disbelieving, she came to a halt as the trail ended. She must have missed the road. The Indian trail surely would have crossed it. She turned slowly in a circle, heart sinking. She would have to retrace her steps and look more carefully. But how far off the route had she wandered? How many needless miles and hours had she added to her journey?

Fighting despair, she closed her eyes and whispered a prayer for courage. Uncle Jacob expected fugitive slaves to make this journey, men and women and even children who had not that morning left the comfort of their home and family, who could not expect a cordial welcome at any farm in the valley. Unless her uncle was a fool, he had known that the people following the symbols in his quilt would be tired, hungry, frightened—and possibly pursued. He would not have made the quilt so difficult to follow. Unless she believed her uncle to be a fool, she would have to trust the message he had left behind.

With her eyes closed, she heard the wind blow through the trees. The few dried leaves still clinging to the trees rustled. Bare boughs squeaked as they scraped against each other. Behind it all, she heard another sound: a gentle, almost musical burbling.

Her eyes flew open and she hurried toward the sound. She recognized it now: the trickling of water. The curving road she sought was a stream, shallow and rocky, nearly frozen over.

She looked down upon it from the snowy bank, laughing aloud from relief even as tears sprang to her eyes. She had found it, she was sure of it, but this was only the third of four landmarks. She could not endure another walk as long as the Indian trail to reach the fourth.

She took a deep breath and gave only one quick, worried glance to the sun nearly touching the horizon. The creek flowed to the east, but instead of following the current, she chose west and hurried on.

She should have started out from home earlier. She should have taken the horse. She should have let her father go instead. Her feet slipped on snow-covered pebbles as she hurried to beat the sunset. The last symbol in the quilt, a square in the upper left corner between the last ring of Delectable Mountains blocks and the sawtooth border, was the most cryptic of all. While piecing it, she had noted the similarities to the Spiderweb block, with its eight slender triangles meeting at a point in the center, but the bases of the triangles were made of narrow rectangles. Surely she could not be looking for something as transient as a spiderweb.

Racing the fading light, she reached the origin of the stream, a broad, fast-flowing creek—not Elm Creek, she was sure, but one that ran from the northwest between cultivated fields. On the other side of the creek was a road, and beyond that, a banked barn and farmhouse. Her hopes rose, and she forgot for a moment the cold and the dull ache of her hands and feet. Though she might not reach the end of her journey before nightfall, she would not freeze to death. Unlike the fugitives for whom the Sugar Camp Quilt had been created, she could seek shelter at one of the farmhouses.

Newly energized, she quickened her pace. Scattered houses appeared more frequently until she was sure she had reached the outskirts of a town. A wagon passed on the road on the opposite shore, but if the driver regarded her curiously, he could not surely consider her behavior suspicious.

Then, suddenly, the sound of the creek altered. She rounded a bend and gasped. Another wagon and a man on foot passed on the road, but she barely noticed them.

Up ahead, turning steadily in the fading light, was the water wheel of a mill. Just beyond it were a bridge and the gray-board buildings of a town.

Relief flooded her. In moments she had reached the road and hastened across the bridge. The sun was nearly gone by the time she pounded on the door of the millhouse, heedless of any passersby who might wonder at her urgency.

The door opened, and a woman with piercing eyes and streaks of white in her dark hair regarded her with concern. "What is it, my dear?"

The moment had come and Dorothea knew not what to say. "I—I'm Jacob Kuehner's niece."

The woman did not hesitate. "Come in. Come in at once and warm yourself."

Muffling a sob, Dorothea stumbled inside.

Chapter Seven

T he woman shut the door and guided Dorothea to a seat by the fire. Dorothea fumbled with her wraps, her eyes tearing from the sudden warmth and light. Her hands were stiff and useless. The woman swiftly removed Dorothea's muffler and coat, then knelt to remove her boots and stockings. Dorothea began to shiver, shaking so uncontrollably that she could not have spoken even if she could have summoned enough strength for words. Within moments the woman placed a cup of hot tea in her hands, and, once assured Dorothea was thoroughly cold but not frostbitten, began to scold her.

"I cannot imagine what your uncle was thinking, sending you out so late and in such cold," she said, using a long-handled hook to pull the iron arm of the kettle crane out of the fireplace.

"He didn't send me." Dorothea drank deeply of the tea, her shaking hands rattling the cup against her teeth. "He is dead."

"I see." The woman stirred the kettle, tasted its contents, and swung the arm back into the fireplace. The aroma of beef stew made Dorothea's head swim and mouth water. "The last passenger told us so, but I had hoped he was mistaken."

Passenger. "You mean Sam. He did come here."

"Yes, riding your uncle's horse. She's in our barn." The woman set out plates and spoons on a wooden table in the center of the room. "You will ride her home, of course, but not tonight. You'll spend the night here."

"Thank you." Dorothea glanced around the large room for a sign of the runaway, but her hostess was not that careless. "Is Sam still here?"

"He continued on north the day after he arrived." The woman gave her a searching look. "We had snow that day. He should have remained with us until the storm passed, but he was terrified to have northerners as well as slavecatchers pursue him. He feared he would be blamed for your uncle's death."

Dorothea thought of her father's suspicions. "Very few know Sam was present when my uncle died. Only one voiced any concern."

"You will have to set that one straight, then. Sam had nothing to do with it."

"Did he tell you what happened?"

"Sounds like an apoplexy, the way Sam described it. He was hidden in the wagon beneath a tarpaulin when the wagon lurched and left the road. Sam peeked out and saw your uncle slumped over in the wagon seat, still holding the reins. He drove the wagon right off the path and into a river—some tributary of the Juniata, I suppose."

"It was Elm Creek," said Dorothea softly, picturing the scene. Uncle Jacob must not have died instantly after all. She wondered if he had lived long enough to realize what was happening to him.

"That horse of his is a capable creature. She didn't buck or panic when the wagon overturned, but waited patiently for someone to unhitch her." The woman set a loaf of bread and a ball of butter on the table. "Your uncle wasn't breathing, nor did his heart beat. Sam spied a cabin and considered asking for help there, but instead he took the horse and gave it its lead home."

"He was wise not to knock on the door of that cabin. The man within would have turned him over to the next band of slavecatchers to pass through the valley."

"They pass through far too frequently these days." The woman sighed and settled into a chair opposite Dorothea's. "We never used to see more than one group every two or three months around here."

"Where, precisely, is here?"

The woman's eyebrows rose. "You don't know? You're in Woodfall, dear. You've walked eleven miles, nearly halfway to Clearfield."

Dorothea gave a shaky laugh. "That explains why I'm so weary."

"Indeed," the woman said dryly. "You look hearty enough, but one wonders why your father did not come instead."

"He wanted to, but I thought I would be less likely to raise suspicions."

"Oh, certainly. A young woman wandering about alone on a cold winter's eve. No one would think twice about that." She regarded Dorothea with amusement. "So the children make the rules around your house now that your uncle's gone, do they?"

Before Dorothea could reply, a door on the far wall opened. Dorothea glimpsed the machinery of the mill in the room beyond as a barrel-chested man with sandy hair and whiskers entered. He shut the door and halted at the sight of Dorothea shivering beside the fire. "Well, who's this now?" he asked, his voice deep but friendly.

"This is—" The woman gave a small laugh. "My goodness, I don't know her name."

"I'm Dorothea Granger."

"She's Jacob Kuehner's niece."

The miller's eyes filled with sympathy. He shook her hand and offered his condolences. "Your uncle was a good man," said the miller, whose name was Aaron Braun. "His death is a great loss to the abolitionist cause."

"My parents and I intend to continue to run his station."

The husband and wife exchanged a look. "I see," said the miller slowly.

"This is not a task entered into lightly," said his wife. "To the young it may seem a romantic adventure, but it is a dangerous business."

"The fugitives depend upon us not only for their freedom, but often for their very lives," said Aaron Braun. "And we depend upon each other's secrecy for our own survival."

At once, Dorothea understood the reason for their concern, the dread that lingered not far below their calm exteriors. "My parents and I realize we must scrupulously conceal our activities. We will, of course, rely on your advice."

"What if our advice is to abandon your plans?"

Dorothea straightened in the chair and met his gaze levelly. "Then I would tell you that would be unwise. You have already lost the Carters, and as I have myself discovered, the journey from Creek's Crossing to Woodfall is too far to venture without a safe haven along the way."

A smile flickered in the corners of Mrs. Braun's mouth. "Most slaves are wise enough not to attempt an escape in the dead of winter."

"Some have no choice. Sam, for example."

The Brauns exchanged a look. Dorothea had no idea why Sam had fled to the north in January rather than waiting for spring, but she could imagine various reasons. She felt a flush of shame at allowing the Brauns to believe she knew more than she did, but securing their confidence was too important.

"They already know enough to betray us," Mrs. Braun told her husband after the doubtful silence dragged on unbearably long. "We might as well let them help."

"Our uncle's activities have already exposed us to the dangers we would face as stationmasters," said Dorothea. "We are prepared to face them knowingly, now."

"So it is to be 'in for a penny, in for a pound'?" said the miller, but his voice was kindly.

His wife's expression was graver. "If we allow you to do this, we will be putting our lives into your hands."

"We would die before we would betray you."

"Would you, indeed." Mrs. Braun smiled, but deep grooves of worry appeared around her mouth. "My dear, you cannot make that promise on anyone's behalf but your own. Especially when you will be expected to keep it."

❧

Mrs. Braun beckoned her husband and Dorothea to the table and served them steaming plates of fragrant beef stew with thick slices of fresh bread. Ravenous, Dorothea thought she had never eaten anything more delicious. While they ate, she expected to query the Brauns about the operation of the Underground Railroad, but they put two questions to her for every one she asked them. They asked how she had found the route to the mill and why her uncle had not confided in her family. She told them about the quilt and answered their other questions as honestly as she knew how. By the time the meal was over, Dorothea felt as if her memory had been put through a mangle and squeezed dry. She had learned almost nothing about the Brauns' station. They did not reveal by so much as a word or a glance whether they hid their passengers in the mill itself or their adjacent residence.

It was late in the evening when Mrs. Braun ordered Dorothea to bed, in a motherly way, affectionate but unyielding. When Dorothea protested, Mr. Braun promised her they would continue their discussion in the morning. Dorothea nodded and resolved that it would not, however, proceed in the same fashion. She had only a few hours to learn all she could from her hosts, and she could not do that if they subjected her to more questioning.

Mrs. Braun led her to a small bedroom on the second story. Dorothea undressed to her shift and climbed beneath the layers of quilts, shivering until she grew warm. She fell asleep almost immediately and woke, hours later, to the sound of the low, steady grinding of the mill. The whole house seemed to tremble.

She dressed swiftly, judging from the sunlight outside it was past eight o'clock. Mrs. Braun was already working in the large room downstairs, which seemed to be kitchen, front room, and parlor all at once. The Brauns had eaten their breakfast earlier since Mr. Braun had to run the mill, but Mrs. Braun invited Dorothea to the table and soon placed a hot plate of potato pancakes and sausages before her.

Mrs. Braun poured them each a steaming cup of tea, and as she seated herself, Dorothea said, "There is much my parents and I need to know about running a station."

"Yes." Mrs. Braun sipped her tea. "So a good night's sleep did not clear your thoughts of such foolish notions."

"They are not foolish notions, and like it or not, you need our help. The situation is so desperate I must wonder why you would turn us away."

"Forgive me, but your uncle did not think your parents capable."

Dorothea felt a surge of loyal anger. "He did not know them as well as I. We found you, did we not?"

Mrs. Braun nodded in acquiescence. "*You* did. Very well, then." She set down her teacup and folded her arms on the wooden table. "I will tell you what you need to know."

Dorothea drank in every word as Mrs. Braun explained the coded language preferred by the stationmasters and conductors, how to conceal one's tracks in the forest, various means to convey a fugitive north, and so much else that Dorothea felt she could not absorb it all. There was too much to remember, and as Mrs. Braun gravely recounted stories of friends and acquaintances whose stations had been discovered and what they had suffered, Dorothea felt her confidence wavering. A fine her family could bear, but imprisonment? The seizure of the farm? The responsibility was so great, as were the consequences. If they failed, they could be worse off than when Elm Creek claimed Thrift Farm. They could be rendered destitute. They could fail those who depended upon them.

Then she thought of what Constance Wright had endured until her husband bought her freedom, and what so many others like her endured every day while Dorothea lived in safety and comfort with her loving family.

She inhaled deeply and sighed. Mrs. Braun studied her. "Are you having second thoughts?"

"Of course," said Dorothea. "But how can I refuse to help? Whatever I might face is nothing compared to what the runaways have suffered. I cannot turn my back."

At last, Mrs. Braun smiled with a warmth that lit up her eyes, and Dorothea knew instinctively that she was speaking with a kindred spirit, the sort of woman she would like to become.

"That is precisely how I felt when Aaron and I embarked on this journey together," said Mrs. Braun. "I have never regretted my decision. May you never have reason to regret yours."

They talked at length, until Dorothea felt she was as prepared as she could be for the task her family had undertaken. Mrs. Braun sent her husband's apprentice to saddle Uncle Jacob's horse while Dorothea put on her wraps, bracing for the cold ride home.

"Do not tarry," advised Mrs. Braun. "The air smells like snow coming."

Mr. Braun instructed her to follow a different route home rather than backtracking along the Sugar Camp Quilt trail. The journey home was much swifter on horseback along the main roads, but Dorothea still did not reach home until after noon. Her parents must have been watching the road, for they ran to meet her before she reached the barn. Their relief was so obvious that Dorothea almost wished she had left the Brauns' at daybreak and spared her parents a few hours of waiting, but she had needed that time with Mrs. Braun.

She recounted for them every detail of her journey from the moment she left the sugar camp until she departed the stable behind the mill. Lorena seemed most interested in Mrs. Braun's guidance for running their station; Robert, on the fate of Sam. He seemed to accept that the runaway had had no part in Uncle Jacob's death. Dorothea accepted Mrs. Braun's word. Robert took as evidence the safe return of the horse.

Dorothea's parents had news of their own to report. Cyrus Pearson had called for her earlier that day, and he had seemed most disgruntled to discover her absent. He asked to wait for her, but Lorena invented an ill friend and said Dorothea would be tending her for at least the rest of the day. He left, reluctantly, with a message: His mother was eager to complete the quilt and wanted to know when Dorothea would be willing to bring her blocks so they could finish piecing the top.

For a moment, Dorothea thought he meant the Sugar Camp Quilt, and then she remembered the Authors' Album. She had not thought of the opportunity quilt or the library board since the night Uncle Jacob went missing. For that matter, she had not given a single thought to Cyrus, who had once occupied so many of her idle musings. She might have missed two board meetings, or perhaps three. Cyrus had not come by the farm to fetch her for them or she would have been reminded. He had probably assumed that the family was in mourning and that she would not have gone. Still, it would have been thoughtful of him to pay his respects to Uncle Jacob out of consideration for Dorothea. Perhaps he knew the older man had not liked him and did not want to appear a hypocrite.

"I have only one block left," said Dorothea. "I will finish it tonight and take the blocks to Mrs. Engle's house tomorrow rather than wait until next Thursday." Her mother had not mentioned that Cyrus planned to come for her then, and she was reluctant to ask.

"There is more news," said Lorena, withdrawing a folded paper from her pocket. "Jonathan has sent a letter. He is coming home."

Dorothea scanned the letter eagerly. Jonathan apologized for his absence and declared that he planned to come as soon as he was able. The needs of his patients and the difficulty of winter travel rendered him unable to provide his family with the specific date of his arrival. If he would be delayed more than two weeks, he would send them another letter to tell them so, but otherwise they should expect him before the end of January. Dorothea's happiness at this news dimmed as she read the letter over more thoroughly. He did not say so, but he implied that after the visit, he intended to return to his studies in Baltimore.

"The post must have been delayed," remarked Lorena, indicating the date written at the top of the page. The letter was almost two weeks old. "Jonathan is probably even now on his way."

"Or a second letter apologizing for his delay is," said Dorothea, but she was so pleased by the prospect of his imminent arrival that she could forgive him all the earlier, canceled visits.

The snowstorm the miller's wife had predicted reached the farm while Dorothea and her mother prepared supper. The flakes flew thick and fast, but after the evening chores were done, Dorothea lit a lantern and made her way to the sugar camp. Inside the sugarhouse, snow had blown in through the weathered boards and had collected in drifts in the corners. Uncle Jacob would have immediately set to work finding and sealing the spaces, but Dorothea could not tarry. The cold nipped at her cheeks as she covered a basket of her mother's dried apples with the Sugar Camp Quilt, apparently undisturbed since her last visit. She glanced up at the loft and envisioned a runaway hiding above in fearful silence while she and her mother stirred boiling kettles of maple sap below. She hesitated before climbing the ladder to check, but no one now hid among the stored tools.

As she completed the Album block bearing William Lloyd Garrison's signature that evening, Dorothea pondered the sugar camp and its fitness as a station. Uncle Jacob had chosen it because it provided concealment from other farms and from his own family, not because it was comfortable and safe. Weary fugitives would be far better off in the house, or even in the barn, especially in winter.

She shared her thoughts with her parents, who agreed they must make more suitable arrangements. They needed a place where one or more runaways could rest comfortably, and yet remain entirely hidden from both friendly visitors and slavecatchers.

Lorena shuddered as they all imagined slavecatchers forcing their way into the house. "Perhaps the sugar camp is safest after all," she said, "for both the runaways and ourselves. If they are discovered, we could pretend we did not know they were hiding there."

Robert said nothing, and even Dorothea was at a loss for words. She could not imagine Mrs. Braun disavowing the fugitives in her care.

The next morning, Dorothea hitched up Uncle Jacob's mare and drove the wagon into Creek's Crossing. Elm Creek had frozen over, the ferry stowed ashore in the boathouse until the spring thaw. Only the tracks of horse's hooves and wagon wheels marked the crossing over the ice.

At the Engles' home, the housekeeper took Dorothea's wraps and led her to the parlor. Mrs. Engle bustled in a few moments later. "I do not usually expect callers so early," she said, taking her customary place in the armchair near the front window. "It is not time for tea. Will you take coffee instead?"

"No, thank you. I won't keep you long. I only stopped by to give you my finished blocks for the Authors' Album."

Dorothea opened her satchel and steeled herself for the inevitable shriek of horror when Mrs. Engle discovered the signatures of several authors she had expressly banned from the quilt.

"Give your blocks to me?" Mrs. Engle asked, bemused, giving the satchel the barest of glances. "It would seem you've misunderstood my son's message." She rose and retrieved a muslin-wrapped bundle from behind the divan. "I was not expecting you to come for these until Thursday, but I suppose this is better. Perhaps you will finish the top before our next board meeting."

Mrs. Engle handed Dorothea the bundle before she was ready for it, and it fell into her lap. "Finish the top?" she echoed.

"Most of the blocks are already stitched, but you will need to assemble the top. Including your own blocks, of course, which I assume will bring the total to eighty." Mrs. Engle folded her hands and smiled. "We did not think you would mind, since you missed our last three meetings and the rest of us have done so much more work than you have. This quilt was, after all, your idea. We assumed you would want to have at least some hand in the making of it."

Indignant, Dorothea nonetheless managed a pleasant smile. "You assumed correctly, although I cannot promise I will complete the top by our next meeting."

"Just so long as you attend." Mrs. Engle took her chair again, sitting with a grace that belied her stout form. "We have much to do and the quilting bee is only weeks away. You'll probably want to get started right now."

Dorothea recognized the dismissal and rose. "Of course. Good day, Mrs. Engle."

"Good day," said Mrs. Engle cheerily. "Oh, Dorothea?"

Dorothea paused in the doorway. "Yes?"

"Please accept my condolences on the loss of your uncle."

"You are very kind."

"I understand his will has not yet been read?"

"No." Dorothea tucked the bundle of quilt blocks into her satchel. "My uncle's lawyer prefers to wait until my brother returns from Baltimore."

"I suppose that would be necessary. Well—" Mrs. Engle smiled and nodded. "Good luck, dear."

Dorothea gave her a wordless nod in return and left the room.

❧

Two days later, Jonathan came home, tall and solemn in his black suit, which Dorothea later learned he had borrowed from his mentor's nephew since he had no suitable mourning clothes of his own. Lorena was so happy to see her son that she flung her arms around him, laughing and crying and clinging to him, impeding his progress through the doorway. He felt so good in Dorothea's eyes that she almost ached from it.

Her baby brother had grown taller, his face more thin, but the thick shock of brown curls was the same, forever tousled no matter how much he tried to slick down the locks, giving him the perpetually windblown look of someone always rushing off on horseback.

He wanted to visit Uncle Jacob's grave, but Lorena insisted he eat and warm himself first. "It will be a pleasure to eat good home cooking again," he said, taking off his coat and sitting down at the table in the chair the family still referred to as his although he had not used it in more than a year.

"Doesn't Mrs. Bronson feed you?" teased Lorena, setting a plate before him.

"Yes, and she's a fair enough cook, but I'm usually so busy I take my dinner at the tavern."

Dorothea saw her parents exchange a look. Jonathan quickly added, "I haven't taken to drink if that's what worries you. Taverns are different in the city. The one I frequent is more like an inn."

"You forget I used to live in a city and I know very well what a tavern is like," said Lorena dryly.

Jonathan grinned. "Of course, Mother."

Dorothea and her parents had so many questions and Jonathan so much to tell that they lingered at the table long after he had finished eating. It was late afternoon before he pushed back his chair and reached for his coat. Dorothea offered to accompany him to the gravesite, but he said he preferred to go alone. Dorothea was sewing in the front room when he returned nearly a half-hour later. He paused in the kitchen and as he bent to kiss his mother on the cheek, she said, "We still have a while before dinner. Why don't you ride over to the Claverton farm and call on Charlotte?"

Jonathan straightened, a barely perceptible frown appearing as he shrugged out of his coat. "I don't know that Charlotte would appreciate an unexpected visit."

"Unexpected? You mean you didn't write and tell her you were coming?"

"I came to see you and pay my respects to Uncle Jacob, not to court a thirteen-year-old girl."

"She is fourteen." Lorena dusted flour from her hands and reached for his coat. She helped him back into it, and after a halfhearted attempt to stop her, Jonathan acquiesced. "If you expect Charlotte Claverton to marry you someday, you must at the very least call on her while you're in town."

Dorothea watched surreptitiously as Jonathan, about to protest, heaved a sigh and nodded. He promised to return soon and left, reluctant obedience evident in his every step.

Lorena resumed kneading bread dough in silence. A few moments later, she said, "I suppose he needn't have gone today. He could have waited until tomorrow or the next day, when he would be more inclined to see Charlotte."

She had spoken as if thinking aloud, but Dorothea ventured a reply. "I am not certain he would be any more inclined tomorrow or any other day."

"I suppose you're right. It was just as well I sent him today. Tomorrow we are going to the lawyer, and there may not be enough time for visiting the Clavertons. Jonathan has not said how long he intends to stay, and he could hardly come home without calling on his fiancée, could he? I'm sure he would agree with me."

Dorothea did not know what to say. Deliberately or not, her mother had misunderstood her. Dorothea gave her a thoughtful nod and a shrug, making a noncommittal noise that could be interpreted in any number of ways. If she said what she really thought, there would be an argument, and she did not want an argument to spoil Jonathan's visit.

She spent the afternoon working on the Authors' Album quilt while Lorena carried fresh linens to Jonathan's old bed in the attic and prepared a welcome-home feast. The other members of the library board had evidently used their very best needlework, for each block lay perfectly flat with small, even stitches and precisely matched seams. The green, Turkey red, and Prussian blue calicos gave the quilt a lively, stylish air, and the signatures were as varied and splendid as the people who had inscribed them. The only complaint Dorothea could have made was that one of the quilters had used indigo embroidery thread to backstitch over the inked signatures, while everyone else had used black. She decided the variation added a note of humor to the quilt, and rather than pick out the indigo stitches and do them over in black, she decided to scatter those blocks throughout the quilt so that the differences would appear part of the pattern.

The nine blocks Dorothea contributed brought the total to sixty-one, far short of Mrs. Engle's expected eighty. After considering several arrangements, Dorothea decided to set the blocks on point and separate them with muslin sashing. Before threading her needle, she took pencil and paper from Uncle Jacob's desk and sketched the quilt layout so that she would have a guide to follow while assembling the rows. A sudden memory came to her of working in that same place as she turned Uncle Jacob's drawings into usable templates,

140 🐾 Jennifer Chiaverini

and she felt a stab of regret that she had not known him well enough while he lived. She had never suspected his courage. She would have respected him more had he not kept the best part of himself hidden.

Her drawings completed, she began sewing the rows of blocks together. It was repetitive, painstaking work, but it allowed her time to her own thoughts, since her mother was too preoccupied in the kitchen to chat.

Jonathan returned just as Dorothea was setting the table. He apologized for his lateness, adding, "Mr. Claverton had so many questions for me I scarcely had a moment to speak to Charlotte."

"Did you manage to get her to speak to you in return?" said Dorothea innocently.

Jonathan grinned. "She did, and you don't need to tease me about her shyness. Or her youth. She is a charming girl and she will make a fine wife."

"And the combined lands of the Claverton-Granger alliance will make a fine farm."

"Dorothea," said Lorena reprovingly as Robert came in for supper. "You needn't be so vicious."

"What?" protested Dorothea as she placed the platter bearing her mother's roasted chicken in the center of the table. "I'm merely repeating an observation that you and Father have made many times."

"Charlotte also allowed me to sample an apple tart she had baked and showed me her needlework," said Jonathan hastily, in a poorly disguised attempt to forestall an argument. "She is quite an accomplished seamstress. Do you know she already has seven quilt tops pieced for her hope chest?"

Dorothea smiled tightly as she filled the water glasses. "I do indeed know that, since her mother finds nearly every opportunity to update me on her progress. I wonder. Charlotte started so early but she has yet to reach thirteen finished quilt tops. Perhaps she is wiser than all of us and is sewing slowly to delay the wedding."

"Seven quilt tops is far more than you have been able to complete for your hope chest," retorted Lorena.

"Since my hope chest and the eight quilt tops within it lie at the bottom of Elm Creek, I am forced to agree with you."

Robert looked from his wife to his daughter and back, bewildered. "Dorothea has made far more than seven quilts. She made at least three this year alone."

Lorena took her husband's plate and began to serve him. "We're talking about bridal quilts. Dorothea has none of those, but it doesn't matter anyway because she doesn't need them."

Dorothea set down the pitcher. "I may not be as young as Charlotte Claverton, but I am not a spinster at nineteen."

Jonathan's brow furrowed. "If I had known how much my visit would upset everyone—"

"Heavens, no." Lorena placed a bowl of cucumber pickles on the table with a bang. "You have been away too long as it is. If I had known how rarely you would come home, I might never have allowed you to study under Dr. Bronson. Don't let a silly quarrel make you regret your visit."

"I meant my visit to the Claverton farm," said Jonathan. "But you are right to chastise me for not coming home more often. I should have come for the harvest. Uncle Jacob wrote and asked me even after you gave me permission to remain in Baltimore, but I refused, without bothering to write and tell him why."

The room was still. Eventually Jonathan said, "Mr. Claverton inquired about my studies, but mostly he was curious about Uncle Jacob's will. It is clear he wants to know if I will inherit."

"He is thinking of his daughter's welfare," said Robert. "That is all."

Jonathan picked up his fork, but he merely poked at his food, brooding. "I hope my negligence of my uncle's pride will not give you reason to be disappointed."

"If it has, there is nothing to do about it now," said Lorena. "If we lose this farm, too, we will manage."

Robert nodded and clapped Jonathan on the back in a gesture of reassurance. Dorothea murmured her agreement, ashamed of her spiteful remarks about Charlotte, who, Dorothea had to admit, was a sweet and gentle girl. Charlotte could not be blamed for obeying her parents. Perhaps she even wanted to marry Jonathan. He was handsome and kind, and Charlotte probably saw him as a dashing older man. That is, if she were not too terrified to think of him at all.

Jonathan steered the conversation to other matters, and the rest of the family was gratefully diverted. He told them of his studies, the patients he cared for, and the Bronson family, with whom he boarded—the doctor, his wife, and their seven children. Since the eldest were girls, Jonathan shared a bedroom with the two youngest boys, aged four and two years. He confessed he had always considered sharing a small attic bedroom with his elder sister a great hardship until boarding with the Bronsons gave him a new perspective.

Jonathan talked and his family plied him with questions until long after the last bite of Lorena's sour cream cake had been eaten. It was such a comfort to be together as a family once again, despite the conspicuous absence of Uncle Jacob, that they forgot their quarrel. This time when Lorena asked Robert to play for them, he agreed. They waited in expectant silence as he tuned the long-abandoned fiddle, but when the first pure, sweet notes of a melody flowed from his bow, Dorothea felt suddenly refreshed, as if relieved of a burden she had not known she was carrying. After the second song, Lorena said, "If only we had an organ for Dorothea, so you could play together again, as you did on Thrift Farm." Dorothea knew from her mother's expression that she was thinking of Uncle Jacob's will. Dorothea would not allow herself to hope that Uncle Jacob might have made some small provision for her, so she hurriedly said that she had not played in so many years that she had likely forgotten.

Eventually, their father reluctantly put away his fiddle and went to the barn to get a late start on the evening chores. Jonathan offered to help, so Dorothea and Lorena were left alone to clear away the dishes and tidy the kitchen. They had nearly finished when Lorena reminded Dorothea to check the sugar camp for visitors.

No one had passed through their station since Sam, and recalling Mrs. Braun's remark that most runaways escaped in fairer weather, Dorothea thought nightly visits to the camp might be unnecessary until spring. Leaving food regularly was surely a waste. Still, she put on her wraps, took a lantern from the hook by the door, and ventured outside.

A light flurry brushed her face as she trudged past the barn, but the night was not as bitter cold as it had been. Uncle Jacob would have been consulting his notes, noting the temperature day and night, checking the sugar molds, carving new spiles. The Grangers had done none of those things, distracted by his passing and learning anew how to run a farm without his supervision. Sugar season would be upon them before they were prepared. If they did not need the sugar and the income from the sale of the surplus, Dorothea would not have been surprised if her parents decided not to tap the trees that year.

"Dorothea," called Jonathan, behind her. "Where are you going?"

She hesitated only a moment. "The sugar camp."

She waited for him to ask why, but instead he said, "Want some company?"

"Certainly."

He broke into a trot and caught up to her. They walked side by side through the snow, Dorothea following the path she had broken the evening before, Jonathan wading through the deeper drifts. She realized too late that her brother was sure to notice. After a few paces, he indicated the old trail and said, "You've been to the sugar camp recently."

"Yes. Last night."

"To tap the trees? Already?"

She shrugged. "Just to be sure the camp is in order."

He shook his head, hands buried in his pockets. "It won't seem like sugaring time without Uncle Jacob. So you're going to try to do it without him?"

"I suppose so, assuming we'll be able to keep the farm." Quickly she added, "I'm sure you'll inherit."

He barked out a laugh. "I am not as confident as you. All that our uncle wanted was my attention, and instead I showed nothing but indifference to him and his farm. I don't want to be a farmer. I want to be a doctor."

"Other men have done both."

"But I am happier in Baltimore. If not for you and our parents, I would not care if Uncle Jacob left the farm to a perfect stranger."

She gave him a sidelong look. "If not for me, our parents, and Charlotte, you mean."

"Yes. Charlotte." He was silent a moment. "I wonder if she would like to live in Baltimore."

Dorothea could not believe he was actually considering it, but she said evenly, "If you have been disinherited, or if you relinquish the farm, the impetus for you to marry Charlotte no longer exists."

"She would probably refuse me in any event." Jonathan looked suddenly to the southwest. "What was that?"

"What?"

"Over there, through the maple grove. It sounded like a dog barking." He paused. "There it was again."

That time Dorothea heard it plainly. "A neighbor's dog got loose, I suppose." Her heart began to pound with dread, but she reassured herself that they had heard only one dog, and slavecatchers surely traveled with several. Nevertheless, she quickened her pace. "I'm getting cold, aren't you? Let's have a quick look around the sugar camp and get back inside to the fire."

He agreed, and they hurried on through the snow. Dorothea was almost running by the time the lantern light touched the old kettle stand, the abandoned chain suddenly resembling a hangman's noose. "I'll be just a moment," she called over her shoulder as she ducked into the sugarhouse. There she stopped short and choked back a gasp.

Jonathan called out in reply, but Dorothea did not hear him.

A man sat on the wooden bench, huddled in the Sugar Camp Quilt. He squinted and raised a hand to shield his eyes from the lantern's light. "A dog got me," he said through clenched teeth. He moved the quilt aside to reveal torn trousers soaked in blood. "I couldn't run no more."

"That dog sounds like it's coming this way, fast," remarked Jonathan as he entered the sugarhouse. He halted at the sight of the bedraggled man. "Good heavens."

Swiftly Dorothea set down the lantern and went to help the fugitive to his feet. "We have to get him to the house."

Jonathan's expression plainly showed he understood the urgency. "Can you walk, with assistance?"

The man nodded and gasped in pain as they lifted him. On either side of him, his arms over their shoulders, Dorothea and Jonathan guided him out of the sugarhouse. Outside they could hear the dog barking louder now, nearly in a frenzy. It had surely caught the scent.

They hobbled toward the lights of the house. Dorothea thought in vain of the instructions Mrs. Braun had provided for concealing one's tracks in the snow. There was no time now.

They reached the house and burst into the kitchen. Lorena froze at the sight of them.

"A dog is on our heels," Jonathan told her as they brought the man inside. "It may be merely a stray, but we cannot take chances."

Instantly Lorena snapped into action. "Jonathan, take him upstairs and hide him. Dorothea, run to the barn and warn your father."

Dorothea nodded and fled. The dog's furious barking had drawn her father to the door of the barn, where she breathlessly told him about the runaway. He glanced worriedly toward the southwest, but told her he would finish the chores rather than raise suspicions by leaving them half-finished. "We must go about our usual business," he said. "Tell your mother I will make haste."

Dorothea nodded and ran back to the house. The barking had grown louder, but the dog had not yet appeared. A dog running alone would have reached the house by that time. It must be leashed.

Dorothea hurried indoors and took off her wraps. In the front room, Jonathan had removed his coat and boots and was seated beside the fire, apparently engrossed in the *Creek's Crossing Informer*. Lorena was rocking in her chair, her knitting needles clicking busily. Dorothea sat down across from her and snatched up her sewing basket. Her fingers trembled as she pieced together narrow strips of muslin for the sashing of the Authors' Album quilt. She desperately wanted to know where Jonathan had concealed the runaway, but she dared not ask.

The dog sounded as if it were almost upon them, and all at once came a furious pounding on the kitchen door. "Granger," a man yelled. "I know you're in there. Open up!"

Dorothea and her mother stared at each other, shocked. The voice, though distorted by rage, was familiar.

The pounding on the door came again, more furious. "Granger!" shouted Mr. Liggett. "Open this door or I'll break it down!"

Jonathan began to rise, but Lorena shook her head and stood. "No. Let me."

Dorothea shot Jonathan a desperate look as they heard their mother greet Mr. Liggett, and then say, "If you wish to speak to my husband, he is in the barn." They heard the strain in her voice and a scrabbling of the dog's toenails on wood as if Mr. Liggett were trying to push past Lorena into the house. Jonathan bounded out of his chair and strode into the kitchen, Dorothea right behind. Their mother struggled to shut the door on Mr. Liggett's dog as Mr. Liggett tried to shove it open. Dorothea snatched up the broom and swiped at the snarling cur until Jonathan shoved it outside with his foot.

"What's the meaning of this, Liggett?" said Jonathan. His frame nearly filled the doorway, and Dorothea was suddenly aware of how much he had matured since she had last seen him, how much authority his manner now commanded.

Mr. Liggett's face was red with fury, but he yanked on the dog's chain and ordered him to heel. "You 'uns got a runaway in there. My dog tracked him here clear as anything all the way from my place. Got a piece of his leg, too."

Dorothea swallowed and suppressed a shudder. "There's no one here but us."

He glared at her. "I'll just see that for myself."

"You are not bringing that dog into my house," said Lorena. "Nor will you set one foot in it yourself. My brother told you to stay off his property, and though he's gone, I'll abide by his wishes."

Before Mr. Liggett could retort, Robert emerged from the darkness behind him. "What's going on here?"

The dog lunged at him, but Liggett held fast to the chain. Robert did not even flinch. "You 'uns are hiding runaways," Liggett spat. "There's a reward out for runaways and I mean to get this one."

Robert shook his head, feigning puzzlement. "There aren't any runaways here."

"I saw him. I tracked him here."

"You heard my father," said Jonathan. "You're obviously mistaken."

"Or drunk," said Lorena disdainfully. "Again."

Mr. Liggett shifted his weight and cinched the dog's chain. "I know what I saw. I saw tracks in the snow, and blood besides. There's blood on the floor of that shack at the sugar camp. Then the tracks go here, and my dog led me right to your door."

"Or perhaps you led the dog," said Dorothea. "You were so certain of your destination."

Robert held up his hands in a conciliatory gesture. "We aren't denying that there might be a runaway out there somewhere, but he isn't hiding here. You're welcome to search the farm if you like, but it's a cold night. Why don't you have a drink first?"

Mr. Liggett hesitated. "I saw tracks in the snow. Someone broke a trail."

"I did," said Jonathan. "My uncle was put to rest in the maple grove. I was out that way paying my respects right before you arrived. Perhaps my presence threw your dog off his original quarry."

"He's a better dog than that." Mr. Liggett eyed him, then turned to Robert. "A drink, you say? What're you pouring?"

"Whiskey."

Dorothea almost started. Uncle Jacob forbade liquor. There had never been a drop of it on the farm except for that which was already in Mr. Liggett.

"Maybe I can stay for a minute," Mr. Liggett said, jerking his head in a nod. He wrapped the dog's chain around a tree branch and ordered the animal to sit. "I could use a drop for warmth."

Jonathan lingered in the doorway, frowning, but after a warning look from his father, he stepped aside and allowed Mr. Liggett to enter. Lorena led their unwelcome guest to the front room, and to Dorothea's astonishment, her father reached into Uncle Jacob's desk and pulled out a bottle of amber liquid. She wondered if her parents had purchased it with Mr. Liggett in mind.

Dorothea knew she must endeavor to maintain appearances, so she resumed her seat and took up her sewing. In a moment her mother's knitting needles were clicking away again, and though Jonathan sat scowling at the fire, Robert engaged Mr. Liggett in conversation. Mr. Liggett had little to say about crops or cattle, but he was eager to boast about a new horse he had procured and his plans to breed champions. He stayed much longer than a minute and took far more than a drop. The bottle was little more than a quarter full by the time Mr. Liggett hauled himself to his feet and declared that he needed to resume the hunt before the runaway fled too far. "I would be much obliged if your pretty daughter would see me to the door," he slurred, his eyes red and bleary.

Lorena's mouth tightened, but Robert gave a slow nod, so Dorothea folded the rows of quilt blocks and placed them on her chair. She escorted Mr. Liggett to the back door, opened it, and said, "Good evening."

He smirked. "Good evening," he echoed in a mincing tone. "Miss Granger, may I ask you a question?"

She nodded.

"Do you folks often leave a burning lantern in the sugarhouse?"

"Only on those evenings when we feel most melancholy for the loss of my uncle. You will recall, of course, that the sugar camp was his favorite place on the farm."

He nodded, disappointed, his eyes searching her face, hungry for more. She kept her features smooth and impassive until he frowned, tugged on the brim of his hat, and left the house.

She shut the door behind him too quickly and stood with her hands pressed against it as if to block his return. She looked for him through the kitchen window, but it was too light inside for her to see more than her own panicked reflection in the glass. Surely Mr. Liggett knew they were hiding something.

Back in the front room, her parents and Jonathan were speaking in hushed voices. "He is a greedy fool," Lorena was saying. "He will likely wake in the morning with a dreadful headache and no recollection of what passed this evening."

Robert looked hopeful, but Dorothea shook her head. "He is a drunkard, but he is no fool." She repeated his remark about the lantern.

Her mother blanched. Jonathan said, "He may have believed Dorothea's excuse, but either way, we will have to be extremely cautious as long as that runaway remains beneath our roof."

"Son," said Robert, "we will have to be cautious longer than that."

Jonathan searched his family's faces until his expression began to shift into comprehension.

Lorena said, "We have much to tell you."

"It will have to wait." Jonathan glanced up. "Dorothea, I will need your assistance."

She nodded and followed him upstairs. Inside the attic bedroom, he knelt beside Dorothea's bed and said, "It's all right. You can come out now."

The runaway emerged from beneath the bed, his face wrenched in pain. Dorothea and Jonathan helped him onto the bed. Dorothea went to remove his shoes and saw that he had only wads of burlap wrapped around his feet and tied with twine. She left them as they were and waited while Jonathan dug into his black leather bag.

"That dog—" The runaway's teeth were clenched in a grimace of pain. "He caught me in the woods, but ran off when I got to the creek—"

"He returned with his owner in tow," said Jonathan, grim. "But now they've left."

"They won't be back." Dorothea patted the man's shoulder and tried to smile reassuringly. "You're safe here."

With a groan, the man fell back upon the pillow and let Jonathan tend to his wounds. The worst injuries were the deep gashes in his left calf where Mr. Liggett's dog had sunk his teeth. As Jonathan washed the wounds, applied a salve, and bound them, Dorothea gently removed the burlap wrappings from the man's feet. She washed and rubbed them to get the blood flowing, but the two smallest toes on his right foot looked shriveled and burned. Silently, Dorothea directed Jonathan's attention to them. Her brother took one look and nodded in assent.

Shortly thereafter, Lorena brought a tray of food upstairs. They helped the man sit up and left him alone to eat and rest, retreating to the front room to discuss his condition. Jonathan asserted what Dorothea had feared: The frostbitten toes would have to come off.

"Perhaps when he reaches safety in Canada—" Lorena began.

"He cannot wait that long," said Jonathan. "The putrefaction will spread. He will sicken and die if his injuries are allowed to fester."

"Can you do it?" Robert asked his son.

"I assisted Dr. Bronson in an amputation once." Jonathan hesitated. "I did none of the cutting myself, but—" He nodded.

At Jonathan's request, Dorothea accompanied him upstairs to deliver the news. As the words sank in, the man began to tremble, but his eyes were angry rather than fearful as he said, "Ain't nobody cutting off my toes. I need my feet if I'm going to run."

"You cannot run in this condition," said Dorothea gently.

"I made it this far."

"It is a long way to Canada," said Jonathan. "Perhaps you will not need to run. Perhaps we can contrive some other means to transport you. We have a wagon."

The man shook his head. "No, sir. You're not taking my toes." Gingerly, wincing with pain, he began to rise from the bed. "Thank you for the food and the tending, but I think I best be going."

"There's a man out there hunting you," said Dorothea, incredulous. "You'll never make it to the next station."

"I made it all this way from Alabama on my own two feet, and it's the same way I'm crossing into freedom."

"This is madness," said Jonathan.

"No, you thinking I'm gonna let you take my toes is madness."

Frustrated, Jonathan ran a hand through his unruly locks. "Very well. Stay. Rest here in safety until tomorrow night. I will not treat you if the alternative is to send you out to a certain death."

The fugitive eyed him. "You swear?"

"You have my word."

Satisfied, the fugitive climbed back into bed and drew the quilt over himself. Dorothea and Jonathan returned downstairs.

"You said 'station,'" said Jonathan as they entered the front room. Their parents looked up expectantly. "Can I assume that you are not unaccustomed to events of this sort?"

They told him everything. Lorena even seemed apologetic about their clandestine activities, deferring to her son as the presumptive future master of the farm. He listened, shock and disbelief on his face, as they explained how they had discovered Uncle Jacob's secret, how Dorothea had followed the clues in the quilt to the next station. How they had resolved to continue Uncle Jacob's work.

When the tale had been told, Jonathan looked drained. "We have not satisfied Liggett's suspicions. He will plague you continuously."

"We will be vigilant," said Dorothea. Her brother abhorred slavery. Why did he look so wary? Had so much time in Baltimore rendered him accustomed to slavery? Resigned to it?

"A man like Liggett would do anything for money," said Jonathan. "Vigilance might not be enough."

❧

It was still dark when a hand on Dorothea's shoulder woke her with a jolt. "Dorothea," said her mother, shaking her gently. "It's time to get up."

Dorothea sat bolt upright. *Mr. Liggett has returned,* she thought. *The slave-catchers are here.* "What's happened?"

"Nothing. All is well," Lorena quickly assured her. "We need to make ready. The will. Remember?"

In the excitement of the previous night, Dorothea had forgotten. The will would be read that morning. They were due at the lawyer's office at eight o'clock sharp.

Dorothea told her mother she would come downstairs presently, and as Lorena left, Dorothea rose and washed herself in the basin of water on the nightstand. Her teeth chattered as she bared her skin to the cold air and the even colder water, then swiftly pulled on her red flannels and second-best wool dress. She unbraided her hair, brushed it out, and braided it up again, coiling the long brown braids at the nape of her neck. She had done her hair by herself in the attic before dawn so often she needed neither mirror nor light to complete the task.

The previous evening, they had moved the runaway—whose name was Zachariah—to the larger and more comfortable bed in Uncle Jacob's old room. Jonathan had slept in the front room at his own insistence, to keep watch. Dorothea paused to check on Zachariah on her way to the kitchen and found him still sleeping. Jonathan and Robert were just returning from the barn. Lorena had already finished cooking breakfast, so all that was left for Dorothea to do was set the table.

They ate in near silence. Dorothea could hardly force herself to swallow a bite. The fate of Uncle Jacob's farm would be decided that day, and yet she could hardly think of the will for the images of Zachariah and Mr. Liggett crowding her mind.

Zachariah emerged just as the family was about to depart. He hobbled into the kitchen, bracing himself with one arm against the wall. "You should be in bed," said Jonathan, going to his side.

Zachariah waved him off. "I'll be fine." He winced as he lowered himself into the chair Lorena held out for him at the kitchen table. Dorothea brought him a cup of fresh milk, cooled now, and a plate of food, which he began to eat hungrily, eyeing the Grangers as they put on their wraps.

"We have some business in town," said Robert. "We will be home before noon."

"When we return, I'll have another look at those toes," said Jonathan. "When you're finished eating, you should get back into bed."

"Into bed or under it?" Zachariah grimaced and looked away to Lorena. "Thank you for the food, ma'am."

"You're welcome." Lorena hesitated. "The man who pursued you here yesterday might not have been put off for good. He may return."

"It would be wise for you to remain hidden," said Robert. "He is not above entering our home in our absence."

Zachariah made a humorless chuckle. "I might be safer at the next station."

"You won't be safer traveling in daylight," said Dorothea. "Lock the doors and stay away from the windows. Take my bed in the attic just to be sure. You will be fine."

She forced certainty into the words as she imagined Mrs. Braun would have done, but Zachariah looked dubious even as he agreed to do as they suggested. After they closed the door behind them, she heard the solid thunk of the bolt sliding into place.

Robert had hitched up the sleigh, and as the horses pulled them smoothly over the snow-covered road, Dorothea glanced back at the house. There was no sign anyone remained inside. "Do you think Zachariah will be there when we return?"

Her father shrugged, and the gesture seemed to mirror Jonathan's thoughts. Lorena said, "Of course he will. Surely he knows to wait until nightfall to depart. Besides, I threw out those old burlap rags of his and he hasn't any shoes."

Dorothea recalled the look in the man's eye when he had rejected Jonathan's medical treatment and thought that Zachariah might very well decide to limp off in the snow barefoot, if it came to that. She feared that it might. All the way into town, from the farm that might no longer be theirs, across the frozen creek, her thoughts dwelt on what might be happening behind her. Even at that moment Mr. Liggett might be lurking about their farm, following the trail through the snow, examining the bloodstains on the floor of the sugarhouse, letting his dog lead him again and again to the Grangers' back door. She thought of what might befall Zachariah should he not wait for Dorothea to return and explain to him the secret route stitched into the Sugar Camp Quilt, and how he would fare if he did not consent to Jonathan's treatment.

The meeting with the lawyer, which had loomed large and foreboding in their imaginations for years—the day they would either secure their futures or be forced to leave Uncle Jacob's farm forever—had been diminished by the previous night's events. Even Jonathan's admission that he had not done all he could to secure his uncle's affection did not fill them with dread as it might once have done. Dorothea knew from her parents' distracted expressions that they, too, were preoccupied with thoughts of their hunted guest. Lorena confirmed Dorothea's suspicions when, upon entering the lawyer's office, instead of encouraging her family regarding the possible outcomes of the meeting, she said, "Likely Mr. Liggett will be sleeping off his inebriation well into the afternoon. We will be home before he even rolls out of bed."

Later, Dorothea wondered if they had surprised the lawyer with their lack of elation when he declared that Jonathan Augustus Granger was the sole heir to his uncle's estate, with the exception of a few smaller gifts to his family and his church. The Grangers were so eager to return home that they barely stayed long enough to sign the papers. Only Dorothea managed a laugh when she learned of Uncle Jacob's bequest to herself: his best steamer trunk, three hundred dollars, and a book about the western territories. His plan for her was clear. She mused that if he had wanted to guarantee she follow it, he should not have left the farm to her brother.

The Grangers hurried home. As many times as Dorothea had thought of this day, she had never envisioned her parents quiet and pensive as they returned to what could at last be called *their* house, *their* land. Only once did a sense of triumph overcome Lorena's uneasiness. As the farm came into view, she declared, "From now on we shall call this place Thrift Farm the Second."

Jonathan shifted uncomfortably.

"No," said Robert. "We will call it the Granger farm."

Lorena shot him a look of surprise, but something in his expression silenced her intended protest.

While Jonathan and Robert remained behind in the barn to unhitch the horses, Dorothea and her mother hastened to the house. Dorothea's heart leaped into her throat when her mother tested the kitchen door. It swung open easily. The bolt had been drawn back.

Lorena hurried to check Uncle Jacob's old room while Dorothea raced upstairs. She found Zachariah resting in her bed, the Sugar Camp Quilt spread over him.

"Where else did you reckon I'd be?" asked Zachariah, bemused. "Did you think I was fool enough to go my own way in daylight?"

"The bolt was drawn back. We thought you had left us, or—that you had been taken."

"That bolt locks from the inside," he told her. "If that man did come back and found the door bolted, he'd know someone was in here. I thought it best to leave it as you folks would have."

"What if Mr. Liggett had returned and come inside?"

"What if he'd been watching the house when you came home and saw you folks knocking on the door and calling out for someone to let you in? He'd know for sure you had someone in here."

Dorothea was stumped for a moment, but she said, "At least the bolt would have kept him out until our return."

Zachariah shrugged. "Maybe, unless he thought to kick in a window. This is a nice place, but it ain't a stockade. You can't keep out someone who's bent on coming in, not unless you got a rifle."

"We do not believe in violence."

He snorted. "Just because you don't believe in it don't make it any less real."

Dorothea had no reply to that. She changed the dressing on his leg as Jonathan had taught her and brought him a cup of water, then returned downstairs to help her mother prepare dinner. When her father came in from the barn to inquire after Zachariah, Dorothea told him of their scare. Robert shook his head and said, "We must contrive a better hiding place."

Jonathan went upstairs to check on his reluctant patient, and when he returned he wore a disgruntled expression. He drew on his coat and announced he was going back into town for something for Zachariah's foot.

Not long afterward, when Dorothea carried a tray upstairs to Zachariah, she drew a chair closer and explained the route to the next station, using the quilt draped over him as a guide. "Remember these patterns and you'll remember the way," she told him.

"What about that doctor brother of yours?" he asked. "Think he'll let me go?"

"He would never keep you here against your will."

"Where is he?"

"He went into town for something for your foot."

"What would that be? A hacksaw?"

Dorothea rose and gathered up his dishes. "He means the best for you. You would do well to take his advice."

"It's not his foot. It's not his choice."

"That is certainly true." Dorothea paused and sat down again, the tray on her lap. "You would risk your life rather than sacrifice two toes. Do you mistrust his skill so much?"

"His doctoring don't have nothing to do with it. Don't you know what they do to runaways they catch? They cut off their feet—and not just so they can't run no more. It tells everyone he's a runaway. He's a slave."

"It's just two toes, not your whole foot. Two toes to purchase your life."

"I'm not going to die because of two shriveled toes."

His expression was resolute, and Dorothea knew further argument was futile. "Summon me if you need anything," she said quietly, and left him to rest and memorize the quilt.

She helped her mother complete the day's housework, then settled in the front room to sew while Lorena knitted. Robert passed through on his way to Uncle Jacob's old room carrying his toolbox and an armload of boards of all sizes. All afternoon while Dorothea and Lorena worked and discussed measures they should take to improve their station—in hushed voices as if they expected to discover Mr. Liggett crouched outside beneath a window—the sounds of sawing and hammering came from Uncle Jacob's room. Just when their curiosity could not bear another moment, Jonathan returned with a paper-wrapped bundle beneath his arm.

"What's that?" asked Dorothea.

"Did Dr. Bremigan ask why you needed the medicine?" Lorena added.

"I didn't go to see Dr. Bremigan." Jonathan shrugged out of his coat. "I went to see Mr. Hathaway."

The cobbler? Dorothea and her mother exchanged a look of bewilderment as Jonathan began to tear off the paper wrapping.

"If Zachariah's going to travel on foot, he'll need boots," said Jonathan, holding them up so the women could see. "Before you ask, no, I didn't tell Hathaway why I really needed them."

"But they're too small for you or your father," said Lorena, drawing closer. They were good work boots, solid and warm. If only Zachariah had had them weeks ago. "Even if they did fit you, everyone knows you are not here often enough to need them. Mr. Hathaway is sure to wonder."

Jonathan grinned. "He did wonder. I said they were for Dorothea."

Dorothea laughed. "You must not think much of my sense of fashion if you considered that a credible story. Don't you think Mr. Hathaway will wonder when he does not see me clomping about the streets of Creek's Crossing in these boots?"

"Now that you mention it, Mr. Hathaway did say he didn't remember you having such large feet."

Lorena said to Dorothea, "Between now and the time you buy a new pair of shoes, you will have to think of some reason to explain how your feet shrank."

"That, or purchase my shoes in Grangerville."

"I don't believe that will be necessary. Mr. Hathaway was so glad to have the sale that he didn't question my story." Jonathan grinned at his sister, amused. "One other customer was more curious, though. He overheard our conversation and said that he didn't recall ever seeing you wearing anything so coarse. I believe he said you had much too delicate a foot and too graceful a manner to wear such things."

Immediately Dorothea thought of Cyrus. "What did you say in reply?"

"I said that obviously he had never seen you stomping outside to milk the cows in the winter before dawn, and that you have the most enormous, clumsy feet of any woman alive."

"You didn't," protested Dorothea. "You could have simply agreed with him."

"On the contrary. I'm your brother. Someone has to dispel your suitors' illusions."

"Jonathan," scolded Lorena, feigning displeasure. "Cyrus Pearson has danced with Dorothea many times. He surely saw through your exaggeration."

"He might have, except he wasn't there," said Jonathan. "The man was not Cyrus Pearson."

"Not Cyrus?" asked Lorena.

"Who, then?" asked Dorothea.

"No one I had ever met. The cobbler called him Mr. Nelson."

"You must be joking," said Lorena. "You must mean Mr. Nelson the elder. He must be in town visiting his son."

"This man did not seem more than a few years older than Dorothea."

"Then you must have misunderstood his manner," said Dorothea. "What you interpreted as flattery was certainly intended as sarcasm. Mr. Nelson has never had a kind word for me."

Jonathan's eyebrows shot up. "So I was speaking to Mr. Nelson, the schoolmaster?"

"I know of no other Nelsons in Creek's Crossing." Heat rose in Dorothea's cheeks. Why had her brother felt it necessary to ridicule her in front of a man who would relish her humiliation all too well?

Jonathan frowned, dubious. "This man did not seem as unkind as you have described him. In fact, he rebuked me for speaking about you unfairly."

Dumbfounded, Dorothea said, "He rebuked you?"

"Yes. He said he had seen you dance and that it was grossly inaccurate to describe you as clumsy."

Lorena shook her head at Dorothea in wonder. "Who would have imagined a compliment from that man?"

"I am not so sure it was a compliment," said Dorothea flatly. "Did Mr. Nelson mention he is a former convict? I am sure he is quite capable of lying convincingly."

Taken aback, Jonathan said, "He made a far different impression upon me. He seemed a trifle stern, but he did not seem dishonest. Besides, is he not the son of—"

"His father has a wonderful reputation, of course," interrupted Dorothea. "From what I have seen, his son deserves nothing of it. None of us even knows the crime for which he was imprisoned."

"Considering that he is the head of the school, I hope it was nothing violent," said Jonathan.

Dorothea agreed, but she did not have time to ponder the secrets of Mr. Nelson's past, or why he had spoken so civilly about her to her brother. He was too deliberate a man to have made those remarks casually. Then she remembered: He had helped search for Uncle Jacob that fateful night. Perhaps, out of pity for her loss, he regretted his earlier rudeness.

Just then, her father peered out from Uncle Jacob's old room. "It's finished," he said, and beckoned them inside. "If you cannot find it, I'll consider it a job well done."

Dorothea scanned the room, but it appeared unchanged from when her uncle had inhabited it. Jonathan knelt to look beneath the bed. "I suppose that's the first place anyone would look," he remarked as he rose, brushing dirt from his knees.

Dirt? Dorothea peered more carefully at the floor by her brother's feet. She had swept the room just that morning. While her mother and brother searched elsewhere, she paced slowly through the room, studying the floor carefully.

"What's that you're doing?" asked her father.

Dorothea merely smiled and did not allow herself to be distracted. What at first glance appeared to be dirt was really sawdust. She found traces of it in several places, most likely where her father had worked with his tools. Occasionally she also spotted a larger sliver of wood. She paused where the debris seemed to be most concentrated: directly in front of her uncle's wardrobe.

She pulled open the doors, peered inside, even shifted aside some faded work shirts. She was about to shut the door when her mother said, "Who returned those old shirts? I know I put them in the rag bag."

Dorothea smiled over her shoulder at her father, who was doing his best to look innocent. She reached deeper into the wardrobe and her fingers brushed the wooden back sooner than she expected. Rapping upon the boards, she heard a faintly hollow report. She spun around to her father and announced, "Here. It's here. You made a false back."

She watched as her father's face assumed its old uncertainty, and it occurred to her that she had not seen it since the night Uncle Jacob died.

"You found it so quickly," he said. "You're a clever girl, much cleverer than Liggett, but maybe I should build something else."

"No," said Dorothea quickly. "It is a fine hiding place. If you had swept the sawdust away, I would never have found it."

"The wardrobe is so narrow, no one would think to look for a false back," added Lorena.

"It's more than a false back," said Robert, and he showed them the hidden latch that allowed the false back to fold away, revealing a compartment inside just large enough for two men to stand shoulder to shoulder. On the floor was a handle, which Robert lifted to reveal a hole sawed through the floorboards.

None of them could see anything below but empty darkness. Robert explained that the hole went straight through to the cellar, and that he intended to partition off a small, hidden room below by building shelves, one with hinges to act as a door. A space large enough for two or three people to sit comfortably would be undetectable to all but the most determined searcher. Now fugitives could hide inside the wardrobe if Mr. Liggett or anyone else searched the house, and could pass from Uncle Jacob's bedroom to the cellar and outdoors, if necessary.

"Let us pray it never will be necessary," said Lorena fervently. Silently, Dorothea agreed.

❧

Zachariah remained with the Grangers for two more days, until the wounds from Mr. Liggett's dog had begun to heal. He left at twilight with a sack of bread and dried meat on his back and the new boots on his feet. The night was cold but clear, with a bright half moon providing enough light to find the landmarks by. He assured Dorothea he would remember the symbols in the quilt, but if they failed him, he would "follow the drinking gourd" and make his own way north.

At breakfast, Jonathan announced that he intended to leave the next day. Lorena was dismayed. "But the farm is yours now," she said. "Don't you wish to stay and take charge of it?"

"Mother, we all know that the farm is really yours and Father's."

"But you could stay on here." She reached across the table and clasped his hand. "You've always liked Dr. Bremigan. You can continue your studies with him."

His mouth curved in a rueful half smile. "If you considered him an adequate tutor, you wouldn't have asked Dr. Bronson to take me on."

"Now that we're running a station, we could use your help more than ever," said Robert. "Zachariah is not the only fugitive who will need a doctor's care."

Jonathan rubbed a hand over his jaw. "There is something I need to tell you." He hesitated. "I have been admitted to Harvard Medical College. Dr. Bronson helped me secure a scholarship. I enrolled last week and will begin my studies there after I conclude our business here."

"Harvard Medical College?" All the color drained from Lorena's face. "But . . . that is so far away, and it will take so long. Years."

Jonathan nodded. "And when those years are over, I will be a proper doctor, not merely some well-trained assistant."

"But we need you now," protested Lorena. "No one else can provide the help you can here."

"There is so much I still need to learn," said Jonathan. "Allow me to study at the college. Then I will return and do all you ask of me. I promise."

Dorothea could see that he was resolved, that he would do as he wished regardless of his parents' reply. She saw in her mother's eyes that she knew it, too.

"I will hold you to that promise," said Lorena softly. Then she nodded.

Robert drove Jonathan to the train station early the next morning. The house felt strange and empty with only herself and her mother in it, so Dorothea was glad for the brief walk out to the sugar camp to leave the quilt. She should have taken it earlier, but Zachariah had seemed to find comfort in it, and he had needed to memorize the symbols. Circling the shelter, she found unfamiliar boot tracks in the snow. Only Mr. Liggett could have left them, but there was no way to determine if he had done so on the night of Zachariah's arrival or if he had returned more recently. Suddenly Dorothea felt a crawling sensation on the back of her neck as if she were being watched. She draped the quilt on the wooden bench inside the shelter and hurried back to the house.

Soon afterward, the jingling of sleigh bells called her from her housework to the window. She had not expected her father to return from the train station so soon. "Who is it?" called Lorena from the kitchen as Dorothea looked out upon the front road.

A single horse pulled a cutter and driver up the road. She had never seen the cutter, but she recognized the horse. "It's Cyrus Pearson."

"On a Saturday?" Lorena came to the window, but the horse and sleigh had already passed. She gave her daughter a quick, appraising glance. "Take off that apron. Your dress and hair are fine, but you have a smudge of dust on your nose."

"If he comes unexpectedly, he should be prepared to see me as I truly am," said Dorothea, but she rubbed her nose with the back of her hand and smoothed the skirt of her dress. Thus she was somewhat presentable when she answered Cyrus's knock. He declined her invitation to enter and instead invited her to go riding. Lorena gave her permission, so Dorothea put on her wraps and took Cyrus's hand as he helped her into the cutter. They bundled up beneath the heavy blankets, Cyrus chirruped to the horse, and they rode smoothly off.

"Please accept my condolences on the loss of your uncle," Cyrus began.

"Thank you."

"I would have been by sooner, but I did not want to intrude on a family matter."

"That's quite all right," said Dorothea, thinking of all the neighbors who had not considered their kindness an intrusion. She was suddenly troubled by his long absence. Something in his manner seemed distant, chilly.

"Oh, by the way, how is your friend?"

"My friend?"

"The ill friend you were caring for when I last called for you."

"Oh. She is fine. She made a full recovery." Dorothea silently scolded herself for forgetting the ruse. "I was gone only for the day."

"Then I should have returned sooner." He grinned at her, his good humor apparently restored. "You will forgive me, but I thought you were out driving with some other fellow and had left your poor mother to invent a story to protect you."

"Do you really think I would have done such a thing?" said Dorothea stiffly.

"Of course not. You are goodness itself." Then, with a sudden edge to his voice, he added, "If you tell me you were nursing a sick friend, I will believe you."

"I assure you, I was not out riding with anyone."

He nodded, satisfied. Dorothea buried her chin under the blankets, emotions roiling. Her friend Mary thought a man's jealousy spoke well of his feelings for a woman, but Dorothea felt unsettled and displeased by Cyrus's concern. She was relieved that he seemed to accept her half-truths, but resentful that he had required them.

"My mother sent me with a message about your library business," said Cyrus.

"You could have delivered it in the warmth of our kitchen."

"And deny myself the pleasure of your sole company? I wouldn't dream of it, especially since it seems that our regular Thursday drives will no longer be necessary."

"What do you mean?"

"My mother has decided to cancel the library board meetings now that the event you have been planning for is so quickly approaching. She says everyone's efforts will be better spent preparing for the quilting bee." He glanced away from the horse to grin at her. "You, especially, are expected to spend all your waking hours completing the quilt top. Neglect every other duty if you must, just as long as you bring the finished quilt top to the quilting bee."

"Your mother said this?"

"Not in so many words, but her intention was clear."

Uncertain, Dorothea said, "Doesn't your mother want to see the quilt top ahead of time? I have already sewn the rows together as I thought best, but I expected her to want to examine my work."

"She would like to, but there isn't enough time. She says she has faith in your ability to complete the task as instructed."

Dorothea suppressed a sigh. She had designed the quilt and would not concede that Mrs. Engle or anyone else on the library board had instructed her. Still, while this arrangement would ensure that the banned authors were included in the quilt, she had intended for Mrs. Engle to learn of it well before the quilting bee.

She ought to tell Cyrus what she had done and ask him to inform his mother. She almost did, but then she thought of Mrs. Engle's patronizing manner and Cyrus's annoying jealousy, and said instead, "You're certain your mother wishes for me to finish the quilt top according to my best judgment?"

"I'm sure that would satisfy her."

"Very well." Dorothea could not hide a smile. "I will do so."

Cyrus peered at her quizzically, then shrugged. "I have never understood this fascination with making bedcoverings." He tugged on the reins to turn the horse in a wide circle until the cutter was heading for Dorothea's home. "For purely selfish reasons, however, I regret that this particular quilt is nearly done. I will miss our Thursday drives."

"I have enjoyed them, too. It is pleasant to have an outing to look forward to during the week."

"I hope that means you enjoy the company."

Dorothea decided to exclude that day's drive from her assessment. "I have, indeed."

"Then perhaps we might continue our drives even if they have no practical purpose."

She had to laugh. "My uncle would have said that is too much of an indulgence, but I think my parents would allow it."

"Then I will call for you next Sunday as long as the weather is fair." He paused. "I understand your brother is in town."

"He was. He left only this morning."

"I'm sorry I missed him. Did he return to hear the will read?"

"Yes." A corner of one of the blankets came loose and flapped in the wind. Dorothea tucked it beneath her feet. "We visited the lawyer yesterday."

"Since I did not see your parents loading the wagon, I assume the news was favorable to your family."

Did everyone in the Elm Creek Valley know the Grangers' circumstances? "Yes. My uncle was generous enough to leave his estate to my brother."

"Splendid," enthused Cyrus. Then he glanced at her. "You don't mean the entire estate?"

"Well, no. He bequeathed a substantial gift to the church and provided smaller sums to friends and acquaintances."

Cyrus's smile seemed frozen in place. "And to you? Did he leave nothing to you?"

"As a matter of fact, he did leave me a most impressive steamer trunk, a book on the western territories, and more than enough money to purchase comfortable accommodations on the next train headed in that direction." Dorothea laughed and shook her head. "The message might not be apparent to someone who did not know my uncle well. He thought I should seek my fortune out West."

"Did he."

"He told me so, not long before his death."

"He could not know how hard life out West is for a woman or he never would have suggested it. Surely you need not resort to such drastic measures. Have you no inheritance forthcoming from your father's side, from your relations in Grangerville?"

"I regret that I do not. My father's beliefs put him at odds with the rest of his family long ago. When he and my mother asked for their share of the land to build their earthly utopia, his brothers bought him out of his share of the family farm rather than have such an embarrassing spectacle so close to home. It was a substantial portion, enough to buy Thrift Farm, but of course all was lost in the flood. I am sure you have heard that part of the story."

"Yes," said Cyrus. "That little I knew."

Dorothea tried to make light of the family misfortune, knowing how quickly Cyrus wearied of any tale of woe. "We are, as far as I know, the only Grangers forced to leave in disgrace the town my grandparents founded, the town named after our family. Perhaps my uncle has a point, encouraging me to venture farther afield. But of course, I will not follow his advice. If I were to go anywhere, it would be back East, to a city such as Boston."

"Boston is quite pleasant," said Cyrus. "As for me, I prefer New York."

They had turned onto the road up to the Granger farm—how easily the family had begun to think of it by that name, as if it had never been called by any other, as if Lorena had never suggested they burden it with the title of their first, ill-fated farm. The meeting with the lawyer had indeed changed everything, even though the inheritor was at that moment traveling eagerly eastward to a city and a life he much preferred.

Cyrus brought the horse to a halt a few paces from the back door. He demurred when she invited him in for tea, saying that he had other messages to carry for his mother. So she bid him a cheerful good-bye and returned inside to finish the housework, work she no longer minded now that the house was the Grangers' own.

Chapter Eight

A heavy snowfall prevented Cyrus from coming on Sunday, and when he did not come the next Sunday, either, Dorothea surmised he had decided it was too cold for a long ride. Still, even without the pleasure of an outing, the two weeks passed swiftly. Dorothea managed to finish the quilt top and, with her mother's help, she made over her best winter dress for the dance. Though Dorothea declared it perfect, Lorena fretted over the dress, insisting that Dorothea should have used some of her inheritance money to purchase a few yards of silk brocade for a proper dancing gown. When Dorothea decided Creek's Crossing did not host enough dances to warrant the expense, Lorena said, "You could wear it for other things besides dancing." Dorothea knew she meant it would be a fine wedding dress, but teased her mother by saying she would wear it to milk the cows, and that she knew Mr. Hathaway could help her find the perfect men's work boots to wear with it.

She did spend three dollars of her inheritance to purchase a bronze plate for a shelf for the new library. She had heard from Miss Nadelfrau that nearly twenty plates had sold. If the opportunity quilt earned only half as much, Dorothea would be well pleased.

In all that time, only two other fugitives passed through the Grangers' station. They had come from Virginia, but thankfully had secured warm clothing before entering Pennsylvania. One of the men told Dorothea they had been planning their escape for a year and had intended to wait until spring, but when word came that their master intended to sell them to another plantation owner farther south before spring planting began, they fled. With regret, Dorothea realized she had never asked Zachariah why he had been compelled to flee to the north in the midst of winter. She wondered what had become of him. It was tempting to ride to the Brauns' mill and ask what they knew, but Dorothea knew she must limit contact between their families to divert suspicion.

She also knew that when spring arrived, traffic through their station would increase. Robert completed the secret room in the cellar and rode out to the Wright farm to tell them to direct fugitives to the house rather than the sugar camp. Runaways could rest comfortably in Uncle Jacob's old room, only a few steps away from a secure hiding place should they need it. The Sugar Camp Quilt would adorn the bed, giving the runaways ample opportunity to learn its patterns by heart. Dorothea was relieved to know that her nightly treks to the sugar camp would cease, for she always felt as if Mr. Liggett was watching her from the darkness of the maple grove. Even Lorena acknowledged that the new arrangements were for the best, as the increased safety of the runaways was worth the greater risk to themselves.

On the last Saturday evening in February, Dorothea and her parents rode into town dressed in their finest. Lorena had made a chicken pie for the covered-dish supper, and Dorothea carried a sour cream cake in a basket on her lap. The completed Authors' Album quilt top lay in the wagon, folded and wrapped in a clean muslin sheet. Although Dorothea was tempted to get it in the quilt frame before Mrs. Engle inspected it too closely, she knew it would be wiser to inform Mrs. Engle about the banned authors before she discovered on her own that they had been included in the quilt. Mrs. Engle might not be above ordering Dorothea to rip out stitches even in front of all the assembled guests if she thought Dorothea had intended to deceive her.

Dorothea had not seen any of the other library board members for several weeks, so she was as curious as any other guest to see what the ladies had done to transform the school into a suitable ballroom. Mrs. Collins greeted the Grangers at the door, beaming. The whole town seemed to be turning out for the Quilting Bee Dance, and so many people had purchased tickets for the quilt based on its description alone that they might sell out. Mrs. Collins was so pleased with the board's success that at first she urged the Grangers to enter without paying the admission fee, but they insisted.

"Where is Mrs. Engle?" asked Dorothea, the quilt bundle in her arms. From inside the school came the sounds of people talking and laughing. A fiddle, banjo, and bass were tuning up, and after the barest pause, they launched into a merry tune.

"She's meeting with Mr. Schultz to see how long it would take to print another batch of tickets," replied Mrs. Collins, raising her voice to be heard. "You'll find Miss Nadelfrau's quilt frame in the front corner. Mrs. Engle said for you to put the quilt into the frame as quickly as you can."

"Doesn't she want to see it first?"

"There's no time! Ladies are milling about with their thimbles and nothing to do." Mrs. Collins broke off for a moment to collect money from a small crowd of revelers eager to enter. "She left strict instructions that you are not to waste a moment on anything else until the quilting is under way."

"You had better do as Mrs. Engle wishes," added Lorena, unable to conceal her amusement.

"I guess I'll take this for you, then," said Robert, indicating the sour cream cake he carried for his daughter.

Dorothea thanked him and followed her parents inside. It was too late to do anything else.

They left their wraps in the cloakroom, and while her parents took their contributions to the covered-dish table, Dorothea hurried to the quilt frame. Miss Nadelfrau stood beside it, fidgeting anxiously with her chatelaine, but she heaved a sigh of relief when Dorothea appeared. Swiftly they layered the backing, batting, and quilt top in the frame as a crowd of admirers gathered about them. Dorothea waited for Miss Nadelfrau to mention the banned authors, but in her haste she seemed not to notice.

Four women sat down to quilt as soon as Dorothea and Miss Nadelfrau pulled up chairs. "It seems everyone wants to be the first to put a stitch in," said Miss Nadelfrau, with the first smile Dorothea had seen from her that evening. She smiled back, weakly, and excused herself to find Mrs. Engle.

The room was steadily filling with people, but Dorothea did not spy Mrs. Engle among them. All of the desks had been pushed back against the walls and a few were arranged end-to-end along the back wall to hold the covered dishes, from which delicious aromas wafted. Couples took the floor and the musicians began a schottische. Dorothea saw her parents among the dancers and her best friend, Mary, with her husband, Abner. Mary called out something, but Dorothea could only smile and shake her head to indicate that she had not heard.

Just then she heard Mrs. Engle bark out a command near the back of the room. Dorothea wove through the crowd of onlookers lining the dance floor and steeled herself as she approached Mrs. Engle, who was giving directions to a group of frightened-looking girls apparently drafted into service as servers, judging by their aprons and the speed with which they scurried to the back tables once Mrs. Engle dismissed them.

Dorothea touched her lightly on the arm. "I beg your pardon—"

Mrs. Engle spun about, the skirt of her royal blue velvet dress swirling. "Ah! There you are, my dear. Is the quilt in order?"

"Yes, but there's something I—"

"Let's have a look at it, then, shall we?"

With an indulgent smile, Mrs. Engle turned and made her way toward the quilt frame. The crowd parted before the formidable woman and closed just as quickly behind her so Dorothea was forced to dodge passersby and groups gathered in conversation. She tried to call out to Mrs. Engle, but her voice was lost in the din.

When she finally caught up to Mrs. Engle, she was standing rigid and wide-eyed at the side of the quilt frame. Two other women had joined the original six, and already they had completed a significant portion of the quilt with meticulous, feathery quilting.

Mrs. Engle did not even turn to look at her. "What is the meaning of this?"

"I meant to tell you—"

"As you should have done!" Two spots of red appeared in the plump ivory of Mrs. Engle's cheeks. "I distinctly recall stating that this man—" She jabbed a finger at one block. "—And this man—" The finger again pointed accusingly. "Were not suitable for this quilt!"

The quilters looked up cautiously but did not pause in their work. Dorothea took a deep breath. "You did indeed tell me that, but I thought—"

"You thought?" Mrs. Engle trembled with anger and disbelief, her powdered jowls shaking from the effort of controlling her temper. "You were not placed on the library board to think. You were included because we thought your uncle might make a donation on your behalf!"

Dorothea could not imagine why they had thought such a thing. "I regret that you were disappointed in that regard," she said. "However, you did include me, and therefore I was obligated to do my very best to make this fund-raiser a success. While you do not care for these authors, their works are widely read and respected in the community, and thus their inclusion increases the value of the quilt."

"You do not know the reading habits of our community very well if you believe that," retorted Mrs. Engle. "What am I to do when people demand their money back once they become aware of this—this debacle?"

Dorothea thought of her inheritance. "In the unlikely event that anyone should do so, I will reimburse them for their tickets—up to a certain point."

Mrs. Engle sniffed. "That is the very least you can do. You will forgive me, of course, if I request your resignation from the library board before you can do any more damage."

Stung, Dorothea was suddenly aware of a lull in the noise around them and the watchful eyes of the women waiting for their turn at the quilt frame. Others, men and women drawn by the sounds of argument, peered at the quilt and whispered to one another as if trying to deduce which authors were not supposed to have been included.

"Why, I declare," said a woman loudly. "This Henry Brown here isn't Henry 'Box' Brown, is he?"

Dorothea turned and saw Constance Wright standing on the other side of the quilt frame, indicating the Album block nearest her right hand. Her feet were planted and she regarded Mrs. Engle with defiance.

"The one and the same," said Dorothea, grateful for the distraction.

"That's worth another dollar from me," said Constance. "I'm going to buy myself some more tickets."

"Who is Henry 'Box' Brown?" asked a young man, apparently curious despite being disappointed that Constance had interrupted Mrs. Engle's tirade.

"Why, don't you know?" said Constance. "He was a slave in Virginia who escaped by having himself shut up in a crate and mailed to abolitionists in Philadelphia."

A wave of incredulous laughter went up from the onlookers.

"Utter nonsense," said Mrs. Engle, looking more outraged than ever. "No one could endure it. Furthermore, I would never abide the inclusion of a—"

"As incredible as the story may seem, it is nevertheless true," said Mr. Nelson, emerging from the crowd. "I lived in Philadelphia at the time and it was in all the papers. Mrs. Engle, you are too modest to claim that you were not aware of his name on your quilt. It was a stroke of genius to include people who were bound to provoke interest and discussion. How appropriate for a library full of books destined to do the very same. While we dance, you must tell me how you arranged this."

He held out his hand to Mrs. Engle with such brisk authority that she could only stare at him, dumbfounded, before taking his hand. He led her off to the dance floor without so much as a glance for Dorothea or the quilt that had sparked such controversy. The spectacle over, the onlookers returned to enjoying the dance.

Dorothea joined Constance on the other side of the quilting frame as she took a chair vacated by another quilter. "You arrived at precisely the right moment. If she had gone on much longer I might have said something I truly regretted."

"Don't regret what you say so long as it's the truth. That's what I do." Constance nodded in the direction Mr. Nelson had taken Mrs. Engle. "If you ask me, he's the one who showed up just in time."

"Mr. Nelson? Oh, yes. One can always rely on him to appear at the moment of my greatest humiliation."

Constance had unrolled a huswif on her lap and was frowning thoughtfully at several needles arranged in a neat row. "I'm just glad she's gone." She kept her voice too low for the other quilters to hear, which Dorothea considered wise. Mrs. Engle had friends and admirers everywhere.

Constance selected a needle and asked the woman seated at her left to pass the thread. "I think we both know she was about to say she wouldn't abide no colored folks' names in her quilt. I don't think she would abide one stitching on it, either."

"We're glad for your help," said Dorothea, just as she remembered she was no longer on the library board and ought not to say "we."

"Tell that to the lady at the front door who almost wouldn't let me in."

"Mrs. Collins?" Dorothea's heart sank, but she said firmly, "The library will be for everyone, white and colored alike, and don't believe anyone who tells you otherwise."

Constance regarded her with weary skepticism. "We'll see what happens when the library opens. You know the men told Abel they wouldn't need his help in the building."

"I didn't know that. One would think they would be grateful for an experienced carpenter."

"One might think that if one was a nice young white girl like you who don't know any better." The woman on Constance's left sniffed and abruptly abandoned her seat, her thimble still on her finger. Constance seemed not to notice. "Anyway, I'm here to help so that later, no one can say I can't borrow books because I had no part in the building of the library. We bought a bookshelf plate, too."

Another quilter gathered her things and rose. This time Constance glanced up and followed her with her eyes. "I take it your lessons are going well?" asked Dorothea, hoping to distract her.

Constance shrugged. "Good enough."

"So here is the infamous quilt," said Mrs. Claverton, approaching with her arm linked through her daughter's. Charlotte wore a dress of ivory crushed velvet with a rose velvet sash and a matching ribbon around her neck. Her dark hair hung in thick ringlets upon her shoulders.

"Yes. Quilt upon it if you dare," said Dorothea with a smile. As Mrs. Claverton and Charlotte seated themselves in the vacant chairs, Dorothea clasped Constance's shoulder and promised to speak with her later.

Dorothea left the quilt frame behind and went in search of her parents to tell them what had occurred with Mrs. Engle before a worse version reached their ears. She spotted them in the supper line, but before she could reach them, Mary called out to her and came hurrying over. "I hoped to warn you," said Mary, taking Dorothea's hand, "but I can see from your expression that I'm too late. Please do compose yourself. Don't give them the satisfaction of knowing they have upset you."

Dorothea immediately smoothed the strain from her features. "Thank you, Mary. It is my fault, really. I should have been more forthright."

"Your fault? Why on earth do you believe that?" Mary cast an indignant look over her shoulder. "He's truly despicable, as I seem to recall warning you. I never liked him—well, not in recent years, anyway."

"Are you talking about Mr. Nelson?"

Mary regarded her with utter bewilderment. "What? Of course not. Why would I—" She drew in a breath sharply. "Then you don't know."

"I don't know what? If we aren't discussing Mr. Nelson and Mrs. Engle—"

"Dorothea." Mary bit her lip, put her hands on Dorothea's shoulders, and gently turned her toward the dance floor. "Look over by the window."

Dorothea complied. "Mr. Hathaway is sipping from his hip flask. You're right. It's scandalous."

"Not there. The other window."

Dorothea laughed but obliged. She saw men and ladies circling on the dance floor. Farmers she hardly knew and townsfolk she had known for years sat side by side enjoying the covered-dish supper. Against the far wall couples stood chatting near the center window. Among them she spotted Cyrus with his head bowed near the ear of a pretty red-haired young woman Dorothea recognized from church; all Dorothea knew of her was that she had been several years ahead of Dorothea in school and that her father's farm lay between Creek's Crossing and Grangerville. Cyrus looked up and met her gaze. She smiled and nodded; he returned a quick, closemouthed grimace and quickly resumed his conversation.

Suddenly she understood. "Am I supposed to be jealous merely because Cyrus Pearson is speaking to another young lady?"

"He is not merely speaking to her. Rumor has it they are nearly engaged."

"How can they be nearly engaged when Cyrus took me driving only two weeks ago?"

"He is fickle and she is nearly twenty-seven."

Dorothea laughed. "Oh. Now everything is made clear." She kept her voice light, but a hollow of confusion and disappointment had formed inside her. "I never had any claim on him, and although I am fond of Cyrus, I do not love him. If he has found happiness with someone else, then I will be the first to congratulate him."

"No, you will be the second," said Mary darkly, glaring across the room. "One can tell by the look on his face that he has been congratulating himself for days. Her parents are aged, you see, and she has no brothers and sisters with whom to divide their farm."

"I see." Indeed, Dorothea did, now. "Thank you for the warning, but I assure you my heart has not been broken."

Mary squeezed her hand. "You are too good for him, Dorothea. Don't lose hope. You will meet a man as fine as my Abner someday, I am sure of it."

Dorothea smiled. "If I meet a man even half as fine as your Abner, I will snatch him up so quickly he will not know what hit him."

As Mary peered at her, not certain whether she spoke in jest, Dorothea bade her good-bye and went off to meet her parents, who had carried their plates to a desk near the front of the room. The delicious aromas from the back table no longer appealed to her, but she kept her parents company while they enjoyed their supper. She told them what had passed between herself and Mrs. Engle, but a reluctant embarrassment kept her from mentioning Cyrus.

She resolved not to dwell on Mary's rumors until Cyrus himself had confirmed or denied them. Before long one of Abner's friends invited her to dance, and after him another young man, and after that she was rarely without a part-ner long enough to more than quickly check the progress on the Authors' Album. Already the rails had been adjusted twice to allow an unquilted portion to replace a section already completed. Miss Nadelfrau had remained beside the quilt nearly all evening, and while she seemed anxious to avoid being seen talking to the disgraced former library board member for too long, she expressed sincere approval for the quality of the quilters' work.

After one of these brief examinations of the quilt-in-progress, Dorothea found herself face-to-face with an abashed Cyrus. "Hello, Dorothea," he greeted her. "Would you care for a dance?"

She agreed, so he took her hand and led her to the dance floor as the fid-dler began a cheerful polka. Cyrus was uncharacteristically somber as they danced, which told Dorothea that Mary's tales were most likely true. When the dance was over, Dorothea thanked him and began to move away, but he held fast to her hand.

"I suppose you've heard."

"Indeed." Dorothea smiled brightly. "I understand congratulations are in order."

"Well—" He glanced over his shoulder. Dorothea forbade herself to see if the red-haired farmer's daughter waited there. "Not quite yet, but perhaps soon."

"I see. Well, I will be sure to congratulate you when the time is right and give the lucky girl my best wishes."

"Dorothea, I always said you were kindness itself." His grip on her hand tightened. "I think I should explain—"

"It truly is not necessary."

"But you see, my father left my mother with little more than her personal belongings, and my stepfather has children of his own from his first mar-riage. They will benefit from his success, whereas I will receive nothing." He regarded her with earnest remorse. "A man with property of his own may make choices a man without it cannot."

"I understand perfectly. You need say no more." She placed her other hand upon his, smiled encouragingly, and freed herself. "I wish you the best. I sincerely do."

She turned her back and walked away, willing her features to reveal noth-ing but glad serenity. Then, the absurdity of how badly the evening had gone struck her, and she could only laugh. She touched a hand to her brow and murmured, "I should have remained at home. Things cannot possibly get any worse."

"That is where we differ, Miss Granger," a man's voice spoke at her side. "I believe that matters can always get worse."

She closed her eyes, sighed, and turned to find Mr. Nelson. "I must confess, Mr. Nelson, that at the moment I find myself quite unable to dispute that."

His eyebrows shot up. "And I find myself quite astonished to discover you without an argument at hand."

Mrs. Claverton chose that moment to walk by. "Oh, she is not always as sharp-tongued as she seems. And she is a fine dancer." She gave Mr. Nelson a pointed look. "You ought to see for yourself."

"Thank you, Mrs. Claverton," said Dorothea, "but I would not want to inconvenience Mr. Nelson."

"Nonsense! I saw him twirling Mrs. Engle about not long ago. If he will partner an old married woman he would surely consent to dance with a lovely young girl such as yourself."

Dorothea intended to explain—and to caution Mrs. Claverton not to refer to Mrs. Engle as "old" too loudly given the temper she was in—but Mr. Nelson spoke first. "It would be my privilege to partner Miss Granger."

Dorothea muffled a sigh and agreed. Mr. Nelson escorted her to the dance floor where couples were forming lines. Mary had taken the floor with Abner, and as the musicians began to play, she stood in place staring at Dorothea with astonished sympathy until another dancer bumped into her. Dorothea smiled ruefully in return to show she was resigned to her fate, but she smothered a laugh when she realized that Mr. Nelson had witnessed the entire silent exchange.

She resolved to be civil company until the dance concluded, but Mr. Nelson made even fewer attempts at conversation than Cyrus had. Finally Dorothea spoke up. "I suppose you expect me to thank you for whisking Mrs. Engle off like that."

"I expect nothing from you."

Dorothea did not know quite what to say to that. "Then I will be happy to oblige."

He nodded curtly.

They danced in silence for a time, an isle of cool civility lapped by waves of laughter and happy chatter.

"Mrs. Claverton is wrong about you," Mr. Nelson said suddenly.

"What do you mean?"

"You are outspoken to a fault." He scrutinized her. "I suspect you deliberately provoked Mrs. Engle. Surely you could have found some moment to tell her about the unexpected signatures she would find in the quilt, but you chose to wait until she discovered them on her own, knowing it would be too late for her to change anything."

"That is not true," retorted Dorothea, but when her conscience pricked her, she added, "Well, perhaps it is partially true. I took the blocks to her home once, but she could not be troubled to look at them. I suppose I could have insisted."

"Or you could have omitted the authors she objected to, but I suspect that never occurred to you."

"I did not see any reason to leave them out." She raised her chin and met his gaze defiantly. "And I do not care who objects to their inclusion."

"I see. Raising money for the library was a secondary consideration for you. Nevertheless, I commend you on managing to have your own way on this. I do believe it will result in more money for the library after all."

The dance ended. Mr. Nelson made a perfunctory bow and released her hand. She nodded and left without thanking him for the dance. She was not certain if he had praised or insulted her. It was quite possible he had managed both.

It was no simple matter to avoid Mrs. Engle, Cyrus, and Mr. Nelson in a schoolroom that suddenly seemed much too small, but Dorothea endeavored. Several hours into the dance, a murmur of excitement went up from the people surrounding the quilt frame: The thread of the last quilting stitch had been knotted and cut. Dorothea joined in the work of attaching the binding, and before long Mr. Collins and Mr. Claverton stood upon a small riser at the front of the room and held up the finished quilt for all to see. Dorothea's heart swelled with pride and pleasure that even Mrs. Engle's criticism could not diminish. It was a beautiful quilt and honored the people of Creek's Crossing as well as those whose names had been enshrined upon it—regardless of what Mrs. Engle thought.

Everyone began to clamor for the winner of the masterpiece to be chosen. Mr. Engle brought forth a large locked box with a slit carved into the lid, used as a ballot box in election time. As Mrs. Deakins filled the box with ticket stubs, the other library board members gathered in a half-circle behind her. Dorothea, standing with her mother and father, did not move to join them. Her mother put an arm around her shoulder, but Dorothea felt no need to be consoled. She had already received everything she had sought from making the Authors' Album. She did not need applause and acclaim as well.

Mrs. Deakins deferred to the mayor, who lifted the lid and withdrew a single slip of paper. Dorothea clasped her hands together and hoped.

"And our winner is—" The mayor paused dramatically. "Cyrus Pearson!"

Exclamations of delight and moans of disappointment filled the room. Dorothea watched as Cyrus strode to the front of the room to claim his prize, accepting congratulations as he went. It pained her to remember how he had told her he would pay any amount to have a quilt made by her hands. She wondered if he would have said such a thing if he had not imagined her inheritance to be much greater than it was. She wondered if he had meant anything he had ever said to her, and if he meant what he told the pretty red-haired girl now.

"He is never happier than when he has an audience," said Lorena for Dorothea's ear alone as Cyrus made a show of beckoning his mother to the front of the room. She came willingly at first, but her pace slowed when she realized Cyrus meant to give the quilt to her. She demurred, but as the clapping and whistling of the crowd swelled, she took the quilt, pretended to admire it, and kissed her son on the cheek. No one who had not heard her outburst earlier that evening would have known how much she disliked it, but Dorothea observed the distasteful curl of her lip and the speed with which she folded the quilt and set it aside. Suddenly she realized that with Cyrus nearly betrothed to someone else, she no longer had to worry about Mrs. Engle's good opinion. It was an enormously relieving thought, and it cheered her immensely.

She saw Mrs. Collins take Mrs. Engle and Mrs. Deakins aside, and when they withdrew into the vestibule, Dorothea knew they were going to the cloakroom to count the evening's earnings. Miss Deakins hastily scooped up the Authors' Album quilt Mrs. Engle had left behind.

The fiddler struck up a sweetly melancholy waltz, a tune Dorothea knew well and loved. She listened wistfully, but when she saw Cyrus glide past with the red-haired girl in his arms, she did not feel a single twinge of regret. She liked him, and any woman with eyes to see him must admit he was handsome, but she knew they did not suit each other well for anything more than a weekly ride in the cutter. She was too serious, he too merry. They would be at each other's throats if forced to remain in each other's company for the rest of their lives.

Just then Dorothea felt someone watching her. She looked over her shoulder and was not entirely surprised to find Mr. Nelson there. Too weary to provoke him, she merely nodded and returned her attention to the dance floor.

To her surprise, he said, "If you are not too tired, I would appreciate the favor of a dance."

She was tempted to refuse on the grounds that a woman does not like to hear that she looks tired, especially when she is dressed in her best at a dance, but she merely nodded again and took his hand. She would enjoy the music if not the company.

Mr. Nelson, however, chose to converse, spoiling any chance she might have had of enjoying her favorite waltz. "You were quite complimentary to my students on the night of the school exhibition."

So many things of greater significance had happened that night that Dorothea had to think before she could recollect what she had told him. "Yes. I thought they performed beautifully."

"I think you give them undue praise."

"I think you tend to offer undeserved censure, for your students and everyone else."

He ignored the bite in her tone, but she knew it had not gone unnoticed. "They are not progressing as well as I had hoped."

"Perhaps the job is too much for you," she said innocently. "Perhaps you should resign and allow someone who actually does like children to take over."

"One does not need to like children to instruct them."

"One most decidedly does!"

"At any rate, that is beside the point, because I do like children. Miss Granger, if you would allow me to speak more than one sentence in succession, I would be able to come to the point much sooner."

Dorothea, who had assumed the point was to annoy her, inclined her head to indicate he was free to speak without interruption.

"The number of students and the differences in their ages is significant enough now to warrant dividing the school into two groups. Obviously I cannot teach both simultaneously, so I wondered if you would consider teaching the younger group."

She stared at him, speechless. Finally she managed, "You would ask me this after criticizing my teaching?"

He had the decency to look embarrassed. "It is possible that my criticism was a trifle premature. While it is true that the students had received only a passing introduction to the more advanced subjects and concepts, their understanding of the fundamentals was quite thorough in all their subjects. I did not discover this until after I made . . . several remarks that I now regret."

"Mr. Nelson, if I did not consider you to be entirely without a sense of humor, I might suspect you are playing a prank on me."

"Do you accept the offer or not?"

"We have not discussed wages, and—" She hesitated. "I am not certain the school board would hire me."

"I have already spoken to them. They agreed or I would not have asked you. Your salary will be the same as when you last taught." He regarded her with barely concealed impatience. "Do you accept or must I find someone else?"

"I would like five dollars more each term," said Dorothea. "If that condition can be met, I would be delighted to accept your proposal."

"I will have to consult the school board, but I think they will be agreeable."

"When you know for certain, please inform me."

The last note of the waltz faded away. Dorothea suddenly became very conscious of Mr. Nelson's hand lingering on the small of her back. "Thank you for the dance," she said, and quickly walked away.

Before she could find Lorena and tell her the astonishing news, Mrs. Engle and the remaining members of the library board approached the stage at the front of the room. "We have our final count," Mrs. Engle called out as everyone gathered around to hear. "The library board is pleased to announce that thanks to the generosity of the people of Creek's Crossing and surrounding environs, we have raised five hundred dollars for the founding of a new library!"

A cheer went up from the crowd. Thrilled, Dorothea joined in the applause. Whatever else befell her, at least she would be able to enjoy a library one day soon.

"We will break ground in spring," Mrs. Engle continued. "Every man who wishes to assist in the building will be gratefully welcomed."

Dorothea thought of Constance and Abel and hoped Mrs. Engle spoke the truth.

Mrs. Engle thanked everyone for attending and stepped down from the stage. Before anyone could depart, Mrs. Claverton quickly asked for their attention again. "We have one more announcement. The Authors' Album quilt that the ladies of Creek's Crossing have so beautifully fashioned has been donated to the library board so that it might be displayed in the library for all to enjoy!"

A rousing cheer went up from the people, but Dorothea was too surprised to join in—and, if she was not mistaken, Mrs. Engle was equally astonished. Mrs. Engle quickly regained her composure, however, and graciously acknowledged the applause. Apparently word of Mrs. Engle's revulsion for the quilt had not spread far or the onlookers would not have found her so generous.

After that, the Quilting Bee Dance ended. Dorothea offered to help Miss Nadelfrau disassemble her quilting frame, but Miss Nadelfrau hastened to assure her she had enough help. Thus rebuffed, Dorothea collected her basket and cake plate from the covered-dish table, bade good-bye to Constance and Mary, and left with her parents.

On the cold ride home, Dorothea told her mother and father about Mr. Nelson's offer. Robert was dubious, but Lorena was pleased. "It is about time they realize what a fine teacher they had in you."

"So you plan to accept?" asked Robert.

"If you think I can be spared from the farm. It is nearly sugaring time, and after that, spring planting. With Uncle Jacob and Jonathan gone, we will be shorthanded."

"We will hire hands, as we have done in the past," said Lorena. Her mouth was concealed beneath her muffler, but her eyes smiled. "You can help me with the garden in the mornings and on Saturdays. We will manage."

"Then I shall accept the position, assuming the school board can scrape together the extra five dollars."

Robert chuckled. "I think you asked for that additional five dollars just to spite them, not because you felt underpaid before."

"I will not deny it," said Dorothea. "If anyone else but Mr. Nelson had offered me the position, I probably would have accepted my original wages."

"This has been quite a successful night for you," remarked Lorena. "You have your position back at a higher salary, your quilt was an overwhelming success—"

"Not entirely," Dorothea reminded her.

"It earned a great deal of money for the library and that's what counts."

"It was a successful night for me, too," said Robert.

His wife peered at him quizzically. "How so?"

"From what I hear, I will no longer have to dread Cyrus Pearson becoming my son-in-law."

He shuddered so comically that Dorothea had to join in her parents' laughter, though she was mortified that they had heard through gossip what she was too embarrassed to tell them herself. Worse yet was the genuine relief she detected beneath their sympathetic humor. If they were so disinclined for her to marry Cyrus, why had they not spoken up when he seemed to be courting her?

❧

For all of the unexpected happenings on the night of the Quilting Bee Dance, two more equally astounding revelations awaited her.

The first came two days later. The school board had sent word that they agreed to the requested raise. After dropping by Mr. Engle's office to sign her contract, she paid a call on her friend Mary, who was eager to share an intriguing bit of news. Mrs. Engle had not donated the quilt to the library, nor had Mrs. Claverton erred in saying the gift had been made. According to one of Mr. Schultz's printing customers, who had witnessed the exchange, Mr. Nelson had purchased the quilt from Mrs. Engle for five dollars and had immediately given it to Mrs. Claverton for the library. "Perhaps Mr. Nelson thought Mrs. Engle would donate the five dollars to the library," said Mary, "but she kept it. So in the end, Mrs. Engle came out well ahead."

"Unless you deduct her expenses. She did purchase all the materials for the quilt."

Mary tossed her head scornfully. Dorothea was trying to be charitable, but they both knew Mrs. Engle had spent far less than five dollars on fabric, batting, and thread. Why she had accepted the thanks of the crowd when she had not been the one to donate the quilt—and why Mr. Nelson had not claimed rightful credit for the deed—was a mystery neither Dorothea nor Mary could explain to their complete satisfaction.

The second revelation came in a letter from Jonathan. He had thought about Mr. Nelson often since leaving Creek's Crossing, and his curiosity and concern plagued him so much that he was compelled to send an inquiry to an acquaintance in Philadelphia. "Thomas Nelson was in prison for a crime he did without a doubt commit," wrote Jonathan. "That much was never in dispute. However, I think it will interest you to know that he was convicted of helping runaway slaves."

Mr. Nelson had lived in Philadelphia, but he had often traveled to Virginia on business for his father. He used his frequent travels as a cover for business of his own. He routinely carried with him money, false identification papers, forged bills of leave, and other useful items for slaves determined to run away, which he distributed to plantations and households throughout several southern states. He earned the enmity of influential slave owners who conspired to catch him in the act. He was tried and convicted of forgery and assisting runaway slaves, and he was sentenced to six years in prison. He served two before his father managed to secure his early release on good behavior, with the understanding that any additional infractions would result in a lengthy imprisonment with no chance of leniency from any judge. Most people believed the senior Mr. Nelson had paid substantial bribes in order to have his seriously ill son freed just in time to save his life.

After a lengthy recuperation, Thomas Nelson's father made him swear an oath that he would tell no one the reasons for his imprisonment, and that he would obey the law no matter how much it tested his moral convictions, for following his conscience had almost killed him. After the Carters informed him of their intention to stake a claim out West, the senior Mr. Nelson sent his son to live on the family estate in Creek's Crossing rather than find a new tenant family. It was believed that the father thought his son safer in a place far from his old temptations; it was also said that the senior Mr. Nelson could not bear to watch his son struggle with his decision to obey his father.

"As you can see," concluded Jonathan, "the scholars of Creek's Crossing could do far worse than Mr. Nelson as a moral influence, although I wonder how long a man of his convictions will be able to keep the oath his father wrested from him. Though you might be tempted to speak to him on these matters, I urge you to refrain. Apparently the truth is known to only a few close family friends, one of whom disclosed these facts to me due to my concern about the safety of Thomas Nelson's pupils. By all accounts, both the elder and the younger Nelson are determined to keep the entire unfortunate episode a secret, and it is their fervent hope that no one in Creek's Crossing will ever know what has passed."

Of course her brother was right; the secret must be kept unless Mr. Nelson himself chose to divulge it. Mr. Nelson was fortunate that Cyrus Pearson's inquiries had not uncovered it.

Dorothea wished she could ask Mr. Nelson what part of his secret he considered shameful: that he had helped runaways, or that he had vowed never to do so again.

Chapter Nine

The next morning, Dorothea hurried through her chores, eager to finish so that she could begin planning her lessons. She shivered in the barn as she milked the cow but she hardly noticed, her thoughts on the schoolroom a mile to the south. A few months earlier, Mr. Nelson's offer to teach only the youngest pupils in the choir loft might have insulted her, since she had so recently instructed the entire school on her own. Now the very thought of teaching again, any teaching at all, so gratified her that she refused to see her diminished role as anything but a wonderful opportunity to foster in Creek's Crossing's youngest pupils the important foundation upon which the rest of their education would be built. That she owed her good fortune to Mr. Nelson unsettled her, but not so much that she would reconsider accepting the position. Perhaps, she told herself, her uncomfortable gratitude would remind her to be civil.

As she carried the milk pail back to the house, she slipped on a patch of ice. A wave of white froth spilled over the brim before she could catch her balance. As she brushed the spilled milk from her skirt, she noticed that the ice underfoot had formed in the tracks of wagon wheels. Up and down the road, similar smooth pools of ice filled all the old ruts left in the mud of the previous autumn so that she could trace several distinct trails from the Creek's Crossing road to the barn. Yesterday the entire road had been covered by a half inch of snow.

She ran back to the house and burst into the kitchen, where her mother was frying potatoes for their breakfast. "We had a thaw yesterday and an overnight freeze."

"Yesterday was not the first thaw, either. It is just the first we noticed."

Lorena wrapped a towel around the handle of the skillet and pulled it off the fire. "Your father has already gone to the maple grove. He asks you to bring him his breakfast."

"Uncle Jacob—" Dorothea hesitated. "We should have begun tapping the trees days ago."

"I know that is what Uncle Jacob would have done." Lorena gave her a small, regretful smile. "We were so distracted by the Quilting Bee Dance that we neglected his records and ignored the weather. We will have to make up for lost time."

Dorothea ate swiftly as her mother packed the lunch pail for Robert, silently berating herself for ignoring the changing seasons. How many days of the sap run had they squandered? On her way to the sugar camp, she observed that already the rising sun was warming the earth. The sap would run that day, and they were not prepared.

She found her father in the maple grove, moving swiftly from tree to tree, inspecting old spiles, hanging buckets to catch the drips of sap, drilling new holes where necessary. He thanked her for the food but did not interrupt his work to take it from her. When she realized he had forgotten it, and possibly her, Dorothea set the pail on the ground between the roots of a tree and went to help him.

She had never done this part of the work of sugaring before, had only occasionally seen it done, but did not need her father's silent swiftness to understand the urgency. They hurried to complete the neglected tasks, and before long, Lorena joined them. When they had seen to all but the last third of the sugarbush, Robert sent them to prepare the sugaring house. He came by later with the team to replenish the depleted stores of firewood and load the empty barrels into the wagon.

Despite their haste, it was past noon before Robert returned with enough fresh sap to warrant building a fire beneath the three empty kettles. Evening had fallen before Dorothea and her mother poured off the contents of the last kettle into two sugar molds. They had not stopped to eat or care for the livestock, so Robert decided they would resume sugaring in the morning. After finishing the evening chores, they ate a cold supper of bread and cheese and went off to bed. Just before she fell asleep, Dorothea's thoughts drifted to the school and the lessons she had intended to prepare. She promised herself she would rest her eyes for only a moment before retrieving her schoolbooks, but she fell asleep before she could summon up enough willpower to force herself to rise.

At the sugar camp early the next day, Dorothea and her mother built the fire and awaited Robert's delivery of the first barrels of fresh sap. He turned the team back toward the grove as soon as he unloaded the wagon, reporting, with chagrin and annoyance, that some of the buckets had overflowed, spilling their precious contents onto the ground. "I should have known that the trees I tapped first would have had time to refill their buckets. I won't make that mistake again," he said, giving the reins a shake and chirruping to the horses. As she and her mother poured sap into the first of the three kettles, Dorothea reflected that Uncle Jacob had always insisted upon emptying all of the buckets at the end of the day, even those only partially full. The sap retained its quality if it went swiftly from tree to kettle, he had often said, and he deplored wastefulness. She imagined him shaking his head in disgust at the sight of sap backing up into the spiles, oozing down the sides of the buckets.

They grew more assured in their work as the week passed, but they missed Uncle Jacob's advice and gladly would have endured his curt criticism to have his guidance. The sugar seemed to be as fine in quality as ever, though not as plentiful, and Dorothea felt they worked twice as hard as in previous years to get it. Evenings found her too exhausted to tend to the housework or plan her lessons. When she mentioned in passing that the school board expected her to begin teaching in two days, Lorena exclaimed in dismay for her own forgetfulness and sent Dorothea in early. "I can finish this myself," she said, stirring the second kettle and peering into the third.

Dorothea gratefully accepted her mother's offer and returned to the house and her books. She took the time to build a fire in the oven and prepare a hot meal for the family—the first they had enjoyed all week—then turned her attention to her lessons. She set her work aside only long enough to eat with her parents after they came in from the sugar camp, steam-soaked and weary, and begged off helping her mother with the dishes so she could return to her books.

"The temperature hasn't fallen off much since sundown," her father remarked when he came in from the barn, the evening chores completed late. Dorothea and her mother acknowledged his words with a nod. No other reply was necessary. Nighttime freezes prolonged the sap run. Without them, sugaring season would end.

Though Dorothea's work absorbed her, after her father's statement, she brooded over their first attempt to make sugar without Uncle Jacob. They should have been as conscientious as he. Before she doused the lamp that night, unable to put her thoughts to rest, she stole into his room, the sensation of trespass lingering despite the many times she had made up the bed for runaways. Lorena had stored his papers in his steamer trunk—but it was Dorothea's steamer trunk now; he had bequeathed it to her, and she had every right to lift the lid whenever she pleased.

She found his farm journal and paged through the notes on sugaring. From his records she concluded that the sugaring season had indeed come upon them earlier than usual, but still well within the average. But even in years when a caprice of the weather had resulted in an even shorter sugaring season, Uncle Jacob had still managed to produce more maple sugar than the Grangers had done alone.

Dorothea sighed, closed the journal, and returned it to the trunk. They were not finished yet. The sap run might endure another week or more. They would learn from their neglect and be better prepared the next winter.

As she closed the lid, her gaze fell upon a familiar book with a worn cover of black leather. Her heart leaped as she reached for her uncle's Bible. Until that moment, she had not realized how much she missed his blessings at mealtimes, his silent nightly devotions, those infrequent occasions when he would read aloud a verse and query her about its interpretation. At the time she had resented his intrusion into her reading or quilting, and suspected he hoped to catch her in a mistake. Now she wondered if perhaps she had misjudged him.

She opened the cover and turned the thin, well-worn pages, thinking of her uncle and his mercurial tempers, his hidden depths. Her eyes blurred with weariness; she drew a hand across her brow and closed the book, but something written on the flyleaf caught her eye. Holding the page closer to the lamp, she discovered a phrase written in an elegant female hand: "For dearest Jacob on the occasion of our marriage. Deut. 23:15–16." Below the words was a simple sketch of a forget-me-not in bloom.

Dorothea could not recall the verse; likely it was another of her uncle's favorite precepts regarding the proper conduct of a wife. She found the page and read the line, her breath catching in her throat: "Thou shalt not deliver unto his master the servant which is escaped from his master unto thee: he shall dwell with thee, *even* among you, in that place which he shall choose in one of thy gates, where it liketh him best: thou shalt not oppress him."

She studied the verses, wondering whether the message was a request, a promise, a warning, or a directive to her husband-to-be. She wondered if they were instead an acceptance of a request he had made of her. She wished she knew. She knew that she could never know.

The flickering of the lamp roused her from her reverie. Closing the lid of the steamer trunk, she took up the Bible and the lamp and carried them upstairs to her attic bedroom.

The next morning Dorothea had to break ice in the well bucket, but the day after, she did not. The Grangers would try to coax the last drops of sap from the maple trees, but the sap run was essentially over. In the final tally, they produced little more than half of the sugar they had the previous year. Robert and Lorena worried whether they would have any left to trade after they set aside the usual amount for their own use, but Dorothea refused to dwell on their unsuccessful first outing. She had long prided herself on knowing the natural world of the Elm Creek Valley better than anyone. Next year she would be mindful of the shifting temperatures, as diligent as her uncle and as intuitive as the Shawnee woman who had taught her herb lore. Next year, she would not fail.

Dorothea resumed teaching on the following Monday, and soon grew accustomed to the pleasant rhythm of the days. Each morning she led the twelve youngest children upstairs to the choir loft, where she gave them their lessons and heard their recitations while Mr. Nelson instructed the twenty-eight elder students in the schoolroom below. Her pupils were sweet and attentive, and they seemed pleased to have their very own teacher and a separate place all to themselves. Sometimes while her students were quietly bent over their books, Dorothea listened to the lectures and recitations below. Mr. Nelson apparently preferred the Socratic method in many subjects, which Dorothea had never tried. It did give his students a great deal of practice in logic and reasoning, skills that Dorothea admitted would be more useful to them once they left school than the endless memorization of facts and dates.

In this fashion they proceeded almost as if they led two separate and distinct schools, but when Mr. Nelson lectured in history, Dorothea took her students downstairs so they could listen. At first she had given her own lectures, but when she observed the younger children straining to hear Mr. Nelson's voice over her own, she gave up and decided one history lecture would serve the entire school. She could not deny that Mr. Nelson's university studies had given him a greater depth and breadth of knowledge than her own in many subjects, but in history, especially, he excelled. He brought the stories of the past to life with such detail and intriguing narrative that the students sat spellbound throughout the lessons. Dorothea had never seen the school so quiet, except for when Miss Gunther's gentle monotone had put half the class to sleep.

"You could have been a university lecturer," remarked Dorothea one day after she and Mr. Nelson excused the students for lunch.

"I was," he said, to her surprise. He had been a tutor in the history department at the University of Pennsylvania for two years and had intended to become a professor.

"Why didn't you?" she asked.

"Other events intervened."

He said no more, and Dorothea did not persist in questioning him. She could only imagine all that he had left behind to keep his promise to his father. It was no wonder he had found little to admire in Creek's Crossing or its inhabitants when he first arrived.

The weeks passed. The sun rose earlier each morning, and before long the temperatures grew mild enough for Dorothea to walk the mile to the ferry rather than ride her mother's horse and board him in Mr. Engle's livery stable during the day. Since she was no longer privy to the plans of the library board, she was surprised one morning to discover that a team of men had broken ground on the vacant lot not far from the school. By the size of the foundation they had marked with pickets and rope, they intended the library to be an impressive size, nearly as large as the Lutheran church. Her spirits soared at the thought of how many books could fill such a space. She only hoped that Mrs. Engle would not somehow contrive to have the building named after herself.

On a particularly warm day, upon noticing that her students were gazing wistfully out the windows more often than at their books, Dorothea suggested to Mr. Nelson that they take the children outside for a lesson in the natural sciences. He agreed, and both classes of students gladly followed as she led them on a walk beside the creek, where she pointed out the various geological features the view provided. Upon their return to the classroom, she assigned the students compositions about what they had learned. She was pleased to find that even the youngest had grasped the concepts of erosion and sedimentation. A few of the boys wrote enthusiastically about turbulence and velocity, which made her glad she had not taken them past Widow's Pining, where they might have been tempted to experiment in the dangerous current.

At the end of the day, after the students departed and she and Mr. Nelson were tidying the classroom, he remarked, "That was a very instructive lesson. I believe I learned something today."

She smiled and continued wiping the blackboard. "You are merely being kind."

"Not at all." He paused. "I am never merely kind."

She almost laughed, but she could not deny it. "Perhaps later in the spring we might venture out again to study plants, when there are more to see."

He readily agreed. That very night, Dorothea began preparing her next natural science lesson so that she would be ready when the time came. Spring planting would soon begin, and the eldest boys and even some of the eldest girls and younger children would leave school to work on family farms. Her lesson on the flora and fauna of the Elm Creek Valley could not wait much longer if she wanted all the students to benefit from it. Besides, with so many pupils gone, Mr. Nelson would likely consolidate the two classes and dismiss her until after the harvest.

Fair weather also brought more passengers through the Grangers' Underground Railroad station: a husband and wife from Virginia, whose necks and shoulders bore thick scars from many beatings, fleeing so that their unborn child could never be sold away from them. Two young girls who dressed as boys and walked off the plantation unrecognized by their overseer. A man, promised emancipation upon his master's death, who rode off on a stolen horse when the master's son and heir refused to honor his father's wishes. Their harrowing tales chilled Dorothea to her core, and she often could not sleep at night for thinking of the others, so many others, who could not run away or who had died trying. The Grangers' efforts to help a handful of runaways reach the North seemed pitifully inadequate, no more than a gesture— except to those few who found their freedom. So much more was needed, so much more than they could ever do.

The hiding place Dorothea's father had made in Uncle Jacob's old room was tested twice in the weeks the winter snows melted and warmer winds began to blow from the southwest. Mary and Abner paid an unexpected call on a sunny afternoon, forcing the Grangers to hide a mother and her young son behind the false back of the wardrobe. Dorothea was dizzy with alarm the whole duration of their visit, waiting for the child to wail and betray them. As soon as the unexpected guests had departed, Dorothea and Lorena rushed to the wardrobe to free its occupants. They found the young boy asleep in his mother's arms, the mother herself anxious but calm, and safe.

The second test came a week later as two men scarcely older than Dorothea lay sleeping in Uncle Jacob's room. Someone pounded upon the back door of the kitchen, but before anyone could run to warn the fugitives, the door opened and Mr. Liggett stuck his head in. "Mornin', folks," he said awkwardly, startled to find Dorothea and her mother there. "I didn't think you 'uns were home."

"Are you in the habit of entering our house when you believe us to be elsewhere?" Lorena inquired.

"No, no, but since I came all this way I thought I'd leave you a note."

Lorena stood fast, blocking his view of the rooms beyond. "How fortunate that we are home and you will not have to bother."

"Yeah." Disappointed, Mr. Liggett still tried to peer around Lorena. "I just thought I'd check and see if you 'uns are hiring for the planting. Since your brother never paid me from last year, I thought you could just tack on what I earn this time to what you owe me."

Dorothea saw the line of her mother's jaw tighten. "I do not believe my husband will require your services this year. Thank you just the same."

Baleful, he said, "Then I'll just take what you owe me and go."

He shoved open the door. Lorena protested and grabbed hold of his coat, but he shook loose, knocking her to the floor. Dorothea, too, tried to block his path, but he shoved her aside and stormed into the front room. He scanned it, and, finding nothing, squared his bony shoulders and turned down the hallway toward Uncle Jacob's room.

Dorothea heard her mother choke back a gasp as Mr. Liggett swung open the door and stepped inside. He lifted the Sugar Camp Quilt to peer under the bed; he flung open the doors to the wardrobe and rifled through the old clothes hanging within. Dorothea held her breath as he looked left, right, then backed out of the room and headed for the attic stairs.

When Dorothea heard his footsteps overhead, she dashed into Uncle Jacob's room. The two runaways were nowhere to be found, and the door to the wardrobe was ajar. She closed it without a sound and returned to the hall where her mother stood, her eyes fixed on the ceiling, darting back and forth in response to the creaks of the floorboards. Dorothea linked her arm through her mother's as they listened to Mr. Liggett tearing about upstairs, her mind racing with plans of what to do if Mr. Liggett found any sign of the fugitives. Her father was off in the northwestern fields; he could not come to their aid.

Mr. Liggett stomped downstairs, glowering. "The cellar," he snarled at Lorena.

Her back was ramrod straight, but her grasp on Dorothea's arm tightened. "I cannot comprehend why you believe you have any right to subject us to this search. If it's money you seek—"

"Never mind. I'll find it myself." He disappeared around the corner into the kitchen. They heard the cellar door swing open and the scuff of his boots on the steps.

Dorothea tore free of her mother and ran upstairs. Her small attic bedroom was in a shambles, quilts and clothes and books strewn over the bed and floor. Swiftly she retrieved the book her uncle had bequeathed to her and removed the stack of bills from within the front cover. She counted out some of her inheritance and raced back downstairs. She reached the kitchen just as Mr. Liggett returned from the cellar.

"Here," she said, holding out the money. "The wages my uncle neglected to pay you. Please take it and leave us in peace."

Mr. Liggett snatched the folded bills and thumbed through them. "This ain't enough."

"It's the wage you agreed upon."

"That was a year ago. I want something for my trouble and for the wait."

"That's all I can give you."

He jerked his head toward the front room. "Then I'll just have that whiskey and call it even."

Lorena quickly retrieved the nearly empty bottle from Uncle Jacob's desk and thrust it at him. "Take it and go."

He shook the bottle, scowling to see how little remained, and tucked it into his coat. "Thank you kindly. Good day, ladies."

Lorena slammed the door behind him and slid the bolt in place. "That will remain locked, day and night, from this moment on." She placed a hand on her chest, breathless. "I declare that man is a demon. He was not looking for money, or even for whiskey. That much is evident despite his words."

Dorothea felt a slow churning of anger growing within her. "We should not have allowed him to invade our home like that."

"Allowed him? I do not see how we could have prevented it."

"If Jonathan had been here—"

"They very likely would have come to blows. Your brother would have thrashed Mr. Liggett soundly, making him hate us all the more. Now Mr. Liggett has seen for himself that we have nothing to hide, and he will not return."

Dorothea was not so certain.

They went to the window, expecting to see Mr. Liggett trudging off on foot, but they caught a glimpse of him on horseback before he disappeared into the trees. They hurried down to the cellar and eased open the door Robert had concealed in a row of shelves. In the dim light, Dorothea saw the two men crouched warily, prepared to run.

"He is gone," she said. "It is safe to come out."

"If you don't mind, we'll stay put for a while," said one of the men. The other nodded his assent.

"As you wish." Dorothea handed them some bread, dried apples, and a jug of water, and closed the hidden door.

❧

Mr. Nelson scheduled Dorothea's second lesson in natural sciences for a Friday, on the same morning her father, at breakfast, had announced that the ground was thawed enough for plowing. He had already hired hands to help with the work, and the men would begin the next day. She walked to school that morning slowly, reluctant for the day to begin and speed toward its end. While she welcomed the work of springtime more than in previous years— now that the farm was the Grangers' own—she would miss her students, the daily walks to school, the cordial lunches in the classroom when she and Mr. Nelson would discuss books or the news from back East. She resolved to fill her hours with work so she would not miss the schoolhouse until they needed her again.

After lunchtime recess, Dorothea and Mr. Nelson gathered the children and set off on foot to the meadow and woods southwest of town. Dorothea showed them the early signs of spring pushing up through the earth, natural herbs useful in medicines, berries and roots that were safe to eat, and poisonous plants they must never touch. The children were so inquisitive and interested in all she had to show them that she lost track of time, and they wandered farther than she had intended. When she finally remembered, she apologized to Mr. Nelson and turned the children back toward school, wondering why he had not reminded her that the hour was growing late. The end of the school day was nearly at hand, and he would not have time for his history lecture.

Usually one of them walked at the head of the group and the other at the end, with the children in between, but this time Mr. Nelson followed behind the children with Dorothea, remarking that the students knew the way to the schoolhouse without a guide, and this way, he and Dorothea could both watch them.

"Another fine lesson, Miss Granger," he said. "Raised in the cities as I have been, I never knew what wonders lay on my family's own land."

"Your land?" asked Dorothea. "We walked far, but not all the way to Two Bears Farm."

"Indeed we did. The stand of oaks beyond the far edge of the meadow marks the boundary of our property."

"I had no idea." She and Jonathan had played there often as children, thinking the land belonged to no one.

"You seem to know every species of plant and animal in the Elm Creek Valley."

"Not every one, I'm sure." She brushed a hand along the long blades of grasses growing on the side of the road, plucking one and raising it to her nose. It smelled like fresh, green wheat. "I have lived in the valley all my life, however, and my brother and I explored every bit of it we could."

They reached the town with its hard-packed dirt roads and flat board sidewalks. The children's pace slowed the closer they came to the schoolhouse. "They think we won't notice their attempts to prolong our outing," said Mr. Nelson dryly. He returned to the front of the line and began walking more briskly so that the students were forced to hurry after him. Dorothea muffled a laugh and quickened her pace to keep up with them.

They were only a block from the schoolhouse when a man stepped out from the doorway of a tavern and seized her by the upper arm. Her exclamation of surprise was cut short by the sharply foul odor of liquor and tobacco juice and unwashed skin.

"I know you 'uns are hiding something," Mr. Liggett muttered, tightening his grip as she struggled to free herself. The children continued on to the schoolhouse unaware. "Something you wouldn't want your sweetheart to know about, eh? You pay me again what you paid me last time, and I won't tell him."

Suddenly Mr. Nelson strode toward them. "What is the meaning of this, Liggett? Release her at once."

Mr. Liggett did. Dorothea backed away from him, rubbing her arm. The children had halted and were watching them curiously.

Mr. Liggett ducked back into the tavern. "Don't forget," he called to Dorothea as she ushered the children on their way, fighting to conceal the sickening dread in her heart.

"Perhaps you would care to explain that," said Mr. Nelson in an undertone.

She would not care to at all. "Mr. Liggett had a long-standing disagreement with my uncle. He persists in troubling my family about it."

"He said something about a sweetheart. I assume he means Mr. Pearson."

Dorothea forced a laugh. "I have no idea what he is talking about. Mr. Pearson is certainly not my sweetheart." She gave Mr. Nelson a searching look. "Perhaps you would have some influence with him."

"I? With Mr. Liggett?"

"Why, yes. I understand he used to work for you."

"Mr. Liggett has never worked for me, nor shall he ever. I assumed he was employed by your sweetheart."

"Cyrus Pearson is not my sweetheart," said Dorothea impatiently. Then she stopped short. "Why would you think Mr. Liggett works for Cyrus Pearson?"

Mr. Nelson shrugged. "I have frequently seen them together in town. One occasion was at the bank, where Mr. Pearson made a withdrawal, which he then gave to Mr. Liggett. I assume it was a payment for services rendered."

Dorothea could not imagine what services. Mr. Liggett rarely did any work but farming, and Cyrus had no farm. "Do you recall when this was?"

"Shortly after my arrival in Creek's Crossing."

Dorothea's thoughts flew back to a day when Mr. Liggett had confronted her and Cyrus as they rode to his mother's house. Mr. Liggett had asked Cyrus for money—more money—and Cyrus had seemed not to know what he meant. Suddenly she remembered that it was Cyrus who had told her Mr. Nelson had hired Mr. Liggett. At once came a cascade of other memories: Cyrus saying that Mr. Nelson had questionable opinions on the subject of slavery; Cyrus surprised that Lorena should recommend Abel Wright as foreman of the library construction; Cyrus doubting that any of the Elm Creek Valley's colored families would care to use the library; Lorena questioning what Dorothea knew of Cyrus's opinions and her own assurances that he must share her own well-known views or he would not have sought her company. But of course, it was never her company, or even Dorothea herself, that had interested him most.

"Miss Granger." Mr. Nelson was regarding her with concern. "Are you all right?"

She had never been less so. A man she had considered a friend may have been more deceitful and conniving than she ever could have imagined, and she had been blind to his manipulations. "Yes, I am fine, thank you."

"If you wish, I will speak to him."

"No! No. Please do not trouble yourself. Anything you say will merely antagonize him."

"If he is as troublesome as you say—" Something in her expression made him break off. "Of course. If that is what you wish."

"It is."

They had reached the schoolhouse. Mr. Nelson held open the door and allowed the students to pass inside. When the last straggler had entered, he said, "I am sure you would prefer for Cyrus Pearson or your father to handle this matter."

"Why are you forever bringing up Mr. Pearson? Are you so engrossed in your books that you hear none of the gossip in this town? You were at the Quilting Bee Dance. Were you standing about with your eyes closed? Are you the only person in town unaware that Cyrus Pearson is engaged to someone else?"

He hesitated. "I was . . . not aware of that."

"Well, now you know." She marched past him into the classroom, where her own young pupils beamed down at her curiously from the choir loft stairs and Mr. Nelson's hid smiles as they wrote upon their slates or pretended to be engrossed in their books. Dorothea flushed with embarrassment and wondered how much they had overheard.

Fortunately, only enough time remained in the school day for Dorothea and Mr. Nelson to assign new lessons and bid farewell to those students who would not return the next week. Dorothea went upstairs and cleaned the choir loft thoroughly before helping Mr. Nelson tidy the main classroom. They did not talk as they worked. Mr. Nelson was in a brood, frowning over some matter—possibly how Dorothea might have brought down scandal upon the school with her public altercation with Mr. Liggett.

When she could linger no longer, Dorothea approached him. "Since the classroom seems to be in order, I will say good-bye."

He did not look up from packing books into his satchel. "Until Monday, then."

"But—" Dorothea did not know what to say. "I did not think you would need a second teacher anymore, with so many of the students gone until after the harvest."

"Did you sign a contract for the entire term?"

"Well, yes, but—"

"Are you asking to be relieved of your obligations?"

"Of course not." She took a deep breath and clasped her hands at her waist. "I merely assumed that you intended to consolidate the classes."

"I intended no such thing. However, if you wish to resign, I will not stop you."

"No, Mr. Nelson, I do not wish to resign." In consternation, Dorothea snatched up her satchel. "I will see you on Monday."

She glimpsed his answering nod as she hurried for the door.

She would be grateful for the respite of the weekend, she thought as she crossed the street on her way to the ferry. She and Lorena had mapped out the garden and were eager to begin planting. Lorena had been nurturing seedlings indoors for weeks, waiting until the danger of frost passed. They had been a fortnight now without a freeze, and Lorena decided the time had come to put her plants into the ground.

Dorothea heard the steady clop of horse's hooves on the street behind her as she descended the hill to the ferry crossing. A horse and rider followed her aboard, and to her dismay, she saw that the man was Cyrus.

She forced a nervous flicker of a smile and turned her back to lean on the rail and gaze out at Elm Creek. Cyrus ignored the hint and came to stand beside her. "Good afternoon, Miss Granger," he said quietly, with none of his usual mirth.

"Good afternoon, Mr. Pearson."

"It is a pleasant day for a crossing, isn't it?" Then he made an impatient gesture of disgust. "This is nonsense. For months you have called me Cyrus and I have called you Dorothea. We laughed at each other's jokes and had a jolly time. Can't we be friends again?"

"I would like that," said Dorothea carefully. "But you must understand, I cannot go riding with another woman's fiancé as if we were courting. You can imagine, I'm sure, what people would say about that."

"I never thought you one to tailor your behavior according to what other people think."

"I do so when I agree with them." She hesitated. "If we are to be friends again, however, we must have complete honesty between us."

"Of course, Dorothea." His mouth twisted in a rueful grimace. "I understand perfectly why you would need my assurances on that point."

"Indeed, I have many questions for you, many uncertainties," said Dorothea. "For one, I wondered why you and your mother allowed everyone to believe that she rather than Mr. Nelson donated the Authors' Album quilt to the library."

Cyrus was taken aback, but he quickly composed himself. "I cannot agree that we did any such thing. If I recall correctly, Nelson was given credit for his gift."

"You do not recall correctly. Mrs. Claverton announced the donation. You and your mother accepted congratulations from one and all without a word of thanks to Mr. Nelson."

"I regret the oversight, but Nelson is not one to draw attention to himself. I am quite confident he was relieved not to be hauled onto the stage. Furthermore, my mother and I did not accept congratulations for the donation. If you recall, I accepted congratulations for winning the drawing. My mother accepted congratulations for running a successful event."

"I see."

"What do you see?"

"I see that we are not going to be completely honest with each other after all. Or rather, you will not be so."

He frowned, annoyed. "Any explanation that does not satisfy a conclusion you have already reached must be a lie?"

"I suppose it might seem that way to you. Let us move on, then. Why were you so eager for me to believe that Mr. Liggett worked for Mr. Nelson when in truth you were his employer?"

He studied her for a moment. "That day in the carriage. Of course. I hope you can forgive me a momentary lapse in judgment. I confess I was not entirely truthful. I could not think of any other excuse for Mr. Liggett's behavior, and, knowing how you despise him, I did not want to admit that he worked for me. I valued your good opinion and did not want to lose it."

"That accounts for why you lied, but not this particular lie. Why not simply deny that Mr. Liggett worked for you? Why attribute your own actions to Mr. Nelson?"

"I thought you did not like him, so your own prejudice against him would make my tale more convincing." He spread his palms and shrugged. "You wanted complete honesty. Very well. You shall have it. I also realized that you two had much in common, with your love of books and pursuit of ideals. I did not want you to prefer him to me. I knew that as soon as you discovered he had paid for your friend's father's release—"

"What?"

His eyes widened, and his grin had a hardness to it she had never seen before. "Is it possible you did not discover it?"

"Mr. Nelson paid Mr. Schultz's ransom? How would you know such a thing?"

"I heard it from the recipients themselves. They are . . . men with whom I occasionally do business."

She let that sink in. Cold fingers of certainty and regret clutched her heart. "Cyrus, tell me plainly. Did you hire Mr. Liggett to threaten Constance and Abel Wright?"

Cyrus leaned against the railing and gazed at the approaching shoreline. She thought she heard him sigh. When he said nothing, she knew.

"Why would you do such a thing?" she asked him. "Do you know he could have burned down their barn?"

"I only meant to frighten them away. I offered Abel Wright a good price for his land, but he refused. I confess I can be an impatient man. Rather than wait months or even years for him to realize on his own that he would be happier among his own kind, I decided to encourage him to depart."

"So they would sell to you at whatever price you offered."

"Come now, Dorothea. Let us have complete honesty on both sides. Do you really want their kind in the Elm Creek Valley? You must know Abel has a colored woman living with him now. Soon colored children will be running around in our streets, taking up seats in our schools, and more colored families will think themselves welcome here."

"They *will* be welcome here."

He shook his head, regarding her with lingering fondness. "You can be so innocent, Dorothea. That is an endearing quality in a woman, but it may lead to your disappointment. You do not know the people of Creek's Crossing as well as you think you do if you believe more share your principles than mine."

"I do not believe it."

"Like it or not, it is true. Not only in Creek's Crossing, but in the entire nation." He reached for her hand, but she pulled away. "Dorothea. Reconsider. You will not want to find yourself on the wrong side."

"I will allow my conscience and not public opinion to determine which, for me, is the right side."

"Suit yourself. But be careful. It is not wise to make enemies of your betters. Think on Miss Nadelfrau."

"What do you mean?"

He smiled coolly. "Is the schoolhouse so cozy that you no longer care about the happenings in town? Or is Mr. Nelson such pleasant company that you no longer visit Mary to catch up on your gossip?"

"What has happened to Miss Nadelfrau?"

"I leave that to you to discover. If you are wise you will take a lesson from her example."

The ferry reached the northern shore of Elm Creek. Untying his horse's reins, Cyrus added, "Despite our disagreements, I still care about you, Dorothea. If I had the carriage, I would offer you a ride."

"If you offered, I would decline."

His eyes snapped in anger. "Apparently it will be impossible for us to be friends after all."

Dorothea made no reply. Cyrus led his horse from the ferry and rode off at a gallop without a backward glance.

❧

Dorothea repeated Cyrus's cryptic remarks about Miss Nadelfrau to her parents, but they were just as mystified as she. They were less shocked to learn of his deception than she had been, though, and more incensed by his veiled threats. When Dorothea proposed that they warn the Wrights immediately, however, Lorena assured her that Cyrus was unlikely to persist in his plan to frighten the couple off their land, now that he had been exposed. Dorothea worried that the erratic Mr. Liggett might act on his own, but she agreed that informing the Wrights could wait until the following week, when they planned to meet in town to swap Lorena's sweet potato seedlings for some of Abel Wright's cheese.

Spring planting began. Jonathan had written that he would try to come, but Dorothea and her parents did not expect him, nor were they surprised when in a second letter he apologized and told them of the many fascinating cases and assignments from his professors that compelled him to remain at college. As if to make up for his absence, he sent Dorothea sketches of quilt patterns he had observed before leaving Baltimore. They were made in the same intricate appliquéd style she had used for the quilt top that she had given to Constance. She could not conceive of making such an elaborate quilt twice in one lifetime, but she admired his drawings and tucked them away for future reference and inspiration.

From time to time over the next two days, Dorothea felt a surge of strange, exuberant melancholy as she worked alongside her mother in the new garden. Spring planting always brought with it a sense of hope and expectation, but she missed her brother and, to her surprise, she even missed Uncle Jacob. Her gladness that she would be able to finish out the term at the Creek's Crossing school was tempered by Cyrus's revelations and her fear that he and Mr. Liggett would not cease their maltreatment of the Wrights. Most of all, she was proud of her family's station but anxious that Mr. Liggett would persist in troubling them. If his mistaken belief that Cyrus was her sweetheart was all that restrained him, she dreaded what he would do if he discovered the truth.

Every daylight hour of Saturday and Sunday was filled with tasks of the spring planting, so none of the Grangers could spare the time for a trip into town to inquire after Miss Nadelfrau. Robert, who stated that Cyrus's ability to lie was inversely proportionate to his capacity to love, thought that likely nothing was amiss, and that Cyrus had spoken as he had only to upset Dorothea, knowing that she would not be able to investigate for several days. Dorothea hoped her father was correct, but on Monday morning she left for school early so that she would have time to stop by Miss Nadelfrau's dressmaking shop.

The blinds were drawn but the door was unlocked, so she proceeded inside, where she found Miss Nadelfrau draping sheets over her dressmaker's forms and sewing machine. No lovely finished gowns hung in their usual places in the front windows, and the bolts of satins, silks, wools, and brocades ordinarily artfully arranged in the front of the store to tempt ladies inside were rolled up and stacked in a corner.

Dorothea took in the sight and said, "This looks for all the world as if you are closing your shop."

Miss Nadelfrau looked up, startled out of a mournful reverie. "The shop is not closing. I am just taking the little that is mine and sorting the rest for the new owner."

"New owner?" As soon as the words left her lips, Dorothea guessed. "Not Mrs. Engle."

Miss Nadelfrau nodded. "She is a rather fine seamstress and apparently she is restless with so little to do now that the library benefit is over. She decided her own business was just the thing to satisfy her need to occupy her time and her desire to express her artful impulses."

Miss Nadelfrau's voice was uncharacteristically bitter. "Forgive me," said Dorothea carefully, "but you do not seem entirely pleased by these arrangements. I am curious why you sold to her."

"I had no choice." Miss Nadelfrau made a brittle laugh and dabbed at her eyes with a handkerchief. "I did not want to sell. I have no other livelihood. Unfortunately, when I opened my shop five years ago, I made the mistake of borrowing money from Violet. She charged a lower interest rate than the bank and I thought my future more secure if entrusted to a friend. When Violet decided our friendship had ended, she called in the loan. Of course I did not have enough to pay her in full." She tucked her handkerchief away. "Of course I do not blame you, Dorothea. No true friend would have turned so quickly against me."

Bewildered, Dorothea asked, "Am I the cause of Mrs. Engle's enmity toward you?"

"Oh, unwittingly, I'm sure. That quilt, you know—the Authors' Album. I helped you put it into the quilt frame. I was in such a state of nerves that evening that I did not even notice the names Violet found so objectionable, but since I saw the quilt top and said nothing, she is convinced I knew all along. She accused me of conspiring with you to go against her wishes."

"For this she would take away your livelihood?" exclaimed Dorothea.

Miss Nadelfrau nodded. "But she has allowed me to retain my apartment upstairs."

"How very decent of her," said Dorothea, fuming. "I will speak to her and set the matter straight."

"Don't bother. I am resigned to my fate, and she would not listen to you anyway." Miss Nadelfrau tried to smile. "She has every reason to suspect me, since she has seen works by those very same notorious authors on my own bookshelves."

Dorothea did not know what to say. "Is there anything I can do to help?"

"No, no. I'll be fine. I am glad for your sake that you have no outstanding debts to the Engles."

Dorothea thought of Mr. Engle's position as head of the school board. For all his apparent faith in her abilities as a teacher, Mr. Nelson could not force them to hire her for the autumn term. "What will you do?" she asked.

Miss Nadelfrau shrugged and lined up spools of thread in a neat row on a table. "I have a little money tucked away, and I might be able to take in a bit of sewing from my most loyal customers. If my savings run out before I find another position, my brother in Pleasant Gap will take me in. He has a farm and seven children, but his wife is sickly. They tell me they would be grateful for my help and that I would not be a burden."

"I am sure you would be an enormous help to them."

"And perhaps someday I will try again." She looked around the walls of her shop, teary-eyed. "Who knows? Perhaps Pleasant Gap needs another dressmaker."

Dorothea hugged her and offered the most encouraging words she could manage. It was an outrage that Mrs. Engle saw fit to punish poor, hapless Miss Nadelfrau for some imagined complicity rather than confront Dorothea directly.

Dorothea could not reflect on the unfolding of recent events without considering that it might have been better had she never sewed a single stitch of the Authors' Album. She certainly regretted what had befallen Miss Nadelfrau. Yet she did not regret including the banned authors in the quilt or the results of her choice. The quilt was not to blame for creating the animosity and mistrust on the rise in Creek's Crossing. It had merely illuminated cracks and crevices that had always existed in the shadows. She was disappointed by what she had discovered about Cyrus, Mrs. Engle, and others, but it was better by far that she knew it. The truth was always preferable to a lie.

She hurried on to the schoolhouse, where she discovered Mr. Nelson in a foul mood. He greeted her curtly and called his students to attention as soon as the hour struck, without his usual dry pleasantries. From the choir loft she overheard his increasing impatience with his students' errors, which, she observed, bewildered them into making even more errors. She had come to know that Mr. Nelson was a clever and quick-witted man, but caustic when vexed. When he nearly brought one slow but dutiful older girl to tears as she struggled through her geography lesson, Dorothea wished she could intervene, but dared not compromise the students' respect for their teacher.

An opportunity to speak frankly did not arrive until they dismissed the students for lunch. "You seem especially displeased with your students today," she said after the last little boy ran outdoors.

Her remark seemed to surprise him. "Do I? They are no worse than usual, though regrettably, no better, either."

"Helene is a sensitive girl. She tries her best, but she never even held a book before she started school only two years ago. I found that a gentle approach, with a great deal of encouragement, worked best with her."

He did not bother to look up from unpacking his lunch from his satchel. "Do you know her so well?"

"I was her teacher myself not so long ago, and I would appreciate the courtesy of a respectful reply. I am not one of your students."

Immediately he looked up. "My apologies, Miss Granger. Of course you are right. Helene cannot be bullied into learning."

"May I suggest that most children cannot?" She regarded him. "I do not believe the students are to blame for your ill temper."

"No." He yanked out his chair and sat down, then glanced up as if surprised to see her still standing. "Are you going to eat or aren't you?"

"I think I might prefer to eat outdoors with the children than remain in your delightful company."

He almost smiled. "I'm sure they would enjoy that."

"I would, too." But she did not leave. "If I knew the reason for this foul mood, I might be able to help—for the students' sake."

He scowled. "You cannot help." The venom in his tone astonished her. "You cannot, and I cannot. There is nothing we can do here in this patch of wilderness that will effect any change whatsoever."

"Our students might not be the dedicated scholars you taught in the East—"

"I am not speaking about our students." Abruptly he rose and strode to the window. "A letter came yesterday, from my sister. Her husband is a representative to Congress. Do you know there is a bill before them that would require all law officers to hunt down and capture all runaway slaves and return them to their owners? Not only in the South, but also in states where slavery has been banned. Harboring or assisting fugitives in any fashion would also be against the law."

Shocked, Dorothea said, "But there are already similar laws on the books. People pay them little attention."

"A new law would signify an increased commitment to the perpetuation

of slavery for the entire nation. It cannot and must not be allowed to pass."
He paced back and forth, scowling morosely. "The bill must be fought and
defeated. My sister's husband is doing his part, while I—" He halted, his
shoulders slumped in defeat. "While I reprimand children for not knowing
the major water routes of Asia. What can I do here that will make any difference? Nothing. I am utterly useless."

"You have already done a great deal to ease the suffering of slaves."

He shot her a sharp, curious glance before uttering a brittle laugh. "You
sound like my father. I made my contribution and now must let others carry
on the fight. I tell you, Miss Granger, that resolution suits me very ill indeed."

There are other ways to fight, she almost told him. Two Bears Farm had
been a haven for fugitives once and could be again. Then she remembered
the promise his father had exacted from him and what would befall him
should he break the law again. She thought of Cyrus and how she had once
imagined, wrongly, so much goodness in him because that was what she
wanted to see. What if she had confided in Cyrus as she now wanted to with
Mr. Nelson?

The risk was too great. Instead she said, "That law, if it should come to
pass, does not bind your hands entirely."

"And what am I to do from Creek's Crossing, Pennsylvania?"

"You can vote," she said sharply. That was more than she could do. "You
can put that university education of yours to good use by writing letters,
newspaper articles, books— You could write about your prison experiences,
how your sacrifice was worthwhile because you brought others to freedom.
If that *is* what you believe, because frankly, your true feelings on the subject
are difficult to discern through all this self-pity."

His gaze bored into her. "Is that how you regard me?"

"Mr. Nelson, I confess that self-pity is one of the lesser faults I have
accused you of possessing since first we met."

He paused. "I am quite sure I deserved your censure."

"You did, indeed."

His laugh echoed hollowly in the empty classroom. "At last, Miss Granger,
a point on which we agree."

She managed a smile in return. She did not share with him her disconcerting observation that they had, in fact, disagreed very little recently, and
that they had more in common than she would have imagined possible a few
months before.

Chapter Ten

As the week passed, Mr. Nelson made an effort to moderate his ill humor, but he was not entirely successful. While he was no longer unduly stern toward his students, several times Dorothea caught him in a brood, gazing out the window or paging through a book without seeing what lay before him. She was struck by the similarity of his expression to what she herself had felt on many occasions—when her brother wrote of his studies or when Lorena reminisced about her childhood in Boston.

Mr. Nelson had never been what she would call cheerful, but she could not bear to stand by and watch him sink deeper into gloom. On Friday morning—after asking Lorena to be sure she no longer needed them—she collected older issues of the abolitionist newspaper the *Daily Advocate* and presented them to Mr. Nelson at lunchtime. He was immediately absorbed, and at the end of the day, he was so greatly encouraged that he walked her to the ferry so he could share his ideas about forming a local abolitionist group modeled after the Anti Slavery Society of Pittsburgh. She offered to assist him, but as soon as she spoke, she realized that this was precisely the sort of activity Uncle Jacob would have condemned for drawing unwanted attention to their other activities. She could hardly rescind her offer so soon after making it, however, nor did she wish to. The Grangers' views on slavery were already common knowledge. Helping Mr. Nelson form an antislavery society would not create any new risks for their station's passengers.

On Saturday, Lorena and Dorothea rode into Creek's Crossing to meet Constance in front of the dry-goods store to exchange Lorena's sweet potato seedlings for several wheels of Abel Wright's cheese. Constance also had unexpected news: Two nights before, a conductor had guided a party of six runaways to the Wright farm. Among their number were an elderly man, two men of middle years, a younger woman, and two children. Their astounding means of escape had been nearly two years in the planning. The two younger men, grooms on the plantation, had stolen horses and a carriage from their master, while the woman had taken from her mistress clothing, a trunk, and other accoutrements of southern womanhood. They had fled under the cover of darkness, but once far enough away so their master's horses and carriage would not be recognized, they kept the children out of sight and passed themselves off as a shy southern belle traveling with her servants. The ruse served them well until they reached Maryland, where by a stroke of good fortune the eldest man spotted a posted handbill describing their disguise and offering a substantial reward for the return of the slaves and stolen property. They immediately abandoned their disguises, and ever since they had traveled on foot led by a conductor, a former runaway who had reached Canada but who had chosen to return time and time again to guide others to freedom. He usually traveled along a westerly route through Uniontown and Pittsburgh, but this time he had been diverted into the Elm Creek Valley by slavecatchers hired by the fugitives' determined and vengeful master. The slavecatchers and their pack of hounds evidently had traveled through the Elm Creek Valley before, given their swift progress through what was to the conductor unknown terrain.

Abel Wright and the conductor had made the difficult decision to divide the group in two, send them north along different routes, and reunite them in Canada. The woman would not be parted from the children, nor could the elderly man keep pace with the two younger men, so the groups were determined by practicality. The two younger men would travel to the Granger farm that night. They were in good health and would not need to rest more than a day before continuing northward.

The other four presented a problem. Of necessity their master's horses and carriage had been abandoned in Maryland, and the children and elderly man could not travel swiftly on foot. More troubling, their conductor did not know the routes through the Elm Creek Valley as well as the Wrights and the Grangers, who knew only the stations directly before and after their own.

After much deliberation, the Wrights and the conductor had concluded that their greatest chance lay in another disguise. The handbills warned to search for a colored slave posing as a white woman with her servants, but they said nothing of a freed black woman traveling with her aged father and two children.

If the Grangers could provide one horse, Abel Wright would offer a second as well as his wagon. With false baptismal certificates and a bill of sale for a fictitious plot of land in New York, the fugitives could pass themselves off as free coloreds from New York returning home from a visit with family. If they traveled lesser-known routes, they might avoid confrontation altogether. Enough colored families lived in the Elm Creek Valley that if they acted with assurance, it was possible no one would suspect them of being runaways.

Constance, Dorothea, and Lorena had strolled down the block from the dry-goods store while Constance spoke, but Lorena still glanced over her shoulder before shaking her head and saying, "They ought to conceal themselves and follow the tried and true routes through the valley. I have grave doubts this ruse will be any more successful than their first."

"Their first disguise *was* successful," replied Dorothea. "They made it all the way to Maryland in perfect safety. If their pursuers had not sent word ahead of them, they would be using it still."

"I thought like you did, at first," said Constance to Lorena. "But if Liza can fool folks into thinking she's a pampered white girl too shy to leave her carriage, she can surely make them believe she's a free colored."

Eventually Lorena agreed that they had little alternative. If the four runaways relied on speed and stealth, the slavecatchers would surely overtake them.

A soft rap on the door shortly after midnight signaled the arrival of the two men. Robert led them to Uncle Jacob's old room and showed them the hiding place in the wardrobe in case of unexpected visitors. Lorena quickly brought them food and drink, and while they rested, Dorothea used the Sugar Camp Quilt to teach them the route to the Brauns' mill. It seemed ages ago that she had pieced the unusual blocks under her uncle's stern and watchful gaze, unaware of their significance. Since then dozens of fugitives had journeyed closer to freedom following its secret symbols.

Robert checked the locks on the doors twice before turning in for the night. In her attic bedroom, Dorothea slept lightly as she did whenever passengers rested at their station, her ears tuned to the familiar noises of the house, listening for the creak of a window or the baying of a dog. Whenever an unexpected sound jolted her awake, her first thoughts were of Mr. Liggett. Strangely, though she knew him to be a coward, she was more wary of him than of the anonymous slavecatchers she had never seen. She wished that he would grow bored of watching her family and leave them in peace, but Mr. Liggett's anger at Uncle Jacob ran too deeply for that, and some debts could not be paid in coin.

The next morning, the Grangers treaded softly as they moved about the house so that their weary guests could sleep. The two men emerged from Uncle Jacob's bedroom at midmorning and gratefully ate second and third helpings of breakfast. After racing through her morning chores, Dorothea worked at Uncle Jacob's desk on the counterfeit documents the other four fugitives would need to make their disguises complete. As she added an official-looking scroll to a piece of parchment, Dorothea overheard the two men conversing in hushed voices, anguishing over the decision to go on without the others. One of the men, Liza's husband and the father of her two children left behind at the Wrights, was especially troubled. "Won't mean nothing to me to be free if they get sent back," he told his companion, who tried to reassure him.

"They won't be sent back," said Dorothea. The two men regarded her dubiously. "You will all be together again in Canada. You will see."

"That's right kind of you, miss," said the man, "but those slavecatchers are close behind. They got a good look at Liza and Old Dan outside of Harrisburg. Pretending to be some freeborn family won't fool them."

"They didn't get such a good look," the other man contradicted. "It was dark, they were thirty yards away, and they didn't know it was Liza and Old Dan they was looking at. And they never saw the children."

Dorothea forced confidence into her voice. "You've made it this far. You will make it the rest of the way. You'll see."

"We have a long way yet to go," the father said, but he did look less anxious. It struck Dorothea then that the hope and reassurance the Grangers provided did as much as food, clothing, and directions to enable their passengers to journey on. Of course, the fugitives had no choice. They could not stay, and they could not return, having come so far. Slavecatchers and masters liked to make examples of recaptured runaways.

The two men left after dusk—reluctantly, or so it seemed to Dorothea. She prayed that they would reach the Brauns' mill safely and that they would endure the separation from their loved ones. The rest of the party would be traveling only a few days behind the men, but they would not see one another again for many weeks. Dorothea could not ignore the fact that their reunion was by no means certain.

The next three days passed in a blur of activity—spring planting, teaching, and laboring painstakingly over the documents. Dorothea had apparently inherited her uncle's talent for drawing, for the false papers she created were virtually identical to the real documents she had copied. In addition to the papers affirming Liza and Old Dan's false identities and the bill of sale, she also wrote a letter purportedly from Liza's sister-in-law in Gettysburg imploring her to come visit her ailing brother. Dorothea also contrived a receipt from an undertaker dated several weeks later for the funeral of Liza's fictitious brother. It was a long journey from New York to central Pennsylvania for a social visit, Dorothea thought, but a dutiful sister would willingly travel that distance to bring her father to visit his dying son.

She admired her handiwork, but hoped that Liza and her companions would not be called upon to present the papers to anyone once Dorothea and Constance bid them farewell and they rode off on their own. Then she folded and creased the letter, spilled a bit of tea upon it, and dog-eared the corners. The bill of sale and other papers she crumpled and soiled with ashes from the fireplace, thinking of Uncle Jacob wiping the mud from his boots on the Sugar Camp Quilt. When the papers were suitably aged, she put them in an old leather pocketbook of Lorena's to await the trip to fetch the runaways.

On Tuesday morning, Dorothea rode her uncle's horse to school and boarded him in Mr. Engle's livery stable just as she had in the winter. All day long her thoughts were on the task ahead, bringing the four fugitives across the ferry to the safety of the Granger farm. She was so distracted that once Mr. Nelson asked her sharply if she were ill and needed to go home. She assured him she was fine and endeavored to give him no more reason to be suspicious, but it was a relief when the school day ended and she could quickly tidy the choir loft and hurry on her way, ignoring Mr. Nelson's questioning glance. Usually she stayed to help him straighten up the main classroom, but since his farm lay along the same road as the Wrights, she must hasten to get enough of a head start so that he would not see her and wonder why she was traveling in the opposite direction of her home.

As she drove up to the Wrights' barn, Constance met her and helped her tend to her horse. While they worked, she assured Dorothea that Liza, Old Dan, and the children were prepared for their journey. The adults had rehearsed the children over and over until they knew their roles perfectly.

"Do you think the children will be able to stick to their story even if challenged?" asked Dorothea.

Constance shrugged. "They're fast learners. They've had to be all their lives. They know how to lie to save their skins. Besides, slavecatchers will most likely talk to the grown-ups and ignore the children. If the children break down and cry because they're scared, that won't surprise nobody none."

They went inside the house. Constance told her that the runaways were upstairs, sleeping in a hidden room in the attic, gathering their strength for the long journey ahead. "Paul was their leader," said Constance, referring to one of the younger men, as Dorothea helped her prepare supper. "He was the courage of this group. Liza tries her best to keep everyone's spirits up now that he's gone on ahead, but it's only worked with the children. Something's gone out of the old man like an old tree hollowed out."

Dorothea felt a quiver of nervousness. "You don't suppose he'll put the others in danger?"

Constance glanced darkly to the ceiling as a floorboard creaked overhead. "You're worried about the children spilling the truth? I'm more worried about the old man."

Night was falling as the four runaways crept quietly downstairs and seated themselves around the table. The two children, girls who looked to be about six and eight, stared at Dorothea with wide eyes as Constance made introductions. Dorothea noted that the four wore the sturdy work clothes of a moderately prosperous farm family, not the garb of slaves. Liza gave Dorothea a polite nod, but Old Dan kept his eyes cast down and did not seem to notice her.

Abel Wright urged them all to eat heartily, but only the children willingly obeyed; Liza choked down her food as if it were the bitterest medicine and Old Dan barely took a bite. After they cleared away the dishes, Constance privately told Dorothea to wrap up as much food as she could. The fugitives, though too nervous to eat now, would be hungry later.

Then it was time to depart.

Liza embraced Constance and thanked her for her goodness. Even Old Dan came to himself enough to shake Abel's hand and murmur that he wished he could repay the Wrights someday. Abel went outside to load his wagon with hay and hitch up the team while the runaways soberly put on their wraps and gathered their few belongings, small bundles that, Dorothea guessed, contained more clothes Constance had sewn for them and food for the journey. They could not rely upon reaching a station every night.

Outside, the stars shone in a clear sky just cool enough to make Dorothea grateful for her shawl. The runaways climbed aboard the wagon and concealed themselves in the hay, with only the smallest mew of complaint from the younger girl, whom Liza quickly soothed. Dorothea took up the reins as Constance swung up to the seat beside her, chirruped to the horses, and set out for the Creek's Crossing road.

Dorothea and Constance rode without speaking. Dorothea's mouth was dry, her stomach a knot of worry. For all the fugitives who had passed through the Grangers' station, she had never felt so solely responsible for any runaway's fate as she did at that moment, driving to the ferry. As they passed the entrance to the road that led through the woods to Mr. Liggett's farm, the knot in her stomach tightened, but the only sounds were the clip-clopping of the horses' hooves on the hard-packed dirt road. Constance breathed a sigh as they left Mr. Liggett's land behind and approached Two Bears Farm. Dorothea studied the tall, white-boarded house as they rode by; two lights were burning, one upstairs and one below. She wondered what Mr. Nelson was doing at that moment.

They reached the outskirts of Creek's Crossing without encountering another wagon or rider. Dorothea turned east on a back road to avoid the noise and lights of the taverns and inns on the main streets. It was too much to hope that they could pass through the town entirely unobserved, but she would avoid as many eyes as possible.

The few townspeople they passed did not seem to give the wagon a second glance. The tightness in Dorothea's stomach began to ease as they crossed the last few blocks to the ferry. If they could reach the northern shore of Elm Creek unchallenged—

"What's that?" said Constance, nodding toward the ferry dock. A cluster of men stood by the boathouse, horses tied up nearby. Two carried torches. One loosely held the reins of a pack of hounds, sitting lazily at his feet.

"I don't know," replied Dorothea. She slowed the team as they drew closer. Just then, a carriage turned on to the street two blocks ahead of them and slowed as it approached the ferry. The men carrying torches leaped forward and blocked its way. A third man opened the carriage door and leaned inside, then withdrew and shouted something to his companions.

Dorothea did not wait to see if the four men allowed the carriage to board the ferry. She pulled hard on the reins and swung the wagon west onto Second Street.

"They're searching that carriage," murmured Constance, turning in her seat to look back upon the scene. "They ain't the constable's men."

"Indeed they are not." Dorothea urged the team into a trot. "They are slavecatchers."

"How do you know?"

"I know. But even if they were not, they would search the wagon before permitting us aboard the ferry. That is reason enough for us to turn around."

Constance studied her as the horses pulled them briskly away from the ferry dock. "Are you taking us back to the farm?"

"No." Dorothea fought the instinct to make the horses run. "I know another crossing."

"Not on Liggett's land, like your uncle tried?"

"The creek does narrow there. My uncle would have made it if not for his stroke."

"But Liggett—if he sees us—"

"He won't see us," said Dorothea grimly. "He is engaged at the moment."

For Dorothea had recognized the slight, hunched form of the man who had peered within the carriage, and the golden curls and arrogant stance of one of the torchbearers.

Cyrus and Mr. Liggett, working openly with slavecatchers.

❧

The four runaways must have felt the wagon turn completely around. They must have sensed their increased speed. Dorothea braced herself for a nervous question from Old Dan or the piping voices of the children, but the fugitives remained hidden.

"What if they saw us?" Constance said in a low voice.

"Let us hope they did not." But Dorothea knew it was possible. They had been only two blocks from the ferry dock when they turned west. Surely Cyrus would wonder about a wagon suddenly veering off as soon as their blockade came into view. Dorothea prayed he had not recognized her or Uncle Jacob's mare.

They passed through Creek's Crossing without incident. As the lights of the town faded behind them, Dorothea strained her ears for any sound of pursuit. All she heard was the steady clopping of the horses' hooves on the road headed south and the gurgling of Elm Creek, unseen in the darkness that fell sharply outside the pool of light their lanterns provided. In the distance Dorothea spied lights from farms, small and fragile in the dark.

They passed Two Bears Farm, the house silent on the top of the hill with only the two lighted windows hinting at warmth within. Dorothea and Constance did not speak. Soon even the sound of the creek died away as it curved around the oxbow to the west. The forest grew deeper; if Dorothea had not known the valley so well, she would have missed the turn onto the road to Elm Creek Farm.

The wagon creaked and jolted over the narrow trail, jarring on rocks and tree roots. Tree branches clawed at Dorothea's face; a lantern pole caught on a limb and snapped. Dorothea pulled the horses to a stop so Constance could get out and retrieve the lantern. The tin was dented, but miraculously, the light had not gone out.

"Seems to me this might be a very bad idea," said Constance as Dorothea started the horses again. Constance held out the lantern at arm's length, but it was a futile gesture.

"If you have a better alternative, I'm listening."

Dorothea's voice was strained from the effort of driving the team. The horses pulled at the bit and tossed their heads, annoyed at Dorothea for steering them into the tangled wood. Dorothea urged them forward, and the wagon jerked and bounded deeper into the woods. Constance nervously clutched at the wagon seat with her free hand, but she did not voice her doubts again. Just when Dorothea thought her aching arms could wrestle the team no further, she glimpsed moonlight on water.

"The creek," she gasped, trying to catch her breath. "We can cross up ahead."

Constance held out the lantern and shook her head. "It's too far off the road. The wagon will never make it."

"We have to try."

Dorothea pulled the team to a halt, jumped down from the wagon seat, and led the resistant horses off the trail into the woods. The horses strained and pulled the wagon into the underbrush, over a rotten log that crumbled onto a carpet of fallen leaves. "Good girl," Dorothea praised her uncle's mare quietly, urging her onward and hoping Abel Wright's horse would follow. They reached the top of a small incline that sloped down a steep hill to the creek bed. The crossing was narrower here, as Dorothea had remembered, but she and Jonathan had been on foot in daylight.

"We can't turn the wagon around here anyway," said Constance. "We might as well go forward." She secured the lantern and climbed down from the wagon seat.

Dorothea nodded and took a deep breath, blood pounding in her ears. She grasped the reins and bridles of Uncle Jacob's mare while Constance took hold of her own horse, and together they pulled the team forward. The horses whinnied in complaint but stepped forward once, then twice, and then quicker steps as the wagon began to roll down the slope of its own accord. Muscles straining, Dorothea held the mare in check as the wagon picked up speed. Suddenly Constance cried out as a wheel jolted against a tree root and sent her sprawling to the ground. The leather reins burned Dorothea's palms as they tore free from her grasp. She fell to her knees and scrambled out of the way as the horses and wagon sped past her down the steep slope to the creek. There was a rumble and a crash of breaking branches, and then the wagon fell from sight.

A scream strangled in her throat. She crawled forward and spotted the wagon below, upright and stuck in the creek. One lantern lay on the pebbled creek side, the other extinguished, lost in the darkness. Abel Wright's horse whinnied and bucked, then tossed her head and snorted, pacing, still bound to the wagon and Uncle Jacob's mare. After a moment of horrifying stillness, a child's wail broke the night air.

Dorothea forced herself to her feet, choking back a sob. She made her way to Constance, who groaned as she sat up and clasped a hand to her head. Dorothea helped her stand, and together they picked their way down to the wagon, where the runaways were cautiously emerging from the bed of hay. The youngest girl stretched out her arms for Liza, sobbing. As Liza snatched her up, the eldest girl stood and looked around, dazed and silent, picking hay from her hair.

"Where's Old Dan?" said Constance in her ear. They quickly climbed into the wagon bed, and while Liza comforted the girls, Dorothea and Constance dug through the hay, searching frantically for the old man. Then, a flickering of lantern light drew Dorothea's attention to a limp form half in the creek, half on the shore. Her gasp alerted Constance, and together they jumped from the wagon and raced to his side. Dorothea was afraid to move him, but Constance ran her hands over him as if feeling for broken bones. He groaned as she rolled him over. Blood trickled from his brow.

Sitting on the damp shore, Constance drew him onto her lap and shook her head. Her wordless gaze confirmed what Dorothea already knew: Old Dan could not walk.

She left Constance with the injured man and returned to the wagon, thoughts churning. Liza had calmed the youngest girl, who had quieted her sobs and merely sniffed back tears, thumb in her mouth. "She's more scared than hurt," Liza said quietly. "Please, see to Hannah." She nodded to the elder child, who stood wide-eyed and wordless in the same spot as when she had first emerged from the hay.

Dorothea approached her gently. "Are you hurt?" No response. Dorothea placed a hand on her shoulder. "Are you all right?"

The girl looked up at her, wordless, but did not even shake her head. Dorothea knelt beside her. "Since you seem to be just fine, I wonder if you could help me. I need someone to hold the lantern while I unhitch the horses. Do you think you could do that?"

Hannah hesitated, then nodded. Relieved, Dorothea helped her down from the wagon and fetched the lantern. Quickly she surveyed the wagon: It had thrown an axle and the right side was smashed in. It was not beyond repair, but they had neither the tools nor the time to attend to it. Dorothea unhitched the mare, who tossed her head and snorted as if to declare that she had warned Dorothea not to try to cross there. Dorothea wished she had taken heed.

She thanked Hannah for helping her. The little girl nodded, lowered the lantern, and ran to her mother. While Liza comforted her daughters, Dorothea and Constance gathered the runaways' bundles, then struggled to lift Old Dan onto the mare. He groaned, semiconscious, but did not struggle.

"We will have to proceed on foot," said Dorothea to Constance as they loaded the bundles on the Wrights' horse.

"At least we're across the creek."

"No thanks to me."

"Hey, now. We both thought this would work."

"We should have gone back to your farm and tried again another night. Those men would have eventually tired of their blockade—"

"Only if they'd moved on to searching houses. And where do you think they'd start? Liggett's already got his eye on you folks, and Abel and I are suspicious just because we're colored."

Dorothea nodded, but silently she berated herself and her poor judgment. She tugged on the mare's reins and ordered her forward, steadying Old Dan with her other hand. Constance walked behind her leading her own horse. Liza followed with the children.

With only the moon and a single lantern to light their way, they made slow progress through the forest. Dorothea led them in a wide arc to avoid the cleared acres and Mr. Liggett's cabin. Old Dan drifted in and out of awareness. Hannah struggled bravely to keep up with the adults, but Liza, Dorothea, and Constance took turns carrying her younger sister.

Suddenly, Hannah piped, "Are we lost?"

"No," said Dorothea emphatically. "Not in the least. This is not the way we intended to travel, but we will reach our destination nevertheless."

She gave the child a reassuring grin and was rewarded with a flicker of a worried smile.

But the journey was long. Dorothea estimated that they would need the better part of two hours to cross Mr. Liggett's land, and her heart sank with dismay, though she kept her true feelings hidden from those who followed her.

At long last, they left Liggett's woods and emerged into a clearing, the border of Two Bears Farm. They climbed a fence and stepped out onto cultivated fields, wide and gently rolling terrain, but clear of underbrush. Their passage would be swifter, but their footprints would be easy to follow in the freshly plowed earth. The open field offered them no protection, no place to hide.

In the moonlight Dorothea studied the white house, alone on the hill. The two lights in the windows had been extinguished, and yet the house seemed a haven.

In a low voice meant for Constance's ears alone, she said, "At this pace, we will not reach the station before daybreak."

Constance indicated the forest with a jerk of her head. "Maybe we can build a fire, make a shelter with branches. Hide out 'til tomorrow night."

"On Mr. Liggett's land? What will we do if he comes home and finds the wagon tonight?"

Constance shuddered, and Dorothea knew she had thought of that. For all they knew Mr. Liggett had already discovered the scene of the accident. He might at that moment be in pursuit.

Dorothea nodded to the house. "We can seek shelter here."

Constance shook her head. "This ain't a station no more. The Carters are long gone."

"Mr. Nelson will aid us."

"I thought you hated that man!"

"I don't. He—he's not a friend, but he is an abolitionist. I do not believe he will turn us away."

Constance halted, bringing the mare to a stop. She glanced back over her shoulder at Liza and the children, struggling several paces behind, exhausted. On the back of the mare, Old Dan slumped lifelessly. They would never make it to the Granger farm without rest.

"I reckon we don't have much choice," said Constance. "I guess . . . I guess we might as well pay a call on the schoolmaster."

They waited for Liza and the girls to catch up, then informed them of the latest change in plans. Liza's expression was haggard, but she nodded and passed her younger daughter off to Constance. New hope quickened their pace, but Dorothea felt exposed and vulnerable in the open field. When they reached the road, she handed the reins to Liza, ran the last few yards to the porch stairs, and rapped upon the front door. She waited, listening, and knocked a second time, louder. She heard movement within, and after what seemed to be an interminable wait, the door swung open.

"Miss Granger?" Mr. Nelson, clad in trousers and an open shirt, fumbled to put on his glasses. "What on earth brings you here at this hour?"

"A desperate need for your help." She stepped aside and allowed him to observe the party now gathered at the foot of the porch stairs. Constance had helped Old Dan down from the mare, and he mustered his strength to stand, grasping the porch railing for support.

Dorothea heard Mr. Nelson's slow intake of breath. "Runaways, I presume."

She nodded. "We lost our wagon, and as you can see, we have an injured man and children. We cannot go on." Her voice faltered. "I would not ask it of you—of anyone—except I know what you have done elsewhere. I know what you suffered for your compassion."

His expression was unreadable. "Then you know what I will suffer if I am caught helping you."

She hesitated before nodding.

He opened the door and stepped out. Uncomprehending, she moved aside and watched as he descended the stairs. "Take them inside," he told her. "I will return shortly."

He took the horses' reins and led them toward the barn.

Dorothea tore her gaze away from him and beckoned the others. "Inside. Quickly."

❦

Dorothea swiftly made a fire in the front room fireplace while Constance helped Old Dan, groaning, to the sofa. Liza helped her daughters from their wraps and drew them closer to warm themselves by the fire. Constance dug into one of the bundles and passed around jerky and johnnycake while Dorothea went to the kitchen in search of water. She found a pan of milk and snatched it up as well. The kitchen window looked out upon the southwestern fields they had crossed; Dorothea spared one anxious glance outside before returning to the front room.

The children drank deeply of the milk and ate even the last crumbs Constance rationed out to them. Dorothea tended to Old Dan's injuries as best she knew how. He did not appear to have any broken bones, his cuts and bruises appeared minor, but he had taken a hard fall, and she knew he might suffer from internal wounds. He refused to eat, but gulped the water only to cough most of it back up. She was encouraged by his responses to her questions about the whereabouts of his pain, not only so that she could tend to him but also because they proved the blow to his skull had not addled his mind.

Even so, Old Dan would need time to recover and more medical attention than she could provide. Jonathan would have known what to do for him, but Jonathan was hundreds of miles away.

Dorothea covered the injured man with a quilt folded over the back of the sofa and held his hand until he drifted off to sleep. By the time Mr. Nelson returned from the barn, the children, too, had fallen asleep, curled up under quilts on the floor near their mother. Without a word Mr. Nelson beckoned her from the doorway. She rose and followed him into the kitchen.

"I hardly know where to begin," he said. He kept his voice low enough so that the others would not hear.

"If you mean to scold me, it is a little late for that."

"It would not do any good, anyway." He removed his glasses and rubbed at his eyes, sighing. "You had best tell me everything."

She could not tell him everything, but she told him as much as she dared, including the events of that night. His eyebrows shot up when she described the blockade at the ferry, and she waited for a caustic remark about Cyrus

Pearson, but none came. When she told him of the accident with the wagon, his expression darkened.

"How far off the main road is the wagon?" he asked.

"Ten yards, if that. But the gully provides some concealment, especially in the dark."

"If a trail of broken branches does not lead Mr. Liggett right to it."

She had thought of that, too, but it could not be helped. "We must put our trust in Providence—and our faith in Mr. Liggett's foolishness."

"Quite right. I would not peg him as a crack scout." Mr. Nelson almost smiled. "Let us arrange it so that your friends are well out of harm's way before he stumbles upon the latest wagon to overturn on his property."

"Mr. Nelson—" She hardly knew what to say. "I cannot thank you enough for your kindness."

"That is true, so you need not bother trying." He nodded toward the front room. "We should not disturb the old man now that he is asleep, but I will show the rest of you to more comfortable rooms upstairs."

"I will remain below to stand watch."

"Indeed you shall not. You need your rest if you are to lead your party onward tomorrow night."

"But what if—"

"I will stand watch, Miss Granger." He replaced his glasses, folded his arms, and regarded her with what she took to be weary tolerance. "I could not sleep a wink in any event. Not all of us are as accustomed to such excitement as you are."

"No, I suppose not," she murmured uncertainly. He sounded almost as if he were teasing her. "But there is another problem. My parents will worry if we do not arrive by daybreak."

"Will they worry enough to come searching for you?"

"I told them not to."

"But they may not obey their daughter. Very well. I will take word to them myself in the morning, but now I must insist that you rest."

Perhaps it was her fatigue, but his didactic manner did not bother her as much as it once had. She made sure Old Dan was comfortable before gently picking up Hannah. Constance gathered the younger sister in her arms, and together they and Liza followed Mr. Nelson upstairs to simply furnished but comfortable rooms.

Dorothea had one small room to herself. After bidding Mr. Nelson good night, she went inside, undressed to her shift, and was about to climb into bed when she realized that the window faced the southwest.

She went to the window and looked out. The open fields that had so unnerved her as she and Constance led the runaways to the house now provided them protection; neither Mr. Liggett nor Cyrus nor any of their ilk could approach the house unseen. Beyond them, the woods stood dark and silent and still.

She closed the curtains and returned to bed, drawing the quilt over herself. She thought worry and the unfamiliar room would keep her awake, but fatigue soon overcame her and she sank into sleep.

❧

The room was still dark when a hand seized her shoulder and shook her awake. "Miss Granger." Mr. Nelson's voice was low and urgent. "Riders from the southwest."

Immediately she threw back the covers and snatched up her dress from the bedside chair. Mr. Nelson disappeared into the hallway to rouse the others. Dorothea swiftly dressed and met him and Constance in the largest bedroom, where Liza was waking the children.

"Stay away from the windows and make no sound," said Mr. Nelson. Just then a heavy fist pounded on the front door below. Hannah gasped. Her sister buried her face in her mother's skirt.

"Nelson," bellowed Mr. Liggett. "We know they're inside."

"Send 'em out and we won't hold you accountable," shouted another man, an unfamiliar voice. Dorothea wished she dared peer out a window to see if Cyrus was among the riders.

As calmly as if the men were guests for tea, Mr. Nelson wiped his glasses and straightened his shirt. "I will have to answer."

"No." Dorothea seized his arm. "They will force their way inside."

"No, they will not." He placed his hand over hers, then released himself from her grasp and left the room.

"Under the bed," Constance ordered. Liza and the children scrambled beneath it while Dorothea and Constance adjusted the quilts to best conceal them. With a flash of terror, Dorothea remembered Old Dan. She fled the room and raced downstairs—only to discover the elderly man nowhere in sight. Mr. Nelson stood before the front door with a rifle cradled in the crook of one arm. He looked over his shoulder at the sound of her footfalls and raised a finger to his lips in warning. She halted at the foot of the stairs, clutching the post, heart racing.

"Nelson." The pounding shook the door, rattling the heavy wooden bolt Mr. Nelson had lowered across it. "We ain't fools. I found the wagon on my land."

His voice steel, Mr. Nelson called back, "My wagon is in my barn."

"So is Dorothea Granger's horse."

This voice was cold and deadly calm, and one Dorothea knew well. A chill prickled down her spine. Cyrus.

Mr. Nelson shifted his weight and adjusted his grip on the rifle, and Dorothea knew he recognized the speaker. He turned to her and said dryly, "My apologies for the damage I am about to do to your reputation." He faced the door again and called out, "Miss Granger is my guest. Since you are engaged to another, it is not any business of yours."

"Don't listen to him. Everyone knows them Grangers help runaways," complained Mr. Liggett.

"Shut up, Liggett," ordered Cyrus. Then, in a kinder tone, he called, "Dorothea, I know you're listening. You're a smart girl. I saw you turn away from the ferry. You know you can't escape. Just give up the runaways and we can all share in the reward."

Mr. Nelson quickly held up a hand to warn her not to answer, but her throat was too constricted for speech.

"That's comin' out of your portion," said a fourth man sharply. "I ain't sharing my reward with them nigger lovers."

"Shut up," barked Cyrus.

Heartsick with dread, Dorothea sank to a seat on the bottom step as the door trembled beneath a man's fist. There had to be another way out. Perhaps if they crept out of a back window, carried the children, sprinted for the cover of the oak grove—but even at a dead run, they had acres to cross. Pursuers on horseback would overtake them easily. And what of Old Dan?

The pounding on the door ceased; the men's voices fell silent. Mr. Nelson turned his head sharply, and Dorothea glimpsed a flicker of a torch as its bearer passed a window. She bolted to her feet.

Mr. Nelson crossed the room in two strides and grasped her arm. "Listen carefully," he said. "Get the others and go into the cellar. Old Dan is already hiding below. In the northeast corner you will find a stack of crates. They conceal a tunnel that will lead you from the house to the barn. Leave the barn by way of the smaller door, on the north side, and go to the ditch nearby. Keep low and follow the contour of the slope all the way to the stand of oaks. Keep running if you can, hide if you must."

"Old Dan cannot run."

"He will have to try." Mr. Nelson handed her the rifle so suddenly that she stumbled from its weight. "Do you know how to use this?"

"Of course."

"Then get moving. I will hold them off as long as I can."

"No." Dorothea shoved the rifle back at him. Surprised, he took it. "I could not fire upon a man, not even those men."

"Don't be a fool." He tried to return the weapon, but she drew back. "It may save your life."

"I cannot run carrying both it and one of the children. You will have greater need of it here."

Without another word Dorothea fled upstairs for Constance and the others. She repeated Mr. Nelson's instructions as they raced downstairs and into the kitchen.

"Nelson," came another shout from outside. "Open up or we'll smoke you out!"

Dorothea tore open the cellar door and sent the others racing ahead of her. She spared one last look for Mr. Nelson. He stalked through the front room, grasp tight upon the rifle, as the furious shouts from outside revealed the men's positions. They seemed to have encircled the house.

Glass shattered as a torch smashed through a window near the front door. Immediately Mr. Nelson was upon it, stomping out the flames. He glanced up and spotted her frozen in the doorway.

"Go," he shouted.

She gasped and descended into the cellar, closing the door behind her.

The air smelled of damp earth. Dorothea stumbled down the stairs blindly. When her eyes adjusted to the darkness illuminated by a single lantern below, she found that Constance had uncovered the entrance to the tunnel. Liza entered in a crouch, still carrying the younger girl; Hannah followed on her heels. When Dorothea reached them, Constance had taken Old Dan by the arm and was cajoling him to hasten after them, but he shook his head and pawed at her hand.

"I won't make it," he said. "Just let me be."

"You can't give up now," cried Dorothea.

"I ain't givin' up." With an effort he tore free from Constance and stood proudly, defiantly, before the two women. "I can't run. You can see that plain as day. Somebody's got to put those crates back or those men'll know just where you went."

"I will stay," said Dorothea. She could not leave him to that fate. "They will not hurt me as they would you."

Quietly, Constance said, "No, Dorothea."

"But I cannot—"

"You have to lead us. You're the only one who knows the way." Constance came forward and kissed the man on the cheek. "You're a brave soul, Old Dan." She darted into the tunnel with the lantern.

Overcome, Dorothea hugged him and whispered a word of thanks before following.

The tunnel was low and cramped, braced every few feet by old wooden beams, too narrow to move through except in single file. Dorothea's short stature allowed her to move more easily than the others, save Hannah, and she soon caught up to the group. Constance's lantern bobbed and threw shadows on the earthen walls as they proceeded as swiftly as they dared. Roots brushed Dorothea's cheeks; the soles of her boots slid over dirt and loose stones. The noises from the house cut off abruptly as the crates slid back into place behind them. Dorothea said a silent prayer for Old Dan and urged the others onward.

"I see light ahead," called Liza, in the lead. A few feet later, the tunnel abruptly ended at a makeshift wall of wooden planks. They listened in fearful silence for noises from without, but heard only the whicker of a horse and a cow's low moo. Dorothea scrambled to the front of the group and shoved the planks aside. She peered out cautiously before leading the others from the tunnel. They emerged into an empty horse stall. Uncle Jacob's mare looked down upon her from the next stall and whinnied in recognition.

Dorothea spotted the smaller of two doors and led the others to it. She stole a glance outside before opening the door wide enough for the others to emerge. Constance snatched up Hannah and led the way across the dirt road to the ditch. Liza followed carrying her younger daughter, and Dorothea brought up the rear. Outside the barn, they could again hear the threats the men shouted at Mr. Nelson's closed door. From the edge of the ditch Dorothea permitted herself one look back. In the light of their flickering torches she recognized the thin, hunched figure of Mr. Liggett, the straight, proud back of Cyrus Pearson. Cyrus stood at the front door, posed as if for a portrait with a hand at his lapel and the other gesturing as he called to Mr. Nelson within. A third man crouched low beneath one of the windows, creeping closer. Cyrus nodded and waved him forward. The other man came even nearer to the window, then lifted his rifle as he rose up on his heels—

"Thomas," Dorothea screamed, but her voice was drowned out by the gunshot.

She had time to witness the men's raucous cheers before hands seized her and dragged her down. "Run," Constance said in her ear.

She struggled to stand. "But Thomas—Old Dan—"

"We can't help them no more." Constance held her fast. "Liza and the girls we can help."

Muffling a sob, Dorothea ran along the ditch after Liza and her daughters. She dared not look back, not even after they reached the safety of the oak grove. They paused only long enough to catch their breath before Dorothea picked up Hannah and urged the others onward. Their entrance unencumbered now, Cyrus and Liggett would search the house and find Old Dan and do to him what they had done to Thomas.

Not ten minutes later, just as they crossed into the Craigmiles' land, the women stopped short at the sound of another gunshot. Liza pressed a hand to her mouth to muffle a cry. Dorothea shook with rage and fear as she whispered a prayer for Old Dan's soul.

"Come," she said, shifting Hannah to her back. "We must make haste."

She could not lead them to the Granger farm. When the riders finished searching Mr. Nelson's house, if they did not find the tunnel, they would think of Uncle Jacob's mare and come after Dorothea, thinking she would flee for the safety of home.

She led them instead across the Craigmile farm to the Shropshires' land, moving always under cover of the trees, shying away from roads and open land. She guided her companions north and east through the maple grove to the old worm fence, which they followed north along the border of the Granger farm to the Wheelers' land. She led them northeastward along the Indian trail to the creek, no longer locked in ice and running swiftly, swollen from recent rains. All the while, to keep her spirits up so that she could in turn encourage the others, to block out images of Two Bears Farm from her thoughts, she pictured the Sugar Camp Quilt and the landmarks she had concealed within its stitches. The Crooked Ladder block. The Sideways

Braid. The Drunkard's Creek. The Water Wheel. The patchwork clues would guide her to safety as they had guided others before her.

They walked west along the creek, taking turns carrying the exhausted children. Behind them the sky turned velvet blue, then violet, then rose. The stars faded. Dorothea urged her companions to hurry, but she knew they had drawn on their last reserves of strength to make it that far. They had nothing left to speed their steps.

It was almost dawn when at last the houses and storefronts of Woodfall came into view. Then she spied the water wheel and the bridge beyond.

"Stay hidden until I summon you," she instructed as she found them a hiding place within a copse of bushes not far from the foot of the bridge. Alone, she crossed the bridge and surveyed the scene. Only when she was sure they could pass undetected did she beckon the others. Liza and Constance, the children in their arms, found new strength with their destination so near, and they fairly ran across the bridge. When they reached her, Dorothea turned and ran for the millhouse. She did not pause to knock on the door; she did not think to be sure all was safe within. Only as she swung open the door and ushered the others inside did she think that perhaps their pursuers had taken the road and arrived before them. Perhaps they waited within. But she had remembered caution too late to call back the others, too late to do anything but enter the station.

The miller and his wife looked up from the breakfast table as Dorothea and her companions burst through the door. A fire crackled merrily on the hearth. They were alone.

"Mercy," exclaimed Mrs. Braun, setting down a serving plate with a clatter. "Shut the door before you are seen!"

Dorothea slammed the door and leaned upon it, breathless, closing her eyes to hold back tears of exhaustion and grief.

Mrs. Braun rushed to attend to them.

"You're safe now," said the miller, his deep voice low and reassuring.

Safe, Dorothea thought dully. Liza and her daughters were safe, but not Old Dan, who had given his life to conceal their escape route.

Nor was Thomas Nelson.

Chapter Eleven

When Dorothea gasped that their pursuers might be close behind, Mrs. Braun quickly ushered them from the residence into the mill. There, in an empty storeroom hidden behind a door fashioned from stacks of barrels, she told them to hide until she could be certain it was safe to emerge. A small, high window provided sufficient light and fresh air, but since it looked out upon the river almost directly behind the water wheel, Mrs. Braun assured them they were in no danger of being observed.

Dorothea helped Liza put the children to bed on the low pallets draped with layers of quilts, then sank down to rest, closing her eyes against tears. She could not drive from her thoughts her last glimpse of Two Bears Farm—the man crouched outside Thomas's window, Cyrus's slow, almost indifferent gesture, the rifle shot.

Not long after showing them to the hiding place, Mrs. Braun returned with food and drink. Dorothea drank a dipperful of water, but her stomach turned at the thought of food. The women spoke little, overcome with exhaustion and the instinct for silence, though the rumbling of the mill would have drowned out any sound quieter than a shout.

An hour later, Mrs. Braun returned a second time and closed the door behind her. "If anyone is chasing you, they are taking their time about it," she said, taking a seat on the wooden floor. "But just in case, you should stay hidden. While we wait, you can tell me what happened today."

But Liza spoke first. "Paul and Jack—did they make it here safe?"

"They did, and they moved on a few nights ago. They told me the rest of their group included a woman, an old man, and two children, and that they would arrive by wagon." Her tone softened. "What has become of the old man?"

Liza's face crumpled in anguish. She turned away.

"I believe he was shot," said Dorothea softly, her voice catching in her throat. "He and . . . a man who tried to help us."

She told Mrs. Braun what had befallen them since leaving the Wright farm.

❧

Dorothea and Constance stayed with the Brauns two days and nights. After the first day, Dorothea no longer remained within the hiding place during the day but instead helped Mrs. Braun with her chores in the adjacent house.

While they worked, they made plans for their remaining three passengers. Both Mr. and Mrs. Braun thought it too great a risk to proceed with Abel Wright's original plan for Liza to pose as a free colored woman traveling with her children. She would still carry Dorothea's forged papers in case they were apprehended, but she and her daughters would travel to the next station concealed in Mr. Braun's wagon. The stationmaster there was an innkeeper with ample space for Liza and her girls, and if Liza were spied by a guest, she would easily blend in among his many colored employees. In fact, Mrs. Braun said, runaways were safer there than anywhere in central Pennsylvania. Southerners had learned to spend the night elsewhere after too many of their slaves had been persuaded by the inn's employees to make an escape while their masters slept comfortably upstairs.

Liza and her daughters would remain at the inn until the stationmaster could be certain that their pursuers had lost the trail. Then they would be integrated back into the underground network and guided north through New York State and into Canada.

On the morning of the third day, Dorothea and Constance said farewell to Liza and her daughters and walked back to the Granger farm. They followed the main road as Dorothea had done after her first journey to the Brauns' mill. If they should encounter Cyrus and Mr. Liggett, they would claim to have been visiting a friend and deny any knowledge of the events at Two Bears Farm.

They were nearly a quarter of a mile from Dorothea's house when her parents came running to meet them on the road.

Lorena's cheeks were wet with tears as she embraced her daughter. The

Grangers and Abel Wright had been frantic with worry wondering what had become of them and the fugitives in their care. "We hoped for the best," said Lorena, linking her arms through those of her daughter and Constance as they walked back to the house. "Abel found scuffed footprints in the dirt outside the barn, but when he discovered the team still within, he could not determine whether you had left those tracks upon departing the barn, or if Mr. Nelson had left them there earlier when he took the horses inside."

"Liggett and Pearson came by here looking for you that morning," said Robert. "We knew you had sense enough to stay away, so we told them you were off caring for a sick friend."

Dorothea almost managed a smile. "Another sick friend."

"Of course they did not believe us, but what could they do?" said Lorena. "Now tell us, how are your passengers faring?"

Dorothea took a deep breath. "You know, of course, that Old Dan stayed behind."

"Yes, we know." Lorena put an arm around her shoulder and hugged her comfortingly. "It was a courageous and noble act to sacrifice his freedom for that of Liza and her daughters."

"Sacrifice his life, you mean," said Constance.

"Why, no, although I suppose in a sense they are one and the same." When Dorothea and Constance regarded her in confusion, Lorena said, "Cyrus Pearson's loathsome associates captured Old Dan. Mr. Nelson could not say for certain which direction they took after they left Two Bears Farm, but we assume they will return Old Dan to his master. It is a grievous reward for his sacrifice."

Dorothea stopped short. "Mr. Nelson lives?"

"He is badly injured, but he will recover." Lorena's gaze was piercing. "You didn't know?"

"No." Dorothea felt faint with gratitude. "We heard two shots. We thought—I thought the first ended Mr. Nelson's life, and the second, Old Dan's."

"No, my dear, no." Lorena held her firmly or Dorothea's knees might have given way. "The first shot struck Mr. Nelson in the shoulder, and after that, he was incapable of preventing the men from entering the house. They left Mr. Nelson barely conscious and bleeding on the floor, searched the house, and found Old Dan in the basement. They dragged the poor soul from the house and lashed him to a horse, but before they could continue the search,

Abel Wright came upon the scene and fired a warning shot. Though they outnumbered him four to one, the men fled with their single prisoner. Mr. Wright bound Mr. Nelson's wounds and tended him until he was assured he would not bleed to death. Only then did he ride off to fetch Dr. Bremigan."

"The doctor says he lost a lot of blood, but he should make a full recovery," added Robert. "I don't see how he will be able to finish out the school year, though. You might expect the school board to ask you to take over the whole school, Dorothea."

Dorothea nodded, but she thought of Cyrus and Mrs. Engle and could not imagine that Mr. Engle, the school board president, would appoint her. Unless the entire town united against Cyrus, Mr. Liggett, and their slave-catcher associates, she was unlikely to teach for the Creek's Crossing school again.

Lorena must have guessed what she was thinking, for she said, "The story of Mr. Nelson's injury has spread throughout town already. News such as this cannot be kept quiet."

"What do folks say about what happened?" asked Constance. "I don't suppose they like the idea of my husband riding with a gun after a bunch of white men."

Dorothea's parents exchanged a look. Reluctantly, Lorena said, "The townspeople seem evenly divided between those who admire your husband for coming to Mr. Nelson's defense and those who fear his actions will inspire other free coloreds to take up arms against their white neighbors."

"So they're afraid my Abel might become another Nat Turner." Constance shook her head in disgust. "Folks in this town would side with slavecatchers and the local drunk before they side with a colored man, even though he's a farmer and a good man who saved one of their own. All that for a warning shot! What would they have done if he had killed one of 'em?"

"Let us just be thankful that he did not," said Lorena, but Constance scowled, her mouth set and brow furrowed in anger.

"There is much to be thankful for. If Mr. Wright had not come after you . . ." Robert shook his head. "He told us he had been restless and uneasy from the moment you two left in the wagon, so he decided to follow you. He was on the way to Creek's Crossing when he heard the gunshot from Two Bears Farm. If he had not come . . ."

Robert did not complete the thought, but Dorothea knew. Without Mr. Wright's curious inkling that all was not well, Mr. Nelson would have perished.

❧

Lorena urged Constance to stay for dinner, but Constance was eager to return home to Abel. Robert hitched up Lorena's horse and offered to drive Constance home, but Dorothea quickly said that she would do it. Her parents were reluctant to let her go lest she run into Cyrus Pearson or Mr. Liggett, but Dorothea told them she could not avoid them for long in a town the size of Creek's Crossing, and she refused to let them frighten her. Lorena had said that the town was evenly divided, so Cyrus and Mr. Liggett had to know they did not have everyone's support. They could not do as they pleased without fear of the consequences. Dorothea knew Cyrus well enough to be sure that he would not risk raising a public outcry by assaulting two unarmed women.

Dorothea and Constance rode to the ferry. The pilot's eyes widened at the sight of them, but he helped them aboard without referring to the events at Two Bears Farm. Dorothea was tempted to ask him for his version just to see how repeated tellings had embellished and warped the truth, but she said nothing. Ignoring a rumor starved it of its strength, hastening its demise. It would be better for their future passengers if rumors about the Wrights' and Grangers' involvement with runaways subsided quickly.

They reached the opposite shore and continued through the streets of Creek's Crossing. Cyrus and Mr. Liggett had apparently abandoned their blockade. Dorothea noticed a few curious glances as they made their way west along Water Street, but no one called out to them, either to praise or to censure.

They passed the site of the new library. To the sounds of hammer and saw, men pulled on ropes and raised the board frame of the eastern wall. A breeze carried the scent of sawdust and fresh pine. Dorothea breathed deeply and imagined bookshelves filled with enlightening biographies, inspiring poetry, entrancing novels. Thanks to Mr. Nelson, the Authors' Album quilt would be on display, perhaps hanging on a wall like a great work of art in a museum. She hoped that curiosity would draw new readers to the writings of the authors whose names adorned the quilt, the men and women whose inclusion had sparked such controversy. In the troubled times that were sure to come, she could not allow Mrs. Engle's caustic letters to the editor of the *Creek's Crossing Informer* to be the only influence shaping the minds and hearts and opinions of the people of the Elm Creek Valley.

They turned down Creekside Road and spotted Miss Nadelfrau approaching on the opposite sidewalk, her head down and shoulders hunched over a basket she carried in both arms. She cringed like a dog that expected to be beaten, but she looked up at the sound of the wagon and brightened to see Dorothea and Constance. She called out to them and waved; Dorothea pulled the bay to a halt and waited as Miss Nadelfrau ran across the street to meet them.

"This town is all abuzz about the two of you," she said breathlessly. "Of course, one cannot believe half of what one hears; it's too fantastic. Is it true you shot a slavecatcher?"

"Good heavens, no," exclaimed Dorothea.

"Pity. Be that as it may, I wanted to invite you—" Miss Nadelfrau nodded to Constance. "*Both* of you to an organizational meeting at the schoolhouse tomorrow evening."

"What are you organizing?" asked Constance.

"The Creek's Crossing Abolitionist Society," said Miss Nadelfrau proudly. "I assumed you two would be interested in participating."

Dorothea and Constance exchanged a look of surprise. "We would indeed," said Dorothea. "I think my parents would like to join, too."

"Please tell them they will be welcome." Miss Nadelfrau gave them a cheery wave. "Don't forget. Six o'clock sharp!"

Dorothea assured her they would come and chirruped to the horses.

"I thought she was going to leave town since Mrs. Engle bought her shop," said Constance.

Dorothea shrugged. "I suppose she found reason to stay."

Her heart rose as they turned southwest out of town.

When they arrived at the Wright farm, Abel ran to meet them and climbed into the wagon to embrace his wife rather than wait for her to descend. He held her so long and so tightly that eventually Constance had to ask him to ease up a bit because she could only hold her breath so long. He chuckled and released her, but Dorothea spied tears in his eyes, and he took Constance's hand to help her down from the wagon and held fast to it long after they had entered the house.

They asked about Old Dan, but Abel could tell them nothing more than what he had already told Dorothea's parents. Constance asked about Mr. Nelson; Dorothea held her breath until assured that he was on the mend, being cared for by his housekeeper, who still blamed herself for being away at her sister's that fateful night. "She thinks if she had been there, those men would never have dared to cause so much trouble," said Abel, shaking his head. "Nelson says she's a force to be reckoned with when she has a rolling pin in hand and a noble cause."

They shared a laugh at the image, but their merriment was subdued.

"I am glad you were able to frighten them off in her absence," said Dorothea to Abel. "To think that such violent men would turn tail at a warning shot."

Abel Wright regarded her with surprise. "Is that what folks think? Is that what they say?"

After a moment, Dorothea understood. "You mean to say that you missed."

"Not by much. Cyrus Pearson was using his horsewhip on Old Dan at the time or maybe I would have just fired in the air to get their attention. Instead I nicked the top of Cyrus's ear. I guess with all the blood he thought he was hit worse than he was, 'cause he yelled for his friends to mount up and run for the forest. They did, too, as if I was the devil himself with an army behind me." He laughed again, shaking his head. "A warning shot. I guess I did give him a warning, all right."

"Good thing you aren't sweet on him no more," said Constance to Dorothea. "He won't be quite so handsome with a piece of his ear missing."

The Wrights laughed, but there was an edge to their mirth, and Dorothea found herself unable to join in.

❧

The Wrights invited Dorothea to stay to supper, but she remained only long enough to feed and water the horse. She still had one call to make before returning home.

Two men she did not recognize were working in the fields with a team of horses when Dorothea arrived at Two Bears Farm. She climbed down from the wagon and, almost without realizing she did so, smoothed her skirt and tucked a stray lock of brown hair back into her bonnet. She climbed the porch stairs and knocked on the door.

A short, motherly woman in a floury apron opened the door.

"Good afternoon," said Dorothea, smiling. "I am Dorothea Granger. I came to see how Mr. Nelson is doing."

"Of course. You're the schoolteacher," said the housekeeper. She opened the door and welcomed Dorothea inside. Dorothea removed her bonnet and smoothed her hair. "Mr. Nelson is in the parlor. I will take you to him."

Dorothea thanked her and followed her to the room where only a few days before, Old Dan, Liza, and the girls had warmed themselves by the fire. Mr. Nelson sat in an armchair by the window, a quilt tucked over his legs, an open book resting face down on his lap. His eyes were closed, his glasses folded and lying on a table at his left hand. She thought he was asleep and was about to quietly leave the room when his eyes opened and fixed on hers.

"A Miss Granger here to see you," said the housekeeper. She gave Dorothea a stern look as if to warn her not to tire her patient and announced that she would be in the kitchen.

"Miss Granger," said Mr. Nelson. He made an effort to sit up straighter, and he gestured to a chair. "Please sit down."

She drew closer but remained standing, wishing she had not come. He seemed so pale and ill; she should not have disturbed him. "I stopped by to see how you are faring. I am exceedingly glad that you were not killed."

"A more unusual greeting from a lady I have never received." He allowed his head to rest against the high back of the armchair. "The woman and her daughters?"

"They are safe."

"Good." He coughed, winced, and involuntarily reached for his shoulder.

"Are you in much pain?" she asked, and immediately wished she had not.

"The wound troubles me very little, thank you." He looked away, and she knew he was concealing the truth. "At any rate, I am in far better condition than I imagine Old Dan is at this moment."

Dorothea felt heartsick at the thought of the courageous man, and she had to force herself not to think of him as tears sprang into her eyes. She inhaled deeply, the words she had planned to speak lost to her. "If not for you, the others would have met his same fate. I am grateful to you beyond my ability to describe it. I— I cannot—" Then in a rush she said, "Oh, Mr. Nelson, what is to become of you?"

His eyebrows rose. "I must look far worse than I feel to inspire such alarm."

"I do not mean your wound. I mean—your probation. A runaway slave was discovered in your home. You concealed and defended him."

"Not terribly well, as it happens."

"You did, and it is against the law." She pressed a hand to her stomach in a vain attempt to settle its fluttering. "Will you be sent to prison?"

"Ah." He smiled, faintly. "No need to worry. Two of the witnesses who might accuse me have fled with their captive, and the other two are too busy denouncing each other to waste breath on me."

"What do you mean? Mr. Pearson and Mr. Liggett—"

"Have had a falling out, according to my housekeeper, who has an ear for the gossip of the town. Mr. Liggett is a grasping and greedy man who has learned there is little money to be gained in Mr. Pearson's employ, while Mr. Pearson does not wish to have his name embroiled in a scandal or associated with a man as disreputable and universally disliked as Mr. Liggett. I do not fear that they will conspire to have me arrested."

Dorothea felt a dark cloud lift from her thoughts. "That is good news." She had expected both men to boast of their adventure, but if they had turned on each other, perhaps they would admit little rather than acknowledge their former friendship.

"It is, since I could do runaways little good from inside a prison." He touched his shoulder and pulled a face. "Next time, however, I will endeavor not to be shot."

"There . . . will be a next time?"

"Not another confrontation with slavecatchers, with any luck, but Two Bears Farm will assist any fugitives in need of shelter as long as the need remains. It would be a pity to let the Carters' tunnel go to waste." He looked away. "Especially since Old Dan sacrificed his freedom to conceal its existence."

Dorothea's throat tightened. "If only we could discover where he has been taken. Perhaps we could buy his freedom."

"Even if Pearson or Liggett knows, I doubt they could be compelled to tell you. They would likely deny his existence just as they deny the rest of the truth."

Dorothea nodded, reluctant to release the fleeting hope that she and her friends might somehow rescue Old Dan. But of course, they could expect no help from Mr. Liggett or Cyrus, no matter how viciously they had turned against each other. "If they deny what really happened," she asked, "how do they account for Cyrus's injury?"

Mr. Nelson smiled in grim satisfaction. "Liggett tells of being ambushed by a band of murderous runaway slaves. It is quite a fanciful tale, with himself at the heroic center. I doubt anyone believes him."

"And Mr. Pearson? Has your housekeeper heard his version?"

Mr. Nelson's smile vanished and his gaze fell upon the book on his lap. "She has." He lifted the book, marked his place with a scrap of paper, and set it on the table beside his glasses. "She cannot trace the rumor directly back to him, but it seems he would have people believe I shot him."

"You?" exclaimed Dorothea. "Well, I suppose it makes perfect sense. You would have been defending your household."

"That would indeed have made sense, which is probably why Pearson did not think of it. Apparently we fought over a woman." He paused. "Over you."

Dorothea's breath caught in her throat. "Me?"

"Evidently I became enraged when my rival appeared and declared his undying affection for you." He snorted. "Have you ever heard anything so ridiculous?"

"No," said Dorothea softly. "No one will believe it."

"Pearson's fiancée does, but she seems to be the only one. In any event, his engagement is off, and I understand he intends to find solace for his broken heart in another tour of Europe." He made a sudden, impatient gesture to a chair. "Would you please sit down? Shall I call for some tea? I apologize for being such a poor host. When I think of what I said about you upon the occasion of our first meeting, I cannot consider myself deserving of this visit."

Dorothea forced a shaky laugh as she seated herself. "So much has happened since then, I hardly remember what words we might have exchanged."

"I cannot forget them."

Dorothea flushed and bowed her head. "I have forgotten them, so you must do the same. If we are to keep teaching together, we must attempt to be civil."

"I do not think I will teach again."

"What? Why not?"

He indicated his shoulder wearily. "The term will be over before I am fit to stand all day in front of a classroom, and whatever version of recent events he chooses to believe, I doubt that the stepfather of Cyrus Pearson will be inclined to renew my contract."

"I expect the same for my own contract."

"They will have to allow you to finish out the school year. There is no one else." Mr. Nelson regarded her steadily. "You are a fine teacher, Miss Granger."

"And you are a fine man," said Dorothea. "When I think of all the trouble I have caused you, I regret coming to your door that night."

"Don't. Three people are closer to freedom because of it."

"I wonder why you did not hesitate to let us in, why you did not send us away."

"Do you?" He held her gaze, but his expression was unreadable. "Surely you know I could deny you nothing."

Dorothea did not know what to say.

He cleared his throat. "I am not the sort of man to make pretty speeches. I have always been straightforward with you, and I would ask the same in return."

She managed a nod. "Of course."

"You are too good to trifle with me. While I deserve nothing but your continued enmity—"

"That is not so," said Dorothea. "Where would I have gone that night if not for you? What would I have done?"

"It is only because you knew that you could come here that I speak of this at all. Your knock on the door, the trust you placed in me that night, gave me hope that perhaps you have forgiven me. Perhaps your opinion of me has changed."

"It has changed," said Dorothea fervently. "My opinion has changed— utterly."

"Then I am relieved that we may call ourselves friends." His head fell back against the chair again, and he regarded her in silence for a long moment. "I wonder if I might hope to someday make you love me."

His eyes, large and boyish without his glasses, were full of such affection and longing that she found herself unable to do anything but warm herself in his gaze.

Then she knelt on the floor beside him, brushed the hair from his forehead, and took his hand.

"I would not dream of discouraging such hopes," she said, and pressed his hand to her cheek.

Circle

of

Quilters

Acknowledgments

I am more thankful for the friendship, dedication, and expertise of Denise Roy, Maria Massie, and Rebecca Davis than I could ever adequately express. I am also grateful for Annie Orr's tireless efforts behind the scenes and the beautiful artistry of Honi Werner and Melanie Marder Parks. How fortunate I am to work with such brilliant, talented women!

Hugs and thanks to Lisa Cass and Jody Gomez, who cared for my boys and gave me time to write, and to Anne Spurgeon, who laughs with me, commiserates with me, and answers obscure historical questions with remarkable speed and accuracy.

Many thanks to Brenda Papadakis and Ami Simms for inspiring me with their quilts, creativity, and contributions to the quilting world. Thanks also to Lee Keyser for her suggestions for the romantic date in Seattle that appears in this book, and to Joelle Reeder of Moxie Design Studios, who created my fabulous new website.

Thank you to the friends and family who have supported and encouraged me through the years, especially Geraldine Neidenbach, Heather Neidenbach, Nic Neidenbach, Virginia and Edward Riechman, and Leonard and Marlene Chiaverini.

Above all else, I am grateful to my husband, Marty, and my sons, Nicholas and Michael. Whenever the frustrations, disappointments, and loneliness of the writing life get me down, you remind me that I already have everything I ever wanted.

To Nicholas and Michael Chiaverini.
I love you a million billion.
I love you infinity.

Are You an Accomplished Quilter
Seeking a New Adventure?

Seeking qualified applicants to join
the circle of quilters at the country's finest
and most popular quilters' getaway, located
in beautiful rural central Pennsylvania.
Applicants should demonstrate mastery of two
or more of the following subjects: hand piecing,
machine piecing, machine quilting, pattern
drafting, computer-aided design, quilt history,
quilted garments, hand dyeing, or other notable
quilting technique. Seasonal work, flexible
schedule, and/or live-in arrangement available
if desired. Teaching experience and sense of
humor required. Ability to tolerate quirky
coworkers, emotional turmoil, and the occasional
minor disaster highly recommended. If that
didn't scare you off, send résumé and portfolio,
including sample lesson plans for two courses,
photos of completed quilts, and letters of
recommendation from at least three students to

Elm Creek Quilt Camp
Attention: Sarah McClure
Elm Creek Manor
Waterford, Pennsylvania 16807

ADA EOE

Chapter One
Maggie

Every morning after breakfast, the Courtyard Quilters gathered in the recreation room of Ocean View Hills Retirement Community and Convalescent Center to quilt, swap stories about their grandchildren, and gossip about the other residents. Nothing escaped their notice or judgment, and woe be it to the new resident or visitor who pulled up a chair to their circle uninvited. No one made that mistake twice, not if they coveted the friendship of seventy-year-old Helen Stonebridge, the leader of the circle of quilters and the most popular woman in the facility.

Within days of coming to work at Ocean View Hills—a name she had trouble saying with a straight face considering they were in Sacramento—Maggie Flynn joined the ranks of Mrs. Stonebridge's admirers. Maggie had heard other members of the staff mention the woman as a sort of unofficial leader of the residents, but it wasn't until she witnessed Mrs. Stonebridge in action that Maggie understood how influential she truly was. On that day, Maggie was sorting art supplies in the recreation room not far from the quilters' morning meeting place. Their conversation turned to an altercation in the cafeteria the previous day in which a certain Mrs. Lenore Hicks had knocked over another resident in her haste to be first in line.

"She plowed right into Rita Talmadge's walker," tsked one of the quilters. "Rita tumbled head over heels, and Lenore didn't even stop to help her up."

"Lenore must have seen the banana cream pie on the dessert tray," another quilter explained. "Never get between that woman and pie."

"Rita could hardly dodge out of the way," said the first quilter indignantly. "She's had three hip replacements."

Maggie was puzzling out how someone with only two hips could have three hip replacements when the youngest of the group, Mrs. Blum, piped up, "This isn't the first time Lenore's bumped into a lady with a walker. Remember Mary Haas and the Mother's Day brunch? Margaret Hoover and the reflecting pool? Velma Tate and the Christmas tree?"

The quilters considered and agreed that Lenore did appear to have a habit of barreling into the less agile residents of Ocean View Hills. So far none of her victims had suffered more than bumps and bruises—and in Margaret Hoover's case, an unexpected al fresco bath—but if the pattern continued, it was only a matter of time before someone broke a bone.

"I would be less concerned if these incidents didn't happen so frequently," mused Mrs. Stonebridge. "It's also troubling that Lenore didn't help Rita to her feet. No pie is worth adding insult to injury."

The other ladies waited expectantly while Mrs. Stonebridge deliberated, her needle darting through two small squares of fabric with small, even stitches. Maggie found that she, too, had stopped sorting out watercolor paints in anticipation of the verdict.

After a few moments, Mrs. Stonebridge spoke again. "Dottie, would you please tell Lenore that I would enjoy chatting with her whenever she has a spare moment?"

Mrs. Blum, the spriest of the group, nodded and hurried off. Maggie suspected that Mrs. Stonebridge expected an immediate response despite the casual wording of the request, and sure enough, Mrs. Blum returned several minutes later with a tall, solidly built woman with a slight stoop to her shoulders and a look of puzzled wariness in her eye.

Mrs. Stonebridge greeted her with a warm smile. "Oh, hello, Lenore. Won't you sit down?"

Mrs. Hicks nodded and seated herself in the chair Mrs. Blum had vacated. Mrs. Blum frowned and glanced about for another chair to drag over into the circle, but the only empty seats were heavy armchairs near the fireplace. She folded her arms and stood instead.

"You wanted to speak to me?" asked Mrs. Hicks, anxious.

"Yes, dear," said Mrs. Stonebridge. "You see, I'm worried about you."

Mrs. Hicks, who had clearly expected to be reprimanded for some forgotten offense, relaxed slightly. "Worried? About me? Why?"

"I'm concerned that you might have an inner ear disorder. You seem to have some balance problems. I'm referring, of course, to your unfortunate collision with Rita in the cafeteria yesterday. Anyone can have an accident, but you must have been feeling especially unsteady on your feet to be unable to help Rita up after you had knocked her down."

"Oh," said Mrs. Hicks, uneasy. "Well, I was in a hurry, you see, and her friends were there to help her, so I thought she was all right."

"It turns out she was," Mrs. Stonebridge reassured her. "But I'm sure you saw that for yourself when you went back later to apologize."

Mrs. Hicks said nothing, a guilty, pained expression on her face.

"Oh. I see," said Mrs. Stonebridge, sorrowful. "Well, I'm sure your balance troubles are nothing to worry about, but you should get yourself checked out just in case."

"I'll see the doctor today," said Mrs. Hicks in a small voice.

"And—this is just a thought—since poor Rita is still bruised from her fall, perhaps you could bring her meals to her until she recovers."

"The busboys can do that, can't they?"

"It will mean so much more coming from you, don't you agree?" Mrs. Stonebridge smiled. "Should we say . . . a month? Do you think that would do?"

Mrs. Hicks agreed, and for the next month, three times a day, Rita Talmadge waited at her favorite lunch table while a repentant Mrs. Hicks brought her meals to her on a tray. Mrs. Talmadge was satisfied, and Mrs. Hicks, who received a clean bill of health from the staff physician, learned to be more courteous of her fellow residents.

Maggie marveled at the simple elegance of Mrs. Stonebridge's solution and how well it restored harmony to Ocean View Hills—and at how willingly Mrs. Hicks and Mrs. Talmadge had complied. Over time Maggie learned that conflicts were often resolved with Mrs. Stonebridge's guidance and she found herself thinking that it was a shame the former professor of anthropology could not lend her services to heads of state in troubled regions of the world. Mrs. Stonebridge read the *Sacramento Bee* daily and the *New York Times* on Sunday, and her opinions on world events were always thoughtful and well reasoned. At least Maggie thought so. She had no doubt Mrs. Stonebridge could offer brilliant and graceful solutions to conflicts around the globe if only political leaders knew where to find her—and if those same leaders could be persuaded to submit to her decisions with the same humility and desire for harmony as the residents of Ocean View Hills.

Since Mrs. Stonebridge kept herself apprised of events in the lives of the staff members with the same thoughtful diligence she applied to her fellow residents and to world events, when Maggie's personal life took an unexpected turn, she decided to tell Mrs. Stonebridge right away. She would ferret out the truth eventually anyway, and Maggie would not want to hurt her feelings by having her hear it secondhand.

On the morning after her twenty-fifth birthday, Maggie came into work early so she would have time to deliver the news before her shift started. She found the Courtyard Quilters gathered in the recreation room, their chairs arranged in a circle in front of the windows with the view of the garden, just like always. Mrs. Stonebridge looked up from her sewing to smile at her. "Well, there's the birthday girl. How was your party last night?"

"It was all right," said Maggie. After work, she had met her two best friends for happy hour at La Hacienda, where they filled up on free nachos, sipped margaritas, and discussed the men at the bar—at least her friends did. Maggie merely played along, pretending to admire the cute guy in the tan suit who had smiled at her. She had little interest in meeting someone new a mere four hours after breaking Brian's heart.

"Well?" inquired Mrs. Blum, trying to get a good look at Maggie's left hand, which she quickly concealed in her pocket. "Did he pop the question or didn't he? Don't leave us in suspense."

"He didn't," Maggie said. "We broke up."

The Courtyard Quilters' exclamations of astonishment and dismay brought an orderly running from another room. Mrs. Stonebridge waved him away with a shake of her head and a reassuring word.

"That louse," said one of the quilters. "I always knew he was no good."

"He's a good man," Maggie defended him. "He's just not the right man."

"How can you call him a good man after he broke your heart?" said Mrs. Blum, tears in her eyes. "And I've already started your wedding quilt!"

"I warned you not to," said another quilter. "That's bad luck. Never start a wedding quilt until you've seen the engagement ring on the bride-to-be's finger."

"He didn't break up with me," explained Maggie. "I broke up with him."

This time, the quilters responded with exclamations of incredulity. "It's not because of that sense of humor thing, is it?" demanded one. "Because that's a lot of malarkey. Who cares if a man laughs at your jokes?"

"That's not it." At least, that wasn't the only reason, although Maggie had always been troubled by how out of sync their senses of humor were. She could not remember a single time in three years that any of her small witticisms or amusing anecdotes had made Brian laugh. Smile politely, perhaps, but not laugh out loud in pleasure or joy. If he had no sense of humor at all, she could have excused it, but he laughed loudly enough at movies—even dramas—and at his friends' corny jokes. What made a person laugh spoke volumes about one's way of looking at the world. Brian's stoic response to things that amused Maggie made her feel as if they were gazing upon the same landscape but facing opposite directions.

She understood the Courtyard Quilters' astonishment. In their three years together, she and Brian had occasionally discussed marriage, but Maggie had assumed their discussions were purely hypothetical. They had attended friends' weddings and confided how they intended to do things differently when their time came—but neither of them explicitly said that they were talking about marrying the other. Then came the day Brian's mother invited Maggie to try on her late mother-in-law's emerald engagement ring, a treasured family heirloom. "You'll need to get it sized," she had advised her son as the ring slipped too easily past Maggie's knuckle.

Inexplicably, Maggie had been seized by panic. She quickly removed the ring and replaced it in the jewelry box, managing a fleeting smile for Brian's mother. Had everything been decided without her? Brian's family seemed to assume that he would propose and that when he did, that she would accept. The thought filled her with dread. She liked Brian; she liked him very much. He was friendly and cute and loyal and easy to please—"All qualities one would look for in a golden retriever," Mrs. Stonebridge had remarked only weeks ago, when Maggie confided in her after the engagement ring incident. "But do you love him?"

Maggie wasn't sure. She enjoyed spending time with him and believed they could have a decent, steady life together. But she had to believe there was something more, something greater, in store for her. It was unbearable to think that she had nothing more to look forward to but a good old reliable ordinary life.

She had hoped for more time to sort things out, but as her birthday approached, Brian hinted that he had a very special evening planned. He reserved a table at the finest restaurant in Sacramento two weeks in advance, and she found a bottle of expensive champagne hidden in the back of his refrigerator. Alarmed, Maggie began making excuses not to see him, but he knew her shifts, her haunts, her home so well that he merely showed up wherever he knew she would be, forlorn and determined to put things right.

He was so hurt and bewildered by her sudden, inexplicable coolness that she knew she would never have the courage to turn down his proposal. So she broke up with him before he had a chance to ask. Worse yet, she broke up with him by email, which was so cowardly of her that she couldn't admit it to the quilters.

"What was it, then?" asked Mrs. Blum, bewildered. "Brian seemed like such a nice young man."

"He was. He is," said Maggie. "But he's not the one."

"Maybe he's not the one but he's good enough," retorted one of the quilters, whom Maggie knew had never married.

"Hester, you won't change her mind," said Mrs. Stonebridge. "Maggie's holding out for true love."

"As you should," said another quilter, wistful. She was famous among the residents for her five marriages and four divorces. "I didn't, and look where it got me."

"I did," said Mrs. Blum. "I was blessed that I met my true love when I was only seventeen. He's out there, Maggie dear. You'll know him when you meet him."

"In the meantime, you'll always have us," said Mrs. Stonebridge. And since Mrs. Stonebridge seemed to think Maggie had made the right decision, everyone else thought so, too, and she never heard another word of dismay or disapproval on the subject.

❧

Two days later, Maggie walked home from the bus stop after work, dreading the thought of spending the rest of the evening alone packing up Brian's scattered belongings. He had already returned a carton of her own things—books and CDs, an old toothbrush anyone else would have thrown out. She would have to return the faded green sweater she had borrowed from him so long ago that he had probably forgotten it had ever been his. It had been her favorite, but she could not bear to put it on anymore.

Maggie reached her own street and passed a middle-aged couple cleaning up after a garage sale. More to procrastinate than to hunt for bargains, she browsed through some books and old vinyl albums stacked in boxes on a card table. She found a copy of Brian's favorite Moody Blues album and had to turn away. At the next table were several folded baby blankets in pink and yellow gingham. She moved on down the aisle and had nearly summoned up enough fortitude to go home when a glimpse of faded patchwork brought her to a stop.

It was an old quilt draped indifferently over a table. Intrigued, Maggie studied the patterns as best as she could without moving the tagged glassware displayed upon it. The two quilts she had made in her lifetime—one a Girl Scout badge requirement, the other a gift for her sister's firstborn—by no means made her an expert on quilts, but she knew at once that this quilt was unique, a sampler of many rows of different, unfamiliar blocks. The Courtyard Quilters would probably be able to identify each pattern easily—if they could see the pieces clearly enough through the layers of dirt.

"How much is this?" she called to the woman running the garage sale.

"That?" The woman dusted off her hands and drew closer. "You mean the quilt?"

"Yes, please. Is it for sale?"

The woman looked dubious. "We were just using it to hide an ugly table. I guess I'll take five bucks for it."

Maggie reached into her purse. "Are you sure?"

"Are you?" the woman countered. "Don't you want to take a better look at it first? It's not in very good shape."

Maggie agreed, though she had already decided to take the quilt home. They carefully moved the glassware and lifted the quilt from the table. The woman held it up so that Maggie could examine it. It was filthy; a good shake flung up a cloud of dust but left the surface as grimy as before. The woman apologized for its condition and explained that it had been kept in the garage since they moved to the neighborhood twenty-six years earlier. Her mother-in-law had bought it at an estate auction, and when she tired of it, she gave it to her son to keep dog hair off the car seats when he took his German shepherds to the park. Still, it was free of holes, tears, and stains, and the geometric patterns of the blocks were striking.

Maggie paid the woman, folded the quilt gently, and carried it home. There she moved the coffee table aside, spread the quilt on the living room carpet, and studied it. All one hundred of the two-color blocks were unique, and each had been pieced or appliquéd from a different print fabric and a plain background fabric that might have been white once, but had discolored with age and neglect. Along one edge, embroidered in thread that had faded to pale brown barely distinguishable from the background cloth, were the words "Harriet Findley Birch. Lowell, Mass. to Salem, Ore. 1854."

The discovery astounded her. How had a beautiful 133-year-old quilt ended up as a tablecloth at a garage sale?

The next morning she took the quilt to Ocean View Hills, and on her first break, she hurried to the recreation room to show it to the Courtyard Quilters. They were as excited and amazed as she had anticipated. "This is a remarkable find," said Mrs. Stonebridge, bending over to examine a block composed of sixteen tiny triangles. "What an impressive assortment of fabrics, and what care she must have given to every stitch for the quilt to have held up so well through the years."

"This is a genuine treasure," exclaimed Mrs. Blum. "Here's a LeMoyne Star block, here's a Chimney Sweep. . . . Hmm. Here's one I've never seen."

The other Courtyard Quilters drew closer for a better look, but no one recognized the pattern.

"I wonder who Harriet Findley Birch was," said Mrs. Stonebridge. "She had an excellent sense of proportion and contrast."

The other quilters agreed, and one added, "Maybe if you found out more about the quilt, you could find out more about her. Or vice versa."

"And of course you must find out how to care for such a precious antique," said Mrs. Stonebridge. "Well, my dear, it seems you have yourself a research project, just in time for the weekend."

On Saturday Maggie went to the Cal State Sacramento library to search for books on preserving antique quilts. She found a few books of patterns and others with old black-and-white photos of traditional quilts, but none with the information she sought. A librarian suggested she contact a professor in the art department, so she made an appointment the next day during her lunch hour. After viewing the quilt, the professor put her in touch with a friend, a museum curator in San Francisco named Grace Daniels. Maggie had to take a day off work to meet with her, but the ninety-mile drive from Sacramento was well worth it. The curator confirmed that the quilt was indeed a rare and unusual find. Grace offered to clean it properly for Maggie in exchange for permission to allow the museum's photographer to take a photo for their archives and for information about the quilt's provenance.

Maggie agreed, and the next day she returned to the home where the garage sale had taken place. The woman was surprised to see her again, but invited her inside to talk about the quilt. She called her mother-in-law, but all she remembered was that she had bought it at an estate sale run by an auction house in Bend, Oregon, about 130 miles southeast of Salem.

Maggie returned to the library and searched microfiche versions of all the phone books for the state of Oregon. She listed every Findley and Birch she could find, beginning with the Salem area, then Bend, and then working outward. It was slow, painstaking work that consumed several weekends while she waited for Grace Daniels to finish tending to the quilt.

Starting at the top of her list, she phoned the Findleys and Birches and asked if they knew of a Harriet Findley Birch, a quilter originally from Lowell, Massachusetts. Most said they had never heard of her; a few mentioned other Harriets much too young to be the one Maggie sought. One man said he did not know any Harriets, but he knew several Harrys she could call.

"Why would anyone think information about a Harry Birch would be useful?" Maggie asked the Courtyard Quilters one day when she found time to run down to the recreation room to update them on her progress—or lack thereof. "This is impossible. I should have known I wouldn't turn up anything."

"You can't give up now," protested Mrs. Blum. "Not after piquing our curiosity. Our old hearts can't take it."

"Don't play the 'We're so fragile, have pity on us' card on me," Maggie teased. "I saw you doing the polka in the library with Mr. Maniceaux not two weeks ago."

"Oh." A faint pink flush rose in Mrs. Blum's cheeks. "You saw that, did you?"

"Don't abandon your project so soon," urged Mrs. Stonebridge. "Someone on that list might be a descendant of Harriet Findley Birch. You'll never know if you don't call."

Maggie feared that it would be a waste of time, but she promised the Courtyard Quilters she would consider it.

A week later, curiosity and a sense of obligation to the Courtyard Quilters as well as the museum curator compelled her to resume her calls. Two-thirds of the way through the names and numbers she had collected, she reached a man who said that his great-grandmother's name was Harriet Findley Birch. "When I was a kid," he said, "my grandmother took me to see Harriet Findley Birch's grave, not far from our original family homestead in Salem. It's a tradition in our family, a pilgrimage we make when we're old enough to appreciate her."

Thrilled, Maggie told the man about the quilt she had found and asked him to send whatever information she could about his great-grandmother. He agreed, but the information Maggie received in the mail a week later was disappointingly scanty. Harriet Findley was born in 1830 or 1831 in rural Massachusetts. She married Franklin Birch in 1850 and traveled west along the Oregon Trail sometime after that. She had six children, only two of whom survived to adulthood.

The next week Maggie returned to the museum. The quilt had been so beautifully restored she almost did not recognize it. Her information about the quilt's provenance seemed hopelessly inadequate compensation for Grace Daniels's work, but the curator brushed off Maggie's apologies. She had made a few discoveries of her own after contacting a colleague at the New England Quilt Museum in Lowell, Massachusetts.

The Lowell curator had not heard of the Harriet Findley Birch quilt, but she had posed an interesting theory. The more than one hundred unique fabrics in the quilt suggested that Harriet had ready access to a wide variety of cottons. Though she could have saved scraps for years or traded with friends, it was also possible that she had worked in one of Lowell's cotton mills before her marriage. A mill girl could have collected scraps off the floor that otherwise would have been swept up and discarded, and before long acquired more than enough for a quilt. Grace's colleague was not convinced that Harriet had been a mill girl, however, because existing diaries of mill girls from Harriet's era rarely mentioned quilting as a pleasurable pastime. Instead these young women new to the excitement of the city spent their precious off hours enjoying lectures, exhibitions, and other cultural events outside of the boardinghouses where they lived.

"I don't suppose we'll ever know for certain," said Grace.

Maggie reluctantly agreed they were unlikely to learn more.

She took the precious quilt home and draped it over her bed. She sat in a chair nearby and gazed at it lovingly, but with an ache of regret. The more she learned how rare and precious the quilt was, the more she realized she had no right to keep it.

But the extra print the museum's photographer had made for her was not enough.

She bought colored pencils, graph paper, and a ruler and began drafting the beloved little blocks, imagining Harriet Findley Birch sketching the originals so long ago. Had she worked on her quilt on the front porch of her boardinghouse, enjoying the fresh air after a fourteen-hour shift in the stifling mill? Had she sewn in her parents' front parlor, envying the confident, independent mill girls who passed by her window on their way to work?

One Saturday morning after she had drawn ten blocks, Maggie visited a quilt store the Courtyard Quilters had recommended, the Goose Tracks Quilt Shop, to purchase fabric and sewing tools. She felt too shy to ask any of the busy customers or saleswomen for help, so she wandered through the aisles scanning the bolts for fabrics that looked like Harriet's. She chose ten, carried them awkwardly to the cutting table, and asked the shop owner to cut her enough of each one to make a six-inch quilt block.

"Okay," the woman said carefully, clearly recognizing her as a novice but not wishing to discourage her. "Do you think a quarter of a yard will do? An eighth?"

Maggie had no idea, but just in case, she asked for quarter- yard cuts.

"We have fat quarters over there if you're interested," the woman said, gesturing with her scissors toward stacked rows of baskets full of rolled bundles of fabric. "What are you making?"

"A sampler."

"Bring some of your finished blocks along next time. I'd love to see them."

Flattered, Maggie agreed, but her quilting skills were so rusty she wasn't sure she wanted to show her handiwork to anyone. Fortunately, when she told the Courtyard Quilters about her project, they eagerly offered her a refresher course in the art of quilting by hand. With their assistance, she relearned how to make a precise running stitch, how to appliqué, how to sew perfectly smooth curves, and how to set pieces into an angle. Breaks and lunch hours she usually passed on her own she now spent in the company of the Courtyard Quilters. By the time she finished making her eighth block, she had earned a chair of her own among the circle of quilters.

A few weeks after her first visit to the Goose Tracks Quilt Shop, when Maggie had completed ten blocks and had sketched the second row of ten, she returned for more fabric. This time she knew exactly what she needed and chose from the baskets of fat quarters with confidence. The shop owner recognized her and asked how her sampler was progressing. Maggie placed the ten little blocks on the counter, her pride in her work abruptly vanishing as other customers gathered around to look. "I'm just a beginner," she apologized, fighting the urge to sweep the blocks back into her purse. To her surprise, the other quilters admired her work and insisted they never would have guessed she was a beginner.

"What do you call this pattern?" asked one of the women, indicating a five-pointed star.

"I don't know," said Maggie. "I'm copying blocks I found in an antique quilt."

With prompting from the quilters, the whole story of Harriet Findley Birch's quilt came out. The women marveled at Maggie's lucky find and begged to be allowed to see Harriet's quilt for themselves, so Maggie agreed to meet them at the shop the following Saturday.

In the interim, she completed five more blocks and sketched a dozen more in anticipation of her return to the quilt shop. The women she had spoken to the previous week must have told their friends, because more than twice the number of people she had expected were there, eager to admire Harriet Findley Birch's masterpiece. After seeing the original version, several of the quilters told Maggie that they respected her courage for taking on such a daunting project, which would surely take years to complete. Until that moment, Maggie had not thought of how much time she would need to invest in her replica. She simply wanted one she could keep.

Harriet's quilt began to consume more and more of Maggie's life. She sketched blocks in the morning before leaving for Ocean View Hills. She sewed by hand with the Courtyard Quilters on her lunch hour. After work she made templates, or read books about the mill girls of Lowell, or tracked down leads at the library, longing to know more of Harriet Findley Birch's story. Her work friends complained that they never saw her anymore, so she made time for them when she could. They did not understand her new fascination and tentatively suggested she start dating again. "I don't have time," she told them.

And then came a day she had long dreaded: the day she finished sketching the one hundredth sampler block.

She called the woman from the garage sale and arranged to meet her. She carefully typed up everything she had learned about the quilt, including her unconfirmed theories about the life of Harriet Findley Birch. The woman's eyes lit up when she saw the folded bundle in Maggie's arms. "I was hoping you would bring it by to show me after you restored it," she exclaimed, holding her front door open and ushering Maggie inside.

"I didn't bring it just to show you," said Maggie. "It's worth much more than I paid for it and I think in all fairness I should return it to you. Or, if you're willing, I would be very grateful if you would allow me to keep the quilt and pay you the difference."

"Don't be silly," said the woman. "It sat in my garage for all those years and I did nothing with it. Thank goodness you rescued it before it was nothing more than a rag."

"But . . ." Maggie hesitated. "You could probably sell it for much more than what I paid you."

"Well, certainly, *now*. Thanks to you. You're a sweet girl, but you don't owe me anything for this quilt. You bought it fair and square, and if you decide to sell it for a profit, then more power to you."

Grateful, Maggie told the woman everything she had learned about the quilt and felt herself at ease for the first time in months. But the feeling did not last. The next day she phoned Jason Birch and offered the quilt to him, the only descendant of Harriet Findley Birch she had been able to locate.

"That would be awesome," Jason Birch replied. "I'd love to have that quilt."

"Okay," said Maggie, heart sinking. "Should I send it to you, or would you prefer to pick it up? I would hate to risk losing it in the mail—my heart nearly stops just thinking about it. But if the drive is too inconvenient, I could insure the package for a lot of money to encourage them to keep track of it."

"When you put it like that . . ." Jason hesitated. "I should at least reimburse you for your expenses."

"I bought it for five dollars at a garage sale."

"What? Five bucks? In that case, keep it."

Maggie was tempted to thank him and hang up, but she couldn't. She could not let him turn down her offer because he believed the quilt was an old rag. "I had the quilt cleaned by an expert and I know it's worth much more than what I paid for it. I could have it appraised if you like."

"No. You know what? It's not like my family *lost* Harriet's quilt. One of us chose to sell it, and that choice has consequences. You should keep it. It's obviously important to you. I'll make you a deal: You keep the quilt, but let me know anything you learn about my great-grandmother."

"I'll do that," Maggie promised, grateful.

Now that Harriet Findley Birch's quilt was truly hers, the original impetus for sewing her replica was gone, but Maggie enjoyed her project too much to abandon it. Every week she stitched a few more blocks; every Saturday she met with the regulars at the quilt shop to show off her progress. A few of them asked whether she'd mind if they tried their hand at a few of the patterns. Flattered, Maggie agreed to share her drawings with them. She had completed eighty-four of the blocks and had already begun sewing them into rows.

A year and a half after discovering Harriet's quilt at the garage sale, Maggie completed her quilt top. During her next lunch hour, she layered and basted it on the Ping-Pong table in the Ocean View Hills recreation room. Many of the residents gathered around to admire her work while the Courtyard Quilters threaded needles and helped her baste the top, batting, and backing together. Their enjoyment salvaged what had otherwise been an unpleasant day. At the morning staff meeting, the director informed them that their parent company had sold them off to an HMO, one with a reputation for slashing budgets and cutting staff. Maggie had an excellent record and the faith of her supervisors, but those accomplishments suddenly seemed inconsequential.

When new management took over a few months later, Maggie kept her job, but ten of her coworkers, including her direct supervisor, were laid off. Maggie was shaken enough to consider canceling her long-anticipated vacation to Lowell, Massachusetts, to research Harriet Findley Birch's life, but she had already purchased her airline tickets and people were expecting her. Postponing her trip might help prove her commitment to her job at a critical hour, but with Ocean View Hills in such disarray, the ideal time for a vacation might never come.

"Go," Mrs. Stonebridge commanded. "You've been wanting to do this for so long. You'll regret it later if you cancel your plans."

"We won't let them fire you while you're gone," promised Mrs. Blum. When the other quilters looked at her in exasperation, she quickly added, "Not that you're in any danger. That's just silly."

It didn't seem silly to Maggie, but finally she realized she could not cancel a trip that had been so many months in the planning. In Massachusetts, she spent a week admiring the fall foliage, exploring the local quilt shops, and sharing Harriet's quilt with the curator of the New England Quilt Museum. The curator in turn introduced Maggie to local historians and a professor who had extensively researched the history of the cotton mills. He was able to identify more than twenty of the cotton prints in Harriet's quilt as fabrics made in the early nineteenth century by the Merrimack Manufacturing Company, and he promised to see what else he could find in his university's extensive historical archives.

The visit was over far too soon, but Maggie returned home determined to complete her own quilt. The Courtyard Quilters had identified many of the traditional patterns for her, but there were many others none of them had ever seen, nor could find in any quilt pattern reference book. Maggie invented names of her own, inspired by Harriet's imagined life—Oregon Trail, Rocky Road to Salem, Mill Girls, Lowell Crossroads, Franklin's Choice.

On the same day Maggie finished sewing the binding on her quilt, the staff of Ocean View Hills were offered the opportunity to accept a ten percent pay cut or a pink slip. With great misgivings, Maggie chose the pay cut. She loved her job but wondered how much longer she would be able to keep it.

She forgot her worries for a time on Saturday, when she displayed her completed quilt at the Goose Tracks Quilt Shop. Her new friends were there, as well as many other quilters who had heard through the grapevine that she might bring the finished quilt that day. They admired and praised her work, and took photos—not only of the quilt, but of Maggie posed beside the quilt, and of themselves with Maggie in front of the quilt. Several encouraged her to enter it in a quilt show, but Maggie thought of how far her quilting skills had come since she began the quilt and shuddered to think what a judge might say about her first blocks.

After the group broke up, Lois, the quilt shop owner, came over for a closer look. "It's lovely," she said. "What are you going to call it?"

"My Journey with Harriet," said Maggie. "Do you think that's all right?"

"I think it's perfect, but it doesn't matter what I think. It's your quilt." Lois bent forward to study one of the blocks more closely. "I was wondering if you would be interested in teaching a class here in the shop. So many of my customers have admired your quilt. I'm sure they'd want you to show them how you did it."

"I've never taught quilting," said Maggie. "I'm not even a very experienced quilter. I'm just a motivated beginner."

Lois shrugged. "I don't care if you just started quilting last week. If you can make a quilt like this, you have something to share. I'll pay you, of course."

Maggie thought of her recent pay cut, summoned up her courage, and agreed.

Almost immediately, she wished she had not. What if no one signed up for the class? What if the students mocked her graph paper sketches and cardstock templates? But she needed the extra money, and she understood completely the desire other quilters might have to re-create Harriet's quilt for themselves. If they wanted her help, she couldn't ignore them.

In the month leading up to her first class, Maggie redrafted some of the blocks and designed templates. She wrote lesson plans and made new versions of the first five blocks she planned to teach, this time using popular jewel tones that she thought would appeal more to her students. If she had any. Lois said that the classroom held a maximum of twenty students, but a typical class at the shop enrolled half that number. Maggie fervently hoped for at least five. She would not break even, but at least the classroom would not be completely empty.

On the evening of her first class, Maggie drove to the Goose Tracks Quilt Shop and found the parking lot full. Lois met her at the door, shaking her head. "I warned people to sign up early, but no one ever believes me. The waiting list is already twelve deep, so if someone doesn't show up, let me know right away, okay?"

Struck speechless, Maggie nodded and made her way through the store with her box of quilts, blocks, and handouts. Twenty students awaited her in the classroom. They murmured with expectation as she went to the front and unpacked her box of supplies. She started class by displaying Harriet Findley Birch's quilt and was stunned when the students burst into applause. As she explained the general structure of the course and took in their eager nods, a glow of warmth began to melt away her fears. She was not alone in her admiration for Harriet Findley Birch's magnificent creation. Just like the Courtyard Quilters, the women gathered here felt the same way.

With each week, she felt more assured and confident in front of the classroom. Each week she demonstrated several blocks, which her students began in class and completed at home. When the course ended, her students begged Lois to create an advanced class especially for them, so Maggie agreed to teach them some of Harriet's more difficult patterns while repeating her first course for beginners. After those courses concluded, she added Harriet's Journey III to her schedule. The local quilt guild invited her to speak about the quilt, and she did so, not realizing until they handed her a check afterward that they had intended to pay her. The guild must have enjoyed her presentation, because they recommended her to another guild, who recommend her to another, until it seemed that every quilt guild within two hundred miles of Sacramento had sent her an eager invitation.

Not long after her first class of students began bringing their own completed Harriet's Journey quilts to show-and-tell for her newest students, Maggie received a letter from the history professor she had met during her visit to Lowell two years before. His search to find a record of Harriet Findley Birch's employment at the Merrimack Manufacturing Company had failed, but he had discovered convincing evidence in the *Lowell Offering,* a literary journal for the mill workers. In 1849, a mill girl had contributed a story about a young woman torn between the independence she enjoyed as a mill worker and her love for a handsome suitor. The professor had enclosed a copy.

The story told of a young woman, probably a thinly disguised version of the author, who lamented, "Though earning her own living was reckoned as a suitable accomplishment for a young maid, few would consider it appropriate for a wife to spend her hours thus employed. Indeed, Hannah's own dear William had often declared that no bride of his should weave or spin in the mills when she could be better occupied cooking his breakfast. And yet Hannah loved him, and would cleave to his side, though he would summon her from the friends and life that had become so dear and bid her go with him to distant lands far from home and family."

The author was Harriet Findley.

At last, Maggie filled in the missing pieces of Harriet's story. She had worked as a mill girl until marrying Franklin. When her husband decided to move west, Harriet, the obedient wife, had agreed, though her heart broke to part from her dear friends, many of whom still worked at the mills. Knowing she would no longer be able to trade patterns with her acquaintances, she stitched her masterwork as a record of all the blocks they knew, so that no matter how far west she traveled, she would have a wonderful variety of patterns to choose from when making quilts for her growing family. Scraps she had saved from her own days in the mill intermingled with pieces shared by beloved friends and relatives. She could not have sewn on the seat of a jolting wagon as they crossed the country on the Oregon Trail, so she had likely pieced the blocks in Lowell and quilted the top in Salem. Into the quilt she had stitched her grief, her hopes, her faithfulness, and her memories.

That was the story Maggie told in her classes and lectures, admitting that it was only one possible version of Harriet's life. Her students did not seem to mind the ambiguity, but they often spoke of finding Harriet's home in Lowell and of seeking out the indisputable truth. Wouldn't it be wonderful, they sighed, if they could find an old, sepia-toned photograph of Harriet? A diary in which she had confided her reasons for making the quilt? Letters she had written home to Lowell from the Oregon Trail?

Maggie, too, longed to know the truth, but she was grateful for every cherished scrap of information she had collected over the years and would not demand more.

When Maggie had saved enough money, she bought a new car, choosing a sensible model with a large trunk and excellent gas mileage because of her expanding schedule of speaking engagements. Her first road trip took her north to Salem, Oregon, to Harriet's final resting place. She planted flowers by the headstone, and on the soft green grass nearby, she spread out Harriet's quilt and the four duplicates she had made. She spoke at a nearby quilt guild that evening, spent the night in a bed-and- breakfast run by the guild treasurer, and drove home in the morning after meeting Jason Birch for breakfast. She wished she could have stayed longer, but Ocean View Hills had cut her vacation from two weeks a year to three days, a reduction that would have been considered unfair and damaging to employee morale when she had first begun working there.

Maggie taught nearly every evening at the quilt shop and twice on Saturdays. She was more grateful than ever for the extra income after a second round of budget cuts trimmed the staff at Ocean View Hills by another four employees and a promised cost of living increase fell through. One evening, Maggie tentatively approached Lois about increasing the fee for her classes to cover printing expenses. "We could do that," said Lois, "but surely you don't plan to give away your patterns forever."

The day her pattern book, *My Journey with Harriet: The 1854 Harriet Findley Birch Quilt,* was published, Lois threw a party in Maggie's honor at the quilt shop. Her sister, brother-in-law, and two nieces flew in from Phoenix, and the curator of the New England Quilt Museum sent her flowers. The most able of the Courtyard Quilters attended, and Maggie was finally able to reveal the secret she had been keeping since the day she had begun her manuscript: The dedication of her book read, "To the Courtyard Quilters, who welcomed me into their circle, offered me their guidance, and shared my journey with Harriet from the very first step."

Lois had sold out of copies that night, and the book's brisk sales at Goose Tracks were mirrored in quilt shops across the country. Second and third printings swiftly followed. Maggie taught workshops at quilt guild meetings and lectured at national quilt shows. She moved across town to a larger house with a spacious formal dining room she converted to a quilt studio. Childhood friends with whom she had fallen out of touch contacted her after reading articles about her in their local newspapers. A former teacher phoned after spotting *My Journey with Harriet* featured in a book club supplement of his Sunday newspaper.

But her success was tempered with sorrow. Her beloved circle of quilters, whose numbers and composition had always fluctuated over time according to what Mrs. Stonebridge euphemistically called "natural attrition," began to lose members faster than they could welcome newcomers as concerned family members responded to staffing cuts by transferring their mothers and grandmothers to other facilities. Mrs. Stonebridge's son wanted to move her closer to his home, but she told him she would never leave Ocean View Hills as long as at least one friend remained. Maggie wanted to believe that would be a very long time, but each day her hopes diminished.

❧

When *My Journey with Harriet* went into its twelfth printing seven years later, Harriet wanted to create a revised and updated edition, but all her editor wanted to know was when she intended to write something new. "When I find another quilt like Harriet's," replied Maggie, hoping that would end the discussion.

"How hard have you looked?"

"Not very," Maggie admitted, but she promised to try harder if her editor would agree to consider a new edition. It was an unsatisfactory compromise, so Maggie hung up with the excuse that she had to get to her day job.

She arrived at Ocean View Hills to find the staff fairly roiling with uneasiness. Rumors had circulated for weeks that their HMO was going to consolidate with another health care corporation, and no one in management knew what that would mean for their jobs and their residents. Though Maggie could not help feeling as unsettled as the rest of her colleagues, she reassured herself that her thirteen years of exemplary employment had to count for something.

The blow came at an emergency meeting of all senior management. Ocean View Hills was not going to merge with anyone. The other health care corporation was going to buy them out and shut them down.

Maggie did not understand the reasoning behind their decision. The director, visibly shaken by his own pending unemployment, provided a lengthy explanation about profitability and tax liabilities, but Maggie was too upset to follow the corporate finance intricacies. She struggled to absorb the truth that in six months, her beloved residents would be scattered around northern California wherever their families could find appropriate care for them, and she would be out of a job.

"At least you have your quilt book and your teaching," a coworker grumbled to Maggie in the lounge where the senior staff had gathered to collect their wits before returning to work. They had been sworn to secrecy until a letter could be drafted to the other employees and the residents' families, although Maggie doubted any of them could keep silent for long. The other employees knew about the meeting, and as far as Maggie was concerned, it would be cruel to mislead them.

"I can't live off that income," said Maggie. Worse, she had received only vague assurances from the director that their pensions would be protected. She also had a modest 401(K), but although she was only thirty-eight, she had hoped to take early retirement in ten years and devote herself to quilting and writing full time. That dream, she knew, was over.

In a move that received criticism from some of the residents, the director informed their families first and allowed the family members to tell their parents and grandparents as they deemed best. Some of the Courtyard Quilters felt that Maggie had betrayed them by not telling them about the closure as soon as she knew. "I wanted to tell you, but I couldn't," Maggie said. "The director forbade it."

"What do you care what he says?" glowered one of the quilters. "What's he going to do, fire you?"

"Don't blame Maggie," said Mrs. Stonebridge, kindly but in a manner that demanded cooperation. "She has professional responsibilities that take priority over ties of friendship. What if one of the patients from C Wing overheard us talking before their children had an opportunity to prepare them? Consider how that might upset the poor dears."

C Wing was where the patients with dementia and other serious chronic medical conditions resided. Thinking of them, the quilters relented. Some even murmured apologies, which Maggie accepted although she did not think she deserved them. She had wanted to warn them of what was coming, but she could not afford to give the director any reason to fire her.

"I can't bear to think our circle of quilters will be split up," lamented Mrs. Blum.

"We can try to stay together," said another. "Maybe our children could find a place with room for all of us."

One quilter shook her head. "Not me. My daughter has already decided that I'm moving in with them. The girls will share a bedroom and I'll get the extra." She paused. "It will be wonderful to see more of the kids, but I'll miss my girlfriends."

"We will have to keep in touch as best we can," said Mrs. Stonebridge. "With any luck, two or three of us will end up in the same place."

The Courtyard Quilters nodded, believing their longtime leader by force of habit, or, Maggie thought, as an act of faith.

That evening at the quilt shop, she taught her class so woodenly that Lois thought she was ill and offered to take over. Maggie briefly told her what the real problem was and forced herself to shake off her worries and get through the evening. She could not afford to lose this job, too.

As she packed up her teaching materials, Lois entered the classroom with a magazine in her hand. "I'm tempted not to show you this," she said, opening the magazine as she passed it to Maggie. "I would hate to lose you."

Maggie read the ad Lois had circled in red pen. "A quilt camp," she said. "That sounds like heaven. But it's all the way across the country."

"You could come back to visit. And teach for me."

"Don't worry," said Maggie, hugging her friend. "I couldn't leave California."

"When you see Elm Creek Manor, you'll change your mind."

Maggie doubted it, but she tossed the magazine in the box with her class samples and took it home.

The next morning, she scanned the Help Wanted ads over breakfast. There were several listings for jobs in geriatric care, but none comparable to her current position in either authority or compensation. After a tense day at work, where she comforted more than one tearful junior colleague in the staff lounge and promised to write letters of recommendation for several more, she found Lois's magazine in her quilt studio and gave the ad for the quilt camp teaching position a second look. After supper, she went online and Googled Elm Creek Quilts. She perused the camp's own website thoroughly, but also read evaluations and reviews former campers had posted on quilting bulletin boards and blogs. The comments were unanimous in their praise. Elm Creek Quilt Camp sounded like a wonderful place, though Maggie was not sure how she would fare in winter weather after spending her entire life in California.

With nothing to lose, Maggie put together the portfolio the Elm Creek Quilters had requested and sent it off, hoping for the best.

She also sent out résumés to every retirement community within a hundred miles, but received only three requests for interviews. As the weeks passed, the residents of Ocean View Hills began to disperse as children and grandchildren found them new homes. Going to work became lonelier and more dispiriting as one by one the Courtyard Quilters departed and her closest friends among the staff left for new jobs or retired at a fraction of their pensions.

A month after Maggie submitted her portfolio, Sarah McClure from Elm Creek Quilt Camp called with an invitation to come to Pennsylvania for an interview. As a test of her skills and creativity, Maggie was also instructed to design an original quilt block that could be used as a logo for Elm Creek Quilts. She was so thrilled to have an interview that she would have agreed to anything. She adapted two of Harriet Findley Birch's patterns, a leaf design and a star, and overlaid them to create a new block. Imitating Harriet's flowing script, in one corner of the block she embroidered "Elm Creek Quilts" and in another, "Waterford, Penn."

Throughout the years, Harriet had often felt like a guardian spirit to Maggie, lingering just beyond her vision, offering wisdom, encouragement, sympathy, understanding. Maggie wondered what Harriet would make of her pinning all her hopes on a job on the other side of the country. Perhaps more than anyone else, she would have understood.

❧

The plane touched down at the Pittsburgh airport after a bumpy descent above meandering rivers. Maggie rented a car and drove the rest of the way to Waterford on a winding journey through the Appalachians, whose lush, forested hills cradled patchwork farms in valleys below.

From the highway, the town of Waterford appeared to be everything Lois had warned—remote, rural, and overpopulated by college students. Beyond the outskirts of town, Maggie drove down a rough gravel road through a leafy wood, taking the left fork that led to the rear parking lot as Lois had recommended. The narrow road wound through the trees and emerged into a sunlit apple orchard through which several women strolled. The car passed a red barn, climbed a low hill, and crossed a bridge over a creek. Then the manor came into view—three stories of gray stone and dark wood, its unexpected elegance enhanced by the rambling, natural beauty of its surroundings.

She parked the car, leaving her messenger bag in the trunk with her suitcase. She considered going around to the front entrance, but when three other women entered through the rear door without knocking, she followed them inside. She peered through the first open doorway she passed and found herself in the kitchen. Two women bustled from stove to countertop to refrigerator, too intent on their work to look up. "Summer, would you help me with this?" one of the women asked as she opened the oven to reveal a large roasting pan.

"You're on your own," replied the younger, auburn-haired woman. "I don't eat anything with a face, and I don't help cook it, either. I could have put together a very plausible tofu chicken if you had let me."

The first woman made retching sounds, and Maggie left, reluctant to disturb them. She continued down the hall until she arrived at a foyer with a black marble floor, tall double doors on the far wall, and a ceiling open to the third story. Women of all ages climbed a grand oak staircase that led to balconies on the second and third floor, or passed through a doorway opposite the front entrance. Maggie asked one of the women where she might find Sarah McClure, and was told to try the library on the second floor. At the library, an older woman wearing glasses on a silver chain told her to try the kitchen. Perplexed, Maggie said, "I was just there, and I didn't see anyone but the two cooks."

The woman laughed. "Two cooks? Oh, that's rich. Well, rather than send you on a mission to find Sarah, may I help you instead?"

"My name is Maggie Flynn. I'm here for a job interview, but it's not until tomorrow. Sarah McClure said I should spend the night here."

"Maggie, of course. I should have recognized you from the photo in your book." The older woman shook Maggie's hand briskly. "I'm Sylvia Compson. Have you had a chance to look around?"

Except for getting lost on her way to the library, Maggie had not, so Sylvia proposed a tour. She showed Maggie what seemed like the entire estate, from the library where most of the camp business was conducted to the hallways lined with bedrooms for the campers. Back on the first floor, Sylvia led Maggie into a grand ballroom that had been separated into several classrooms by tall, movable partitions. Voices and sewing machines created a happy buzz, and when Maggie remarked that she wondered how the students avoided being distracted by the sounds from adjacent classrooms, Sylvia said, "Distracted? Oh, they enjoy eavesdropping on one another. We consider it part of the entertainment."

From the converted ballroom they went to the banquet hall, where four young men, three of them surely no more than teenagers, were setting ten round tables for supper. "Michael, don't forget the soup bowls," Sylvia called out. "And close the curtains partway so it's more difficult to see the food."

The eldest looked up from his work and nodded solemnly. "Don't worry. I'll take care of it." Another boy, blond and handsome, snorted and shook his head.

"They're brothers. The younger one has trouble accepting that the elder is in charge," Sylvia confided as she led Maggie from the room. "The other two are new this summer. One is the son of the neighbor of one of our instructors, and the other is the son of one of our instructor's colleagues. They're working off a rather large debt to another Elm Creek Quilter. They're quite a pair of juvenile delinquents, or so I've been told, but Michael and Todd will keep them in line."

Maggie nodded, trying to sort out the tangled relationships. She wondered how much she would be expected to remember for the interview the next day. And why would Sylvia not want the campers to see the food on their plates? Lois, who had attended the camp twice, had praised the cooking. Her only complaint was that she had gained two pounds from the rich desserts.

The tour turned to the grounds of the manor, which Sylvia seemed to believe were just as essential to the camp as the classrooms and dining facilities. They passed several quilt campers who recognized Maggie, and a few of them asked if she had come to Elm Creek Manor to teach a class. Grateful for the perfect timing of their praise, Maggie told them she had come for an interview, but she would be thrilled to become an Elm Creek Quilter.

By the end of the day, she realized that was true—and not only because she desperately needed the work. She longed to be a part of the world these amazing, inspiring women had created. It was a haven in the central Pennsylvania countryside, a place of respite and healing. If they offered her a job—whether as teacher or office clerk or scullery maid—she would gratefully sign up for a lifetime term.

Sylvia left her to explore the estate on her own until supper, when she joined the staff and campers in the banquet hall for a delicious meal of roast chicken, sautéed vegetables, and an amazing spicy chickpea soup served with warm flatbread. Five women introduced themselves as the other Elm Creek Quilters and made her feel as welcome as if they had known her for years. After supper, she toured the north gardens with Sarah McClure, the woman she had mistaken for the head chef earlier that day. Sarah told her about the manor's history, from its founding in 1858 by Sylvia's great-grandparents and its role as a station on the Underground Railroad to its rebirth as a retreat for quilters. When Sarah mentioned that Sylvia's ancestors had left behind quilts and a journal from the manor's earliest days, Maggie thought of how long she had yearned to discover a similar record of Harriet Findley Birch's life. She hoped that Sylvia treasured these gifts and wished she could be invited to see them.

As twilight approached, Sarah escorted her back to the manor for the evening program, a fashion show of the campers' quilted clothing. Afterward, Sarah showed her to a charming room on the third floor with a private sitting area and a sampler quilt on the bed, and bade her good night.

Weary from travel and the extended effort to impress, Maggie slept soundly.

The next morning after breakfast, she repacked her suitcase and dressed in her new tan slacks, a crisp white blouse, and a blue blazer, hoping that they would not mark her down for not wearing a suit. Her only suit, a black, somber ensemble she wore to funerals and board meetings, summoned forth too many memories of unhappy occasions to be worn on a day when she needed every ounce of confidence.

Carrying her small suitcase and messenger bag, she went downstairs to the first floor to find the parlor where she was supposed to officially meet the Elm Creek Quilters. On her way across the foyer, she heard a frustrated sigh drift down to her from somewhere above. She looked up and spotted a white-haired woman seated in an armchair on the second-floor balcony.

"Are you okay?" called Maggie. "What's wrong?"

"Oh, it's nothing. I just can't appliqué a smooth curve to save my life, that's all."

Maggie glanced at her watch and saw that she had a few minutes to spare. "Want me to take a look?"

When the older woman gratefully agreed, Maggie returned upstairs and demonstrated her variation of the needle-turned appliqué technique. The older woman took a few awkward stitches and shook her head in frustration. "I still don't understand."

Maggie showed her again, but more quickly this time, mindful of the waiting Elm Creek Quilters. Then she apologized and explained that she was late for an appointment.

"That's all right, dear." Behind her pink-tinted glasses, the older woman's blue eyes beamed with satisfaction. "I think I've learned all I need to know."

Maggie hurried back downstairs to the parlor and knocked on the door. Sarah McClure invited her inside, where some of the other Elm Creek Quilters were seated on the far side of a coffee table, across from a single armchair.

"Gwen couldn't make it," said Sarah as Maggie seated herself. "She has a class. But this is really more of a formality, since you've already met everyone."

"Almost everyone," said a pretty blonde Maggie did not recognize. "I had to go home and feed my family last night, so I missed the supper party. I'm Diane."

"Maggie Flynn." Maggie rose to shake Diane's hand, which felt smooth and cool, though Diane squeezed a fraction harder than necessary.

Sarah began with a few perfunctory questions about Maggie's employment history. When Sylvia asked her to tell how she came to publish a book, Maggie told the story of discovering Harriet Findley Birch's quilt and how that one chance encounter had changed her life. At another Elm Creek Quilter's request, Maggie showed them the block she had designed. Everyone complimented her pattern and handiwork—everyone except Diane, who took a page from a folder on her lap and frowned at it. Giving it a surreptitious glance, Maggie recognized the paper as a color copy of a photograph of her original My Journey with Harriet quilt. With a quaking heart she thought of her first few blocks, those first stumbling efforts that had eventually launched her career, and wondered if Diane was marking her mistakes. Surely a missed stitch or two would not be evident in a picture of that resolution.

Then Diane set down the photocopy and tapped two squares with her pen. "I thought your original block looked familiar."

Maggie did not like the emphasis Diane placed on "original block," but she nodded. "I adapted two of Harriet Findley Birch's patterns to create my own. Since I'm best known for documenting her quilt, I thought that would be appropriate. Was I wrong?"

"Your block is fine," the youngest Elm Creek Quilter assured her.

Diane did not look as if she agreed. "I was wondering, too, why you didn't send us any pictures of your other quilts."

Maggie hesitated. "I sent twelve photos."

"Yes, but all twelve are of the same quilt. You haven't made twelve different quilts; you've made twelve versions of the same quilt."

"They aren't exactly the same," said Maggie. "I've used different fabrics, color palettes, and techniques with each variation. Each version was made for a specific purpose." She reached into her messenger bag and pulled out copies of the same photos she had included in her portfolio. "This one, my third Harriet's Journey, was an exercise in contrast and value. The blue and white version I made entirely by machine just to prove to some of my reluctant students that it could be done. I personally prefer hand piecing."

"You do seem capable of adequate handwork," said Diane, "which makes it all the more disappointing that you sold out to the machine mafia."

"I don't understand."

Diane gestured to the photo. "You said it yourself. You prefer one technique, but you pandered to lazy advocates of an easier method to reel in more students, to sell more books."

Taken aback, Maggie replied, "I don't consider it selling out to encourage a quilter to try a project that is more challenging than what she's previously attempted."

"Of course not," said Sylvia briskly. "Does anyone else have a question for our guest?"

Summer glanced at her notes and looked up with a smile for Maggie. "How do you account for your continuing interest in this one quilt? It's not just about the patterns, is it?"

"No," said Maggie. "Although I'm awed by Harriet's sense of geometry, balance, and proportion as well as her technical skills, my fascination has always been with the quilter more than with her creation. Who was she? Why did she make this quilt? Did anyone help her? What did she think about as she sewed? Did she have a good marriage? Was she happy? Was she lonely? Did she regret leaving Massachusetts for the West? There's so much I'll never know about her, but working on this quilt makes me feel closer to her."

Some of the Elm Creek Quilters nodded, encouraging her to continue. "Over the years, I've made several visits to Lowell to try to retrace Harriet's steps. I've found tantalizing clues to her past—a baptismal record, a bill of sale for a plot of land that her father owned, a few other facts relating to her ordinary daily life. But a collection of facts isn't the truth. I think Harriet's truth lies in the story her quilt tells, and that's the story of a woman who was creative, resourceful, and steadfast. I'll never know for certain, and that mystery compels me to make sure she is remembered, not only for her sake, but for all those other women whose sacrifices built this country but whose names never made it into the history books."

Sylvia smiled. "If only we had more time, I have some quilts in my attic I would love to show you. I think you would appreciate them."

Sarah took that as her cue to wrap up the interview, and Maggie was surprised that she was no longer eager for it to end. For all that she had promised Lois she could never leave California, she had seen enough of Elm Creek Quilt Camp to know that she would feel at home there. Aside from Diane, the Elm Creek Quilters had been kind and welcoming. She knew she would enjoy working with them and becoming their friend.

Now she could only hope that the impression she had made over the previous twenty-four hours would be enough to dispel any concerns Diane might raise after she left.

Sarah rose to show her to the door. Maggie shook their hands, even Diane's, and told them she hoped to hear from them soon. She collected her bags and left the parlor to find that someone had arranged a row of folding chairs along the wall just outside the door.

The white-haired woman she had tried to help earlier was in the hallway leading to the west wing. She brightened and seemed about to speak, but Maggie was spent from the interview and did not want to talk. She turned quickly and hurried to the tall double doors that marked the front entrance, though her car was parked around back.

As she stepped out onto the veranda, she saw a younger woman dressed in an interview suit struggling up the stairs with an oversized stroller and two little boys in tow. Maggie could only imagine how Diane would react at the sight of the children, and although this woman was the competition, she was moved to sympathy, knowing what was in store for her.

"Watch out for the blonde," Maggie warned as they passed on the stairs. The young mother paused, but Maggie had a long drive to Pittsburgh ahead of her and a flight to catch, so she hurried on her way.

Chapter Two
Karen

I f Nate had not been too busy to go to the grocery store as he had promised, Karen would not have been forced to load the boys into the car and drive to the store in the rain. If she had not had to endure the boys' nonstop begging for sugar-frosted junk marketed by cartoon characters, she would not have felt entitled to a reward. If she had not been so annoyed at Nate, she would not have tossed the Modern Quilter magazine into the shopping cart on her way to the checkout line, and if she had not bought the magazine, she never would have seen the ad. So, in a way, everything that resulted, all the embarrassment and stress and frustration, was Nate's fault.

If she had not felt guilty about the purchase, she would have learned about the job that same day, but as she unpacked the groceries she imagined her husband's lament at the sight of the magazine. "Think of all the trees that died for those pages," Nate would say. "Don't they have an online version you could read instead?" Nate had cancelled his last newspaper subscription while still in graduate school, and Karen had allowed hers to lapse after they had dated for six months and she realized his anti-newsprint stance was not a passing phase. They had not had a magazine in the house since the subscription to *Parents* they had received as a baby shower gift ran out four months after Ethan was born. If Nate came home and found a magazine in her hands, he might keel over in shock. She could not do that to him, so she hid the magazine in her fabric stash, taking it out only when Nate was at work and the boys were asleep. Those two events coincided only rarely, so it was not until two weeks after purchasing the magazine that she discovered Elm Creek Quilt Camp was hiring.

She postponed telling Nate about the job not only because she would have to admit how she had heard about it, but also because she was not sure she ought to apply. It was not as if she had an abundance of free time. Even with Ethan in nursery school three mornings a week, she still had plenty to do tending to his increasingly active little brother. Her house looked like the before photo in a redecorating makeover, and come to think of it, so did she. She didn't need more work; she needed a month alone at a tropical spa with daily massages and handsome cabana boys to bring her fruity drinks with little paper umbrellas in them while she relaxed on the beach.

But to work at Elm Creek Manor . . . She wistfully remembered the week she had spent at quilt camp a few months before Ethan was born, a time when she had naively considered herself accomplished and capable because her children had not yet taught her otherwise. The week's stay had been a gift from Nate, who had secretly made all the arrangements after she had mentioned that she had been seized by an irresistible urge to make a quilt for her firstborn. Maybe she had been under the influence of the breathtakingly adorable pictures in the clandestine stash of baby magazines she had secreted in her underwear drawer, because none of her friends or family quilted, and she had not grown up with quilts around the house. She had no one to teach her, and she was afraid what would result if she tried on her own. Then she happened across an arts program on cable featuring an interview with a male quilter from the Pacific Northwest whose work was exhibited in galleries across the country. The baby quilt Karen envisioned was nothing like his wild, abstract creations, but she figured that if a man could quilt, so could she.

As she and Nate shopped for the nursery, Karen told him she wished she knew how to quilt without expecting anything more than sympathy. But Nate's understanding of quilting was that it involved reusing scraps of worn fabric that would otherwise end up in a landfill, so he was all for it. He found Elm Creek Quilt Camp on the Internet and surprised her with a week's stay, no doubt pleased to foster her budding environmentalist frugality. Soon after she returned home, however, he learned that quilters need new fabric just as painters need paint and sculptors need clay, and he regarded her steadily increasing stash with concern and resignation as it threatened to outgrow the linen closet and spill into the hallway.

If Karen were more experienced, she might have put her application in the mail immediately, but she had quilted for only five years. She had tried to teach quilting only once, to her best friend, who had eagerly chosen a pattern and purchased fabric but had never actually cut out any pieces. It was a less than exemplary record, one she was certain the other applicants would far surpass. She pictured the Elm Creek Quilters passing her application around a long table, marveling at her hubris before tossing her file into a paper shredder.

That image made her wish she had never seen the ad. If she ever returned to the manor, it would be as a camper, not as an Elm Creek Quilter.

❧

Monday night blurred into Tuesday morning. Lucas woke twice to nurse, and Karen dozed uncomfortably in the rocking chair until he drifted off to sleep. She returned him to his crib and stumbled back to bed, but on the second return trip, she stepped on a Tickle Me Elmo doll, which promptly burst into giggles, waking Ethan. She told him to go back to sleep, but not long after she lay down and pulled the quilt up to her chin, she felt the mattress shake as Ethan crawled into bed between her and Nate. Twice before sunrise Karen was jolted awake by her son's feet in her ribcage, a sensation oddly reminiscent of her pregnancy, though far less entrancing than when he had been on the inside.

In the morning, Nate shut off the alarm clock and muttered something about sleeping in—a lovely idea in theory, but impracticable for the parents of young children. Lucas rose at his regular hour, calling out for milk. Half asleep, Karen brought him into the master bed to nurse as she lay curled protectively around him. She drifted back to sleep stroking his downy blond hair, his sweet baby softness warming her heart, the fragrance of baby shampoo soothing her into slumber. Later she woke to the sound of the shower running. The sliver of the bed Nate had occupied was empty, Ethan was snoring, and Lucas was sitting up in bed, smiling at her. "Poo poo," he announced, and held up his hands. While she slept, he had removed his diaper and fingerpainted the sheets with the contents.

In the summer, the boys' playgroup met at the park every Tuesday and Thursday morning, but on Tuesdays Ethan had a swimming lesson first. "Did you feed the boys?" Karen asked Nate as she raced into the kitchen after a quick shower and a scramble through the unfolded clothes in the laundry basket for something to wear.

"Lucas had cereal and toast."

"What about Ethan?"

"He said he wasn't hungry."

"If he doesn't eat now, he'll want something five minutes before his swimming lesson starts."

Nate shrugged. "I can't force him to eat."

"Did you pack the swim bag?"

"I thought you did it."

Silently, Karen counted to five. Every Monday night she asked him to pack the bag, and every Monday night he agreed. Every Tuesday morning, he assumed she had already taken care of it. Did he think she had squeezed it in between Lucas's midnight and predawn feedings? "Could you please pack the bag so I can grab some breakfast?"

"Sure, honey." He rose and kissed her, coffee mug in hand, and went upstairs. She tracked his footsteps from Ethan's room to the main bath to their room, hastily spooning down a bowl of muesli while standing at the sink. She had just finished when Nate returned with the blue nylon bag and put it on the kitchen table between his plate of toast crusts and Ethan's cereal bowl.

"Did you remember everything?" asked Karen, clearing away the dishes.

"Yep." He gave her a quick kiss. "I have to go. I have student conferences."

"Did you remember the swim cap?"

"Uh huh." Nate took his lunch from the refrigerator and stuffed it into his backpack.

"Towel?"

"Yes."

"Coffee cup?"

He paused. "What?"

"Coffee cup. When you went upstairs, you were carrying a coffee cup."

"Oh. I think I left it on the dresser." He glanced at his watch. "Do you want me to go get it?"

"That's all right. I'll get it."

"Okay. I'll see you later." He went into the living room to say good-bye to the boys, then hurried off with a cheerful wave.

After the door to the garage closed behind him, she tried not to open the bag to make sure he had remembered everything. She hated feeling like she always needed to check his work, but the urge was insistent. Towel, swim cap, and goggles were tucked inside the bag just as Nate had promised, but the swim trunks were old, faded from chlorine, and size 3T. Karen had no idea where Nate had found them, since they should have been packed away in the basement with the other clothes Ethan had outgrown and Lucas could not yet wear. If Ethan managed to squeeze into them at all, the waistband could quite possibly cut off his circulation.

Can't he read a tag? Karen wondered as she hurried upstairs to Ethan's room. *Does he not know his son's size? Didn't he recognize the right pair from last week?*

She took a deep breath and tried to let it go. Nate was in a hurry, students were waiting for him, and how many dads knew anything about their kids' sizes? He had tried to help, and that was what mattered.

She retrieved the coffee cup from the bathroom counter on her way back downstairs, finished packing the swim bag and the diaper bag and the lunch bag for the park later, and called for the boys to come and get ready to leave. Ethan came at once, but Lucas ran away, laughing, and hid by climbing behind the armchair and covering his eyes with his hands.

"We can still see you," his older brother said.

"No see," Lucas insisted.

"And we can hear you. Mom, tell him he's not hiding right."

"Time to go." Karen reached behind the chair and lifted Lucas to his feet. He promptly went limp, forcing her to haul him out into the open. She wrestled the boys from their pajamas into their clothes and cajoled them into holding still while she slathered them in PABA-free sunblock. She had barely finished one of Lucas's arms when he grabbed the pink bottle and flung it behind the piano.

"No pool," said Lucas. "No pool, please?"

"Honey, we have to go to the pool." Karen dropped to her hands and knees and strained to reach the sunblock. "Your brother has a swim lesson."

"No pool. No swim!"

"You don't have to swim," said Ethan reasonably. "Just me."

"I swim. I swim!" Lucas tugged at Karen's T-shirt. "I swim, please?"

"When you're a big boy, you can take lessons, too."

Lucas sent up such a wail of dismay that she had to promise him a treat from the club's vending machines just to get him to calm down. When Ethan protested, she had to assure him that he could buy something, too.

"Treat," said Lucas happily as she buckled him into his carseat.

"I'm going to get Cheetos," said Ethan.

"Cheetos," shouted Lucas. "Cheetos, too!"

Karen muffled a groan. Nate would have a fit. She would have to scour the boys' fingernails clean of all traces of blaze orange cheese residue before he came home from work. What did it say about her that she so quickly resorted to bribing her sons and hiding the evidence from her husband?

"Mom," said Ethan as they pulled into the parking lot of the swim club. "I'm hungry. Can I have my treat now?"

"Treat," echoed Lucas.

"No, honey, we don't have time."

"But I'm starving."

"You should have eaten breakfast."

"Daddy didn't give me anything."

"I'm sorry, sweetie." They were already five minutes late. "You'll have to wait until after your lesson."

Ethan grumbled as she rushed them into the locker room and threw him into his swim gear. To her dismay, the exchange had given Lucas the impression that snack time was imminent. "Chee-tos," he cried plaintively as Karen carried him while she led Ethan from the locker room to the pool. The room smelled of chlorine and wet cement, and Lucas's every wail echoed off the walls. Karen left Ethan with his instructor and hurried Lucas into the waiting room. Catching sight of the vending machine, Lucas struggled in her arms until she had to set him down. He ran across the room and flung himself at the Plexiglas. "Cheetos! Cheetos!"

Three mothers sitting near the tinted glass overlooking the pool broke off their conversation and stared at him, then looked daggers at Karen. Smiling weakly, Karen hurried over and wedged herself between her son and the vending machine. "Lucas, honey. After your brother's lesson. Remember?"

"No! No! Now!"

Bewildered, she picked him up and winced as she avoided his flailing limbs. This was so unlike him, the mellow kid, the one who made her and Nate realize just how challenging Ethan had been. "Honey, calm down. It's okay." She held him close and patted his back as he squirmed in protest. "We talked about this. Remember? We'll have a treat after your brother's lesson— if you're a good boy."

"Cheetos, Mama," he wept. "Please."

It was pitiful to watch. "All right. Okay." She set him down, a howling mass of fury and tears and despair on the blue industrial pile carpet. She dug around in her back pocket for change and came up with a quarter and two dimes. With a sigh of relief she slipped the change into the slot, pressed the buttons, and waited for the snack to dispense—cheerfully narrating each action in a vain attempt to assure Lucas his precious Cheetos were on the way. His misery abated only after she placed the open bag in his hands.

"There." She straightened and rested her hands on her hips. "All better?"

He smiled wanly up at her. Only then did she become aware of the conversation by the window. The other mothers were not trying to keep their voices low, and although they did not look at her, she suddenly had the impression that they wanted her to overhear.

"I can't believe she rewarded that tantrum—"

"I pity that child's teachers in a few years—"

"—that's what a diet of junk food does to children—"

"—someone needs a parenting class—"

"—yes, a lesson on how to redirect negative impulses—"

After the moment Karen needed to realize the women were talking about her, she scooped up Lucas, yanked open the door to the locker room, and ducked inside. The door closed too slowly to block out the derisive laugher she had left behind. "Stupid, gossipy bi—" Just in time, she remembered Lucas's rapidly developing vocabulary and clamped her mouth shut around the word.

This was not the first time she had earned outright disdain from mothers like these, women who managed to handle, apparently effortlessly, the tasks of motherhood and look good doing it. They made their own baby food from organically grown fruits and vegetables. They wore white cashmere twinsets knowing their children would never dream of spitting up on them. They had shiny hair and manicures and wore their prepregnancy clothes within six weeks of their deliveries. They found time to iron. Their children had never tasted a trans-fatty acid. They read all the current books and articles on the latest trends in child development. Having stepped off the fast track for the noble art of motherhood, they pursued their new profession the way they had once pursued advanced degrees and corner offices. They scorned and pitied mothers who stuck their kids in day care and regarded with bewilderment mothers such as Karen's best friend Janice, mother of four with one on the way, who seemed not to know when to say when, and Karen, scattered and disorganized and unable to pull herself together. When Karen had resigned from her job within a week of returning from her eight-week maternity leave, she had tried to befriend such women at Kindermusik and library story hour, but they smelled her desperation and gave her polite but chilly rebuffs. They did not know that she had once been as successful and confident as they. What was it about motherhood that made her doubt everything she had once admired about herself?

"One, Mama?" offered Lucas, holding a gnarled orange twig of Cheeto to her mouth.

"No, thank you." She redirected the offering and looked up at a sudden movement in the mirror. On the other side of the locker room, a smiling, slender woman in a perfectly tailored suit turned away from a locker, a gym bag slung jauntily over her shoulder. Karen nearly choked. With Lucas balanced on her hip, she swiftly turned toward the nearest locker, ducked her head, and spun the dial as if she knew the combination.

The click of black pumps on concrete paused beside her. "Karen?"

Reluctantly, Karen turned around. "Oh, hi, Lucy."

"Karen! I can't believe it's you." Lucy's makeup was flawless, and she looked well rested and refreshed. Karen dimly remembered feeling like that once, long, long ago. "You're looking—" Lucy sized up Karen in a swift glance. "Wow! How long has it been?"

Karen rose and instinctively tucked loose strands of hair behind her ears. "Um . . . almost five years now. Four and a half."

"It's hard to believe it's been so long." Lucy smiled at Lucas. "He's gotten so big! Is something wrong, little guy? You look sad."

Karen took in his tear-streaked face and runny nose and cringed. "This is actually my youngest, Lucas. You met my older son, Ethan."

"You had another one! How great is that? Two boys. He is just so cute." Lucy pressed a hand to her chest, as if it ached from adoration. "You know, every time I see all the precious little girl clothes at Neiman Marcus, I think I should have a baby, too."

Karen nodded, her face straining from the effort of maintaining a pleasant expression. Why couldn't she have taken five more minutes before leaving the house to fix her hair and put on makeup? "So, how have you been? Are you still seeing Eric?"

"Eric?" Lucy laughed. "You *have* been gone a while. I haven't seen him in years."

"Is that right?" For some reason Karen found this enormously depressing. They had seemed so in love. "What's new at work? How is everyone?"

"Don't get me started. Last year we moved into the new building—you probably heard that—but hardly anyone's happy with the office assignments. Riegert retired last fall, Donnie got married—" Lucy waved her hand. "You know. The usual."

Karen nodded, though she did not know and desperately wanted to. For years she had spent most of her waking hours with these people, but four and a half years ago, they had abruptly vanished from her life.

"But what about you?" said Lucy, concerned. "How do you like the whole stuck-at-home-mom thing?"

What could Karen say? "It's everything I hoped it would be, and so much more," she enthused, forcing a grin. "It was definitely the right choice for me. And . . . we usually go by stay-at-home mom, not stuck-at-home. It feels more voluntary that way."

"That's wonderful," said Lucy, relieved. "I really admire you. I could never give up everything I've worked so hard for."

"You'd be surprised what you can do when you believe it's right for your family."

"I suppose so. I admit sometimes I envy you. It must be so nice not to have to work."

Karen kept her smile fixed in place and nodded.

❧

Despite the swim lesson, Karen and her boys were not the last of the play-group to reach the park. Janice and her four children did not arrive until more than twenty minutes after Karen parallel parked her compact car between the minivans already lined up along the curb.

Janice's three eldest children ran for the playground as Janice followed, carrying the oversized tote bag with their lunches and balancing her one-year-old on her hip. Though she was only five months into her pregnancy, she could easily pass for eight, a fact that had panicked her until an ultra-sound confirmed that she was not carrying twins. Janice had said that whenever she took all of the kids to the grocery store, other shoppers regarded her with either profound sympathy or alarm. Once, a well-meaning elderly woman had taken her aside and kindly encouraged her to discuss birth control options with her physician, secretly if she had to, if her husband disapproved. At her last prenatal appointment, a pregnant woman struggling to amuse her bored two-year-old in the waiting room remarked that Janice was either very brave or very insane. Janice laughed as she recounted the stories, but Karen knew she had begged her husband to get a vasectomy two children ago. Whenever she was especially annoyed with him, she threatened to perform the operation herself.

"Sorry I'm late," said Janice, panting, as she spread out her blanket and settled herself and the baby upon it. "I got trapped in a phone call with the food police."

"What was it this time?" asked one of the other mothers, who was changing her three-year-old's pull-up pants on a nearby blanket. "Peanut butter?"

"No! God forbid. Even I know enough not to bring peanut butter. Peanuts can kill."

"You forgot to cut the grapes in half," guessed Karen, who had committed that same infraction on her first turn to provide the morning snack for Ethan's nursery school class, earning herself a lecture on hidden choking hazards from the room parent.

"Your school is strict," remarked Connor, the only stay-at-home father in the playgroup. "We can bring anything except candy and soda."

"The food police aren't official representatives of the school," said Janice. "The peanut rule is a school policy, and understandably so, but the others have been tacked on by a few overzealous parents with too much time on their hands."

"So what did you do?" said the oldest mother in the group. She and her husband had been surprised by a late-in-life third child, and she regarded with bemused skepticism the innumerable new parenting rules that had sprung up since her first two children passed through the preschool years.

"I brought the wrong kind of milk."

"Buttermilk?" asked one of the mothers. She was an uncertain parent who often described her child's development in terms of the dog obedience classes she had put her standard poodle through a few years before. "Chocolate?"

"Spoiled?" said Karen.

"No! Honestly, do you really think I'm that bad? I brought milk. Fresh milk, regular nonchocolate milk. However, I failed to select organic, BGH-free milk."

"What's that?" asked the oldest mother.

"One more thing to worry about," said Connor, who regularly regaled them with magazine articles on subjects such as pesticide residues in applesauce.

Janice smote her brow in mock dismay. "I thought I brought those children something healthy, but apparently it was not quite healthy enough. Tell me, where am I supposed to find organic, bovine growth hormone–free milk? And how much more than regular milk does it cost?"

They all laughed, except for Connor, who looked ready to defend the food police, and Karen, who knew exactly how much that kind of milk cost and where to find it because it was the only kind Nate allowed in the house other than soy.

"Some kids are allergic to dairy," one of the mothers warned, then excused herself to chase down her youngest daughter, happily wandering from the playground.

"I promise I'll take soy next time," Janice called after her. Then, all at once, every child seemed to need something: a push on the swing, a snack, a referee, a cuddle. The conversation broke up in a scramble of caregiving, as most of their conversations did. Few of their chats were as long in duration as this one had been. They had learned to converse in bits and snatches.

Later, as Karen and Janice pushed their youngest ones on the swings, Karen told her about her morning with the coven of mean swim moms and her former coworker. Janice interrupted with incredulous laughter when Karen repeated Lucy's statement that Karen did not work. "Oh, of course we don't work," said Janice. "We just sit around and let our feral children scavenge for food and clothing in the streets."

"When working mothers imagine our days—if they imagine them at all— they think of playdates at the park, hugs and kisses and peaceful naptime on spotless cotton crib sheets. Hours of maternal bliss and fully requited love. They have no idea what it's really like."

Janice nodded emphatically and Karen did not bother to continue. Janice, mother of four and a half, already knew very well what life as a stay-at-home mother was like. That was one of the reasons they got along so well. Each admired the other for simply managing to shower, dress, and get out of the house once a day. Sometimes Karen felt as if Janice was the only person she knew who demanded nothing more of her.

Karen adored her children. She loved them beyond measure. However, if pressed, if forced to admit the truth, she would confess that she structured her entire day around coordinating the boys' naps so that she could have a half hour to collapse in a chair and catch her breath. Some days she could almost weep just thinking of the mind-numbingly repetitious nature of her daily routine. And while she claimed the playgroup was for the boys, it was really for her, because if she did not have a conversation with someone above the age of four at least once during the day, she sincerely believed she would go stark raving mad.

Worst of all was the knowledge that someday she would have to give it all up.

"Motherhood is the only job in the world where your every decision is questioned and doubted and criticized," said Janice. "No matter what you do, no matter what choice you make, someone somewhere is convinced that you are doing irreparable harm to your children. And she probably has a vocal, militant group of like-minded mommies on the Internet backing her up."

"Maybe not the only job," said Karen. "What about President?"

"Okay, maybe President. But he's well compensated for it."

"And we all know that if you don't get paid for it, it isn't work." Karen had been guilty of that assumption before she had children, and now, thinking of the millions of working women who still operated under that misconception, she could not feel angry, or indignant, or even frustrated. She simply felt tired, much too tired to try to enlighten them.

Janice pushed her son's swing for a moment in silence. "Speaking of paid work . . ." She paused. "There's no delicate way to phrase this. I'm getting a nanny."

Karen stared at her, forgetting to push the swing or move out of the way. Lucas bumped into her. "Mama, Mama, no no no," he complained as he twisted in the swing.

She straightened out the chains and gave Lucas another push. "You're serious," she managed to say. "Why do you need a nanny?"

Stupid question. Who needed a nanny more than Janice?

"Don't hate me," said Janice. "I'm going back to work. In a manner of speaking, since I'll work out of the home. Remember the birthday parties I ran for Elise's and Jayne's girls?"

Karen nodded. Janice, a former producer of children's public television programs, threw legendary birthday parties complete with themes, costumes, and games that could only be described as enchanting. When her eldest daughter turned five, Janice arranged a fairy tea party like something out of a movie, with cute little girls dancing around the backyard in ballerina skirts and delicate wings made from wire and tulle. Even Ethan, the only boy, wore a pair of emerald green wings and ran around calling himself a dinosaur dragonfly. The photos would surely mortify him in years to come, although he had enjoyed the party as much as the girls.

"I've helped so many other moms with their parties that I finally decided to make it official," Janice explained. "I can do something I enjoy, still be with my kids, and make a little money, too."

"I'm sure you'll make tons," said Karen, forcing a smile. "Enough for a Mercedes with built-in car seats. Congratulations."

She asked for more details, reminding herself that Janice was her closest friend, the only friend who understood her anymore, and she ought to be delighted and encouraging for her sake. Instead, she was so stunned and envious that she soon gave up responding with anything more than wordless murmurs. *I am a bitter, mean, little person,* she thought. *I nag my husband and I can't be happy for my best friend.*

It seemed a long time before Janice finished explaining the specifics of her new job and discussed her family's need for extra income with the new baby coming and five college tuitions to plan for, as well as her own ache for some kind of life of her own apart from bottles and diapers and nursery rhymes.

"You never needed a life before," said Karen lightly, watching the older children running and climbing and tumbling over the playground like a pack of happy puppies. "You were as committed to the calling of maternal drudgery as the rest of us."

Janice laughed, but as her eyes followed Connor as he raced to stop his youngest from pouring a bucketful of pebbles down the front of her sundress, her smile faded. "I want my own income. There's no such thing as job security anymore. Or marital security."

"What?" exclaimed Karen. "Is something going on with Sean? His job, or . . . you two?"

"No. Not yet. But sometimes you never see it coming."

"Janice, no." Karen shook her head. "Sean would never leave you. He adores you. He would never be interested in someone else. He can hardly keep his hands off you."

Janice gestured to her round belly. "That much, at least, is true."

"Please don't tell me you're taking this job as an insurance policy in case Sean leaves you. I've never seen a man so in love with his wife, and that includes my own husband, as much as I hate to admit it."

"What are you talking about? Nate worships the ground you walk on."

"You're half right. He worships the *ground.* I know he loves me and he loves the boys, but the reason he'll never leave me is that he knows he'll never find anyone else who will agree to wash and reuse aluminum foil."

"I don't think Sean will leave me for another woman, either," Janice acknowledged. "But it's not just about the money. I need this. Don't get me wrong. I love being a mom. You of all people know I do. But I need something else. Something that's just for me. Sometimes . . ." Janice gestured to the playground, where Connor had all but disappeared beneath a shrieking, laughing pile of children. "Sometimes I feel that the woman I was before I became a mother is drowning, and if I don't reach in and hold her above the waves long enough for her to take a breath, she won't make it."

Karen did not know what to say. In silence they watched the older children play until their two toddlers kicked their dangling legs and fussed, indignant at being forgotten in the swings.

❧

They ate lunch at the park and played for an hour more before a chain reaction of toddler meltdowns set in, signaling the end of the play date. Karen drove around for a half hour before Ethan and Lucas fell asleep in their car seats. Then she turned the car toward home, torn between guilt for the waste of precious fossil fuels and giddiness at the thought of perhaps as much as an hour to spend as she pleased. Miraculously, she was able to carry Lucas to his crib and Ethan to the living room sofa without waking either boy.

After checking the answering machine and the mail, she hurried downstairs to the basement. If they ever saved enough money for a larger house, Karen would insist upon a home with an extra, above-ground room she could claim as her own, a quilting room that could double as a guest room. For now, a desk salvaged from a garage sale, a second-hand sewing machine, and two stacks of milk crates for storage served as her quilt studio.

She switched on the baby monitor and pulled out the magazine, settling herself down on a metal folding chair in front of the desk. She had read the ad so often that the magazine fell open at the proper page, and she read the requirements again although she had nearly memorized them. The Elm Creek Quilters wanted someone accomplished, but they were not asking for the impossible. Karen knew how to piece and quilt by hand as well as by machine, and she considered herself especially adept at foundation paper piecing, which ought to qualify as a "notable quilting technique." She met the requirements. Other applicants would probably far exceed them, but Karen could not let the potential competition discourage her from applying.

The logistics of returning to work would make the competition for the job seem like a breeze. Ethan would need to be transported to and from nursery school three mornings a week. Lucas was still nursing, and she didn't relish the thought of hauling a breast pump to Elm Creek Manor. She would just have to wean him. If she'd had any backbone at all, she would have stopped nursing him months ago, but it was less exhausting to simply give in to his demands. Eighteen months was definitely old enough for her to wean him without guilt, and it would be easier once she had a strong motivation to stick to it.

But who would care for the boys in her absence? She had heard too many alarming reports of day care centers to contemplate one for her children, but Nate's job was secure—and would become more so, once he had tenure—and they could afford a nanny. Her heart quaked at the thought of peeling her sobbing babies from her legs and handing them over to a grandmotherly woman with a crisp British accent and her hair in a bun, but she quickly turned her thoughts to the beautiful estate where the quilt camp was held, the friendly, encouraging faculty, the joy of creativity and camaraderie she longed for in her daily life but had not truly felt since quilt camp. At the time, in the middle of her first pregnancy, she had laughingly described her week at Elm Creek Quilt Camp as one last opportunity for fun before the demands of motherhood took hold. A few months after Ethan was born, she finally understood why the other mothers at the Candlelight welcoming ceremony had nodded knowingly instead of smiling at her joke.

She would hire the best nanny in the world, she told herself. A Penn State student majoring in elementary education or premed with a concentration in pediatrics. Mary Poppins. The nanny would be so nurturing and affectionate that the children would not even realize Karen had left the house until she returned home in the evening. They would run to meet her at the door as they ran to meet Nate, and they would beg cuddles and kisses as they told her about their fun, educational, and enriching day. They would probably cry when Nanny said good-bye. They would probably cling to her and beg her to stay for supper. On weekends, they would ask why Nanny had not come, and if they fell and scraped a knee, they would sob for Nanny rather than their mother.

She had not even mailed in her application yet, and already guilt and jealousy had set in.

She brushed the thoughts aside and plugged in her laptop. She had nearly finished updating her résumé—she had very little to add—when Lucas's cry pealed over the baby monitor. After scrambling to conceal all evidence of her activity, she ran upstairs to her younger son, vowing that she would tell Nate her intentions that evening as soon as he came home from work.

She procrastinated by waiting until after supper, for that brief period of relative calm after the boys finished eating and ran off to the living room to play and before they returned to ask for popsicles. Karen insisted on clearing the table while Nate finished his water, realizing too late that this was a sure sign she wanted something from him. They never waited on each other except on birthdays, after arguments, or when one was feeling amorous and was hoping to overcome the other's desperate need for sleep.

Until Karen quit her job, they had always divided their expenses equally. Even on their first date, she had insisted on paying half of the check. Nate had put up a modest fight, but eventually his desire to convince her he was a modern, sensitive, egalitarian male overcame his instinct for chivalry. They were students, with students' modest incomes. Frequent dating would quickly bankrupt him if they didn't split the costs, and neither wanted anything to stand in the way of seeing each other again.

Karen had never expected a simple blind date for lunch to turn out so well, even though her roommate and her roommate's boyfriend had been trying to set them up all semester. For months, heavy course loads and a general reluctance to find out exactly why their mutual friends considered them an ideal match prevented them from arranging to meet. Eventually they ran out of excuses and agreed to meet between classes for a quick bite to eat. Karen skipped her favorite seminar to stay for a dessert she really didn't need and more amazing discoveries of all she and Nate had in common—a fervent belief in the musical genius of Paul Simon, an inability to care about professional sports, an almost embarrassing depth of knowledge of *Buffy the Vampire Slayer* lore. Nate's earnest charm and warm sense of humor had quickly erased Karen's doubts about their four-year age difference and the gap between Nate's graduate student status and her own as an undergraduate junior. He had already confessed his environmentalist leanings, and after he walked her to her car and saw a late model, low-emission, fuel-efficient Volvo at the curb, he seized her hand and kissed it. Karen was suddenly very glad her parents had insisted she take her mother's car instead of her father's Cadillac to college, and forever after wondered what Nate would have done had she come on bicycle.

"What's on your mind?" asked Nate as she filled the sink and squeezed dish soap into the stream from the faucet. They had a dishwasher, but Nate disputed the manufacturer's claim that it used less water and energy than hand washing. So they used it to store the trashcan and the recyclables bin instead.

"Nothing," said Karen quickly. "Well, okay. Something. Sit down," she added, as he began to rise. She retrieved the magazine from the diaper bag on the counter, where she had placed it in anticipation of this moment. She returned to her seat and set the magazine on the table before her. "Please don't panic."

"Panic?" He looked warier than she had ever seen him. "Why should I panic?"

She gestured to the magazine. "Because I allowed one of these into the house."

"What?" He glanced at the magazine. "This? That's what all this is about?"

She nodded.

He strangled out a laugh. "You nearly gave me a heart attack. I thought you were going to tell me you were pregnant again."

He of all people ought to know there was little chance of that. Karen flipped the magazine open and placed it before him. "I think I'd like to apply for this job," she said after giving him a moment to skim the ad. "It's not my traditional line of work, but I think I'd enjoy it more than any other part-time work I could—"

She broke off at the sound of a thud from the living room. She paused, but when neither of the boys howled in pain or outrage, she returned her attention to Nate. "So. What do you think?"

"Sounded like something hit the wall."

"No, honey. About the job. Look." Karen pointed to a line of type. "It says seasonal work and flexible hours are available."

"But it's all the way in Waterford."

"That's an hour drive at most."

"What about the kids? Won't you miss them?"

"Of course I'll miss them, just like you miss them when you go off to work in the morning." She had expected objections to the magazine, but she had not prepared any counterarguments to concerns about the job itself. "Elm Creek Quilt Camp is open only March through October, so I would be working less than if I tried to get a teaching job someplace. We always said I would go back to work when the kids were old enough—"

Another thud sounded from the living room, followed by an ominous crash.

Nate twisted in his chair. "Ethan, what are you boys doing in there?"

"Nothing!" Ethan shouted. "Lucas threw his sippy cup at the lamp again."

"Why?"

"He needs a reason?" asked Karen.

"Because the first time he missed," called Ethan. "It fell off the table and rolled under the sofa. I can't reach it."

"Just leave it alone. I'll get it."

As he rose, Karen placed a hand on his arm. "May we finish this conversation later?"

"Sure." He pushed back his chair. "First chance we get."

Karen watched him go, muffling a sigh. She waited, but when she realized he was not returning anytime soon, she got up and finished cleaning the kitchen.

Later that evening, she bathed the boys while Nate checked his email and graded exams. He shut down his computer long enough to read the boys a story and tuck them into bed, but soon after she kissed the boys goodnight and turned off their lights, the phone rang. She snatched it up, praying that the boys would sleep through the noise. It was one of Nate's undergraduate students, frustrated with a particularly difficult section of code he was trying to write for a class project. While Nate patiently talked him through it, Karen returned to the basement and finished her résumé. She printed out a copy and took it upstairs to seek Nate's advice, but found him in the recliner, feet propped up, computer on his lap, eyes riveted on the screen.

Rather than interrupt him, she returned to the basement and put in a load of laundry. She switched on the baby monitor and worked on a foundation paper–pieced Pickle Dish quilt in between shifting loads to the drier and folding the clothes. By the time she carried the basket of warm, crisp, neatly folded laundry upstairs, Nate had fallen asleep. She made sure to save all of his documents before shutting down the computer and carefully setting it on the table beside him. It was a warm night, but she drew a light quilt over him and shut the windows before turning off the lamp and going upstairs to bed, laundry basket balanced on her hip.

"Karen?"

She left the laundry basket on the landing and returned to the living room. "I thought you were asleep."

Nate turned on the lamp and reached for something on the floor beside his chair. It was the *Modern Quilter* magazine, and when he placed it on his lap, it fell open to the ad. "Do you want to talk about this job now?"

Karen was so tired that all she wanted to do was close her eyes and crawl into bed, but she had laundry to put away, bills to pay, and three unanswered emails from her mother waiting on the computer. She needed eight uninterrupted hours of sleep, not a lengthy, overdue conversation, but she got down the laundry basket and nodded.

"Do you really want to work at a quilt camp?" asked Nate. "Would you— I mean, I thought your quilting was just a hobby. When you said you wanted to teach, I thought you meant—"

"You thought I meant teaching undergrad business courses at Penn State," Karen finished. "I know this isn't what I went to graduate school for, but I loved quilt camp and I think I'd enjoy working there. It would be fun."

He studied the magazine for a moment before closing it with a sigh. "I guess life hasn't been much fun for you for the past four and a half years."

"No, honey, that's not true." She loved her life with Nate and the boys. She had never laughed so much or thought herself so utterly necessary to another human being. "But I do want something more. Something . . . separate. Something where I can be just me again and not someone else's mom. You know, almost everyone I've met since Ethan was born knows me not as Karen Wise but as 'Ethan's Mom' or 'Lucas's Mom.' Isn't that sad? Even other mothers don't bother to learn mothers' names."

"So you want to get a job to prove there's more to you than motherhood?"

"That's part of it, but not everything." She hesitated, wondering how to explain without hurting his feelings. It wasn't because her best friend had found a job and she resented being left behind. She had earned her own money ever since accepting her first baby-sitting job at thirteen, and she hated depending upon someone else's income. She hated that guilty feeling of spending Nate's salary, even though she knew he considered his earnings to be hers as much as they were his own. In theory she agreed; he would not be able to be both a father and a tenure-track university professor if someone else were not willing to care for his children during the day. Karen agreed with that philosophy, and yet, she still wished she had a little part-time income to spend as she pleased, guilt-free.

"I'm sure I'll want something full-time when the boys are in school," she told Nate. "But in the meantime, a part-time job like this one would help support my quilting habit."

"Then you should apply."

"What about the kids? We'll have to get a nanny or day care or something, and we'll have to work out a schedule to cart them around to their activities."

"We'll figure something out." He lowered the footrest of the recliner and beckoned her to curl up on his lap. "If other families can manage, we can. First, get the job. We can work out the other details later."

❧

Karen had never taught quilting, but in her previous life, she had taught introductory marketing courses as an MBA student at the University of Nebraska. Before the boys woke the next morning, she searched the basement for the carton holding her old graduate school papers and books, still taped tightly shut from their move to Pennsylvania eight years before, when Nate accepted an assistant professorship in Penn State's School of Information Sciences and Technology. She hoped some of her undergraduates' teaching evaluations would qualify as letters of recommendation from former students. Her students had graduated long ago and she had no way to track them down before her application package was due.

She drafted sample lesson plans after taking Ethan to nursery school, typing with one hand while cradling a nursing, dozing Lucas on a pillow on her lap. She doubted she had the sort of employment history the management of Elm Creek Quilt Camp expected of their applicants. What would they think of her four years as an associate director in Penn State's Office of University Development? Would they have any idea what that meant, or should she work into her cover letter pertinent details such as the size of her office in Old Main or the fact that she had been the youngest associate director in the history of the university?

How would she reply when they asked her why she had abandoned such a promising career?

The truth was that she had fallen passionately in love with Ethan the moment she held him in her arms in her hospital bed. She stayed awake throughout the night holding him, marveling at him, rather than miss a single moment of his first hours in the world. The nurse scolded her and threatened to whisk him off to the nursery, telling her she would be sorry later that she had not taken advantage of the chance to get some rest. She would have ample opportunity to admire her baby later, every day until he left for college if she so desired. Karen refused to hand over her son and compromised by sleeping with Ethan in the bed beside her. The nurse did not approve, but fortunately her shift ended at six in the morning, and the nurse who replaced her believed that a newborn could never be held too much.

As her last trimester drew to a close, Karen had written detailed notes for her colleagues and assistant so they could carry on smoothly in her absence, and she had reassured her superiors that she would be back on the job eight weeks to the day after she gave birth. She and Nate managed to obtain a place for Ethan in the most sought-after day-care program in town, the Child Development Laboratory operated by the College of Health and Human Development right on the Penn State campus. Karen knew Ethan would be well cared for, but as the eight weeks of her maternity leave raced by in a blur of wonder and exhaustion, she grew less certain she would be capable of leaving him. She spent every evening of the last week crying in the glider rocker as she nursed Ethan to sleep, as Nate sat on the edge of the bed worriedly watching her and assuring her that everything would be fine.

On her first day back to work, she put on the least obvious of her maternity ensembles, having not yet managed to fit into her prepregnancy suits. She kissed Nate good-bye and offered him a ride as she had hundreds of times before, but this time she loaded a breast pump in the car along with her briefcase. She left her precious baby sleeping in the arms of a competent-looking caregiver and made it all the way back to her desk in her beloved office in Old Main before racing back to the Child Development Lab with a hasty excuse for the first colleague she passed on her rush out the door. Remorseful and relieved, she buckled Ethan in his car seat and drove home.

During Ethan's afternoon nap, she phoned her most understanding supervisor, apologized, and promised to return in the morning. This time she did not even manage to leave the Child Development Lab before hurrying back for her baby. The following day she turned the car around before reaching College Avenue. That day, after meeting Nate in his campus office for a tearful discussion, she phoned her supervisor and told him that the next time she returned to Old Main would be to submit her letter of resignation. He replied—rather cheerfully and not at all surprised, or so it had struck her then—that he had assumed as much. They had already cleared out her desk and would interview her potential replacement the following morning.

Unfortunately, every embarrassing, graceless misstep was part of her employment record and fodder for a job interview. Given her history, the Elm Creek Quilters might be justifiably wary of hiring a woman who had intended to return to a job she loved but found, at the very last possible moment, that she could not bring herself to leave her baby. They might also be concerned that she would quit Elm Creek Quilt Camp if she became pregnant again. But what could she do? She could not retract her choices, and despite the hassles and the loss of income, she never regretted stepping off the career track to stay at home with her boys. She could not help it if the Elm Creek Quilters held her indecisive wavering against her, but she would tell them the truth and hope for the best.

Nate had given her a digital camera for her birthday, so it should have been an easy matter to photograph her quilts for her portfolio. It would have been if the boys had not been so eager to help. Ethan insisted on holding up the quilts for her, but although he stretched his arms high above his head and stood on tiptoe, even the smallest crib quilts dragged on the ground. When reasoning with him failed, she pretended to take pictures his way, but suggested they also hang the quilts in case they needed extras. Ethan agreed that this sounded like a good idea, but then he insisted on posing in front of each quilt and smiling brightly while she took the picture. Bribes or threats were powerless to persuade him to step out of the shot. Meanwhile, Lucas flung her other quilts into the air and danced upon them where they landed on the floor, apparently mistaking them for the parachute at Gymboree.

When she finally gave up, she had wasted an hour and squandered the last bit of her carefully conserved patience. She stuck Lucas in his playpen, handed out Veggie Booty, and put on a Dragon Tales DVD before locking herself in the bathroom with the quilt magazine. Ten minutes of deep breathing and art quilt inspiration later, she emerged with a renewed sense of resolve and purpose—only to find Lucas asleep on one of her quilts with his little diaper-clad rump sticking in the air and Ethan engrossed in the adventures of Zak and Wheezie. Karen abandoned her project for the rest of the afternoon rather than jeopardize the miraculous calm. After supper, she prevailed upon Nate to distract the boys while she quickly hung the quilts and snapped pictures during fifteen precious, uninterrupted minutes.

The lesson plans took her two weeks to complete, since she could work only when the boys were asleep and after Nate came home from work. Second-guessing every decision, she edited and revised her portfolio repeatedly and might have continued to do so except she ran out of time. Though not completely satisfied, she made an eleventh-hour sprint to the post office and sent the portfolio next-day express, return receipt requested. If she never heard back from Elm Creek Quilters, she did not want it to be because her portfolio had been lost in the mail.

Nate told her that, having done her best, she should now put the application out of her thoughts. Pacing and worrying would not hasten their response. Karen grit her teeth and promised him she would try. It was so easy for him. He left every morning for a job he enjoyed in a department that seemed eager to grant him tenure. At the end of an interesting day, he returned to the boys' joyous welcome, their favorite playmate grown even dearer in his absence. He could tell her not to worry because if the Elm Creek Quilters never contacted her, his life would clip jauntily along as it always had, unaffected by her disappointment.

Two weeks passed with no reply except for the postal service's confirmation that her portfolio had indeed reached the mailroom of Elm Creek Manor. She wished she could vent to Janice about the excruciating wait, but something held her back, even as Janice waxed enthusiastic about how she and her husband were converting the living room into a home office. Karen was unsure why she concealed her own tentative step back into the working world, except, perhaps, because it was so tentative. She had applied for the job at Elm Creek Manor and that job only. She did not peruse the want ads in the *Centre Daily Times* or submit her newly updated résumé to online services. A foray into the safe, nurturing world of quilting was just about all she could handle, and she wasn't completely confident she could manage that.

On a Friday morning more than a month after she submitted her portfolio, Karen was trying to coax some oatmeal and bananas into Lucas when the phone rang. "Hello?" she asked, pressing the receiver tightly to one ear. Nate had already left for work or she would have asked him to take the call upstairs.

She could not make out the reply over her children's clamor. Lucas was cheerfully banging his spoon on the table and exhorting her in language he alone understood, and Ethan was running around the house shouting, "Efan to the rescue!" As he sprinted past, she saw that he wore nothing but the cape to his Superman pajamas and a pair of socks.

"Hello?" she said again, prying the spoon from Lucas's hand. "I'm sorry, I didn't catch that."

"May I speak with Karen Wise, please?" asked a woman who sounded close to her own age.

"I'm Karen. Sorry for the noise."

"Don't worry about it. This is Sarah McClure from Elm Creek Quilt Camp."

"Oh, hi!" Karen made a frantic gesture for Ethan to quiet down.

He stopped running and strained to reach the phone. "Who is it, Mommy? Can I talk to him?"

"No, sweetie. It's for Mommy."

The woman on the other end laughed. "It sounds like you have company. Is this a bad time?"

"No! No, this is great." Karen desperately did not want her to hang up. "I'm glad you called."

"Can I talk?" pleaded Ethan. "I'll use my good manners."

"My colleagues and I were very impressed with your portfolio," said Sarah.

"Thank you." Karen turned her back on Ethan and covered the mouthpiece with her hand. "Honey, please. I can't hear."

"Mommy! Mommy!" Ethan punctuated each shout with a leap for the phone. "Please, Mommy! Let me talk, too!"

"We haven't taught many classes in paper piecing, so your experience would complement us nicely." Sarah paused. "Would it help if I talked to your son?"

Karen was mortified. "Oh, no. That isn't necessary. He's all right."

"Really. I'd be happy to."

"Well—" Karen thought quickly. "Okay. Here he is."

Thrilled, Ethan held the phone to his ear. "Hello? Who's this?" A pause. "Oh, I thought you were Daddy." He looked up at Karen. "Efan." A slight pause. "No, not Efan. E-Fan," he said, emphasizing each syllable. "My baby brother's name is Lucas. I use the big boy potty but Lucas still goes in his diaper. Once after his bath Mommy couldn't get his diaper on fast enough and he peed on the rug."

"Okay, honey, thank you, that's enough." Karen snatched back the phone and took a quick, deep breath before putting it to her ear. "Hi. Sorry about that."

"That's all right. Sometimes it's easier to just give them what they want, so long as it won't hurt them."

"That's the truth. Do you have kids?"

"No, but I know many childish adults. Back to the job—if you're still interested, we'd like to invite you to Elm Creek Manor for an interview."

"I'm definitely still interested." Karen ducked as a blob of oatmeal sailed past her ear. Lucas crowed for joy as she scrambled for a pen and paper to take down the date and time of the interview.

"One more thing," said Sarah after Karen assured her she knew the way to the manor. "We're asking all of the applicants to create an original block design and bring it to the interview."

"What sort of design?" Karen's heart sank a little. Somehow Sarah made "all of the applicants" sound as if there were hundreds.

"A new logo for Elm Creek Quilts. Use whatever techniques showcase your talents best."

"Any particular size or colors?"

"You know, you're the first person to ask. Let's make it a twelve-inch block, and use whatever colors you prefer. I suppose I should call everyone else back and let them know."

Or not, Karen thought. Then the other two hundred applicants might get it wrong and be disqualified.

After they hung up, Karen gripped the counter, exultant and yet slightly queasy. She had an interview. Even Ethan's interruption and potty talk had not scared away Sarah McClure from Elm Creek Quilts. She had an interview. Not only that, she had but one week, two days, and four hours from the time she hung up the phone in which to design and make an original quilt block.

Karen knew this quilt block would be the most important pattern she ever designed. She had never taught quilting, published a pattern, or won a ribbon in a national quilt show. It was something of a miracle that Sarah McClure had requested the interview at all, considering how many expert quilters would give their entire fabric stashes for an opportunity to become an Elm Creek Quilter.

Still, Karen knew from her stay at Elm Creek Quilt Camp that the women who worked there were more than close friends. They were a family, and selecting someone to join a family was a far more complex and difficult matter than selecting an employee. They surely had any number of qualified instructors from which to choose, but they would be seeking something more, someone who understood what Elm Creek Quilt Camp meant to quilters worldwide, someone who would cherish Elm Creek Quilts as much as they did.

Karen knew this single quilt block could be her best opportunity to prove she was that person.

She chose bright, cheerful cottons from her fabric stash and stacked them on the kitchen counter for inspiration, hoping a passing glance as she cooked or hauled laundry upstairs from the basement would encourage an idea to spring forth from her subconscious. As she took the children through their daily routine, a part of her thoughts were elsewhere, sketching, considering, revising. With two days to go, she stayed up late into the night armed with a pencil, a ruler, graph paper, and a pot of coffee. The kitchen table was covered in eraser crumbs by the time she finally went upstairs to bed, but her pattern was finished and, unlike her portfolio, she thought it was well done.

The next morning, she dragged herself from bed for Lucas's second feeding, deeply regretting her decision to forego sleep the night before. Lucas dozed as he nursed but became suddenly alert as soon as she tried to return him to his crib, so she put on her slippers and carried him downstairs to the kitchen, where Nate was reading a Dr. Seuss book to Ethan over breakfast.

She asked Nate to hold Lucas so she could shower, and as she handed him off, she glanced at the kitchen counter. "Where's my block?"

"Your what?" asked Nate, settling Lucas on his lap.

"My quilt block." Karen searched through the pile of mail, glanced at the floor, and opened the dishwasher to check the trashcan. "I left the pattern right here last night."

"Daddy spilled coffee," volunteered Ethan, spooning cereal into his mouth.

Karen turned an inquiring look upon Nate, who shook his head. "There weren't any quilt blocks there, just some papers and junk mail." His mouth twisted into a sour frown around the last two words. A forest of credit card applications filled their mailbox every week despite Nate's attempts to remove their address from mailing lists.

"Those papers were my quilt patterns." Karen checked the trashcan a second time and noticed that a new white plastic bag lined it. "Did you take out the trash?"

"It's at the curb," he said, but, having guessed the answer, she was already hurrying past him to the front door. Grass clippings stuck to her bare feet as she padded down the driveway and lifted the lid of the nearest garbage can, recoiling at the stench. Grimacing, Karen pulled out one bag, unfastened the tie, and peered inside. A man passed walking a pair of black labs, who sniffed the trash and then Karen before continuing on. The man deliberately averted his eyes, and Karen suddenly remembered she wore nothing but panties and Nate's extra-large Cornhuskers T-shirt, shrunken and faded from many washings. She tugged the shirt down as far as it would stretch and continued digging through the bag with her free hand. After a while she abandoned the first bag and tried the second, then frantically reached for the third when she heard the garbage truck shifting gears down the block. She had almost given up hope when she spotted a few pieces of paper, now wadded into a ball and soaked through with coffee. She shook off an orange peel and a few soggy Annie's Cheddar Bunnies only to discover that she held a crumpled piece of waxed paper. Her drawings were nowhere to be found.

She returned the trash bags to the can just as the garbage truck came into view. A low whistle followed her as she scurried up the driveway back to the house. It occurred to her that, aside from Sarah's praise for her portfolio, it was the first compliment she had received in months.

Nate was feeding Lucas in his highchair when Karen entered, trailing grass clippings and coffee grounds. "I couldn't find them, and now the garbage truck has come and gone, so that's that."

Nate looked as if he knew that whatever he said next was bound to get him in trouble, but he had no choice. "Did you check the recycling bin?"

"The recycling bin?"

"It was paper," he explained carefully. "I always recycle paper."

She knew that, but somehow coffee-soaked paper did not seem to qualify for recycling. "Why didn't you tell me that before I dug through the trash on the curb?"

"I thought you were going upstairs to shower. I didn't think you'd go outside dressed like that."

Karen yanked open the dishwasher and found her drawings buried under bottles and cans in the recycling bin. "Great," she said, as the pages dripped coffee.

"I'm sorry," said Nate. "I thought they were your rough drafts or I wouldn't have thrown them away."

Karen spread paper towels on the counter and lay the ruined pages upon them. She would have to do them over, but at least she could refer to her original drawings rather than working from memory. Sighing, she went to the sink and scrubbed her arms from fingertips to biceps using hot water and antibacterial soap. "I suppose once they absorbed all that coffee, they probably did look like rough drafts."

"I really am sorry."

"He's sorry, Mommy," said Ethan, and Lucas babbled out a few earnest syllables in agreement.

"Okay. Fine. He's sorry." Relenting, Karen added, "I'll just do them over after supper. You're still planning to take the boys to the park, right?"

Nate took a sip of coffee and shook his head. "I can't. I have a meeting at five-thirty."

"But you said you'd be home at five so we could eat early and I could have the evening to sew my quilt block."

"I'm sorry, honey. The department chair dropped a curriculum review on us at the last minute."

Karen shut off the water and snatched up a towel. "But I was counting on you. I need the time more than ever now that I also have to redo my drawings."

"Can you wait until Saturday? I'm sorry, Karen, but I can't come home early. I don't have a choice. You remember what it's like to work."

Karen stiffened. "Yes, actually, I do."

"Mommy's mad at Daddy," observed Ethan to no one in particular.

"I'm not mad," said Karen, though she was.

"I'll redo the drawings for you this weekend," offered Nate.

"No, you can't." Karen flung the towel onto the counter, but picked it up, folded it, and hung it on its usual wall hook when she remembered Ethan watching her. "It's a test for the job interview. I have to do it myself."

Just like everything else around here, she thought.

❧

On the morning of her interview, Karen showered and tried on some of her suits from her Office of University Development days. With some effort, she managed to fit into her loosest, most forgiving suit. The skirt was a bit too snug around the hips and thighs and the jacket was surprisingly snug at the bosom, thanks to Lucas's sustained nursing. If she got the job and convinced Lucas to wean, she would shrink back to B cups in a matter of days. She studied her transiently ample profile in the mirror and decided the suit fit well enough for the interview. It had to, since her only other options were yoga pants or maternity jeans.

She hung up the suit, making a mental note to iron it later, pulled on her sweats, and went downstairs to have breakfast and kiss Nate before he bicycled off to work. "I have to leave by two," she reminded him, following him out to the garage with Lucas riding her hip.

"I'll leave campus no later than twelve-thirty," he promised, strapping on his helmet.

"Can you make it noon, so you can watch the boys while I get ready?"

"Sorry, I can't. I have a meeting. I'll leave as soon as it's over."

"Twelve-fifteen?"

"The second the meeting's over, I'll be on my way home. Promise." He gave her a reassuring wave good-bye as he pedaled down the driveway and out into the street, his overloaded backpack giving him the appearance of a precariously balanced turtle.

Karen had time for a quick cup of coffee and bagel before taking Ethan to nursery school. Lucas fell asleep in the car on the way home, so once she had him settled in his crib, she gathered her maps and directions, the quilt block and pattern, and a copy of her portfolio. She packed all the papers into her briefcase and put everything in the car, just in case Nate came home later than anticipated and she had to rush out the door at the last minute. Lucas thoughtfully slept longer than usual, so she had time to iron her suit and find a pair of nylons without any runs. She rehearsed the interview in her mind, posing questions to herself and answering them aloud.

Lucas woke as soon as she lay down on her bed to rest so she would be fresh for the interview. Sometimes she suspected a device hidden in her bedsprings triggered an alarm in the children's rooms, because somehow they always knew as soon as her head touched the pillow. She took Lucas from his crib and tried to persuade him to nurse lying beside her on the bed so she could grab a few minutes of rest, but he fussed and complained until she took him to the rocking chair.

Afterward, Karen and Lucas played with blocks and stuffed animals until it was time to pick up Ethan from school. Although she had warned him they would need to leave right away, Ethan begged to stay and play with his friends, and since Lucas was squirming in her arms and gesturing desperately toward the playground, she agreed. She chatted with the other parents and kept careful track of the time, remembering to give the boys a ten-minute warning, and then five, and then two. Somehow Ethan still managed to be astonished when she told him that it was five minutes past noon and they needed to leave. Lucas did not want to leave, either, but he was still small enough to be carried against his will—unlike Ethan, who retreated to the farthest corner of the climbing structure and refused to budge. Mindful of the teachers and the other parents observing her, Karen projected loving sympathy as she reasoned, coaxed, and finally begged him to come down, all to no avail. After ten minutes, another mother offered to hold Lucas while she climbed the ladder, pried Ethan's fingers from the monkey bars, and took him down the slide on her lap, since she knew there was no way she could wrestle him down the ladder.

"Say good-bye to your teachers," she said cheerily when his feet finally touched pea gravel. She took Lucas back from the helpful mother and reached for Ethan's hand. Instead of taking hold, Ethan burst into tears and reached for her with both arms.

"Someone's tired," remarked the other mother. Karen replied with a tight smile and a nod. She bent down and hefted Ethan onto her right hip, and, balancing Lucas on her left, she managed to shuffle across the playground and out the gate.

Once out of sight of the playground, she abruptly set Ethan on the sidewalk. "Okay, that's enough. I need lots of cooperation today."

Tearfully, he sniffled, "Please pick me up."

"Honey, I know you're tired, but I can't carry both of you all the way to the car." She took his hand, and he reluctantly held hers. He dragged his feet, but he came. Suddenly she felt overwhelmingly weary. They went through this at least twice a week. Almost every other child in Ethan's class spotted their mother at the gate, cried out "Mommy!" and went running for a hug. Only Ethan acted as if a stranger had come to drag him off to the deepest circle of hell. Karen could only imagine what the teachers and other parents thought went on in the Wise home to evoke such a reaction.

As soon as she buckled Ethan into his car seat, he brightened and began chattering about his day at school as if nothing had happened. His mood could turn on a dime, leaving her dazed in the wake of his emotions. Lucas fell asleep again, which surprised her considering how long his morning nap had lasted, but he woke as soon as they pulled into the garage. She had hoped to find Nate waiting for her, but had not really expected him to be able to leave so early.

She fixed the boys their lunch—peanut butter and jelly sandwiches and sliced bananas—and stood at the counter while they ate, too nervous to swallow a bite herself. She had not been on a job interview in eight years. She had not had a sustained conversation with any adult other than Nate, Janice, or her mother in more than four. What if she had forgotten how to talk about anything but her children?

At a quarter to one, she began glancing out the window, watching for Nate on his bike. Ethan finished eating and went into the living room to play, but Lucas pushed the pieces of his sandwich around on his plate and mashed his bananas into a sticky paste. At ten minutes to one, she phoned Nate's office. He did not answer, so she left a message on his voice mail and decided to take his absence as a good sign; he must already be on his way home. She did not try his cell, knowing that he could not answer it while riding his bike.

"Sweetie, are you going to eat your lunch?" she asked Lucas absently, standing at the window. In response, Lucas picked up a peanut butter and jelly triangle and dropped it disdainfully on the floor.

Sighing, she unbuckled him from his booster seat and washed his face and hands. When he toddled off to join his brother, she cleared the table and wiped up the mess on the floor, keeping one eye on the clock. It was one o'clock. If he had left campus at twelve-thirty, the latest he promised her he would leave, he should have arrived home already. Even in bad weather, he never needed more than a half hour to bike home from the office.

She called his office again, and then tried the cell. After five rings, he answered in a low voice. "Hello?"

"Where are you?"

"I'm stuck in this meeting," he griped in an undertone.

"You mean you haven't even left campus yet?"

"Honey, I can't talk right now. I'll call you back as soon as I can."

"But—"

"I'm sorry, but I have to hang up. Bye."

She fumed as the line went dead. She hung up the phone and began pacing. At a quarter past, Lucas ran back into the kitchen and reached for her with his head tilted to one side, his sign that he wanted to nurse. She carried him back to the living room, settled on the recliner, and nursed him, glancing at the clock on the mantel and starting a slow burn.

At half past she knew she could not wait any longer. "I'm going upstairs to get dressed," she told Ethan, and carried Lucas, still nursing, to her bedroom. Lucas stomped his feet and wailed in protest when she set him down on the floor, and he would not be consoled with cheerful talk and smiles as she hastily showered, blew her hair dry, and squeezed into her suit. He clung to her legs as she put on her makeup, so she picked him up and fixed her hair as best she could with only one hand. At one-thirty she returned downstairs. Nate was nowhere to be seen.

"I can't believe this," she muttered, setting Lucas down on the kitchen floor. Instead of searching out his brother, he opened the pantry door and began taking out the boxes and cans on the bottom shelf and lining them up on the floor. She called Nate's cell phone again, hanging up with a bang when he did not answer. Maybe he was on his way. He had said he would call first, but maybe he had run for his bike as soon as the meeting ended rather than wasting time on the phone.

He was more than an hour late. He had better be on his way.

"Mama?" Lucas held up the familiar yellow box hopefully. "Chee-woes?"

"I already made you a yummy sandwich and you threw it on the floor," she snapped. She took a deep breath and reminded herself that she was not angry with *him*. "Sorry, honey. Of course you can have some cereal."

She buckled him into his booster seat and handed him a spoon so he could bang away happily on the table while she poured cereal and milk. "Ethan, how are you doing in there?" she called when it occurred to her she had not heard from him in some time.

"Fine," he called back, and something in his tone made her go to the doorway and look. He had turned on the television and was staring at a cartoon in which a vile-looking slime monster made deep-voiced threats to a shapely blonde girl wearing a cut-off shirt and military cargo pants. An indeterminate rodentlike creature was gnawing through the ropes that tied the girl to a metal barrel marked "Toxic Waste."

"What is this?" cried Karen, quickly switching off the television. "That is not PBS Kids."

"PBS Kids had Mr. Rogers. I don't like Mr. Rogers."

"You mean you don't like his show. Mr. Rogers was a very nice man." Karen shook her head. That wasn't the point. "You know you're not supposed to watch TV without asking."

Ethan's eyes were fixed on the dark television screen. "Can I watch TV?"

"No. Read a book."

"I can't read!"

"*Look* at a book." She returned to the kitchen where Lucas, still strapped into his booster seat, strained to reach his bowl of Cheerios on the counter. "Sorry, sweetheart." She snatched up the bowl and set it before him.

He peered into the bowl warily and looked up at her with a face full of doubt.

"It's Cheerios, honey, just like you wanted." She picked up his spoon and began feeding him. He took two bites before clamping his mouth shut and turning away. "Not hungry after all?" She rose and picked up his bowl. He let out a howl of protest that nearly made her drop it. "Okay, okay. Here it is." She set it down again and placed the spoon in his hand. He smiled angelically and began to eat.

She checked the clock. Ten minutes until two.

She blinked back tears of frustration and practiced her Lamaze breathing. She pulled the phone closer, sat down beside Lucas, and tried Nate's numbers one last time. It rang so long she was sure his voice mail would pick up, but instead Nate answered.

"Please tell me you're on your way home," she said.

"I'm not, honey. I'm still in the meeting. I can't talk—"

"Don't you hang up again. You'd better talk to me."

"Hold on." She heard muffled voices, a moment of quiet in which she feared he had hung up on her, and then Nate's voice at a normal volume. "Okay. I'm in the hall."

"Are you coming home?"

"No, Karen. I have to go back into the meeting."

"But I have to get to my interview. You promised you'd be home by twelve-thirty."

"I know. I know. I'm sorry. I had no idea this was going to run so long. We haven't even taken a break for lunch."

"Oh, poor you."

"Karen—"

"You're supposed to be here, right now, with the boys. I should already be on the road."

"I'm sorry. How many times can I say it? Can you call the quilters and reschedule?"

"Are you kidding me? This is a job interview. What kind of impression will that make?"

"Well . . ." Nate sighed. "Let's just hope they'll be reasonable and accommodate a working parent."

And if they didn't? So much for her dreams of becoming an Elm Creek Quilter. "Nate, if you come home now, I might still make it on time."

"I can't walk out of this meeting. It's too important."

"More important than a job interview?" cried Karen. "It's a meeting. You have a dozen meetings every week. They won't care if you miss the last twenty minutes of one meeting."

"It might run longer than that, and they will care. My whole tenure committee is here. I couldn't leave even if I wanted to."

"Surely they'll understand that you have a family emergency."

"This isn't an emergency and you know it."

"But it's just one meeting!"

"It's more than that. They'll consider it indicative of my commitment to the department."

"What about your commitment to me?"

"That's not fair."

"Not fair? I asked for one day. Not even a whole day. Just one afternoon for something I care about. And you promised."

"It's a job interview, Karen. Be realistic. What's the worst that could happen if you don't go to that interview today? And what's the worst that could happen if I don't get tenure? I'll lose my job, I'll have to find something else as if that won't be next to impossible as a failed assistant professor, we'll have to sell the house and uproot the kids and move God knows where. Listen. I'm sorry I've let you down, but this is my job and I can't leave just because you want me to."

"Nate—"

"I don't have a choice."

"You do have a choice."

"You're right. I do. And I've made it. I'm sorry."

She said nothing, stunned.

"Look," said Nate. "Call the quilters and see if you can reschedule for Friday or Saturday. If they won't, call someone else—Janice or one of the other moms. Someone will help you out. But I've got to go."

He hung up.

After a moment, Karen pressed the button on the receiver, waited for the dial tone, and called Janice.

"Hello?"

The voice was girlish, too young for Janice and too old for her daughters. "Um, hi. Is Janice there?"

"I'm sorry, she's not available at the moment. Would you like to leave a message?"

Then Karen recalled that Janice had mentioned hiring a baby-sitter to watch the kids while she and her husband went for an ultrasound. "No, thank you," she said, and hung up.

She called every other parent in the playgroup. Half were not home; the other half were either on their way out, or the background noise in their homes radiated so much chaos and confusion that Karen could not bring herself to ask them to take on two more children. She clutched the phone, racing through her mental list of baby-sitters and friends and people who owed her favors. She heard Ethan turn on the television and watched as Lucas began to fling soggy Cheerios out of his bowl using his spoon as a catapult. One sailed past her ear and stuck to the window; another landed on her sleeve. Immediately she brushed it off and snatched up a napkin to press the milk out of her clothes. Fortunately it was a dark suit. The spot would dry on the way to Waterford.

Sick to her stomach, she turned to the clock. It was a quarter past two.

Swiftly she unbuckled Lucas from his booster seat and snatched him up. "Ethan, honey, please go potty," she shouted toward the living room as she raced upstairs to change Lucas and put him in more presentable clothes.

"Why?"

"We're going for a ride."

She changed Lucas's diaper at a record pace and dug around in the laundry basket for a clean pair of overalls and onesie. All the while she strained her ears, praying that she would hear the door open and Nate calling out apologies.

"Mom?"

Karen glanced over her shoulder to find Ethan lingering in the doorway. One look told her she would have to change his clothes, too, since he had apparently used his shirt for a napkin after eating his peanut butter and jelly. "Did you go potty, honey?"

"I don't have to go."

"You should try to go. We're going to be in the car a long time."

"I don't have to pee. When I have to pee I feel a tickle in my penis and I don't feel one right now."

"I would like you to try. Just try. If you try and no pee comes out, that's fine."

Reluctantly, Ethan dragged himself from the doorway. She heard the sound of the toilet seat banging against the tank, and, a moment later, the boy who did not have to go potty doing exactly that.

"Okay, sweetie, you're done," she said, pulling on Lucas's socks. She coached Ethan through washing his hands and rushed him into a clean pair of jeans and a polo shirt. He complained about the collar and buttons, which

he despised, but Karen insisted. She brushed their teeth and hair and ushered them downstairs to the foyer and into their shoes. She checked the diaper bag for supplies, tossed in a few snacks and drinks, and snatched up her
purse and car keys.

"Where are we going?" asked Ethan as she rushed them outside to the car.
A reasonable question. "To my job interview."

Ethan climbed into his car seat glumly. "I don't want to go."

"Believe me, honey, this is not my first choice either." She gave him a sympathetic smile and a quick kiss.

He peered at her. "Mom—"

"What is it?" she said, struggling for patience. "We're in a very big hurry."

Whatever it was, he thought better of it. "Never mind. I love you."

Stabbed by guilt, she silently vowed to make it up to them. Later. She
closed Ethan's door and hurried around to the other side of the car, but as
she leaned over to place Lucas inside, she caught a whiff of his bottom. Muffling a groan, she told Ethan she would be right back and raced inside to
change Lucas's diaper again.

They set out a full half hour later than Karen had originally intended. She
might still make it, she thought grimly as she drove down Easterly Parkway
toward 322, only slightly faster than the law permitted. She had no idea what
she would do with the boys when she got there, but she would try to figure it
out on the way.

"Muk," said Lucas. "Mama, muk."

"He wants milk," translated Ethan.

"Hold on." Keeping one hand on the wheel, she dug into the diaper bag on
the front passenger seat and grasped his sippy cup. Straining to reach behind
her, she asked Ethan to take the cup and hand it to his brother. She heard
Ethan take a sip, and then something struck the back of her chair.

"No!" shouted Lucas. "Muk!"

"He wants *your* milk," Ethan clarified. "And I'd like some music, please.
Wasn't that nice of me to say please?"

"Yes, honey. Very nice." She turned on the CD player, struck by a sudden
and alarming vision of her sweet elder son becoming the most notorious,
ingratiating teacher's pet in the history of elementary education.

"Muk!"

She really should have weaned Lucas a long time ago. "I'm sorry, sweetie,
but I can't nurse you while I'm driving."

Lucas wailed.

"No, sweetie. Don't cry," she begged. "Come on. Sing with Mama. 'The wheels on the bus go round and round, round and round, round and round.' Ethan, help me."

Ethan joined in. "The wheels on the bus go round and round, all through the town!"

To Karen's relief, Lucas quieted down. As long as she kept singing, he was content, but if she paused to check the directions or change lanes, he broke into tears again. Even the break between songs was enough to make him whimper.

Twenty minutes later, Ethan had turned his attention to a picture book, she had become a hoarse solo act, and a glance in the rear view mirror revealed that Lucas's eyelids were starting to droop. She began singing louder, desperate to keep him awake. She knew her only chance at Elm Creek Manor would be if he slept through the interview, but he had already napped twice that morning and a third nap would guarantee active wakefulness for the rest of the day.

The motion of the car proved irresistible, and ten minutes later, Lucas was asleep. Karen switched off the CD player and wished she had thought to bring a bottle of water for herself. The singing had left her dry-mouthed and thirsty. She dug around in the diaper bag for a juice box and managed to puncture the foil with the straw without driving the car into a ditch or pouring apple juice down the front of her skirt.

"Mommy?" asked Ethan from the back seat. "What does 'tuck you' mean?"

"You mean like 'tuck you into bed'?" asked Karen. Ethan was always asking her to define words that he used every day, words whose meanings were, to Karen, so self-evident that she struggled to explain them without using the word itself in the definition. The other day he had asked her, "What is a bird?" She listed the standard details about feathers, nests, and eggs, to which he had replied, "No, Mommy. What *is* a bird?" Either he was a budding Zen master or he was trying to drive her insane.

"Mommy?"

"I'm thinking. Well, it means to snuggle your blankets and quilts around you so that you're warm and cozy in bed."

"What does it mean when there's no bed?"

"No bed?"

"What does it mean when you're mad at someone? Does it mean they should go to bed right now?"

Karen paused. "Honey, I don't understand."

"Like when someone takes your animal crackers at snack time and you hit them and they yell, 'Tuck you!' Does that mean they think you're naughty and you have to go to bed even though it's still daytime?"

"One of the kids at school said that?" gasped Karen. "Who?"

Ethan was silent.

"Who, Ethan? Who said that?"

"Well . . ." said Ethan slowly. "It definitely wasn't Graham. And he definitely didn't say it to Owen."

Ah. Graham. She should have guessed. Ethan had come home with several interesting Graham stories over the past school year. "That's a naughty thing some people say when they're angry. I don't want to hear you saying that, okay?"

"Okay," said Ethan, disappointed.

"Muk," murmured Lucas in his sleep.

Karen put in another CD.

She did not know whether to be grateful or alarmed when Ethan, too, drifted off to sleep. She was glad for the peace and quiet in which to collect her scattered thoughts, but she knew any chance that the boys would sleep peacefully in the tandem stroller while she chatted with the Elm Creek Quilters was long gone. If nothing else, they at least ought to be well rested and cheerful.

Both boys woke about fifteen miles from Waterford. She had made good time and wanted to press on, but Ethan's announcement that he had to go potty abruptly altered her priorities. Out of options, she pulled into the parking lot of McDonald's, and Ethan cheered in joyful disbelief at the sight of the golden arches. "Do *not* tell your father we came here," she instructed Ethan as she rushed the boys inside to the bathroom. She waited outside the stall trying to prevent Lucas from tipping over the garbage can while Ethan sat, asked for knock-knock jokes, told her another hair-raising Graham story, asked for fries and a shake, and did everything but go to the bathroom.

He looked up at her, swinging his feet, and his smile turned quizzical. "Mommy?"

"Honey, please, are you going to go or aren't you?" She checked her watch. "We are in a humongous hurry."

"Ooh-kay," he said, drawing out the word. "I guess I'm done."

"You may have fries but no ketchup," she said, wiping his bottom and quickly washing both boys' hands and her own. She made good on her promise, but the stop had cost them precious minutes. She would need a minor miracle to make it on time.

If she had not been to Elm Creek Manor before, she might have missed the turn completely, but she hit the brakes hard, turned the steering wheel sharply, and drove into a dense forest. The boys complained as the little car bounced over the gravel road. "Look! See? There's the creek," she said brightly as the water sparkled into view through the trees. She could not afford to put them in a bad humor now. "Just wait until you see the manor. It looks like a castle."

"Really?"

"Fwy!" shouted Lucas. A french fry whizzed past Karen's shoulder and landed on the dashboard. He had a remarkable arm for a toddler.

At a fork in the road, Karen took to the right. The left fork led to the parking lot behind the manor, but she would save time by parking closer to the front entrance.

They passed over Elm Creek on a narrow bridge, and soon afterward, they emerged from the midday twilight of the forest into sunshine. The gravel road gave way to a smooth, paved drive that gently curved across a broad, gently sloping green lawn. At last, just ahead, Karen caught sight of the three-story, gray stone manor graced by tall white columns. It was such a welcome, comforting sight that she let out a sigh of relief and forgot the clock for a moment.

The road ended in a circular driveway directly in front of the manor. "Look at the horse," exclaimed Ethan, pointing as they drove around a fountain of a rearing stallion in the center of the drive.

"Hort!" cried Lucas.

Karen pulled up to the curb as close to the manor as she dared. She didn't see any signs marking it as a fire lane, but with her luck, her car would get towed. "Yes, it's lovely, isn't it?"

"It *is* a castle," declared Ethan. "You were right, Mommy." Lucas babbled something that might have been agreement.

Karen turned off the car and glanced at her watch. She had exactly one minute before her interview was scheduled to begin. "Okay, boys. Lots of cooperation, remember?" She bounded from the car, briefcase and diaper bag in hand, and took the stroller from the trunk. Ethan stood by patiently as she tried to pry Lucas out of her arms and into the stroller, but he had had quite enough of sitting for one day and not nearly enough nursing, and he clung to her like a barnacle on a whale. She compromised by holding him and using the stroller to trundle the briefcase and diaper bag to the nearest of the two semicircular staircases leading from the driveway to a broad veranda. Too late, she remembered the wheelchair ramp at the rear entrance.

She managed to dislodge herself from Lucas, who stood at the bottom of the stairs wailing as she hefted the stroller up the stairs. Just then, one of the tall double doors opened and a tall, slender woman exited the manor. She wore a blue blazer and tan slacks, and her light brown hair hung in gentle waves to her shoulders. Her large brown eyes looked startled, and perhaps even annoyed. Karen guessed that she was probably somewhere in her late thirties.

Their eyes met, and for a moment, Karen thought the woman was going to offer to help. Instead she said, "Watch out for the blonde," and hurried past. Surprised, Karen turned to watch her go, but the boys and the stroller needed her attention. What blonde? Lucas? She *was* watching out for him, although from the sound he was making, an outsider might think he was neglected. Why did everyone feel obliged to comment on her parenting?

On the veranda, she set down the stroller and dashed back downstairs for the boys. Carrying Lucas, holding Ethan's hand, and propelling the stroller along with her hip, she crossed the veranda and paused at the entrance. "Okay, boys," she said, catching her breath. "This is very important to Mommy. I need you to be on your absolute best behavior. Understand?"

Lucas didn't, of course, but Ethan nodded solemnly. Karen took a deep breath to steady herself and pulled a funny face to make Ethan grin. Then she pushed the door open and went inside.

She had remembered the grand foyer, with its ceiling open to the third story and the balconies adorned with quilts, but she had forgotten the steps dividing the black marble floor into the entranceway and the foyer proper. This was as far as the stroller would go. She nudged it out of the way against the wall at the bottom of the stairs, released Ethan's hand, and picked up her briefcase and the diaper bag. Ethan seized as much of her hand as he could reclaim, clinging to her fingertips and shoving the handle of the briefcase over her knuckles.

"Do you need a hand?" a woman called.

Karen wished that she had been able to find a moment to freshen up first, wished that she had been able to make a more graceful entrance, but it was too late now. She fixed a confident smile in place and turned to find a white-haired woman in pink-tinted glasses gazing down at her from the top of the stairs. She held a sewing basket in one hand and a small bundle of fabric in the other.

"Hi. I'm Karen Wise. I'm here for an interview." Karen studied the woman, certain she had seen her before. "You're one of the Elm Creek Quilters, aren't you?"

The woman let out a tinkle of a laugh. "Oh, aren't we all Elm Creek Quilters at heart? Camp's in session, you know. I'm just on my way outside to work on my quilt block in the fresh air." She nodded to a row of chairs lining the wall just outside the hallway leading to the west wing of the manor. "I saw Sylvia Compson and some of the others go into that parlor just around the corner. I believe if you wait outside in one of those chairs, someone will come out for you soon."

"The thing is . . . I'm a little late."

The woman shrugged cheerfully. "Seems to me they are, too, or someone would be standing here waiting for you." She came down the stairs and smiled at the boys on her way to the door. "Adorable."

"Thank you," said Karen. She hoped the Elm Creek Quilters agreed.

"Mommy?" asked Ethan after the white-haired woman went outside. "Can we go home now?"

"Not yet, honey. We just got here." She took the boys up the marble stairs and stood for a moment in the center of the foyer. Through the doors in front of her, she heard the murmur of voices and sewing machines coming from the ballroom turned classroom. She seemed to recall that the administrative office was in the second floor library, but the thought of hauling the boys, diaper bag, and briefcase up that grand oak staircase was too daunting. "Let's wait over here," she said to the boys instead, hoping for the best, and she led them to the chairs the woman had indicated.

Ethan had no interest in sitting after the long drive, but Lucas cuddled in her lap while his older brother invented a game involving jumping from one marble square to another in a pattern only he could discern. "Muk," said Lucas insistently, wriggling into position. Karen unbuttoned the three lowest buttons on her suit jacket, untucked her blouse from her skirt, and felt him latch on.

Ethan stopped leaping from square to square to observe them. "Aww. He's so cute. He looks just like a little caterpillar."

Curious, Karen asked, "How so?"

"You know. Because he's nursing."

"Caterpillars are insects, honey. They don't drink milk."

"Oh." Ethan reconsidered. "I mean, he's just like a little baby calf, and you're the big mommy cow!"

"That's exactly right." She managed a wan smile. "Thanks for that, honey."

Perplexed, he regarded her for a moment before the sound of an opening door drew their attention. A woman in a tan pantsuit entered the manor and glanced around before climbing the marble stairs. She carried a quilted tote bag on her shoulder and a plastic container in her other hand. She looked to be a year or two older than Karen, a few inches shorter, and more than a few pounds heavier. Her dark brown hair was gathered into a thick French braid that hung to the middle of her back.

"Hi," Ethan called out enthusiastically.

"Hello," the woman said, sounding equally delighted. She glanced questioningly at Karen. "I'm here for the job interview?"

"I think this is the line," Karen said, gesturing to the chairs beside her.

"Oh." The woman flashed an apologetic smile. "I guess I'm early."

"And I'm late," said Karen ruefully, realizing too late that it might not have been wise to acknowledge that point to the competition.

The woman seated herself two chairs down from Karen, set her bag at her feet, and politely averted her eyes from Lucas as he enjoyed his snack. "Babysitter cancel?"

"Husband had other priorities."

The woman tsked and shook her head. "Men."

Karen nodded emphatically. Lucas chose that moment to pop off the breast and beam at the newcomer. Milk spurted on his face and on Karen's skirt.

"Oh, no," she exclaimed. She would have brushed off the droplets before they soaked in, but her arms were full of Lucas. When she tried to set him down, he drew his knees up to his chest and refused to put his feet on the floor.

"Here. Let me take the little guy." The woman reached for Lucas, and Karen, red-faced with embarrassment, automatically handed him over. She restored bra, blouse, and jacket, then found a cloth diaper in the diaper bag and began blotting the dark spots on her skirt.

Just then, the door to the ballroom opened and a stout woman with long, gray-streaked auburn hair rushed past. "Sorry, sorry, it's my fault," she told them, then disappeared into the parlor with a bang of the door.

"Who was that whirlwind?" the woman asked Lucas in the musical, cheerful voice adults use when they address children but are really speaking to the other adults in the room.

"She's Gwen Sullivan, one of the teachers here. I took one of her classes a few years ago." Karen stood and tried to smooth out the wrinkles in her skirt with her hands. Why did she bother? She was a mess. She never should have come.

Lucas reached for her, and when she took him, he regarded her solemnly and patted her cheeks. "Mama. Sor-sor, Mama."

"It's all right, honey." She kissed him and closed her eyes as he rested his head on her shoulder. She was the one who should apologize. She never should have applied for this job. She was underqualified and overextended. The boys would miss her and she would worry about them. If she left now, the Elm Creek Quilters would forget about her canceled interview and by next summer she could face them again—as a camper.

"Would you like a cookie?"

Karen's eyes flew open. "Beg your pardon?"

"Would you like a cookie?" The woman opened the plastic container to reveal three dozen beautifully frosted sugar cookies, decorated to resemble quilt blocks. "I made more than enough. If you don't take some I'll eat them all myself, and I really can't afford to."

"I'll help," Ethan piped up.

The woman smiled at him. "Ask your mommy first."

Karen agreed, reminding him to say thank you. The woman insisted she take two cookies for each of them, so Karen did, tucking the extras into the diaper bag for the ride home, or for bribes during the interview should bribes become necessary. Her own cookie, a Double Nine-Patch, was the best sugar cookie she had ever tasted.

If she had any sense, she would take the boys and leave right then. She was no match for a woman who arrived early and brought homemade cookies.

The door to the parlor swung open. A woman who looked to be in her midthirties smiled at them, her eyebrows rising slightly at the sight of the children. "Hi," she greeted the two women. "I'm Sarah McClure. Thanks for coming. Sorry for the delay." She glanced down at the file folder in her hand and back to Karen. "Karen Wise?"

"That's me." Karen rose, surreptitiously brushing crumbs from her lap, and gathered up baby, diaper bag, and briefcase. "Ethan?"

He ended his game with one last, emphatic leap and joined her at the parlor door. "Hi," he said, beaming up at Sarah. "I'm Efan and this is my baby brother Lucas and this is my mommy Karen."

Sarah's smile widened. "Yes, we spoke on the phone. It's nice to meet you in person, Efan."

"Not Efan. E-Fan."

"I'm so sorry about this," Karen interjected. "My husband was supposed to come home in time to care for them—I promise this would never happen on a regular work day, but—"

Sarah guided them into the parlor. "Don't worry about it. Stranger things than this happen around here all the time. Trust me."

Karen managed a smile as Sarah shut the door behind them and indicated a high-backed, upholstered chair facing six women seated on sofas and chairs on the other side of a low coffee table. With its sharp corners and gleaming polished surface, it was naturally a magnet for the boys. With a quick, apologetic shrug for the Elm Creek Quilters, Karen settled her sons in a corner, pulled out soft toys, crackers, and sippy cups from the diaper bag, and quietly begged Ethan to keep Lucas amused while Mommy talked to the nice ladies. Then she took her seat as Sarah McClure made introductions. Most of the women looked at least vaguely familiar from her week at quilt camp. The silver-haired woman seated in an armchair much like her own was unmistakable—Sylvia Compson, award-winning Master Quilter, teacher, and member of the Quilters' Hall of Fame.

Sylvia peered at Karen over her glasses, and she was not smiling. "Well. What's this?"

"Karen had some child-care issues this morning," said Sarah. The woman on one end of the sofa—Judy—caught her eye and nodded understandingly.

"They're wonderful boys and they won't be any distraction," Karen promised.

"I can see that," said Sylvia dryly as Lucas toddled over to Karen and rested his head on her knee.

Karen smiled weakly and stroked his hair. "I know these are unusual circumstances for an interview, but I'm delighted to be here. It's an honor just to be considered for this position."

"I wonder . . ." Sylvia's gaze was piercing. "Did you feed your children directly before coming here?"

"Well . . ." Did she look like the kind of mother who forgot to feed her children? Forget to leave them at home, yes, but forget to feed them? Never. "They've eaten, thanks. If they get hungry, I brought snacks."

"Anything good?" asked Gwen, peering at the diaper bag. Karen, grateful for the levity, smiled at her.

"Your résumé is very strong," remarked Sarah. "You have impressive marketing and teaching experience."

"Have you ever actually taught *quilting,* though?" asked an attractive woman with blonde curls.

Karen considered her failed attempt to teach Janice and decided not to mention it. "No, but I'm confident my teaching skills will serve me well with any curriculum. Once you've taught required core courses to reluctant college freshmen, you can thrive in any classroom."

To her relief, most of the women smiled, but not Diane, and not Sylvia Compson. Karen felt her courage falter. She had admired Sylvia as long as she had been a quilter. Karen had been too shy to introduce herself during her week at quilt camp, but she had observed Sylvia at mealtimes and during the evening programs. Why was she frowning? And what was with that odd, impatient gesture she kept making, as if she were brushing loose strands of hair off her forehead?

Lucas struggled to climb onto her lap. Automatically Karen reached for him as the youngest of the women, Gwen Sullivan's beautiful auburn-haired daughter, asked her how she began quilting.

"I began here," Karen said. As she told them how she had longed to learn to make a baby quilt, Lucas tugged at her lapels and struggled with the buttons of her suit. Then Sarah McClure posed a question to her, and one from Gwen followed. All the while Lucas peppered the conversation with demands for "Muk!" ever increasing in volume and insistence.

At last she gave up and pleaded, "Lucas, honey, wouldn't you like some milk in a cup?"

"I think he wants milk in a shirt."

She started to hear Ethan's voice at her elbow, the last to discover he had crept silently closer rather than be the only one left out of the interview. "Honey, would you please go look at your book until I'm done?"

"Lucas is over here with you."

"Oh, just go ahead and let him nurse," said Gwen good-naturedly. "We're all friends here."

The blonde woman shot her a look. "Don't be ridiculous. Look at how big he is. He doesn't want to nurse. He's just fidgety." She turned to Karen. "Right?"

"Well," Karen managed to say, wrestling with her toddler, "actually—"

"He nurses all the time," said Ethan. "That's all he does. Nurse, nurse, nurse. And go poop in his diaper. He doesn't talk much. But he's very cute."

"How old is he?" asked the blonde woman, appalled.

"Eighteen months," said Karen. Lucas whooped with delight as he managed to unfasten a button.

The blonde woman shook her head in disbelief. "When they can walk over and ask for it, it's time to cut them off."

"Oh, Diane, please." Gwen rolled her eyes. "Breastmilk is the best, most natural food in the world. In some cultures, children nurse until they're four years old. It's only in western societies that we've so sexualized the female breast that we've forgotten what they're really there for. Breastmilk is full of antibodies and proteins that simply can't be reproduced in formula, no matter what the corporate manufacturers claim."

"Did you know that a child's IQ increases by five points for every month he or she nurses?" added Sarah.

The Elm Creek Quilters stared at her. "And why have you been studying up on breastfeeding?" inquired Gwen's daughter.

Sarah turned beet red. "No reason."

"I nursed Summer for almost three years," said Gwen with pride.

"I could tell," said Diane.

"How? Because she's so intelligent? So healthy?"

"No. Because that's exactly the sort of thing you would do. I'm just surprised you haven't bragged about it earlier." Diane fixed her attention on Karen, though it was obvious she was trying not to see Lucas, now happily suckling away. "So tell us. What makes you think you're qualified for this job, aside from your obvious ability to multitask?"

"Well, I'm a quilter, of course," said Karen. "I enjoy designing my own quilts, and I've mastered many of the techniques you listed in your ad." She probably could have put together a more cogent answer if she didn't have a baby at the breast. "I also have a sense of humor, and being a mother has definitely taught me how to deal with occasional minor disasters."

"And a few major ones," remarked Gwen, "if your experience is anything like mine. No offense, kiddo."

"Of course not, Mom," said Summer, as if she had heard it all before.

"I have another question," said Diane. "What kind of mother are you?"

Karen blinked at her. "What kind? Well, I suppose I'm attentive, loving, patient—most of the time—a bit of a worrier, creative—"

"That's not what I meant," Diane broke in. "I mean, what kind of mother *are* you, to even contemplate taking on a job outside the home when your children obviously need you?"

"I don't think this line of questioning is appropriate," said Sarah.

"I don't think it was even a real question," said Judy.

"It's a legitimate concern," said Diane. "For her and for us. She and her boys clearly have a strong attachment. If we hire her, we are forcing her to stick those two precious children in a day care center. How can we be a party to that?"

"I went to day care when I was a child," said Summer. "I turned out all right."

Diane waved that off. "That's different. Gwen's a single mother. She didn't have a choice."

"Ms. Wise's child-care arrangements are her concern, not ours," said Sylvia.

"They will be our concern if she cancels classes because she can't get a baby-sitter."

Karen was about to assure them that she would never cancel class, but she hesitated. She could not be sure that she would never miss a day because of the boys. What if Lucas had an ear infection? What if Ethan had a day off school?

"I think it's against the law to discriminate against a job applicant because she has children," said the dark-haired woman named Bonnie. "If it isn't, it should be."

Sylvia raised a hand. "Let's get this conversation back on track. I believe Sarah has several more questions on her list, and we don't want to keep Ms. Wise and her sons any longer than necessary."

"Just one." Sarah looked up from her copy of Karen's portfolio and smiled. "I wondered if you would read to us from the cover letter you submitted with your application. I have it here if you need it."

"That's okay. I brought one." Karen withdrew the letter from her briefcase, wondering what Sarah had in mind. Didn't each Elm Creek Quilter have her own copy, and wouldn't they have read it already?

"Start with the third paragraph from the top," said Sarah.

Karen nodded and read aloud:

"Please note that the nearly five-year gap in my employment record is voluntary, as I left my last position to raise my children. In all honesty, I had no intention of returning to the work force so soon, but when I saw your ad, I immediately reconsidered. I enjoy staying home with my children, but I could not pass up this opportunity to become an Elm Creek Quilter. I think every former camper considers herself an Elm Creek Quilter to some extent, but I feel that to deserve that title, and to deserve the privilege of joining the staff of Elm Creek Quilt Camp, a person must possess more than excellent technical skills and teaching abilities. In my time as a camper, I discovered teachers who passed along knowledge but also were willing to learn from their students, who honored the traditions handed down through the generations but were not afraid to push the art beyond its traditional boundaries. I encountered women committed to creating a supportive environment where quilters of all levels of experience could challenge themselves artistically without fear of ridicule or failure, because every risk honestly and courageously attempted is looked upon as a success. I learned about valuing the process as well as the product, and about honoring every piece's contribution to the beauty of the whole. Elm Creek Quilt Camp celebrates and honors the artist inside every woman, and I would consider it a great privilege and honor to join your circle of quilters."

Karen was almost afraid to meet the Elm Creek Quilters' eyes after she finished reading. Too much information, she decided. They probably thought she was a font of ingratiating rhetoric, spouting praise in order to win herself an interview. What they could not know was that she meant every word of it. That letter had been the easiest part of her application to complete because she had written from the heart.

"Thank you," said Sarah. "Does anyone else have anything to ask Karen?"

Karen took a deep breath to steady her nerves as Gwen continued the interview. She answered the remaining questions with Lucas on her lap and Ethan by her side. Occasionally Ethan piped up with responses of his own, which were invariably more insightful and wittier than her own. Lucas took a liking to Gwen's daughter and initiated a game of peek-a-boo, burying his face in his mother's shoulder, peeking out to catch Summer's eye, laughing, and hiding his face again. At Sylvia's prompting, Karen showed them her Elm Creek Quilts pattern and quilt block, which they added to her portfolio. She felt a glimmer of pride when they praised the artistry of her design and the ingenuity of the foundation paper piecing construction, but she doubted that that small demonstration of competence would be enough to win them over.

They shook hands all around at the end of the interview, but Karen did not bother to ask when she might hear from them. She packed the diaper bag and led the boys from the parlor to a bathroom a few doors down, in the west wing, where she changed Lucas's diaper and asked Ethan to try, just try, to go potty before they returned to the car.

As she washed her hands, she looked at herself in the mirror over the sink to see if she looked as hopeless and miserable as she felt. That was when she saw the Cheerio clinging to her bangs, slightly off-center above her forehead.

She gasped and brushed it out of her hair. How long had it been there? Immediately she guessed it: since Lucas's lunch. She had sat there on the phone trying to reach Nate, paying no attention as Lucas flung cereal across the room.

That explained Sylvia Compson's odd question about whether she had fed her children and her inexplicable gestures at the start of the interview.

"Why didn't anyone tell me?" she wailed. Sylvia's all too subtle gestures aside, everyone she had seen since lunchtime had allowed her to walk around with cereal clinging to her bangs.

"Tell you what?" asked Ethan, drying his hands on a paper towel.

"That I had a Cheerio in my hair! You must have seen it. Why didn't you tell me?"

"I tried to."

"When?"

"When you buckled me in the car and when I was on the potty at McDonald's. You seemed busy and mad so I didn't want to talk."

Karen closed her eyes and sighed, remembering. "Honey, I know I was impatient then, but I really, really wish you would have told me."

"I thought maybe you wanted it there."

"Why would I have wanted a Cheerio in my hair?"

He shrugged. "It looked pretty."

Karen could not think of any possible response to that, so she shook her head in disbelief and led the boys from the bathroom. When they passed the friendly woman in the tan suit on their way to the front doors to the manor, the woman said, "I hope your interview went well."

"I hope yours goes better," Karen replied wearily. The woman peered at her inquisitively and seemed on the verge of speaking, but just then the parlor door started to open. Karen quickly scooted the boys outside rather than face any of the Elm Creek Quilters again, pausing only long enough to fetch the stroller.

"Mommy, can we play in the water?" Without waiting for an answer, Ethan raced across the veranda and down the stairs toward the fountain in the center of the circular driveway.

"Look both ways before you cross," Karen called after him, although the driveway was lightly traveled compared to the road leading to the parking lot behind the manor. Her car was the only one parked in the circle. The other applicant, whom Karen could not help thinking of as the Cookie Lady, must have parked in the rear lot as Karen was supposed to have done. The Cookie Lady was probably at that moment making a wonderful impression on the Elm Creek Quilters. She would never know how Karen had set the stage for her, how she had made herself the ideal act to follow.

She set down Lucas and struggled to collapse the tandem stroller so that it would be easier to carry downstairs.

"Oh, dear."

At the sound of the voice, Karen glanced down the veranda and spotted the white-haired woman who had greeted them when they first arrived at Elm Creek Manor. She was seated in an Adirondack chair a few yards away, a quilt block in one hand, a threaded needle in the other.

"Is something wrong?" asked Karen as she carried the stroller to the grass below.

"I can't for the life of me figure out what I'm doing wrong," the white-haired woman said, holding up the quilt block and shaking her head in consternation.

Karen checked on Ethan, who was happily throwing leaves into the fountain and following their progress through the whorls of water. Assured that he was occupied, she scooped up Lucas and went to see what was the matter. "Maybe I can help."

"Oh, would you try, dear?" The woman smiled gratefully before gesturing to the center of the block. "I can't get this edge to lie smooth no matter what I try."

Karen pulled up a chair beside her, set down Lucas, and leaned over for a closer look. "I'm not that great at hand appliqué," she said apologetically, studying the Rose of Sharon block. Despite the woman's frustration, the block seemed nearly halfway completed. "I'm more of a fusible-webbing, machine-zigzag stitch kind of appliquér. But maybe . . ." She reached for the block. "May I?"

"Of course." The woman handed it to her.

Karen flipped it over and examined the stitches on the back. They were tiny, neat, and even. "I don't think the problem is your needlework. Your stitches are excellent. Maybe it's the appliqué. Did you baste the edges of the circle in place before you began sewing?"

"Of course."

"As I said, I'm no expert, but whenever I appliqué circles, I always cut a template out of cardstock, and then cut a circle from my fabric an eighth to a quarter of an inch larger. Then I place the template on the wrong side of the fabric, thread my needle, and take small running stitches in the fabric circle all the way around the edge, leaving longer tails at the beginning and the end." Karen demonstrated the movements with an imaginary needle and the woman's cloth. "Then I pull gently on the thread tails, drawing the fabric circle around my template. That makes a circle with perfectly smooth edges."

"What an ingenious idea," exclaimed the woman.

"I can't take credit for it. I read it in a book or a magazine somewhere. After I have my circle, I press it flat with a hot iron and use my sewing machine to baste the edges in place until I appliqué the circle to the background fabric."

"Do you sew right through the cardstock with your machine when you baste?"

Karen shrugged and returned to the quilt block. "I might not if I had a top of the line machine, but mine is secondhand and tough—built to withstand just about anything, but without all the fancy computerized stitches. There's not much I can do to hurt it."

"Well, thank you very much." The woman patted the quilt block as if to reassure it all would be well. "I will have to try that."

Rising, Karen nodded to the front doors of the manor. "I'm sure one of the Elm Creek Quilters could show you how."

"I've no doubt one of them could. Have a safe trip home, dear."

"Thanks." Karen scooped up Lucas and carried him on her hip as she went to join Ethan at the fountain, pushing the stroller along before her. Why had she bothered to bring it? It was one more bead on a string of bad decisions. Her sense of failure and impending rejection, which had ebbed as she chatted with the white-haired woman, suddenly returned in a torrent. Discouraged, she allowed the boys to play near the fountain for a few minutes longer, concealing her disappointment and weariness behind smiles and encouragement for their game. Then she coaxed them back into their car seats and drove home.

The boys had slept too much that day to fall under the spell of the car's motion another time, so although Karen longed to be alone with her thoughts, she gave in to Ethan's requests for stories and sang along with the CD as they wished. She owed them after dragging them through that debacle. She also owed them supper, and she was not in any hurry to get home.

When they reached the outskirts of State College, she pulled over at an Eat 'N Park and treated all of them to buttermilk pancakes. The boys bounced happily on the padded vinyl seats of their booth and made sticky messes of themselves with the maple syrup, but they charmed the waitress as well as several nearby diners and Karen's heart lifted each time they made her laugh. She even ordered a Dutch apple pie to go before remembering that Nate did not deserve his favorite treat, not that day and possibly not for the rest of their marriage. But she was not bold enough to ask the waitress to remove the charge, so she paid the bill, cleaned the boys with wet wipes, and took them home.

Nate was waiting for them on the front stoop. As she drove past him into the garage, she glimpsed his expression, somehow both wary and resolute. He met her at the car door before she turned off the engine.

"How did it go?" he asked, backing away from the door as she opened it.

"How did it go?" She could not even look at him. She opened Lucas's door and unbuckled him from his car seat. "I had to take two small children on a job interview. How do you think it went?"

Nate went around to the other side of the car for Ethan. "If I could have gotten out of that meeting—"

"You could have." Carrying Lucas, she reached into the front seat for the pie. She brushed past Nate and went into the house. "Like you said, you made your choice."

"I put an existing full-time job ahead of a potential part-time job. I'm sorry, but from where I stand, that looks like the only logical choice."

She slammed the pie box on the kitchen counter and glared at him. He carried the diaper bag and her briefcase, which he set on the floor. He reached for Lucas but she would not hand him over.

Ethan followed a pace behind his father. "We were good, Mommy. Even Lucas. Except for the Cheerio. You said."

His words abruptly drained the force of her anger. "Yes. You were both as good as I could have expected. You did what I asked and you used good manners. Thank you."

Ethan beamed and ran off to the living room. A second later, she heard PBS Kids on the television. Lucas squirmed until she set him down, and he toddled off after his brother.

"Karen, I said I was sorry."

"If you don't want me to work, why not just say so?"

A muscle in his jaw tightened and relaxed. "I did not deliberately sabotage you and you know it."

"One day, Nate. I asked for one day."

"And I had every intention of giving it to you, but I couldn't. Honey—"

He reached for her, but she avoided his touch and fled downstairs to the basement, where she sat on the folding chair in front of her sewing machine and covered her face with her hands so the boys would not hear her cry.

Chapter Three
Anna

Olive oil, roasted red pepper, rosemary, basil, sea salt, a pinch of white pepper, and—and what? What had she forgotten? With no time to rummage through her notes, Anna closed her eyes and willed the recipe to emerge from her subconscious. It wasn't her fault she was unprepared. This was supposed to have been her night off, but when her boss called and asked if she would be willing to take over the provost's dinner for several important college donors, she told him she would be there in ten minutes. For months she had begged him to entrust her with a special event like this one. She had assisted senior chefs for years and was eager to try her hand at the head chef position. As she raced from her apartment to the kitchen of the banquet room of Nelson Hall, where the guests were due to arrive in less than two hours, she ran through the menu given to her over the phone. It was not difficult, and she was confident she could handle it even on such short notice. Then she arrived at the kitchen to discover that two of her work-study students had failed to show and the fresh vegetables her predecessor had requested from the College Food Service's prep room in South Dining Hall had arrived frozen. By the time she sorted out that mess, she was a half hour behind schedule. Ordinarily she thrived on improvising in the face of unexpected complications, but today, the additional stress made her head ache.

Ideally, she should set the sauce aside for a half hour to allow the flavors to blend, but she had run out of time and would have to serve it as is—if she managed to finish it at all. "What did I forget?" asked Anna, thinking aloud, not really expecting an answer.

"Thyme," replied her favorite work-study student, almost at her elbow. "You added thyme when you made this for Junior Parents' Weekend."

"Of course. Thyme." Anna measured the last of the herbs into the processor and punched the blend button. "Thank you, Callie."

"Whatever," said Callie, trying unsuccessfully to conceal a grin of pleasure. Unlike the rest of the crew on duty that night, Callie had a passion for food and was not simply putting in hours to earn textbook and beer money. She watched everything Anna did and asked admiring questions, making Anna feel almost as if she had a protégé. Sometimes Anna was tempted to encourage Callie to enroll in a culinary institute after graduation, but she worried that Callie might be insulted. Just because Anna had no idea what anyone would do with a degree in American Studies did not mean that it was not useful. What would she know about it? She had known she wanted to be a chef since the seventh grade and had never explored other options. According to her boyfriend, Anna had a disgraceful tendency to be skeptical of any education that was not immediately practical, but she was working on it.

"The provost set down his salad fork," remarked another student, peering through the round window in the kitchen door instead of stirring the chocolate sauce for the raspberry tarts even though Anna had already asked him twice. He was a business major and considered such mundane tasks beneath him because he believed he was destined to become the CEO of a major international corporation before reaching his thirties. He didn't need to learn how to cook; he needed to observe the wealthy donors dining with the college provost because one day he would be among them.

Make yourself useful, Anna silently ordered him, but she said, "Do they look like they're ready for the main course?"

"I . . . think so."

"Okay. Just a minute." Anna took the pitcher of herb sauce and hurried to the gleaming stainless-steel counter where her assistants were spooning wild rice pilaf and sautéed vegetables onto warmed plates, assembly line fashion. "Where are the salmon fillets?"

"Here," said Callie, removing the first of several trays from the broiler.

Anna gestured to Callie and the laconic observer by the door. "Callie and Rob. Get the salmon on the plates." Something in her tone made even Rob promptly obey. As soon as each fillet was in position, Anna dressed it with sauce. "Okay. Servers, come and get 'em. And take care of the head table first this time, please?"

She had little time to talk except to issue instructions or urge a server to hurry. She had scarcely enough time to monitor the progress of the meal in the banquet room on the other side of the door, but she found moments where she could. Her position in Waterford College's College Food Services could rise or fall depending upon the diners' response to her entrée.

Occasionally Rob returned to the window in the door to describe the progress of the meal. "The provost just tried the fish. He's smiling. So is the guy next to him."

"On which side?"

"Um, his right. Our left."

Anna closed her eyes and breathed a deep sigh of relief. That "guy" was the college's most generous donor. If he was happy with the meal, she could consider it a successful evening even if the kitchen caught on fire.

She couldn't relax until after dessert was served, when all she had to worry about was keeping the servers circulating with coffee and making sure they refilled the cream pitchers and sugar bowls and didn't confuse regular with decaf. Despite its inauspicious beginning, the banquet appeared to be a success.

Afterward, the provost came into the kitchen to congratulate Anna on a job well done. "Glad to help," she said, and she was pleased when he continued on through the kitchen, where her student workers were busy cleaning up, to thank them as well. It was common knowledge on the Waterford College campus that working for food services was the lowest of the low as far as work-study jobs were concerned—minimum wage for menial tasks and, except on special occasions such as this, the indignity of cleaning up after their more fortunate classmates in the dining halls. A word of thanks and a handshake from the provost was a nice perk, and Anna was so relieved to have survived the evening that she intended to provide her students with another: all of the extra desserts they could carry back to the dorms.

Before leaving, the provost paused at the door, scrutinized Anna, and said, "Are you new here? I don't think you've been in charge of any of my dinners before."

"This is my sixth year at Waterford College," said Anna. "I've worked some of your other events, but always as an assistant."

"This is your first banquet as head chef?"

Anna nodded. "The head chef assigned to your event called in sick. I guess I'm the understudy."

"Understudy or not, you've done an exemplary job," the provost said. "I wasn't even aware of any emergency. Your dishes were intriguing, and your response to the situation is the very definition of grace under pressure."

Anna glowed. She knew that a successful banquet with delicious food and excellent service could mean that next year's faculty salary increases would be paid for by donations rather than tuition increases. "Thank you."

"What's your name again?"

"Anna. Anna Del Maso."

"Well, Anna Del Maso, I'll be asking for you again." He nodded a good-bye and left the kitchen.

As she walked home after the banquet, Anna wished she could share her triumph with Gordon. She wasn't sure if she should call him. When she called off their dinner plans, they'd had—not a fight, exactly—more like a heated disagreement. "Can't they get someone else?" he had griped when she called from her cell phone, already hurrying down the stairs of her apartment building on her way to the job.

"They could, but I don't want them to," she said.

"Don't you all use the same recipes? Can't they call that woman you work with—Sandra? Mandy? She's worked there almost as long as you."

"Andrea," corrected Anna. "She started here two years after I did and I don't think she wants the responsibility. I do. This is for the provost. This could be my big break."

"Oh, come on. Big break? In College Food Services?"

Anna paused to wait for the crosswalk, annoyed by the sneer in his voice. "If I prove myself, I could finally get promoted to head chef."

He was silent so long she thought the connection had broken. "Is that what you really want?"

It wasn't her ultimate career goal, no, but it was a significant step in the right direction. The light changed and she hurried across the street. "Of course."

"Do you really think it's a good idea for you to be working more banquets? All those heavy sauces, the rich desserts—"

"I'll renew my gym membership."

"Don't be so defensive. I'm just saying it would be easier to eat healthy if you're working the dining halls."

And easier still if she left the profession altogether. Gordon had made that point before. "I'm almost there, Gordon, I've got to go." She hung up without waiting for a good-bye and immediately regretted it. Gordon was easily offended and never accepted an apology unaccompanied by a humbling show of atonement. She would have to make it up to him tomorrow night with a dinner as impressive as the provost's.

The central, bewildering puzzle about Gordon was that, although he liked delicious food as much as the next person, he did not want his girlfriend to be a chef. Or maybe it was not such a puzzle—if she were thin, her choice of profession might not bother him at all, especially if she also had a Ph.D. to hang on her wall to impress his friends. Like Gordon, they were liberal arts graduate students and aspiring intellectuals with whom Anna had very little in common. Anna would never admit it to Gordon, but his friends intimidated her, and she was relieved that he rarely suggested they go out with them.

Anna had never dated anyone who wasn't thrilled that she enjoyed cooking, not until Gordon came along. She thought Gordon ought to appreciate her job, if not for all the delicious, home-cooked, gourmet meals, then for the fact that her work had brought them together. They had met the previous year at a dinner given by the English department to honor a retiring professor. It was the first week of the semester and they had not yet hired enough work-study students, so Anna had to help carry serving trays to the buffet table. A bearded, stocky man not much taller than she had followed her into the kitchen to compliment her on the marinated mushrooms and had stuck around to chat. She was flattered by the attention of someone so well spoken and knowledgeable about world affairs, especially since most academics ignored her, so she accepted his invitation to go out for coffee the following afternoon. His topics of conversation differed so drastically from what she and her friends talked about that she feared she would bore him, but he did not seem to mind that she mostly listened, asking occasional, carefully constructed questions to reveal as little of her ignorance as possible.

Apparently she had made a good impression because that date led to another, and soon they were seeing each other steadily. He was often too busy with his teaching and research to take her out, but several times a week he managed to stop by her apartment on his way home from the library for a late supper. It wasn't an ideal arrangement, but he promised her things would improve once he had his degree and no longer had to hit the books sixteen hours a day. She was pleased by this hint that he thought they had a future together, because he usually brushed off her hesitant attempts to discuss the direction of their relationship. Most often, he said that he hoped she agreed that modern relationships needed to throw off their patriarchal tendencies and allow all parties room to be. To be *what,* she wasn't sure, and in this case she didn't want to reveal her naïveté by asking.

She paused to shift her purse; the strap kept slipping off her shoulder and bumping into the paper grocery bag she carried, heavy with carefully wrapped containers of salmon in fresh herb sauce, grilled vegetables, and raspberry tart with chocolate glaze. College Food Services officially discouraged employees from taking leftovers home, but to discourage was not to forbid, and Anna hated to see all that food go to waste. It pained her to throw away good food when she had to monitor her own grocery budget so carefully. If she splurged on luxuries now, she might never have enough money saved to open her own restaurant.

She had the place all picked out—Chuck's, a diner across the street from the main gate of campus. Its excellent location guaranteed it a steady business, even though the current owner was nearing retirement and lately had put only a halfhearted effort into running the place. He had sent his two children to Waterford College in hopes that they would take over the business, but they left Waterford for good as soon as they received their degrees.

Anna hoped he would hold off his retirement for a few more years, just long enough for her to have amassed a down payment. She had an excellent credit rating and ought to be able to get a small business loan to cover the rest. And then she would say good-bye to the dining hall and hello to her own menus and the freedom to work with ingredients that did not have to be purchased in bulk quantities.

The short walk from campus to her three-story red brick walk-up on the eastern end of Main Street always seemed longer at the end of a grueling shift in the kitchen, and hauling the grocery bag up three flights left her winded. She set the bag on the floor outside her apartment door and dug in her purse for her keys.

A door opened behind her. "Oh, hey, Anna. Just getting off work?"

Anna glanced up. "Hi, Jeremy. Just going out?"

Jeremy shook his head, scrubbing a hand through his dark, wildly curly hair. "Not to do anything fun, if that's what you mean. I have an exciting night planned with my dissertation. I'm going down to Uni-Mart for a snack and something caffeinated. Want me to bring you anything back?"

"Don't waste your money on junk food," protested Anna, reaching into the grocery bag. It was a wonder he had any taste buds left. "Here. I brought home extras from the provost's party."

"Any meat?" he asked, his eyes hopeful behind round, wire-rimmed glasses.

"Does fish count?"

"Fish always counts. Just please don't tell Summer."

Anna laughed and agreed, amused by his guilty expression. Jeremy's girl-friend was a vegetarian, and although she didn't insist that Jeremy also avoid meat, he did so when dining with her to spare her feelings. "Take this," she said, loading his arms with College Food Services containers. "Salmon, veggies, plus dessert."

"Chocolate?"

"There's chocolate sauce for the raspberry tart."

"You are the best neighbor in the world," he said fervently, peeking in the container holding his dessert. "Thank you for this. Once again. I swear I wasn't waiting by the door for you to come home."

Anna smiled and found her keys. "You do seem to have a strange way of knowing which nights I work a banquet and when I'm just at the dining hall."

"Can I at least get you a cup of coffee?"

"No, thanks, I'm fine." She unlocked her apartment and carried her bags inside. "See you later."

Anna had hoped Gordon would be waiting for her, but she was not surprised to find the apartment dark and quiet. She was disappointed, but not surprised. Graduate students kept long hours, and she had not yet called him to apologize. Besides, she had already given away his share of the leftovers.

She flipped on the light with her elbow and placed her burdens on the kitchen counter beside the answering machine, whose light was definitely not blinking to notify her of a message. The kitchenette was wholly inappropriate for a chef—no bigger than a walk-in closet with a small refrigerator, a single sink, a two-burner electric stovetop, and an oven too small to accommodate her jellyroll pan. "Someday," she said aloud. Someday when she had her own restaurant, she wouldn't care what her kitchen at home looked like. Someday, when Gordon finished his degree, they could move in to a wonderful new home with a state-of-the-art kitchen where she would cook him romantic dinners and serve him marvelous breakfasts in bed.

"Someday," she said again, setting the table for one.

After supper, she washed the dishes, checked the phone for a dial tone to make sure it was working, and decided to unwind before bed by quilting for a little while. After taking her sewing machine from the closet to the kitchen table and retrieving her cutting board from beneath the day bed, she laid the quilt top in progress on the floor and pondered it from atop a chair. "Somehow everything in my life ends up being about food," she murmured, frowning thoughtfully at the blue circles appliquéd on a background of white and brown. There was no escaping it. What she had intended as an abstract arrangement of circles of varying sizes and hues set against two contrasting forms in brown and white now resembled nothing so much as a cascade of ripe blueberries falling from an overturned bucket into a pool of rich cream. At least it would complement her strawberry pie quilt, her eggs Benedict quilt, and her chocolate soufflé quilt. If anyone asked, she would say that the resemblance was intentional. She could claim the quilts were a series: Quilts from the Kitchen.

Not that anyone would ask, since it was unlikely that anyone would ever see them. Anna had shown her quilts to Jeremy and his girlfriend once, but since Summer moved out of his apartment and into Elm Creek Manor, Anna rarely saw her anymore.

She wouldn't show her quilts to Gordon, either. Gordon knew she quilted but wasn't interested—although it might be more accurate to say that her quilting perplexed him. After he told her that she was too intelligent to spend her time stitching away pointlessly, she had learned to conceal her quilting projects as soon as she heard his key in the lock. When he had quoted some eighteenth-century woman's essay denouncing women who had nothing better to do than sit around "stitching upon samplers," Anna had felt wounded. The wound had stung even more when Gordon had added that Theresa taught that insulting essay in her creative nonfiction class.

Gordon's roommate Theresa had been a part of their relationship from the beginning. Even on that first night as Anna and Gordon talked in the kitchen while the rest of the English department enjoyed dessert in the other room, Gordon found ways to bring Theresa into the conversation. When he did it again on their first official date at the coffee shop, Anna asked him if he and Theresa were dating or if they had broken up. He laughed and said that he and Theresa were "special friends," but they had never had a romantic interest in each other. "Romantic love is mere biochemistry, anyway," he said, waving a hand dismissively. Anna nodded to indicate that she understood, though she wasn't sure she did. It seemed a rather cynical attitude for a first date.

More than fourteen months had passed since then, and Anna had yet to meet the mystery woman. She felt certain she would recognize Theresa if she saw her, though. She must be brilliant and alluring; nothing else could explain Gordon's preoccupation. Anna envisioned a tall, willowy, raven-haired woman with artistic hands and haunting eyes. Since she was a poet, she probably dressed all in black, or maybe she draped herself in yards of wildly colored ethnic print fabric. Theresa definitely wouldn't be twenty pounds on the wrong side of plump, like Anna, and she would never fear that her boyfriend was ashamed of her job or her lack of a graduate degree or her double-digit dress size. No, Theresa's mind would be focused on loftier affairs.

"But she probably can't even boil water," Anna said aloud.

She waited until it was too late for Gordon to call. Only then did she put away her quilting, turn out the lights, and go to bed.

❧

When she woke the next morning, Anna decided to take her day off seriously and eat a meal prepared by someone else for a change. She considered going to the Bistro, a favorite spot for breakfast and lunch for local residents and college faculty, a popular student hangout in the evenings when the bar opened. She would probably run into some friends there, so she would not have to dine alone. L'Arc du Ciel was another possibility; although the most exclusive restaurant in town far exceeded her usual budget for dining out, their Sunday brunches were sublime and she could pick up a few ideas.

She quickly settled upon a far less gastronomically pleasing option, but one that had become her favorite dining spot nonetheless: Chuck's. She tucked a tablet of graph paper and a pencil into her purse and walked a few blocks down the street to the restaurant that would hopefully one day be hers.

She ordered a chocolate cappuccino and a blueberry muffin, seated herself at an inconspicuous corner table, and, while she waited for her breakfast, drew a floor plan of the restaurant on the graph paper. Since she had never been in the kitchen and could see very little of it through the window where the cooks placed orders for the servers to pick up, she left that part of the drawing blank. By the time her breakfast arrived, she had sketched a rough blueprint of the dining areas and entryway. As she ate, she studied her drawing and compared it to her surroundings, drawing new lines and erasing others. She would remove the counter and the seven stools to make room for more tables. Where the order-up window was now, she would install a brick oven, as much for atmosphere as for cooking. She would replace the wood paneling with off-white stucco to brighten the room and make it more inviting. The entry should be extended to create a small foyer between the outside door and the door to the dining room. Currently there was only one door, and it led directly outside. That wasn't a problem now, in midsummer, but she recalled from previous visits that in less temperate weather, every new customer brought in the cold and sometimes even drifts of snow. In January she had seen customers leave rather than take a table near the door.

A merry jingle reminded her of another change she would make—lose the bell over the door. It was fine for a diner, but not for the intimate but friendly, elegant yet casual restaurant she intended to create. She added a quick note to her drawing, then glanced up in time to see the couple who had entered. As the man smiled at the woman and gestured to an empty booth, Anna went motionless from surprise. He was Gordon.

Instinctively, she put her graph paper on the floor beside her chair and set her purse on top of it. She held still as the couple approached, and when Gordon's expression didn't change, she realized that he had not noticed her.

"Hi, Gordon," she said when they had almost passed her table.

Gordon stopped short. "Anna? Well, hello. What a surprise."

"Yes. It is." Anna tried not to stare at his companion. This couldn't be Theresa, the mysterious, glamorous Theresa. This woman was shorter than Anna and not much thinner, and wore thick glasses with black plastic rims. Her frizzy brown hair hung almost to her waist and was held away from her face with an elastic band. A bit of white fuzz clung to her left eyebrow.

Gordon turned to the woman. "Theresa, this is my friend, Anna. Anna, this is my roommate, Theresa."

"Nice to meet you." Theresa leaned forward and extended her hand.

Awkwardly, Anna shook it. "Nice to meet you, too, finally. Won't you join me?"

Gordon glanced over his shoulder. "Actually, we were just—" He broke off when he saw that Theresa was already pulling out a chair and sitting down. He shrugged and took the seat beside her.

"I've heard a lot about you, Theresa," Anna said. "All good, of course."

Theresa's thick eyebrows shot up. "Really? From whom?"

Anna paused. "From Gordon, of course."

"Oh." Theresa flashed him a quick grin before returning her attention to Anna. "How do you and Gordon know each other?"

Anna looked from Gordon to Theresa and back, puzzled. "Well, I'm sure Gordon's already told you how we met at an English department function, and since then we've been seeing each other—"

"All over campus," interrupted Gordon. "Just like this morning. That's what happens at a smaller college. Wherever you go, you see people you know. Right?"

"Right," echoed Anna, uncertain.

Theresa rested her elbows on the table and scrutinized her. "So, which department are you in? Are you a grad student or on the faculty?"

"Neither. I'm a chef for College Food Services."

"Anna graduated from Elizabethtown College," added Gordon quickly. "You've probably heard of it. It's highly regarded for an undergraduate liberal arts education. Anna hasn't decided upon a graduate school yet."

Anna looked at him, speechless. She had already completed all the post-baccalaureate study she needed at the Culinary Institute of New York.

"It's often best to take time off before returning for a graduate degree." Theresa sat back, a fond smile playing on her lips. "For three years after I earned my A.B. in English Language and Literature from the University of Chicago—"

"Summa cum laude," interjected Gordon.

Theresa rolled her eyes. "If you must. Summa cum laude from the University of Chicago, I wandered the continent with some of my more hedonistic friends. It was a wonderful opportunity to explore my own depths, gather grist for the mill. But now it's back to work. What degree are you going for, Ann?"

"It's Anna. Actually, I don't really need a graduate degree for my work."

Theresa pondered that briefly. "I suppose I don't, either, technically. You either are a poet or you aren't; no amount of training can modify the soul. If I want to teach at the university, however, I have to have my MFA. That's the system. That's the price we all pay."

"An MBA would be useful, right, Anna?" Gordon persisted.

"I guess so," said Anna reluctantly. "Marketing, management—sure. An MBA would be helpful, I suppose." She looked at Gordon to see if she had said the right thing. He smiled his thanks, visibly relieved.

Somehow she managed to get through the rest of the encounter. Gordon and Theresa drank seemingly endless refills of coffee until they were wired from the caffeine. Anna sat quietly as they talked to each other, laughing at each other's jokes, gossiping about departmental politics, discussing writers she had never heard of whose works she had never read. Finally it ended, and she was able to walk home, alone and very annoyed.

It was after ten o'clock at night when Gordon finally called. "Anna, about today."

She broke in before he had the chance to make excuses. "Why haven't you told Theresa about me?"

"Why should I have told her?"

"Because we're involved, and she's your roommate and a friend. My friends know about you."

"That's different."

"How so?"

"I prefer to keep my personal life private."

Her throat tightened. "You're ashamed of me because I'm not in graduate school. Because I'm not going to be some tenured professor in an ivory tower some day."

"How could you say such a thing? That's ridiculous. I also might add that it's not fair of you to resort to cheap stereotypes about academics."

"Not fair? Do you really want to talk about not fair?"

"Anna—"

"Gordon, I'm proud of my career. I've worked and studied very hard to get where I am. What I do is just as creative as Theresa's poetry."

"I know. I know. I was an idiot. I was wrong. After breakfast I told Theresa all about us. She liked you. She thought you were great."

"Am I supposed to feel honored?"

"I said I was sorry. Can't you forgive me?" said Gordon. "How can you not forgive me after I admitted I was wrong?"

He persisted, and eventually she gave in. He wanted to come over and continue the apology in person, but she refused. She was too tired to make up in the way he meant, and she had to get up early the next morning.

❧

Conflicting work schedules kept them apart for the next two days, but on Wednesday, Anna hurried home from her lunch shift at South Dining Hall and baked Gordon a seven-layer chocolate hazelnut torte as an apology for her outburst on the phone. She packed it carefully in a bakery box and walked to campus to catch the bus to the east side. Having never visited his apartment, she had needed to look up his address in the campus directory and check the bus schedule to see which route to take. His answering machine picked up when she called to let him know she was on her way, but she decided to go even though he was not there. He usually went home for supper, so he would probably arrive before she did.

As she rode the bus, her purse on the seat beside her and the cake box balanced on her lap, she began to have second thoughts. Uninvited and unexpected might not be the best way to make her first visit to Gordon's apartment. Whenever her friends expressed their bewilderment at his failure to invite her over after fourteen months of presumably exclusive dating, Anna had always managed to find a plausible excuse for him, but the encounter at the diner had left her rattled. Maybe she should leave the box outside his door. Or maybe she should get off at the next stop and take the first bus back toward campus. Surely Gordon would come to see her within a few days, while the torte was still reasonably fresh. She could wait until then to present it.

But she was his girlfriend. She pulled the wire to signal her approaching stop and got off the bus. They had been dating for more than a year. Surely a guy wouldn't complain if his girlfriend of almost fourteen months decided to stop by his apartment, especially to make up after an argument, especially bearing a seven-layer chocolate hazelnut torte.

She found his address and climbed the stairs to the second floor apartment. Theresa answered her knock.

"Hi," Anna said, forcing a smile. "Is Gordon home?"

"Not at the moment." Theresa glanced over her shoulder as if to make sure. "Do you need something?"

Anna kept the smile firmly in place. "I'm Anna. Gordon's girlfriend? We met Sunday at Chuck's Diner?"

"Oh, right, right." Theresa opened the door wider and waved her in. "Did you want to wait for him to get home? I think he has office hours until six."

"That's all right." Anna looked around the cluttered room. Books and newspapers were stacked on every horizontal surface. "I'll just leave this in the kitchen and go."

"Good enough." Theresa led her into the adjacent kitchen and cleared a space on the counter. "I would have cleaned up, but Gordon didn't mention you were coming."

Anna set down the box. "It's a surprise." She lifted the lid and let Theresa peek inside.

Theresa's eyes lit up. "Oh, I get it. Chocolate for love, right? That's great. Too bad it's not heart-shaped. Gordon loves the irony of bourgeois kitsch."

"It's not a quiche. It's a chocolate hazelnut torte."

Theresa burst into laughter. "Oh, Anna, you're priceless. I can see why Gordon likes you."

Anna's smile felt tight and strained. She had said something wrong, or funny, or both, but she wouldn't let Theresa know it was unintentional.

"Where did you get this?" Theresa asked, inhaling the delicious aroma. "That bakery on the west side?"

"No, I made it."

"Really?" She shook her head in regret. "You're so lucky. I wish I had time to bake. I haven't cooked in years. I'm always too busy."

"I'm a chef. It's what I do."

"Oh." Theresa nodded. "That's right. But you're really just, like, a lunch lady, right? Not a real 'chef' chef, as in a restaurant, right?"

Anna could not think of a reply that would suffice.

"Not that there's anything wrong with that," Theresa added. "Someone has to feed the students' bodies while we feed their minds, isn't that so?"

"There's a lot about what you said that isn't so," said Anna. "I'm not a server on the cafeteria line, if that's what you think. I develop recipes, direct the cooks, supervise my student workers—and that's just in the dining halls. I also prepare banquets and special events, sometimes for the provost himself."

"Of course you do," said Theresa encouragingly. "You absolutely should feel good about what you do. Never forget that every contribution to the academy is important, from the president to the lowliest custodian."

"I do feel good about what I do," said Anna. Something in Theresa's tone, in direct contradiction to her words, suggested that she should not.

"Absolutely," said Theresa again, nodding.

They stood there looking at each other in strained silence. Anna couldn't think of anything else to say, so she stammered something about having to catch the bus and left.

As she rode home, she felt tears of embarrassment and anger gathering. How dare that woman make her feel inferior? Theresa was "too busy" to bake; important people like her never had time to cook for themselves. Only insignificant people like Anna could afford to waste time over pots and pans. People with doctorates hired people like Anna to save themselves from such menial tasks.

"You're really like, just, like, a lunch lady, right?" Anna muttered, imitating Theresa. "Not a real, like, 'chef' chef, right?" For a poet, Theresa was amazingly inarticulate. She was also a snob, and Anna hated that she had been too surprised to defend herself properly. What was worse, though, was the sinking suspicion that if Gordon had been there, he would have agreed with every word Theresa had uttered.

They were perfect for each other.

Anna ought to face the facts: She and Gordon were a mistake. She had never doubted herself or her life choices before they got involved, but now she did little else. What precisely did he find so offensive about Anna's cooking and quilting? She was hardly a throwback to the Dark Ages just because she enjoyed traditionally female pursuits. She was not about to stop voting and driving and she defied anyone to try to stuff her into a corset. Admittedly, Gordon and Theresa knew much more about feminist theory than Anna ever would—their English department offered entire courses on the subject—but it hardly seemed very liberating to expect Anna to become ashamed of her talents just because they did not meet other people's expectations.

What on earth was wrong with being a chef?

Gordon had known what she did for a living from the very first. Why had he asked her out if he was ashamed of her? Unless those feelings had come along later, courtesy of Theresa's influence.

Anna walked home from the bus stop dejected and lost in thought. Jeremy, descending the apartment stairs in a rush, almost ran into her. "Sorry, Anna," he said cheerfully, but a second glance stopped him short. "Hey. What's wrong?"

Anna just shook her head.

"What did Gordon do now?"

How did he know? She never complained about Gordon to him. She had a sudden, frantic worry about the thickness of the building's walls. "It's nothing like that," she said. "I'm just—I don't know. I'm just tired."

"Uh huh." He leaned against the banister, studying her. "Maybe you're tired of Gordon."

"I'm not tired of him, but maybe I am tired of some of the things he does."

"What's the difference?"

She did not want to pursue this line of questioning, knowing where it would lead. "There must be a difference. What a person *is* is not the same as what they *do*."

And that was precisely what Gordon would never understand.

Jeremy still looked concerned. "If you ever need to talk—"

"I know. You're right across the hall." She continued upstairs. "See you, Jeremy. Thanks."

Upstairs, she checked her answering machine—Gordon had not called—and washed her cake pans and batter bowls in the tiny sink. She had a sudden craving for a rich dessert and wished she had kept the torte for herself. Gordon would not appreciate it. He and Theresa would make it the subject of a research paper for an academic journal: "Tortes and the Chauvinistic Female in Contemporary American Society." They would probably win an award and Anna would end up assigned to the English Department's celebratory banquet.

Rather than make and devour an entire second torte, Anna brought out her sewing machine and worked on the blueberry quilt. Sending the fabric beneath the needle with the pedal all the way to the floor was as effective a form of therapy as eating, and much better for her.

A few hours later, she heard a pounding on the front door over the cheerful, industrious buzz of the sewing machine. She finished a seam and went to the door. Through the peephole, she saw Gordon standing in the hallway, his hands behind his back.

She resisted the instinct to rush around to conceal all evidence of her quilt. She opened the door. "Hi, Gordon."

"Hi," he said. "Thanks for the cake. Theresa and I tried it. It was delicious."

She stood in the doorway, her hand still upon the knob. "I'm glad you liked it." She could not care less what Theresa thought.

"May I come in?"

She let him enter, and after she closed the door behind him, he held out a bottle of wine and a ribbon-tied scroll. "For you. A token of thanks."

Wine she recognized, but she eyed the scroll warily. "What's this?"

He held out the scroll until she took it. "It's a poem. A sonnet. I wrote it for you."

"You wrote me a sonnet?" She untied the ribbon and carefully unrolled the paper. "That's sweet. No one ever wrote me a poem before."

"I hope you like it."

She read the lines, trying to make sense of them. "Come, Sleep; O Sleep! the certain knot of peace," it began, and became even less clear as it went on. Maybe it was the old-fashioned language he had used, but the poem didn't seem very romantic. It sounded more like someone complaining about insomnia.

Gordon must have sensed her doubt. "It's about a man who begs for sleep to overtake him so that he's no longer tortured by thoughts of the woman he cares for."

"Thoughts of me torture you?"

"No, no. What I mean is, thoughts of not being with you, not being able to have you. Thoughts that you might be angry at me." He gestured to the paper. "That's why in the poem I'm so eager to fall asleep, because then I can dream about you."

"Oh. 'Livelier than elsewhere, Anna's image see.' That's the dream."

"Exactly." He placed his hands on her shoulders and kissed her on one side of her face, close to her mouth. "I'm sorry I wasn't home when you came over. Theresa said you left in a huff."

"I did not," said Anna. "And even if I had, I had every reason to, after what Theresa said."

"What did she say?"

"She called me a lunch lady."

"Did she?" Gordon considered. "Don't you prepare lunch in the dining halls?"

"Yes, but my job title is not 'lunch lady.'"

"Did you tell Theresa your job title?"

"I . . ." Anna tried to remember. "I think I told her I was a chef. I can't remember."

"If you can't remember, how can you expect her to?" He kissed her other cheek, lingering. "Just forget it. Theresa loved the cake. I loved the cake. Let's not fight anymore." He kissed her on the lips.

She returned the kiss, and as she did, she reminded herself that she was annoyed with Theresa, not him. Gordon did love her, even if he never said it in those exact words.

Suddenly it occurred to her that she and Gordon both wanted the other to be something they weren't. If it was wrong for Gordon, it was wrong for her, too. She had to accept him as he was and hope he would learn to do the same.

But how could she get Gordon to appreciate *her* for who *she* was? Distracting his attention away from Theresa couldn't hurt. It was a pity Theresa didn't have a boyfriend of her own. If Gordon saw that Theresa was happily involved with someone else, he might lose interest.

Maybe that was the answer: find someone for Theresa. But whom? Theresa would probably want someone well educated and interested in the arts, but most of the men Anna knew who fit that description were confirmed bachelors nearing retirement age or already married.

Except for one. The perfect one.

After that flash of inspiration, Anna was so eager to get started with her plan that she could not get rid of Gordon fast enough. As she guided him to the door, he protested mildly until she reminded him about his upcoming candidacy exam, when he perked up and agreed that he ought to get to the library. She watched from the window as he strolled down the block and turned the corner; then she hurried across the hall and knocked on Jeremy's door. Jeremy was the ideal prospective boyfriend—cute, considerate, smart, funny. If Anna were not already attached, she might ask him out herself.

Anna gave him her brightest smile when he answered the door. "Hi, Jeremy. Listen. I have a huge favor to ask."

"Sure. What is it?"

"Would you go out on a double date with me, Gordon, and Gordon's roommate, Theresa?"

"Go where with whom?"

"I know it's a lot to ask. Double dates can be awkward if everyone doesn't know everyone else and blind double dates are even worse. But if you could do this for me, I would make it up to you, I swear. Chocolate desserts every night for a month."

"Seriously? Every night?" Then he shook his head. "Wait. Hold on. Anna, you know I have a girlfriend."

"But I thought . . ." Anna hesitated. "When Summer moved out, I thought you broke up. I thought she was going away to graduate school in a few months."

Jeremy shifted his weight and shrugged. "She did, we did, and she is, but we're back together and planning to stay that way. At least that's what I'm planning."

"Oh." Anna considered. "Well, do you think she would mind?"

"I think she might."

"What if all four of us agreed that we were just going out as friends?"

"Anna, you're making my head hurt."

"I'm sorry. I know this sounds strange, but Gordon has this—I don't know what to call it—this strange fixation on his roommate. Fixation isn't the right word. He's letting her influence him too much. I think it would be healthier if she met some other guys, and, and, maybe—"

"Found her own boyfriend so she'd leave yours alone."

"Yes." Anna gave him a feeble grin. "That's it exactly."

He tried to hide a smile. "So, knowing I'm already seeing someone, you want to hook me up with someone you don't even like."

"I wouldn't have put it exactly that way."

Jeremy laughed. "Anna—"

"I know. I'm out of my mind. But is there any way you could do it? You're the most perfect guy I know."

"For Theresa?"

"For anyone. If they had a contest, you would win. But even if you don't become Theresa's boyfriend—"

"I won't. That's a promise."

"Even if you don't, you'll still show her that there are men other than Gordon in the world. You'll encourage her to start looking around."

He regarded her with amused patience. "Do you really expect me to believe anything you say after you call me the most perfect guy you know?"

He had to pick the most honest part of her request. "That's not mere flattery."

"So you say." He sighed and ran a hand through his unruly curls. "Okay. I'll do it. For you."

"And for the desserts."

"And for the desserts, sure. As long as there are no expectations beyond one night out."

"I promise to present it as a night out with friends. Just friends."

"All right." Jeremy looked as if he regretted it already. "I hope Gordon is worth all this."

"Of course he is," said Anna staunchly.

"Anyway, I'm glad you came over. I have something to tell you." He opened the door wider and beckoned her inside. His apartment, like all of those on his side of the building, was larger than hers, with two bedrooms and a substantially larger kitchen and living room. "Since Summer's going away, there's an opening for a quilt teacher at Elm Creek Quilts. Two openings, actually, since another teacher is leaving, too."

"Really?" Anna watched as he dug into his backpack and took a sheet of paper from a folder. "Are they looking for someone whose quilts are similar to Summer's? Because mine are sort of . . . different."

"They're unique," he agreed, handing her the page. One glance told her it was ad copy. "Here's what you need to know. I've already told Summer you might apply, so they'll be looking out for you. I know it's not the same as running your own restaurant, but it might be fun."

"I'm sure it would be. Thank you." She had told him once that she might look for a second job to help her build up her savings more rapidly, but she had not expected him to remember her off-hand remark. Gordon did not even know of her plans, and Jeremy had already found her a promising lead.

Now she really owed him.

Back in her own apartment, she read the ad, carefully noting the job requirements. She never sewed anything by hand, but she could machine piece, appliqué, and quilt very well, at least in comparison to the quilts displayed at the Waterford Quilting Guild's annual show in the college library. She always drafted her own original patterns, and as for possessing the ability to tolerate quirky coworkers, emotional turmoil, and the occasional minor disaster, she had finely honed that skill thanks to her years in professional kitchens. Seasonal work with a flexible schedule was exactly what she needed from a second job.

Over the next week, she planned the double date and assembled her application for Elm Creek Quilts. Her old résumé was so outdated that she started over from the beginning, wishing that she had more quilting-related qualifications to mention. Although she had quilted for more than fifteen years and had worked part-time in her aunt's Pittsburgh quilt shop during high school, she had never taught quilting. She was not quite sure what to do about the ad's requirement for three letters of recommendations from former students. The ad didn't say they had to be *her* students. Maybe any former students of quilting would do.

Anna gave away almost all of her quilts as soon as she sewed on the bindings, but fortunately, she had taken photos of each to send to her aunt, who had retired to Arizona with her second husband after the overwhelming success of a local competitor, Quilts 'n Things, put her out of business. Anna found the negatives buried in a box at the back of her closet and had five-by-seven reprints made at a camera shop next door to Chuck's Diner. She did have to take new snapshots of her more recent, abstract "food" quilts, which she had not yet photographed since she did not really consider them complete. Still, she thought it only fair to show the Elm Creek Quilters the direction her quilts seemed to be taking, since they were so different from the traditional patterns with which she had begun. She also thought it wouldn't hurt to show as many quilts as possible, a little padding to compensate for the areas where her qualifications were a bit thin.

Arranging the double date proved to be more difficult. At first Gordon balked, claiming that he was uncomfortable socializing with people he did not know, but when she pointed out that he knew everyone but Jeremy and that she had attended that awful English department Holiday Gathering in December, where everyone brooded into their cocktails and hardly anyone spoke to her, he relented. Recalling that event, Anna wondered briefly if Gordon would have asked her to come had Theresa not stayed home with a bad cold that night. He had, after all, invited her at lunch on the same day, claiming that he had forgotten about it until a fellow student had mentioned it in the mailroom that morning. Everyone was supposed to bring an international hors d'oeuvre to share, but Gordon had told her not to trouble herself; he would heat up a couple of boxes of frozen egg rolls. He would have brought chips and salsa, but the student from the mailroom was bringing that. Appalled, Anna had insisted upon bringing her own Thai chicken peanut satays, which turned out to be the hit of the buffet table. For Anna, the diffident praise of her cooking was the only pleasant note of the entire discordant evening.

But this night out with just the two couples would be nothing like that. After several days of phone tag and trips across the hall to Jeremy's, Anna finally found an evening that accommodated everyone's schedules. The four would dine out at a popular chain restaurant two weeks from Friday.

In the meantime, Anna finished her application portfolio and sent it off to Elm Creek Manor. In lieu of the letters from former quilting students, Anna included three letters from supervisors at College Food Services and three additional letters from work-study students, including Callie, to give the interviewers a sense of her teaching abilities in the kitchen.

For the next few days, work kept her too busy to worry about Gordon or the job at Elm Creek Quilts. With the new school year approaching, College Food Services had begun preparing for the usual frenzy of welcome banquets and new faculty orientation luncheons. Anna had been assigned to the Freshman Orientation banquet—a stressful event requiring the college to reassure worried parents and impress their bored progeny, who always felt oriented enough by that time and would much prefer for their parents to be on the road home so they could sneak off for a little underage drinking at a fraternity party somewhere. She didn't see Gordon until the weekend, and that was only for a few short hours on Saturday night. He said both he and Theresa were looking forward to going out on the upcoming Friday.

Late Friday afternoon, after Anna rushed home from work to dress for the date, Summer Sullivan called from Elm Creek Quilts. She sounded so genuinely pleased that Anna had applied for the job that Anna was immediately seized by guilt and almost blurted out a confession. Fortunately she managed to restrain herself, as it was highly unlikely that Summer would have invited her to Elm Creek Manor the next week for a job interview if Anna told her of her plot to use Summer's boyfriend to distract another woman from her own boyfriend. The more Summer talked, the more Anna realized that her plan was actually a very bad idea. It was underhanded and unlikely to succeed. It was a wonder Jeremy had agreed to be any part of it.

But it was too late to back out now.

She finished the call, thanking Summer and promising to see her at Elm Creek Manor the following Wednesday. Then she quickly showered and dressed in a pink, short-sleeved mock turtleneck and an A-line denim jumper that fell just below the knee. It was not fancy, but it happened to be the most flattering item in her wardrobe. She considered putting her hair into the usual French braid, but decided to wear it down instead. The ends curled in a gentle wave where they brushed her shoulders, and although her chef's instinct was to tuck her hair out of sight beneath a tall white toque, she thought she looked surprisingly pretty. If only she didn't have those extra twenty pounds. Unfortunately, weight gain was an all-too-present occupational hazard. If she were any less careful, she could put on five pounds a year.

Jeremy knocked on her door about ten minutes before they were due at the restaurant. He wore a navy oxford shirt and light tan slacks, and although he did not seem his usual, easygoing self, he told her she looked beautiful and that he was looking forward to the evening. She thanked him with misgivings, suspecting that he was really looking forward to having the evening end.

"Summer called," Anna told him as they walked to the restaurant, and immediately regretted it when he shot her a look of guilty alarm. "To ask me to come for an interview at Elm Creek Manor, I mean. I'm also supposed to design an original quilt block, something to represent Elm Creek Quilt Camp."

"That's great. I'm sure you'll impress them."

"So you didn't tell Summer about tonight?"

"No." He paused. "Did you?"

"No."

"Good." Then he caught himself. "I don't mean that I'm concealing this from her, and I definitely don't mean that I'll ever ask Theresa out, but . . . some things just defy explanation. I thought the less I said, the better it would be."

Anna nodded, feeling terrible. She almost told him to forget the whole thing, that she would tell Gordon and Theresa that he had fallen ill and had to cancel, but they had come within half a block of the restaurant. Gordon and Theresa, waiting outside while Theresa finished a cigarette, had already spotted them.

"I didn't know she smoked," murmured Anna, knowing how Jeremy hated the smell. He often placed the assignments of his chain-smoking students in the apartment hallway to air out overnight before grading them.

"Don't worry about it," Jeremy replied, but his smile was strained. "It's just one dinner with friends."

They joined Gordon and Theresa, who wore black corduroys, a black turtleneck, and a black wool felt vest embellished with intersecting lines of white rickrack. Gordon, Anna was pleased to see, had dressed up in his one pair of navy dress slacks and a white shirt with a tie, an actual tie. She made introductions, everyone shook hands, and they entered the restaurant, where Anna was quick to request the nonsmoking section. They made small talk as they waited to be led to their table for four. It soon came out that each of them had eaten there before; in a town the size of Waterford, there were not many choices. Anna had chosen the restaurant because of its reputation as a nice place to take a date: pleasant atmosphere, moderate prices, typical American cuisine. If the quality of the food had been her primary concern, she would have cooked for them at home.

She was pleased to see that Jeremy and Theresa seemed to be getting along well. He talked about his research for the history department, Theresa talked about her poetry, Gordon talked about Theresa, and Anna said hardly anything. She didn't need to. The others were all liberal arts grad students and had plenty in common. Though Anna was the person who had brought them together, they didn't need her to guide the conversation.

Even the food was fairly tolerable, although even without tasting them

Anna could list at least a dozen improvements she could make to each dish that was set before them. Her mind wandered as Gordon, with a couple of beers in him, began reciting Irish poetry and Theresa chimed in with explanations of the metaphors. Jeremy, to his credit, asked a few questions about the historical context of the poems, but Anna was not sure if he was genuinely interested or merely being polite. She supposed if she, who knew Jeremy was there under false pretenses, could not tell, Gordon and Theresa were unlikely to become suspicious.

The evening passed better than Anna could have anticipated until Theresa mentioned that Gordon would be taking his candidacy exam soon.

"I don't envy you," Jeremy said, grinning. "I'm glad that's behind me."

"Hear, hear," Theresa said. "No more exams for me, either."

"You still have to finish your dissertation and defend it," said Gordon. "You too, Jeremy."

As the others commiserated, Anna smiled and took a sip of water.

"We're all so overworked." Theresa sighed in mock despair. "I suppose the only one of us who has any leisure time is Anna."

For the first time that evening, everyone turned to look at her. It startled her so much that she almost choked on her water. She coughed and tried to speak, then set down the glass.

"I'm not exactly free," she said, managing a smile. "I'm gainfully employed, full-time. During our busy seasons, I might work up to sixty hours a week."

Jeremy nodded, but Theresa said, "That's a quantitative response to a comment that required a more qualitative analysis."

This time Gordon nodded. Annoyed, Anna said coolly, "If you speak to anyone who's dined at one of my banquets, I'm sure they'll tell you my work is of the highest quality."

"I said 'qualitative,' not 'quality.'" In an aside to Gordon, Theresa added, "A garbage man can work sixty hours a week, but it's still just tossing trash into the back of a truck no matter how well he does it. It's not exactly intellectually demanding."

"Working as a chef is intellectually demanding," said Jeremy. "Physically demanding, too. You're on your feet in a hot kitchen, directing cooks and servers, and racing to meet one deadline after another." The smile he offered Theresa was a pleasant mask. "If you have any doubts, you should try it yourself."

"Me?" She laughed. "I'm too busy. Who has time to cook anymore?"

"I have time to cook because it's my job," Anna pointed out. Again. For all her education, Theresa seemed unable to grasp the obvious.

"True," Theresa shot back. "But you can't seriously argue that you're as busy as a graduate student. I mean, come on. You have time for hobbies."

"Hobbies?"

"You know. That embroidery or whatever it is you do. Gordon says you've made some cute little crafts for your apartment." Theresa laughed. "You're going to make someone a great housewife someday."

She said housewife as if she considered it only a few steps above lunch lady on the rank of human endeavor. Anna refused to look at Gordon, which she supposed relieved him. He sat so stiff and wide-eyed in his chair it was as if he believed stillness would allow him to blend in to the background, camouflaged by his cowardice.

"Are you talking about Anna's quilts?" asked Jeremy.

"Quilts! That's what it was." Theresa rested her arms on the table and smiled indulgently at Anna. "You know, my grandmother made quilts."

Anna managed a tight-lipped nod. "Mine, too."

"Anna's quilts are true works of art," said Jeremy. "She won't brag about them, but she should."

Anna threw him a grateful look, but he might not have seen it because Theresa suddenly regarded him with new interest. "You know how to quilt? That's fascinating, a man pursuing the domestic arts."

Anna could not resist rolling her eyes. Suddenly, when practiced by a man, quilting was elevated from cute little craft to domestic art.

As Jeremy struggled to explain how he knew so much about quilting without mentioning that he was dating a founding member of Elm Creek Quilts, Anna fixed her gaze on Gordon. He simultaneously developed an urgent need for the waiter, or so his craning of the neck, shifting in his chair, and looking in every direction but Anna's suggested. Finally she caught his eye, but when she raised her eyebrows at him, he offered only a meek shrug. She picked up her wineglass and took a sip, shooting him a more pointed look over the rim, willing him to say something, anything, in her defense.

At last he caught the hint and spoke. "Anna's not planning to stay in the kitchen forever. She'll find out what busy really means when she goes back to grad school for her MBA."

An inch above the table, the glass slipped from her hand and hit the surface with a loud clunk. Somehow it stayed upright.

Puzzled, Jeremy said, "You're going to open your own restaurant *and* return to grad school?"

"Not all in the same week," Anna said, forcing a shaky laugh.

"This is an interesting turn of events." Theresa interlaced her fingers and rested them on the table. "So tell us the whole story. Where are you going? When do you start?"

Anna looked daggers at Gordon, who was studying his ribeye intently. "Let's just say I don't have any definite plans yet."

"Oh," Theresa said, drawing the word out, conveying in one syllable comprehension and pity, perhaps scorn. "And I suppose this plan to own your own restaurant is in a similar state of flux?"

"Those plans are actually a little further along." It would be difficult for them to be otherwise.

Jeremy looked from Anna to Gordon and back, but said nothing.

In his first helpful move all evening, Gordon brought up some gossip that had been spreading around campus, and soon he and Theresa were dissecting the latest developments with the rapid enthusiasm of soap opera fans during sweeps month. The topic of conversation did not return to Anna or her future plans, but the damage had been done. Theresa ignored her for the rest of the evening, and when Gordon spoke to her, his tone was hesitant and apologetic. At least he apparently realized that he had not provided the help she had needed, but it was no comfort.

Afterward, the couples parted outside the restaurant as they had arrived, although Gordon gave Anna a quick kiss and Theresa and Jeremy shook hands. Gordon and Theresa drove away in her car, and Jeremy and Anna walked back to their apartment building.

They climbed the stairs to the third floor and paused outside their doors. "When do you want your first dessert?" Anna asked Jeremy as she dug around in her purse for her keys.

He shook his head. "Forget about it. You don't have to."

"But the deal was a dessert every night for a month."

"I was just kidding. Who could eat that much dessert?"

Anna could, if she allowed herself. "So what did you think of Theresa?"

"She's nice when she's not being completely evil." He waited a moment before adding, "She and Gordon get along well."

Too well, Anna thought, and she knew that was Jeremy's point. "Do you think you'll ask her out sometime?"

He shrugged. "Maybe."

"And by 'maybe,' you mean 'no.'"

"Right."

Anna couldn't help smiling at the apologetic look on his face. "That's okay. I figured out a long time ago that this wouldn't work. Summer's a very lucky girl."

"Gordon's a very lucky guy, but he obviously doesn't realize it. You're beautiful, you're nice, and man, the way you cook—"

"Yeah, I'm nice and I'm a great cook," said Anna, suddenly depressed. "Too bad that's not enough. Gordon's afraid I'm going to blow up like a Thanksgiving Day parade balloon if I don't find myself a sugar-free, low-fat career."

"I wondered what was going on with that." Jeremy stepped forward and before she knew it he was wrapping her up in a bear hug. "Anna, you're good enough for anyone. Don't ever let Gordon make you feel otherwise. He is out of his mind not to realize how wonderful you are."

"Said the man dating a skinny girl."

Abruptly Jeremy released her. "What?"

"You call me beautiful to be polite and you say I'm good enough for any-one, but would you ever date someone who looked like me?" She heard the anger in her voice and knew she should stop. "What size is Summer? Four? Two?"

"I honestly don't know," said Jeremy. "I didn't fall in love with Summer because of her size."

"But if she had been my size, would you have been attracted to her? Would you have asked her out?"

Without pausing to consider it, he said, "If she had been the exact same person on the inside with twenty extra pounds on the outside? Yes."

"Oh, please."

"What?"

"You say that, but it's not true."

"How do you know it's not true?"

"Because fat girls don't get the cute guy."

He shook his head, incredulous. "I can't believe this. You're deluded. Fat girls get the cute guy every day."

"In what alternate reality?"

"In this reality. Okay. You want the truth? Yes, Summer is thin and pretty.

Go ahead and call me shallow for noticing and appreciating that. But I didn't fall in love with her because of that. I fell in love with her for her warmth and her strength and her smile, her kindness and her confidence and the way she can find the humor in any situation. That's what makes her beautiful to me." He looked at Anna closely, exasperated. "It's kind of insulting that you don't get that. And that you don't think there's anything more to Summer than her looks."

Contrite, Anna said, "I've met Summer. I know she's a wonderful person."

"And so are you. And that's another thing I didn't say just to be polite."

Anna felt mean and guilty. Why had she vented at Jeremy, and after he had been so nice to her? "I'm sorry," she said. "The good news is you scolded the self-pity right out of me."

He frowned and shook his head. "If Gordon has said anything to make you feel this way about yourself—"

"Don't blame him," said Anna quickly. "This goes back long before I ever met him. He's a good person. Really. I guess we're just better by ourselves than with groups. Everything's fine when it's just the two of us."

"If you say so. You know him better than I do." Jeremy turned to unlock his door. "But don't forget what I said, promise?"

"Promise."

"Good."

They entered their separate apartments. Anna closed her door and watched through the peephole until he closed his.

🐝

On the morning of her interview, Anna woke filled with the same nervous energy that accompanied her throughout the day of an important banquet. She had taken the day off work, and with nothing to do until it was time to catch the bus out to Elm Creek Manor, she decided to bake cookies. She had to run down to Uni-Mart for a shockingly overpriced pound of butter, but the rest of the ingredients were already in her cupboard—Madagascar cinnamon, Penzey's pure vanilla extract, organic flour. She mixed the sugar cookie dough and let it chill while she ironed her tan suit and organized her interview materials. Back in the kitchen, she rolled out the dough and cut cookies in the shape of quilt blocks using the cutters her aunt had sent as a souvenir of her trip to the Road to California quilt show the previous January. She decorated them with pink, yellow, and lavender tinted frosting, which hardened while she dressed and braided her hair. She packed the cookies carefully in a plastic storage bin with a snap-on handle, put her papers and Elm Creek Quilts block in a tote bag, and met her bus at the stop on the corner.

Uncertain how long the bus ride to Elm Creek Manor would take, Anna left home two hours before her interview. Only three other passengers rode her bus, and they remained on board after Anna disembarked at a remote spot along the main highway where a gravel road led into a forest. The place looked exactly as Summer had described it, but Anna still eyed the shadowed path warily before venturing forward. She picked her way through the loose stones, grateful she had worn her lowest heels but aware too late that she should have packed them in her tote and worn tennis shoes for the walk from the bus stop.

The road was narrow and winding, with no shoulder for her to scramble onto if a car came along. She passed a burbling creek, crossed a bridge, and was relieved when she finally emerged from the leafy wood onto a broad, green lawn divided by a paved road leading to the gray stone manor. If she did get the job and had to make this trip every day, she might finally get in shape.

She had seen pictures of Elm Creek Manor in the *Waterford Register,* but the real thing was far more impressive. It was easily larger and grander than the most impressive fraternity house near campus, although the comparison was probably not fair, considering that the quilters were not obligated to nail four-foot-tall Greek letters to the façade and adorn the veranda with spent kegs and beer cans.

Three women in workout clothes emerged through the tall double doors, descended the gray stone steps, and strode briskly along the front of the building, disappearing down a path through the trees. Another pair sat in Adirondack chairs on the veranda while a third woman held up a quilt block for them to admire. Anna considered going inside, but she was more than an hour early and did not want to annoy the Elm Creek Quilters by throwing off their schedule. She decided to explore the grounds on her own to get a feel for the place.

She wore a run in her nylon knee-highs from walking in the inappropriate shoes, but she enjoyed herself, stopping to chat now and then with some of the quilt campers, admiring the abundant fruit trees in the orchard, and relaxing for a while in a gazebo in a secluded garden. She followed a group of campers into the manor through the rear entrance and couldn't resist peeking into the kitchen, which turned out to be larger than her own, but not at all what she expected to find in what was essentially an inn. How they managed to feed fifty-plus people three meals a day with that four-burner gas stove was a mystery. The pantry was well stocked, but she shook her head at the state of the cooking utensils. The whisk looked to be at least fifty years old, which she could have excused had it not been so bent out of shape. The hand mixer had rust, actual rust, on the handle. A sudden noise from an adjacent room startled her back out into the hallway before she could peek in the refrigerator. Realizing that it would probably not work in her favor if she were caught snooping, she quickly left through the back door, lost herself in a crowd of women crossing the parking lot, and walked around the manor to the front entrance.

On the stone staircase, she hesitated. She was still more than forty-five minutes early. Punctual was one thing; unable to tell time, quite another. If not for the blister developing on her heel and the sense that she ought to gather her thoughts before venturing inside for the interview, she would have made a second tour of the estate.

She glanced down the veranda. The group of three women had left, and now one white-haired woman sat alone, bent over a quilt block. As Anna watched, the woman shook her head and exclaimed to no one in particular, "I ought to just throw it in the scrap bag."

"What's wrong?" asked Anna. She sat down next to the woman, setting her tote bag and container of cookies on the floor. After all that walking, that Adirondack chair felt very good.

"I've been fussing with this silly block all day and haven't accomplished a thing." The woman flung the block onto her lap with an exasperated sigh. "I honestly don't know why I bother."

"It can't be that bad," said Anna. "Want me to take a look at it?"

The woman handed her the block, a traditional floral appliqué pattern Anna had seen before but whose name she could not remember. She examined the block, front and back, and tried to figure out what the woman was complaining about. Most of the quilters who had taken classes at her aunt's quilt shop would have been thrilled to master such tiny, even stitches. "I'm not quite sure what the problem is."

"This piece here," said the woman, indicating a small, leaf-shaped piece half attached to the background fabric. A small indentation marred the perfect smoothness of the curve, but not enough that anyone would notice it in a completed quilt.

"I think you're being too hard on yourself," said Anna cautiously, not wanting to offend. "Why don't you set this project aside and work on something else for a while? You can always come back to this when you're feeling less frustrated."

The woman regarded her with astonishment. "Of all the techniques you might have recommended, I never expected you to suggest I give up."

"That's not what I meant," said Anna. "Quilting is supposed to be fun. It's supposed to bring you joy. It shouldn't be such a struggle. If it's making you miserable, it's time to move on. Some quilts were born to be UFOs."

"UFOs?"

"You know. Unfinished Fabric Objects."

"Of course." The woman smiled. "I believe I've accumulated enough of those already. The trouble is, as much as I might like to try my hand at something else for a while, I must finish this block. It's for a guild exchange and I can't let the other ladies down."

"Oh. That's different." Anna took a second look at the block. Based upon what the woman had already sewn, Anna did not understand why she was struggling so much with that one particular, relatively easy piece. "I prefer to machine appliqué, but it wouldn't look very pretty if you switched in the middle of the block. Can I watch you sew for a few stitches?"

"Certainly, if you think it will help." The woman took a few labored, clockwise stitches around the curve of the leaf.

Anna watched and immediately spotted the potential problem. "Have you tried sewing in the other direction?" The woman peered at her inquisitively through her pink-tinted glasses. "You're right-handed, but you're sewing in a clockwise direction. It's a more natural movement for right-handers to sew counterclockwise."

"Why, I never thought of that." The woman rotated her block and turned her needle. "I think that might just do the trick once I get used to it. Thank you, my dear."

"In all honesty, you were doing just fine before I came along." Anna glanced at her watch, glad to see the conversation had used up another fifteen minutes. "Are you hungry? Would you like a cookie?"

"A cookie?"

Anna opened the container. "I baked three dozen. Help yourself."

"Oh, how charming. An Ohio Star." The woman took a cookie, her eyes alight with pleasure. "And a LeMoyne Star, too. These are far too pretty to eat."

"No, you have to eat them." Anna handed her a second cookie. "They taste even better than they look."

"If you insist, I will eat them, and I'll enjoy every bite." The woman smiled. "You are definitely going to make a wonderful impression. On whomever the lucky recipient of these cookies is, I mean."

"I didn't do it to make a good impression. When I'm nervous, I get this compulsion to bake, and it's either share the treats or eat them all myself. Not a good idea."

"I understand completely." The woman nibbled a point of the Ohio Star. "Delicious."

Anna thanked her for the compliment and bade her good-bye. She returned the lid to the cookie container and entered the manor through the tall double doors. The foyer was grand and imposing, but Anna's attention was immediately captured by a young boy leaping from one black marble square to another, while a woman not much younger than herself nursed a toddler in a nearby metal folding chair.

The little boy looked up from his game and smiled at her. "Hi!"

"Hello," she answered, and glanced at his mother uncertainly. Campers wouldn't bring kids along, so she must be one of the Elm Creek Quilters. "I'm here for the job interview."

The woman gestured to the row of metal folding chairs next to a closed door. "I think this is the line."

"Oh," said Anna, embarrassed by her mistake. "I guess I'm early."

"And I'm late."

That seemed to be the least of the young mother's problems. The kids were cute, but it turned out the other woman had not intended to bring them along; when Anna asked if her baby-sitter had canceled, the mother implied that her husband had backed out at the last minute. Anna felt immediate sympathy. She tried to help, holding the baby when milk squirted all over his mother's clothes, making polite chat, and offering them all cookies. She avoided looking too directly at the other woman rather than have her curious glance be misinterpreted as a critical glare. It came as no surprise, though, when her efforts made little apparent difference to the young mother's stress level.

Anna wondered what the mother planned to do with her boys during her interview but was reluctant to ask. She considered offering to watch them, but they didn't know each other and the last thing this mother needed was some strange woman acting overly eager to watch her kids.

Not long after one of the Elm Creek Quilters dashed past them and disappeared inside the room, the door opened again and a woman around Anna's age peered out. "Hi. I'm Sarah McClure," she said. "Thanks for coming. Sorry for the delay." She glanced down at the file folder in her hand and looked at the mother. "Karen Wise?"

The mother rose, collected her belongings and children, and followed Sarah into the room. Anna leaned her head back and closed her eyes, her sigh echoing in the suddenly silent foyer. She wondered how many other quilters had applied for the job, and whether knowing Jeremy and Summer would give her an advantage. Perhaps their acquaintance had helped her land the interview, but she doubted it would mean much when the final selection process arrived. For all she knew, the Elm Creek Quilters had already eliminated her and had only agreed to see her as a courtesy to Jeremy.

Anna took a deep breath to settle her anxiety and rehearsed responses to potential questions. After less than an hour, the door opened and Karen ushered her boys down the hallway in the opposite direction. From the corner of her eye, Anna watched them go and wondered if they had gotten lost, but they soon reappeared and headed to the front door. The boys seemed happy enough, but Karen looked miserable and defeated.

"I hope your interview went well," said Anna, meaning it, but doubting it.

"I hope yours goes better," said Karen, leading the boys outside without waiting for a reply.

A few minutes later, Sarah McClure opened the door. "You must be Anna Del Maso."

"That's right." Anna rose and shook Sarah's hand before picking up her belongings. "Thank you so much for granting me this interview."

"It's our pleasure. I loved your quilts."

"Really?" Anna was pleased. "I know they've become a little unusual in recent years."

"They're brilliant. The photos you sent truly revealed your development as an artist."

An artist. Anna had never thought of herself as an artist. She wished Gordon and Theresa had been there to hear it. Of course, Gordon and Theresa's presence would have been so wildly unsettling that Anna surely would have made a mess of the interview.

Sarah escorted her into a parlor decorated in the Victorian style, but comfortable rather than fussy. Summer and five other women sat facing one lone armchair on the opposite side of a coffee table. Sarah invited Anna to sit there before taking her own place upon a loveseat closest to the door. Anna glanced at Summer and was heartened to see her smiling encouragingly.

Sarah introduced her fellow Elm Creek Quilters and began with a few questions about Anna's quilting history. Anna was glad to see a few nods when she mentioned that she had been quilting since her aunt had taught her at age fifteen. One dark-haired, ruddy-cheeked woman sighed wistfully as Anna spoke of her experiences working in her aunt's quilt shop, completing sample projects for her classes, assisting customers, and helping her aunt select new notions, books, and fabric lines at Quilt Market each fall in Houston.

"But lately you've been working in a different profession entirely," remarked Sylvia, studying her résumé.

"That's true. I have." Anna told them about her experience with College Food Services, and perhaps influenced by Theresa's derisive comments, she focused much more on her banquet work than on the daily tasks of the dining halls.

"I always wanted to be able to make a gourmet meal," said Sarah.

"Let me guess," said Anna. "You're too busy to cook."

"No, I just don't have the skills. Or the terminology. What's the difference between folding and braising and blending? When I see so many unfamiliar terms in a recipe, I panic and slam the cookbook shut." Sarah shook her head. "I wish I had a talent like yours. Ledgers I understand. Payroll taxes give me no trouble. Food? Forget it. It's a wonder I haven't starved to death or poisoned myself."

"You can't be that bad," said Anna.

"No, she really is," interjected the pretty blonde woman Sarah had called Diane.

"I could teach you a few things," said Anna, quickly adding, "I mean, if I get the job. Not that I wouldn't anyway, but if I get the job, I'll be around. Not that I would take time away from teaching quilting to cook."

Summer came to her rescue. "Did you bring your Elm Creek Quilts block to show us?"

Anna reached for her tote bag, and the sight of the plastic container reminded her of the cookies. "I brought these, too," she said, removing the lid. She handed the cookies to Sarah and placed the quilt block flat upon the coffee table. She told them about the evolution of her design as they passed the cookies around. Each Elm Creek Quilter took one, except for Gwen, who took two, and Diane, who handed off the container without looking inside to admire the cookies as the others had done. Anna did not take offense, guessing from Diane's trim figure that she had not allowed sweets to pass her lips in more than twenty years.

"These are elm leaves drifting on the breeze," continued Anna after describing her raw-edged appliqué method. "This is Elm Creek splashing over some pebbles, and this is the sun, or the warmth of sisterhood, or the light of illumination teachers pass on to their students. I thought I would leave that open to your interpretation."

Most of the Elm Creek Quilters chuckled, but Diane frowned and leaned closer for a better look. "It looks like a tossed salad."

"Diane," admonished Sylvia.

"You'll have to excuse her," said Gwen. "She has absolutely no appreciation for anything other than traditional blocks pieced by hand."

"I see the elm leaves," said Summer. "And that's definitely a creek."

"No, she's right," said Anna, suddenly seeing it. "It looks exactly like a tossed salad."

Diane gave Anna a sharp look, and Anna suddenly realized that the last thing Diane had expected was for her to agree.

"It's a lovely block," said the dark-haired woman who had seemed so engrossed by Anna's stories of her aunt's quilt shop.

Diane had composed herself as she paged through Anna's portfolio. "Looking through your material, I wondered . . . Have you ever taught quilting?"

Anna had been expecting the question. "No, I haven't."

"I see." Diane made a check mark on her notes. "You realize, of course, that all of the other applicants have taught at least a few classes."

"Not all of them," said Summer.

"I've never led a quilt class, but I have taught," said Anna. "In my current job, I've taught many student workers how to prepare food, how to follow safe kitchen practices, and other things. Years ago, I also assisted my aunt in classes at her quilt shop."

"But it's not the same, wouldn't you agree?" said Diane.

Anna hesitated. "It's not exactly the same, but I think it's relevant."

Diane's slight frown deepened. "I'm reluctant to suggest that the only reason you were granted this interview was because you're Summer's boyfriend's neighbor—"

"That is absolutely not true," said Summer.

"That's reassuring," said Diane. She studied Anna's résumé and shook her head. "I'm curious. When did you decide to become a quilting teacher? Based upon your education and employment history, I never would have guessed you were interested in quilting as a career."

"Well, actually . . ." Anna knew she would stumble if she wriggled out of the question with an evasive lie, so she decided to give Diane the truth. "Someday I want to own my own restaurant. That's why I'm looking for a second job, so I can save up the money faster."

"So this would be your second priority, not your first," said Diane, with a glance at Sylvia.

"I said second job, not second priority."

"There's nothing wrong with Anna taking on teaching responsibilities here as a second job," said Summer. "Our ad did mention that seasonal work and flexible hours were available. In fact, Anna's schedule could work to our advantage."

"We can discuss that later," said Sarah, meaning not in front of Anna. "Let's move along. Anna, I was intrigued by your lesson plan for the machine appliqué class. Would you tell us more about how you would run the class?"

Anna did, eager to switch to a safer topic. She answered the Elm Creek Quilters' other questions as best she could, but it was still a relief when Sarah rose and thanked her for coming.

"Thanks for the cookies, too," added Gwen.

"Yes, indeed," said Sylvia. "They were scrumptious."

"Here, have some more," said Anna, passing around the container again. "So I have fewer to carry home."

All but Diane gladly helped themselves to more cookies. Sarah offered to give her a tour of the grounds, but Anna assured her that she had already shown herself around.

The metal folding chairs were empty as Anna crossed the foyer, and the white-haired woman had left the veranda. Anna walked down the front drive toward the woods, going over the interview in her mind just as she always ran through the highlights and missteps of a banquet as she cleaned the kitchen afterward. She wished she had responded more articulately to Diane's queries. With just a few, pointed questions, Diane had dug out Anna's weaknesses for the position, and Anna had not defended herself well. She should have said more about the teaching role she assumed with her student workers in the kitchen, her experience helping shoppers at her aunt's quilt shop, her creative inspiration. Thanks to Diane, the Elm Creek Quilters probably had no idea how badly Anna really wanted the job, not just as a source of revenue for her restaurant fund.

She made her way back down the gravel road to the main highway, arriving twenty minutes before the bus was due. She leaned against a small wooden sign and set her tote bag and cookie container on the ground at her feet, looking up every time a car passed. A blue midsized four-door car, so shiny it had to be nearly new, passed her once, disappeared around a bend, then returned and stopped on the shoulder, motor idling.

"Excuse me," the driver called. His dark hair and beard were sprinkled with gray, and he looked to be in his midforties, handsome except for a deep sadness in his eyes. He did not look like a salesman, at least not a prosperous one; his blue suit seemed a few years too old and his hair, though neatly trimmed, lacked the shiny, coiffed appearance Anna associated with salesmen. Likely he was one of the Elm Creek Quilters' husbands.

"I'm looking for the road to Elm Creek Manor," the man said, disproving her theory. "Do you know where it is?"

Guiltily, Anna jumped away from the sign and pointed into the woods. "It's that way. Sorry for blocking the sign."

The man smiled, and all trace of sadness disappeared. "It's not your fault. This isn't the first time I've missed it. Thanks."

He waved, turned onto the gravel road, and drove off into the woods. Anna watched his car disappear into the trees. *What a novelty,* she thought. *A man who asks for directions.*

❧

While she was gone, Gordon had left a message on her answering machine. Anna changed out of her suit and called him back.

"Where were you?" he asked. "I stopped by after my eleven o'clock class but you weren't home. You said you were taking the day off."

"I took the day off to go to a job interview."

"Oh. Right." He paused. "I walked all the way over there and had to settle for calling your answering machine on my cell."

Anna wanted to point out that he could have used that same cell phone to call before dropping by if the walk was too much for him, but when that petulant, spoiled child tone crept into his voice, she had to handle him carefully. "I'm sorry. I should have reminded you."

"Or left a note on the counter."

"Or that." She was suddenly uncomfortable at the thought of Gordon wandering about her apartment when she was not home. She had given him a key so he could let himself in when she was expecting him, and it had never occurred to her that he might use it at other times. But that was unfair; she had never told him the key came with restrictions. "I'm sorry," she repeated.

"I guess it's all right."

"My interview went well," she said, wishing he had asked. "Maybe we could do something to celebrate."

"Should we invite Theresa and Jeremy to join us? Theresa enjoyed meeting Jeremy. She's considering asking him out."

"That's nice," said Anna, wondering if she should warn him. "But I meant just the two of us."

"In that case, I can't make it tonight. What's your schedule like for the rest of the week?"

"Um, well, let me see." Anna took her pocket calendar from her purse and checked. "I have the usual weekday things, a dinner Saturday evening, and a brunch on Sunday."

"I'm busy every night next week. How about the next Saturday?"

"I'm free."

"Let's do something special a week from Saturday, then. Just the two of us."

"Great," she said, pleased. "What did you have in mind?"

"Oh, I don't know. You know I'm the spontaneous type. Surprise me."

"Oh." Her pleasure vanished. "Okay."

"So it's a date?"

"Sure. A week from Saturday."

Anna hung up the phone with a sigh. At least he wanted to have a special evening, just the two of them. It didn't matter who planned it.

By Tuesday evening she still had not decided how to spend their Saturday evening date. She was in the kitchen making a mug of cocoa and pondering her options when Jeremy knocked on the door. She was glad to see him, since they had hardly spoken since the double date. "I'm making some cocoa," she said, inviting him inside. "Want some?"

"Hot cocoa in summer?"

"People drink hot coffee in summer," she said, a little defensive. She shouldn't have to explain her chocolate addiction to someone who loved it almost as much as she did.

He shrugged. "Good point. Sure."

She cleared the kitchen table of her sewing machine and fabric while the kettle boiled, then fixed two mugs of cocoa and carried them to the table. "Have a seat."

"Thanks." Jeremy sat down and took a sip. "This is great. How did you make it?"

"Are you serious? It's the powdered mix from the grocery store."

"You don't put anything extra in it?"

"No."

"It never tastes this way when I make it." Jeremy took another drink, then set down his mug. "Have you heard anything from Elm Creek Quilts?"

"Not yet. Why? Should I have heard something by now? Did Summer mention something?"

"She hasn't said a word. That's why I'm curious." He took another sip, and she had the sudden impression that he was stalling for time. "I also wanted to see how things were going with you since the date with Theresa wasn't exactly a resounding success."

"Things are fine," said Anna, stirring her cocoa. "In fact, Gordon suggested we go out Saturday and celebrate my job interview."

"You mean the job interview you had last week?"

"He's been busy. And that's just as well because I'm having trouble thinking of where we should go."

"*You're* having trouble." He mulled it over. "If he wants to celebrate your successful job interview, why doesn't he just take you out? Why should you have to plan everything?"

"That's the way we like it," said Anna. "Gordon says it's sexist if he makes all the decisions."

"I see," said Jeremy. "When's the last time he made any decisions of this type?"

"Well—"

"When's the last time he did anything special for you?"

Anna took a sip, but the cocoa felt like chalk in her mouth. She set down the mug and met Jeremy's skeptical gaze evenly. "He wrote me a poem a few weeks ago. A sonnet."

"A sonnet?" echoed Jeremy. "I thought Theresa was the poet."

"She is," said Anna, hiding her sudden distress. "But Gordon knows a lot about poetry, too. Don't forget he's working on a Ph.D. in English literature. Anyway, why are you so upset about this? It's not any of your business."

"You're absolutely right." Jeremy stood up and pushed in his chair. "None of my business. But I still can't stand to watch him use you."

He left the apartment without another word.

Anna watched him go, heart constricting. Jeremy didn't know what he was talking about. He was completely out of line to insinuate that Gordon had not written the sonnet himself. Theresa *never* would have written a romantic poem for Gordon to give to Anna.

She knew it was a flimsy bit of evidence on which to place her trust.

❦

Something about Jeremy's strange visit made her resolve to make her special date with Gordon a romantic evening at home. She would prepare for him the most elegant meal in her repertoire—at least, the most elegant meal that he would like, she could afford, and her minuscule kitchen could handle. She would adorn the table with fresh flowers and tall candles and play his favorite classical music in the background. Afterward they would go for a starlit stroll, observing the beauties of late summer on the campus grounds and sharing intimate conversation. When they returned they would curl up on the sofa with cappuccino and biscotti, and she would ask Gordon to tell her about his latest discoveries in the library and his progress on his thesis. He would love it.

She planned the menu and went well over her budget shopping at the organic market on Campus Drive. Hoping to appeal to Gordon's spontaneous side, she told him only that he should arrive around seven o'clock on Saturday.

All that day she worked, baking and preparing, cleaning and arranging, until she was satisfied. An hour before Gordon was due to arrive, she set the table and changed into her dressy black capris and a pink silk blouse. At seven, she lit the candles, turned on the CD player, and admired the scene. It was perfect. Gordon would be overwhelmed.

She jumped at a knock on the door, even though she had been expecting Gordon and he was right on time. She hurried to answer, struck by a sudden wild fear that he had brought Theresa along, and a second fear that Jeremy would happen to step out into the hallway just in time to witness everything.

She flung open the door, eager to usher Gordon inside before Jeremy saw them.

Gordon stood in the hallway, entirely alone and dressed in jeans and a sweatshirt from a Canadian Shakespeare festival he had attended five years before.

He looked her up and down. "You dressed up. I didn't think you wanted me to dress up."

"That's okay," Anna said, waving him inside. "It doesn't matter." She led him into the apartment and gestured to the beautiful table. "What do you think?"

He took in the flowers, the candles, the music, and the delicious aromas wafting from the kitchenette. "Anna, kitten, you did all this for me?"

"No, I called a caterer. Of course I did it."

Gordon shook his head. "You must have worked all afternoon on this."

She shrugged, smiling, and went to the oven. "Everything's about ready. Five more minutes for the entrée and then we can eat. Do you want to pour the wine?"

He followed her into the kitchenette and took her hands in his. "Anna, you shouldn't have done all this."

"Of course I should have." She freed one hand and touched his face, delighted with his reaction, which was even stronger than she had hoped. "We wanted to have a special date, right?"

He took her hand again and for the first time she noticed the regret and concern in his expression. "I know, but I feel tremendously uncomfortable about this."

"Uncomfortable?"

"Anna, I can't bear to think that you feel I'm shoving you into some traditional gender role. I don't want you to conform to a stereotype of womanhood out of some misguided belief that it's what I want for you."

"I just thought you might want a nice dinner."

"I do. But I don't think you should have to cook it."

"But I'm a chef. I don't understand what's wrong about me cooking for you. You're a literature student and you wrote me a poem."

"It's not the same thing." He steered her out of the kitchenette. "Let's go to my place. I'll cook for you."

"But—"

He raised her hands to his lips. "Please. Let me do this for you."

She thought about the days of planning and preparation, and about the delicious meal going to waste in the kitchen. She remembered Jeremy's criticism. What would he think now, with Gordon at last offering to do something special for her?

"Please?" he implored.

"All right," she said in a small voice. "Let me turn off the oven and clean up first. Will you wait for me outside?"

Gordon agreed and kissed her swiftly, grinning with relief. "Sure, okay. I'll be out front. Don't be long."

After he left, Anna stood fixed in place until the oven alarm roused her. She took the beef tenderloin en croûte from the oven, turned off the burners beneath the sautéed vegetables and the wild rice soup, and covered the chocolate mousse cake. She shouldered her purse, blew out the candles, and went across the hall to knock on Jeremy's door. Jeremy looked surprised to see her, but Anna didn't give him a chance to ask questions. "I made supper for me and Gordon, but we had a change of plans. We're going to his place. You should come over and eat so it doesn't go to waste. Or take it to your place and I'll get the dishes later. Maybe you can call Summer over, too. Wait—better not. It's beef."

"But—"

"Please lock up when you leave." Anna hurried down the stairs before she had to explain further.

Gordon was cheerful and talkative as they drove to his apartment. When they arrived, Theresa was sprawled out on the living room floor, wearing a gray sweatshirt and jeans frayed at the ankles. Anna felt prim and overdressed.

"Hey, Theresa," said Gordon. "We're going to make dinner. Are you hungry?"

"Sure." Theresa climbed to her feet. "What are we having?"

Gordon shrugged and turned toward the kitchen. "Beats me."

Anna followed, and as Gordon and Theresa pulled open cabinets and the refrigerator joking about how little food they had in the house, she leaned against the kitchen counter and watched them. Finally Gordon found a box of macaroni and cheese and held it up triumphantly. Theresa applauded and laughed, then dug up a dusty pot, rinsed it in the sink, and set water on to boil. As the pasta cooked, Gordon and Theresa bantered back and forth about department politics, but this time Anna made no attempt to follow the conversation. They had no colander to drain the macaroni, so Gordon tried to pour out the water in small trickles through a tea strainer, which sent Theresa into gales of laughter. Gordon and Theresa added margarine and milk and powdered orange cheese to the pasta, then stirred it all together and placed the pot in the center of the table with much ceremony. Anna found a diet soda in the refrigerator for herself and chose a seat at the end of the table. Gordon took the other end, and Theresa sat on his right.

Anna had not eaten since breakfast, but she found herself with no appetite. She took small bites of the rubbery pasta, forcing herself to smile and nod at appropriate intervals. Then suddenly, desperately, she wanted to leave the room.

"Will you excuse me?" she said. They broke off their conversation long enough to acknowledge her departure.

"Down the hall to the left," Theresa called after her. "You passed it on your way in."

Anna went to the bathroom and turned on the fan to drown out the noise from the dining room. She went to the sink to splash her face with water, and when she closed her eyes, she pictured the evening she had originally planned. She saw herself and Gordon gazing at each other over the wild rice soup, feeding each other bites of tenderloin en croûte, sighing with pleasure as the wineglasses reflected the candlelight.

She opened her eyes and caught a glimpse of herself in the mirror. The water had made her makeup run, and the towel racks were empty.

She sighed and blotted her face dry with tissues.

She left the bathroom, but instead of returning to the dining room, she turned in the opposite direction. She strolled down the hallway studying posters and photographs, touching a picture frame, fingering a plastic bowl of potpourri, allowing the laughter and talk to fade into the background. Each step took her farther from the dining room, and each step made it easier to continue. Then she was at the front door, which shut out the noise completely when she closed it behind her.

She descended the flight of stairs and left the building. She paused on the sidewalk to inhale deeply, and although the August evening was only pleasantly cool, she detected the scent of a wood-burning stove. The end of summer meant fewer salads and berry desserts, more meats and cream sauces. Harvest dishes—pumpkin soup, apple cobbler. Turkey with cranberry cornbread stuffing. Gnocchi in mushroom broth. When she opened her restaurant, she would design her menu around the four seasons, using locally grown organic produce and her own secret recipes, refined from years in the college's huge kitchens and her own tiny kitchenette.

Chuck's Diner was open until ten. Tonight she would take a table for one, order a sandwich, and plan. One day that restaurant would be hers, and on the night of her grand opening, she would look back on this evening and marvel that she had ever allowed anyone to convince her to trade wild rice soup and beef tenderloin for powdered orange cheese pasta.

Chapter Four
Russell

Russell met Elaine at the Torchlight Run at Seafair. He had run the race every year since relocating from Indiana, but this was the first time he had signed up as part of a team from work. A coworker had talked him into it, insisting that Russ was the computer systems engineers' key to finally snatching victory from the marketing department's team, whose names had been engraved on the winners' bronze plaque in the employee lunchroom three years in a row. A techie team had never won, except for the year that an overly competitive manager in the software division had hired three college track stars as summer interns, which didn't count.

The self-appointed coach of Russ's team told him and their other two teammates that their best strategy was to stick together, shadowing the marketing guys until the last four hundred meters, when they could sprint ahead to the finish line. Rather than hold their faster runners back, Russ thought they each ought to strive for a personal best time and gamble that their average would beat the marketing guys', but he saw some merit in staying together so they could push one another. Then he spotted Elaine a few yards away in the pack, and all thoughts of the competition vanished. He instinctively slowed to get a better look.

"Move it, Russ," the coach called as he fell behind.

"Okay," he called back, weighing victory against getting a second look at a very attractive racer. He quickly decided bragging rights were just not that important and feigned a sore hamstring.

When his friends pulled too far ahead to witness his sudden recovery, Russ maneuvered through the pack toward the woman in the pink tank top, close enough to see the freckles on her pale shoulders. Her black hair was cut so short it barely moved in the breeze, but what struck him most was that of all the runners surrounding them, she was the only one smiling.

They crossed the finish line at nearly the same time, and he stayed close enough so that he did not lose her in the crowd at the postrace party. He squeezed into the buffet line behind her and handed her a plate as she gathered her napkin and plasticware. She thanked him, which gave him enough encouragement to speak to her. "You must love to run," he said, immediately regretting it. They had just finished a 10K race. Russell McIntyre, Master of the Obvious.

To his relief, instead of bursting into derisive laughter, she looked up at him, curious. "What makes you think so?"

"You were smiling exactly like that even at mile five."

She turned away to continue moving through the buffet line, but she seemed pleased. "I must have been thinking about how glad I was that the race was almost over. I really pushed myself today. I usually go at a slower pace."

"Were you after a personal best time?" Since they were technically in a conversation, Russ did not think she would mind if he accompanied her as she chose a table and sat down. "Or just this carbo-loading feast of pasta?"

"Definitely the carbs," she said. "No, I really just wanted to make sure I got here before my kids did, so they wouldn't worry that I had collapsed somewhere along the way."

"Your kids?"

"Yes, my kids. They're meeting me." A small, knowing smile played on her mouth. "They're legal in this state, you know. You don't even have to have a license."

Russ quickly recovered. "Are they with their baby-sitter? Or . . . your husband?"

"No husband, no baby-sitter. My daughter's sixteen, so she can drive when I'm sufficiently motivated to allow it. She dropped me off at the starting line and she and my son will pick me up later." She glanced at her watch. "In about an hour."

Sixteen? Russ was flabbergasted. Without thinking, he said, "How old were you when you had her, twelve?"

He was halfway through a hapless apology when he realized she was laughing.

Although he would catch grief from his coworkers on Monday for costing their department a bitter loss to those smug jocks from marketing, before Elaine left to meet her kids, Russ had her phone number and an invitation to call.

❧

They met the next Friday evening for dinner at Elliott's Oyster House on Pier 56. They watched the ferryboats depart and arrive as the sun set behind the Olympic Mountains and shared their life stories. It turned out Elaine was twenty when she had Carly, twenty-two when she had her son, Alex, and twenty-eight when she and her husband divorced. Her ex, a chief financial officer for a dot-com, had decided he needed a new wife to go with his new lifestyle once his company's stock options made him a millionaire. Under California law, Elaine was entitled to half of his wealth, but she chose to accept a lower settlement in exchange for uncontested full custody of Carly and Alex. "I didn't want his money for myself anyway, not after what he did," she said breezily, dismissing his betrayal. "I'm so obstinate I wanted to refuse child support, too, but my lawyer talked me out of it. I'm glad he did. Do you know what college costs these days?"

Russ thought a better question was how any man could be deluded enough to believe any trophy wife could surpass Elaine. There was a moment when he was unsettled by their six-year age difference, but he quickly shrugged it off. She was so full of life and—and she just had a way about her that made her more attractive to him than most women his own age.

She worked in public relations for a local nonprofit, which meant that she spent her days trying to convince the wealthy and upper-middle class citizens of Seattle to write checks to support unwed, pregnant teenagers. "There's not a lot of money in that," she remarked once. "Orphaned babies? Sure. They're cute and innocent. You can always find someone willing to help cute little orphans. Teenagers, though, are not so cute, and if they're pregnant, conventional wisdom says they must not be so innocent. Some say these girls got what they deserved for their irresponsible behavior. If people only knew what these girls have been through, they might believe differently, but they don't know, and frankly, far too many of them don't want to know."

Her ex-husband's new wife had once been a spokesmodel for Toyota, but since her marriage, she had devoted herself full-time to promoting her husband's career and raising their baby boy. Elaine had met her successor only once; Carly and Alex saw her as the destroyer of their parents' marriage and rarely asked to visit their father at his new home. If they were frosty to their stepmother, they were fortunately only chilly to Russ, with promising warming trends as the months passed.

In December, Russ's best friends from college, Charlie and Christine, came down from Olympia to do some Christmas shopping and meet Elaine. Charlie was obviously relieved Russ was finally dating again after breaking up with his almost-fiancée, a fellow engineer he had left behind at his former employer when she decided she liked her job too much to follow him to the West Coast. Christine's opinion mattered more somehow, possibly because she was the more astute of the pair and also because Russ had once been half in love with her. They had met in history class the first semester of sophomore year, had shared notes, met for lunch, and studied for the midterm together. If Russ had not made the mistake of inviting her to the football tailgater where she met his roommate, she might have become his girlfriend instead of Charlie's. He had watched with dismay as she and Charlie hit it off better than he had expected, but he hid his feelings when she later asked him if he would be upset if she went out with Charlie.

What could Russ say? He didn't own her. He had never even kissed her. "Why would I mind?" he said. "Charlie's a great guy."

She beamed at him with such warmth and sweetness that he would have been filled with bliss had her happiness sprung from any other source but Charlie.

Still, Russ clung to a thin shard of hope: Charlie always moved on to a new girl every few weeks, leaving her bewildered, jilted predecessor with nothing but vague promises that he would call. Usually Russ felt sorry for the girls Charlie dumped, but this time he hoped that it *would* happen, and soon, because when it did he would be there to comfort Christine.

But even Charlie recognized what he had found in Christine. They dated exclusively for the rest of their college years, and eventually Russ resigned himself to their romance. It was impossible to avoid them—not that Russ tried very hard, because he liked Charlie, and his admiration for Christine increased as his infatuation diminished. Before long she, too, became a close friend. Still, Russ knew when he was welcome and when they wanted to be alone, which was probably why the three of them got along so well.

Christine tried to set him up with some of her friends, but although they were all friendly, smart, pretty girls, he never really clicked with any of them.

Once, after an exam week all-nighter turned into a predawn breakfast off campus, the three friends' conversation turned from their sadistic professors to the dismal state of Russ's love life. That was when Christine delivered her devastating verdict: Russ was doomed because he was "too nice."

"Great," said Russ gloomily, loading his fork with pancakes. "So I should become a jerk?"

"That's not what I meant," said Christine.

"Are you saying that I'm not nice?" Charlie asked her, wounded. "I open doors for you. I remember birthdays. Your mother loves me."

"Of course you're nice, honey," said Christine, but when he wasn't looking, she rolled her eyes at Russ.

"Russ's problem is that he's waiting for the girl of his dreams," said Charlie. "Once he figures out that no such girl exists, he'll settle for a real girl."

Russ could tell from the pointed look Christine gave Charlie that she took in all that this implied and was not pleased, but she didn't rebuke him. Instead she turned to Russ and said, "Keep looking, Russ. You'll find her."

And in Elaine, he thought he had. She and Christine struck up a friendship immediately, and as soon as Charlie got him alone, he said, "Russ. Marry her. Marry her now. Don't give her the chance to get to know you better or she'll never have you."

"Very funny," said Russ, but he couldn't stop grinning. It meant the world to him that his best friends liked Elaine, because he was falling in love with her.

They married a year and a half after meeting in the road race. Charlie was the best man and Elaine's sister was the matron of honor. Carly and Alex, the only other attendants, tentatively approved of the marriage. They even consented to spend a week with their father so Russ and Elaine could honeymoon in the California wine country. They had mixed feelings about leaving their home to move into Russ's, but Elaine decided the sacrifice of next-door friends and a familiar school was worth it for a larger house in a better neighborhood on the other side of the city. Russ, eager for Elaine's children to feel welcome, offered to help them repaint their new rooms, choose new furniture—anything they wanted, anything that would make them feel at home. They thanked him politely and took him up on the offer, while a subtle nonchalance in their voices told him they would tolerate these new arrangements only because their mother loved him and they would be moving out soon anyway.

Elaine was thrilled with her new surroundings, not only because her kids would finish up high school in a much better district, but also because Russ agreed to let her turn the spare bedroom into a sewing room. Elaine was a quilter, and although Russ had known that about her, he had not entirely understood what that meant until moving day when she enlisted his help in carrying box after box of carefully folded fabric into her new sewing room.

"What's all this?" he asked, wondering how it would all fit and secretly concerned that she might ask to move their bed into the spare room so the master suite could become her sewing room.

"My stash, of course."

"Your stash?" It sounded vaguely illegal. "Do you think you'll have enough room?"

"I'll make it fit," she said cheerfully, and somehow she squeezed everything into the closet. Her sewing table took up the entire length of one wall, across the room from two bookcases stuffed full of books on quilt patterns and quilting history. She hung a large, flannel-covered board on another wall. As she designed a new quilt, she would press fabric shapes to it until they stuck, then stand back and study the arrangement, sometimes for twenty minutes at a time.

But helping Elaine set up her new sewing room, or "quilt studio," as she preferred to call it, was only the beginning of his initiation into the world of marriage to a quilter. The whirr of her sewing machine woke him in the morning, and she stitched by hand on the sofa beside him while they watched television at night. Before ironing his shirt and slacks every morning, he had to remove stacks of quilt squares from the ironing board. At least once a week, a quilt magazine turned up in their mailbox. Little bits of thread clung to everyone's clothing; fashion conscious Carly ran a lint brush over herself every morning before going to school at an age when most girls had probably never seen a lint brush. Elaine communicated via the Internet with other, similarly obsessed quilters from around the world; she peppered their dinner conversation with references to friends she had never seen in person, ladies who identified themselves by such names as "Quiltlady" and "Scrappbagg." He learned the hard way not to walk around in bare feet after she pin basted a quilt on the living room floor. Every vacation, every excursion to a new city turned into a quest to spend at least twenty dollars at every quilt shop within a ten-mile radius. He also discovered that one does not ask a hard-core quilter to sew on a loose button.

The first and only time he did so, Elaine stared at him in astonishment. "Would you ask Picasso to paint your living room?"

"I might," he said, "if he owned a three-thousand-dollar Bernina painting machine."

Elaine gave her sewing machine an affectionate pat. "It was only fifteen hundred, used, and worth every penny."

"I wouldn't have asked except you love to sew. You have enough fabric in here to outfit the entire Spanish Armada in full sail. What's one little button?"

She laughed, patted his cheek, and agreed to sew on the button. Unfortunately, she placed the shirt and the button on her worktable and promptly forgot about it. Eventually the shirt migrated to her stack of unfinished projects, and later he spotted it buried within her fabric stash. He knew any chance of having the shirt restored to its former usefulness had passed when his birthday came and she gave him a new shirt, identical in every way to the one trapped beneath an avalanche of cotton in her closet except that all of its buttons were intact.

Russ enjoyed teasing her about her quilting, partially because in this, he, Carly, and Alex shared common ground. Her quilting actually did not bother him at all. She never ignored him in favor of a quilt project, and quilting seemed therapeutic for her, helping her to relieve the stress of her emotionally demanding job. He loved her for the joy she took in making quilts for each of his nieces and nephews, and he loved coming home from work to find that she had hung a new quilt on a bare wall "because the wall looked cold." But it was when he overheard her on the phone with a friend from her quilting bee, marveling about how supportive he was of her quilting compared to her ex, that he vowed she would never hear a word of complaint from him about her quilting, no matter how many lost pins he found with the soles of his feet.

They wanted children, and as Elaine's thirty-ninth birthday approached, they decided not to wait any longer to start a family. "Continue the family," Elaine corrected. "We're already a family."

Russell agreed, for although Carly and Alex often seemed frustratingly indifferent to him, he loved them as if they were his own. He had shared more of the challenges and conflicts of their teenaged years than their own father had. After they had made the transition to college, the house seemed too big and quiet without a youngster around. Russ and Elaine understood they would face challenges as new parents at their ages, if they were fortunate enough to conceive at all, but they decided to try.

A year passed. Elaine halfheartedly suggested they see a fertility specialist, but they had long ago discussed whether they would be willing to take extraordinary measures to conceive and had decided they would not. They had begun to investigate adoption when Elaine surprised him one morning with the exciting news that she had missed her period. When a home pregnancy test came back negative, her face twisted with unshed tears, but she said that perhaps it was too early for the test to detect anything. When she failed a second test a week later but her symptoms persisted, she made an appointment with her ob-gyn, because she felt bloating and pressure in her abdomen, and she was certain the pregnancy tests were wrong.

When the diagnosis came back positive for ovarian cancer, Russ could not believe it. Elaine's mother and an aunt had died of breast cancer, and she was meticulous about her self-exams and annual mammograms. It was breast cancer that had been stalking them, breast cancer she had been keeping at bay. Russ was so certain that the diagnosis was wrong that he stormed from the doctor's office and went outside to sit on the curb until the dizzying blackness left his head. Before he was able to return, Elaine finished her appointment and joined him outside. He was ashamed that in her hour of horror and fear, *she* had had to comfort *him*. He knew he had failed his first real test as a husband.

The women of her quilting bee rallied around her as she underwent surgery and discovered that her cancer was already at stage II. At least three times a week, a quilter stopped by with a casserole ready to stick in the oven, with explicit cooking directions for Russ to follow. Her Internet quilting friends sent packages of fabric, quilt blocks, and chocolate. Everyone who knew and loved Elaine—and Russ was proud of how many, many people this included—prayed for her.

As she underwent chemotherapy, she began a new quilt. She took angry reds and sickening greens and blacks as deep as oblivion from her closet stash, cut jagged shapes, and pressed them to her design wall. She frowned at them from a chair, too weak to stand as long as she needed, a red polka-dot scarf covering her baldness, her eyes circled in dark shadows, her lips thin and pale.

"What are you making?" he asked her once, gently, wishing she would put this garish project aside in favor of the quilt she had been working on before her diagnosis, a pattern of golden stars and log cabin strips. The warm colors and familiar motions of sewing would cheer her up, he thought. Staring at the design wall seemed so bleak and despairing that he wished he could take her by the arm, lead her from the room, and shut the door on that quilt.

She rose from her chair with an effort, eyes fixed on the design wall. "This is my cancer quilt."

"This is what cancer looks like?"

"This is what cancer feels like." She shifted a red triangle to the right three inches. "This is what it feels like in me."

He held her at night when she cried. She exacted endless promises from him that he would take care of Carly and Alex, that he would show pictures of her to her future grandchildren, that he would not withdraw from the world after she had gone. He begged her not to ask him to plan for a life without her, but she insisted, and to placate her, he agreed to all that she asked.

Then, unexpectedly, she began to feel stronger. Her hair grew back; she bought new running shoes and began taking morning walks through the neighborhood. She left the cancer quilt undisturbed on the design wall and joined a round-robin quilt project with her Internet friends. She talked about getting a dog and returning to work, and she suggested they spend a long weekend in California's Napa Valley, enjoying some of the places they had discovered on their honeymoon. Most of all, she wanted the two of them to run in the Swedish SummeRun, a 10K race through Seattle and a fund-raiser for the Marsha Rivkin Center for Ovarian Cancer Research. It was a serendipitous event for Russ and Elaine, she said, since they had met in a road race and she definitely supported the research.

Russ was conflicted. He was thrilled that she felt well enough to begin running again and he was a fervent supporter of ovarian cancer research, but to run in a race with Elaine, especially for this cause, seemed to frame their relationship, putting a full stop at the end of their story. But if she meant to enter the race, he was determined to run beside her, to celebrate her triumph or to support her if she faltered.

A few days after they sent in their registration forms, Elaine told him that she wanted to reschedule her follow-up appointment with the oncologist to an earlier date. When he asked her why, she shrugged and said, "Just a feeling."

He had learned to trust her intuition, but he refused to believe that it was necessary to see the doctor sooner than planned. If they did not believe in her remission, trust in it entirely, it would cease to be. Then he was filled with a terrible fear that cancer cells might be even then growing and dividing within her, and that his superstitious delay might kill her. "Call," he urged her. "It's probably nothing, but call."

When tests confirmed that the cancer had resurfaced in her lymph nodes, Russ was flooded with feelings of rage and betrayal and despair so intense it made his head swim. Elaine, in contrast, seemed to have expected it. She grew still in the chair beside him as the doctor spoke about trying to join a clinical trial, nodding silently and stroking Russ's back to comfort him.

Even in the worst days of their mother's treatment, Carly and Alex had seemed certain that she would ultimately overcome the disease. Russ had marveled at their conviction and tried to follow their example once he saw how much their confidence heartened their mother. Now their certainty was shattered, and disbelief quickly shifted to despair. Carly, recently engaged, moved back home to help Russ care for Elaine. Alex drove down from his new job in Vancouver nearly every weekend. Even their father called once, near the end. Elaine wore a bemused expression as she listened on the phone, then laughed when he offered financial help and told him that if he really wanted to make a difference, he should give to Childhaven's Crisis Nursery instead. Russ never learned if he did.

The women of Elaine's quilting bee surrounded her with love. They brought food, laughter, and hope into the house and always seemed to appear right when Russ felt the most helpless and exhausted. He had taken a leave of absence from his job to care for Elaine, but he still felt as if there was never enough time, never enough that he could do for her.

Elaine's oncologist called in some favors and got her enrolled in a clinical trial. Russ convinced himself that this would cure her. Even as Elaine contacted Hospice and got her affairs in order, Russ clung to his faith in the power of her new meds. Then came the day when Elaine told him she had placed all of her important papers in the fireproof box in the closet so he would not need to worry about searching the whole house for them.

"I won't need to search for them because if we need them, you'll tell me where they are," he said firmly.

She looked at him with affectionate amusement. "I see. You're still in the denial stage."

"But the treatment," he said. "Your new medication. Why would they keep treating you if you weren't getting better?"

"Oh, sweetheart," she said, pressing her thin cheek to his. "Clinical trials aren't for the patients in them. You know that."

He knew it.

Elaine was determined to participate in the Swedish SummeRun. Russ saw to it that she did. He pushed her the entire route in a wheelchair, but even this exhausted her. "All of this effort is going to pay off someday," she told him as they approached the finish line, smiling despite her fatigue. He nodded, unable to speak out of fear that he would start sobbing. It would pay off someday, but not soon enough to save Elaine. He remembered how full of life and happy she had looked running just ahead of him on the day they met. Now she was again moving ahead of him, away from him, but this time he could not follow.

Elaine died surrounded by Russ, her children, her sister, and her dearest friends. Her last words were for her children, gentle whispers for them alone that left them sobbing and smiling and choking out assurances. But before she turned to them, she asked Russ to hold her. "Thank you," she said. "I'm sorry."

"What do you mean?" he said. He meant, what in the world was she apologizing for? He was the one who was sorry, sorry that he could not save her, sorry that he had not been a better husband, sorry if he had ever disappointed her in any way for even a moment.

"Thank you for loving me," she answered. "Thank you for loving my children. They didn't always make it easy. They're going to need you. Their father will try to comfort them, but he'll just upset them."

Gently, his voice barely above a whisper, he asked, "Why did you say you're sorry?"

"I'm sorry I'm leaving you. I'm sorry we didn't have a baby together. I know how much that disappointed you."

"Oh, Elaine." He wanted to press her hard against him, but she was so delicate in his arms, like a broken bird. "You have never disappointed me. There's not a minute of any day since I've known you that I would change. Not one single minute."

He had so much more he wanted to say, but he was fighting back tears, trying not to let her see his anguish. She wanted him to be strong for Carly and Alex. He must let her think he could be, though he was convinced his grief would kill him.

It was not a relief when she finally passed. He had heard some families from the Hospice say that in the end it was a relief when their loved ones were finally released from their pain. For Russ, Carly, and Alex, nothing could be further from the truth.

Elaine had planned well. "That's Mom," said Carly when they discovered that she had planned her own funeral down to the last note of music and the suit she wanted Russ to wear. Somehow word got out on the Internet that she had died, and dozens of mourners introduced themselves to Russ and the children as friends from one quilting list or another. Even if they had not come, the church would have been full, as coworkers, residents of the Catholic Worker House where Elaine had once lived, and an astonishing number of young mothers with babies came to pay their respects.

"See how many lives your mother has touched," Russ said to Carly and Alex. They looked and saw through their tears, and they nodded.

After the Mass, Russ and the members of Elaine's quilting bee fulfilled her final request. They held up her quilts one by one as Bach cantatas played in the background, carried them down the aisles so that all could witness her artistry, then draped the quilts over the few empty pews until the back of the church was awash in color. Russ took in the quilts hungrily, seeing them as a reflection of Elaine's affectionate nature, her boundless humor, her compassion for the less fortunate—everything she was and had become over the span of more than twenty years the quilts had captured.

Afterward, Russ distributed the quilts as Elaine had instructed: one to a college roommate, another to her sister, one each to the members of her quilting bee. Her friends were grateful, and they hugged their quilts with eyes closed against tears or held them reverently as if cradling Elaine herself. Russ should have been comforted by their gratitude and appreciation, but each giving pained him as if pieces of Elaine were being carved from his memory.

❧

The weeks passed, and somehow Russ endured them. His family leave ran out and he returned to work, where he went through the motions of his job and nodded numbly when people told him how sorry they were for his loss.

Carly had put her wedding plans on hold, but she decided to return to her own apartment so she could be closer to work and her fiancé. "You don't have to leave," Russ told her, dreading an empty house.

"I do have to," she told him. "If I don't move back in soon, my roommate will find a replacement for me. Besides, this is your house. It was never really ours."

That pained him. "Yes, it was. It was to me. I wanted you and Alex to feel at home here. I thought you did."

Carly looked away, and Russ recognized her indifferent shrug from her teenage years, the gesture with which she tried to disguise shame. "It was more of a home than our father's house ever was."

And Russ was grateful.

Before Carly moved out, she helped him go through her mother's belongings, sorting heirlooms and cherished keepsakes from items to be donated to one of Elaine's many causes. Carly took her mother's jewelry and a leather jacket Russ had given to her one Christmas. She divided family photographs into a set for herself and one for her brother. They folded her clothes carefully and placed them in paper sacks to deliver to the women's shelter. Russ had a sudden vision of himself walking in downtown Seattle and spotting a stranger standing in a doorway, carrying a bag of groceries, wearing Elaine's favorite sweater. He had to force himself to continue packing the clothes.

Last of all, they went to her quilt studio. When Russ opened the door, the sight of the cancer quilt staggered him. He could almost see Elaine there, arranging the red of blood, the green of disease, the black of oblivion. He couldn't bear it. He pulled the door shut and leaned against it as Carly stared at him.

"What is it?" she asked.

"No," he muttered.

"What's wrong?"

I can't, he thought, but said, "I'm too worn out to tackle that room today."

"Okay." She studied him, concerned. "But I'm leaving tomorrow. I don't know when I'll be able to come back to help."

"I'll take care of it on my own."

Carly followed him downstairs. "But there's so much to sort through. It's too much for one person."

"I said I'll take care of it," he said harshly. Carly raised her hands in a small gesture of surrender and shook her head as if to say it made no difference to her.

❧

Carly returned two weeks later with a carload of boxes and garbage bags. Russ was pleased to see her and agreed that they should get started on the quilt studio, but he was actually just about to leave for Pike Place Farmer's Market. He would be glad for her company if she wanted to join him. Carly assented, and they spent the day seeing the sights and shopping for ingredients for their supper, which they prepared together. Russ asked her about work and her fiancé, and circumspectly asked if they had resumed planning their wedding. Although Russ had long privately considered Carly too young to get married, Elaine would not have wanted Carly to postpone her happiness for the year of mourning Carly seemed to believe was necessary. For his part, Russ saw no point in observing a symbolic year of mourning to suit social conventions. They would always mourn Elaine. One year or two years or ten years later, they would still mourn. To pretend that everything would be resolved on some arbitrary date was ridiculous.

"If you're postponing the wedding because you're having second thoughts, that's one thing," said Russ, after Carly gave a tearful account of her fiancé's bewildered unhappiness at her reluctance to set a new date. "You should take that time. But if you're doing it for your mother, I really think you ought to reconsider."

"I know I want to marry him," said Carly. "I just can't imagine getting married without Mom there. How can I celebrate when she's gone?"

"We'll have to figure out a way," said Russ quietly. "Your mother would be very annoyed if we never celebrated anything ever again just because she's not here to enjoy it."

Carly actually managed a laugh. "She'd be furious. Can you imagine what she'd say?"

"All too well."

They laughed together. Carly wiped her eyes and said she would call her fiancé as soon as she got home so they could choose a new wedding date.

They washed the dishes side by side. Afterward, Russ walked Carly to the door to say good-bye. Unexpectedly, she hugged him.

"I never thanked you for marrying my mother," she said, her voice muffled as she buried her face in his shoulder.

"Well . . ." Russ patted her on the back. "It's not something you need to thank me for. I was glad to do it. Thank you for letting *me* marry *her*."

"It's not like I could have stopped her." Carly lifted her head so he could see that she was teasing. "I'm glad she was married to you when this happened. If she had still been married to my dad—well, he would have been totally useless. But you saw her through. You eased her way."

His throat constricting, Russ held Carly tightly.

When Carly opened the door to leave, she spied her car in the driveway and, through the windows, the boxes she had brought. She shot him a look that was mildly accusing. "We were so busy, we forgot about Mom's quilt studio."

"I guess we did. I'll get around to it. Maybe you could leave the boxes."

She did, and a few days later, she called to ask if he had sorted out the quilt studio yet. *Sorted it out?* Russ thought. He could not even open the door. "I haven't had a chance," he told her. "I've had a lot to do, catching up at work after the time off. You know."

"Yes, Dad," she said. "I know."

The last time she had called him Dad was at her high school graduation.

When he returned home from work the next day, he found a tentative, apologetic message on the answering machine. Elaine had been participating in a round robin quilt project with some friends from the Internet, the caller explained. When a member received another member's quilt block, she was supposed to add a border and mail it on to the next quilter in the circle. The person after Elaine had not received any packages in months, and three of the round robin quilts were missing. They had heard about the "recent trag-edy," and hated to bother him about something so trivial, but they wondered if perhaps the quilt tops could be located among Elaine's belongings and sent on their way. The caller left an address.

Russ searched through the pile of unopened mail on the credenza in the foyer and found one large, padded envelope addressed to Elaine. Inside was a red, brown, green, and ivory quilt, partially completed, with a complicated star in the middle and two surrounding borders, one of squares, one of flow-ers and leaves. Russ tore open every envelope addressed to his dead wife, and although some contained fabric or quilt blocks, none but the first met the description the caller had left on the answering machine.

He climbed the stairs, touched the door to her quilt studio, and let his hand fall to his side. Then he went to his bedroom and dialed the phone.

"Hello?"

It was Christine, not Charlie. That made it easier. "Christine." He cleared his throat. "Christine, it's Russ. I need your help."

❧

She arrived early the next morning, before he had eaten breakfast. That was his fault, not hers; he had sat at the table lost in thought without taking a bite for at least a half hour before her car pulled into the driveway. He scraped his clammy eggs and bacon into the trash and let her in.

Christine gave him one long, wordless hug, then held him at arm's length and gave him a searching look. "You stopped shaving?"

His hand flew to his jaw. "Yeah. Well. Sometimes I forget."

"You look like you're growing a beard." She smiled, wistful and sad. "It looks good on you."

He mumbled a thank you and led her upstairs. Christine pushed open the door to the quilt studio without giving him a chance to prepare himself, as if ignoring his need to steel himself would make the need vanish. "Should we find the round robin quilts first?" she asked, standing in the center of the room. Her gaze fell upon the design wall and lingered there.

"Sure," said Russ. He went to the stack of envelopes on the table beside Elaine's sewing machine. They held letters full of condolences and well-wishes and assurances of the senders' prayers. They turned Russ's stomach and he threw them in the trash.

Christine soon found the round robin projects neatly folded on Elaine's worktable. Russ set them aside to mail later and began assembling the collapsed cartons Carly had left. He opened the closet door, scooped up armfuls of folded fabric, and dropped them into an open carton. Christine did the same with the shelves of quilting books.

"What do you want to do with all this?" asked Christine when they had filled several cartons.

"Donate it. Give it away. Throw it away. I don't care."

He was conscious of Christine's silence, but at that moment he truly did not care what became of his wife's treasured accumulation of fabric and patterns. Now that he had finally broken through whatever had kept him from entering that room, he wanted to strip it bare of anything that reminded him of Elaine. She had called the quilt studio her haven, her sanctuary, but it had not saved her. She had not even been able to climb the stairs to reach it in the end.

He packed her sewing machine into a box and stuffed smaller pieces of fabric around it for protection. Sorting out her unfinished projects was harder, especially when he came upon the partially completed quilt with the log cabin blocks and the stars, the last quilt she had begun before her diagnosis. He recognized pieces from quilts he knew well—two for his nieces, one for Alex, one for their own bed—extra or imperfect blocks she had not been able to use but had been unwilling to discard. He found a stack of twenty small quilt blocks made up in old-fashioned looking material, each pattern different, from a class she had taken years before. Christine discovered a binder Elaine had kept of useful tips her Internet quilting friends had exchanged by email.

"Email," said Russ, suddenly remembering. He switched on the computer and checked her account. She had more than fourteen hundred email messages waiting. The last was a warning from her ISP that her account was full.

"I can't write back to all these people," he said.

"You don't have to," said Christine. She sat down and began typing. He hesitated, but returned to his own work, and before long Christine announced that she had sent one message to everyone in Elaine's address book letting them know that she had died. "There's no good way to deliver this kind of bad news," she said. "I hope this doesn't come as a shock to anyone."

"Most of them probably know already," said Russ, sealing a carton with heavy tape. "I think someone posted a link to her obituary on a message board."

The hours passed. They took a break for lunch; Russ made sandwiches and listened to Christine's news about Charlie and the kids. Christine seemed to want to tell him something else, but hesitated on the brink of speaking. He was getting used to that. Everyone wanted to comfort him, to find the right words that would bring him solace. He knew there were no such words.

It was harder to return upstairs than he had expected. He had thought the shock of pain would wear off from the sheer physical effort of putting away a life. Instead he had to force himself through the doorway of the room. And suddenly he understood why: The cancer quilt gaped like an open wound from the design wall.

Angrily, he snatched the fabric pieces one by one and stuffed them into a plastic bag.

"Careful," said Christine.

"Why?" He scraped the last pieces to the floor roughly. "What's the point? What was the point of any of it?"

"Oh, Russ. You don't mean that."

But he did. He wished he could articulate his anger, his demand for some divine justification for what had happened. Elaine's death was beyond unfair. God should not allow someone who had devoted her life to easing the suffering of others to die in pain. God should not have brought Russ and Elaine together just to shatter his heart by taking her away. All their dreams, all their plans, every word of tenderness, every gesture of affection, every kiss, every hope, every moment had been an empty promise, a tease, a waste.

Hollow and cold and helpless, he closed his eyes and let the bag of black and red and green fall to the floor.

Christine took it up. He watched as she gently picked up the remaining pieces of the quilt from the floor, brushed them off, and placed them carefully into the bag. She zipped the bag shut and put it in one of the last open boxes, where it quickly disappeared amid the abandoned quilting tools.

At last they finished. They packed up the last carton and sealed it, and as he straightened, Russ realized that he was exhausted, flooded with the kind of bone-aching weariness that usually followed a much more physically arduous day.

"What should we do with these?" asked Christine, gesturing to the cartons and boxes they had carried downstairs and stacked in the foyer. He wondered if she knew it was a different question than the one she had asked before.

Christine had driven her minivan, so he said, "If I help you load, will you take them?"

"Take them where?"

"Goodwill. St. Vincent de Paul's. Wherever."

"But Russ . . ." Christine looked around, then gestured to the box containing Elaine's sewing machine. "What about that? Don't you want to save that, at least?"

"What for?"

"I don't know. Mending? Maybe you should save it for Carly."

"Carly already took what she wanted to keep. If you want it, take it."

"I don't want it. I just thought . . ." She shook her head. "Quilting was such an important part of Elaine's life. I thought maybe you would want to keep something of that."

"I don't." He hefted the largest box in his arms and carried it out to her minivan.

❧

He woke shortly after two A.M., shaking and sick at heart. The covers were soaked in sweat. He pushed them aside and stumbled downstairs to the kitchen, where he poured a glass of water and tried to stop shaking. He ached for Elaine.

Back in bed, he struggled for sleep. At seven the alarm clock roused him from a restless doze. He showered and dressed for work, but his heart seemed to be pounding unnaturally hard, as if he had sprinted up four flights of stairs. In the hallway, he paused by Elaine's quilt studio. The door was ajar; he pushed it open and took in the emptiness. Only the design wall remained, white flannel marked with a faint blue grid. A wave of grief swept over him and he pulled the door shut.

He needed to fill that space, he told himself as he drove to work. An exercise room. A home theater. Storage. All day he forced himself to consider alternatives rather than imagine the room without Elaine.

Two nights he wrestled with insomnia, fighting off memories of Elaine. On the third morning, he woke to the sounds of his own weeping. Ashamed, he snatched up the quilt and wrapped himself in it as he sat on the edge of the bed. He buried his face in the quilt and imagined he could still smell Elaine in it.

He picked up the phone and called Christine. The oldest boy answered; Russ asked for his mother with his teeth clenched to keep them from chattering. When she finally came to the phone, he said, "Where did you take them?"

"Russ?"

"Do you remember?" Three days had passed since Christine had driven off with the boxes. Elaine's possessions were surely scattered by now; he had no hope of gathering them together again. "The cartons. Her quilting things. Where did you take them?"

"Russ—"

"I need to find her cancer quilt. You put it in a green and white carton that used to hold copier paper. Did you donate it or throw it out or—"

"Russ," said Christine. "I have it."

❧

She had kept everything for him, every box, a safeguard against future regret. Later that day, Charlie returned them. He helped Russ carry the boxes upstairs but left quickly, mercifully, before Russ began unpacking.

He searched for the cancer quilt first just to assure himself that it had not disappeared. He pressed each jagged piece to the design wall exactly as Elaine had arranged them, exactly as they had been indelibly seared into his memory.

He set up the sewing machine, found the manual, and read it cover to cover. The machine was capable of producing more stitches than he had known existed. He doubted he would need them all. As far as he could recall, Elaine had used only the one that went in a straight line and the one that zig-zagged.

It took him four tries to thread the machine properly, but once he did, he proceeded slowly and methodically through a few practice seams. Elaine had always whizzed through everything, hacking off pieces that were too large or steaming them with the iron and stretching them if they were too small. That was her way in many things. Had been her way.

He hesitated before taking pieces of the cancer quilt from the design wall. How Elaine would have marveled at the sight of him. She probably would have smothered a laugh before diplomatically coaching him through his first few clumsy stitches.

He sewed a green triangle to a red, added a black pentagon, then stuck the assembled pieces to the design wall and stepped back to take a look. It didn't look like much. He took a few more pieces, sewed them together, and then a few more. He interrupted his work to set up the ironing board; he pressed all the sewn sections flat and discovered that they adhered to the design wall better. "What do you know," he said aloud, rearranging a few pieces, then immediately shifting them back to Elaine's original placement. It was her quilt, her last quilt. Nothing he did could improve upon it.

He sewed late into the night, and he worked on the quilt every week-end and every evening after work until the top was completed. Tentatively pleased, he stuck it to the design wall and studied it. The sight struck him like a punch in the gut. It was all sharp angles and angry colors; it was shat-tered glass and anguish. This is how Elaine had felt.

He had to leave the room.

When he returned to the quilt studio a few days later, he unpacked the boxes of books and returned them to the shelves. One title caught his atten-tion: *All About Quilting from A to Z*. That sounded promising. He set it aside and referred to it later as he layered and basted the quilt top.

The book provided an entire section on machine quilting, but Elaine had never quilted any other way but by hand. Russ had often watched as she sat on the sofa beside him, quilt hoop on her lap, the rest of the quilt's layers bundled around her. The book said machine quilting could be sturdier and faster, but he decided to stick with what was most familiar.

He found Elaine's lap hoop in the largest of the cartons, put it around the center of the quilt, and tightened the screw until the three layers were secure and smooth. Carrying it downstairs so he could quilt during the Mariners game, he stepped on a corner of the quilt, tripped, and stumbled down several stairs before grabbing hold of the handrail. He swore softly, envisioning his skull cracked open upon the tile floor of the foyer. Untangling himself, he discovered that he had not torn the quilt, but had stepped on the hoop and broken one of the thin wooden circles.

The next day, he spent his lunch break at Elaine's favorite quilt shop, wandering the aisles in search of replacement parts for quilt hoops. He found new hoops and more gadgets for machine quilting than he would have imagined necessary, but no replacement parts. Occasionally an employee or another shopper, invariably female, would smile indulgently at him in passing. No one offered to help, but he suspected that was not because he looked like he knew what he was doing.

His lunch hour half over, Russ went to a large island in the middle of the room where a shop employee was cutting fabric. She smiled at him as he approached, but she immediately returned her attention to her work.

"Excuse me," said Russ. "I'm trying to find some replacement hoops."

"Oh, I'm sorry." The woman set down her rotary cutter. "I just assumed you were the husband of one of our customers."

"No." Not quite.

"I'd be happy to help you. What did your wife send you in to buy?"

Inwardly, Russ winced. "She didn't send me. I broke the inner wooden circle of her quilting hoop and I was hoping to find a replacement."

"Before she finds out?" said the woman, amused.

"No," said Russ. "I need it to finish one of her quilts."

"Finish one of . . ." The woman's eyebrows rose. "Do you think that's a good idea? Maybe you should ask her first. I know if my husband started poking needles into my quilt, I'd really let him have it."

"If my husband did, I'd take away the scissors before he hurt himself," remarked a passing customer.

"Can you point me in the right direction?" asked Russ patiently.

"We don't sell replacement parts for quilting hoops," said the woman. "In fact, I don't know anyone who does. It probably wouldn't be very cost effective. You can buy a new hoop pretty cheap. Do you want me to show you where they are?"

"No, thanks. I remember." Annoyed and embarrassed, Russ purchased a hoop similar to the one he had broken and left the shop as quickly as possible.

He quilted in the evenings in front of the television, as Elaine used to do. Something about the repetitive motions of quilting allowed his mind to disconnect from himself, to float on a stratum out of reach of his anger and the slow, steady ache of loneliness. In those moments he could remember Elaine without pain.

Working on the cancer quilt became a way to fill the empty hours between work and sleep. The quilt became a tribute to her, a link to her. Sometimes he felt as if she were watching over his shoulder, encouraging him to persevere, shrugging off his mistakes. At first his stitches were huge, crooked, and scattered, as if someone had spilled a bag of long grain rice on the quilt. As the weeks passed, they became smaller and more precise, falling into a distinguishable pattern of loops and scrolls.

He finished the quilt a few weeks shy of the first anniversary of Elaine's death. Following the instructions in her books, he attached a hanging sleeve to the back of the quilt and hung it in the living room. It clashed with the rest of the furnishings, but he didn't care. In fact, he respected the disruption. He figured that was part of the message of the quilt.

On the night that marked one full year without Elaine, Christine and Charlie came into the city to distract him with dinner at his favorite restaurant. They didn't tell him that was the reason, of course, but he knew. When they came over to pick him up, they stopped short at the sight of the cancer quilt. Christine sucked in a breath; Charlie let out a low whistle.

"Interesting choice in . . . art, buddy," said Charlie dubiously.

"Elaine designed it," Christine warned in an undertone.

"I mean, it's great," said Charlie quickly. "It's . . . Wow. Elaine did good work."

"Elaine started it. I finished it."

Two pairs of eyes fixed on him. Then Charlie laughed. "You finished it?"

"That's right." Russ studied the quilt for a moment. "And I'm thinking about starting another."

"Why?"

Russ shrugged. "Something to do."

Charlie and Christine exchanged a look. Christine delicately changed the subject, and no one mentioned the quilt for the rest of the evening.

❧

Elaine's books listed what must have been thousands of quilt patterns—stars and baskets and geometric designs with names like Shoo-Fly and Lone Star and Snail's Trail. Russ leafed through the pages and tried to pick one or two he wouldn't mind attempting, but cutting out precise pieces and sewing from point to point and making the same block over and over did not appeal to him. He liked the way Elaine's last quilt just fell together.

He needed something to fill the nights and weekends. Elaine had left an inexhaustible supply of fabric to experiment with, so he decided to improvise. It wasn't as if anyone else would see the quilt, unless he decided to hang it on the wall just to provoke another reaction from Charlie.

Russ had grudgingly admired Elaine's rotary cutter from the time he first saw her slicing through fabric, years before. It was sharp, fast, and metal—in short, it was a guy tool. After sorting her fabric stash by color, he took about a yard of green and a yard of blue, stacked them on top of the cutting mat, and, using Elaine's longest acrylic ruler as a guide, made four arbitrary slashes across the whole width of the fabric from left to right, varying the angle of the cut and the distance between them. He then turned the ruler and made four more slashes from top to bottom. He swapped every other green piece for blue and sewed the pieces together, checkerboard fashion. It was quick and satisfying, but the green and blue fabrics, so distinct and different when seen alone, blended into one mass when sewn together.

He tried again, this time choosing a deep green and a dull copper. Layering the fabrics as before, he cut more strips, some wide, some narrow. He swapped colors and sewed them together, for the first time racing along with something approaching Elaine's speed. When he put the quilt top on the design wall and stepped back to examine it, he let out a dry chuckle. Looking at the quilt was like looking out at a lush green field through the metal bars of a cage. Only one small opening at the bottom where the bars did not completely reach the edge allowed for an escape.

❧

He returned to the quilt shop, ignoring the curious stares of the employees as he picked out batting and an iridescent quilting thread unlike anything in Elaine's sewing box just because it looked interesting. He came back a few days later after reading in one of Elaine's reference books that such thread was meant for machine quilting only. He intended to exchange the thread for something more suitable for hand quilting, but he left the shop with the spool of thread still in his pocket and a new sewing machine foot especially for free-motion machine quilting.

His first attempt was a disaster. The bobbin thread bunched and knotted on the back of the quilt, the stitch length on top of the quilt varied from minuscule to long enough to catch on the presser foot, and he could only sew a minute or two before the top thread stretched and snapped. He took a perverse pride in being responsible for what was probably the worst example of machine quilting ever produced. The only thing he did right was to practice on junk fabric first.

When he thought he had learned all he could from books and practice, he committed his quilt top to the needle. The results were mixed. The quilting stitches brought out an interesting depth and dimension to the flat surface of the quilt top that he liked, but the finished quilt had somehow become distorted from true square. Obviously he was doing something wrong, but he had no idea what or how to fix it.

Finally he called one of Elaine's quilting friends, Francine, a woman not quite his mother's age who had organized the delivery of casseroles and cookies in the weeks following Elaine's surgery and chemo. "You want help doing what?" she asked after he explained the purpose of his call.

"Free-motion machine quilting."

"Why?"

"Because I can't figure out what I'm doing wrong."

"You're trying to make a quilt?"

"Yes," he said, impatient. Why was it such a shock that he wanted to quilt? These quilters, who were so generous and encouraging to other women who wanted to learn to quilt, acted like he was demanding the right to use women's public restrooms.

"Why?"

Russ did not have a good answer for that. "Never mind. Thanks anyway."

"Wait!" commanded Francine. He returned the receiver to his ear. "Don't hang up. Our quilt guild has a machine quilting workshop coming up this weekend. There are still a few spots open. Ordinarily you have to be a guild member to sign up, but I think we can make an exception for you, as the husband of a longtime member."

"You mean, take a class with other people?"

"You're not afraid of us, are you?"

"No, but—" He doubted he would be any more welcome there than at the quilt shop. "I was hoping you could just give me a few pointers over the phone."

"It's much easier to learn by watching. We're meeting on Saturday at ten in the community center rec room, same place as always. Do you have a sewing machine?"

"There's Elaine's—"

"Don't forget to bring it. And some fabric to practice on. I'll sign you up and you can just pay at the door. See you then."

She hung up before he could refuse.

All week long he intended to call Francine back and cancel, but somehow, Saturday morning found him lugging Elaine's sewing machine into the community center. It appeared that all the other workshop participants had arrived early to set up their workspaces, but he found an unoccupied place near the back. Most of the women ignored him, but a few threw him curious stares as he searched for someplace to plug in Elaine's Bernina. After a while, a grandmotherly woman wearing her long gray hair in a bun helpfully pointed out the nearest power strip. He thanked her and sat down, already regretting that he had come.

But by the end of the afternoon, he had figured out where he had gone wrong with his first attempt at free-motion machine quilting; apparently, an uneven amount of quilting in different sections of the top could pull it out of shape. The instructor had also demonstrated a few techniques he had not seen in any of Elaine's books, and she talked about how different kinds of thread could produce different effects. Then he caught himself taking mental notes of ideas to share with Elaine when he got home, and all interest in the workshop drained from him like air from a punctured tire.

Francine approached him afterward and asked him how he had fared in the workshop.

"Not bad." He felt fairly confident about his machine quilting now, but none of the other quilters had talked to him during the breaks, and they all kept shooting him furtive, suspicious glances.

"You should join the guild."

"Me? Oh no. I don't think so. I wouldn't fit in."

Francine was a retired high school principal, and at this remark, she gave him a look that made him feel like a truant sophomore. "Why? Because you're a man?"

"To be honest, yes."

"Oh, please." She thrust a guild newsletter at him. "Don't be such a coward. You have a lot to learn, and a guild is the best place for that. You'll get a discount on future workshops, too. You're not the only man who quilts, you know."

He wasn't? Russ took the newsletter, gave it a quick look, and stuffed it in his pocket. "Maybe I can make a meeting now and then."

"Good. See you next Wednesday."

"I didn't say I'd come for sure."

"I know." She waggled her thick fingers at him over her shoulder as she departed.

He did go to the meeting, drawn by curiosity and hopeful that he would meet another male quilter. The lecture on Civil War era quilts was more interesting than he had expected, but the social break was a hassle, full of conversations that stopped as soon as he approached and more of those suspicious looks. It was a relief when Francine came over and, in her imposing way, asked if he was enjoying himself.

"Sure," he said. "But I was hoping to meet some of those other men quilters you mentioned."

"There aren't any men in our guild yet."

"But you said—"

"I said that male quilters exist, not that they are members of our guild. Of course, you could join and change all that."

Russ looked around at the other quilters, all women, all studiously ignoring his conversation with the guild president. "I don't think so."

He stuck around for the second half of the meeting, but left as soon as the motion to adjourn had been approved. Elaine had always enjoyed her monthly quilt guild meetings, so he had expected a warmer welcome, a friendlier crowd. Then again, Elaine always brought out the best in people. She could have warmed up even that chilly bunch. But a quilting guild was clearly no place for him.

❦

Quilting was the first thing he learned to enjoy without Elaine, and for a long time, it was the only thing. Then he began to run again, to go out for a beer with some of the guys from work every so often, to take in an occasional Seahawks game with Charlie. But always he returned to quilting. He alternated between completing one of Elaine's unfinished quilts and one of his own designs. Trying to buy anything at the quilt shop, where he was alternately ignored and patronized, was such a demeaning experience that he started ordering his supplies through the Internet. One evening, web surfing after a purchase, he followed a shop's link to a quilt museum to a fabric designer to a quilt block archive, where he stumbled upon an online quilting guild.

Intrigued, he read the messages other members had posted. A neophyte would pose a timid question; a flurry of encouraging responses from more experienced quilters would follow. Someone would post a celebratory note announcing a quilt finished or blue ribbon won and the others would shower her with praise and congratulations. A frustrated quilter would ask for advice on a challenging seam or an impossible block arrangement and receive it. Here, at last, he had found that elusive quilting community Elaine had often spoken of—and he realized that, courtesy of the anonymity of the Internet, he could participate.

He signed on to the quilting list just to see what would happen. For the first few months, he was a "lurker," a member who read but never posted. Then he began to post brief replies, signing them with only his initials. No one knew he was a man and no one cared.

Then one day, as he checked his email after breakfast, he discovered a thread someone had started that just about knocked him out of his chair: "I just found this list and I'm wondering if there are any other men quilters out there? Not that I mind talking quilts with you ladies, but I was just wondering if I am the only guy—again." The message was signed, "Jeff in Nebraska."

The first response was from a woman who assured Jeff that there were several men in the group. The next four messages were from men announcing that they were proud to call themselves quilters and longtime members of the list. Another woman followed with a list of websites featuring the work of well-known male art quilters. A man from Australia wrote that he and his wife made all their quilts together. A man from Vermont wrote that he and his partner were male quilters and quilt shop owners. A woman who contributed at least one post to every discussion on the list chimed in, "Howdy, Jeff!

We don't care if you're male, female, or a three-horned purple hermaphrodite from Saturn! You're welcome here as long as you quilt!"

Naturally, someone then wrote in claiming to be a three-horned purple hermaphrodite from Saturn who enjoyed quilting as well as embroidery, and the conversation deteriorated from there. But enough of the original thread remained to compel Russ to introduce himself.

"Hi," he wrote. "I guess it's about time I explained that RM stands for Russell McIntyre. I'm a man and a quilter. I started quilting when I wanted to complete one of my late wife's UFOs and I found out I enjoyed it. I've been quilting for almost three and a half years now and I've made nine quilts. (Four of my wife's, five of my own.) I don't know any men quilters in real life so it's great to finally meet some online."

For the first time he signed off using his full name.

He shut down the computer and went to work. By the time he got to his office and checked his email again, he had five personal messages welcoming him belatedly to the group. Three were from other men, two were from women, and each offered condolences on the death of his wife. They brought tears of renewed grief to his eyes, but he blinked them away, dashed off responses, and settled in to work.

Over the next few years, the five people who first responded to his introduction on the quilting list became close friends. They corresponded almost daily, swapped fabric and blocks through the mail, and met up at the Pacific International Quilt Festival each October. When one of the men started up a separate Internet group for men quilters, Russ signed on, but still retained close ties to the original group that had befriended him. To his surprise, he discovered that while some other men quilters had been ignored or patronized at quilt shops and guilds just as he had, others' experiences of the quilting world were quite different. Many admitted to enjoying preferential treatment in their guilds as the only man among a host of women, and others said they were treated no differently than any other quilter. Russ could only imagine what that would be like.

His style evolved in part because of inspiration from his online friends. He continued to layer, slash, and swap fabric, but he experimented with fabric dyed in gradients and curved cuts instead of straight lines. Through his Internet contacts, he was invited to submit a piece for an exhibit at the Rocky Mountain Quilt Museum featuring work by men quilters. Invitations to teach his unique style of quilting followed, as did requests to submit articles to quilting magazines.

On his fortieth birthday, he sat down with his financial advisor and discovered that he could retire early and live off his Athena Tech stock options quite comfortably for at least another forty years. Finally he would have enough time to work on that book proposal an editor had begged him to submit after observing his workshop at the American Quilter's Society show.

Soon after his book, *Russell McIntyre: A Man of the Cloth,* was published two years later, Russ had a solo exhibition in an eclectic art gallery in downtown Seattle. Carly and Alex came home a few days ahead of time so they could watch the exhibit being hung. Alex teased Russ at the gallery and at their celebratory dinner out afterward, calling Russ his stepdad, the great artiste, but the proud grin never left his face. On the morning before the exhibit debuted, Carly took Russ shopping and helped him pick out a new suit and tie. They both knew but did not acknowledge aloud that Elaine would have insisted upon it had she been there.

Even Charlie and Christine came up from Olympia, marking the first time they had seen his work in such an impressive setting. Christine was obviously thrilled for him, but Charlie seemed perplexed by all the fuss. "They're just quilts," Russ overheard him tell Christine. "They're nice, I guess, but they're not even big enough for a bed."

"Don't embarrass me," said Christine, exasperated. "This is art. They aren't supposed to fit a bed."

Russ was surprised to hear her snap at him, and he turned away so they would not know he had overheard. He stopped short at the sight of Francine, tilting her head as she examined a quilt. He made his way through the crowd to greet her. "Hello, Francine," he said, unable to conceal his surprise. "Thanks for coming." He had sent an announcement to the guild, but he had not expected anyone who remembered his fumbling attempts to join the guild to come.

"It's good to see you," she said. She had grown thin and her hair was grayer, but she had lost none of her imposing manner. "You've come a long way."

He shrugged. "I had a long way to go. You were right years ago when you said I had a lot to learn."

Francine eyed the quilts displayed on the gallery walls and indicated the many admirers with a nod. "Apparently you learned it. And to think I assumed you gave up quilting when you snubbed the guild."

"I snubbed the guild?" said Russ, incredulous. "You're kidding, right? They gave me the cold shoulder."

"You came to one meeting, and did you even bother to introduce your-self?" countered Francine. "Everyone adored Elaine. If they had known you were her husband, they would have made you feel at home."

"So that's what it takes for a man to be accepted in that guild."

"No one knew you were a serious quilter. Most of the members assumed you were there to meet women."

Russ almost choked. "That's a strange assumption, but it's not even the worst prejudice I've run into in the quilting world. You have no idea what it's like to go into a quilt shop or a quilt show and have everyone there assume I'm a blundering idiot who has to be watched carefully so he doesn't break something."

"Oh, I think I have a fairly good idea what that's like. I face it whenever I walk into an automobile repair shop."

His indignation promptly deflated. "Right. It's exactly like that."

She smiled. "Well. At any rate, I came to enjoy the show, but also to let you know that we would be thrilled if you would give the guild another try."

"Thanks. I'll think about it." He had no idea how he would find the time, but he would reconsider.

"I also feel compelled to mention that while I liked your book, I did not care for the title."

"It wasn't my choice," he said automatically, as he had done hundreds of times since the book came out. "The marketing department thought it was a clever play on words."

"Nonsense. It makes you sound like you've joined the clergy."

That was exactly what he had told his editor.

He and Francine parted ways. A few minutes later, he caught the arm of the gallery director and asked for a word. "Anything for you," she said, but her smile quickly faded when he asked her if she had considered his pro-posal to put on a retrospective of Elaine's work.

"Russ, darling," she said. "Your late wife's quilts are charming, and you are a dear to want to show her work. But I've gone over the schedule and I just don't think we can squeeze in another exhibit in the foreseeable future."

That was her euphemistic way of telling him she was not interested. "Thanks anyway."

"Oh, Russ." She gave his arm a squeeze. "Don't let this ruin your day. You've made three sales already and I overheard Bill Gates's representative asking you about a commissioned work for the corporate headquarters."

"For his house, actually," replied Russ, but his thoughts were of Elaine's quilts, hanging on the walls at home where hardly anyone ever saw them.

"Even better." She gave him a quick kiss on the cheek and moved off to greet an important patron who had just arrived. Beyond her he saw Charlie and Christine approaching. From their grins he knew they had seen the kiss.

"It doesn't mean anything," said Russ, rubbing his cheek with the back of his hand in case she had left traces of scarlet lipstick. "She does that to everyone."

"She got me twice already," admitted Charlie reluctantly. Russ knew he was dying to tease him, and Christine would have been thrilled to see him interested in someone new, even someone twenty years younger with multiple piercings and jet black hair dyed shocking pink at the tips. Almost seven years had passed since Elaine's death. He was forty-two, a year older than she had been when she died. Sometimes he could not believe that he had been her widower longer than her husband.

"Elaine would have loved this," said Christine. "She would have been so proud of you."

"Thanks," said Russ. He felt Elaine's presence so strongly then that he could not manage to say more.

❧

Two weeks after the exhibit closed, Russ heard about an opening at Elm Creek Quilt Camp from a posting on the QuiltArt Internet list. Grace Daniels, a friend who was a museum curator in San Francisco, attended camp there every summer and gave it glowing reviews. He checked out their website and mulled it over for a few days before deciding to apply. He had all of the materials they wanted, so it was easy to assemble the application packet and send it off. A few weeks later when they called to invite him to Pennsylvania for an interview, he was away from home, teaching a series of workshops in Oregon and Idaho. He returned the message from the road; he and an Elm Creek Quilter named Sarah McClure quickly settled upon a date for the interview.

Sarah McClure also gave him an assignment: to design a quilt block pattern suitable as an emblem of Elm Creek Quilts. He didn't have the slightest idea how to begin. While he had many original designs saved on his computer, it would take a huge stretch of the imagination to believe any represented a quilters' retreat.

He went to Elaine's quilt studio and studied her fabric stash, hoping inspiration would strike. Elms meant leaves, bark, twigs—he pulled shades of green and brown from the shelves. A creek meant flowing water, whorls, eddies, pebbles on a creek bed—he selected blue, white, and gray. He tossed the folded fabric bundles onto the floor at random, taking in the colors and thinking.

The obvious answer was to put together some kind of pictorial appliqué block with elm trees, a creek, and a big stone manor like the one in the photograph on the website, but he had never tried that kind of appliqué and doubted a project so important should be his first attempt. Besides, the Elm Creek Quilters were probably familiar with his signature style and wanted to see how he could adapt it to their request and to the significantly smaller canvas. This was a test of his imagination and versatility, and he would lose points if he took an easier way out.

Since everyone else would probably appliqué elm leaves and creeks, he ought to focus on another aspect of Elm Creek Quilt Camp. Above all else, his Internet acquaintance who attended each year praised the camaraderie that developed among all the quilters, strangers as well as old friends. He knew something about that. It had not been easy to break into the traditional female world of quilting, but once he had, he had forged strong friendships there. Without them, he might never have survived the aching loneliness of life after Elaine.

After a few aborted attempts, he struck upon a design that represented, to him at least, the power of quilting to forge community. He chose shades of green, blue, and brown, layered them with white, and cut narrow strips on the diagonals. He swapped out fabrics and sewed the squares and rectangles together in a design that resembled banners of those four colors flowing from the corners of the block to the center, where they met and appeared to weave together. To him, the pattern symbolized the power of quilting to draw together people of disparate ages, races, nationalities, socioeconomic backgrounds, and genders, united by their passion for their art.

It occurred to him that his design might be too abstract for the Elm Creek Quilters' purpose; he could not imagine them actually using it as a symbol for the quilt camp. He had already failed the assignment in that respect. Still, it was an honest response to what the ideal of Elm Creek Quilt Camp meant to him, so he decided it was good enough.

A few weeks later, he flew into Pittsburgh, rented a car, and drove through the rolling, forested Appalachians into the valleys of central Pennsylvania.

Though he had lectured in Lancaster twice, he had never been to this part of the state, and he now understood why Grace had warned him to allow plenty of time and to bring a map. Sarah's directions were fine until he left the interstate, but they fell apart not long after the Waterford city limits. He was supposed to look for a rural road through the woods marked by a small wooden sign for Elm Creek Manor. The turnoff had no name that Sarah knew of, so she had warned him to watch his odometer and go by the mileage rather than road signs.

When he arrived at the place where the gravel road was supposed to be, he found nothing but dense woods. He drove another mile, then turned around and backtracked until he started seeing signs for Waterford College again. Sighing in frustration, he turned the car around and drove back the other way, monitoring the odometer more carefully and driving more slowly as the mile approached. This time, a young woman stood on the grassy shoulder between the road and a narrow gravel driveway where the road to Elm Creek Manor ought to be, but he saw no sign.

"That can't be it," he muttered, driving on. Sarah had said that the road was not paved, but that strip of dirt and rocks couldn't possibly accommodate the kind of traffic a thriving business would generate. It must be the young woman's driveway, he thought, glancing at her in the rearview mirror. And if it was, he thought, turning the car around yet again, she ought to know the right way.

"Excuse me," he called to the young woman, slowing the car nearly to a stop. She was strikingly pretty, with big brown eyes and dark brown hair pulled back into a thick braid that hung to the middle of her back. She looked to be in her early thirties. "I'm looking for the road to Elm Creek Manor. Do you know where it is?"

The young woman bit her lip and stepped aside, revealing the missing sign. "It's that way," she said, gesturing to the narrow strip of gravel leading into the woods. "Sorry for blocking the sign."

"It's not your fault," said Russ, smiling. "This isn't the first time I've missed it. Thanks."

She nodded and gave an apologetic wave as he drove into the woods. The road wasn't as bad as it had looked from the highway, but it still was only barely passable. If an oncoming car suddenly appeared, one of them would have to pull off into the trees. He decided he would volunteer. His car was a rental.

The pretty girl standing by the sign . . . He wondered what she was doing there, waiting alone by the side of the road in the middle of nowhere. Was she a camper? He should have offered her a ride to the manor just in case. He felt a sudden surge of protectiveness for the girl. Something in her wary manner made him instinctively associate her with Carly, though they looked nothing alike. When he had first met Carly she had been so defensive, so purposefully aloof, so bruised by her father's abandonment. She had needed years to accept that Russ would not also leave her. Now she was a mother herself, and her little son called him Pop-pop, for grandpa.

He wished Elaine could have been there to hold her first grandchild within an hour of his birth, as Russ had.

The narrow road wound through the trees and opened into a clearing, an orchard to the west, a red barn built into the side of a hill on the right. Russ followed the road up the low slope and around the barn until it ended in a driveway at the rear of the manor. He parked the car, took his briefcase in hand, and climbed the back stairs to the rear door. It swung open before he could knock. A woman exiting the manor glanced at his raised hand and smiled. "Just go on in," she said. "Everyone does. You don't need to knock."

Russ took her advice and found himself in an empty hallway that dead-ended into another passage a few yards ahead. A frenzied buzz drew his attention to a doorway on his left, which turned out to be the entrance to the kitchen. A timer complained on the countertop, and the aroma of baked chicken filled the room. Next to a 1940s era stove, he saw a doorway leading to a brightly lit room.

"Hello?" he called. "Uh . . . your timer went off." When no one responded, he crossed the kitchen and peered inside a small, sunny sitting room. No one was within.

He turned off the buzzer and hesitated, wondering if he should take out whatever was inside the oven or at least turn down the heat. He might end up ruining the meal rather than salvaging it, though, so he left it alone and went to look for the missing cook.

He strode down the hallway and took a right at the intersection. He had almost reached an impressive front foyer when a door opened in front of him. A tall, silver-haired woman with just the slightest stoop to her shoulders stepped into the hallway, chatting with a much younger woman with glasses and long brown hair.

"Excuse me," said Russ.

The two women stopped so suddenly that someone else trying to leave the room crashed into them from behind. "Ouch," complained the woman Russ could not see.

"May I help you?" inquired the older woman.

Russ jerked a thumb over his shoulder. "I just passed by the kitchen. A timer was going off."

"My chicken," exclaimed the younger woman. She sprinted past Russ toward the kitchen.

The older woman sighed and turned to address someone behind her. "We can't manage like this much longer."

"We're pitiful," said a shorter, stockier woman as she emerged from the room. Her long red hair was streaked with gray. "It's only been a week and we're falling apart. Oh. Hello," she said, spotting Russ. "You must be Russ."

"How did you know?" he asked. He was sure he had never met her before.

"We don't get your kind around here much. And I recognize you from the photos in your book." She extended her hand. "I'm Gwen Sullivan, Elm Creek Quilter."

He shook her hand. "Russ McIntyre."

"Mr. McIntyre," said the older woman. "What a pleasure it is to meet you. Welcome to Elm Creek Manor. I'm Sylvia Compson."

"Thank you. Please, call me Russ."

The woman smiled graciously. "Russ it is, then. Allow me to introduce my colleagues." She introduced him to four other women as one by one they entered the hallway. Each shook his hand and greeted him in a friendly way, except for a pretty blonde who scowled and squeezed his hand too hard as if she had something to prove.

Great, he thought as he shook her hand and forced a cordial smile. Another woman quilter who resented men for invading her domain.

Sylvia Compson explained that they were taking a break after interviewing other applicants and that she would have just enough time to show him around the estate while the other Elm Creek Quilters returned to their classrooms. "Perhaps we should start there," she suggested, and led him across the three-story tall, marble-floored foyer into a large ballroom that had been subdivided into classrooms by movable partitions. When Grace had described the arrangement in her last email, he had had some concerns about noise levels and space. As he looked around, he observed students setting up workstations in some of the classrooms, talking and laughing together, clearly enjoying themselves. They didn't seem bothered by the lack of isolated classrooms; if anything, the arrangement seemed to foster a more collegial atmosphere.

Part of the ballroom had not been partitioned off. Beyond the classrooms, Sylvia showed Russ an open gathering space framed by tall windows and a raised dais along the far wall. A group of women had gathered there, and they sat listening attentively to a slight, gray-haired woman in a gray skirt and blue cardigan. One of the Elm Creek Quilters, Russ assumed, watching as the older woman gestured to a quilt the other women held outspread and talked about its design. He waited for Sylvia to introduce them, but when she just watched the woman, quietly thoughtful, he examined the quilt, a traditional block repeated in a traditional horizontal setting. If this was the kind of quilt Elm Creek Quilts expected from its teachers, he was out of luck.

The older woman glanced over her shoulder at them once, but did not break off her conversation or otherwise acknowledge Sylvia except for a slightly guilty look she threw her before turning back to the campers. Russ thought that a bit odd, but Sylvia did not seem to mind. Instead she resumed the tour, taking him next to the dining room, where more than a dozen tables had already been set for dinner. "Sarah did invite you to stay for supper, didn't she?" she asked.

"She did, but I have to leave right after my interview to catch a flight home."

"You mean you won't even spend the night?"

Russ shrugged. "I wish I could, but I have a few speaking engagements in California beginning tomorrow."

"My goodness, you're popular. Not even a day off to rest between trips."

"I can rest on the plane. But that's part of the appeal of working here. I could let the students come to me for a change."

Sylvia nodded thoughtfully and continued the tour of the first floor, then led him up a carved oak staircase to show him an example of their guest rooms and the business office, a large library spanning the entire width of the south wing. Light spilled in through tall diamond-paned windows on the east, west, and south walls. Between the windows stood tall bookcases, shelves heavy with leather-bound volumes. A stone fireplace nearly as tall as Russ's shoulder dominated the south wall. Two armchairs and footstools sat before it, while more chairs and sofas were arranged in a square in the center of the room. Nearby, parallel to the western wall, was a broad oak desk cluttered with paperwork and computer peripherals, a tall leather chair pulled up to it.

The library, Sylvia told him, was where the Elm Creek Quilters conducted camp business, but it was primarily Sarah McClure's domain. She handled all their finances, marketing, and operations, allowing her co-director, Summer Sullivan, to concentrate on curriculum, faculty, and anything associated with the Internet. "But Summer is leaving us for graduate school soon," said Sylvia with a sigh. "We will miss her dearly."

Russ nodded and made a mental note to mention his considerable Internet experience during the interview.

Next Sylvia showed him the estate grounds, which included the barn he had passed as he drove to the house, most of the woods, the orchard, and several gardens. He was amazed to learn that the estate was tended by only one caretaker and a few seasonal gardeners. *At last, other men,* he thought with relief as Sylvia introduced him to Matt McClure and his staff. It was probably too much to hope that one or two of them quilted.

Nearly a half hour passed before they returned inside for his formal interview. Sylvia escorted him to the room where they had first met, a fancy sitting room with too many doilies, throw pillows, tassels, and breakable knickknacks for him to feel entirely comfortable. When Sylvia said that the Elm Creek Quilters conducted camp business in the library, he had assumed his interview would take place there.

The other Elm Creek Quilters soon arrived and took seats across from him. The break between interviews had clearly not improved the mood of the blonde, Diane, who frowned as she took her place in an armchair. She opened up a folder, took out several pages of notes, and fixed him with a look of challenge.

He resigned himself to failure as far as winning her over was concerned. She had already made up her mind, and nothing he said would impress her. He would concentrate on the others.

Sarah McClure began the questioning by asking him how he became a quilter. He was glad to tell them how Elaine had inspired him, and not until he finished his response several minutes later did it occur to him that maybe he had gone on too long. "Sorry," he said with a self-deprecating smile. "I tend to ramble when talking about my late wife."

They smiled sympathetically—except for Diane. "Our students generally don't like instructors who ramble," she said, checking off an item in her notes with a flick of her pencil.

"Russell, you're clearly an experienced teacher and you're apparently willing to go anywhere in the country to lead workshops," said Sylvia, without a glance at Diane. "Staying in one place from spring through autumn would be quite a change for you. Won't you miss the travel?"

He recognized a softball question when one was lofted his way; Sylvia had already gleaned an answer from their conversation during the tour. "Quite the opposite," he said. "Working for Elm Creek Quilts would allow me to teach more students more efficiently. Instead of traveling, I'll be able to develop new courses and make my own quilts. In the winter, when camp is out of session, I can resume my usual schedule of quilt guilds and conferences."

"So you aren't willing to make a year-round commitment to Elm Creek Quilts," said Diane.

"We don't need him for the full-year," said Summer, an edge to her voice. "That's why the ad said seasonal work available."

"If you need me year-round, I could do that," said Russ. "I didn't think it was an option."

"It isn't, yet," interjected Sarah as Diane prepared to speak. "Someday we may go to a full-year schedule, but not soon."

"We could do it soon if we weren't losing two founding members of our teaching staff," Diane shot back.

"Which brings us to the purpose of Mr. McIntyre's visit," said Sylvia. "Russ, would you please show us the Elm Creek Quilts block we asked you to design?"

He took it from his briefcase and explained his creative process as they passed it around the circle. "I know it's kind of abstract," he said.

"Kind of?" murmured Diane, her pretty features screwed up in bafflement as she examined his block, holding it right side up, upside down, at an angle. She finally gave up, shook her head, and passed the block on to Summer.

"I like it," said Summer. "It's different. And I, for one, can grasp the symbolism."

"Symbolism? Is that what it is?" said Diane. "I'm not so sure. I doubt anyone would look at this block and think 'Elm Creek Quilts.'"

Russ said nothing. If he were to be honest, he would have to agree.

"You would certainly bring a very different perspective to our faculty," remarked Sylvia, studying his résumé.

"I believe so," said Russ. "I think part of the reason my quilts have been received so well is that as a man, an outsider to the traditional quilting world,

I don't feel as constrained by the accepted norms of what is and what isn't permitted in a quilt."

Sylvia allowed a brief flicker of a smile. "I was referring to your status as an acclaimed contemporary art quilter, but you're quite correct to say that your perspective as a man who quilts is also rare. And potentially valuable."

"Wait. Let's go back to something he just said," Diane broke in. "Do you mean to say that women quilters are constrained by accepted norms? We all just make the same quilts every other woman makes, like a mindless herd of cows?"

"That's not what he meant at all," protested Gwen. "Cows don't quilt."

"And they're not mindless," said Summer, with a pointed look for Sarah. "Which is why we should not eat them."

Bewildered, Russ tried to sort out the sudden shift in conversation until Diane caught his attention with a sigh of disappointment, as if she had hoped for so much more from him. "That's what I find so frustrating about men quilters. You come in at the last minute, jump on the quilting bandwagon, and assume that you can do it better than generations of traditional women quilters who have come before you simply because you have a penis."

"Diane," exclaimed Sylvia.

"I can't believe she said that," said Gwen in an aside to Summer. "She must be off her medication."

"I don't take medication," snapped Diane.

"Maybe you should start."

Sylvia shook her head. "Diane, I have no idea what has gotten into you today, but if you cannot control yourself, you will be banned from the remaining interviews."

Interesting, Russ thought. Apparently Diane hated everyone—or at least every applicant for the job she had seen that day.

With a stern look of warning for Diane, Sarah said, "Obviously, Russ, you don't have to respond to Diane's wholly inappropriate remark."

He thought for a moment. "I'll respond to a variation of it. First off, I don't think men are intrinsically better quilters than women, and I don't think I personally am better than traditional quilters simply because I'm a man. I said my perspective was different. Not better, not worse, just . . . different. Just like men and women are different."

"But equal," said Gwen.

"Of course, equal. Look, I'm not trying to make a big political statement here, but artists are shaped by their life experiences, and men and women have very different experiences in the world. I can be as empathetic as humanly possible, but there are some things about being a woman that I will never understand. Being a husband and father taught me that. And there are some things about being a man that women will never understand."

"What's to understand?" muttered Diane. "Beer. Football. Nascar. Duct tape. Fart jokes."

"Honestly, Diane," said Sylvia, exasperated. "Russ, I'm truly sorry."

But Russ had heard enough. "If that's the Elm Creek Quilts perception of male quilters, that could explain why none of the campers I've seen here today are men. That's an untapped and potentially lucrative market for you, but why should men come where they aren't welcome? From what I've seen today, men quilters could benefit a lot from a place like Elm Creek Quilt Camp, but you could learn a lot from them, too." He picked up his briefcase and stood. "But apparently only women can break into your circle of quilters. Thanks for inviting me. I know the way out."

"Nice going," said Gwen to Diane as he strode to the door.

Nice going, Russ told himself, disgusted, as he left the parlor and headed for the back door. *Brilliant strategy. Righteous indignation always wins over potential employers.*

Sarah followed him into the hallway. "Russ, please don't go. Diane—"

"It's not just her." Russ stopped and allowed Sarah to catch up. "But for what it's worth, I'm sorry I stormed out of there."

"You can come back. We can start over."

Russ shook his head. He knew nothing else he did or said would erase their negative impression of his outburst. "I don't think it will work out. If the faculty doesn't support a male colleague, why should your campers?"

"We would support you. You have an excellent reputation and we'd be fortunate to have you join our staff. I know men and women alike would sign up for camp just to meet you."

"Well . . ." Russ took one last long look around the manor. During Sylvia's tour, he had imagined himself living there, teaching there, creating, finding peace in surroundings that did not underscore Elaine's absence every time he passed from one room to the next. But thanks to Diane, he had blown his chance.

"Next time you're hiring," he said, "give me a call. Maybe the climate will be different."

Sarah nodded.

He made his way down the hall toward the back door. His hand was on the doorknob when he heard quick footsteps behind him. "Wait," a woman called. "Just a moment!"

Russ turned around to find a white-haired woman in pink-tinted glasses pursuing him, breathless. "Is something wrong?"

"I'm just . . ." She placed a hand on her hip and held up a finger as she caught her breath. Russ waited. "I'm having a little trouble with this quilt block."

"Uh huh." Baffled, he gestured down the hall toward the frilly parlor. "Back that way, there's a roomful of Elm Creek Quilters who would be glad to help you."

"Oh, I'm sure they're too busy." The elderly woman came closer and thrust a quilt block at him, panting. "You, on the other hand, seem to be free."

Studying her with increasing concern, he automatically took the block. "Maybe you should sit down."

"No, no, I'll be fine. But the quilt block. What do you think?"

He turned it over. It was a traditional, hand-appliquéd block, probably a Rose of Sharon variation. It looked fine to him. "Sorry. I don't do hand appliqué."

"But you're an experienced quilter. Surely you can recommend something."

"To be perfectly honest, I can't even spot the problem."

He held out the block, but she wouldn't take it back. "Oh, come now," she said. "You're just flattering me."

"No, really. It looks good to me." He glanced at his watch. "I'm on my way out. I have to catch a plane. Are you sure you don't want me to get you a chair, a glass of water, something?"

"No, thank you." Disappointed, she took her quilt block. "Thanks just the same."

Shaking his head in amazement, Russ left quickly before anyone else could stop him. He could not remember a stranger day spent in the company of quilters, and contrary to all stereotypes, they were not generally a sedate bunch.

❧❧

He drove back to the Pittsburgh airport, dropped off the rental car, and added himself to the standby list for an earlier flight to Seattle. He spent an hour wandering idly through the stores on the concourse mall, passing most of that time testing gadgets at Sharper Image and wishing he had handled Diane's confrontational questioning better. When the announcement came that the earlier flight to Seattle was boarding, he went to the gate and received a seat assignment. "You're in luck," the ticket agent said as she issued him a new boarding pass. "It's wide open."

He took his seat on the aisle in the middle of coach, found a paperback in his carry-on, and settled in for the cross-country flight. Weary from the long, round-trip drive earlier that day, he dozed off and woke an hour later to find the plane at cruising altitude. He stretched, picked up his fallen book from the floor, and wished he had brought something more engrossing to read or that domestic flights still showed movies. Then, a few rows ahead, he glimpsed a woman working on a quilt block.

He watched as the fabric patches came together beneath her fingers. She had long, elegant hands and held the needle as if she were accustomed to it. The contrast between the contemporary batik fabric and the traditional appliqué pattern intrigued him. At least he assumed it was a traditional pattern, since she was sewing by hand; for all he knew, it was her own original design, but it did look familiar.

After a while, curious and with plenty of time on his hands, he put his book away and moved to the empty seat across the aisle from the woman. "Hi," he greeted her. "What are you working on?"

She seemed surprised by the question. "Oh. Nothing. It's just a block for a quilt."

"I can't place that pattern. Is it traditional?"

Her eyebrows rose. "Do you quilt?"

"Now and then," he said. "But I don't know much about appliqué. I do everything by machine."

She considered that, then gave a little shrug. She had long waves of light brown hair held back by a tortoiseshell barrette, and hazel eyes set into a soft oval face that suddenly reminded him of a sepia-toned photograph. "You could easily adapt this pattern to machine appliqué, but I prefer handwork. The process is more soothing, more contemplative."

"More portable," added Russ, indicating the cramped space of their coach-class seats.

"That, too." She smiled, and although he was certain she couldn't be more than four or five years younger than he, she suddenly seemed half her age, coltish, a girl. Maybe it was the sprinkling of freckles across her nose and cheeks, or the shy way she lowered her eyes back to her sewing after she spoke. Then she looked up at him again, her gaze open and friendly. "What kind of quilts do you like to make?"

If he had not left his carry-on back at his original seat, he would have shown her a copy of his book, impressed her, feigned nonchalance. If he ran back for it now, he would just look too eager to please. "They're more contemporary," he said instead. "I use a lot of color and contrast effects, rotary cutting, intersecting lines and so on. Mostly wall hangings."

She considered. "That sounds like the work of an art quilter I met at a conference once. He's very well known." She bit her lower lip, brow furrowed. "I have his book at home. What was his name again?"

Reluctantly, Russ said, "Michael James?" Everyone had heard of Michael James. Sometimes Russ thought he was the only male quilter anyone knew by name.

"No, but he's good, too. It's Ross—no, Russ. Russell McIntyre."

"We've met before?"

"You're Russ?"

He nodded.

"Really?" She studied him. "Your beard was longer then."

He rubbed his jaw absently. "I've been keeping it shorter for the past year or two. When did we meet?"

"We sat at the head table at the awards banquet at the AQS show in Paducah. It was years ago, and there was this huge flower arrangement and a podium between us. I'm so sorry I didn't recognize you."

"That's okay. I didn't recognize you." He wrestled in vain with his memory. "You are . . . ?"

"Maggie Flynn." She held out her hand for him to shake. It was warm and smooth, except for a few quilting calluses on finger and thumb. "I did the Harriet Findley Birch book. The My Journey with Harriet quilts?"

She looked at him hopefully, and he was fervently grateful when his faulty memory suddenly kicked out the details. "Of course. Maggie Flynn." Now he realized why her appliqué pattern had looked familiar. Elaine had taken a My Journey with Harriet class at a weekend retreat with her quilt guild. Russ still had the twenty or so little blocks in reproduction fabrics she had made from Maggie's patterns. "You have a legion of followers. You're a genuine celebrity."

"Only in the quilting world," she said, but he could tell she was pleased.

"Are you teaching for a guild in Seattle?"

"No, I'm on my way home. I'll be in Seattle only long enough to catch a connecting flight to Sacramento. How about you?"

"Seattle's home for me. I'm just returning from a job interview." Instinctively, he shook his head to clear it of the memory.

Her eyes widened. "Job interview? Not at Elm Creek Quilt Camp?"

He paused. "You, too?"

She nodded.

"Oh."

"This is awkward."

"It shouldn't be," Russ quickly assured her. "I don't stand a chance. Believe me, I'm no longer in contention for the job."

"Your interview must have gone better than mine. There was this one woman—"

"Diane?"

"Yes! The blonde. What was her problem?"

"I have no idea. I thought she just hated men quilters."

"Don't worry; it's not that. She doesn't like women quilters, either." Maggie frowned and laid her quilt block on her tray table. "Or maybe just me."

Russ couldn't imagine how anyone could dislike Maggie. "Maybe it was a set up. Maybe she was there to be the devil's advocate." Which meant, of course, that he had fallen for it and failed the test entirely. "Are you a full-time instructor?"

"No, only part-time. I'm a geriatric care manager at Ocean View Hills—it's a senior citizens' home in Sacramento."

"It must be a very tall building to have an ocean view from Sacramento."

She smiled. "I've always thought the name was a bit silly. It won't matter for much longer, though. It's closing."

"That's too bad." Russ found himself hoping Maggie had made a better impression on the Elm Creek Quilters than she thought. "You'll probably get the Elm Creek job. I would think they'd be glad to have you on their staff. Your style is so versatile, and you could lecture on quilt history as well as teach quilting."

She gave him a rueful half-smile. "That's what I tried to tell them, but I think Diane was more persuasive."

"Trust me. After meeting me, Diane probably decided you could be her new best friend."

"I would put in a good word for you, but that would probably do you more harm than good."

Russ laughed.

Maggie stared at him, wide-eyed. "You have a nice laugh," she said softly, and quickly turned her gaze to her sewing, as if embarrassed by what she had said.

Russ was suddenly very glad that he had left Elm Creek Manor early.

He remained in his new seat for the rest of the flight. He and Maggie rejected the painful subject of their interviews and turned to their quilts, favorite quilt shops, industry gossip, quilting friends they had in common, their families. As the plane touched down they exchanged business cards and agreed to have lunch the next time they were scheduled at the same quilt show.

Russ intended to walk Maggie to her gate, but he lost her in the disembarking crowd after returning to his original seat for his carry-on. He was disappointed, but at least he had her card. He would email her from home.

He was almost to the security checkpoint when he turned around.

He found her flight on the monitor and raced to the departing gate. "Maggie," he called, finding her in the line to the jetway.

She looked his way, and her face lit up with surprise and, he hoped, pleasure. "Russ?"

"I'm coming through California this week on a teaching tour," he said. "Can we get together? Coffee, or dinner, or something?"

"I'd like that," she said. "Call me. Or email me. One or the other."

"I will."

She nodded and turned away to hand her boarding pass to the gate attendant. She glanced over her shoulder at him and waved, hesitating a moment before disappearing down the jetway.

"I'll see you next week," Russ called, but she was already gone.

Chapter Five
Gretchen

Gretchen rose carefully so she would not jostle her husband, still asleep on his side of the bed, supported with pillows to relieve pressure on his lower back. As she dressed, she paused to study his face, so dear to her even after forty-two years of marriage. Even in sleep Joe wore a slight grimace of pain. He was so handsome as a young man that all her friends had envied her. On their wedding day, she had considered herself the luckiest woman alive. She still considered herself blessed to have shared so many years with the man she loved, but she no longer believed in luck, good or bad. People made choices and lived with the consequences. Through the years she had discovered that some people had certain advantages that allowed them to escape the worst consequences of their bad decisions, but she wouldn't call that luck. If she did, she would have to wonder why good luck and bad had not been distributed more equitably, and dwelling upon that was the quickest route to bitterness.

By the time she started cooking breakfast, she heard Joe climbing out of bed—pushing himself to a seated position, swinging his legs to the side, grasping the back of the bedside chair, hauling himself to his feet. Morning was the worst time of the day for her husband, muscles stiff, medication yet to be taken. He hated for her to see him gritting his teeth and struggling to rise, so if he did wake first, he would feign sleep until she slipped downstairs. He didn't know she knew.

She set his eggs and sausage on the table as he entered the kitchen. "Morning, sweetheart," he said, kissing her. His cheeks were shaved smooth, his hair carefully combed. He looked as prepared for a day at work as any other husband on the street, even though his commute took him only as far as the garage.

"Morning to you, too." She poured his coffee and took her own seat to his left. It was a small table, just big enough for two plates, two cups, and a serving dish. Their dining room table sat four comfortably, six if they didn't mind getting a little cozy. When it was just the two of them, though, it was too much trouble to clear off her fabric and sewing machine three times a day.

"I forgot to tell you," said Joe, buttering a slice of toast. "Clyde came around yesterday to see if we wanted to meet him and Jan at the fish fry at the VFW tonight."

"I can't," said Gretchen. "Heidi's having a party. She wants me to come by and help out beforehand."

Joe frowned. "Will you still be on the clock or is this volunteer work?"

"Oh, Joe, don't start."

"All I'm saying is that she can afford to hire help. She doesn't need to draft you into service unless she's going to pay for it."

"I work for Heidi and you know it." Gretchen tried to sound reasonable, but it was exasperating that they still argued over this. "My family has always worked for hers. I don't think she could manage without me."

"Darn right she couldn't, which is why she should pay you what you're worth." He set down his coffee cup with a bang, a mulish look in his eye. "If I could work, you could quit your job and tell Heidi to stick it where—"

"I like my job," Gretchen reminded him. "I don't want to quit working. The quilt shop is like a second home to me."

"At least you could drop all the extra fetching and carrying and cleaning."

Gretchen bristled with annoyance—in part because she knew he was right. She liked Heidi, but it was often inconvenient to pick up Heidi's dry cleaning on her way in to work, or collect her mail and newspapers while her family was away on a Caribbean cruise, or to help the housekeeper clean Heidi's grand home in Sewickley for a party to which Gretchen would never be invited as a guest. "It's all part of the job," she said. "I prefer to think of it as helping out a friend."

Joe grunted, and Gretchen knew what he was thinking: In Heidi's eyes, Gretchen was closer to a servant than a friend.

🦋

Perhaps Heidi did not consider Gretchen a friend, but through the years, Gretchen had learned that a shared history was as important as affinity. Perhaps more so. As people who had known her since childhood grew scarcer, they became more precious, even if they were not the same people who made her laugh or whose company she most enjoyed. And if nothing else, Gretchen and Heidi shared a history, one that had begun before they were born.

When Gretchen's grandmother emigrated from Croatia, she lived with a cousin's family and found a job at a butcher's in the strip district in Pittsburgh. Because she was pretty, clean, and good with sums, she was occasionally told to ride on the wagon to make deliveries to the fine houses in Sewickley on the other side of the river. On one occasion she met Heidi's great-grandmother, who sized her up as a quiet, industrious sort of girl and hired her to replace her second housemaid, whom she had recently fired for theft. Gretchen's grandmother was almost let go herself when the lady of the house discovered she spoke only rudimentary English, but she relented at the recommendation of the housekeeper, who appreciated a hardworking girl who would not talk back. Gretchen's grandmother was relieved to stay; the work was hard, but no more so than at the butcher's, and in the Albrechts' house, she had her own bed in a small, third-floor room she shared with the other housemaid.

Years later she married, but continued to live with and work for the Albrechts until well into her first pregnancy. When her own children were old enough, she returned to work as a housekeeper for her original employer's daughter, now married with a baby of her own. Gretchen's mother left school after the eighth grade to work alongside her mother, eventually taking over her position when her mother grew too old for the arduous labor. She married a steelworker and moved into a small house on a hill in Ambridge, where Gretchen was born a year later.

Gretchen was six when Heidi was born, and she remembered her mother leaving before dawn to catch the bus to Sewickley, where she bathed Heidi, fed her breakfast, and, in later years, escorted her to school. While Heidi was at school, Gretchen's mother tended the Albrecht home, hurrying to finish the work before it was time to walk Heidi home and prepare the family's supper. She returned home to her own family after dark, exhausted, but still eager to hear about her daughter's day. As soon as Gretchen was old enough, she learned to start supper early so her mother could put up her feet for a little while before Gretchen's father returned home from the steel mill.

Gretchen listened with amazement to the stories her mother told of little Heidi: the extravagant birthday parties, the closets full of dresses, the ridiculously inappropriate gifts Mr. and Mrs. Albrecht showered upon her. "A string of pearls for a four-year-old," she marveled one Christmas, "when all the poor little dear wants is their attention."

Gretchen did not think Heidi was a poor little dear. Heidi had everything— pretty clothes, a big house, and Gretchen's mother at her beck and call. If that wasn't enough for her, she was just being selfish.

Perhaps her mother sensed Gretchen's feelings, because when school ended for the summer the year she turned twelve, her mother received permission to bring Gretchen along with her to the Albrecht home. Mrs. Albrecht may have assumed Gretchen was there to begin learning the duties she would one day take over, but Gretchen knew her mother wanted to teach her only that Heidi's life was not one to covet. It was true that the Albrechts had come down in the world somewhat since Gretchen's grandmother's day, but they still lived in a large, luxurious house in one of Sewickley's most prestigious neighborhoods. Gretchen's mother as well as a cook, gardener, and driver waited upon them.

Six years Heidi's elder, Gretchen was more of a caregiver than a playmate to the younger girl, and she learned quickly to give in to Heidi's demands rather than try to teach her to share or to play nicely. The first time she told Heidi not to boss her around, Heidi burst into tears and fled to her mother, who was entertaining guests and was greatly annoyed by the interruption. It was Gretchen's mother she scolded, however, rendering Gretchen heartsick with shame. She did not make that mistake again, and eventually she convinced herself that Heidi could be a happy, charming girl if given her own way.

Since Gretchen was six years ahead of Heidi in school and an able student, she naturally slipped into the role of Heidi's tutor. It was then that Heidi's mother began to take more notice of her, complimenting a flattering change in hair style or suggesting she "smarten herself up a bit." "You're becoming a young lady," she said once. "Why don't you take some of your wages and buy yourself a pretty dress?" Relieved to have Heidi taken off her hands, she hurried off without waiting for a reply. Gretchen would have explained, if Mrs. Albrecht had let her, that the clothes her mother sewed for her suited her just fine, and she preferred to save her money for college. After discovering how much her tutoring had helped Heidi, she had contemplated becoming a teacher.

Gretchen made the mistake of confiding her plans to Heidi, who immediately decided that she wanted to be a teacher, too. Her declaration mystified Mrs. Albrecht, who could not fathom how such an idea would have entered her daughter's head. To her credit, Heidi did not reveal the source of her inspiration, not to spare Gretchen a reprimand but for the thrill of keeping a secret from her parents. Gretchen should have known better than to mention her private wish in Heidi's presence. Whenever she invented a game or made a joke, Heidi claimed it as her own, embellishing it for her parents, who praised her for her cleverness. If Gretchen happened to admire a dress in a storefront window, within days she saw Heidi wearing a younger girl's version of it to school. Gretchen's mother told her she ought to be flattered that Heidi admired her so, but Gretchen quietly resented Heidi's mimicry. Heidi honestly seemed to believe that the ideas and tastes she picked up from Gretchen originated in her own mind, or worse, that Gretchen's ideas naturally belonged to Heidi, just as Gretchen's family belonged to the Albrechts.

At eighteen, Gretchen graduated from high school and won a partial scholarship to college, where she intended to major in elementary education. This news astounded Mrs. Albrecht, who sat her mother down for a serious chat about Gretchen's future. In a conversation Gretchen overheard from another room, she explained how Gretchen's parents would be far wiser to direct her down a more practical path than to indulge an imprudent dream. "You want to be kind, I understand that," said Mrs. Albrecht sympathetically. "But you must think of how much more hurtful it will be later, when she discovers that one cannot rise above one's station in life."

Gretchen's mother thanked Mrs. Albrecht for the advice, and on the bus home that evening, she tentatively suggested that Gretchen reconsider. Gretchen adamantly refused, but over the next few days, her mother's worried expressions and tearful arguments wore her down. She agreed to compromise: She would major in elementary education and home economics. Her mother's thankful relief at this promise filled her with a cold, angry helplessness that worsened when Mrs. Albrecht congratulated her for making such a sensible decision.

Two years into her program, she still would not admit aloud that her home economics courses were among her favorites. She learned to sew and design garments even better than her mother, and she especially enjoyed the creative outlet her quilting class provided. The instructor, a graduate of the college's art education program named Sylvia Compson, spiced her lectures about patterns and stitches with stories of the etymology of quilt block names, the role of the quilting bee in the lives of early American women, and commemorative quilts that promoted justice and social change. Gretchen took to quilting as if she had learned at her grandmother's knee, as most of the other students in the class had done. The small class size fostered the creation of deep friendships, strengthened by the teasing they endured from their fellow coeds who thought both home economics and quilting trivial subjects, pursuits in which no woman who wanted to be taken seriously would engage.

Perhaps that was why Gretchen rarely spoke of her inspirational teacher or home economics program to anyone but Joe, the handsome young man she had met at church and the one person with whom she felt she could be completely honest and free with her opinions. He was a wonderful dancer, a machinist at one of the steel mills, polite and respectful to her parents. He wanted to marry her right away but agreed to wait until she had taught for a few years, although sometimes after a date, when they had to tear themselves away from each other, breathless and dizzy from fervent kisses in the shadows of the pine trees obscuring her parents' view from the house, Gretchen considered abandoning her education and marrying him soon, tomorrow, that very night, because the wait seemed unbearable when he held her in his arms.

Even in those days, Joe did not like the Albrechts. He called Heidi's parents rich snobs who took advantage of Gretchen's mother, and his mouth turned in a skeptical frown whenever Gretchen had to cancel a weekend date to help Heidi with one crisis or another. He said nothing when Heidi went off to an exclusive New England college with plans to earn a teaching degree. His raised eyebrows and knowing look conveyed his meaning with perfect clarity, as it had when Mrs. Albrecht remarked that she and her husband could not be prouder of their daughter, for didn't it reveal Heidi's tremendous strength of character that she was so passionate about educating the less fortunate?

Joe had plenty to say, however, a few years after he and Gretchen married. As Heidi's own wedding approached, she asked Gretchen to make her a nearly identical gown, but of silk instead of cotton brocade and with lovely seed pearl accents. When Gretchen stayed up past midnight for the third night in a row in order to finish the gown in time, he folded his newspaper, flung it on the table, and said, "You be sure to keep track of your hours and charge her a living wage. No more favors for Princess Heidi." Then he stormed upstairs to bed.

Joe was not a temperamental man. Gretchen knew he wished the beautiful silk gown was for her, and that he could have afforded to buy it for her.

He hated that she needed to pick up occasional work from the Albrechts to supplement his wages from the plant and the small salary she received for teaching at a Catholic primary school. He did not want her to have to work, period, but he knew she enjoyed teaching, even on days when her more outspoken girls rolled their eyes when she assigned a sewing project and declared that they ought to be allowed to take metal shop with the boys instead. He took as much overtime as he could, but every time they saved up a promising sum, the car broke down or the furnace went out or the roof needed to be repaired. But they were frugal and found their happiness within each other, and as they slowly built up a nest egg, they were hopeful that more prosperous times would come their way.

Then came the dark morning when the principal came to Gretchen's classroom and in a hushed voice informed her that the plant foreman had called. Joe had been taken to Allegheny General Hospital after a support beam fell and pinned him to the floor. His back was broken and he was not expected to live.

When he survived that first night and regained consciousness the next morning, Gretchen seized that faint glimmer of hope and would not allow the doctors' grim predictions to dispel it. Stubborn to a fault and determined to prove his doctors wrong, Joe lived when they said he would die and fought to learn to walk again after they concluded he never would. They urged Gretchen to convince him to accept their diagnosis, to encourage him to let go of false hope, but Gretchen refused. Let the rest of the world condemn him to a wheelchair; someone had to believe in him. Joe needed her to believe in him.

Bedridden for months and in almost constant pain, Joe struggled to regain use of his legs—and to accept that for the time being, he must allow his wife to do things for him that a grown man ought to do for himself. Gretchen quit her job to care for him. Their modest savings quickly disappeared, but Gretchen made ends meet on a small monthly stipend from Joe's union.

When that proved insufficient, she paid a call on Heidi and asked for work. Heidi grandly offered her a job cleaning her house on Saturday mornings, when Gretchen could arrange for a neighbor to check in on Joe.

She knew from his silence that he hated to see her going hat in hand to the Albrecht family, but he did not lash out at her as some husbands might have done. He redoubled his efforts to recuperate, and within months he could sit up in bed unassisted. Soon he could move from the bed to the chair on his own, and within a year, he could stand. From the kitchen below she would hear him attempting slow, shuffling steps across the bedroom floor, but she resisted the temptation to dash upstairs to watch, knowing his pride would suffer. For Joe, it was bad enough that she had to work to support them, a fact of their married life they both accepted but did not discuss. If he did not want her to watch him struggle to walk, she would leave him alone until he was ready.

There were no more Saturday night dances or Sunday matinees with friends. Instead, they entertained themselves in the evenings by listening to the radio or reading aloud to each other. Most often, Joe would read aloud while Gretchen quilted. His voice, as strong and deep as before the accident, comforted her, and the piecework drew her attention from the shabby furniture, her made-over dresses, the diminishment of their expectations, the loneliness and isolation of their lives. Gretchen's scrap quilts brought warmth and beauty into their home, allowing them to turn the thermostat a little lower or to conceal a sagging mattress and threadbare sofa cushions. Gretchen knew Joe appreciated the softness and bright colors, since he rarely left the house except to go to church.

Gretchen was glad that Joe admired her quilts, for it seemed that no one else did. No one she knew quilted anymore. Her women friends were taking on jobs outside the home, enrolling in community college, competing in local elections, and declaring that women could do anything men could do. Gretchen had known that for a long time, but it was quite another thing to watch from the sidelines as other women her age and younger broke into realms from which they had traditionally been excluded. Even Heidi, who had given up teaching after one unfortunate semester, had worked her way onto boards and committees that a generation ago would have pleasantly but firmly steered her toward a woman's auxiliary instead of allowing her to be a part of the decision making. Gretchen watched with awe and admiration as other women's lives became busier and fuller, and she nodded vigorously when former coworkers talked about equal pay for equal work and valuing woman's contributions. It took her time to realize that they were not referring to many of the contributions she valued most.

Other women had abandoned quilting, but not because they were too busy. Quilts had become old-fashioned, the craft of the poor and the unsophisticated, an unwelcome reminder of the limitations of their mothers' and grandmothers' lives. Quilting, with its inherent association with the domestic sphere and the traditional "woman's work" of housekeeping and family tending, was something for women to avoid tripping over as they strode into the male world of work that mattered.

Gretchen refused to apologize for her love of quilting, but she decided to stop discussing it one Saturday morning at Heidi's house. Heidi had set Gretchen to work clearing out some old cartons from the basement, where she stumbled across a box of old fabric scraps, half-sewn patchwork blocks, and an envelope stuffed full of brittle, yellowed quilt patterns clipped from the newspaper. The envelope bore Heidi's great-grandmother's name and the address of their older, grander house. Gretchen immediately hurried off to report the find to Heidi, who regarded her with bewildered skepticism as she described the treasure trove downstairs.

"Do you think it's worth anything?" asked Heidi when Gretchen had finished.

"As a memento of your grandmother, of course," said Gretchen, taken aback. "I don't think it's something you could sell. I suppose a historical society might be interested in the donation . . ."

"I doubt it. Just toss it out."

"But—" Gretchen hesitated. "The fabric is still usable, and the blocks are charming."

"What would I do with them? Sew them together? Make a quilt?"

"That's what I would do."

Heidi laughed. "You're still quilting? Honestly, Gretchen, I don't see how you of all people can afford to waste your time that way. Think of how much you charge an hour and how many hours it takes to make a quilt. You could buy the best comforter at Gimbel's or Kaufmann's for less that that. It's a bad return on your investment."

"Quilting is not just about saving money."

"You are so right. It's also about what we consider truly important. We aren't chained to the kitchen anymore, and we can't let anyone forget it. If we women don't insist upon spending our time as thoughtfully as we spend our money, we'll never be considered equal to men."

Stung, Gretchen nevertheless nodded. "What should I do with the box, then?"

Heidi shrugged dismissively. "If you want it so badly, you take it."

Gretchen did exactly that, but as she pieced a dozen pastel Dresden Plate blocks into a lap quilt, she brooded over Heidi's words, an echo of a more prevailing message that Gretchen was out of step with her times. She did not understand why. In an era where the work of women was expanding and being recognized and earning greater respect than ever before, why was "women's work" so denigrated? Gretchen did not want quilting and cooking and caring for children to be respected *despite* the fact that they were tasks traditionally accomplished by women, but *because* of it.

But she knew no one else who shared her opinion, so she kept her quilting to herself. She quilted to add beauty to her life, to give purpose to her hours, to distract her from the unfairness of fate.

Her longtime prayers were answered when Joe began to walk again; tears came to her eyes whenever she recalled his proud demonstration of his new, halting gait across the kitchen. He had hoped to return to work, but he never fully recovered his old strength, and an accidental jolt could leave him gasping from pain. His dream of returning to his former occupation faded, and with it, his hope.

It broke Gretchen's heart to see him turning in upon himself, giving up, growing old before his time. Before long, she realized that it was beyond her powers to cheer him up, but she resolved not to sink into despair with him. She found a new job as a substitute teacher, and while it was not steady work, it did help pay off some outstanding debts and it gave her a chance to get out of the house. In the evenings after a day away, she found she could be more cheerful with Joe, and she had more interesting stories to tell him.

Gradually he returned from his melancholy. He resumed seeing old friends, even though they thoughtlessly ribbed him about loafing and living off his wife's earnings. He planted a garden in the small patch of land behind their house and learned how to preserve the harvest. Then one evening, he paused in the middle of the chapter he was reading aloud and said, "You sure seem to get a lot of pleasure out of your sewing."

She smiled. "We've been married six years and you only just noticed?"

"What is it you like so much? It's not just having a pretty quilt at the end, is it?"

"I suppose I just like working with my hands. Keeping busy."

Joe was quiet for a moment. "Maybe I should try that."

"You want to quilt?"

"No, no, not quilting. Something else."

The next day he went on his usual slow walk around the neighborhood and returned accompanied by a boy pushing a white wooden rocking chair in a wheelbarrow. It looked to be at least fifty years old, with a split armrest and a few missing spindles on the back. Gretchen watched from the window as the boy unloaded the chair on the sidewalk. Joe gave the boy a coin from his pocket, sent him on his way, and dragged the chair out of sight into the garage.

She gave him fifteen minutes, then went outside to find out what was going on. She discovered him on one knee beside the chair, vigorously rubbing off the peeling white paint with sandpaper.

"Where did you find that old thing?" she asked.

"On the Gruebers' curb. They threw it out."

Gretchen could see why. "What are you doing?"

He turned stiffly to face her, straining the limit of his back's flexibility. "Fixing it."

"It needs a lot of fixing." She folded her arms over her chest. "And when you're done?"

"I'm going to sell it, unless I get so attached that I can't part with it."

"I see." She watched as he returned to sanding the chair. "Tomato soup and grilled cheese sandwiches for lunch sound all right to you?"

"Suits me fine."

"I'll call you when it's ready." She left him to his work.

True to his word, Joe repaired and finished the chair beautifully and sold it for twenty dollars. He took on a bureau and matching chest next, and sold both to a shop in Sewickley for fifty dollars. Within months, neighbors and strangers alike were stopping by the garage at all hours of the day to browse through the finished pieces on display or to schedule an appointment to drop off worn or damaged furniture for him to refurbish. Joe made a sign and hung it above the entrance to the garage: "Joseph Hartley: Fine Furniture Repaired and Restored." He worked when he felt able, rested when the strain on his back and legs became too much. He checked out library books on cabinet making and woodworking, and soon he began designing and building his own original pieces. An antique shop in downtown Sewickley began carrying his work. After the *Pittsburgh Post* ran a half-page article on him, customers from as far away as Harrisburg commissioned custom-made pieces.

Two years after bringing home that old rocking chair, Joe surprised Gretchen with the gift of a new sewing machine. "Joe," she exclaimed, running her hand over the gleaming new Singer. "What's the occasion?"

"Don't you like it?"

"Of course I like it, but—" Then she saw how proudly he beamed, how he could barely contain his delight, and she caught herself before asking if they could afford it. "I love it. Thank you."

He put his arms around her. "I saw it on the store shelf and it occurred to me that good things come from your quilting. You ought to have the right tools for the job."

✿

The sewing machine was well broken in a year later when two teenage girls knocked on the door. Gretchen did not recognize them, but she guessed they were sisters. Both wore their straight blonde hair long and parted down the middle, denim jeans that flared at the ankle, and loose peasant blouses. The elder of the two had appliquéd a black-and-white peace emblem over her heart with such large, uneven stitches that Gretchen had to hide a wince.

"What can I do for you girls?" she asked, smiling at the two youngsters on her doorstep. "Are you looking for the furniture man?"

"No, we're looking for you," said the older girl. "Mrs. Johnson lives next door to us and she says you know how to make patchwork quilts."

"Why, yes, I do." Gretchen had made a baby quilt for Trudie Johnson's son, now six years old or thereabouts. She was pleased Trudie remembered.

"Could you teach us?" asked the younger sister.

"Teach you how to quilt?"

The girls nodded. "Yes, please," said the older girl.

"Does your mother know you're here?"

They nodded again, and the younger girl added, "She says it's all right with her as long as we aren't a nuisance."

"Why do you want to learn?" asked Gretchen. "Is this for Girl Scouts?"

"No," said the elder girl. "We just want to know how."

Gretchen hesitated, considering. Their request sounded very odd to her, two girls she had never seen before coming around the house seeking quilting lessons. The girls must have interpreted her puzzlement as reluctance, because they exchanged a worried look. The elder girl quickly blurted, "We could trade you. We could help you around the house and you could give us lessons."

"That's an intriguing thought." They certainly seemed sincere in their interest. Kids these days seemed to do as they pleased, with few responsibilities and an endless supply of amusements. Anyone from their generation willing to do chores in exchange for something must truly want it.

Gretchen opened the door wider. "Very well," she said, welcoming them inside. "You can start with the dishes."

The Hellerman sisters came for their lessons every Saturday morning and Wednesday afternoon after school. Gretchen usually saved them a token amount of housework, but they were such a pleasure to have around that she would have taught them regardless. They were eager to learn, so cheerful and inquisitive, that Gretchen enjoyed instructing them in the making of templates, the matching of colors in calicos and solids, the small and precise motions of the running stitch. She was astonished to learn from them that traditional handicrafts fascinated all of their friends, who were learning quilting, knitting, weaving, candle making, soap making, preserving, and a whole host of other domestic skills that had almost entirely skipped their mothers' generation. When Holly and Megan had finished their sampler quilts, Gretchen agreed to teach a few of their friends. She was asked to teach a Saturday workshop for a group of Girl Scouts, and a few weeks later, a high school class studying the pioneers invited her as a guest speaker.

One afternoon, Gretchen ran into one of her quilting pupils at the grocery store with her mother. The mother thanked Gretchen for sharing her talents and said, "Susan makes quilting seem like so much fun. Do you think someday you might teach a class for adults?"

"I honestly hadn't considered it," said Gretchen. "I don't think there would be enough interest."

"I think you're wrong," the woman declared. "If you ever do start up an adult class, please let me know."

A week later, the woman called to tell Gretchen that she had a list of six friends who would gladly pay Gretchen to teach them how to quilt. Surprised and flattered, Gretchen agreed. She reserved the public meeting room at the Ambridge library for each Wednesday evening at seven and dug out her old lesson plans from her home economics teaching days. On the first day of class, she distributed a list of supplies her students needed to purchase for the following week. They would each make a six-block sampler quilt, choosing the blocks they liked best from a collection of thirty patterns. The blocks were interchangeable, and by adding sashing and borders, the quilts would be large enough for a twin bed. In this way, each new quilter could create her own unique project without departing too much from the standard curriculum. Gretchen was thrilled to be in front of a classroom again, so when her students asked if they could bring friends along, she consented. Before long, her class doubled in size.

Some of the women owned sewing machines and had made their own clothes once upon a time; others barely knew how to thread a needle. Together they learned to choose patterns and fabric, to draft patterns and make templates, to sew a running stitch and set in pieces. They shared confidences as they quilted, as Gretchen imagined women had at quilting bees a hundred years ago and more. She was so grateful for the company of other quilters that when they finished their sampler quilt classes, she suggested they continue their weekly meetings as friends.

At one meeting of the Wednesday Night Stitchers, as they called themselves, a member hurried into the room digging into her tote. "You'll never believe what my sister-in-law sent me from Colorado," she announced. "A magazine about quilts!"

Everyone crowded around to see. Gretchen, who had envisioned something on the order of *Life* magazine with a photo of a brilliantly colored quilt on the cover, was somewhat let down by the few pieces of paper stapled together with the words *Quilter's Newsletter Magazine* on the masthead. But when it was her turn to leaf through the pages, she felt a stirring of excitement and belonging that she had not felt since that long-ago home economics education course in college, with the admired instructor who was as passionate about precise piecing as she was about the storied heritage of American quilting. For so many years she had felt that her love for quilting isolated her until at last she discovered a small group of like-minded friends. Now she realized that they were not alone, that they were part of a larger community, a circle of quilters that had kept quilting alive and were passing along their skill and wisdom as generations of women had before them.

Over the years, Gretchen observed that interest in quilting was slowly and steadily growing. *Quilter's Newsletter Magazine* began running full-color photographs and acquired some competitors. Fabric manufacturers began creating a wider variety of prints than the traditional floral calicos.

Quilting guilds like the Wednesday Night Stitchers began cropping up in cities and towns across the nation. Then, in 1976, this interest blossomed into a veritable quilt revival. The Bicentennial created a surge of renewed interest in American history, inspiring people to search for family heirlooms in their attics and closets and under their beds. Suddenly, quilts were spoken of as if they were more than just bed coverings; they were art to be displayed on walls, historical artifacts to be studied, time capsules reflecting the social, political, and aesthetic milieu of their makers—just as Sylvia Compson had asserted in the classroom so many years before.

Gretchen knew quilting was back to stay when Heidi phoned, suggesting she come in to work early the next Saturday morning so she could show Heidi how to quilt. "I thought I'd make a quilt out of flannel," she said. "Warm and cozy, to use at the cabin. What do you think?"

Gretchen did not want to come in to work any earlier than usual, nor had she ever heard of piecing a quilt from flannel, but she did not want to discourage Heidi. "How about if I stay later, instead?"

"I can't. I have a fund-raising luncheon at the Sewickley Academy."

Gretchen thought for a moment, and then, with misgivings, said, "Do you want to come to my quilt club meeting on Wednesday? We all pitch in to help newcomers."

"I was really hoping for private lessons . . . but I suppose that would be fine."

"All right," said Gretchen, already regretting her offer. She waited until Heidi found a pen before dictating the time, date, and directions.

"I'll see you there," said Heidi. Suddenly she laughed. "You sure were clever all those years ago when you talked me out of my great-grandmother's quilting materials, weren't you? If I had only known how much they were worth."

She hung up before Gretchen could reply.

When Gretchen went to the garage to repeat Heidi's comment to Joe, he looked up from staining a sleigh bed and shook his head. "You never should have asked her to join you and your friends."

"I know." But it was too late now. "I can always hope that she'll have a miserable time and never come back."

Joe laughed shortly. "Not Heidi. If it's yours, she wants it, and she'll try to take it. That's the way she's always been."

"Heidi has everything," said Gretchen, trying to make a joke of it. "She doesn't need my little bit."

"Who said anything about need? I said want, and Heidi has a way of getting what she wants."

Joe turned out to be all too prescient. Heidi never mentioned her great-grandmother's quilting again, but instead set about learning to quilt with more diligence than Gretchen had known she possessed. She charmed the other women with her enthusiasm and infectious humor, and if she referred to Gretchen once too often as her cleaning lady, no one seemed to think less of either of them for it. Besides, Gretchen *was* Heidi's cleaning lady, and there was no sense in being too proud to acknowledge it.

Heidi absorbed everything the other women taught—everything but their rules. She mixed plaids and stripes. She shunned small-scale floral calicos. Instead of selecting a multicolored focus fabric and choosing other fabrics to match, she enthused about color wheels, complementary colors, and split-complementary color schemes, jargon she had picked up in a painting class. She combined cottons with polyesters and wools. She refused to prewash. And although Gretchen secretly predicted—and perhaps even hoped—that Heidi's reckless ways would result in disastrous quilts, somehow her collisions of incongruous methods worked, earning the grudging admiration of the Stitchers' most conservative traditionalists.

It was Heidi who suggested that the Wednesday Night Stitchers write up bylaws and officially declare themselves a quilt guild. It was Heidi who was selected as the first president. And as the other members celebrated their transformation from a group of friends to a recognized nonprofit organization, Gretchen smiled and agreed that these changes certainly were remarkable, while silently she mourned the passing of an era.

Not all of the changes Heidi inspired made her long for the old days. One of her first acts as guild president was to organize a directory of quilting guilds in Pennsylvania, West Virginia, and Ohio. The guilds shared information about quilt shows, guild activities, and teachers willing to travel. When Heidi defied alphabetical order and placed Gretchen's name at the top of the teachers' list, she received more invitations for speaking engagements than her schedule could accommodate. She felt obliged to thank Heidi, since the money she saved from her speaking fees enabled her to buy a new color television for the living room. Her gratitude evaporated when, in front of three other Wednesday Night Stitchers, Heidi replied, "It was my pleasure. I just hope the fame doesn't go to your head or my toilets will never be clean again!"

Gretchen could have died when the other women laughed.

"You shouldn't take that from her," said Joe when she told him about it. "After all you've done for her, she still acts like a spoiled brat. She'll never grow up, and you shouldn't put up with it."

"What am I supposed to do?" said Gretchen. "If I talk back, she could fire me."

"So? Let her fire you. I'm making decent money now. You have your quilt teaching. We'll get by."

But Gretchen, who balanced the family checkbook, knew that the wages she received from Heidi often made the difference between ending the week in the black or in the red.

❧

Gretchen celebrated her fiftieth birthday by splurging on an airline ticket to Houston to attend the International Quilt Festival. She had never seen so many glorious quilts in one setting—and even more thrilling was the sense of being surrounded by other women as passionate about quilts and quilting as she was. She took classes with some of the brightest stars in the quilting world, attended lectures, struggled to stick to her budget in the merchants' mall, and enjoyed many spontaneous conversations with quilt lovers from around the country.

One seminar in particular, "From Quilt Lover to Quilt Shop Owner," resonated so strongly with her that she reread her notes every evening after she returned to her hotel room, footsore and exhausted but brimming with inspiration for new quilts. Joe was the only person who knew that the prospect of attending this seminar was what had convinced her to come to Houston. For the past year they had examined their finances, studied their budget, investigated local average rents, and planned, and hoped. Joe wanted her to find an alternative to working for Heidi; Gretchen longed to fulfill a fond wish to earn a living doing what she loved best.

On Gretchen's first night home, she and Joe stayed up late into the night discussing their options, papers covered in notes and figures spread across the kitchen table. Shortly after one in the morning they concluded that they could do it. Gretchen could run a quilt shop, and considering how many quilters lived on their side of the river, how many new quilters joined their ranks every year, and how under served their area was, it could be a very successful quilt shop.

One significant obstacle stood in the way: the enormous up-front expenses necessary just to open the shop doors. She could purchase some inventory on credit, but she would still have to pay for remodeling, advertising, wages, insurance—the list went on much too long for their savings. Gretchen would have to apply for a business loan.

"It should be a piece of cake," Joe assured her. They had no outstanding debts except for their mortgage, but their monthly payments were reasonable and they would have it paid off in another eight years.

Gretchen first applied at the bank where she and Joe had held accounts since they married. They had been very good clients, never bounced a check, rarely dipped below the minimum balance, so Gretchen was crushed and bewildered when the bank turned down her application. "I don't understand," she said to the loan officer. "We have good credit."

"You have satisfactory credit," the younger man said, nodding, though he had not really agreed with her. "But you don't have a business credit record. Once you have that established, we will gladly reconsider your case."

Gretchen thanked him and left without explaining that until she opened her quilt shop, she would not be able to establish a business credit record. Until she had the loan, she could not open her quilt shop. Joe had never sought a loan for his woodworking, so she doubted he had much business credit, either, so he could not take out the loan on her behalf.

She applied elsewhere, was rejected and tried again, until every bank in Ambridge, Sewickley, and Coraopolis had turned her away. When her last application met with refusal, she tearfully broke the bad news to Joe. He tried to comfort her as she finally admitted defeat. "It was a foolish dream," she said. "I never should have allowed myself to get my hopes up."

"What kind of talk is that?" protested Joe. "What happened to the housekeeper's daughter who paid her way through college to become a teacher? What happened to the girl who told a husband with a broken back that he could walk again if he didn't quit?"

She grew up, Gretchen thought. She grew up and wised up and learned that life doesn't always reward persistence. But she hated to disappoint Joe. "I suppose I could apply to a bank in Pittsburgh," she said, though she had assumed a smaller, hometown bank would be more amenable.

"We could take a second mortgage."

"No, Joe," said Gretchen. "Absolutely not. I won't do it. I won't risk our home, not even for this. No matter how well I've planned, the shop might fail. There's always that chance."

He knew better than to argue when she got that tone in her voice, but his brow furrowed and he regarded her with fond sympathy. "If that's what you told the loan officers, no wonder they turned you down."

Joe's encouragement strengthened Gretchen's resolve, but she knew she would run headlong into the same problem at any other bank she tried. If she were ever to make her dream a reality, she had to swallow her pride and seek help from the one person to whom she did not want to become further indebted.

The following Saturday, she lingered after collecting her paycheck and asked Heidi if she had a moment. Seated in the parlor she had dusted so many times, Gretchen outlined her plans for opening a quilt shop in Ambridge. She gave Heidi a copy of her business plan and explained the problems she had encountered trying to secure a small business loan.

"I just don't know, Gretchen," said Heidi. "I agree this could be a marvelous business opportunity—and a potentially lucrative investment—but I'm leery about lending such a large sum to a friend. Money quarrels can destroy a friendship."

"We won't have any reason to quarrel," Gretchen assured her. "We'll have everything in writing, in a contract just as if the loan was made through a bank. I'll pay the going interest rate, of course."

"Of course," echoed Heidi. "I'll need to think about it and talk to my husband. Do you need an answer right away?"

"No," said Gretchen, although she had hoped for one. "Take whatever time you need."

They shook on it, and Gretchen left feeling hopeful and just the tiniest bit anxious. Heidi's husband was tightfisted and suspicious. He was likely to complain even though the money for the loan would come from Heidi's trust fund, a bequest from her grandmother that was, according to Heidi, none of his concern.

A few days later at the meeting of the Wednesday Night Stitchers, Heidi behaved normally, as if unaware that Gretchen's future happiness rested on her decision. Gretchen waited all evening for her to mention the loan, unwilling to seem like a nag by bringing it up herself. On Saturday morning, she could wait no longer and had barely closed the back door behind her when she asked Heidi if she had discussed the loan with her husband.

"He's still looking over a few details," replied Heidi. "I'll have some news for you in a few days."

Her smile meant to encourage, but Gretchen felt faint with nervousness. It was unlike Heidi to need an entire week to convince Chad to agree to something she was determined to do. Was he balking at a flaw in her business plan? Was Heidi herself uncertain if she should help Gretchen? The waiting and the worry troubled her sleep and made her short-tempered with Joe, until she almost wished she had consulted every last bank in Pennsylvania before approaching Heidi.

At last, on Wednesday evening, Heidi began the new business portion of the guild meeting by declaring that she was about to make a very important announcement. Although she only glanced at Gretchen, seated in the back, Gretchen knew at once that the answer to her request was forthcoming. Not even Heidi would decline a friend's request for a loan so publicly, so Gretchen straightened in her chair, heart pounding as if it would burst with happiness. In the moment Heidi paused to allow the murmurs of expectation to build, Gretchen envisioned the Stitchers' response to the good news: their exclamations of delight, their congratulatory embraces, their promises to become her shop's best customers. She was still lost in a joyful reverie when Heidi announced that she intended to open a quilt shop in downtown Sewickley by summer and hoped they would all turn out for the grand opening.

Gretchen sat stunned in her chair while her friends showered Heidi with applause and the exact good wishes she had imagined for herself. Heidi needed a good five minutes to quiet them so she could proceed with the meeting. Not once did she look Gretchen's way.

Gretchen left the meeting at the social break without speaking to anyone.

Joe was furious. "She stole your business plan," he thundered. "She took all your ideas, all our research, and kept them for herself. She can't be allowed to get away with this."

But Gretchen did not know what to do. Had Heidi broken any laws? Without a doubt, what she had done was sneaky and underhanded—unethical, yes, but illegal? Heartsick, Gretchen could not even begin to pursue that question. She hardly saw the point. Even if she obtained a loan elsewhere, she could not open a quilt shop in Ambridge with Heidi's shop practically next door in Sewickley, not if she expected it to succeed. And Heidi would have known that.

Gretchen dreaded Saturday morning. For the first time in her life, she deliberately arrived late to work, hoping Heidi would have already left for a tennis lesson or board meeting or garden society brunch. Unfortunately,

Heidi was waiting for her just inside the back door. "We should talk," she said before Gretchen was out of her coat.

"All right." Gretchen set down her purse and regarded Heidi evenly. She felt strangely calm. "Let's talk about how you pretended to consider my request for a loan to distract me while you stole my idea."

"How could you say such a thing?" exclaimed Heidi. "That's not what happened."

Gretchen stared at her, amazed. Did Heidi really believe she could bluff her way out of it? "I showed you my business plan and the next thing I know, you're opening a quilt shop."

"That's not fair. I didn't follow your plan. For one thing, my quilt shop will be in Sewickley, not Ambridge. I admit the timing is unfortunate, but I've been planning this for a long time. You don't really think I could have set everything in motion in one week, do you?"

It had been a week and a half between Gretchen's request and the announcement at the guild meeting, a more than sufficient amount of time for someone with Heidi's connections. "I hardly know what to believe. If you were already planning to open a quilt shop, why didn't you tell me when I asked for the loan?"

"I can explain." Heidi sank into a chair at the kitchen table and gestured for Gretchen to sit. "I've wanted to run my own company for years. You know that. You've heard me talk about it."

Gretchen shrugged and sat down, reluctantly. Heidi had mentioned an interior decorating service, a wedding planning service, and a myriad of other businesses throughout the years, but she had never seemed serious about any of them.

"When I first mentioned a quilt shop to Chad, he dismissed it just as he had all my other ideas." A frown of annoyance briefly cut Heidi's face and disappeared. "Worse, he thought it was silly and frivolous, a waste of my time. So when you asked for the loan, I did seriously consider it. I thought that if I couldn't have a shop of my own, investing in yours would be the next best thing. You did write up an excellent plan. It was very professional."

"Joe helped a lot," said Gretchen quietly.

"A lot of credit goes to you both, then, because when I showed Chad everything you had presented to me, he realized that there was much more to 'this quilting thing' than he had thought. All I wanted was for him to agree to the loan, but instead he told me I should go ahead with my original plan to open my own shop."

Gretchen studied her for a moment. Heidi's expression was so open and guileless, her clear blue eyes pleading for understanding and forgiveness. "You never mentioned wanting to run a quilt shop."

"Of course not! No one pays any attention to my career plans anymore. Who can blame them? I've thrown out so many ideas and haven't stuck with any of them."

Gretchen wondered why Heidi seemed so convinced that this time would be any different. She did not know what to say. How could she convey to Heidi her disappointment, her sense of loss? Could she persuade Heidi to step aside, forget her own shop and grant the loan for Gretchen's dream instead?

Heidi broke the silence. "You know, you could still get a bank loan and open your own quilt shop."

Gretchen knew Heidi was wrong on at least two counts, but she was too frustrated and defeated to argue. She shook her head.

"I'm sorry," said Heidi, reaching for her hand. "But in a way, I'm glad you won't be setting up a competing shop. I had hoped you would come and work for me."

Gretchen yanked her hand free. "You have a lot of nerve."

"Gretchen—"

Standing, Gretchen waved her to silence. "Don't. I can't talk about this anymore. I have work to do."

She left the kitchen with Heidi staring after her in astonishment.

Quilts 'n Things opened three months later. Lingering doubts about the truth of Heidi's explanation kept Gretchen away for the first two weeks, but eventually her curiosity overcame her resistance. Heidi greeted her excitedly, bounding over to her from behind the cash register and giving her an impulsive and entirely unexpected hug. "I'm so glad you came," she said. "I wanted your opinion so many times, but—" She shrugged. "You know."

Gretchen nodded, taking in the scene. "Congratulations," she said, more impressed than she cared to admit. The former shoe store had been decorated to resemble a country farmhouse, with bolts of brightly colored fabric arranged in antique armoires and pie cupboards. In the center of the room, an old kitchen table had been transformed into a cutting table. A partial wall that resembled the entrance to a one-room schoolhouse separated the back of the room from the main sales floor; through the doorway, Gretchen spied several rows of wooden desks and a blackboard hanging on the wall. Everywhere she looked, Gretchen found enticing displays of the latest fabrics, notions, patterns, and products to satisfy any quilter's heart's desire.

Heidi regarded her expectantly. "What do you think?"

"It's wonderful," said Gretchen. Even when she had envisioned her own quilt shop, she had not imagined anything so warm and enchanting. It was the kind of shop in which she could gladly spend an entire day and half a paycheck. "I'm sure it will be an enormous success."

"I'm so glad you feel that way." Heidi took her hand and led her to a small office tucked away in a back room, all but invisible from the shop floor. "I'm sure you noticed my classroom space. I would like you to be my first teacher."

"I don't know . . ."

"Not just a teacher. A partner." Heidi indicated a sprawl of paperwork on the desk. "I haven't forgotten your business plan. I know you have some capital. You asked me to invest in your shop, and now I'm asking you to invest in mine."

Gretchen felt a small glimmering of hope. "I would be a partner?"

"A junior partner, but still, part owner. We would run this place together." Heidi squared her shoulders as if to summon up an inner reservoir of resolve. "All right. You're forcing me to do something I know I'm going to regret. You're fired."

"What?"

"You're fired. As my cleaning lady. Now that you're unemployed, I'd like to rehire you as my quilting instructor and junior partner." Heidi placed a sheaf of papers in Gretchen's hands. "Here's a contract. You'll have two weeks of vacation each year and a health care plan. Including dental."

Through Chad's insurance company, no doubt, with a high deductible. But still . . . "Why?" she asked. Heidi knew many other perfectly capable quilting instructors. Was this her admission of guilt? Her apology? Nothing Heidi did could compensate for stealing Gretchen's dream, intentional or not.

"I need you," said Heidi in a small voice.

Gretchen was about to retort that nothing she had seen that day gave her that impression, but something in the younger woman's expression stopped her short. It was the look of the little girl she had tutored, the one who wanted to dress like her and be a teacher like her, the little girl who had wanted so badly to be loved and admired.

"You don't need me," said Gretchen. Heidi didn't, not really. "But . . . I think I would like to work here."

Heidi beamed.

❧

Over the years, as the junior partner of Quilts 'n Things, Gretchen was able to accomplish everything she had hoped to as owner of her own shop. She loved every part of her day, from opening the cozy shop in the morning to selecting stock, helping customers, making sample quilts to display on the walls above the fabric bolts, and teaching, especially when she introduced new quilters to the craft. She still cleaned up Heidi's messes, but she would rather sweep up thread and put away fabric bolts than scrub bathrooms. She had come to appreciate Heidi's creative imagination, which not only manifested itself in her quilt designs, but also in the way she ran the shop. She would hold spontaneous one-day sales that had the store packed with shoppers from the time they unlocked the doors in the morning until long after their usual closing hour. She would throw parties based upon the silliest themes—"Three Months Until Christmas Day" or "Fabric Appreciation Week"—to the delight of their customers, who willingly seized upon any excuse to buy more fabric. She held an annual quilt show in the store where customers could vote for the Ugliest Quilt of All Time. Gretchen was appalled when Heidi first announced the contest, and she could not believe that anyone would humiliate herself by putting her name to any quilt entitled to that dubious honor. But ten brave souls entered that first year, and the winner was crowned while wearing a paper bag over her head. She had to be led by the hand to the front of the store to receive her prize, a basket of fat quarters and a gift certificate to one session of classes at the shop. Every year the contest grew, the entries becoming ever more abominable, until Heidi had to put her foot down and exclude any quilts that were deliberately made badly, so that only the truly and unintentionally awful would be considered for the grand prize.

Most winners used their gift certificates to enroll in a Quilting for Beginners course, and most made dramatic improvements. They all bought fabric, books, and notions at Quilts 'n Things, and many signed up for more advanced classes. Gretchen never would have thought to increase class enrollments by demonstrating to potential customers how sorely they needed the help.

"I wonder if this is how Ami Simms attracts new students," Gretchen remarked once.

Heidi did not look up from the rack of quilt patterns she was arranging—not in alphabetical order as Gretchen would have done, but according to season. "Who?" she asked absently.

"Ami Simms. I said, I wonder if she uses her contest to get more students to enroll in classes, but I was only joking. She probably has so many students she has to turn some away."

Heidi glanced over her shoulder at Gretchen, puzzled. "What contest?"

"The Worst Quilt in the World contest. She's been running one for years. I assumed that's where you got the idea."

Heidi shook her head and shrugged, turning back to her work. "I've never heard of her, or her contest. Maybe she took the idea from us."

"Never heard of Ami Simms?" repeated Gretchen, dubious. "Of course you have. We carry her books. We met her at Paducah three years ago."

Heidi made a helpless, apologetic gesture as she filed patterns. Gretchen watched her in disbelief. Why on earth would Heidi pretend she had never heard of Ami Simms? Was she that unwilling to admit she had taken inspiration from Ami's contest rather than invent it herself?

Gretchen already knew the answer to that one.

Although she and Heidi did not always agree, Gretchen liked to think they complemented each other: Heidi brought the imagination and spark to the business, while Gretchen understood how to turn her partner's outlandish ideas into workable plans. Heidi was energetic and inventive; Gretchen, steady and practical. They were two halves of an excellent management team, and neither could have succeeded as well without the other. Gretchen often thought, however, that although they were both essential to the success of Quilts 'n Things, Heidi seemed to have most of the fun.

As the years passed, the quilt shop thrived, riding the surging wave of the quilting revival. Gretchen wasn't sure whether Heidi was a trendsetter, putting forth styles and products she liked best and taking a chance that others would share her tastes, or if she was simply quick to perceive the sways and swells of popular opinion and could adapt quickly to match them. Either way, Quilts 'n Things earned a reputation for being the place to shop for everything new and innovative in the quilting world. Heidi advocated rotary cutter techniques and establishing a presence on the Internet when Gretchen was still worrying about how to best provide templates for their block-of-the-month kits. Heidi invested in a longarm quilting machine and charged customers by the hour to use it at a time when Gretchen and her friends were still wrestling with the question of whether a machine-quilted top could be considered a true quilt. Before long, Gretchen began to notice a clear division within their clientele: the younger, newer quilters brought their questions to Heidi and ignored Gretchen, while the older, longtime quilters sought Gretchen's advice and assumed Heidi was her less experienced assistant. Gretchen, to her secret shame, never clarified the reality of their arrangement.

Sometimes Heidi went too far. Gretchen was shocked and angered when she returned from her day off to discover that her partner had replaced all the shelves of her beloved floral calicos with brightly colored, exotic batiks. "Our customers will love these," Heidi protested, bewildered by Gretchen's reaction.

"Our customers love the calicos," insisted Gretchen.

"They can still have them," Heidi hastened to reassure her, and compromised by relocating the remaining bolts to the back shelves where they stored clearance merchandise. But hardly anyone bothered to look for them because they had usually reached their spending limits by the time they made it that far into the store. Taking inventory at the end of the month, Heidi remarked that only about five yards of the calicos had sold, and that she had been right to move them to make room for the highly popular batiks. When Gretchen pointed out that Heidi's decision had become a self-fulfilling prophecy, Heidi merely shrugged. She did not need to perpetuate the argument; she had had her own way and she was selling fabric. For the sake of workplace harmony, Gretchen masked her annoyance and contented herself with making sure her fellow calico lovers knew exactly where to find the bolts and by placing baskets full of floral calico fat quarters at the checkout line to encourage impulse purchases.

Their educational philosophies differed even more than their tastes in fabric. Gretchen instructed aspiring quilters as she had been taught, learning the fundamentals of quiltmaking while making simple blocks and moving on to more difficult patterns and new skills when the basics were mastered. Heidi believed that contemporary women did not have time to quilt as their grandmothers had. If they were going to spend an entire Saturday at a quilting workshop, they wanted to have a finished top at the end. Her classes emphasized rotary cutting, quick piecing, working with prepared patterns, and machine sewing every stitch. "Look at how many of my students finish their workshop quilts, bring them back to show us, and sign up for another class," said Heidi when they were planning the next session of courses and were trying to efficiently divide up the classroom time.

"That's true," said Gretchen. It was easier to win over Heidi if she agreed with her first. "But at the end of the semester, my students can look at any quilt block, figure out how it's constructed, design their own quilts, and draft their own patterns. Your students can make that one quilt. They make it quickly and well, but they can only make that one quilt. They might vary the colors or size, but it's always the same."

"That's what they like," countered Heidi. "They want certainty. They enjoy the feeling of accomplishment. They like having finished quilts to put on beds or give to grandchildren for Christmas. Their friends see the quilts and sign up for the next class. Maybe your students can decipher any pattern, but they also have closets stuffed full of UFOs."

Gretchen knew her students did finish quilts—perhaps not as many as Heidi's, but the quilts they did complete were unique, each one an original creative expression of its maker. The mass production of Heidi's students could not compete. Of course, she would never say so aloud. Heidi's students were lovely women and they enjoyed quilting as much as Gretchen's favorite pupils did. But their sole focus on reproducing other quilters' patterns underscored another important difference between the two partners: Gretchen was most concerned with process, Heidi with product.

For many years, their partnership weathered minor disagreements and occasional full-blown arguments. They always reconciled, in part because Gretchen never failed to appease Heidi when she became tearful and melodramatic, but mostly because Quilts 'n Things was too important to them both to sacrifice its success to petty squabbling.

Just in time for its tenth anniversary, Quilts 'n Things was selected to appear in a special issue of *Contemporary Quiltmaker* magazine titled "The Best Quilt Shops of the Millennium." Privately, Gretchen and Joe agreed that the title smacked of hyperbole and really ought to be amended to "The Best American Quilt Shops Currently in Operation That Carry Our Magazine," but neither would have suggested they decline to participate. For all her self-deprecating jokes, Gretchen was honored to be included, and Heidi was thrilled with the prospect of so much free publicity.

The three days the team from the magazine spent in Sewickley was as close to stardom as Gretchen figured she was ever likely to get. Their stylist helped her select an outfit and did her hair and makeup for the photo shoot at the store. A reporter interviewed her at length, twice on her own and once more with Heidi and their two part-time employees. As he inquired about her vision for the shop, the inspiration for her quilts, and her history as a quilt-maker, Gretchen was struck by the realization that no one had ever asked her these questions before. She had quilted most of her life, and now, finally, someone cared enough to ask. Best of all, the reporter represented tens of thousands of readers who also cared.

A few months later, the magazine arrived from the printer's and was arranged with much fanfare on the new book display at the front of the quilt shop. Gretchen knew that the reporter had interviewed Heidi just as thoroughly as her, and yet she was stunned when she turned to the article and discovered a full-page photo of Heidi beaming out at her. A caption identified her as "Heidi Mueller, owner, creative inspiration, and driving force behind the finest quilt shop in western Pennsylvania." Scattered among the photos of customers browsing through the shop were some of Heidi smiling over a cup of coffee in her kitchen, lecturing to an adoring class in the schoolhouse, wearing a look of thoughtful introspection as she arranged bolts of fabric—and one small group photo of Heidi standing with her arms folded in the foreground as Gretchen and the two other employees smiled admiringly at her from behind the checkout counter. Amid the paragraphs about how Heidi launched the shop and kept it running with the help of her "able assistants" was one quote from the lengthy interviews Gretchen had given the reporter. "Our customers tell us every day how much the shop reflects Heidi's creativity," Gretchen had told him. "She has a true gift for inspiring new quilters to take up the needle."

If not for that quote and the small staff picture, Gretchen would have not appeared in the article at all. No one who read the magazine would suspect her true role at Quilts 'n Things.

Heidi was throwing a Publication Day Party, so Gretchen could not slip on her sweater and walk home to sort things out on her own. Dazed, she moved through the celebrating crowd, accepting their congratulations, autographing the small group picture, helping customers with their purchases, and keeping up appearances. The cash register rarely paused in ringing up sales. The magazine had indeed brought out the quilters, which ultimately was the most important thing. The success of the shop, she reminded herself when she was finally able to escape home, was more important than personal recognition.

Joe did not entirely agree.

He read the article and might have stormed off to the shop to give Heidi a piece of his mind if his old injury had not been acting up, forcing him to lie prone on the sofa and restrict his movements. "How did she do it?" he asked, eyes glittering with barely suppressed rage. "How did she pull this off? You talked to that reporter for hours."

Gretchen felt dull and tired. "I suppose I didn't sing my own praises enough."

"And Heidi exaggerated hers." He winced as he shifted to his side. "You ought to call that magazine and set them straight."

"What good would that do?"

"They might print a retraction."

"And again, what good would that do?" The quilting world ran largely on goodwill. Anything she said against Heidi would make Gretchen seem small and spiteful, and Quilts 'n Things would suffer for it.

"It would set the record straight. Heidi's taken all the credit."

"She can have it," said Gretchen wearily. "I'm still a partner, no matter what the rest of the world thinks."

But she soon discovered that Heidi was all too willing to believe her own press. In the shop, her requests took on the air of commands. She ignored Gretchen's recommendations when it came time to order new fabric. She adjusted their schedules so that Gretchen worked every weekend instead of alternating with her as they had always done before. She slipped so naturally into the role of manager that it was difficult to disagree with her without seeming petty. Their other employees did not seem to object to the shift in power, if they even noticed it. Gretchen was struck by the alarming possibility that from their perspective, perhaps nothing had changed. Perhaps this was the way it had always been, and Gretchen was just the last to know.

Gretchen's love for the quilt shop endured, but she was no longer content. Enjoying her work took more effort, but she put a smile on her face and reminded herself how much better off she was now than she had been as an itinerant quilting instructor and Heidi's housecleaner.

But she was well aware that Heidi deliberately failed to reorder bolts of Gretchen's favorite floral calicos unless a customer made a specific request. She also altered the teaching schedule, assigning more classes to herself and fewer to Gretchen. Gretchen found it difficult to criticize the changes. From an economic standpoint they made perfect sense, as an increasing number of their customers preferred Heidi's methods. And yet she missed the old days, when she felt more useful, more relevant.

When Heidi began self-publishing a line of original patterns under the Quilts 'n Things name, Gretchen welcomed the new direction for their partnership, hoping that it would renew her creative spark as well as her interest in the job. She missed that sense of anticipation that something unexpected and delightful would be waiting for her when she went into work each day. But when she approached Heidi with two designs that she wanted to publish, Heidi balked. "These are nice quilts," said Heidi, returning the drawings with an apologetic shrug, "but they don't really have the right look for the line."

"What do you mean?" asked Gretchen, hurt.

"Well, they're kind of old-fashioned, don't you think? The first three Quilts 'n Things patterns were for brightly colored, fun, modern quilts. Yours are more . . . retro. You're locked into this blocky-blocky sampler style, and most quilters have moved beyond that." Heidi spoke gently, but that took none of the sting from her words. "Why don't you try to make a more contemporary design, and maybe we can consider publishing that?"

Gretchen tried to convince Heidi that many quilters still enjoyed making samplers, as evidence pointing to the brisk sales within their own shop of books like *Dear Jane, Quilted Diamonds,* and *My Journey with Harriet.* Their customers' requests that they stock more reproduction fabrics indicated that the "retro" look appealed to quilters as much as contemporary designs did.

When Heidi continued to refuse, Gretchen grew indignant. "I am as much a part of Quilts 'n Things as you are," she declared. "A pattern line using the Quilts 'n Things name should represent my style as well as yours."

Heidi turned away, shaking her head. She busied herself with paperwork on the desk and muttered under her breath.

A word caught Gretchen's ear. "What did you say?" The office door was open and passing customers might hear, but she did not care.

"I said that you're the *junior* partner," said Heidi. "You apparently need the reminder. I can't put my store's name to anything I'm not proud of. If you don't like it, my daughter would be happy to buy out your share, or you can be a silent partner and not come into the shop anymore."

Shocked, Gretchen could not reply. Heidi studied her for a moment, took her silence as submission, and left Gretchen alone in the office.

Gretchen went home without a word for anyone. She called in sick the next morning and was relieved when one of the part-time employees answered so she did not have to speak to Heidi. Heidi would consider her excuse a lie, but it was not. Gretchen *was* sick—sick at heart, sick and tired. Worst of all was the sinking suspicion that Heidi's decision was justified. Gretchen's quilts *were* old-fashioned. She had branched out from her beloved floral calicos in recent years to tone-on-tones and graphic prints, but her quilts were still composed of traditional blocks in traditional layouts. They were beautifully and exquisitely made, if she did say so herself, with perfect points and graceful curves, each tiny piece in its precise and perfect place. But in an age of raw edge appliqué and fusible webbing, none of that seemed to matter anymore.

It was time she faced facts: The quilting world had passed her by. She felt like a mother who had nurtured a child from the utter dependence of infancy through the awkward teenage years only to watch her child suddenly blossom into a Phi Beta Kappa cardiologist or Supreme Court justice or rocket scientist too busy and too important to call home anymore. She had loved quilting at a time when few others did, but it had grown away from her, and she could not change to keep up with it. A woman like her was fortunate to have any connection at all to the wider quilting world beyond her own sewing machine and lap hoop. She would be a fool to throw that away.

And she had Joe to think about. The years had not been kind to his old injury, and there were days when his back was so stiff and painful that he could not manage his tools. For years he had spoken wistfully of retiring to the country, where he could enjoy his woodworking without the pressure to complete pieces for clients. Gretchen longed to grant him that wish, but they knew they had to remain in the city so Gretchen could work. Retirement was a long time off for both of them. It might never come.

When Gretchen returned to the quilt shop, chastened and resigned, she and Heidi continued on as if their confrontation in the office had never occurred. Perhaps as a conciliatory gesture, from that day forward Heidi worked on the Quilts 'n Things patterns away from the shop, on her own time, and never asked Gretchen to hang the pattern packs on the display rack or to fill Internet orders. Occasionally, Heidi would admire a quilt Gretchen had made and agree to consider it for the Quilts 'n Things pattern line; she must have thought she was being supportive and encouraging, but the sketches and instructions always ended up in Gretchen's employee mailbox with a brief note of rejection providing only the vaguest of explanations why they were not suitable. Gretchen found Heidi's ongoing interest painful to bear. It would have been a relief had Heidi stopped asking for submissions they both knew she would eventually reject.

It would have been a greater relief if Heidi had limited their contact to the hours they spent within the store, but apparently that was not to be. Gretchen had worked for Heidi for so long that she could hardly refuse to help when asked, not without putting greater strain on an already troubled relationship. And if Heidi more frequently asked her to do unpaid favors outside of the quilt shop, Gretchen never acknowledged that she complied because she was the junior partner, or because Heidi's daughter was waiting in the wings to buy out her share.

❧

On the afternoon of Heidi's party, Gretchen left one of the part-time employees in charge of closing the shop and ran Heidi's errands at the dry cleaner's, the bakery, and the florist. Then it was off to the Muellers' large home in an arboreal neighborhood of Sewickley, where she found a caterer's truck in the driveway behind a van bearing the logo of a professional housecleaning service. A bit put out, Gretchen went around to the back of the house to her usual entrance, wondering why Heidi had asked her to come over when she apparently already had sufficient help.

Heidi was in the kitchen instructing the two caterers. "Gretchen, finally," she greeted her, taking the dry cleaning. "I'll run these clothes up to the master suite so you can get started."

"What do you need me to do?" asked Gretchen. "You seem to have everything covered."

"You're right. I'm probably fine, but you know how stressed out I get over Chad's business parties. It's easy to throw a get-together for friends, but when the purpose is to impress potential clients . . ." Heidi ran a beautifully manicured hand through her dark brown pixie cut and sighed. "I still have to shower, and dress, and—well, since you're here anyway, would you mind taking a walk through the house to make sure everything is spotless? You never know how hired help is going to perform. My mother always said they do worse on important occasions out of spite."

Gretchen winced, but the caterers and the middle-aged woman scrubbing Heidi's tile floor did nothing to indicate they had overheard, although they could not have avoided it. "Of course," she agreed. Heidi thanked her and hurried off, the recently pressed dress and suit slung over one shoulder, their thin plastic sheathes rustling crisply.

Feeling foolish, Gretchen strolled through the house going through the motions of inspecting the cleaners' work. Heidi could easily handle the task herself, but perhaps she sought Gretchen's professional opinion. She found only two problems so minor that they hardly qualified as problems: The shortest of the four cleaners had neglected to dust a high shelf that Gretchen, too, had occasionally missed back in the day, and an old copy of *Quilter's Newsletter Magazine* had slipped beneath a sofa cushion in the family room.

On a closer look, Gretchen discovered that it was not an old issue, after all, but the most recent. The address label indicated that it was the store copy, from the subscription Heidi had ordered for Quilts 'n Things so the four employees would leave the copies for sale in pristine condition on the racks. They had a long-standing agreement that no one could take the store copy home until everyone else had read it, but Gretchen had never seen this issue. Apparently the rule was flexible where Heidi was concerned.

"Oh, you didn't need to be that thorough," said Heidi, entering the room and finding her replacing the cushion. "I can't imagine our guests will peek under there."

"Do you mind if I borrow this?" asked Gretchen, holding up the magazine. "The cover quilt is exquisite."

Heidi's eyebrows rose in muted incredulity. "It's a little beyond you, don't you think?" She gestured for the magazine. "I'm in the middle of an article. I'll let you have it when I'm finished."

Gretchen reluctantly handed it over. "The other girls might wonder why it's not in the break room."

"Only if you tell them." Then Heidi smiled. "Oh, come on. I'm not the first to bend the rules a little. I promise I'll bring it back as soon as I'm done. There's a quilt I might want to teach next session. I need to study it for a while and make a sample top."

"You could just photocopy those pages."

"Gretchen! I'm surprised at you. That's a violation of copyright law."

Gretchen thought the situation was covered under the Fair Use provision, but she did not want to make a fuss that would delay her return home to Joe. She dropped the subject, told Heidi that the cleaners were progressing nicely, and left before Heidi could assign her another errand.

On Monday morning, she opened the store alone and put on a pot of coffee for early bird shoppers. Heidi's weekends off had extended into Mondays, but Gretchen did not mind. She rather looked forward to days when Heidi was unlikely to stop by. The shipment of *Quilter's Newsletter Magazine* arrived midmorning, so Gretchen unpacked the boxes and stocked the shelves, admiring the cover quilt anew. She wondered how long Heidi would hold on to the store's copy and thought of how they always had one or two of the previous month's issues left over when the new edition arrived.

Surely they could spare one copy, just this once.

At lunchtime, Gretchen left the shop in the care of the part-time helpers, discreetly took a copy of the magazine from the rack, and retired to the break room with her ham sandwich, apple, and pint carton of skim milk. The cover quilt was indeed beyond Gretchen's abilities, as Heidi had rightly noted; the Grand Prize winner of the Tokyo International Great Quilt Festival had taken its maker nearly eight years to complete. Gretchen would have to content herself with admiring the photograph of the original.

She spent a half hour pleasantly browsing through the magazine, lingering over the classified section, where she often picked up ideas from other shops or found a bargain. A quarter-page ad immediately caught her attention, and she held her breath as she read that Sylvia Compson's Elm Creek Quilt Camp was seeking two new teachers.

Elm Creek Quilt Camp. What a lovely, enchanted place it had seemed to Gretchen five years earlier when she and Heidi had visited. Fortunately, Heidi had declared it a research trip and deducted their tuition and fees from the Quilts 'n Things account or Gretchen would not have been able to afford to go. Heidi had heard about the marvelous success of the Elm Creek Quilters and was exploring the possibility of creating a similar quilters' retreat closer to home. Gretchen had had a wonderful time, but was not surprised when Heidi concluded that they could not possibly reproduce what Sylvia Compson and her associates had created. "If I had inherited an enormous mansion in the middle of the countryside, I could do it, too," she grumbled as they drove home. Gretchen refrained from pointing out that Heidi had inherited something very much like it, along with an impressive trust fund. What Heidi lacked was a group of close quilting friends she could rely upon to help run the business as Sylvia had in the Elm Creek Quilters. For all the people who admired Heidi and enjoyed her company, Gretchen was the only person she consistently relied upon.

How wonderful it would be to become a teacher at Elm Creek Quilt Camp, to work side-by-side with the marvelous woman who had inspired her in college so many years before. She envied the lucky women who would be invited to join that remarkable circle of quilters.

Then she thought some more. Well, why not? Why couldn't she be one of those lucky quilters? In fact, this job, coming along at precisely the right time, could be an answer to her prayers. She could make a break from Heidi and yet remain within the quilting world. The ad said a live-in arrangement was possible; living at Elm Creek Manor would fulfill Joe's dream of retiring to the country. The estate was large enough that they could surely find a place for him to set up a woodworking shop—perhaps in that red barn the caretaker used.

Gretchen pulled hard on the reins of her wildly galloping imagination. She had not even applied and she was already packing the moving van. It would not be easy to move from the home she and Joe had shared throughout their married life, and at their ages, it would be challenging to put down roots someplace new. When it came right down to it, Joe might not want to try. She would speak to him before allowing her hopes to rise.

But she already knew that she would gladly take the least desirable classes at the worst times of the day for the opportunity to become an Elm Creek Quilter.

At the end of the workday, she bought the magazine and hurried home to show it to Joe. "Huh," he said, scanning the ad. "What do you know."

"Is that all you're going to say?"

"Well . . ." He searched her expression for the right answer. "Looks like they're hiring in Waterford. Too bad it's hundreds of miles away. That's a long commute."

"We could move."

He shrugged. "I suppose we could."

"Joe, I want to apply for this job."

He studied her, and she knew he could tell she was serious. "Well, all right then. Give it your best shot. They'd be lucky to have you."

The best thing about Joe was that he sincerely believed that.

Gretchen had not typed a résumé in more than twenty years. She no longer even owned a working typewriter. When Joe agreed that neatly printing her application materials by hand looked unprofessional, she went in early to Quilts 'n Things every day for a week to use the store's computer unnoticed, though she suffered pangs of guilt for using company resources to obtain another job. She had many lesson plans from which to choose, while three of her favorite students wrote letters of recommendation and promised not to divulge her plans to anyone. Joe was an able photographer and had taken pictures of all Gretchen's quilts throughout the years. She wished he had not insisted that she pose with them. Compared to the glossy, perfectly lit photos in the quilt magazines, hers always looked like amateur snapshots—which, she supposed, they were. An amateur photographic record of how her quilts had remained timeless while she had aged.

She sent off her application with a hope and a prayer.

Six weeks later, just as she was beginning to wonder if her package had been lost in the mail, a young woman from Elm Creek Quilt Camp phoned to invite her for an interview. She also asked Gretchen to design an original quilt block to represent Elm Creek Quilts. Gretchen planned her design as she made supper that evening: She would take the traditional Oak Leaf block, alter it to resemble elm leaves, and place a Little Red Schoolhouse block in the center. It was so literal and obvious she worried that other applicants might come up with the same idea. She would have to rely upon her precise handiwork to give her the edge.

It was far more difficult to summon up the courage to ask for the time off so she could travel to Waterford. Gretchen did not know what to tell Heidi.

"That's easy," said Joe. "Lie."

"I couldn't do that," said Gretchen, surprised that he would suggest it. "I don't want to and I can't do it convincingly anyway."

"If you tell her you're going for a job interview, she'll either fire you or make you so miserable that you'll wish she would."

Gretchen knew that, too. She could not risk the job she had for the one she wanted. Together she and Joe worked out a solution: Gretchen would say she needed the time off for professional development to improve her teaching opportunities. That was true. Misleading and incomplete, but true.

"Professional development?" asked Heidi dubiously a few days later when Gretchen asked for the time off.

Gretchen nodded. The phrase was a holdover from her substitute teaching days, the reason many teachers had given for needing her services.

"You never needed 'professional development' before."

"I needed it," Gretchen clarified. "I just never asked for time off for it."

Heidi shrugged and granted her the days off, perhaps hoping that

Gretchen would return prepared to embrace the way of quick-pieced, rotary-cut, one-day quilts.

On the day of the interview, Joe offered to drive her to Elm Creek Manor. As much as Gretchen longed for his company and moral support, she knew three hours in the car would leave his back in painful knots. He stowed her overnight bag in the trunk, kissed her, and held her for a long time.

"Do you have your maps?" he asked, after her gentle reminder that she had a schedule to keep.

"Yes, honey, but I remember the way." She gave him one last hug and climbed into the car.

"Do you have your triple A card?"

"Yes, and my AARP card and my charge card." She buckled her seat belt. "And my driver's license and registration."

"Do you have change in case you need to call me?"

"I have four quarters in my purse," she assured him. "Don't worry so much. I'll be fine."

She blew him a kiss as she pulled out of the driveway. He followed the car to the sidewalk and was still standing there when other houses and street signs blocked her sight of him in the rearview mirror.

Gretchen had not taken such a long car trip alone in many years, not since she gave up traveling to teach at other quilting guilds. A book on tape she had checked out from the library kept her company as the car wound through the familiar, forested hills of western and central Pennsylvania until she reached Elm Creek Manor, nearly two hours before her interview. She parked in the lot behind the manor and listened to the tape until the end of the chapter, then shut it down and wondered how to fill the time. She decided to stroll through Elm Creek Manor and see if anything had changed since her visit.

Entering through the back door, Gretchen passed by the kitchen and stopped short at the sight. It was in a state of utter disarray, with cupboard doors hanging ajar, dirty pots and pans loaded into the sink, and dishes cluttering every countertop. It was nothing like the warm, busy, cozy place she remembered, and she could not imagine Sylvia Compson standing for it. She hoped the rest of the camp had not experienced a similar decline.

To her relief, the rest of the manor seemed to be in perfect order. Smiling campers passed her in the halls, chatting with one another or lost in thought as they contemplated the day's classes. A peek into the banquet hall revealed four young men clearing away the lunch dishes. One dark-haired young man seemed to be in charge, but the others seemed to follow his direction only grudgingly. If they were the new kitchen staff, that would certainly account for the state of the kitchen.

Gretchen moved on to the ballroom, her favorite place in the manor and where she had spent most of her time during her week at camp. The room bustled with activity, and every glance into a classroom revealed quilters working busily as their instructors demonstrated techniques or strolled past tables checking their students' progress. A murmur of nostalgia and longing tugged at her. *If only,* she thought. If only she could get the job, she would belong here. This was where she was meant to be. She could not bear to spend the rest of her days dissatisfied and unappreciated at Quilts 'n Things, or worse yet, set adrift with only the purchase price of her share in the store to sustain her.

She had lingered long enough in a doorway for the instructor to glance up and catch her eye. "Would you like to come in?" the dark-haired, ruddy-cheeked woman invited.

Gretchen shook her head in apology and moved on. She left the partitioned section of the ballroom for the dais where, she remembered, a few quilters would often gather to work on their projects when they were not scheduled to be in class. If she could engage them in conversation, she might be able to glean some information about the state of the camp that might help her in her interview.

Five women had pulled up chairs in a half circle and worked on projects of their own as they offered advice to a younger woman hand piecing a nine-patch block. Gretchen quickened her step; sharing some of her hand-piecing secrets would allow her to join the conversation. But as she drew closer, the quilt draped over another woman's lap drew her attention.

"That's a lovely quilt," she said, wondering why it looked so familiar.

The five women looked her way. "Thank you," said the woman Gretchen had addressed, adjusting her lap hoop to offer a better look. The sense that she was looking upon something she knew well increased, but at first Gretchen could not explain why. Of course she recognized the traditional Dogtooth Violet block, because four years earlier, she had made her own Dogtooth Violet quilt and taught it as a class for advanced quilters. Her fingers had memorized the shape of every triangle, the thickness of the folded seam allowances where they met in the middle of each edge, the precise way to hold the central star when attaching the corner triangles so that the bias edges would not stretch and distort the block.

But it was more than just the familiar block. Gretchen stifled a gasp. The plum, green, gold, and black batiks that the other woman had used were much more vivid than the muted florals Gretchen had chosen for her version, but otherwise it was the same quilt. Gretchen quickly scrutinized the other woman's features and dismissed the obvious explanation that she was a former student. Gretchen had taught the class only once; after the first time, Heidi had banned it from the schedule with the excuse that such small classes barely paid for themselves. Gretchen would have remembered if this woman had been one of her eight students.

But how was it possible that someone she had never met had duplicated her quilt so precisely, down to the size and number of the blocks and the outer border of isosceles triangles alternating in height to echo the Dogtooth Violet shapes? They were traditional patterns; she had not invented them. It was possible that someone else could have made a quilt similar to hers—but identical in every detail except for the fabric?

The woman misinterpreted her stunned silence. "It's not as difficult as it looks," the woman assured her. "The quilt pictured with the pattern was hand pieced, but I machine pieced mine."

"Pattern?" echoed Gretchen.

The woman nodded. "A friend of mine took a class at a quilt shop a few years ago. I kept calling to see if I could sign up for the next session, but they never taught that class again. The quilt shop owner said her teacher wasn't interested."

"She said that?"

The woman nodded. "So my friend gave me her pattern. I could make a copy and mail it to you if you like."

"Thank you, but that's not necessary," said Gretchen. "I designed it."

The other quilters regarded her with new interest, but the woman who had made the Dogtooth Violet quilt looked worried. "I hope you don't mind that we copied your pattern without permission."

Other quilters might, but Gretchen thought one copy was negligible—and the woman had certainly tried to enroll in her class. "I don't mind at all. In fact, I'm pleased that you liked the pattern so much. Your fabric selections are so different from my own that at first I didn't even recognize it as my design."

"Do you have a book?" asked one of the other quilters. "I'd buy it for more patterns like this one. This is exactly the kind of quilt I like: traditional, but versatile enough that I can spice it up with the fabrics I like best."

The others nodded in agreement. "I'm afraid not," said Gretchen.

"You should really think about doing one."

Gretchen smiled. If it were that easy, she wouldn't have been so discouraged by Heidi's refusal to publish her patterns under the Quilts 'n Things line. "Maybe someday."

"Tell us about your quilt," urged another of the women. "What inspired you? How did you get the points so perfect? Did you use foundation paper piecing?"

"I hand pieced mine," Gretchen told them, and she went on to explain how she had made her quilt, from the selection of the block, which she had first seen in a collection of antique patterns, to the choice of the perfect floral calicos and solids, to the layout and piecing of the top. She felt as if she were back in the classroom again, using the new Dogtooth Violet quilt as a visual aid to help explain her process. Midway through her impromptu presentation, the women looked past her as if momentarily distracted. Without breaking the thread of conversation, Gretchen glanced over her shoulder and spotted an elderly woman and a younger, bearded man pausing to watch as they crossed the ballroom a few yards away. She recognized Sylvia Compson at once, but since Heidi had insisted they keep a low profile during their week at Elm Creek manner—and since Gretchen had felt too guilty about their spy mission to introduce herself to Sylvia as a former student—Gretchen doubted Sylvia recognized her. With a pang of worry, she considered ending her talk rather than look like a show-off, but she could not be so abrupt to her new acquaintances. She took a breath and persevered, hoping Sylvia would not think Gretchen had made herself too comfortable at Elm Creek Manor, that she presumed too much.

After she heard Sylvia and her companion continue on their way, Gretchen wrapped up her little talk and bade the quilters good-bye. She left the manor, returned to her car, and sat in the driver's seat watching campers pass in and out of the back door, reflecting upon the chance encounter with a beautiful quilt she had, in a sense, helped create. But how different it appeared from her own quilt and from those of her eight Dogtooth Violet students! She had encouraged them to use floral calicoes and solids in class, and her most daring student had only ventured as far as a geometric, tone-on-tone palette. As a result, her students' quilts resembled differently hued versions of her own rather than an entirely new expression of their individual creativity. What might they have created if she had not steered them toward her own preferences? What might she have learned from them?

Had her resentment of Heidi's rejection of her favorite traditional fabrics blinded her to an entire world of artistic possibilities?

For years, she had clung stubbornly to her favorite blocks and fabrics as if she had to fight Heidi for the right to use them. Would they have remained her favorites if not for that? Would Gretchen's tastes have evolved naturally over time if she had not felt obligated to defend her first choices?

Had her refusal to capitulate to Heidi allowed her to stagnate as an artist?

It was an uncomfortable thought, but she forced herself to face it. For years, she had defined her quilts in opposition to Heidi's instead of striking out on her own independent path. Her designs were fine; the chance encounter in the manor had proven that. But what might her quilts be today if not for her relationship with Heidi? In the very act of struggling to avoid Heidi's influence, she had allowed Heidi's tastes to define her own.

With still more than an hour to go before her interview, Gretchen ate the sandwich and apple she had packed for lunch, wishing she had remembered to bring along something to drink and that she had not left home so early. With too much time to fill, her thoughts bounded from her new uncertainty about her growth as a quilter to the heightened importance of her forthcoming interview until her stomach was in knots.

A continued tour of the manor seemed out of the question, not that Gretchen really believed she was likely to run into anything else as disconcerting as she had already experienced that day. Still, she could not remain in the car working herself into a state of nerves or she would be in no condition to meet the Elm Creek Quilters. She left the car, shutting the door firmly behind her, and strode briskly away from the manor, across the bridge over the creek, past the red banked barn, and into the orchard, where already fruit was ripening. The fragrance of the apples and the sound of birdsong restored her sense of calm, and she resolved to put forth her best effort in the interview.

She prepared for their questions as she wandered among the rows of Red Delicious and Jonathan apple trees, rehearsing possible answers and points she intended to raise if the interviewers did not. With still more than a half hour to go, she returned to the manor in time to witness the back door open with a bang and the bearded man from the ballroom emerge, briefcase in hand. He strode across the parking lot and climbed into a newer model blue car, shaking his head in either disgust or disbelief. She instinctively turned aside as he drove past, but he did not appear to even notice her, much less recognize her as the presumptuous woman making herself too much at home at the front of an impromptu Elm Creek Quilt Camp class.

With any luck, Sylvia would have the same reaction. Gretchen stopped by her car for her purse and the accordion file containing her Elm Creek Quilts block, steeled herself, and returned to the manor. When she passed the kitchen, she glimpsed two of the young men from the banquet hall scrubbing pots halfheartedly while another swept the floor. Her fingers itched to take the broom and demonstrate the proper technique, but she left him to it.

Assuming that one of the Elm Creek Quilters would expect to meet her at the front door, she headed toward the front foyer, but just before she reached it, she heard voices coming from a room on her left. She glanced through the open doorway and discovered the Elm Creek Quilters gathered within a charming Victorian parlor. She paused and rapped twice on the open door.

"Hello," she greeted them, smiling as they looked up from an intense conversation. "I'm Gretchen Hartley. I've come for an interview. I realize I'm a bit early. Should I wait outside?"

"No, come right in," said a brunette in her thirties, whom Gretchen recognized as Sarah McClure, one of the founders of Elm Creek Quilts. "Our last interview ended early."

She said the last with a disapproving frown for an attractive blonde woman at least ten years her senior, who responded with a pout of injured innocence.

"Please sit down," said Sylvia Compson, gesturing to an armchair on the other side of a coffee table from the Elm Creek Quilters. Gretchen nodded and took her seat. She waited nervously during the few moments the Elm Creek Quilters took to rearrange papers and files. Before long, Sarah looked around the group, noted that everyone was ready to begin, and turned to Gretchen with a smile and a request to describe her quilting experience.

At sixty-six, Gretchen had a lot of history to share. She told them about the old days, when she felt as if she was the only woman who quilted anymore, and how the quilting revival had brought her new opportunities to teach and lecture. She described the founding of Quilts 'n Things, carefully selecting details to avoid any appearance of conflict with Heidi. She reflected upon how she had traveled to quilt guilds, conferences, and trade shows—to teach and to learn, to observe shifting trends in the modern quilting world, and to pass on the traditions that previous generations had bequeathed her. This wealth of experience made her uniquely qualified to become an Elm Creek Quilter.

Or at least that was what she tried to tell them. Joe had made her promise to promote herself as if she were praising her best friend, but Gretchen had been brought up to believe that no one liked a woman who bragged, that confidence was often mistaken for arrogance, and that it was always best to err on the side of modesty and allow others to sing her praises on her behalf. She struggled to articulate how much she had to offer Elm Creek Quilts, but to her own ears her voice sounded meek and humble, as if she felt undeserving of the honor of their presence, as if she knew she were only Heidi Mueller's cleaning lady suffering delusions of grandeur. For the first time since childhood, she wished she were more like Heidi, who never allowed anyone to see her disturbed by a moment of self-doubt.

"I'm familiar with the Quilts 'n Things pattern line," said Sarah. "Have you published any of your designs?"

"No." Compelled to be completely honest, Gretchen added, "I have submitted designs to my business partner, who makes the selections, but she didn't believe my quilts fit in with the rest of the line."

"And yet your patterns are being distributed by your former students and enjoyed by others," remarked Sylvia. "Or so I overheard earlier today. I'm surprised you didn't mention it."

Gretchen shrugged. "I didn't think that counted. And—I didn't want to brag."

Several Elm Creek Quilters exchanged smiles of amusement. "This is an occasion when bragging is perfectly acceptable," Sarah told her.

"I understand," said Gretchen. "But bragging isn't something that comes naturally to me."

"That much is apparent," said Sylvia, the corners of her mouth turning in the barest hint of a smile. "In fact, you must be the most inappropriately unassuming quilter I've ever met. You talk about how the quilting revival gave you so many opportunities, and yet never once do you point out that without quilters such as yourself nurturing and passing on the traditions of quilting, that revival never would have come to be. Elm Creek Quilt Camp itself likely never would have existed without quilters like you."

For a moment, the praise from her former teacher left Gretchen speechless. "And quilters like you," she said to Sylvia when she had recovered.

Sylvia nodded her thanks, and a look of understanding passed between them.

"That's all well and good," said the pretty woman with the blond curls, "but let's not overstate things."

"By all means, let's hear it," declared Gwen, whom Gretchen recalled as an outspoken woman inclined to make innovative, artsy quilts of the sort Heidi preferred. "You certainly haven't minced words with any of our other applicants. Why start now?"

"Because she made our last applicant flee for his life," said Judy, gesturing toward the door.

Diane raised her hands in appeasement. "I admit I've challenged our applicants. We should. We're Elm Creek Quilts. We ought to have the most rigorous hiring procedure around."

Sylvia regarded Diane sternly over the rims of her glasses. "Thorough questioning is important, dear, but so are respect and diplomacy."

"Of course," said Diane, a faint flush appearing on her cheeks as she studied a copy of Gretchen's résumé. "I agree that you deserve some credit for keeping quilting alive through a long dry spell, Gretchen, but isn't it true that your style never really left the late seventies?"

Gwen shook her head and sighed.

"Diane," warned Sarah. "Tread carefully."

Gretchen forced herself to remain perfectly still in her chair, against her better instincts that were shouting at her to follow the previous applicant's example and flee for the door. "If you're suggesting my quilts are traditional, I accept that. Willingly. But I must add that my traditional quilts and traditional ways appeal to many quilters. My students' achievements and my full lecture schedule are proof of that."

"You say traditional," said Diane. "I say old-fashioned. If I had not been warned to use tact, I might have said dowdy or frumpy instead. I definitely would have said boring."

"That is quite enough," said Sylvia. "Do I have to ask you to leave?"

"I won't leave before asking her about this." Diane pulled a sheet of paper from the file on her lap. Gretchen could not read what was printed upon it, but it brought uncertainty to the Elm Creek Quilters' expressions. "You might not like my tactics, but you have to admit this raises doubts about her qualifications to teach for us—and her truthfulness."

Gretchen could not imagine what she was talking about. Every detail of her résumé was true, if understated. Her students' letters of recommendation praised her so highly that she had almost been too embarrassed to include them in her packet.

"Even if you don't care for my quilts," said Gretchen, breaking into the sudden silence, "I hope you can agree that my artistic style and my teaching ability are two very different things. My skills are sound whether or not you like what I do with them. I have taught for a very long time, and I've taught many different types of students successfully."

"Not everyone thinks so."

Gretchen stared at Diane in confusion. What on earth could she mean?

"Allow me to share a few excerpts from an employer evaluation." Diane frowned at the page in her hand. "'Mrs. Hartley runs her classes in a strict, didactic fashion and is impatient with questions. . . . She is short-tempered and sarcastic with anyone who suggests modernizing her patterns or techniques. . . . Her classes are the least popular of those offered at our shop and the drop-off in attendance each week is significant.' Shall I go on?"

Gretchen felt tears welling up in her eyes. The letter had said "our shop." *Heidi* had written those hateful things about her. "You called Quilts 'n Things?" she managed to say. "You told them I'm applying for this job?"

Diane regarded her incredulously, and Gretchen realized that the first words from her lips should have been an emphatic denial. Now it appeared that she agreed with the evaluation and was distressed only because the Elm Creek Quilters had discovered the truth.

"Of course we called the shop," said Diane. "We had to check your references. You only had two, and everyone from your era retired from the Ambridge School District a long time ago."

Gretchen blinked back the tears and cleared her throat. "I have no idea why my employer said those things, unless she's angry that I'm looking for another job. All I can tell you is that those—those things are simply not true."

"Indeed," said Sylvia dryly. "One wonders why she has kept you on so many years if you are so dreadful a teacher."

"One wonders something else," said Sarah, studying Diane. "Why would you of all people want to undermine Gretchen's chances for this job? You're an old-school quilter yourself. For years you've been telling us to offer more hand-piecing classes, more hand-quilting workshops. I've heard you say that only quilts made entirely by hand are true quilts. And here we have an applicant who is everything you say you want. Why aren't you begging us to offer her the job?"

"That's right," said Summer, her expression taking on a new light of understanding. "You're not only nasty to the quilters you don't want to hire. You're nasty to everyone."

Warily, Diane looked around the circle of suspicious quilters. "I'm just a nasty person."

"True," cried Gwen. "You heard her admit it. I didn't say it this time. She said it herself."

Sylvia sighed, rose from her chair, and sat beside Diane. "The jig is up, my dear," she said gently, taking Diane's hand. "Why don't you tell us what this has been all about?"

Diane maintained her expression of wide-eyed innocence for only a moment before it crumpled into distress. "I don't want to hire anyone."

"Of course, dear." Sylvia patted Diane's hand. "I understand."

Gretchen didn't, and by the look of things, neither did the other Elm Creek Quilters, who seemed to have forgotten her. She was so relieved that the subject had shifted from Heidi's malicious letter that she sat motionless in her chair rather than remind them of her presence.

Diane ran her index finger below her eyelids to prevent her mascara from smearing. "It was working," she told Sylvia defensively.

Sylvia shook her head, smiling in amused sympathy. "No, dear, I don't believe it was."

"I get it," said Summer. "You thought that if we couldn't hire any replacement instructors, Judy and I wouldn't leave."

"You wouldn't," retorted Diane. "You'd never leave knowing how much we still need you. I've told you both a hundred times that you can't be replaced, and you won't be replaced, if I have anything to do with it."

"I'm sorry," said Judy to Diane. "I've accepted another job. I'll miss all of you very much, but I'm still going."

"And I start school next semester," said Summer. "I couldn't postpone my enrollment, not after they accepted my application past the usual deadline."

"Brilliant strategy," remarked Gwen. "Too bad it was doomed to fail on the grounds of sheer silliness. You do realize you've left us worse off than before, right?"

"What could be worse than Summer and Judy leaving us?" said Diane.

The dark-haired teacher who had invited Gretchen into her classroom sighed. "Judy and Diane leaving us with two openings on our staff that can't be filled because you've insulted and intimidated every applicant."

"I'm still interested in the job," said Gretchen.

All eyes fixed on her.

She shifted uncomfortably in her chair. "If . . . if I'm still in the running. I know my employer gave me a terrible review, but—"

"Oh, please," said Diane. "Anyone can see she's just resentful that you were invited for an interview and she wasn't. How stupid does she think we are?"

Gretchen stared at her. "Heidi applied for the job?"

"We really shouldn't discuss the other applicants," Sarah broke in quickly. "I think we've covered everything, don't you?" The other Elm Creek Quilters nodded. Diane sniffed miserably, accepting the box of tissues Gwen passed her. "Is there anything you'd like to add, Gretchen?"

"Well, there's my block—"

"Of course. Please, show us."

Gretchen quickly brought out the Elm Creek Quilts block she had created and handed it to Sarah. They passed it around the circle, nodding and murmuring in appreciation—even Diane, who had abandoned her show of disapproval. When the block had traveled all the way around the circle, Sarah asked if anyone had any more questions.

"I have one," said Sylvia. "You remind me of one of my star pupils from very early in my career. She was also named Gretchen, but her last name was not Hartley. You wouldn't be her, by any chance, would you?"

Gretchen glowed. Sylvia had called her a star pupil. "Hartley is my married name. I was in your home economics course in college."

Summer stared at Sylvia. "You taught home ec?"

"Only because they wouldn't hire me to teach quilting in the art department." Sylvia fixed her gaze on Gretchen. "Why didn't you mention that you're one of my former students?"

Gretchen fidgeted and gestured to the copy of her résumé in Sylvia's hand. "I described my educational background in some detail."

"Yes," said Gwen, amused, "and you somehow managed to omit that one important fact."

"I honestly didn't think Sylvia would remember me," confessed Gretchen.

"I didn't want to seem as if I was taking advantage of an earlier acquaintance, especially since it was so long ago. It didn't seem fair to the other applicants."

"All's fair in love, war, and job interviews," said Sylvia, smiling faintly. "In the future, I hope you won't be so reluctant to sing your own praises."

Gretchen smiled back, her spirits rising. "I'll remember that."

After that the interview wrapped up quickly. Sarah waited while Gretchen retrieved her overnight bag from the car and then led her upstairs to a comfortable suite on the second floor where she would spend the night.

After unpacking her things and hanging up her change of clothes in the wardrobe, Gretchen returned downstairs to call Joe from the campers' phone in the converted ballroom. She passed a white-haired woman perhaps not quite ten years older than herself sewing in an armchair in the foyer.

Suddenly the woman set down her work. "I'm going to flunk out of quilt camp. I just know it."

Gretchen paused. "I don't think you need to worry about that," she said. "The teachers here don't grade your work. All they ask is that you try."

"That's the problem. They'll think I haven't been trying very hard when they see this Rose of Sharon block. They'll think I've been sleeping in class."

"Nonsense. They'll think no such thing." The woman looked unconvinced, so Gretchen added, "Do you want some help?"

"Yes, please. If you have time."

Gretchen didn't, not really. She wanted to call Joe right away so she would have time to properly prepare for dinner with the Elm Creek Quilters, where they would surely continue to evaluate her even though the official interview had ended. It was too bad she had not run into this woman before her interview, when she had so much time to fill. "I'm in no hurry," she said, crossing the foyer.

The woman handed her the Rose of Sharon block, and Gretchen quickly spotted what had so frustrated her: a slight bulge in the side of an appliqué leaf where a perfectly smooth curve should have been. "Your stitches are excellent," remarked Gretchen, inspecting the underside of the block. "The problem must be in the preparation of the appliqué. From the feel of it, I'm guessing you used freezer paper. Did you place it wax-side up on the wrong side of the fabric and iron the seam allowance down so it stuck to the wax?"

The woman nodded. "That's right."

"You might want to try placing it wax-side down instead and ironing it so the whole appliqué sticks to the wrong side of the fabric."

"Wax-side down?" echoed the woman, puzzled.

"That's right. Then take a little glue stick and glue the seam allowance to the smooth side of the freezer paper. Your edges will be smoother and they'll stay put until your appliqué is sewn in place on the background fabric. When you want to remove the paper, just cut through the back as you ordinarily would, and press the block with a damp cloth between the block and your iron to loosen up the glue. The paper will come right off."

Gretchen returned the block to the woman, who was staring at her. "That's very clever."

"I've found it to be a very useful technique."

"I have honestly never heard of that method, not in all my years of quilting."

"I didn't invent it," said Gretchen, startled by a curious look in the woman's eye. "I just picked it up along the way."

"Even so," said the woman, rising. "Even so. Thank you very much, Gretchen."

Gretchen nodded a good-bye and watched as the white-haired woman disappeared into the parlor where the Elm Creek Quilters were still conferring, or perhaps comforting Diane. Only then did Gretchen realize that she had not told the woman her name. She was almost completely certain she had not.

Curious, she almost knocked on the parlor door on the way to the ballroom but decided against it. As she hurried off to tell Joe about her day, she thought of Diane and her desperate, misguided, and rather poorly conceived plan to prevent her friends from leaving. How wonderful it must be to work with friends who loved you enough to risk utter foolishness to keep you close.

The place where one worked and the work one did was not enough. Without the company of good friends, even the most interesting job could become drudgery, something to be endured rather than enjoyed. No wonder Gretchen had been dissatisfied with Quilts 'n Things, a place that most quilters regarded as the mortal world's closest equivalent to heaven.

Whatever else happened, Gretchen knew she could not go back to work for Heidi. Their partnership had fractured beyond repair, and it was long past time for Gretchen to move on. She had made her decision and nothing would change her mind. She did not need to talk it over with Joe, who had been encouraging her to quit for years. She did not need to rehearse her departure speech, or spend hours writing and rewriting a letter of resignation, or worry about what other people would think of her or how Heidi would explain things to their customers after she was gone.

Tomorrow she would stop by Quilts 'n Things on her way home and break the news to Heidi.

Whatever the Elm Creek Quilters decided, Gretchen's days at Quilts 'n Things were over.

Chapter Six
The Elm Creek Quilters

Perhaps to convince Diane that nothing could prevent them from leaving, Summer and Judy wanted to begin discussing the candidates right away, but Sylvia thought they needed some time alone to reflect—and in some cases, to allow their tempers to cool. She announced that they would meet in the parlor the following day between supper and the campers' evening program to deliberate.

Before dismissing them, Sylvia instructed the Elm Creek Quilters to evaluate the applicants based upon everything they had presented since the selection process began, and not only upon the applicants' performances in the interview. It was fair to say that, thanks to Diane, the applicants would have fared better in a classroom with only the questions and problems of real students to confront them.

"We must consider all of the applicants' qualities," said Sylvia. "Not only how many years they've quilted, or how much teaching experience they have, or how many awards and accolades their quilts have won, but all of those things, and more. Why do they want to work here? What will they bring to our circle of quilters, beyond their technical expertise? How will they fit in with us, and how will they complement one another? What will their presence here mean for the future of Elm Creek Quilt Camp? Our choice will say as much about us and what we want for Elm Creek Quilts as it says about those we decide to hire."

"Can't we just draw straws?" grumbled Diane.

Sylvia smiled. "No, dear. I'm afraid there's too much at stake."

Heidi's eyes went wide. "You can't mean that."

"I do," said Gretchen. Already the office felt like a stranger's. "Please ask your daughter to contact me about purchasing my share of the business. If she isn't interested, I'll find someone else."

"But—but what about the shop? Who will cover for you?"

"I'm sure one of our part-timers would be glad to go full-time."

Heidi's expression was both lost and trapped. "But we've been together so long."

"Perhaps too long." Gretchen shouldered her purse and rose from her chair. "Good-bye, Heidi."

She turned and left the office with her head held high, prouder of herself than she had been in many years.

But she could not deny the small ache of regret that a longtime friendship was over, and that something that had begun with so much promise had ended in disappointment.

❧

The morning after her disastrous interview, Karen woke to a soft rapping on the door to find sunlight streaming in through the window. She sat up with a gasp and frantically searched the bed beside her for the baby. Lucas was not there, nor could she remember getting up in the night to nurse him.

"Good morning, honey." The door eased open and Nate entered, carrying a tray. She caught the aroma of coffee.

"Where's Lucas?"

"Downstairs in the kitchen."

"Alone?" She threw back the covers.

"No, honey, stay in bed. He's not alone. Ethan is keeping an eye on him."

"Our four-year-old is keeping an eye on the baby?"

"Just for a minute. They're eating oatmeal. They're fine."

"When did Lucas wake up?"

"Around four, four-fifteen."

"I didn't hear him. He was in his crib crying for"—she glanced at the clock—"four hours, and I didn't hear him?"

Nate shook his head. "He wasn't crying. I got up with him and gave him a sippy cup. He fell asleep and I put him back in his crib. He slept until about a half hour ago."

"You're telling me he willingly went back to sleep without nursing?"

"And now he's downstairs having breakfast with his brother. I think you're up to date now, just in time for your own breakfast." He unfolded the legs of the tray and set it across her lap. "I made waffles."

"Breakfast in bed." She sat up as Nate placed a pillow behind her back. "Looks like the sufferings of a guilty conscience."

"You could just say thank you."

"Thank you," she said, after a moment. "But you know this doesn't make everything all right."

"I know." He sat down on the edge of the bed. "What will?"

She studied the tray he had prepared for her—waffles in maple syrup, coffee with soymilk, veggie faux sausage, and orange juice. "I don't know."

"I'm sorry I ruined your shot at the job."

She shrugged and picked up her fork. "They haven't said no yet." But she knew it was only a matter of time.

"Daddy!" came Ethan's shout from downstairs.

"Da-Da!" echoed Lucas.

"I think you're being summoned."

Nate nodded and turned to go, but already they heard footsteps scampering on the stairs. Nate snatched up the tray and moved it to the dresser just in time to avoid the two little boys who ran into the room and hurled themselves at Karen. "Mama," cried Lucas, delighted, as he and his brother tumbled over her, burying her in hugs and kisses.

"Hello, Lucas. Good morning, Ethan," she said, hugging Lucas and tousling Ethan's hair. "Did you have a good night?"

"Pretty good. Are you still mad at Daddy?"

She glanced up at Nate, who looked back at her anxiously. "Not so much. And how about you, pumpkin?" She kissed Lucas on his soft cheek. "You were such a good boy, going back to sleep for Daddy so nicely."

"Good," agreed Lucas, snuggling closer for another kiss. He patted her chest. "Muk."

"Oh, muk, is it?" she growled, tickling the boys, who shrieked in delight and tried to get away. "That's all I am to you people: milk in a shirt!"

Nate stood outside the play, closed off from them, watching, but Karen did not draw him in.

※

Mrs. Stonebridge kept her promise to stay at Ocean View Hills as long as at least one friend remained, but two days after Mrs. Blum left, her son arrived to take her to a new residence near his home in Santa Cruz.

Mrs. Stonebridge was in her eighties now. She had acquired a walker and white hair and aches and pains in her hands that made quilting a challenge, but to Maggie she was the same admirable, diplomatic leader, sorting out differences and disagreements with grace and humor. She had comforted her departing friends and had organized a round-robin quilt project among the Courtyard Quilters. In the days leading up to their separation, each quilter sewed a sixteen-inch block in her favorite pattern. Before the first of many departures, they exchanged blocks. Each quilter would add a border of her own favorite blocks to the center she had received, and on the last day of the month, she would mail the growing quilt top to the next quilter in the circle. After each quilter had added a concentric border to every other quilter's center block, the tops would be returned to their owners in their new residences, a keepsake of dear friends.

In this way their circle of quilters would endure even though they could no longer gather every morning in their favorite chairs by the windows with the view of the courtyard garden.

When it was time for Mrs. Stonebridge to go, Maggie escorted her outside and waited while her son loaded her belongings in the car. "I'll miss you," she said, hugging the older woman. She was startled by how thin and fragile Mrs. Stonebridge felt in her arms.

Mrs. Stonebridge patted her on the cheek. "You take care of yourself, my dear."

Maggie nodded and blinked back tears as Mrs. Stonebridge's son helped her into the front seat. Just as her son started the car, Mrs. Stonebridge rolled down the window. "I forgot to tell you," she called over the noise of the engine. "Guess who's going to be down the hall from me?"

"I don't know," Maggie replied. "Who?"

"Lenore Hicks."

The car pulled away from the curb. "Don't get between her and pie," Maggie shouted.

Mrs. Stonebridge laughed and waved to her through the window until the car turned onto the main avenue and drove out of sight.

🦋

Anna did not hear from Gordon for almost a week after the macaroni and cheese dinner at his apartment. She wondered if he had been waiting for her to apologize or if it had simply taken him that long to discover she had left.

She had her answer when she returned home from working as the lead chef at a banquet for the provost, who had requested her by name. Gordon's voice on the answering machine was clipped and irritable. "You were inexcusably rude to sneak out like that without even telling us you were going. Theresa's feelings were hurt. We may not be able to cook like you, but we did our best. Call me if you want to apologize."

Anna didn't. She erased the message and went across the hall to share the banquet leftovers with Jeremy. She hoped Summer had told him whether the Elm Creek Quilters had made their decision, but he had not heard anything.

Two days later, she discovered another answering machine message: "Anna, kitten. I'm not mad anymore. Give me a call and let's talk."

Once again she hit the erase button and did not return his message. She was growing accustomed to his absence and found she did not mind it.

As the days passed, his messages became more worried, more forlorn. "I miss you," he said once, and, "I'm sorry." He did not elaborate, and she suspected he did not know exactly why he ought to be sorry, just that saying so might bring her back.

Maybe it would. He seemed genuinely remorseful, if not for the right reasons. But how would she know for certain unless she gave him another chance?

One afternoon, she came home from work to discover that Gordon had visited her apartment in her absence. He had left a dozen roses in a vase on the kitchen table and a heartfelt note asking her to call and let him know she was all right. In the postscript, he added the last lines of the sonnet he had written her: "Thou shalt in me, livelier than elsewhere, Anna's image see." The memory of a happier occasion pained her.

The sight of the roses had startled her so much that she had left the apartment door ajar, and as she stood gazing at the note and wondering what to do, Jeremy peered in from the hallway. "Nice flowers."

Quickly Anna returned the card to the envelope. "No one's ever given me a dozen red roses before."

"Very romantic."

"You don't have to be sarcastic. He's trying."

"Have you called to thank him?"

"Not yet."

"Are you going to?"

"I don't know." Anna tossed the note onto the table and touched a rose petal. "He hasn't paid so much attention to me in months."

"Take my advice and don't call. That bouquet doesn't mean anything. Anyone can buy flowers. I could buy you flowers."

"It's not just the flowers," Anna insisted. "Gordon cares about me. He gave me a gift—a gift from the heart. He wrote me a sonnet. How many guys do you know who write their girlfriends a sonnet?"

"None," said Jeremy flatly. "And I say that having met Gordon. Let me see this alleged sonnet. I bet it came out of a greeting card."

"I don't have it on me," said Anna, flustered. "Anyway, it's private."

He gestured for her to hand it over. "Come on."

She hesitated, but he was resolute, and she wanted to prove to him that Gordon had written her a poem. Unless Theresa had written it—but she squelched that thought and went to her bedroom for the poem. Reluctantly, she gave it to Jeremy, who unfolded the page and read the words with a deepening frown.

"It's not from a greeting card," she told him.

"I know," he said, and he looked as if he were sorry he had asked. "It's by Sir Philip Sidney, a sixteenth-century English poet. Gordon just changed the woman's name from Stella to Anna. Every undergraduate English major knows this poem."

Anna felt faint. She had been seconds away from calling Gordon to apologize and forgive him everything.

The Elm Creek Quilters were so divided in their opinions about the applicants that the evening of deliberation Sylvia had arranged quickly proved to be insufficient. If they could have chosen by a simple majority vote, they could have selected their two finalists within a day, but Sylvia insisted their decision be unanimous. It would not do to admit someone into their circle of quilters unless everyone could give the newcomer an unqualified welcome.

"But that doesn't mean Summer and I aren't leaving if we can't agree," said Judy.

"I know that," said Diane so quickly that they all knew Judy had interrupted her in the midst of plotting an interminable filibuster.

Within four days they reached their first decision: Karen Wise would not be one of the two finalists. Diane thought that anyone incapable of finding a baby-sitter for a job interview was not resourceful enough to handle the various crises Elm Creek Quilters faced every day. The others considered this view too harsh, but they agreed that although Karen was a fine quilter, she was less experienced than the other applicants. Elm Creek Quilt Camp students expected a great deal from their classes and workshops, and it might be unfair to them—and to Karen—to give them a novice teacher.

"She's never taught quilting, not even at a quilt shop," said Diane, echoing an earlier concern. "I'm not sure why we invited her to an interview."

Because of her letter, Sylvia explained. No other applicant had so perfectly articulated the spirit of Elm Creek Quilts. Sylvia had thought Karen deserved to make her case for that reason alone. If she had taught even a single class at a quilt shop, Sylvia might be willing to take a chance on her, but her teaching experience was too different from what she would face at quilt camp. Karen was simply not ready.

"In a few years, perhaps, but not now," said Sylvia, and with some regret, placed Karen's portfolio on the pile with the other eliminated applicants.

Everyone loved Anna, and not only for the delicious cookies. "I ranked her first out of all the applicants," said Bonnie. "If we ever open a quilt shop here in the manor, her experience at her aunt's store will be invaluable."

"Her aunt's store went out of business," reminded Diane.

"I'm sure that wasn't Anna's fault."

"Gretchen has more relevant quilt shop experience than Anna," said Sarah, who privately was not convinced that the manor ought to include a retail store. "But our most immediate need is for teachers. Anna has taught quilting, but not recently."

"Anna has other talents," remarked Sylvia.

The Elm Creek Quilters exchanged questioning looks. Then Sarah caught on. "Oh, yes. Please. Hire her today."

Summer looked uncertain. "But she applied for a teaching position. Would she be insulted if we asked her to take a different job?"

"It won't hurt to ask," said Gwen.

"Indeed," said Sylvia. "She can always refuse."

She set Anna's portfolio aside.

The Elm Creek Quilters needed another week to decide the fates of the remaining three candidates, who were so well-qualified in different ways that it was difficult to choose. All three had years of teaching experience, each had designed original quilt patterns, each had developed a following that might help boost camp enrollment. Each possessed qualities that made the Elm Creek Quilters eager to welcome them into their circle of quilters, and each raised questions about how they would fit in.

For all Maggie's skill and depth of knowledge of quilt history, she was not very versatile in her style. Would she be willing and able to teach other classes if their campers were not interested in reproducing the Harriet Findley Birch quilt?

"She has taught other classes," said Sarah, reading from Maggie's résumé. "Machine and hand appliqué. Machine and hand piecing. Hand quilting. The list goes on."

"So does her list of upcoming speaking engagements," said Diane. "How committed to us can she be if she's going to be traveling all the time? Are we ever going to get to know her if she just shows up to teach her camp classes and then heads out to a quilt guild as soon as camp is over?"

"I didn't get the impression that she intended to continue her exhausting travel schedule," said Sylvia. "I believe that's why working for us appeals to her so much."

"Anyway, Russell McIntyre has the same problem," said Sarah.

Everyone acknowledged that this was true, and the debate turned to him. All agreed that Russell was an accomplished art quilter who had developed his own style and techniques. As a man in a predominantly women's field, he would indeed bring a new and valuable perspective to Elm Creek Quilts. But he seemed to know very little about quilting history and traditions, and out of all the applicants, he had been the only one to fail Agnes's test.

"It wasn't a fair test in his case," reasoned Gwen, who had placed Russell at the top of her list. "He doesn't do hand appliqué. We knew that."

"He didn't fail the test by not knowing how to help me," said Agnes, removing her pink-tinted glasses and rubbing her eyes wearily. "He failed by not wanting to help."

"But he was on his way out, and he wanted to leave as quickly as possible," said Gwen. "Diane had insulted him."

"Diane insulted everyone," Judy pointed out. "Russell was the only one to leave before the interview was over. He was the only one who refused to help Agnes."

"But . . ." said Gwen, then shrugged. "Never mind. You're right."

Gretchen, on the other hand, had soared through Agnes's test. Not only had she been willing to take the time to help a stranger, she had offered a solution Agnes had never heard of before. "We should hire her at once," said Agnes. "She has so much to offer our students."

"But for how long?" asked Diane. "I like that she's a traditionalist. No one loves quilting by hand more than I do. But isn't Gretchen getting a little close to retirement to make such a drastic career change?"

"It's not that drastic," said Judy. "She's been quilting and teaching for decades."

"Maybe too many decades," said Diane, sparing a furtive glance for the elder Elm Creek Quilters.

"We can't discriminate on the basis of age," said Sarah.

Diane held up her hands. "I'm just saying we need to think of how long the people we choose are likely to stay with us."

Agnes regarded her coolly. "I'm older than Gretchen. Is my job in jeopardy?"

"Of course not," said Diane. "Forget I mentioned it."

But they could not forget, and as the intermittent discussion wore on, the Elm Creek Quilters pieced together a solution with as much care as if it were a quilt they hoped would become a cherished heirloom.

Their first unanimous vote came in favor of Maggie, whose strengths as a quilter, teacher, designer, and historian set her slightly ahead of the other two. After that, their second choice became clear. Most of Gretchen's strengths overlapped with Maggie's, but Russell possessed other skills and experiences Maggie did not. As a pair they complemented each other well, better than Maggie and Gretchen did.

The second unanimous vote came nearly three weeks after the interviews. Once Sylvia was assured all were at peace with their decision, she instructed Sarah to call the applicants.

When the phone rang, Maggie eagerly picked up, hoping the caller was Russell. Since his visit the previous weekend, he had called almost every evening from the road. His quilt guild tour was winding down and he was supposed to return home that afternoon. She had not expected him to call until later, but she was glad he had. She wanted to tell him that she had decided to accept his invitation to visit him in Seattle the following week. She was not sure why she had hesitated, prompting him to add that she should think about it and let him know. No hard feelings if she couldn't come. The guest room would be ready either way.

But the voice on the line belonged to a woman. "Maggie?"

"Yes?"

"This is Sarah McClure from Elm Creek Quilts."

"Oh, of course." Here it came: the moment of rejection she had dreaded. "How are you?"

"Fine, thanks. I'm calling with good news. On behalf of all the Elm Creek Quilters, I'd like to offer you the teaching position. We would be delighted if you would join our faculty."

"I—" Maggie sat down. "Really? You're really offering me the job? But I did so badly in the interview. Are you sure?"

Sarah laughed. "Are you trying to talk me out of it? Of course we're sure. You won't need to begin teaching until the new camp season in March, but we'd like to have you out here no later than January. Does that sound all right?"

"That sounds fine. Better than fine. It sounds wonderful." Then Maggie thought of Russell, and suddenly relocating to Pennsylvania lost its appeal. "I don't suppose you could tell me who the other new teacher is?"

"I really shouldn't, not until I've notified the other applicants."

Maggie felt a thrill of delight. She was the first new teacher Elm Creek Quilts had called.

She hesitated only a moment, a moment in which she considered Russell's qualifications for the job and decided that if the Elm Creek Quilters had chosen her, they surely also intended to make an offer to someone like Russell. Even if they did not, she could not afford to throw away the job offer of a lifetime all because of one marvelous weekend and a dozen phone calls with a man she had only just met. No matter how wonderful he seemed. No matter how much she already liked him. No matter how readily he laughed.

She thanked Sarah and told her she would begin planning her move to Pennsylvania. Sarah promised to be in touch.

As soon as Maggie hung up, she dialed Russell's number. The line was busy.

Maggie smiled as she replaced the receiver. Very likely, he was on the line with Sarah McClure at that very moment.

❧

Russell heard the phone ringing as he unlocked the front door. Dropping his bags on the porch, he bounded inside and snatched up the phone just as the answering machine clicked on.

"Hold on a moment," he called over the outgoing message, fumbling for the off switch. "Okay, sorry about that. Hello?"

"Hello, Russell McIntyre?"

A woman, but not Maggie. "Yes?" he said, disappointed. He should have let the machine get it.

"This is Sarah McClure from Elm Creek Quilts."

"Oh, hi." He had never expected to hear from them after storming out of the interview. The memory of it still embarrassed him.

"I'm calling with good news. After considering all the candidates, we've decided to offer you one of the teaching positions. You won't be expected to teach until the new camp season begins in March, but we'll need you here by January so we can prepare. How does that sound?"

"Uh—" Russell's thoughts flew to Maggie, to her warming smile, the feel of her hand in his, and knew he could not move so far away from her. "I'm curious. Who else did you hire?"

"I'm afraid I can't say. Not all of the applicants have been notified."

"Oh. Right." Russell considered. Maggie was convinced that she had failed miserably in the interview. She had told him she was certain that she would not be offered the job. He decided to believe her. "I'm afraid my plans have changed. I'm no longer able to accept the job."

"You don't want the job?"

She sounded incredulous, and with good reason. "I'm truly very sorry it didn't work out."

"Is this because of a certain overzealous interviewer?" asked Sarah. "I assure you, our decision to choose you was unanimous, and she's eager to make amends."

"It's not that," said Russell, although he was satisfied to hear it. "I've decided that I want to stay on the West Coast, that's all."

"All right, then," said Sarah, still sounding as if she did not believe he was turning her down. "Would you consider joining us as a visiting instructor on occasion? I still believe we have a lot to offer each other."

"Thanks. I'll consider it," said Russell. "I'm sure we can work something out."

But he was impatient to get off the line. He would rather work out travel arrangements for Maggie's visit to Seattle than for some future, hypothetical visit to Elm Creek Quilt Camp.

※

"I can't believe it," said Sarah, hanging up. "After all that, he doesn't want the job."

Sylvia shrugged. "After what Diane put him through, I suppose we can't be too surprised."

"I'm surprised," said Sarah. "We aren't the least bit turn-downable. Now what are we supposed to do? Call an emergency meeting and have another vote? Deliberate another two weeks? That's just enough time for all of our applicants to find other work or to become so irritated at us for taking so long that they'll brush off our offer just like Russell did."

"I don't think that's necessary," said Sylvia. "There's really only one other choice, don't you agree?"

※

After two weeks with no word from Elm Creek Quilts, Gretchen was tempted to call and ask how the selection process was going and if she was still in the running. She refrained, in part because she did not want to nag, in part because she was too busy working out the final details of her separation from Quilts 'n Things. Heidi's daughter, submitting to pressure from her mother to decline Gretchen's offer to sell her share of the store, had come around only after other potential buyers surfaced. Rather than allow control of the store to leave the family, Heidi relented, and her daughter eagerly made Gretchen a fair market bid. Now all that was left was the paperwork.

Naturally, all the local quilters were astonished when the news broke that Gretchen was leaving Quilts 'n Things on unpleasant terms. A frenzy of gossip circulated through the quilting bees, spurred on, no doubt, by Heidi's embellished version of recent events. Gretchen refused to demean herself by carrying on her disagreement with Heidi through the rumor mill. When mutual acquaintances asked her what had happened, she told them, simply and without acrimony. Then she left them to make up their own minds. It was too soon to tell which friends would stand by her, which would abandon her out of loyalty to Heidi, and which would try to balance precariously between them, in hopes that one day they might make amends and everything might go back to the way it was before.

Gretchen knew that would never happen. She also knew—and this was a nagging worry—that she would have to find some work to occupy her time and pay the bills. The sale of her share of Quilts 'n Things would carry her and Joe a little ways, but it would not last forever.

When Sarah McClure finally called, Gretchen's heart leaped and she eased herself into a chair, holding her voice carefully neutral. She could not tell from the young woman's greeting if she intended to deliver good news or bad.

Thankfully, Sarah got right to the point. When she asked Gretchen if she could be available by January, Gretchen said, "I could be available next week if you like. If you need a substitute teacher, I'd be delighted to fill in anytime. Just say the word."

How fortuitous that she had already cleared her calendar by resigning from the quilt shop.

Joe waited nearby until Gretchen hung up. "Well?" he asked.

She flung her arms around him. "How soon can you pack up your workshop? We're moving to Elm Creek Manor!"

❧

Karen was in the kitchen fixing the boys a snack of soynut butter and strawberry jam sandwiches when the phone rang. Sylvia Compson was kind and regretful as she delivered the bad news Karen had expected since leaving Elm Creek Manor.

"I'm very sorry," Sylvia said.

"That's all right." Or it would be, if Karen thrived on disappointment and rejection. "I expected as much when I couldn't find a baby-sitter and the interview turned into a debate on the merits of extended breastfeeding."

"That wasn't the reason at all," said Sylvia. "We appreciate a rousing discussion as much as anyone. We simply found that some of our other candidates had more teaching experience. Perhaps if you teach at your local quilt shop, the next time we hire, you'll be among the most qualified."

"Thank you for the suggestion," said Karen, although she doubted there would be a next time.

When she hung up, she found Nate listening in from the doorway. "Who was that?"

"Sylvia Compson from Elm Creek Quilts."

"And?"

Karen shook her head.

"I'm sorry, honey." Nate wrapped her in a hug, and she rested her head on his chest. "I know you really wanted that job."

"It's all right," said Karen, and she meant it. In a way, it was even a relief. She had no idea how she would have managed working outside the home and raising the boys without driving herself to the brink of exhaustion.

"But I know how much it meant to you." Nate hesitated. "I know you want a paying job so that you can feel like you're doing something important."

"That's not it." Karen pulled away and picked up the knife, slicing Lucas's sandwich into squares and Ethan's into triangles, the way they preferred. "I think that what I do now is important. Not making sandwiches, but all of it. What could be more important than raising my two children to be self-confident, compassionate, moral adults? I just wish other people respected what I do. I know I shouldn't care what other people think, but I wish other people thought that what I do is important."

"And by 'other people,'" said Nate, "you mean me."

She set the knife in the sink and tightened the lid on the strawberry jam jar. "Yes, Nate. I mean you."

"I get it," he said. "I get it."

She doubted he did. If he did get it, if he really understood how she felt—but how could she expect him to understand when she herself could barely sort out her conflicted feelings? She loved her children dearly. They were more precious to her than any job could ever be. But one moment she felt utterly fulfilled by motherhood, and the next as if she were trapped, spent, finished. Old and ugly, tired and used up. She missed feeling special. She missed that sense of anticipation that everything lay ahead of her, anything was possible, that she could do anything, be anything, be admired and cherished and beloved. She missed feeling wanted for herself, for the woman she was and not merely the housekeeping chores she performed. At the same time, she knew that taking care of her children was her duty and her calling and whatever she did or failed to do in the boys' early years would affect them so profoundly that nothing else she ever did would leave such a mark on the world. She was angry that no one appreciated the importance of the task appointed to her and ashamed that she wished she could escape its drudgery. She felt both taken for granted and selfish. She was ashamed that she could not simply enjoy her beautiful sons, children any parent would be grateful to have, and that what seemed to come so naturally to other women was a continuous uphill struggle for her. She felt like a failure, hopelessly inadequate to a task that was far too important to entrust to anyone else.

If she could have joined the circle of quilters at Elm Creek Manor—that would have made her special again. She knew how foolish it was to feel that way, but she could not help it. If Nate only knew how fortunate they both were that she had sought fulfillment from a new job rather than another man. But it didn't matter now.

"I'm sure you honestly believe you do understand," she told Nate, and called the boys for lunch.

Nate said nothing. He left the kitchen frowning, but not in anger. He frowned as he did when wrestling with an especially difficult piece of computer code.

Later, while the boys napped, Nate found her in the basement where she worked on the last block for her Pickle Dish quilt. "I made a spreadsheet," he announced.

"That's great, honey," she said, not really listening. It was hardly a revelation. He made spreadsheets all day long.

"No, I mean I made one for us." He turned her chair and placed a thin stack of papers in her hands. She glanced at them, curious. "It's a schedule. A new, revised family schedule."

"Can something be both new and revised?" she asked dubiously, paging through the sheets. She paused at the sight of a block of time labeled in blue. "What's this?"

"That's 'Mom Time.'"

She could read; she just didn't know what it meant. "That's when I do my mom work? Because there's no way I can fit everything into two and a half hours after supper."

"No, that's when you're *not* allowed to do any mom work. See? I'll come home at five-thirty every night. No exceptions. We'll have supper, and then from six until eight-thirty, you do whatever you like. Read a book, talk on the phone with your mom, take a long bath—"

"Speaking of baths, if I'm reading or talking, who—"

"*I'll* give the boys their baths. I'll get them their snacks, play with them, brush their teeth, read stories, all the things you usually do so you can have time for yourself." He shrugged. "Maybe you could even use that time to teach a class at the quilt shop so you can get the experience the Elm Creek Quilters are looking for."

"But you've always needed the evenings to work. Won't you go through laptop withdrawal?"

"If I can't get my work done during the day, I can finish after the boys go to bed."

She shook her head, skeptical. "Taking care of the boys doesn't mean parking them in front of the TV, you know."

"I know that. Karen, I want to help, but you have to let me."

He had a point; she knew it. Now that he had finally offered to share more of the parenting load, she couldn't refuse because he would not do everything as well as she did. She'd had years of practice. He would need time to catch up, to learn how to care for the boys his own way, because her way was not the only right way.

Perhaps she would look into teaching a class at her favorite quilt shop.

Perhaps someday she would have a second chance to join the circle of quilters at Elm Creek Quilts.

❧

Maggie called Russell twice more before reaching a ring instead of a busy signal. When he answered, she breathlessly said, "Was that Elm Creek Quilts on the line?"

"Maggie?"

"Yes, it's me. Hi! How was your trip? You had a busy signal. Were you speaking with Sarah McClure?"

"How did you know?"

"Because they called me, too, right before you. I knew they'd offer you the job. I knew it! You couldn't possibly have done as badly in the interview as you said."

"You mean they offered you the other teaching position?"

"Yes! Won't it be fun to work together?"

Russell let out a heavy sigh.

"What's the matter?" asked Maggie. "Didn't Sarah call to offer you the other job?"

"Yes. She did."

"Then what's wrong?" Suddenly Maggie had a horrible thought. He did not want to work with her. Or see her again. She had completely misinterpreted his signals. It wouldn't be the first time. "If you're worried that I might—you know, expect to see you all the time, I wouldn't. I just thought—"

"Maggie, that's not it. I turned down the job."

"Why?"

"Because I didn't want to move so far away from you."

His words warmed her heart—for a moment. "You didn't think I'd get the job?"

"*I* thought you would, but *you* said you didn't stand a chance."

"And you believed me?"

"Yes! Yes, I did. I have a terrible problem with that. When people tell me something, I tend to believe them."

Maggie burst into helpless laughter. It would have been flattering if he had assumed she would be offered the job, but it was even more revealing that he had turned down his offer in order to be closer to her. "What do we do now?"

She held her breath, fearful that he would suggest she reject her offer, too. She couldn't. She couldn't afford to even if she wanted to.

"I'll call Sarah back," said Russell. "Maybe it's not too late. I'll tell her I changed my mind."

"Call me right back and let me know what she says."

"I will. I promise. I have to hang up now."

"I know."

"I'll call you right back."

"Okay."

"You hang up first. I can't hang up on you."

"Russell, you're being silly." But she was tickled. "Okay. I'll hang up first."

And she did.

❧❧

Cursing himself, Russell raced to his office, dug his notes on Elm Creek Manor from his files, and punched in the phone number. Another young woman answered, and he asked for Sarah. He paced impatiently around the room as far as the phone cord would allow while he waited for her to pick up the extension.

Finally she answered. "Russell? Sorry for the wait. What can I do for you?"

"I've reconsidered and I'd be happy to accept your offer," blurted Russell. "I can start whenever you like."

"I'm sorry," said Sarah. "I've already given the job to someone else."

In less than thirty minutes? "Then I'm too late?"

"I'm afraid so. The other applicant has already accepted the job." Sarah sounded sincerely regretful. "I know it's not the same, but we would still like to have you as a visiting instructor."

"Yes," said Russell quickly. "Anytime. For as long as you like."

"We won't have our schedule ready until late winter. I'm not sure what we'll have available. It might not be more than two or three weeks throughout the whole camp season."

"I'll take any openings you have. All of them."

"Sure," said Sarah. He knew she was wondering what had inspired his new enthusiasm. "We'd be glad to have you."

He hoped so. He intended to become Elm Creek Quilt Camp's most frequent visiting instructor.

❧

On Saturday afternoon, the Elm Creek Quilters bade their campers goodbye and settled back to enjoy their one evening off before the next group of quilters began to arrive on Sunday. They completed their last chores of the week together, relieved to have reached the end of their search for new teachers, full of anticipation for what the newcomers would bring, and saddened by the approaching departure of two dear friends. They would not have many more days like this one, when all of the original Elm Creek Quilters were together, celebrating the end of another successful week.

When the work was finished, they lingered on the veranda rather than returning to their own homes and families right away. They chuckled about the week's mishaps, made plans for the next session of camp, and mulled over Russell McIntyre's inexplicable change of heart.

"I hope we made the right choice," said Diane.

"Time will tell," said Sylvia. With a sigh, she rose stiffly from her chair and rubbed her hands together. She noted ruefully that they seemed to have become permanently waterlogged. "In the meantime, I have a sink full of dirty dishes awaiting me."

"I'll help," said Summer, rising. "I'll be glad when Anna can start."

Sarah gasped.

All eyes turned to her.

"You did call her, didn't you?" asked Gwen.

Sarah shook her head. "I was so thrown by Russell's refusal that I forgot."

"Never mind," said Sylvia. "I'll take care of it."

❧❧

"I'm sorry," said Anna. She never should have answered the phone. "But I can't."

"Please," begged Gordon. "Just give me another chance."

"What good would it do?" asked Anna. Why didn't he see it? They were unsuited for each other. They did not make each other happy. If she took him back, nothing would change. Forcing themselves back into couplehood would not resolve their differences. She would always worry that he considered her inferior; he would always nag her about her weight and her lack of interest in Derrida. She would always wonder if he preferred Theresa; he would forever hope in vain that she would take an office job in a building without a kitchen, a lunchroom, or even so much as a vending machine.

"It won't work," she told him firmly. "We don't work."

"I can change. Tell me how and I will."

She didn't want him to change for her any more than she wanted to change herself for him. "Good-bye, Gordon."

"Wait," he cried as she began to hang up. "'Come, Sleep; O Sleep! the certain knot of—'"

"Stop right there," said Anna. "I can't stand all that silly unrequited courtly love stuff. It's so annoying. You're not Sir Philip Sidney and I'm not Stella. Don't dream about me, don't plagiarize poems for me, and, whatever else you do, don't call me."

She hung up the phone with a crash. Almost immediately, it rang again. Irritated, Anna snatched up the receiver. "I mean it. If you don't stop calling, I'm going to block your number."

"I beg your pardon?"

"Sylvia?" gasped Anna. "I'm so sorry. I thought you were someone else."

"I certainly hope so. I can't imagine what I might have done to warrant that greeting."

"I really do apologize." Anna groped for an explanation. "Boyfriend trouble."

"Of course. It usually is. Well, whatever the young man has done, I believe I have some news that might cheer you up."

"Really?"

"When you visited the manor, you may have noticed the state of our kitchen."

How did they know? "I did sort of sneak a peek in passing."

"Our chef recently retired, and his replacement quit after only a week. We've been at loose ends ever since trying to take care of all the cooking in addition to teaching and managing the camp. In your interview you mentioned that you hope someday to own your own restaurant. The position I can offer you is not quite the same, but you would be in charge of all of our food service—planning the menus, preparing meals, purchasing supplies, and so forth."

Anna sat down so suddenly that she landed hard on the arm of her chair. "I would be in charge? I would be the head chef?"

"Why, yes. In fact, you would be our only chef."

Anna's thoughts whirled. Working for Elm Creek Quilt Camp would be very much like running her own restaurant. No more cafeteria lines, no more indifferent student employees to prod along, no more lunch lady jokes. She would be the head chef of—of a hotel. A resort. And she already knew she would like her coworkers.

"We offer room and board in addition to your salary, if you wish," said Sylvia, adding dryly, "and we could arrange for caller ID on your phone extension."

"I'd love to be your chef," said Anna. "On two conditions. First, I'll need to hire a few assistants."

"Our previous chef had assistants. I would not expect you to do without. What is your second condition?"

"We remodel your kitchen," said Anna. "At the very least, you'll need a six-burner stove and a double oven. Your pantry is fine, but you need more counter space and a much larger refrigerator. I don't know how you've managed, considering all the people you feed."

"You seem to have given this a great deal of thought for someone who took only a quick peek into the kitchen in passing," remarked Sylvia.

"It might have been more than a peek. You really do need to expand. How often do you use that little room off the kitchen?"

"My sitting room?" asked Sylvia. "Well, not as much as I used to, I suppose."

"If we knocked out that wall . . ."

"Oh, my. I had no idea you had such extensive changes in mind." Sylvia considered. "However, I must admit you're right. We are long overdue for an upgrade. Our last chef was miserable with the state of the kitchen, but he was less determined than you to ask for what he needed."

Anna smiled and did not mention that this was a rather recent upgrade of her own.

Cradling the phone between her shoulder and ear, she dug in her tote bag for her pad of graph paper and a pencil. She flipped past the floor plan of Chuck's Diner and began a new sketch, planning the kitchen of her dreams with her new boss.

Anna couldn't wait to show that circle of quilters—*her* circle of quilters—all she could do.

The Quilter's Homecoming

Acknowledgments

I am very grateful to Denise Roy, Maria Massie, Rebecca Davis, Annie Orr, Aileen Boyle, Honi Werner, Melanie Parks, and David Rosenthal for their ongoing support for—and contributions to—the Elm Creek Quilts series throughout the years.

Many thanks to Tara Shaughnessy, nanny extraordinaire, who lovingly cares for my boys and gives me time to write.

I thank Lou Kirby and Susan Robb at the Stagecoach Inn Museum in Newbury Park, California, who generously provided historical details that helped shape two important settings in this novel; Ross E. Pollock of the B&O Railroad Historical Society for advising me regarding rail travel in the 1920s; and Jeanette Berard, special collections librarian at the Thousand Oaks City Library, who directed me to invaluable research sources. I am also indebted to Mary Kay Brown, a fine quilter and storyteller, for sharing her perspective of Southern California farm life, and to the late Patricia A. Allen, whose chronicles of life in the Conejo Valley informed the research for this novel. It was my great privilege to know Pat when we both worked at the Thousand Oaks City Library years ago. Her love for local history inspired my own.

Thank you to the friends and family who have supported and encouraged me through the years, especially Geraldine Neidenbach, Heather Neidenbach, Nic Neidenbach, Virginia Riechman, and Leonard and Marlene Chiaverini. My late grandfather, Edward Riechman, encouraged me until the end.

As always, I thank my husband, Marty, and my sons, Nicholas and Michael, for everything.

To Nan Bawn,
Quilt Maker,
Book Lover,
Friend,
and Honorary Elm Creek Quilter

Chapter One

1924

As her father's car rumbled across the bridge over Elm Creek and emerged from the forest of bare-limbed trees onto a broad, snow-covered lawn of the Bergstrom estate, Elizabeth Bergstrom was seized by the sudden and unshakable certainty that she should not have come to this place. She should have stayed in Harrisburg, Pennsylvania, to help her brother run the hotel, even though business invariably slowed during the holiday week. Or she should have offered to help care for her sister's newborn twins. Even celebrating Christmas alone would have been preferable to returning to Elm Creek Manor. Her lifelong feelings of warmth and comfort toward the family home had suddenly given way to dread and foreboding. She would have to pass the week next door to Henry, knowing that he was near, and waiting in vain for him to come to her.

As Elm Creek Manor came into view, Elizabeth watched her father straighten in the driver's seat, his leather-gloved fingers flexing around the steering wheel of the new Model T Ford, an unaccustomed look of ease and contentment on his face. He never drank at Elm Creek Manor, nor in the days leading up to their visits, which made Elizabeth wonder why he could not abstain in Harrisburg as well. Apparently he craved his brothers' approval more than that of his wife and children, not that anyone but Elizabeth ever complained about his drinking.

"We're almost home," Elizabeth's father said. Her mother responded with an almost inaudible sniff. It irked her that after all these years, her husband still referred to Elm Creek Manor as home, rather than their stylish apartment in the hotel her father had turned over to their management upon their marriage. Second only to her father's flagship hotel, the Riverview Arms was smartly situated on the most fashionable street in Harrisburg, just blocks from the capitol building. It was a good living, much more reliable and lucrative than raising horses for Bergstrom Thoroughbreds. On his better days, George remembered that, but his insistence upon calling Elm Creek Manor home smacked of ingratitude.

But in this matter, if nothing else, Elizabeth understood her father. Of course Elm Creek Manor was home. The first Bergstroms in America had established the farm in 1857 and ever since, their family had run the farm and raised their prizewinning horses there, building on to the original farmhouse as the number of their descendants grew. They had lived, loved, argued, and celebrated within those gray stone walls for generations. But it was her father's fate to fall in love with a girl who loved the comforts of the city too much to abandon them for life on a horse farm. He could not have Millie and Elm Creek Manor both, so he accepted his future father-in-law's offer to sell his stake in Bergstrom Thoroughbreds and invest the profits in the Riverview Arms. Still, though he had sold his inheritance to his siblings, Elizabeth's father would always consider Elm Creek Manor the home of his heart.

And so would she, Elizabeth told herself firmly. Though Elm Creek Manor would never belong to her the way it would her cousins, every visit would be a homecoming for as long as she lived. She would not mourn for what was lost, whether an inheritance sold off before it could pass to her, or the love of a good man whose affection she had taken for granted.

Her father parked in the circular drive and took his wife's hand to help her from the car. Elizabeth climbed down from the backseat unassisted. A host of aunts, uncles, and cousins greeted them at the door at the top of the veranda. Uncle Fred embraced his younger brother while dear Aunt Eleanor kissed Elizabeth's mother on both cheeks. Aunt Eleanor's eyes sparkled with delight to have the family reunited again, but she was paler and thinner than she had been when Elizabeth last saw her, at the end of summer. Aunt Eleanor had heart trouble and had never in Elizabeth's memory been robust, but she was so spirited that one could almost forget her affliction. Elizabeth wondered if those who lived with her daily were oblivious to how she weakened by imperceptible degrees.

Suddenly Elizabeth's four-year-old cousin, Sylvia, darted through the crowd of taller relatives and took hold of Elizabeth's sleeve. "I thought you were never going to get here," she cried. "Come and play with me."

"Let me at least get though the doorway," said Elizabeth, laughing as Sylvia tugged off her coat. She had hoped to linger long enough to ask Aunt Eleanor—casually, of course—if she had any news of the Nelson family, but Sylvia seized her hand and led her across the marble foyer and up two flights of stairs to the nursery before Eleanor could even give her aunt and uncle a proper greeting.

Elizabeth would have to wait until supper to learn no one had seen Henry Nelson since the harvest dance in early November, except to wave to him from a distance as he worked in the fields with his brothers and father. Elizabeth feigned indifference, but her heart sank at the thought of Henry with some other girl on his arm—someone pretty and cheerful who didn't spend half her time in a far-distant city writing teasing letters about all the fun she was having with other young men. It was probably too much to hope Henry had danced only with his sister.

❦

By the next morning Elizabeth had persuaded herself that she didn't care how Henry might have carried on at some silly country dance. After all, since they had said good-bye at the end of the summer, she had attended many dances, shows, and clubs, always escorted by one handsome fellow or another. Her mother worried that she was running with a fast crowd, but her father, who should have known better since his own hotel had a night-club, assumed Elizabeth and her friends passed the time together as his own generation had—in carefully supervised, sedate activities where young men and women congregated on opposite sides of the room unless prompted by a chaperone to interact. Elizabeth's mother had a more vivid imagination, and it was she who waited up for her youngest daughter with the lights on until she was safely tucked into bed on Friday and Saturday nights.

Every summer, Elizabeth surprised her mother by willingly abandoning the delights of the city for Elm Creek Manor. Millie, oblivious to the appeal of the solace and serenity of the farm, always expected Elizabeth to put up more of an argument. Elizabeth certainly did about everything else. She wanted to bob her hair and wear dresses with hemlines up to her knee. She plastered her bedroom walls with magazine photographs of Paris, London, Venice, and other places she was highly unlikely to visit, covering up the perfectly lovely floral wallpaper selected by Millie's mother when the hotel was built. She chatted easily with young men, guests of the hotel, before they had been properly introduced. Millie shook her head in despair over her daughter's seeming indifference to how things looked, to what people thought. Why should anyone believe she was a well-brought-up girl if she didn't behave like one?

Yet every year as spring turned to summer, Elizabeth found herself longing for the cool breeze off the Four Brothers Mountains, the scent of apple blossoms in the orchard, the grace and speed of the horses, the awkward beauty of the colts, the warmth and affection of her aunts and uncles and grandparents. She felt at ease at Elm Creek Manor. Her meddling mother was far away. She was in no danger of walking into a room to find her father passed out over a ledger, an empty brandy bottle on the desk. There was only comfort and acceptance and peace. And Henry.

Once he had been only Henry Nelson from the next farm over, a boy more her brother's friend than her own. All the children played together, Bergstroms and Nelsons meeting at the flat rock beneath the willow next to Elm Creek after chores were done and running wild in the forests until they were called home for supper. They met again after evening chores and stayed out well after dark, playing hide-and-seek and Ghost in the Graveyard. One hot August night on the eve of her return to the city, Elizabeth, her brother Lawrence, Henry, Henry's brother, and the Bergstrom cousins climbed to the top of a haystack and lay on their backs watching the night sky for shooting stars. One by one the other children crept off home to bed, but Elizabeth felt compelled to stay until she had counted one hundred shooting stars. Secretly, she had convinced herself that if she could stay awake long enough to count one hundred stars, her parents would decide that they could stay another day.

She had only reached fifty-one when Lawrence sat up and brushed hay from his hair. "We should go in."

"If you want to go in, go ahead. I'll come when I'm ready."

"I'm not letting you walk back alone in the dark. You'll probably trip over a rock and fall in the creek."

The darkness hid Elizabeth's scarlet flush of shame and anger. Lawrence never made any effort to disguise his certainty that his youngest sister would fail at everything she tried. "I will not. I know the way as well as you."

"I'll walk back with her," said Henry.

Lawrence agreed, glad to be rid of the burden, then he slid down from the haystack and disappeared into the night.

Elizabeth counted shooting stars in indignant silence.

"Thank you," she said, after a while. She lay back and gazed up at the starry heavens, hay prickling beneath her, warm and sweet from the sun. After a time, Henry's hand touched hers, and closed around it. Warmth bloomed inside her, and she knew suddenly that after this summer, everything would be different. Henry had chosen her over her brother. Henry was hers.

She was fourteen.

After that, whenever Henry came to Elm Creek Manor, Elizabeth knew she was the person he had come to see. They began exchanging letters during the months they were separated, letters in which each confided more about their hopes and fears than either would have been able to say aloud. Whenever they reunited after a long absence, Elizabeth always experienced a fleeting moment of shyness, wondering if she should have told him about her dreams to visit Paris and London and Venice, her longing to leave the stifling streets of Harrisburg for the rolling hills and green forests of the Elm Creek Valley, her shame and embarrassment when her father stumbled through the hotel lobby after returning home from his favorite speakeasy, her frustration when the rest of the family turned a blind eye. But Henry never laughed at her or turned away in disgust. In time, he became her dearest confidant and closest friend.

As the years passed, Elizabeth wondered if he would ever become more than that. He never drowned her in flattery the way other young men did; in fact, he was so plainspoken and solemn she often wondered if he cared for her at all. Sometimes she teased him by describing the parties she attended back home, the flowers other young men brought her, the poems they sent. She casually threw out references to the movies she had seen in one fellow's company or another's, the dances she enjoyed, how Gerald preferred the fox-trot but Jack was wild about the Charleston and Frank seemed to consider himself another Rudolph Valentino, the way he danced the tango. She hoped to provoke Henry into making romantic gestures of his own, or at least to do something that might indicate a hidden reservoir of jealousy.

In her most recent letter, she had described a Christmas concert she had attended with a young man whose determination to marry her had only increased after she declined his first proposal. She had worn a blue velvet dress with a matching cloche hat; her escort had given her a corsage with three roses and a ribbon the exact shade of her dress. They had traveled in style in his father's new Packard. The next day, their photo appeared on the society page of the Harrisburg *Patriot* above a caption that declared them the most handsome couple in attendance. Elizabeth included the newspaper clipping in her letter and asked Henry for his opinion: "Do you think this will encourage him to think of us as a couple? I should discourage him, but he's such a sweet boy I hate to seem unkind. I imagine many girls are eventually won this way. Persistence is admirable in a man. If he doesn't become impatient waiting for me, maybe someday I will come to think of him as more than a friend."

Satisfied, she sent off her letter and awaited a declaration of Henry's true feelings by return mail.

It never came.

As the days passed, she began to worry that instead of stirring him into action, she had driven him away. Henry was, after all, a practical man. He would not pursue a lost cause, and she had all but declared the inevitability of her marriage to another more persistent, more expressive man. Henry had endured her teasing stoically through the years, but to repay him with musings that she might fall in love with someone else might, possibly, have been going too far.

Henry had never said he loved her. He had made her no promises. He had never kissed her and rarely held her hand except to help her jump from stone to stone as they crossed Elm Creek at the narrows, or to assist her onto her horse when they went riding. She had it on very good authority that he had not sat around pining for her at that harvest dance. How dare he end a ten-year friendship and five-year correspondence when she quite reasonably asked his opinion about the man who seemed most interested in marrying her? He ought to be flattered that she thought so highly of his opinion, especially since he seemed to lack any romantic instincts whatsoever. She would have done better to consult Lawrence.

Henry had given up too easily. If he loved her, he would have written back. He would have been waiting for her on the front steps of Elm Creek Manor to demand that she turn down Gerald or Jack or any other fellow who came too close. He would have done something.

He hadn't, and that told her the truth she did not want to know.

Two days before Christmas Eve, Elizabeth tried to lose herself in the joyful anticipation of the holidays. She played with little cousin Sylvia, threaded needles for Great-Aunt Lucinda as she sewed a green-and-red Feathered Star quilt, and helped Aunt Eleanor and the other Bergstrom women make delicious apple strudel as gifts for neighbors. Perhaps she should offer to take the Nelsons' to them at Two Bears Farm on the chance that she might see Henry—but what then? How pathetic she would seem, hoping to win him back with pastry. It was very good pastry, but even so. She had her pride.

She was reading a Christmas story to Sylvia when a cousin came running to the nursery to announce that Elizabeth had a visitor. She almost knocked Sylvia out of the rocking chair in her haste to see who had come.

She hurried downstairs to find Henry in the kitchen talking companionably with her father and Uncle Fred. Her heart quickened at the sight of him, taller and more handsome than she remembered, fairer and slighter of frame than the Bergstrom men but with the hardened muscles and callused hands of a farmer. She was pleased to see he had since summer shaved off his seasonal mustache because she had never liked the way it hid the curve of his mouth. He smiled warmly at her, but she was struck by a newfound resolve in his eyes.

She knew at once that he had come to tell her he had fallen in love with someone else.

He invited her to go for a walk. Together they crossed the bridge over Elm Creek, passed the barn, and strolled along the apple grove, the trees bare-limbed and bleak against the gray sky. "What did you think of my last letter?" Elizabeth asked when she could endure exchanging pleasantries no longer. "You never answered, unless your reply was lost in the mail."

He was silent for a moment; the only sound was the crunching of their boots upon snow and the far-off caw of a crow. "I'm always glad to get your letters. I'm sorry I didn't have a chance to write back. I've been busy with . . . some business matters."

She smiled tightly. December was not usually a busy time around Two Bears Farm. "I asked for your opinion and I was counting on you to offer it."

"I wasn't sure what you were asking," said Henry. "Do I think this friend of yours considers you two a couple? I'd bet on it, if you haven't told him otherwise. Do I think you should discourage him? That depends."

"It depends?" Elizabeth stopped and looked up at him. "It depends on what?"

"Do you want him to think you're his girl or not? I never thought you were the type to marry a fellow because he wore you down, but if you are, maybe you should save him the time and trouble and marry him now."

"Thank you for the suggestion," said Elizabeth. She resumed walking, faster now, to put distance between them. "I'll consider it."

Henry easily caught up to her. "It wasn't a suggestion."

"Then what *do* you think?"

"Do you love him?"

"He asked me to marry him, and I refused, didn't I?"

Henry caught her by the elbow. "That doesn't answer my question. Do you love him?"

"No," Elizabeth burst out. "I don't love him, but at least I know how he feels about me, which is more than I can say about you."

❧

She did not expect to see Henry again, but he returned the next afternoon. By that time, most of her anger had abated. Though the memory of her outburst and subsequent flight embarrassed her, she was determined not to apologize. She agreed to another walk, mostly out of curiosity. She had puzzled too long over the mystery of Henry's feelings to send him away when he had apparently decided to divulge them.

He waited until they had crossed the bridge, out of earshot of both the house and the barn—unless they shouted, which was perhaps not out of the question. "I thought you knew I loved you."

The gracelessness of his declaration sparked her anger. "How would I know, since you've never told me?"

"Would I write to you for five years if I didn't love you? Would I come to Elm Creek Manor and see you every day you're here?"

"I don't know. Maybe."

"No, I wouldn't," he said emphatically, and Elizabeth knew it to be true. Another man might, but not Henry.

"Well, say it, then," she told him.

He hesitated. "Why do I have to say it?"

"Because I need to know. Because you never lie, and if you say you love me straight out, I'll have no choice but to believe you."

He shrugged. "All right, then, I love you."

Elizabeth nearly laughed, incredulous. "Is that the best you can do?"

"What else do you want me to say?"

"I've received four proposals—five, counting yours—and I have to say that this one was by far the least romantic. It might very well be the least romantic proposal of all time."

"I wasn't proposing. I was only trying to tell you that I love you."

"Oh." All the blood seemed to rush to Elizabeth's face. "Oh. I didn't mean—"

"Elizabeth, wait." His voice was low and gentle, with a trace of embarrassment. "I'm coming to that part."

She took a deep breath, ducked her chin into the collar of her coat, and waited for him to continue.

Henry took a thick envelope from his overcoat pocket. "I know you want to see the world. I know you wish you had land to call your own the way your aunt and uncle have Elm Creek Manor. I know you're tired of your father's hotel and of Harrisburg." He thrust the envelope into her hand. When she just stared at it, he said, "Go on. Open it."

She withdrew several sheets of thick paper, folded into thirds, and three photographs of an arid landscape of rolling hills dotted with clusters of oaks. She unfolded the papers, and as she scanned the first, Henry said, "Yesterday I told you I couldn't answer your letter because I was occupied with some business. That's the title to a cattle ranch in southern California."

"The Rancho Triunfo," Elizabeth read aloud. "You bought a ranch?"

"With every cent I've earned and saved since I was twelve years old. It's about forty-five miles north of Los Angeles. They say it's like paradise, Elizabeth. Summer all year round, orange trees growing in the backyard—"

"It's so far away." And he had purchased the ranch without knowing whether she would want to go with him.

"Aren't you always saying you want to leave Harrisburg?"

"Well, yes, but . . ." She had wanted to see the world and then come home to Elm Creek Manor. She never meant to stay away forever. "It's on the other side of the country."

"That's the point." Henry took her hands, crumpling the papers between them. "If you'll marry me, I want to give you land of your own in the most beautiful part of the country I could find. If you won't marry me, I want to put a continent between me and the chance I might ever see you in the arms of another man."

Elizabeth felt breathless, light-headed. As far as she was concerned, the most beautiful part of the country was right here, all around them. "What about Two Bears Farm? What will your parents think?"

"They have my brothers and sister to help them work the place and take it over for them one day. If I go, there will be one less person arguing for a piece of the same pie."

And what of her family? Her mother and father expected her to marry a nice young man from Harrisburg who would come to work for her father in the family business. That was what her mother had done. Millie had shrieked in outrage when Elizabeth refused Gerald's proposal. Gerald, who would fit so neatly into Millie's plans for the hotel—and who drank nearly as much as her father and seemed constitutionally incapable of fidelity.

It was Henry Elizabeth wanted, although when she had imagined them together it had been at Two Bears Ranch, so close to Elm Creek Manor that it was almost as good as coming home. A ranch in southern California might be beautiful, but it would not be home.

But Henry was going, with or without her.

"Yes," she told him softly. "I'll marry you."

He kissed her. The papers and photographs fell to the snowy ground, forgotten.

❧

As Elizabeth had expected, her parents were dismayed to hear of their plans to move so far away. Millie could not disguise her anger that they had come to inform them of a decision already made, and not to seek advice and permission. George did not share his wife's outrage, but admitted surprise that the prudent, steadfast Henry had acted so impulsively. "If you're tired of farm life, you can come and work for me," he offered. "I wanted to open a second hotel, and with you to help me, I could do it. It would be advantageous to both of us. Why go to the ends of the earth when you can make a decent living here?"

"I don't intend to make only a decent living, sir. I intend to make a fortune."

Henry spoke in such frank seriousness that Elizabeth could not help but believe him, but her father looked dubious. "A man doesn't become a farmer to get rich."

"Your grandfather did, sir."

Elizabeth's father smiled grudgingly. "That was a very different time. There are fortunes to be made every day, but not in farming, not anymore. The land isn't worth what it used to be. My brothers have prospered because they raise prize horses. They cater to wealthy customers, and I can tell you those customers aren't farmers. The place for an enterprising young man these days is business."

Henry shook his head. "I intend to raise cattle, sir, not corn, not oats. I'll be raising beef. All those wealthy businessmen who buy your Bergstrom Thoroughbreds want beef for their tables. Providing it will make me a rich man."

Elizabeth's father sighed, knowing the argument was lost before it had begun. "Farming is the only industry I can think of riskier than opening a new hotel across the street from your strongest competitor. If you come work for me, you'll still make your fortune. It may take time, but you'll get there."

"With all due respect, sir," said Henry carefully, "and I do value your opinion, but I could never live away from the land."

Elizabeth's father, who had given up his share of the Bergstrom land for a love that had not flourished with the passing of time, nodded and said no more, except to offer the couple his blessing.

When the family gathered for Christmas Eve supper the next evening, Elizabeth's father announced their engagement. Everyone but little Sylvia welcomed the news with great joy, which made it more difficult to announce their plans to move away. The family accepted the couple's decision with surprise, but steadied themselves with the knowledge that most Bergstroms who left the Elm Creek Valley eventually returned.

Henry's family was far less sanguine. His sister, Rosemary, broke down in tears and begged him to reconsider. His brothers, who had assumed he would always be there to help them run the farm, voiced cautious support, shot through with shock and betrayal. His father was concerned that his ordinarily prudent son had purchased land without examining it firsthand, but after he studied the documents and photographs, he admitted everything looked to be in order. If the land was indeed as the agent had described it, Henry had made a sound investment, a sensible purchase.

But Henry's mother took Elizabeth aside. "You can still talk him out of this," she beseeched in a whisper. "Henry adores you. He will stay here if he knows that's what you want."

"I'm afraid it's too late for that," Elizabeth told her gently. "I don't think he could get out of the sale even if he wanted to."

What she did not say was that despite the small seeds of doubt Henry's father had planted with his concerns about the sight-unseen purchase, Elizabeth had no intention of talking Henry out of it. She had become as eager as Henry to embark on their adventure, and in idle moments she would take out the photographs, search them for tiny details she had previously overlooked, and murmur, "Triumph Ranch." The very name rang with promise.

Elizabeth had little time for romantic musings, for there was much to do before the wedding. The Pittsburgh landbroker from whom Henry had purchased the ranch assured him that the former owners would be willing to remain on the ranch and tend the livestock until the end of April, but he could make no guarantees after that. At first, Henry suggested he and Elizabeth leave the week after New Year's and marry when they arrived in California, but Elizabeth firmly refused. Her family put great stock in propriety and tradition, and she would not deny them the pleasure of a traditional Bergstrom wedding.

The scant three months of preparations raced by in a blur of dress fittings, china pattern selections, and private lectures from all of her aunts, including her unmarried great-aunt Lucinda, about what she could expect from married life. Some of their advice was amusing, but when the lessons dismayed and alarmed her, she allowed her mind to wander. Hadn't she already learned everything she needed to know about being a good wife by watching her mother, grandmothers, and aunts?

When the time came to pack for their journey west, the enormity of their undertaking began to sink in. She felt almost as if she and Henry were among the early pioneers, setting out for the West with grand dreams to meet an unknown fate, uncertain whether they would ever return home. Silently she chastised herself for such foolish worries, for so much homesickness before they even left Pennsylvania, and this from the girl who all her life had longed to see the world. Once she and Henry were established, they would surely be able to leave the Rancho Triunfo in the care of trusted ranch hands long enough for a visit home. Still, she did not know how soon a return trip might come, and she had to swallow a lump in her throat every time she thought of spending years without seeing Elm Creek Manor and those who lived there.

She took comfort in the handmade gifts the Bergstrom women gave to her as the wedding approached. In addition to lovely new clothes, they made her several quilts to use in her new home. Great-Aunt Lydia doubted that quilts would be necessary in so warm a place as southern California, but Aunt Eleanor declared that they would be a beautiful touch of home nonetheless. One of Elizabeth's favorites was a bridal quilt in the Double Wedding Ring pattern, embellished with beautiful floral appliqués. All the women of the family had sewn together the arcs and wedges of the pieced rings, and whenever Elizabeth looked upon the quilt she recognized the work of individual quiltmakers: Great-Aunt Lucinda's precise piecing, Aunt Eleanor's intricate appliqué, Great-Aunt Lydia's painstaking stipple quilting, her grandmother's perfectly mitered binding. As the finest quilt Elizabeth owned, it should have been saved for company, but as soon as she saw it, she decided it must grace the bed she would share with Henry.

As lovely as the bridal quilt was, a second quilt was somehow more precious to her, even though it was only a sturdy scrap quilt meant for everyday use. Great-Aunt Lucinda had sewn it in the evenings after the day's work was done, rocking in her favorite chair in the parlor and hiding the pieces whenever Elizabeth entered the room. Elizabeth pretended not to notice since it was obvious Great-Aunt Lucinda intended the quilt to be a surprise, but her curiosity was piqued and she could not resist a little surreptitious observation of her aunt at work. One day a few weeks before the wedding, Sylvia gave Elizabeth the perfect opportunity. She had just been scolded by her father for some minor offense intended to prevent the marriage—telling Henry she hated him, perhaps, or pretending she had the plague so the house would be quarantined—and she had sought out the comfort of Great-Aunt Lucinda's lap for her sulk. Elizabeth listened just beyond the doorway as Great-Aunt Lucinda told Sylvia about the quilt, made in a pattern of concentric rectangles and squares, one half of the block light colors, the other dark in the fashion of a Log Cabin block.

"This pattern is called Chimneys and Cornerstones," Great-Aunt Lucinda explained. "Whenever Elizabeth sees it, she'll remember our home and all the people in it. We Bergstroms have been blessed to have a home filled with love from the chimneys to the cornerstone. This quilt will help Elizabeth take some of that love with her."

Silence prompted Elizabeth to draw closer and peek into the room. Sylvia was watching Great-Aunt Lucinda as she ran her finger along a diagonal row of red squares, from one corner of the block to its opposite. "Do you see these red squares?" asked Lucinda. "Each is a fire burning in the fireplace to warm Elizabeth after a weary journey home."

"You made too many," said Sylvia, counting. "We don't have so many fireplaces."

"I know," said Lucinda, smiling in amusement. "It's just a fancy. Elizabeth will understand. But there's more to the story. Do you see how one half of the block is dark fabric, and the other is light? The dark half represents the sorrows in a life, and the light colors represent the joys."

"Then why don't you give her a quilt with all light fabric?"

"I suppose I could, but then she wouldn't be able to see the pattern. The design appears only if you have both dark and light fabric."

"But I don't want Elizabeth to have any sorrows."

"I don't either, love, but sorrows come to us all. But don't worry. Remember these?" Lucinda touched several red squares arranged diagonally across one block. "As long as these home fires keep burning, Elizabeth will always have more joys than sorrows."

Little Sylvia's brow furrowed as she studied the quilt. Suddenly she brightened. "The red squares are keeping the sorrow part away from the light part."

"That's exactly right," Great-Aunt Lucinda praised. "What a bright little girl you are."

Pleased, Sylvia snuggled closer to her great-aunt. "I still don't like the sorrow part."

"None of us do. Let's hope that Elizabeth finds all the joy she deserves, and only enough sorrow to nurture an empathetic heart."

When Great-Aunt Lucinda gave Elizabeth the quilt the day before the wedding, she said nothing of the quilt's symbolism or how much Elizabeth would be missed. Lucinda had stitched her farewells and hopes for her grandniece into the quilt, and as Elizabeth held the soft folds of cloth to her heart, she understood everything Lucinda could not say. For a fleeting moment she feared that leaving Pennsylvania would be a terrible mistake, bringing down upon her all the sorrows that Great-Aunt Lucinda wanted the fires of home to protect her from. Then she thought of Henry, and how in all her hopes of future happiness, she imagined herself by his side. She knew she could not stay behind.

She wrapped their new china in the precious quilts for protection and placed them in her sturdiest trunk, a gift from Lawrence. Then, at last, all was ready.

The wedding itself passed in a blur. She had always heard that a wedding day was the happiest in a young woman's life, but she was sure she would remember hers only in glimpses: her mother helping her arrange her golden hair into long corkscrew curls swept back from her face by her headpiece and veil, her father walking her down the aisle of the same church her parents had married in, Henry's encouraging smile as she murmured her vows, a whirl of celebration back at the manor. She could not swallow more than a few bites of the delicious feast her mother and aunts had prepared, but her first dance with Henry as husband and wife filled her with the warmth of pure happiness. She knew with a certainty she could not explain that she and Henry would weather whatever storms came their way—not that they were likely to face many in sunny southern California.

ℜℓ

1875

Isabel ran up and down the length of the front porch, her bare feet padding on the smooth oaken boards, pausing only briefly when Mami and Abuelo crossed her path carrying boxes from the house to the wagon. Abuela waited on the front seat, holding Isabel's little sister on her lap. Her back was tall and straight, and she would not turn around no matter how often Isabel called out to her to look, to see how fast she could run.

Swinging her doll by the arm as she darted back and forth, Isabel stumbled and ran headlong into her mother's legs. "Will someone keep this child out of my way?" her mother cried. And she was crying. Horrified, Isabel watched as her mother struggled to balance a box of dishes on her hip while wiping tears from her eyes.

"I didn't mean to hurt you," said Isabel. She did not think she had struck her mother so hard. She had not hurt herself even one little bit.

"You didn't, *mija.*" Mami forced a smile and continued down the porch steps to the wagon. "Go and play for a little while longer."

Worried, Isabel wandered away from their cabin home and into the backyard, wishing her brother would come and play, but he had gone with Papi up to the big farmhouse to collect Papi's pay. Her father would come home happy. He always did on paydays. Sometimes he brought her little treats, too—candy or a ribbon for her hair.

She sat on a rock drawing patterns in the dirt with a stick, listening to her mother and grandfather loading the wagon, unseen on the other side of the cabin. They had been working all morning, and everyone was sad except for the baby. Abuela had not started dinner, working the cornmeal with her hands and frying the tortillas as she usually did at this time of the day. Isabel was hungry. When were they going to eat?

She went to find her mother but found her grandfather first. "I'm hungry," she told him, slipping her hand into his.

He hesitated and looked back at the cabin. Mami was somewhere inside; Isabel heard a door open and close. "We're almost done," he said. "Can you wait?"

Isabel shook her head.

Her grandfather smiled kindly down at her. "Very well. Let's see what we can find."

Together they went around back to the pair of orange trees that grew side by side a few yards from the cabin. They searched the branches, but found no ripe oranges, only hard, green fruit too bitter to eat. Her grandfather thought for a moment. "We will have to search a little ways from the house," he told her. "Can you walk that far?"

Isabel nodded, although she was not sure how far he meant to go.

Hand in hand they walked up the hill, leaving the cabin behind. Before long Isabel's legs grew tired, but she did not complain. She was relieved when her grandfather finally halted, but surprised that he had chosen the apricot orchard for their rest. Isabel and her brother were strictly forbidden to play there, lest they accidentally harm the trees.

The branches were heavy with plump, ripe fruit. Already Papi and the other hired hands had stuck the posts deep into the ground where every year they set up the cutting shed. The harvest would start soon. Even Mami and Abuelo worked the apricot harvest. Someday Isabel would, too.

"Would you like one?" her grandfather asked, gesturing to the nearest tree.

"Mami says we aren't allowed," Isabel said, though the sight of the fruit made her mouth water. "She says we should never, never take the apricots without permission."

"On an ordinary day, I would say that is very good advice," her grandfather replied. "But today is a special day, and just this once, you may have any apricot you choose."

He hoisted her up onto his shoulders and moved so close to the trees that she felt hidden within the branches like a little bird. Giggling, she searched and searched until she found the perfect apricot—rosy and plump, without a single blemish. She plucked it, wiped it on the hem of her dress, and bit into the soft flesh. The sweet juice trickled down her chin, warm from the sun. Sometimes her father brought home the dried, cured apricot slices at the end of harvest, but Isabel rarely tasted the fresh fruit, and never straight from the tree.

She picked a second apricot for Abuelo, and then one for Mami, Papi, Abuela, and her brother. She took one for the baby, too; she could suck on it even though she didn't have any teeth. Isabel expected her grandfather to tell her to stop, to warn her that she was taking too many, but he let her continue until she could carry no more. Only then did he lower her to the ground.

They walked slowly back to the cabin. Isabel held up her hem to make a basket of her skirt, carefully cradling the fruit. Abuelo offered to help, but she insisted upon carrying the apricots herself. She had picked them; she would bring them home to the family.

"Abuelo?" she asked. "How long are we going away?"

His dark, graying eyebrows rose. "How long?"

"When are we coming home?"

He watched her for a moment, his rich brown eyes full of sympathy. Then he sat down and drew her onto his lap. *"Niña,"* he said, "we aren't coming back. You know that. Your mami and papi have found a new home for you and your brother and sister."

"What about you?"

"Abuela and I will be right next door."

"But I don't want to go." She loved the orange trees, the shady front porch, the cozy room she shared with her brother and baby sister. When her parents had taken her to see their new home on the western side of the valley near the grocery store, she never thought they were meant to live there forever.

Her eyes welled up with tears.

"Oh, no, we can't have tears," said her grandfather sternly. "You're a big girl and you mustn't cry. You must be proud. Remember that this land once belonged to our family, from those high hills to the east and as far as you can see to the west. The king of Spain gave all this to my grandfather as a reward for his courage. You must be as brave as he was."

Isabel gulped air and dried her tears. She understood now why her grandmother had turned her back upon the cabin where they had spent so many happy years. It was already a part of their past.

Chapter Two

1925

Elizabeth and Henry almost missed their train. They had planned to arrive at the Harrisburg station in plenty of time to make the 10:05 night train, but after the car was packed and the last farewells said, Elizabeth discovered that her shoes were missing. At first she thought she had merely misplaced them in the excitement surrounding the wedding, but little cousin Sylvia couldn't hide her grin of satisfaction, refusing to help in the search or give the grown-ups a single clue as to their whereabouts. Elizabeth had to bite the inside of her cheek to keep from laughing, but when Henry glanced at his watch and checked the car for the hundredth time, she took pity on him.

"I suppose those shoes are gone for good," she said, rising with a sigh and smoothing the skirt of her traveling suit, a gift sewn by her aunt Eleanor and great-aunt Lucinda. "They were my favorite pair, too. I'll suppose I'll have to do without until we reach California."

While Sylvia looked on suspiciously, Elizabeth bade farewell to each cousin, aunt, uncle, and grandparent in turn, exchanging hugs and kisses and promises to write. Last of all, Elizabeth said good-bye to her parents. Her father was too overcome to speak, but he hugged Elizabeth and held her so long she wondered if Henry might be forced to pry her loose. Her mother, tears filling her eyes, choked out a few last-minute warnings about the dangers of travel. Elizabeth nodded, but the words scarcely registered. Shoes or no shoes, she really was leaving.

She took Henry's arm and left Elm Creek Manor, chasing away thoughts that she might be crossing the threshold for the last time. Gingerly she picked her way across the veranda in her stocking feet, greatly exaggerating the discomfort.

"You can't go all the way to California like that," protested Sylvia.

"I could lend you my boots," said Henry.

Elizabeth raised her eyebrows at him, surprised that he had decided to play along. "I don't have any choice," she told Sylvia. "If Henry and I don't reach the ranch before the former owners leave, who will take care of the animals? They'll be hungry and lonely, the poor things."

Elizabeth knew Sylvia loved animals too much to bear the thought of one neglected. Sure enough, the little girl scowled, disappeared into the manor, and returned moments later carrying Elizabeth's black leather Mary Janes. "Here," she said sullenly, thrusting them at her cousin.

"Oh, you found them," exclaimed Elizabeth, slipping them on. "What a clever girl."

Sylvia did not smile at the praise. She flung her arms around Elizabeth for one last, fierce hug and ran back into the manor without a word.

Elizabeth held Henry's hand tightly as Elm Creek Manor disappeared behind them. She held her gaze on the photographs of Triumph Ranch, lingering over the beautiful landscape that she and Henry would soon call home. Yet Two Bears Farm would always mean as much to Henry as Elm Creek Manor did to her. Two Bears Farm had been in the Nelson family since before the Bergstrom family came to America, and its history was just as renowned. Henry's great-grandparents, Thomas and Dorothea Nelson, had run an Underground Railroad station out of the old farmhouse, and the Nelson children loved to retell the story of how Thomas had been shot defending the home from slave catchers. Dorothea had run the farm, raised a child, and edited an abolitionist newspaper while Thomas was off fighting in the Civil War. The farm had sustained Henry's family for generations. If only Triumph Ranch would prove as bountiful.

Because it was their honeymoon, Henry splurged on a compartment for the eighteen-hour-and-five-minute trip from Harrisburg to St. Louis on Train 17. The accommodations were small but well appointed, but most important, they were private—which was in Elizabeth's opinion essential for a newlywed couple. Their compartment boasted two facing seats, an ingenious washbasin that folded into the wall, and a covered toilet in the corner. Elizabeth immediately decided that she would send Henry out into the corridor whenever she needed to use it. Married or not, there were some activities she had no intention of sharing with him.

The night porter helped them settle in with their hand luggage and then converted one of the seats into a double bed, where Elizabeth and Henry snuggled beneath the covers. As Henry held her and kissed her to the swaying of the train, Elizabeth wished their wedding quilt was not packed away with their china in the luggage car. She had meant for them to sleep beneath it every night of their marriage.

The next morning she and Henry had breakfast in the dining car. Afterward they explored the train and settled in the observation car, where Henry wanted to enjoy the view as the forested hills of Pennsylvania gave way to the low mountains of West Virginia and the flat farmlands of the Midwest. Elizabeth preferred to observe their fellow passengers. She was fascinated by the knee-high hemlines of the ladies' dresses, the dropped waists that gave their slim figures a boyish look, the lipstick carefully applied to mimic the effect of a bee sting. "Every one of them has her hair bobbed," Elizabeth whispered to Henry, envious. Her parents had forbidden her to cut hers. "They look like they stepped out of a Hollywood fashion magazine."

"I love your hair," said Henry. "Don't cut it off to chase a fad. You're prettier than any of these girls."

Pleased, Elizabeth rewarded him with a kiss on the cheek, glancing over his shoulder at a woman with a sleek, dark bob who held her cigarette holder elegantly as she pored over a recent issue of *True Story*. With a flash of inspiration, she rose and excused herself. She hurried back to their honeymoon suite, as they had nicknamed it, and unearthed her sewing box. The jolting of the train at first made it difficult to thread her needle, but she soon altered the hem of her dress with swift, deft stitches.

"Perfect," she declared, admiring the fall of the skirt and the daring show of leg.

As for her hair . . .

She braided it into two golden plaits, took a deep breath, and raised the scissors. Quickly, before she could change her mind, she cut off the braids and immediately shut her eyes, setting the scissors down as if the metal scalded.

Not that she regretted what she had done; she would look like a blond Clara Bow, only prettier. Henry would love it.

Elizabeth opened her eyes and peered into the mirror. Her gentle ringlets had given way to wild, uneven curls.

She gulped and pressed a hand to her stomach. Her hair would grow back.

It would take years for it to regain its former length, but it would grow back. In the meantime, she would wear fashionable hats.

She left the sleeper and made her way back to the observation lounge, taking her time and rehearsing her entrance. With any luck, Henry would be so distracted by her higher hemline that he wouldn't notice her hair. Yet whom should she pass in the narrow corridor but the woman with the enviable, sleek, dark-haired bob. "Jeez!" the woman exclaimed. "Didya forget your beautician's birthday or something? 'Cause it looks like she saved the dull scissors for you."

Elizabeth promptly burst into tears.

"Oh, hey, hey there, honey. I didn't mean nothing by it." She patted Elizabeth awkwardly on the shoulder. "You look fine. I mean—well, not fine, but it'll grow back, right?"

Elizabeth took out her handkerchief and tried to compose herself. "I was just trying to bob—bob—"

"Another bob gone bad," said the woman, shaking her head. "Well, I've seen worse. Do you want me to fix it?"

"Can you? I didn't think it could be fixed."

"Sure. It won't be as good as new, but it'll be swell. Don't you worry."

The woman, whose name was Mae, followed Elizabeth back to her compartment. "Nice digs," she remarked, glancing around as Elizabeth dug in her sewing box for the scissors. "You sure know how to travel in style."

"We splurged," Elizabeth explained, handing her the scissors. "It's our honeymoon."

"You don't say." Mae gestured for her to take a seat. "I guess the fun's over for you, honey."

"On the contrary, I think the fun has just started."

"You must've married one hell of a fella to feel that way." Mae studied Elizabeth's mangled locks. "Say, wait a minute. I saw you two in the observation car. That sandy-haired looker is your husband?"

"That's right," said Elizabeth, cringing slightly at the sound of the scissors snipping away near her right ear.

"He seems . . ." Mae paused. "Awful serious."

"I suppose he is, but he knows how to have a good time, too."

"Don't get me wrong, honey. A guy like that is the right sort of fella when you're ready to settle down." Mae sighed. "Sure wish I could fall in love with one of those. You don't know how lucky you are."

But Elizabeth did know, and she felt a surge of love and pride for her new husband. "Henry's one in a million, all right."

Mae snorted. "So's Peter, but I don't think I mean that the same way you do."

"Is Peter your husband?"

"No, and I tell him he won't be until he proves he can keep a job for more than two months running. And I mean a decent job, too."

"He probably just hasn't found his niche yet," Elizabeth said.

"Oh, he's found his niche all right. There's only one thing he's any good at." Mae thought for a moment. "Okay, two things, but he sure can't make any money doing the other. I would have to put my foot down, if you know what I mean."

Elizabeth had no idea what she meant, but she murmured a vague agreement. At last Mae handed the scissors back to Elizabeth. "It's not bad for a makeshift barbershop on a moving train," she remarked, looking pleased with herself. "You're a regular jazz baby now."

Elizabeth leapt to her feet and snatched up the mirror. "I can't believe it," she exclaimed, tossing her short curls. It was a perfectly shaped bob, light and carefree. "You're a miracle worker."

"I know," said Mae, "but I still don't want to be around when your husband sees you for the first time."

Elizabeth tugged on her cloche and returned to the observation car, where Henry's eyes widened as they traveled from her raised hemline to her bobbed hair. In that instant, she knew exactly how to play it. "Like it?" she asked, snatching off her cloche. She shook her bobbed curls, sat down beside him, and smiled.

"Your . . . hair," Henry managed to say. "And . . . your dress."

"Enjoy the view?" she asked playfully, crossing her legs at the knee and swinging her foot in his direction.

"Of course I enjoy it." He lowered his voice. "I just don't know if I want everyone else to enjoy it."

Elizabeth laughed. "Don't be silly. Don't you think I'm pretty?"

"Of course. You're beautiful. You'll always be beautiful. But . . ." He struggled for words. "Why?"

Elizabeth shrugged. "I thought it would be more practical. It's going to be hot in southern California, and we're going to be awfully busy on the ranch. Bobbed hair is cooler and easier to care for. I don't want to waste a minute on my hair that could be spent helping you run the ranch."

Henry looked as if he didn't quite believe her, but she smiled and settled back with a copy of Willa Cather's *A Lost Lady* someone had abandoned on an adjacent seat. Later, back in their compartment, she would alter another dress or two before they repacked their bags and changed trains in St. Louis. By the time they reached California, she could make over her entire wardrobe.

❧

A few hours later as they were sitting down to lunch, Elizabeth spotted Mae entering the dining car on the arm of a red-haired man in a finely cut double-breasted wool flannel suit. He was a few inches shorter than the willowy Mae, with a small mouth, a pencil-thin mustache, and a large mole on his left cheek.

Elizabeth caught Mae's eye and beckoned her to join them. Mae hesitated before speaking quietly to her companion, whose glance in the newlyweds' direction, Elizabeth had the distinct impression, took in more than it seemed, down to guessing within a dollar the number of bills in Henry's wallet.

Mae and Peter strolled over to their table. "You don't have a black eye, so I guess he liked the hair," Mae greeted her. She extended a hand to Henry. "Hi, Henry One-in-a-Million."

Startled, Henry rose slightly from his chair to shake her hand. "Hello."

"Henry, this is Mae," said Elizabeth, "and I assume you're Peter?" When he inclined his head in acknowledgment, Elizabeth smiled and gestured to the two empty seats beside her and Henry. "Will you join us for lunch?"

"We don't want to intrude on your honeymoon," Peter demurred.

"That's all right," said Henry. "It's a long trip. I don't want Elizabeth to get bored with only me to talk to."

Mae laughed and pulled out the chair beside Henry.

"How long a trip?" asked Peter as he sat down beside Elizabeth, across from Mae.

"All the way to California," said Elizabeth. "We're changing trains in St. Louis."

"Well, what do you know?" said Mae. "We're on our way to California, too. Peter goes at least twice a year, but this is the first time he's taken me. And it's not even my birthday."

"Maybe we'll be on the same train," said Elizabeth.

"Unlikely," said Peter, as the waiter approached to take their orders. "We're stopping over for the night in St. Louis on business."

"But once that's out of the way, we'll be on our way to Los Angeles," said Mae. "Orange groves, palm trees, Hollywood— Say, why are you going to California, anyway? It's a long way from Pennsylvania even for a honeymoon."

Surprised, Elizabeth said, "I never mentioned that we're from Pennsylvania."

"No, but you got on in Harrisburg and you have those accents."

Elizabeth and Henry shared a look of amusement. It was Mae who had the accent—a thick New York accent just like an actor playing a big-city cabbie on a radio program. Peter didn't, Elizabeth suddenly realized. His accent was more polished, as if that same actor had taken elocution lessons from the man who sold the sponsors' products between programs.

"We're not going only for a honeymoon," explained Elizabeth. "We're staying. Henry's bought a ranch."

Peter regarded them, intrigued. "You don't say."

"One hundred and twenty acres of prime southern California ranchland," said Elizabeth. "Over two hundred head of cattle, the farmhouse, a bunkhouse, and even a stream, a tributary of the Salto Creek."

"Never heard of it," said Mae.

Peter seemed more impressed, and he looked to Henry for confirmation. Henry's pride won out and he explained, "It's called the Rancho Triunfo. It's about forty-five miles north of Los Angeles in the Arboles Valley."

"Actually," added Elizabeth, "the proper name is 'El Triunfo del Dulcisimo Nombre de Jesús,' but we're going to call it Triumph Ranch."

"Or we'll just stick with the Rancho Triunfo, since that's what it says on all the maps," said Henry good-naturedly.

"Triumph Ranch," said Mae. "That sounds like a sure thing, doesn't it?"

"There's no such thing as a sure thing," said Henry. "I have every intention of succeeding, but our only guarantee is that we're in for a lot of hard work."

"You don't say," said Mae, with a glance for Elizabeth that inquired if she still believed the fun was just beginning, because it certainly didn't sound like Henry thought so.

To change the subject, Elizabeth asked, "What line of work are you in, Peter?"

"Sales and distribution."

Mae choked on her water. She set down her glass, wiped her lips delicately with her napkin, and nodded to the table behind Elizabeth and Peter. "Don't make a big show of it, but take a look."

As inconspicuously as she could, Elizabeth glanced over her shoulder at the middle-aged man in a black pinstriped suit and bowler hat, dining alone. He had unscrewed the brass handle of his walking stick and was surreptitiously pouring a clear liquid into a glass of tomato juice.

"I'm shocked," remarked Peter in a low voice, shaking his head. "Absolutely shocked."

"Because he's flouting the law so publicly?" asked Elizabeth, not at all shocked. She had seen worse in the hotel back in Harrisburg, in the dining room as well as her father's private study.

"No, because he's drinking that rotgut. By the cut of his suit, he can clearly afford something smoother, as well as a decent flask to carry it in. That wooden cane can't be doing much for the taste."

The waiter arrived and set their plates before them. "You must really know your liquors to be able to tell rotgut from the best Russian vodka at this distance," said Henry.

"It's the most obvious conclusion. If it were the finest Russian vodka, he would either make a show of drinking it to impress everyone with his wealth and connections, or he'd drink it at home, alone, in the privacy of his study. He wouldn't ruin it by storing it in a cane."

"It's hard to argue with that logic," said Henry.

"Tell me, Henry." Peter paused to taste his pork chop. "What is your opinion on the issue of Prohibition?"

Henry thought for a moment, sparing a glance for Elizabeth. "I think it was well intentioned, but it's created more problems than it's solved. From what I've seen, it hasn't done much to stop people from drinking."

"What do you expect?" said Mae. She sounded almost pleased. "Booze is forbidden fruit now. If you want to make something seem a lot more fun, make it illegal."

"Oh, I agree completely. Back in Harrisburg, girls who would never set foot in a saloon sneak off to speakeasies every Friday and Saturday night and drink nearly as much as their dates." At a surprised look from Henry, Elizabeth quickly added, "Not that I have any firsthand knowledge of such places."

"Of course not," said Mae. "Me, neither."

"Back where we come from, most of the farmers have been making their own home brews just as their German ancestors did generations ago," said Henry. "Who am I to say they should stop?"

"The law says they should," said Peter.

"Maybe it's a misguided law."

Peter smiled. "Then I gather you're not planning to turn in the gentleman seated behind me?"

"No. Live and let live, I say. He's no danger to anyone as far as I can see." Henry regarded Peter curiously. "Why, are you planning to report him?"

"Of course not. It's none of my business." Peter picked up his fork and continued eating. "Besides, he'll drink away the evidence before the authorities meet the train in St. Louis. It would be our word against his and a waste of everyone's time."

Henry merely shrugged and finished his coffee.

After lunch, the two couples went their separate ways. Elizabeth and Henry went to the observation car, where Elizabeth altered the hemline of a poplin housedress and Henry read a farming journal. The flat farmlands of central Indiana sped past the windows, the first early shoots of corn and wheat wafting a light green haze to the horizon.

"I wonder," said Henry suddenly, in a voice too low for anyone else to overhear, "what it is exactly that Peter sells and distributes."

Elizabeth looked up from her sewing. "What do you mean?"

"He said he was in sales and distribution. I'm just curious what his product is. He seems to know a lot about alcohol."

Elizabeth smothered a laugh and resumed her work. "You're right, he did. He also seems to know a lot about canes. That must mean he's either a cane salesman or a bootlegger."

"You can laugh," said Henry. "But don't you think it's interesting that he noticed we got on in Harrisburg? Out of all these passengers, he remembered that about us?"

"All that means is that he's observant. Doesn't a salesman have to be? And anyway, it wasn't Peter who said that but Mae."

"Right. Mae." Henry brooded in silence. "I bet she knows a lot more about speakeasies than she lets on."

"Well, obviously."

"Maybe you should steer clear of her for the rest of the trip."

Elizabeth set down her sewing. "Henry Nelson, you might be my husband now but you can't tell me who my friends should be. Mae was kind to me when I needed someone to salvage my hair and I'm not going to give her the cold shoulder just because you're suspicious of her boyfriend."

"Salvage your hair?" Then her words fully sank in. "You mean they're not married?"

"Oh, for goodness sakes. So what if they aren't? That doesn't mean anything. Didn't you suggest that we should wait to get married until we arrived in California?"

"I'm glad you talked me out of it. I wouldn't want anyone to get the wrong idea about you."

"Just like you're probably getting the wrong idea about Mae and Peter." Elizabeth hated to argue with Henry on their honeymoon, so she gave him a fond smile and said, "They're getting off in St. Louis, so it doesn't matter anyway. After a few hours, we'll never see them again."

Henry nodded and raised her hand to his lips in apology, yet it seemed the train could not reach St. Louis soon enough to suit him.

About an hour outside of St. Louis, someone rapped on their compartment door. Thinking she was admitting the porter, Elizabeth was startled to discover Peter standing in the corridor, hands in his pockets. "May I speak with your husband?"

Elizabeth nodded, beckoned to Henry, who joined Peter outside, leaving the door ajar. "I wondered if you might be amenable to a business proposition," she heard Peter say, while she pretended to be intent on her sewing.

"All of my savings went into the ranch," said Henry. "I can't afford any other investments right now."

"I'm not asking for money. I'm offering you the chance to earn some. A good amount, in fact, with little or no effort on your part."

"Sounds too good to be true."

"I assure you, it's not," said Peter. "I have friends in southern California who are interested in expanding their business. Your ranch lies in an area that is of particular interest to them."

"I've been told there's little in the Arboles Valley besides ranches and farms."

"Its location makes it important," said Peter. "The valley lies between Los Angeles and the cities of Oxnard and Santa Barbara. My acquaintances have had . . . let's call it distribution problems conveying their wares from Los Angeles to cities farther north. The route through those hills can be treacherous—and I'm not speaking only of the terrain but of highwaymen and other unsavory types. Entire shipments have been stolen along the way, or the shippers have been forced to abandon their cargo to preserve their own lives."

"I've been warned about highwaymen," said Henry slowly. Elizabeth resisted the urge to shoot him a sharp look. He had said nothing to her about such dangers. "What would your acquaintances need from me?"

"They need a place where they could store their shipments in case of emergency. They need an honest fellow willing to allow them to use a remote corner of his property and not ask any questions. In exchange for a regular fee, of course. We can call it rent."

"I see," said Henry.

"At lunch I discovered that you're not a man to meddle in another's business. I saw that you're willing to look the other way. That's what my associates want. I assure you, they're discreet. You'd never even know they were there, except for the payments delivered to your door on the first of each month, in cash. They can also offer you . . . protection, should these highwaymen or anyone else cause trouble around your ranch."

"Your associates will protect *me*?" asked Henry. "They seem to have trouble protecting themselves."

Peter gave a low chuckle. "I wouldn't worry about that. They know how to handle people who cross them. So tell me, what's your price?"

"Sorry, but I can't help you." Henry stepped back into the compartment.

"You're passing up a great opportunity," Peter cautioned, blocking the door with his foot. "Regular cash payments, powerful friends, and your hands stay clean. Think about it."

"I don't need to think about it. I've made up my mind. Thanks, but no thanks."

Henry stood firm until Peter retreated.

"What do you think he was talking about?" said Elizabeth when they had shut and locked the door. "Bootlegging? Guns?"

"I don't know and I don't want to know. Whatever it is, I don't want any part of it on our ranch." Henry held Elizabeth's gaze, apprehensive. "Elizabeth, I don't want to make an enemy of Peter, but I think we should avoid your new friends for the rest of the trip. I also think we should keep our business in California to ourselves from now on."

"I won't breathe a word of it until we reach the land office," said Elizabeth shakily.

They remained in their compartment until the train reached St. Louis. As they pulled into Union Station, Elizabeth glanced through the window and spotted a dozen uniformed police officers lined up along the platform. "Is this a typical Missouri welcome?" she asked Henry as they gathered their bags.

"I doubt it," he said grimly.

They were about to disembark when suddenly Elizabeth felt a whiff of perfumed air on her cheek as Mae came swiftly up from behind them and linked her arms through theirs. "Let me leave with you," she said in a low, urgent voice. "Just until we cross the Midway. Act natural. We're old, dear friends traveling together."

Elizabeth was too surprised to say anything, Henry, too reluctant to make a scene, so they allowed Mae to lead them off the train, down the platform, and past the waiting policemen. After they rounded a corner and ducked out of sight between a cigar shop and a newsstand, Mae released their arms and breathed a deep sigh of relief. "Thanks, kids," she said. "That was a close one."

"Listen," said Henry, his voice stern but too low to draw attention. "If you're in trouble with the law—"

Mae's eyes went wide. "Me? I haven't done anything. It's Peter they want. I'm just afraid of getting dragged down as an accomplice."

"*Are* you his accomplice?" asked Elizabeth.

"Of course not," said Mae reproachfully. "But that's not what it looks like, and that's all the Feds care about. I'm his girl, aren't I? That's enough to condemn me right there."

"What did Peter do?" Henry quickly shook his head. "Never mind. I don't want to know. If you say you weren't involved, we'll take your word for it."

"Thank you."

"What are you going to do?" asked Elizabeth.

"I can't go back for my luggage, that's for sure," said Mae, regretful. Then she smiled. "Don't worry about me. I have a little money tucked away—" She patted her leg, close to where her garter probably was. "I'll find work and earn the fare back to New York. With any luck, they'll spring Peter soon and he'll come home to me."

"Are you sure you want him to?" asked Henry. "Whatever he's done, he's obviously trouble."

"I know it doesn't make any sense." For a moment, Mae's mask of surety slipped and a more wistful, vulnerable woman looked back at them. "But Peter's the only man for me." She touched Elizabeth's shoulder and gave her a quick kiss on the cheek. "Good luck to you both. I hope California suits you." She darted off and lost herself in the throng of people passing to and fro on the covered transfer area.

After a moment, Henry took Elizabeth's hand. "Come on," he said. "We don't have much time before our next train."

As they crossed the Midway, they passed within two yards of Peter being led away in handcuffs. His gaze slid past them as if he had never seen them before.

✎

1885

Isabel was fifteen when illness forced her mother to quit her job cleaning rooms at the Grand Union Hotel. The lump beneath her arm had become so swollen and sore that she could not sweep or scrub floors without pain. Isabel's father insisted upon taking her to the doctor in Oxnard, who told them that she had a cancer of the breast and less than three months to live.

The doctor gave them medicine for the pain and sent them home with little hope. Friends and neighbors brought food and said prayers. Isabel's father wept on the back stoop at night while he thought the children were asleep.

A day came when Isabel's mother called her to her bedside, gripped her arm, and told her to visit her cousin in San Mateo. She was a *curandera,* a healer, and she would know what to do. She would know more than that doctor, a man, how to treat a woman's illness.

Isabel hitched a ride to San Mateo and found the address of the *curandera.* Her mother's cousin, an old, wizened woman with long gray hair and gnarled hands, offered her coffee and listened intently as Isabel described her mother's symptoms. "Your mother's cancer is caused by grief and longing," she said. "Has she lost a child? Has her husband strayed?"

"No," Isabel told her.

The *curandera* said she could prepare a remedy, but unless they could figure out what secret grief festered in her mother's heart, the cancer would return.

The *curandera* sent Isabel home with a list of ingredients she must gather: a bottle of holy water blessed by her mother's confessor, wild raspberry leaves from a plant growing no more than a hundred paces from where her mother slept at night, and fifty seeds from fifty freshly picked, unblemished apricots.

Two weeks passed while Isabel waited for the harvest to begin, two weeks while her mother's pain increased until even the doctor's medicine could not abate it. "What did my cousin say?" she demanded. "Has she nothing for me?"

"She says you must not ask questions or her cure will not work," Isabel lied. "She's working on a poultice. In the meantime you must keep saying the rosary twice a day, at morning and at night."

When harvesttime came, Isabel slipped into the line of men and women seeking jobs at the orchard. To her surprise, the hired hand who issued her a punch card did not react when she gave him her name. Yes, she had expected to be compelled to explain, I am Isabel Rodriguez, whose parents once owned all the land you see from the eastern hills to the Salto Canyon. But the hired man either was not paying attention or he had never heard the story of how her father had sworn that neither he nor his descendants would ever again toil for those who had stolen their land. He merely waved Isabel toward the cutting shed and told her to take a place at one of the tables.

A girl she knew from school glanced at her in surprise as Isabel took an empty place at her table, but she said nothing. Isabel took up her knife as a man left a box of apricots beside their table. Isabel worked in silence with her eyes downcast, unwilling to draw attention to herself as she carefully chose unblemished fruit, swiftly cut out the seed, and placed the apricots cut -side up on the table. A bag sat on the table for collecting the seeds; Isabel brushed the bag with her hand as if she were dropping the seeds within, but instead she tucked them into her apron pocket.

Suddenly a hand closed around her wrist so hard she dropped the knife. "What are you doing?" a young woman said in her ear.

Isabel jerked her arm free and stepped back. "Nothing." She recognized the brown-haired girl, although she wasn't sure Hannah knew her. They had played together as young children, in the cabin as well as in the yard of the farmhouse where Hannah lived with her family.

"I saw you put something in your pocket," Hannah said in a low voice. Her discretion came too late; already the other cutters had stopped working to watch them. "Are you stealing apricots?"

"Of course not."

"Then why are your pockets bulging?"

Slowly, aware of all the eyes upon her, Isabel reached into her apron and withdrew a handful of seeds. When she opened her palm, Hannah barked out a laugh. "What in the world are you going to do with those? Plant your own orchard?"

"Of course not," said Isabel. "My family has no land for an orchard."

Hannah flinched. Perhaps she recognized Isabel after all. "You can't eat the seeds, you know," she said sharply. "They're poisonous."

No, Isabel thought. They are medicine. "That's what I need them for," she said. "Poisoning rats. We grind up the dried seeds and sprinkle them on the floor, in the corners."

"I never heard of that."

"You probably never needed to know. I doubt that you have to worry about rats in your home."

Hannah fixed her with a hard stare for a moment before looking away. "Take all the seeds you want. If you need food, ask first."

Isabel nodded and resumed cutting fruit, her face hot with shame. She needed no charity from Hannah or her family. She had only taken what was needed to save her mother, something that otherwise would have been discarded.

At the end of the day, she collected her wages and told the hired man she would not be back.

The next morning, Isabel returned to the *curandera* and waited while she prepared the medicines for her mother. Others waited in the parlor—an old man with a pain in his chest, an angry mother with a nervous girl not much younger than Isabel, a sad woman with the first streaks of gray in her hair and no wedding band on her finger. The old man, wheezing and spitting, told Isabel that she was lucky—*muy afortunada!*—that the *curandera* had agreed to help her. "Her power never fails," he confided. "You will see, my girl. All will be well."

The *curandera* returned from the back room with two parcels wrapped in cheesecloth for Isabel, one large and one small. The first was a poultice for her mother to wear upon the skin between her arm and her breast. It would draw the cancer to the surface, roots and all, where it would be expelled by the body. The smaller parcel was a tea. Isabel's mother should drink a strong brew of it every morning upon waking, then take the leaves from the bottom of her cup and mark a cross upon her heart.

"How long until she will be better?" Isabel asked. A month, perhaps two. If the cancer had not been expelled by the end of the second month but her mother yet lived, Isabel should return for a stronger poultice.

That evening, Isabel helped her mother tie the poultice to her arm to keep it in place while she slept. For the first time in weeks, her mother smiled.

"The poultice has a familiar smell," she said as Isabel drew her favorite quilt over her. It was one Isabel's grandmother had sewn as a young bride-to-be, and it seemed to remind Isabel's mother of more hopeful times.

Her mother slept well. In the morning Isabel brewed her a cup of the tea and brought it to her in bed. Her mother sat up, thanked her, and sipped from the steaming cup. A slight frown clouded her face. "What do I taste?" she asked, inhaling deeply.

"It's better not to ask," said Isabel. "As long as it works, it doesn't matter how foul it tastes."

"It tastes of raspberry leaves," said her mother. She brewed a similar tea to ease her monthly pains. "But also of apricots. I haven't tasted apricots in years."

Isabel busied herself with folding bedclothes that had fallen to the floor.

"Isabel," her mother said, her voice rising. "Are there apricots in this tea? In this poultice?"

"You would have to ask the *curandera*. She made them in a back room. I wasn't watching."

"But I know she gave you a list of ingredients to gather. I know you took them to her. What was in that bag you carried?"

"Just drink the tea, Mami. It will make you well."

"It was harvesttime that week. Were you there? Are these apricots from the ranch?"

Isabel could not lie to her so she said nothing.

Isabel's mother set the cup aside and tore off the poultice. "I want nothing from those people. Their apricots are poison to me."

"What does it matter where the apricots came from?" cried Isabel. "The apricots don't know who owns them."

"But I know. *I* know."

Isabel argued and fought with her mother until they were both in tears, but her mother was resolute. She ordered Isabel to carry the offending medi-cines far away and bury them deep within the ground.

Isabel obeyed, her heart brimming over with helpless anger. Without the *curandera*'s remedies, her mother would die.

If only they had never left the cabin. If only Hannah's family had not made them go.

If they lived there still, her mother never would have refused the gift of the land.

Chapter Three

1925

Henry gripped Elizabeth's arm tightly as they left the Midway for the Headhouse. "This way," he said, guiding her beneath the Grand Hall's gothic arches. Elizabeth marveled at the cathedral ceilings and stained glass windows. Her traveler's eye was drawn to a tableau of three train stations—the castle-like structure of St. Louis's Union Station framed by the New York and San Francisco rail hubs, all rendered in lead and glass. Her gaze continued upward until it settled upon the Whispering Arch she had heard tell of on board the train. A person could reputedly speak softly at one end of the arch and be heard with perfect clarity at the other end, nearly forty feet away. Elizabeth had intended to try it out for herself, but Henry looked determined to quickly and cleanly distance them from her new friends.

The Headhouse contained the ticket office, a hotel, and a restaurant, where Henry and Elizabeth joined the queue at the door. The brakeman had taken the passengers' orders earlier that day before they crossed the Mississippi and had wired them ahead to the restaurant.

"This is a marvel of convenience," Henry said as he sampled his dinner. "Tasty, too."

"It's quite good," said Elizabeth. They were the first words they had exchanged since leaving Mae, and purposefully innocuous, until she forged ahead. "I feel like Saint Peter at the high priest's palace."

"You can't be serious," Henry replied in an undertone. "Allowing them to face the consequences of their actions is hardly denying Jesus three times. If they've done something wrong, they need to face up to it. If Peter's innocent, which I doubt, he'll be released. If anyone asks, we'll tell the truth. We've done nothing wrong." He hesitated. "Except in letting Mae go. We probably should have turned her in."

%

After finishing their meal, Elizabeth and Henry hurried down the Midway to catch the *Pacific Coast Limited* to Los Angeles.

Their encounter with Peter and Mae had left them wary of other passengers, so they remained in their compartment throughout the trip except for visits to the dining car. Eventually their unease faded, but they had come to enjoy their comfortable isolation and ventured out only rarely. Elizabeth had to laugh one morning when she caught Henry tipping the porter extra to straighten their bedcovers but not fold the bed away.

As the train crossed the Central Plains, the flat landscape stretched and rolled into hills and mountains. Although Elizabeth relished the undivided attention they were finally able to give each other, she noticed that Henry grew more pensive the farther west they traveled. He seemed fully at ease only when he held her in his arms.

"What's wrong?" she asked him one evening as the train crossed the Arizona desert. "Are you still upset about Peter, or are you just sorry that our honeymoon's nearly over?"

Henry gave her a brief smile and laced his fingers through hers. "As far as I'm concerned, the honeymoon is never going to end."

"Then what's wrong?"

"I just want the ranch to be perfect for you." He hesitated. "Maybe I should have come out to inspect it myself before buying."

She was reluctant to point out that he probably could not have afforded an additional round-trip, cross-country journey. "You saw the pictures, didn't you? You have the surveyor's map."

"It's not the same as seeing it with my own eyes. I'm also wondering how I'm going to manage the ranch crew. I've never farmed with anyone but my father and brothers and hired hands I've known all my life. Now I'll be giving orders to men who understand that ranch better than I do. Why should they listen to me?"

"Because you're their boss, that's why," said Elizabeth with more certainty than she felt. "You're a natural leader, and if you show them confidence, they'll cooperate. Consult them about their knowledge of the land and then make the best decisions you can. The men will respect you if they know you respect them."

Henry smiled. "Asking you to marry me was the best decision I ever made."

"I couldn't agree more. Don't you see? Once the hired hands meet me, everyone there will know you're a man of sound judgment. Of course they'll listen to you."

She was rewarded by Henry's rich, rare laughter, but even that could not put her own nagging worries completely to rest.

They reached Los Angeles by midafternoon the same day. Their last train would not depart until the following morning, so Henry had arranged for them to spend the night in a modest boardinghouse not far from the station. Elizabeth was eager to see the ocean, though she was surprised and somewhat disappointed to learn that not every place in Los Angeles was convenient to the ocean.

"You could take the trolley to Venice," their landlady suggested.

"Venice?" said Henry, grinning. "That's for us. My wife has always wanted to see Venice."

"I meant Venice, Italy," said Elizabeth, amused. "Not Venice Beach, California."

"It was my Harry's favorite place," said their landlady. "He used to take me there on weekends. We always had a grand time—dancing under the stars, riding the roller coaster, poling along in a gondola. . . . But that was before our favorite pier burned down. And before the Great War." She made an abrupt gesture to a framed photograph on the mantel. A sailor in uniform regarded the camera with steady pride. Flanking the photograph were a folded American flag in a triangular wooden case and a smaller frame enclosing two medals.

Their landlady watched them hopefully, awaiting their reply.

"I didn't know they had real gondolas," said Elizabeth. "I wouldn't miss that for the world. Henry, please say you'll take me."

Their landlady brightened and gave them directions. From the station a few blocks away, they rode a Pacific Electric Red Car southwest out of the city, marveling at the sight of streets washed in sunshine and lined with palm trees. Elizabeth wished she had a camera so she could capture the scenes for the worried folks back home. Never had she imagined such a bright and promising place.

They disembarked at Windward Avenue. Following the breeze off the ocean, they strolled along canals filled with couples in gondolas and children paddling canoes toward streets of shops and restaurants. Elizabeth gasped at the sight of roller coasters looming above the amusements. "We have to ride one," she exclaimed, seizing Henry's hand and pulling him in the direction of the nearest.

"Hold on," said Henry, pausing at the entrance of the Great Dipper. "I thought you wanted to see the ocean."

"I do." She tugged at his hand when he did not budge. "We will. Let's try this first."

"Sweetheart, we're running low on money. It's ten cents apiece."

"We can spare twenty cents."

"Not if you want ice cream and lemonade on the beach."

"You just don't want to ride. You're afraid you'll sick up and embarrass yourself."

"How do you know *you* won't sick up?" he countered. "You've never been on a roller coaster."

Elizabeth considered, scanning the height of the lacy wooden structure. She jumped and clutched her hat in place as a car full of screaming riders hurtled overhead, swirling sand and debris in its wake. "All right," she said shakily. "You can have your way this time, but only because I love you and I don't want an upset stomach to spoil your day."

"Thanks," said Henry, struggling to hide a grin. "That's kind of you."

They strolled along Ocean Front Walk past cafés and beach houses, where the breeze off the ocean was strong and cool.

"I'm going in," Elizabeth declared.

Henry watched with alarm as she peeled off her stockings. "You're kidding."

"I'll only dip my toes in," she assured him. "I want to tell the folks back home that I set foot in the Pacific Ocean. Don't you want to be able to say that?"

"I'd rather have dry feet."

Disappointed, Elizabeth handed him her shoes and stockings. "Then you can watch these until I get back."

She marched unsteadily across the beach toward the water, then stood on the wet sand and let the ocean come to her. The first wave upon her toes shocked her with its coldness. She gasped from surprise, and then, as she grew accustomed to the cold, she waded in up to her ankles. A second wave swept up to her knees and tugged at her gently, beckoning her forward into the deeper water.

She laughed aloud and took a step back toward dry land, but a sudden wave rushed forward and seized her, knocking her off balance. A firm hand on her arm caught her before she fell. "Careful," said Henry, his voice carried away by the wind.

He had removed his shoes and socks, but the rolled cuffs of his trousers were soaked through. As he helped her regain her footing and led her from the water, sand collected on his cuffs in a layer that thickened as they crossed the beach.

When they reached the pavement of Ocean Front Walk, he tried to shake his cuffs free of sand. "I'm sorry," said Elizabeth. "It's my fault you're such a mess."

"Never mind." He handed her her shoes and stockings, which he had left beside his own on a bench. "I'm sure I'm not the first man to walk the streets of Venice covered in a good portion of the beach."

"It was sweet of you to come along after me."

He sat down and brushed sand from his toes. "I wanted to be there to witness it if you decided to dive in headfirst."

Elizabeth laughed. She had never been happier, not even on their wedding day. She had waded in the Pacific Ocean, something no one in her family had ever done. She had seen sights they had never seen. Every day of the rest of her life would be an adventure, with Henry nearby to steady her if she should stumble.

❧

Walking out on the Venice Pier—past the Flying Circles aerial ride, the Dragon Bamboo slide, and the Ship Café—Elizabeth and Henry came upon two dozen couples in just that predicament. On the maple floor of a spacious dance hall, partners dragged their feet to a lively Irving Berlin tune. Some of the women slung their arms about their partners' shoulders and clung to them to keep themselves upright. Several of the men had apparently nodded off with their heads on the shoulders of their smaller partners, who struggled to keep them on their feet. Suddenly a woman appeared to faint; at first her partner grappled to catch her but then he too collapsed onto the hardwood floor. Three men rushed out to drag them out of the way while the other couples danced on, oblivious and glassy-eyed.

"How long have they been at it?" Henry asked a man who stood near the orchestra pit sipping a ginger ale.

"Three days," said the man, shaking his head in amazement.

"How do they stay on their feet?" marveled Elizabeth. "I'd want to pass out."

"Some of them do." The man indicated a man at least six feet tall dancing with a petite, red-haired woman. "See that couple over there? That's my brother and his girlfriend. They soaked their feet in brine and vinegar for two days straight beforehand. They'll be going strong for a long time yet, you just wait and see. They'll take home that thousand-dollar prize sure enough."

"A thousand dollars?" Elizabeth touched Henry's arm. "Isn't it a shame we didn't arrive in time to enter?"

"It's a shame, all right," replied Henry, sounding not at all disappointed. "Do you want to stay and watch the action, or see more of Venice?"

"Let's stay for a while. Maybe we'll see who wins."

"Probably not," said the man. "Some of these marathons last a week or more."

Henry, looking ever more pleased they had arrived too late to compete, offered to get them some drinks while Elizabeth found a place to sit and watch the marathon.

"I bet you could dance circles around them all," a man spoke close to her ear. Startled, she drew back as he pulled out the chair beside her and sat down. "You look like a girl with energy to spare."

"Not that much," she admitted. "I like dancing, but in smaller doses."

"I'd ask you to dance, but the floor is reserved for the marathon."

"I'd have to refuse," she told him. "I'm married."

He made an exaggerated show of looking around. "I don't see any husband. If you were my wife, I wouldn't let you out of my sight."

Elizabeth laughed politely and watched as a dancing woman frantically waved smelling salts beneath her partner's nostrils. She shrieked and burst into tears as he staggered into a table at the edge of the dance floor, sending glasses of lemonade and ginger ale flying.

"That'll disqualify him," the man remarked. His hair was parted down the middle and combed down neatly. When Elizabeth nodded, he suddenly peered at her curiously. "Say, aren't you that actress, the one from that movie—what was it? No, don't tell me. *The Thief of Baghdad*?"

Elizabeth smiled. "No, that wasn't me. I'm not an actress."

"Are you sure?"

"I think I would know."

"You're pretty enough to be an actress. Have you ever thought about being in the movies?"

"No, I can't say that I have," said Elizabeth. "But I've been in California only a day."

"Well, let me tell you, sister, girls not half as pretty as you are making movies every day." He reached into his breast pocket and pulled out a business card. "I'm a producer myself, always on the lookout for new talent. Where are you from? Ohio? Indiana?"

"Pennsylvania."

"Same difference. You've got that wholesome, midwestern look the camera just loves. I have half a dozen scripts on my desk with roles you'd be perfect for."

"But I've never acted before," Elizabeth said, fingering the business card. "I wouldn't know the first thing to do."

He shrugged. "We have an acting coach on staff. It's easy. You're a smart girl. You'll pick it up. My number's on the card. Just call me at my office—"

"My wife won't have time to be in your picture," said Henry, directly behind them. "We're ranchers, not movie stars."

The producer jumped up in surprise, nearly knocking over his chair. He eyed Henry's strong farmer's build before taking a step back and saying, "She looks like a girl who can answer for herself."

"I can," said Elizabeth quickly, as Henry glowered. "And my husband's right. I'm going to be much too busy to be an actress. I'm sorry, but thank you anyway."

"Suit yourself." Grumbling, the man walked off and disappeared into the crowd of observers lining the dance floor.

"You didn't have to be so rude," said Elizabeth as Henry took the vacant chair and set two glasses of lemonade before them. "He might have put me in a movie. It would have been fun."

"I doubt he was a real producer."

"He had a business card." Elizabeth held it up. "See? Grover Higgins, Golden Reel Productions, Hollywood, California."

Henry jerked his thumb toward the entrance. "Back out on the midway, I can buy a copy of *Life* magazine with my picture on the cover. I don't think a fake movie mogul would have any trouble making fake business cards."

Insulted, Elizabeth turned away from him and studied the exhausted dancers. When Henry reached over to touch her arm, she scooted her chair out of reach.

"Sweetheart, don't be like that," he said. "Even if he was the real thing, that's not the life for us. You never even thought about being an actress until he came along."

"Maybe it never occurred to me that it was possible," she retorted. "You know I love the movies. Why couldn't I be an actress?"

"Because the day after tomorrow, you and I are going to be in the Arboles Valley running the Rancho Triunfo."

Elizabeth had nothing to say. Why was it so impossible to believe that a genuine movie producer thought she had talent?

They sipped their drinks in silence until Henry abruptly drained his and stood. "Come on." He held out his hand, and by force of habit she took it and rose. "You want to go to Hollywood? I'll take you to Hollywood."

On the way to the door, Elizabeth tightened her grip on Henry's hand—and slipped the business card into her pocket.

&#

On the way back to the trolley station, Elizabeth persuaded Henry to stop and allow her to shop for souvenirs. He owed her that much, she figured, for his unwillingness to consider the possibility that she could be the next Clara Bow or Mary Pickford. As she browsed through racks of purses and jewelry at a shop on Windward Avenue, Henry's willingness to please her despite their dwindling funds made her feel demanding and unreasonable, and ashamed of herself. She was a married woman now, not some Sheba with a string of boyfriends who only accepted apologies in gift boxes. If she told Henry she had changed her mind about choosing a souvenir, he would never believe it, so she settled for a postcard of the midway at Venice Beach with a view of the Giant Dipper roller coaster and the Bamboo Dragon slide to send to little cousin Sylvia and a silk scarf with the words *Venice Beach, California* printed upon it in curved letters that reminded her of the crash of ocean waves upon the sand.

From Venice Beach they took the Red Car trolley north to Hollywood, where they strolled along the sidewalks lined by shops and businesses built in an eclectic assemblage of Beaux Arts, Spanish Colonial Revival, and Art Deco architectural styles. They stopped at Sardi's on Hollywood and Vine for a soda, then continued down Hollywood Boulevard to Grauman's Egyptian Theater. The name alone prepared Elizabeth for the hieroglyphics and decorative carvings, but the front courtyard also boasted columns larger around than her favorite stately trees along Elm Creek back home. She and Henry marveled over the tiled murals and a fountain, enormous planters filled with exotic flowers, and a twelve-foot statue of an Egyptian idol with the head of a dog. "All this before we pass through the front doors," Elizabeth exclaimed. Henry laughed and squeezed her hand.

Halfway through the first feature, *Trouble at Rocky Ranch,* Elizabeth leaned over to Henry and whispered, "Do you think our ranch will be anything like this one?"

"Considering that we've already seen three men shot, a bank robbed, and two women kidnapped by Indians, I sure hope not."

Elizabeth smothered a laugh and settled back to enjoy the movie, savoring every bit of pleasure from the lavish theater and the company of her dear, wonderful husband. She knew this would be one last day of fun before the real work began. In the morning they would take the train northwest into the Arboles Valley, or at least as close as they could come to it. Henry had shown her on the map how the railroad actually ran through a valley to the east, where they would disembark and hire a cab to take them the rest of the way. They would spend one night in a hotel, but the next morning they would go to the land office and take possession of Triumph Ranch.

After so much waiting and planning, only the last stage of their journey still lay ahead of them. They were almost home.

❧

1886

After her mother's death in late summer, Isabel left school to care for her younger brother and sister and keep house for her father. Her closest friends did not forget her. Every day after school, they gathered on her small back stoop to gossip and help Isabel with her chores. Isabel's heart lifted when her friends were near, but all too soon summer came, and her friends' visits ceased. She soon discovered the reasons for their absence. Most had to work their family farms; others had taken summer jobs in the sugar factories in

Oxnard. If they had forgotten her, it was only because they had become as busy with responsibilities as she.

Even her father had taken a second job delivering milk. Every morning he rose well before dawn to walk to the dairy farm two miles away. Before the sun rose, he was crisscrossing the Arboles Valley in a wagon loaded with milk and butter and cheese. Isabel would have his breakfast waiting for him when he returned. He would bolt down whatever she put in front of him, thank her, and give her sleeping brother and sister quick, gentle kisses before leaving for his regular job as a handyman at the Grand Union Hotel. He returned home in time for supper, exhausted, with little to say. The children crept quietly around the house when their father was home, heeding Isabel's warnings to let him sleep. Although her father had never raised his voice to them, Isabel slowly came to understand that they were fearful of the stoic, silent man who worked so hard to provide for the family. She wished they had known the father she remembered, the man he had been before her mother died.

On her birthday, Isabel's father gave her a dollar to spend as she pleased, so she decided to take her brother and sister to the Arboles Grocery for ice cream. She bought them each an Eskimo Pie, pocketed the change, and took them outside to enjoy their treats in the shade of the live oaks.

As her brother and sister chattered happily, Isabel heard through the open store window a conversation in Spanish. "Who's the beautiful widow?" a young man not much older than herself asked.

"Who?" another man replied.

"The pretty widow who just left. You saw her. She bought ice cream for her boy and girl."

The second man laughed. "Widow? Are you crazy? That's Isabel Rodriguez. She went to school with us. She was in the same class as your sister."

"That's not Isabel Rodriguez. She's much prettier than Isabel."

"I'm telling you, that's her. She's a friend of my cousin. That was her little brother and sister with her, not her kids."

The men argued good-naturedly as they left the store and approached the three siblings. Isabel pretended not to see them, but they strolled over, all too casually. "*Buenos días,* Isabel," her friend's cousin greeted her. "Do you know my friend, Miguel Diaz?"

Miguel, whom she recognized as a boy a few years ahead of her in school, smiled in a friendly, hopeful way, but Isabel returned an icy glare. "Only by what one overhears."

Miguel winced, but his friend grinned.

"It's Isabel's birthday," her younger sister piped up. "You should tell her happy birthday."

"Feliz cumpleaños, Isabel Rodriguez," said Miguel, with a regretful look that begged for an apology. She was only sixteen, but the past year had not been kind to her. Someone she barely knew thought she looked old enough to have children ages ten and thirteen. Isabel hardened her heart, gave her friend's cousin a curt nod, and took the children home.

She sent her brother and sister out to play while she put beans on to soak and made tortillas. She ached for her mother. She longed for her to walk through the front door, smile in her fond and gentle way, and tie on her apron. She wished her mother could be beside her, teaching her all the treasured family recipes she had learned from her own mother. On Christmas, Isabel had tried to make tamales the way her mother had always done, but her brother complained that they tasted nothing like Mami's and her sister left hers untouched on her plate. Nothing was right without their mother. Nothing had been right since they had left the little cabin on the ranch so many years before. She wished she were still that five-year-old girl, safe and happy within the lie that all would be well in her world, that she would always be loved and protected and happy.

Chapter Four

1925

Elizabeth woke in the middle of the night, shivering. She groped around at the foot of the bed for the comforter that she had folded out of the way when she first climbed beneath the covers, certain she would not need it, not in California. She drew it over herself and snuggled closer to Henry, who put his arm around her and slept on. The landlady had told them she kept extra quilts in the cedar chest at the foot of the bed, but Elizabeth was too cold to climb from beneath the covers to find one. She wished again for her wedding quilt, still tucked away in the trunk her brother had given her, bundled protectively around their fine china. Elizabeth puzzled over the curious cold snap until she grew warm enough to fall back asleep.

It was still early when she woke again. Henry had already risen and was sitting on the edge of the bed, pulling on his shoes. He saw that she was awake and leaned across the bed to kiss her. "Good morning," he said. "Better get up soon if you want breakfast before we go to the station."

Elizabeth would have gladly done without breakfast if it meant reaching the Arboles Valley sooner, but their tickets were for the midmorning train and it wouldn't do them any good to wait on the platform for hours. She threw back the covers and quickly washed and dressed. It took only moments to repack her suitcase, and soon they joined several of the other guests in the dining room, where their landlady was serving breakfast.

"You folks leaving so soon?" inquired a traveling salesman seated across the table. "You won't find many places on the road as hospitable as this."

"Flatterer," scoffed the landlady, but Elizabeth noticed that she added an extra pancake to his stack.

"If we weren't expected elsewhere, we'd be happy to stay another night," said Elizabeth, with a smile for her hostess. "We're on our way to the Arboles Valley."

The salesman turned an inquiring look upon Henry. "What do you plan to do all the way out there? The most popular tourist attractions are around the city. I hope you didn't buy a bogus map. You have to be careful around here. People take advantage of tourists."

"We're not tourists," said Henry. "We've come to stay. We're farmers."

"Farmers?" The salesman smiled at Elizabeth. "You're much too pretty to be a farm wife. If you want work, you should get into the movies."

"You're not the only one to think so," said Elizabeth, deliberately avoiding Henry's eye. "Perhaps someday."

"Not likely," said Henry. "I don't think you'll be running into many movie producers in the Arboles Valley."

"You'd be surprised," remarked their landlady. "Movies shoot on location up that way all the time."

Elizabeth threw Henry a triumphant grin. Perhaps the movie producers would come to her. Besides, as long as she had one producer's card in her pocketbook, she didn't need to meet any others.

"We'll be too busy," Henry reminded her. "Don't get your hopes up."

"I won't, but I also won't dismiss the possibility entirely," said Elizabeth. "Isn't California the land of opportunity? Anything can happen."

The salesman nodded in approval of her optimism. The landlady beamed, and why shouldn't she? Someday she might be able to brag to her friends that she had hosted the famous Elizabeth Nelson on her first night in California. Henry merely scowled and continued eating.

"Take care on the route north," cautioned an older guest, who had introduced himself as a civil engineer visiting Los Angeles to study the aqueducts. "It's a dangerous road through those hills. Highwaymen stop automobiles, wagons—anyone traveling alone. They'll steal anything of value they can find and they're not above roughing up women. Begging your pardon, miss."

Elizabeth gave him a quick smile to reassure him that his words had not upset her, although they had, a little. After what Peter had said, the engineer's warning carried more weight than he knew.

"The Sheik Bandits have been at it again," said the landlady. "It's in the paper this morning. They robbed a bank and left the poor cashier tied up in the vault. They were last seen heading north."

"The Sheik Bandits?" echoed Elizabeth.

"A gang of three or four men, always sharply dressed," said the salesman. "A couple of years ago, they held up a post office just over the Los Angeles County line. They bound and gagged the postmistress and made off with nearly five hundred dollars cash."

Elizabeth shuddered. "My goodness. The poor woman."

"Anyone can disappear in those rugged hills," said the engineer. "Rumor has it the bandits hide out in the old Indian caves. No one should drive that road without a loaded firearm at his side. You're not safe until you're within the Oxnard city limits."

"It's not that bad," said the salesman, but unconvincingly. "The Arboles Valley is perfectly safe. It's just getting there that's the trouble. You young folks won't be traveling after dark, will you?"

"We're traveling by train to the Simi Valley and driving over the grade from there," said Henry.

Around the table, the other guests visibly relaxed. "In that case, you'll be fine," said the engineer.

Elizabeth managed a brief, shaky smile, wondering what other plans Henry had made without explaining their imperative to her. She had assumed he had chosen the train for its speed and directness, not because their lives depended on it.

❧

For the relatively short trip to the Simi Valley station, Henry had purchased two seats in coach and paid an additional fee for their excess luggage. Their seats were quite a change from the comfortable private compartments they had enjoyed on the first two legs of their journey, but Elizabeth was so eager to reach their final destination she did not mind.

At last the conductor called out the Simi Valley station. Almost before the train halted, Elizabeth and Henry leaped to their feet to collect their bags. As they waited for their trunks to be unloaded from the luggage car, Elizabeth paced along the platform, taking in the sights and unfamiliar smells, breathless from excitement. The station lay in a broad, flat valley surrounded by low, arid mountains. Just over the ridge was the Arboles Valley.

Henry set Elizabeth to counting their pile of trunks and suitcases while he went to hail a cab. She sat down on the largest trunk and watched arriving passengers being met by family as outgoing passengers climbed aboard the train. The conductor called out his warning; shortly after, the engine started up again and the train chugged out of the station. Elizabeth sat alone on the platform.

She rose, shaded her eyes, and looked around for Henry, but all she saw was a man working inside the ticket booth. In a moment, even he disappeared from view. Elizabeth began pacing again, but did not stray far from their belongings. Finally Henry appeared. "There's not a cab anywhere."

"Well, we *are* out in the country."

"Sure, but this is a train station. We can't be the only passengers who arrive here without anyone to pick them up."

Elizabeth glanced around the platform but decided not to point out that they certainly seemed to be, at least for that train. "Could we send word to the ranch? If they know we've arrived, I'm sure they'd send someone for us."

"If we had someone to send word to the ranch, we'd have our ride."

"Of course," Elizabeth murmured. She sat down on the trunk again, planted her elbows on her knees, and rested her head in her palms.

"I'll find us something to drink," said Henry in a kinder tone, as if to apologize for his impatience. He went off again and returned with two paper cones of cool water. Elizabeth drained hers quickly and wished for more, but Henry was in such a sour mood she didn't want to inconvenience him.

A few minutes passed and Henry went off to try again to find a cab. Elizabeth wished him good luck with more cheerfulness than she felt. Nearly an hour had passed since their arrival, and a trickle of people had begun to gather on the platform to await the next train. Before long Henry hurried back, grinning. "I helped a farmer unload his cargo in exchange for a ride," he said. "Our hotel for tonight is out of his way. Let's hurry so we don't delay him any longer than necessary."

Elizabeth quickly rose and took two of the lighter suitcases in hand while Henry hefted a trunk onto his shoulder. She followed him off the platform and around the corner, where a tall, thin man in faded overalls and a plaid shirt waited beside a wagon, holding the reins of two draft horses. The weathered lines of his face spoke of hard times and disappointment, but his gaze was steady, though unsmiling. Henry hurried through introductions, and while Elizabeth shook Lars Jorgensen's hand, her husband returned to the platform for their remaining luggage.

"Can you hold a team?" Lars Jorgensen asked Elizabeth gruffly. When she nodded, he helped her up onto the wagon seat and handed her the reins. One of the horses stomped an enormous hoof and shook his shaggy mane. The farmer said something to him in a language Elizabeth did not recognize and went off to assist Henry.

The Nelsons' belongings took up nearly half of the wagon bed, much more territory than that claimed by the few wooden crates of supplies and cans of kerosene Lars Jorgensen had already stowed there. Lars took the reins from Elizabeth, who moved over to make room for him on the seat. Henry climbed into the back with the cargo. "Thank you for the ride," he said to their host. "We're obliged to you."

"Yes, thank you very much," Elizabeth added. Lars nodded and shook the reins to start the team forward. The wagon lurched and headed off down the road toward the west.

Elizabeth expected the farmer to be curious about strangers traveling with so much luggage, but he said nothing until the train station had disappeared behind them. "So you're a Nelsen?" he said, and then added a few words in the same language with which he had addressed the horses.

"Sorry," said Henry ruefully. "I know very little Swedish, barely enough to say hello and good-bye. My family always spoke English at home."

"That was Norwegian," said Lars dryly. "Many Norwegian families live in the Arboles Valley. Why did you say you were a Nelsen? You must be a Nel-*son.*"

Henry gave a small, baffled shrug. "That's right. Sorry."

"Norwegian settlers?" said Elizabeth. "I had expected Spaniards."

"We got some of them, too. Mostly Mexican, though, not Spanish." Lars fell silent for a moment, as if contemplating how much to tell them. "Most of the Arboles Valley belongs to five different families—the Olsens, the Pedersens, the Kelleys, the Borchards, and my people, the Jorgensens. Other families have smaller farms and ranches scattered thereabouts. We still got more sheep than people in the valley, but I expect that'll change in days to come."

Elizabeth wondered why he had left the former owners of Triumph Ranch off the list. "You have cattle, too, isn't that so? I understand this is an excellent region for raising cattle."

Lars shrugged. "Some folks have done all right with cattle. Sheep fare better here."

At the risk of alarming Henry by divulging too much of their secret, Elizabeth persisted. "You must know the Rodriguez family, I'm sure."

He gave her a sharp look. "Yes, I know them. Of course I know them. Their people have been around here for generations."

And yet he was not aware of the Rodriguez family who ran a thriving cattle ranch? Elizabeth wondered if the Arboles Valley was larger and more populous than Henry had led her to believe. She was about to jog the farmer's memory when Henry spoke up. "What crops do you raise on your farm, Mr. Jorgensen?"

Elizabeth recognized his attempt to change the subject and let the matter drop.

"I work my brother's farm," replied Lars. "He raises sheep, barley, and apricots. Sometimes he tries his hand at another crop just to see how it fares, but sheep, barley, and apricots are our mainstays. That was a load of wool bound for Los Angeles you helped me unload back at the station."

Suddenly the wagon pitched as a wheel rumbled over a pothole in the hard-packed dirt road. Instinctively Elizabeth gasped and clutched the seat. Lars glanced at her, and something that could have passed for a smile briefly appeared in the tanned leather of his face. "Road's a little rough in parts," he said. "It'll smooth out once we cross over the grade."

"I don't suppose there are any plans to improve the road?" asked Elizabeth, her teeth rattling with each jolt of the wagon. In the wagon bed, Henry muffled an exclamation as a trunk slid into him. China rattled. Elizabeth hoped fervently that the quilts the Bergstrom women had made would see the precious wedding gifts safely the remaining few miles of their journey.

"You're looking at the improvements," Lars replied. "Folks used to have to come over the Old Butterfield Road to the Camarillo Valley to haul our crops to the train. It was even steeper than this, and when it rained the wheels would stick in the mud so you'd lose half a day getting your wagon free. Everyone knew it was only a matter of time until a wagon overturned and someone got killed. So a farmer named Nils Olsen donated the land, and all the Norwegian families worked together in their spare time for two years to carve this route through the hills. They did it all on their own, with no help from the government except for the money the county gave them to buy dynamite to blast the boulders too large to move." Lars regarded the road before them with pride. "They call this the Norwegian Grade in honor of those families."

"They must be very proud," said Elizabeth faintly. If this were the safer pass, she prayed she would never be required to take the Old Butterfield route.

The team pulled the wagon over the grade. At the summit, Elizabeth forgot about the rough road as she gazed out upon the Arboles Valley, a patchwork quilt of green and brown bathed in warmth and sunlight and framed by mountains. Behind her, Henry rose to his knees in the wagon bed for a better look. Elizabeth beamed at him as he took her hand, but she quickly returned her gaze to the breathtaking sight. She wished she knew which of the patchwork farms and ranches was theirs.

"What's that?" asked Henry suddenly, indicating a shadow cutting into the gentle roll of the valley floor.

"That's the Salto Canyon," said Lars. "The Salto Creek runs through the bottom. Best source of water in the valley. The only reliable source when the rains don't come."

The description of their land included a creek; perhaps it was this one. Elizabeth shaded her eyes with her hands and eagerly searched the region around the canyon for landmarks from the photographs the land agent had given Henry, but from their vantage point, one cluster of oaks resembled every other. She wished Henry would take out his map and locate Triumph Ranch while they could still enjoy the view of it from above, but he would not risk divulging their secret too soon, even to one taciturn farmer.

They descended from the hills into the valley, and as Lars had promised, the road grew considerably smoother. They passed other farms and had a first glimpse of their new neighbors from a distance. Farmers labored in fields; a pair of dogs chased the wagon for an eighth of a mile before giving up and going home, tails wagging.

They had nearly reached the opposite side of the valley before the first real signs of a town appeared. They passed the Arboles Grocery, a modest, one-story wooden structure with a single gas pump out front. Farther down the road was the Arboles School, a newer, whitewashed building with a bell in a high cupola. Children played in the short, brown school-yard grass.

"Where's the post office?" asked Henry. Elizabeth knew he really wanted to know how to find the land office, which was located within the post office, not an unusual arrangement for a town this size.

"John Barclay runs it out of his front room."

"The post office is in his house?" asked Elizabeth.

Lars shrugged. "He is the postmaster."

"How do we get there?" asked Henry. "And how early does he open?"

"Take the El Camino Real north from your hotel, turn right at the first road east, and you'll go right past it. Barclay's likely up at daybreak to care for his livestock. If you go to see him that early, you'll find him in the barn. If you want him to leave his chores to take care of post office business, you should offer to help him or he's liable to take his own sweet time just to spite you."

"I gather Mr. Barclay's a difficult man," remarked Elizabeth.

"No more than any other man who's well acquainted with trouble. Some folks might say he's brought his troubles on himself—and I might be one of them—but what hurts him hurts his wife, and she surely doesn't deserve any more heartbreak."

Lars broke off and frowned deeply as if startled by his own frankness. Elizabeth wanted to ask him what manner of trouble and heartbreak had afflicted the Barclay family, but the set of his jaw made it obvious that he had said all he intended to say. She glanced over her shoulder at Henry, who was mulling over Lars's words in bemused concern. Henry would not be content until the deed of trust was in his hand, and if what Lars said was true, acquiring it depended upon the goodwill of a temperamental man.

Surely Mr. Barclay would fulfill his professional obligations, bad temper or not. Surely the citizens of the Arboles Valley would not have chosen him as their postmaster if he was the sort of man to disrupt official business on a whim.

The wagon topped a low rise and approached an intersection with a broader, more recently paved road. "There it is," said Lars, gesturing toward a two-story building on the other side of the street, high above them on a foothill of the scrub-covered mountains that rose dramatically behind it. "The Grand Union Hotel."

It was the tallest, most stately building they had seen so far in the valley, freshly painted, with a broad wraparound porch, tall windows, and a second-floor balcony with a railing of turned spindles. Tall, leafy oaks lined the cobblestone drive leading up to the hotel, where Mr. Jorgensen brought the horses to a halt. The front walk was neatly kept, and the garden boasted several magnolia trees in full bloom. Around the side of the hotel, Elizabeth spotted a grove of orange and lemon trees with a walking path and a gazebo. Suddenly she felt a sharp, painful longing for home. Somehow this hotel, smaller and so different in appearance from Elm Creek Manor, reminded her of that beloved place.

Henry jumped down from the wagon and assisted her to the ground. While Lars helped Henry unload their belongings, Elizabeth took in the view from the porch and tried to peek inside the curtained windows. Then Lars tugged on the brim of his hat, wished them well, and turned the horses back down the cobblestone drive.

Elizabeth's attention was drawn to the windowsill, which was pockmarked by many small holes. "What creature made these, do you suppose?" she asked Henry when he joined her on the porch. "An insect? A woodpecker, perhaps?"

Henry studied the holes. "That's buckshot."

"What?" said Elizabeth. "You mean someone shot at our hotel?"

"A long time ago," Henry quickly replied. "Those are old scars. This is an old hotel. I'm sure it's perfectly safe now."

"Perhaps, or perhaps some of Peter's business associates paid a recent call."

"It's safe." Henry opened the door and gestured for her to precede him inside. "I wouldn't put us up anywhere that wasn't safe."

"Not knowingly, you wouldn't."

"Elizabeth—" Henry waved her inside impatiently. "It's safe. Go on in."

She obeyed, reluctantly, and only because she did not think they had any other choice. Lars Jorgensen was long gone, and they had nowhere else to stay for the night.

Inside the lobby, the front desk was unoccupied, but Elizabeth heard voices and the clinking of glassware somewhere beyond. To her right was the doorway to a barroom, with a long bar that seemed to run the entire length of the building. Three or four men sat on tall bar stools, their backs to the lobby. Elizabeth wondered what they were drinking. If alcohol filled their glasses, they were making no effort to conceal it.

She looked to her left, through a second doorway leading into a Victorian parlor, which appeared to be unoccupied. Between the lobby and the parlor was a polished hardwood staircase spindled even more ornately than the balcony outside. The same small holes that marred the windowsill also riddled the banister. Elizabeth, hearing quick footsteps approach, gestured at the holes and raised her eyebrows at her husband to be sure he had taken note of them. Henry smiled weakly and shrugged just as a woman in her sixties entered through a doorway behind the desk. Her two dark braids threaded heavily with gray were coiled at the nape of her neck, her manner officious but cordial. "Welcome to the Grand Union," she greeted them. "Do you need lodgings for the night or shall I show you to the dining room? Or perhaps you'd like refreshments in the bar?"

"We'll be staying the night." Henry reached into his breast pocket and pulled out a letter. "I'm Henry Nelson and this is my wife, Elizabeth. I wrote to you last month."

"Oh, yes, of course. The newlyweds." The proprietress smiled briefly as she skimmed the letter. "I'm Gertrude Diegel. Your room is upstairs. Do you need help with your luggage?"

When they explained that most of their luggage sat outside on the front porch, Mrs. Diegel suggested they store the heavy trunks in the staff area off the kitchen. Elizabeth and Henry agreed, and after summoning a porter, Mrs. Diegel led them upstairs. The staircase divided at a landing; they followed Mrs. Diegel up the right-hand stairs to the east wing, down a narrow hall past several closed doors, and to their own room close to the end.

"It's a single bed," Mrs. Diegel warned them as she opened the door. "It will be cozy, but perhaps as newlyweds you don't mind. Or would you care to take a second room?"

Peering inside, Elizabeth saw that the room was only about eight by ten feet, with a narrow dresser, a ladder-back chair pulled up to a table scarcely large enough to hold the vase of flowers set upon it, and a bed no wider than a single berth on the *Pacific Coast Limited*. It was smaller than Elizabeth had expected, but she did not want to spend the last night of her honeymoon apart from her husband, especially since their funds were dwindling and they had barely enough left to pay for the single room. Henry must have been thinking the same, for they both quickly assured Mrs. Diegel that a second room would not be necessary. Mrs. Diegel nodded, reminded them that supper would be served at five o'clock, and left them alone in the small room.

Elizabeth promptly went to the washbasin and pitcher on a dresser near the window, eager to freshen up and explore the citrus grove before supper. With a creak of bedsprings, Henry sat down and unfolded the map on the quilt, smoothing out the creases. "I think this is an older map," he said after a moment. "None of the names of the families Lars Jorgensen mentioned are marked on any of the farms and ranches bordering our property."

Elizabeth dried her face and hands and retrieved her brush from her handbag. "Is the hotel on the map?"

"No, but that doesn't mean anything. This map only shows property boundaries, not buildings."

Elizabeth ran the brush through her bobbed curls, unconcerned. "Land changes hands. Families change names through marriage. We'll sort everything out at the land office tomorrow."

"I'd rather go today." Henry refolded the map, frowning. "I'd go this minute if I could."

"They aren't expecting us until tomorrow."

"But John Barclay will be there, won't he, if the office is in his house?"

"I suppose so, but if he's as cranky as Lars Jorgensen implied, he probably won't be happy if we show up early. What's your hurry? Triumph Ranch is already ours. Waiting half a day won't make a difference."

"The sooner I can see the place with my own eyes, the better I'll feel."

"Really, Henry, what are you so worried about? Say we show up at the ranch and the cattle are sickly and the barn roof is half caved in. We can fix whatever's wrong, and if we can't, we'll sell the land to recover our costs and go back home to Two Bears Farm. That's the worst that could happen, and you have to admit that isn't so bad."

He looked up at her with such unexpected bleakness that she immediately regretted her flippant tone. She sat down on the bed beside him and kissed him on the cheek. "I'm only joking," she said. "Everything's going to be fine. Cheer up, won't you? This is the last day of our honeymoon, we're almost out of money, and tomorrow the real work begins. Let's have fun while we still can."

Henry closed his hand around hers and gently stroked her cheek. "You're right," he said, but the worry did not completely leave his eyes.

❧

Elizabeth persuaded Henry to join her on a stroll along the walking path that wound through the orange and lemon trees. They found a stone bench beneath a shady oak and sat down to take in the view of the Arboles Valley, less dramatic than from the Norwegian Grade, but still lovely. Henry's old confidence returned as he pointed out the direction of Triumph Ranch and what he thought was the western boundary of the property.

"Tomorrow we're going home," he promised. "We'll have lunch in the kitchen of the Rancho Triunfo and sleep in a comfortable bed."

"And we'll sleep beneath our wedding quilt," Elizabeth promised in return. "It's too beautiful to save for only special occasions."

Henry laughed. "Any other woman would say that it is too beautiful to use every day."

"Things don't become more beautiful locked away in a trunk," protested Elizabeth. "I say if one can surround oneself with lovely things, one should."

Henry smiled and kissed her. "That's why you belong here in California. You are too beautiful yourself not to be surrounded by beauty every day of your life."

At five o'clock, they met Mrs. Diegel in the dining room just off the parlor Elizabeth had seen from the lobby. Beyond it lay the kitchen, from which delicious smells wafted. Elizabeth had not eaten since breakfast back in Los Angeles, so she eagerly sat down when Henry pulled out her chair. Six other guests had already seated themselves, four men traveling on business and another married couple about ten years older than the Nelsons. The guests introduced themselves and chatted while Mrs. Diegel served chicken and dumplings with a salad of sliced tomatoes and cucumbers. As they had in the Los Angeles boardinghouse just that morning, the Nelsons found themselves forced to be evasive when confronted by their fellow guests' friendly curiosity. This time, however, their usual reply that they were farmers who had come to the Arboles Valley to settle down met with puzzlement.

"You're planning to buy a farm?" asked one man, who, to Elizabeth's consternation, happened to be in the real estate business. "I wasn't aware that there were any farms for sale in the valley. Or should I say, farms for sale that are going to remain farms."

"Don't tell him what land you have your eye on," advised another man jovially. "Milton here will buy it out from under you and subdivide it into a dozen lots before you have time to grab your coat and hat."

"It's an honest living," replied Mr. Milton, apparently unoffended.

"We aren't looking to buy a farm," said Henry. It wasn't a lie; he had already purchased a ranch.

Mr. Milton regarded them with new interest. "Then perhaps you've come to look at Meadowbrook Hills? I apologize, but I don't remember a Mr. and Mrs. Nelson on my list of appointments. No matter. I have a few hours free tomorrow afternoon after I take the Crewes out." He nodded to the other married couple. "I'd be happy to show you the remaining lots after they have their turn."

"Maybe the Nelsons came to see Oakwood Glen," suggested Mrs. Diegel as she passed through the dining room with a pitcher to refresh their water glasses.

Mr. Milton frowned. "I never thought I'd say this about any plot of land, but that development would be better off plowed and seeded with alfalfa."

"You only say that because Mr. Donovan is your biggest competitor," said Mrs. Diegel airily. "I happen to know you tried to buy the Lindstrom farm, but Mr. Donovan made a higher offer."

"We're not interested in Oakwood Glen," said Elizabeth hastily as Mr. Milton's scowl deepened. She wished Henry had agreed to tell everyone that they were merely newlyweds on their honeymoon.

"What sort of development are you talking about?" asked Henry. "New businesses coming to town?"

"No, although I'm sure that will follow." Mrs. Diegel regarded the Nelsons with surprise. "All this time, I had you two pegged as another young couple looking to buy homes in these developments Mr. Donovan and Mr. Milton are building."

"Perhaps I can still persuade you," said Mr. Milton, passing Henry a business card. "I still have several half-acre lots with scenic views available."

"The views are scenic *now*," said Mrs. Diegel. "They won't be forever if you and Mr. Donovan have your way. Leave these young people alone and let them finish their dinner. They clearly aren't in the market for one of your homes."

To Elizabeth's surprise, Mr. Milton chuckled. "Say what you will, I know you're happy we're improving those empty acres of farmland. You'll thank me when you prosper from all the new residents. These developments will make up for everything the stagecoach and the train never delivered."

Elizabeth had no idea what he meant. She exchanged a look with Henry and knew that his thoughts mirrored her own: They were very fortunate to have purchased the Rancho Triunfo before Mr. Milton or Mr. Donovan heard the land was up for sale.

That night, hours after Henry had fallen asleep beside her, Elizabeth climbed carefully from the narrow bed and slipped a robe over her nightgown. Her thoughts were too full of their plans for the next day to allow her to rest. Lighting the lamp, she took paper and pen from her bag, wrapped a blue-and-white Nine-Patch quilt around herself, and settled into the ladder -back chair to write letters home. She wrote to her parents first, assuring them she was safe in California and describing their journey west in the best possible terms. Of Peter and Mae she said only that she and Henry had met an interesting couple traveling from New York on business, but she did not expect to see them again since they disembarked in St. Louis and she did not think to get their address.

She wrote to little Sylvia about the train ride west, wading in the Pacific Ocean at Venice Beach, and the glamorous Egyptian Theater. To Aunt Eleanor she wrote of all these things, but also described her encounter with Grover Higgins, movie producer, and how quickly her excitement had turned to disappointment when Henry chased him off. "Please don't tell my mother about the movie producer," she added in a postscript. "Henry disliked him at first sight (I think he was jealous) and I doubt my parents would approve. Still, wouldn't it be marvelous to have even a small role in a movie—perhaps with Rudolph Valentino as my leading man? I confess that as we sat in the dark of that sumptuous theater, I imagined myself up there, in a glamorous costume, enthralling the audience. Perhaps it's nothing more than a silly fantasy, but let's not forget that I never dreamed I would one day live on a ranch in California, or see any place lovelier than Elm Creek Manor, or visit a town any more exotic than Pittsburgh. Now I am a rancher's wife and I've seen the Pacific Ocean. Who knows what else the future might hold?"

She wrote a last quick letter to her brother Lawrence, telling him—almost defiantly—that she and Henry had arrived safely and were having a marvelous time. She finished up with envelopes and stamps—and glanced over at her husband, slumbering peacefully, while she felt not the least bit tired. Tomorrow morning, she would regret not following his example.

Her mother always recommended warm milk as a cure for sleeplessness, but Elizabeth had never heeded her advice. Privately, she knew that she would have tried it long ago if her aunt Eleanor, and not her mother, had offered the suggestion, so she decided to stop spiting herself and do as her mother instructed for a change. Her mother would never know. Elizabeth doubted any of the kitchen staff would be awake at that hour, but she didn't see anything wrong with helping herself as long as she tidied up afterward and remembered to tell Mrs. Diegel to add it to their account.

She descended the oak staircase in darkness. Her hand slid along the banister, polished to a glossy smoothness with age except where it was riddled with bullet holes and buckshot. A dim glow came from the parlor, and to her surprise she found Mrs. Diegel seated in a chintz armchair piecing a simple nine-patch quilt block by the light of a single lamp.

The proprietress looked up at the sound of Elizabeth's footfalls. "Good evening," she said, resting her sewing in her lap. She did not seem to think it unusual for a hotel guest to be wandering about at that hour. "Or rather, good morning. Did you need something? An extra blanket, perhaps?"

"No, thank you." Elizabeth had not been warm enough until she threw an extra quilt on the bed, but the room was comfortable despite the close quarters. "I couldn't sleep."

"Did the ghost wake you?"

Elizabeth felt a chill on the nape of her neck that had nothing to do with the unseasonably cool night—if it *was* unseasonable. She was beginning to suspect it was not. "Ghost?" she said. "You're joking."

Mrs. Diegel shrugged and resumed sewing. "His name is Pierre—Duval or Duvon, the stories aren't consistent. He was shot and killed in the barroom back in the eighteen eighties. I've never seen him myself, but some guests claim to have woken in the middle of the night to discover a man with a handlebar mustache staring at them from the foot of the bed and suddenly vanishing. He slams doors and rearranges the furniture from time to time, hides keys and hairbrushes when you most need them. He's more of a nuisance than a fright, as far as I'm concerned."

"I don't believe in ghosts," said Elizabeth firmly.

"Most people don't until they see one. Our postmaster didn't believe, either, until he saw the ghost of his dead mother-in-law wandering the mesa near the Salto Canyon. Or so he says. It nearly unhinged him." Mrs. Diegel looked up and smiled. "I don't suppose this sort of talk will cure what ails you. Would you like a glass of warm milk or a cup of tea?"

"A glass of warm milk, please. If it isn't too much trouble."

"Not at all." Mrs. Diegel set aside her sewing and left the parlor. Unsure whether she was meant to wait or to follow, Elizabeth hesitated a moment before trailing after her hostess to the kitchen. She sat down at a broad oak table while Mrs. Diegel poured milk from a glass bottle into a saucepan and heated it over a burner of the gas stove.

Mrs. Diegel stirred the saucepan with a wooden spoon, her expression thoughtful. "So you and your husband aren't in the market for one of Mr. Milton's houses," she remarked after a time. "You say you're farmers and that you've come to the Arboles Valley to live, when as far as I know—and I would know—there aren't any farms for sale in the valley at present."

She glanced over her shoulder at Elizabeth, who responded with an uncertain nod.

"I suppose it wouldn't do any good to ask you what your business here is."

"I can't tell you today," said Elizabeth. "Tomorrow afternoon I'll be able to say more."

"I can wait that long." Mrs. Diegel filled a coffee cup with steaming milk, stirred in a dash of vanilla, and set it before Elizabeth. She pulled up a chair across the table and regarded her speculatively.

Elizabeth thanked her, picked up the cup, and took a sip. The warmth of the milk and the fragrance of vanilla were soothing. "I hope you won't think I'm prying," she said. "But I've been wondering what Mr. Milton meant earlier today when he said that the neighborhoods he is building will make up for what the stagecoach and the train didn't deliver."

"So that's what's keeping you awake tonight?" said Mrs. Diegel, amused. "He was referring to the history of this old place. James Hammell built the Grand Union Hotel in 1876 and welcomed his first guests on July Fourth. It was a grand place, comfortable and beautifully decorated, an oasis for weary travelers taking the Coast Line Stage from Los Angeles to points farther north. He stood to make a fortune, but then the stagecoach line switched its route from the Arboles Valley to the Santa Clara and took his customers with it. He might have endured that blow if not for the terrible drought of seventy-six and seventy-seven. The valley saw only three inches of rain in all that time. James Hammell wasn't the only one to lose everything in those years. He was forced to sell, and my grandfather bought the hotel and about a thousand acres of farmland at a sheriff's auction." Mrs. Diegel sighed and shook her head, remembering. "There were rumors that a train connecting Los Angeles and Oxnard would run right through the Arboles Valley. My grandfather had a friend in the transportation department who assured him this was so. He was certain he would become rich from the travelers who had eluded Mr. Hammell. But as you know, the railroad companies chose the Simi Valley instead."

"So the stagecoaches and trains brought only disappointment," said Elizabeth.

"No, not only that. Enough travelers ventured this way for my grandfather to stay afloat, and our farmers benefited from the train as much as anyone. Still, when another drought struck years later, my grandfather was forced to choose between selling the hotel or selling the farm. He received a better price for the farm, so he sold it and kept the hotel. My family has run it ever since."

"What happened to the farm?"

"It's changed hands several times since, so I suppose my grandfather made the right choice." For a long moment, Mrs. Diegel cupped her chin in her hand and stared off into space. Then, suddenly, she fixed Elizabeth with a steady, appraising gaze. "For more than fifty years, my family has welcomed fortune-seekers to the Arboles Valley. Within a few years most newcomers pack up and leave—as soon as times get tougher than they expected. It takes a strong will and a good dose of luck to make it here. Many folks go broke, give up, and move away, while others stay, endure, and wait for better times. I wonder which kind you and your husband are."

Elizabeth, secure in the knowledge that Triumph Ranch awaited them, replied, "We're the kind to hang on."

"Everyone thinks that or they wouldn't come in the first place." With a sigh, Mrs. Diegel rose and carried Elizabeth's empty cup to the sink. "Only time will tell."

"Our families have always been farmers," said Elizabeth. Mrs. Diegel did not need to know that Elizabeth's experience was limited to a few summers of helping her aunt and uncle on their horse farm because her father had given up the land to marry her mother. "They've endured floods and accidents and every other imaginable hardship. I assure you, we're the kind of people to hang on."

Mrs. Diegel gestured to the doorway. "Then you'll need your rest."

Elizabeth followed Mrs. Diegel from the kitchen, through the dining room, and back into the parlor, where Mrs. Diegel paused to pack up her sewing. As she folded her Nine-Patch quilt block and tucked it into her sewing basket, Elizabeth glimpsed scraps of a familiar fabric.

Impulsively, she asked, "May I see that?"

"The quilt block?" Mrs. Diegel unfolded it and smoothed out the creases on her open palms. "It's just a simple Nine-Patch. I'm not much of a quilter, but I must keep my guests warm."

"It's very well done," said Elizabeth generously, sparing a once-over for the block before peering into the basket. "Would you be willing to swap scraps? I could bring my sewing basket to breakfast and let you take your pick of my collection."

"There's no need to trade." Mrs. Diegel folded back the lid of the basket and held it out to Elizabeth. "Take whatever you need if you can put it to good use."

Elizabeth took the basket, hesitant. "Are you sure? I wouldn't want you to run out."

"I have plenty of scraps already. These are too small for the quilts I make, but I'm too frugal to throw them out. I'm glad to find a better use for them."

"Thank you." Elizabeth took out two pieces each of three different cotton prints—a shirting fabric, a demure floral, and a cheerful blue-and-white check.

"You're very welcome." Mrs. Diegel closed the basket. "Now, don't stay up all night sewing this quilt of yours. I suspect you have a busy day ahead."

Elizabeth promised she wouldn't, an easy promise to keep because she hadn't nearly enough fabric to begin the quilt that a glimpse of Mrs. Diegel's scraps had inspired her to make. As soon as Elizabeth spotted them in the sewing basket, she knew they must be left over from the innkeeper's sewing for the Grand Union Hotel. The brown-and-white pinstriped fabric matched the shirtwaist dress Mrs. Diegel had worn when she welcomed the Nelsons in the lobby. The pretty chintz floral was identical to the pillowcases in the little room she and Henry shared. The blue-and-white check must have been trimmed from the tablecloth in the dining room where they had enjoyed their first meal in the Arboles Valley, sharing a delicious chicken and dumpling supper with the other guests. Each of those scraps held a special memory for Elizabeth. She would collect others—a piece from the silk scarf she had bought at Venice Beach, the trimmings left over from when she hemmed her skirts on the train west—and stitch them together into a patchwork of memories, a record of their journey. It would be only fitting for such a quilt to be the first she would make on Triumph Ranch.

❧

1889

It took Miguel Diaz three years to convince Isabel to marry him. The first year went to making up for the bad impression he had made on her sixteenth birthday. Once he persuaded her to tolerate him, he needed a second year to win her heart. He rejoiced the day she confessed she loved him, too, unaware that this did not mean she would agree to become his wife. One more full year passed in which he felt as if he were taking her by the hand and cajoling her to take small steps out her front door and into the sunlight.

Her father was no help. Whenever the couple brought up the subject of marriage, her father spoke of how much her brother and sister needed her. How would they manage without Isabel to care for them? How would *he* manage? He had no wife. He worked from daybreak to sunset to provide for his family. Without their mother, without Isabel, the family would fall apart.

Whenever her father spoke this way, Isabel reluctantly set aside any thought of leaving. Miguel wanted to admire her loyalty, but he was becoming impatient. Would he have to wait for the old man to die—God forgive him for such a thought—before he could make Isabel his wife? Miguel promised her they would live close enough that she could check on her father and sister and brother every day if she wished. He would welcome her father into their home if that was what he had to do. Isabel listened to his assurances and told him, wistfully, that they needed to wait, to wait and see. Perhaps someday the time would be right.

The day finally came on her sister's birthday. "She's sixteen today," Miguel remarked, watching from the kitchen chair as Isabel mixed up batter for a birthday cake. "She's the same age you were when I saw you buying ice cream at the Arboles Grocery."

Isabel smiled, remembering. "Yes, that's right." Then her smile faded.

"Maybe I shouldn't have reminded you," said Miguel ruefully. "After working so hard to make you forget it—"

But Isabel did not seem to hear him. "At her age, I was taking care of the whole family. I had left school. I was so lonely."

Not like her sister, who excelled at school, flourished in her circle of friends, and insisted that after graduating, she would go to college and become a teacher. Miguel wondered what dreams Isabel had cherished in her heart at sixteen, dreams that she had been unable to fulfill. Did she hope someday to make them come true, or had she abandoned them?

"Your brother and sister are old enough to take care of themselves now," he told her.

"Yes, but my father—" Her spoon clattered against the side of the mixing bowl. "Don't you see? If I leave, my sister will take my place. There will be no graduation for her, no college, no classroom of her own, no love of her own. I can't do that to her."

"Isabel, listen to me." Miguel took her hands. "Your father can look after himself. Your sister knows that. She won't fall into that trap."

Isabel tore her hands from his. "Is that how you see me? I'm not trapped. This is my choice. My family needs me. I can't walk away from my duties. This is what my mother would want."

"Would she?" asked Miguel gently. "You *are* locked in a trap, and you're carrying the key in your own pocket. Are you sure that's what your mother would want?"

Miguel's words haunted Isabel long after he went home. She could not bear to think that he pitied her. She did not want him to think that caring for her family was a burden. It was not the life she would have chosen, but neither would her mother have chosen to die.

Isabel was so subdued during the family birthday party for her sister that her brother asked if she was feeling ill. "I am, a little," she said. "I think I'll go to bed early."

The next morning, she remained in bed long after she should have risen to fix her father's breakfast. She heard him moving around the kitchen but feigned sleep when he came to her doorway. Finally he rapped softly on the door. "Isabel," he whispered. "Are you all right?"

"I'm not feeling well." It was no lie. She had not felt well since Miguel told her she was trapped.

Her father hesitated in the doorway. "Can you make breakfast?"

Annoyance flared. "No," she said, a trifle harder than a sick woman should have been able to manage.

After a significant pause, her father shuffled off to the kitchen to find something to eat. Silently Isabel wished him luck, rolled over, and went back to sleep.

She woke to sunlight streaming through the windows. After stretching luxuriously beneath her favorite quilt, the one her mother had made as a young bride-to-be, she was struck by the realization that her brother and sister had allowed her to sleep in rather than waking her to fix their breakfasts, pack their lunches, and send them off to school. They would not have risen until after their father had left for the dairy, so he could not have told them Isabel was very sick. Perhaps they had assumed as much, because Isabel had never let illness keep her in bed before. Or perhaps—and this was a more troubling thought—they had let her sleep in because, like Miguel, they felt sorry for her.

She ate a light breakfast on the back patio and spent the rest of the day working on a Double Nine-Patch quilt she was making to use up scraps. It was bright, colorful, and cheerful, and when she had begun piecing the first blocks, she imagined spreading it over the bed she would share with Miguel after they married. How quickly she had sewn those first dozen blocks, as if that would speed her wedding day. Now she knew that unless she stood firm, she would have all the time in the world to complete her wedding quilt—all the time, and none of the necessity.

When she expected her brother home from school, she put the quilt away and hurried back to bed. He checked in on her, feeling her forehead and offering to bring her a glass of orange juice, as she always did for him whenever he did not feel well. He was so sweet and courteous that she felt guilty for deceiving him, but a sudden recovery would raise too many questions, so she stayed in bed.

Her sister came home soon after, toting an armload of books. She perched on the edge of Isabel's bed and asked about her symptoms, frowning studiously at Isabel's carefully worded, vague replies. She only wanted a day off, not a diagnosis that would alarm the people she loved.

Her father came home just as the sun was going down. Isabel listened to his footfalls from her bedroom and heard him come to an abrupt halt in the kitchen. The sight of an empty table where he had always found a meal waiting before had apparently confounded him.

When he came to her doorway, she pretended to be asleep. Rather than disturb her, he moved on to the front room, where her sister was curled up in a chair with a biology textbook on loan from her teacher.

"I'm home," he told her, somewhat mournfully.

"Hi, Papi. How was your day?"

"Good, good. Busy." He hesitated. "It's suppertime."

"I'm not hungry. I ate when I came home from school."

"Well, I'm hungry, and I'm sure your brother is, too," he said. "Will you make us something to eat?"

"Sorry, Papi, but I have to finish this book tonight. My teacher has to return it to her college's library tomorrow."

"Oh. Of course." Papi respected teachers and was proud of his bright daughter's achievements. He would never ask her to set a schoolbook aside. "Well . . . I guess I'll fix myself something."

Before long, Isabel heard the frying pan sizzling on the stove and her father call her brother to the table. They even washed the dishes afterward.

The next morning, Isabel was miraculously cured. She prepared breakfast cheerfully and sent her siblings off to school, then hurried off to see Miguel. By the time her family returned home to supper waiting on the table like always, she and Miguel were engaged.

They married three months later. Her father turned out to be a fine cook, and fairly good at keeping house and doing laundry. At Christmas, he prepared tamales from memories pieced together of his wife and mother and grandmother in their kitchens, taking two days to cook enough for the family and to share with friends. Isabel's brother swore they were much better than Isabel's and nearly as good as those their mother had once made.

Isabel, who had not finished her wedding quilt in time after all, was happy to agree.

Chapter Five

1925

The next morning Elizabeth rose at dawn full of anticipation and as energetic as if she had slept soundly the entire night. Henry had risen even earlier and dressed in his second-best suit. He sat on the bed going over their papers for Triumph Ranch while Elizabeth quickly washed and dressed. They were the first guests to the breakfast table and the first to finish eating. Afterward, Henry arranged for Mrs. Diegel's handyman, Carlos, to drive them to the post office. They would take their overnight bags with them and arrange to pick up the rest of their luggage later that day.

Cool mists shrouded the hotel grounds when the Nelsons met the handyman in the garage, but he assured them they would burn off by midmorning. "They always do," he said. "Except during the winter. Then they might linger all day—or turn into rain."

"You have winter here?" asked Elizabeth as she climbed into the car.

"*Sí,* we do." Carlos grinned. "Maybe not so bad as what you have back east, but we do have winter, even here."

"Does it ever snow?" asked Henry.

"Only on the mountaintops."

"Then it can't be too bad," said Elizabeth, hoping it was so. "Perhaps California winters only seem cold to you because you're used to Mexican winters."

Carlos was silent for a moment. "That might be so, except I was born in the Arboles Valley. I am a sixth-generation Californian on my mother's side."

"I beg your pardon," said Elizabeth, abashed. "From your appearance and accent I assumed— Please forgive me. I have this terrible habit of making a fool of myself by speaking on subjects I know nothing about."

"I'm not offended," said Carlos, with a tolerant chuckle. "You're not the first to make that mistake and I doubt you'll be the last."

The car rumbled over the cobblestone driveway and back onto the road they had taken across the valley the day before. They turned north at the intersection instead of heading back east toward the Norwegian Grade. It was a smooth, gently descending ride from the foothills though oak groves and past the outer pastures of farms. After a mile or two, Carlos turned east onto a dirt road.

"Do you know Mr. Barclay well?" Henry asked.

Carlos shrugged. "He's married to my sister."

Elizabeth took it as a bad sign that he did not continue. "Is he an able post-master?"

"He fulfills his duties competently."

"I would have expected higher praise from a brother-in-law."

Carlos gave her a sidelong glance before returning his attention to the road ahead. "You're right."

"About what?"

"You do have a terrible habit."

Henry let out a loud guffaw. Elizabeth was about to protest when a small, one-story farmhouse, a larger barn, and several smaller outbuildings came into view. Carlos turned the car onto a narrow, dirt road in poor repair. Elizabeth saw his gaze leap from a broken fence to a half-plowed field. "He plows later each year," Carlos grumbled softly, as if to himself. "And fewer acres."

He said nothing more as they topped a low rise and pulled up in front of a tidy wood and adobe structure. ARBOLES VALLEY POST OFFICE proclaimed a sign-post hammered in the ground beside a walkway of worn wooden planks. Two little girls about four and twelve years old played jacks on the hard-packed earth near the front steps, where another girl of about eight sat watching them listlessly. Their floral calico dresses appeared handmade but deftly stitched, and their dark brown hair was neatly braided. The girls were a solemn-eyed welcoming committee, but they brightened at the sight of Carlos. Somewhere inside the house, a toddler wailed weakly.

"Your nieces are beautiful," said Elizabeth, and in his proud smile she saw that her earlier gaffe had been forgotten.

"I'll wait here with *mis pequeñas preciosas* while you conduct your business," said Carlos as the two jack players came running. He scooped up the youngest and swung her high in the air as the older girl flung her arms around his waist. On the steps, the middle girl sat up straighter and beamed at her uncle, barely registering the Nelsons' approach.

Henry rapped on the front door. "Papi's in the barn," said the middle girl, her gaze fixed on her uncle.

At that moment, the door opened and a woman holding a baby on her shoulder peered cautiously outside. "Yes?" she said, her wary gaze darting from Henry's face to Elizabeth's. With her dark lustrous hair and regal features, she looked to be no more than ten years older than Elizabeth, yet her eyes seemed to have witnessed all the grief of the world. She would have been beautiful if not for those eyes. The baby, a tiny bundle with a dark cap of black curls, lay limply upon his mother's shoulder.

"Good morning," said Henry. "We have business with the land office."

The woman did not seem to hear. Her gaze rested upon Carlos, playing with his two nieces in the dusty yard. "*Buenos días,* Carlos," she said to him, so quietly that Elizabeth doubted he would have heard.

But Carlos halted and turned to face her, his expression unreadable. "*Buenos días,* Rosa." His eyes fell upon the baby on her shoulder. "Miguel has fallen ill?"

His sister shrugged and attempted a smile, but it was a bitter grimace. "He is two. He had two blessed years."

Anger flashed in Carlos's eyes. He muttered something in Spanish but broke off abruptly at the sight of his nieces. Sick at heart, Elizabeth looked upon the tiny child with shock and dismay. At his age, Elizabeth's cousins had been twice his size, and his illness, whatever it was, had apparently not been unexpected.

"Have you called the doctor?" asked Carlos in a flat voice.

"Of course, but what good will that do?" Suddenly Rosa seemed to remember the Nelsons. "My husband is in the barn. If you care to wait here, I'll get him for you."

"That's all right," said Henry quickly. "We'll find him ourselves."

Rosa nodded, withdrew into the house, and shut the door. Elizabeth trailed after Henry to the barn, mulling over the short exchange between brother and sister, wondering why Carlos had not gone inside with Rosa.

They found John Barclay in the barn, wrench in hand, tightening bolts on a tiller. He looked up when the Nelsons entered and wiped his hands on a rag. Henry introduced himself and Elizabeth and explained that they had come to collect the deed of trust that was being held for them in the land office.

John Barclay looked puzzled. "I'm not holding any deeds of trust at the moment," he said. "What did you say your name was again?"

"Nelson. Henry Nelson. From Pennsylvania. Back in December, I bought the Rancho Triunfo from Vicente Rodriguez through J. T. Simmons, a land agent from Pittsburgh."

"Aw, hell, not again." John Barclay flung his rag down in disgust. "I suppose you have some documents to show me?"

Henry nodded and retrieved them from the pocket of his suitcoat. John looked them over, shaking his head. Elizabeth tried not to wince at the greasy fingerprints he left on the parchment.

"There's no good way to say this, so I'll just tell you straight out." John thrust the papers back at Henry. "You've been had."

Henry returned a blank stare. "What?"

"You've been had. There's no Rancho Triunfo, at least, not anymore. Vicente Rodriguez was my wife's great-grandfather. He died years ago. The land you paid for has been in the Jorgensen family for three generations."

"But . . ." Henry seemed to struggle for words. "We have a signed contract. A map. Photographs."

"Forgeries." John rustled the worthless papers. "Go on. Take them. They won't do me any good."

Numbly, Henry did.

"You said, 'Not again,' " said Elizabeth.

"This J. T. Simmons character sold this property to two others before you. First fellow was from South Bend, Indiana. Second was from Cleveland. I guess he's working his way east." John spat into the dirt and took up his wrench again. "I swear I'd throttle him if I could get my hands on him. Why he chose to make this my problem, I surely don't know."

"Your problem?" echoed Henry in a strangled voice. "I gave every cent I owned to that man."

John Barclay hesitated, scratched the back of his neck, and frowned in what might have been sympathy. "I hate to say it, but you can kiss that money good-bye. Though I guess it's too late for that, since it's already gone." He eyed them for a moment. "Unless you folks have a letter to mail, I've got work to do."

With trembling hands, Elizabeth gave him the letters she had written the night before. John stuffed them into his pocket and was back to turning wrenches before the Nelsons left the barn. Outside in the yard, Carlos took one glance at their stunned expressions and shooed his nieces toward the house. "Are you all right?" he asked.

Henry said nothing. As if in a daze, he went to the car, climbed inside, and shut the door.

Carlos turned to Elizabeth. "What happened? Did you collect your letter? Was it bad news from home?"

"We weren't here for the post office." Elizabeth craned her neck to watch her husband, but all she could see was his head, slumped wearily in his hands. "I'm afraid we've had a shock. We thought we had bought a ranch, but our papers were forgeries. We've been robbed."

"*Dios mio.* Not El Rancho Triunfo again."

Elizabeth nodded.

Carlos scowled. "That swindler should be tried and hanged."

"He has to be caught first." Suddenly dizzy, Elizabeth pressed a hand to her forehead. "God help us. We've lost everything."

Carlos caught her by the arm and helped her to the car. The Nelsons sat wordless from shock as he started the car and left the Barclay farm behind. "Do you have family?" Carlos asked. "Someone who can wire money, enough to get you home?"

"No," said Henry shortly. "I won't go hat in hand to my father. It was my mistake that got us into this mess. I'll get us out of it."

Carlos glanced at Elizabeth to see if she might respond differently, but she would not humiliate Henry by contradicting him.

"What do you want to do?" Carlos asked her. "Should I take you back to the Grand Union?"

"I suppose." They had nowhere else to go. With a sudden jolt, Elizabeth realized that they could not afford a second night in the hotel.

They drove along without speaking until Carlos broke the silence. "The Jorgensens are decent people. Every farm in the valley is glad to have extra hands. They might offer you work, good work, until you can get back on your feet."

Henry said nothing.

"Henry?" Elizabeth prompted. "It would be a start. Just until we can make a better plan."

"All right," he said dully. "All right."

Carlos pulled the car onto another dirt road that gradually turned toward the east. It occurred to Elizabeth that they were crossing through the landscape they had admired from the citrus grove the day before, but its beauty was lost on them. Everything they had planned for and dreamed about for the past four months had vanished in an instant, burned away like the ocean mists beneath the brilliant California sun.

Elizabeth recognized the Jorgensen farm from the photographs of Triumph Ranch, although there were several additional outbuildings and the yellow farmhouse with white shutters had a new wing. Chickens scratched in the front yard. Petunias grew in window boxes; a young woman and a girl hung laundry on a line. Beyond the house, Elizabeth glimpsed row after orderly row of trees in full leaf, pink and white blossoms newly emerging. It was a cheerful, prosperous farm, as ambitious and industrious as the Barclay farm had been despondent.

It should have been theirs.

Henry's gaze followed a team of sowers laboring in a newly plowed field. Elizabeth wondered if he was imagining himself among them.

"Spring planting has just begun," said Carlos. "This is a good time to be seeking work. You have worked a farm before?"

"Since before I could walk," said Henry.

"Then the Jorgensens are fortunate you have come. I hear they pay a good wage, the best in the valley. They offer room and board, as well."

Carlos was doing his best to raise their spirits. Somewhere in the depths of his shock and disappointment, Henry must have recognized this, for he managed a nod and a tight-lipped smile.

Carlos parked the car outside a machine shed and called to a man inside working beneath the hood of a truck. They exchanged a few words in Spanish. "Oscar Jorgensen and his brother are in the barley fields," he reported. "My friend says they're shorthanded."

"Then let's go meet him," said Henry grimly.

Carlos suggested that Elizabeth wait by the car; she was not sure if that was because her shoes were not fit for a trek through the mud or because it was not fitting for a man to ask for work with his wife by his side. She strolled around the front yard, keeping out of sight of the woman and girl hanging laundry. A mother and a daughter, she decided. They were laughing and talking as they fastened men's flannel work shirts to the rope line with clothespins. White sheets billowed in the breeze. Elizabeth felt a sudden, painful ache for her aunt Eleanor so intensely that she had to sit down on the fender and catch her breath.

Before long the men returned, Carlos beaming, Henry holding his head high though a muscle worked in his jaw. "They offered you a job?" Elizabeth exclaimed, relieved. She had not dared to think about what they would do if the Jorgensens refused.

"I can start immediately," said Henry. "Lars Jorgensen told his brother how I helped him unload the wool at the train station yesterday. Oscar hired me on his brother's recommendation."

"There's more good news," said Carlos. "Oscar said they need help around the house. There's work for you, too."

"I'll take it," said Elizabeth quickly. If she worked hard enough, the Jorgensens might never know she had been raised in the city.

"No," said Henry. "This is my fault. You don't have to work to pay for my mistake."

"We'll earn money twice as fast if we both work." Well, perhaps not twice as fast. She doubted she would earn as much working as a domestic as Henry would as a farmhand. "Besides, what else am I going to do all day? Sit around like a lady of leisure? I doubt even Oscar Jorgensen's wife can do that. I'd rather help with chores than die of boredom, so I might as well be paid for it."

She could tell from his expression that he didn't like it, but he couldn't come up with a reasonable argument against it. After unloading their suitcases from the car, Carlos took Elizabeth around back to the kitchen door while Henry found a place to change from his second-best suit into work clothes.

A sturdy, brown-haired woman in her late sixties answered Carlos's knock. "Yes, Carlos?" She gave Elizabeth a quick once-over but did not otherwise acknowledge her. "What can I do for you?"

"This is Elizabeth Nelson," said Carlos. "She's Henry Nelson's wife. Oscar just hired him as a farmhand and he thought that you might have work for Elizabeth."

"I could always use extra help around here." Mrs. Jorgensen folded her arms over her blue gingham apron and studied Elizabeth. "I need a girl who's a decent cook and can keep a house clean. Have you worked a farm kitchen before?"

"Yes, at my aunt and uncle's horse farm back in Pennsylvania. I've also worked at my father's hotel for many years."

Her eyebrows rose. "What brings you to the Arboles Valley if you have a family farm and a hotel back east?"

Elizabeth hesitated. "My husband's other plans for employment fell through."

"So working for us is not your first choice. Well, at least you're honest about it." Mrs. Jorgensen looked past the visitors on her doorstep at the approach of the younger woman and the girl carrying the laundry basket. "Mind you keep an eye on those clouds," she warned the eldest. "You should have had that laundry hung an hour ago. If it rains on my sheets you'll have to do them over."

The younger of the pair, a girl of about twelve, abruptly stopped smiling, but the elder tossed her head and laughed. "It's not going to rain, Mother Jorgensen. Look at that sky! It's a beautiful day. Hello," she greeted Elizabeth suddenly. "I'm Mary Katherine Jorgensen. This is my daughter, Annalise. And you are?"

"Elizabeth Nelson." Elizabeth shook her hand and flashed a quick smile at Annalise.

"Elizabeth and her husband have just hired on," said Mrs. Jorgensen. "Perhaps you can show her around while I get back to work."

Her eyes on Elizabeth, Mary Katherine said, "Have you settled on a wage yet?"

As Elizabeth shook her head, Mrs. Jorgensen said, "We don't have time for that at the moment. We can take care of it at the end of the day."

"Oh, let's just take care of it now, get it out of the way." Mary Katherine waved a hand dismissively. "What were you thinking of paying Elizabeth, Mother?"

"Twenty-five cents a day is a fair wage for a new kitchen helper."

"I agree completely, but as soon as Elizabeth finds out that the Russells are paying fifty cents, she'll quit and go work for them. I think we ought to pay fifty just to be safe, don't you?"

Mrs. Jorgensen frowned. "I suppose so."

"And if we would like her to help in the garden occasionally—" Mary Katherine touched Elizabeth lightly on the forearm. "You don't mind gardening, do you?" Elizabeth shook her head. "Then we ought to pay seventy-five. That's the going rate on the Kelley farm."

"This is not the Kelley farm."

Mary Katherine shrugged. "No, I suppose it isn't. Elizabeth, honey, do you have a place to live?"

"I'm afraid not," said Elizabeth.

"Then we'll have to provide room and board as well. And Sundays off."

"Of course she'll have Sundays off," said Mrs. Jorgensen, indignant. "But room and board will have to come out of her wages. Ten cents a day."

"Very well," said Mary Katherine. "Sixty-five cents a day plus room and board and Sundays off. But Elizabeth can't live in the bunkhouse with the men. We'll have to make other arrangements for her and her husband. How about the yellow room off the parlor?"

"You can't mean the guest room," said Mrs. Jorgensen.

"Why not? It's rarely used."

"I can't ask guests to sleep on the sofa because two hired hands have the only spare bedroom. We can fix up the quarters over the carriage house."

"It will take weeks to make that place habitable."

"Then I suppose they can have the cabin." Mrs. Jorgensen drew herself up and looked Elizabeth squarely in the eye. "It's small, but it has a kitchen and a front room and two bedrooms. There's no running water, but the well has a pump. Will that do?"

"It sounds fine. Thank you."

"Very well." Mrs. Jorgensen turned to go. "Change into more suitable clothes and meet me in the kitchen."

"Just a moment," said Mary Katherine. "Let's shake on it."

Mrs. Jorgensen halted and peered over her shoulder at her daughter-in-law. "What?"

Mary Katherine's eyes were wide with innocence. "Isn't that what Oscar does to seal a business agreement?"

Her mouth pressed in a sour line, Mrs. Jorgensen thrust a hand toward Elizabeth, who shook it. "Thank you," Elizabeth added for good measure.

"When you've changed, I'll take you through the house," Mrs. Jorgensen replied. She returned inside, the screen door banging shut behind her. When they could no longer hear her footsteps, Annalise let out a nervous giggle.

Mary Katherine gave her a warning look, but it quickly melted into a grin. "Go help your sister in the garden. I'll catch up," she said. As Annalise ran off, to Elizabeth she added, "Don't let Mother Jorgensen intimidate you. She likes to think she's still the lady of the house."

Elizabeth nodded. "My suitcase is outside. Could you show me where I can change?"

"Of course." Mary Katherine accompanied her outside for the suitcase and then showed her to a modest bedroom with yellow roses on the wallpaper and a yellow-and-white Grape Basket quilt on a bed with a cherry headboard. After Mary Katherine departed, Elizabeth swiftly changed from the traveling suit Aunt Eleanor had sewn for her into a cotton housedress and sturdy shoes. She was grateful to Mary Katherine for negotiating a higher wage and better room and board, but it was not lost on her that Mrs. Jorgensen had made the final decision—or that Carlos had taken Elizabeth to the elder Mrs. Jorgensen to ask for work, when it would have been easier to go to Mary Katherine, who was already outside. Perhaps Mrs. Jorgensen retained the role of lady of the house despite what Mary Katherine thought.

She met Mrs. Jorgensen in the kitchen, where she had time for a quick look around before her new employer sent her running downstairs to the root cellar for a bushel of potatoes, which she washed and sliced in preparation for lunch. Mrs. Jorgensen spoke little as they worked, issuing directions or asking for assistance, but not indulging in friendly chat. Elizabeth supposed that was just as well. She could not bear to be forced to explain how she and Henry had ended up in this state. She still could not believe they had fallen so low so quickly, although she had the waterlogged hands and frying oil splatters on her apron to prove it was no dream.

Henry came in at lunchtime with the men, as sunburned, tired, and hungry as they were, but with a stunned, disbelieving look in his eyes that set him apart. Lars Jorgensen offered her a nod of recognition and welcome, but said nothing to indicate that he thought it odd for the Nelsons to be respected guests of the Grand Union Hotel one day and hired hands the next. The men ate swiftly, barely pausing between bites to discuss the condition of the fields or to plan for the afternoon. Oscar Jorgensen did most of the talking, consulting his brother, who sat at his right hand at the long, redwood plank table that took up most of the kitchen. Despite his thinning blond hair, Oscar resembled his mother—sturdily built, serious, and direct of expression— and seemed years younger than weathered, somber Lars. His face broke into a smile whenever his gaze fell upon his daughters, and Mary Katherine regarded him affectionately as she served the meal. He grinned up at her as she passed the plate of fried chicken, and Elizabeth suspected he might have pulled her adoring face toward his for a kiss if there hadn't been so many people watching.

The men had barely cleaned their plates when Oscar gave the order for them to return to the fields. Elizabeth could not get Henry alone long enough to ask about his morning or offer encouragement. In the few words they managed to exchange in passing, he said stoically that the field work was no worse than back home in Pennsylvania, and that he hoped the Jorgensen women had been pleasant company for her. Elizabeth assured him that everyone had made her feel right at home, although that was not entirely true. Mrs. Jorgensen was not unkind or short-tempered, but she kept her thoughts to herself, making Elizabeth long for the warmth and cheerful banter of the kitchen at Elm Creek Manor, where her grandmother and aunts teased and gossiped and laughed as they prepared meals for the family.

After lunch, she washed the dishes while Mrs. Jorgensen dried them and put them away. Later Mrs. Jorgensen took her through the house, instructing her what to clean and how often. Elizabeth's spirits faltered as she learned about the house that she had meant to call home. She imagined her wedding quilt spread on the four-poster bed in the master bedroom. A smaller bedroom beside it would have made a perfect nursery. The comfortable chair by the window in the front room would have been a lovely place to sit and quilt after the day's work was done. On holidays, Henry could have sat at the head of the walnut table in the dining room. If little cousin Sylvia visited, she could have slept in the yellow guest room off the parlor—although she probably would have crawled into bed with Elizabeth in the middle of the night and nudged Henry farther and farther aside until he gave up and retired to the guest room himself. But it was not to be, none of it.

After the house tour, Mrs. Jorgensen sent Elizabeth out to help Mary Katherine, Annalise, and a younger daughter, Margaret, in the garden. The girls were so cheerful, their mother so friendly, that at last some of Elizabeth's heartache began to ease. She told them about her family back in Pennsylvania, Elm Creek Manor, and her parents' hotel in Harrisburg, but provided only vague answers to Mary Katherine's probing questions about how she and Henry had ended up in the Arboles Valley. Perhaps when she knew them better, if Mary Katherine became a friend and not just an employer, Elizabeth would confide in her. For now, she was too ashamed of their gullibility and foolish optimism to tell them about the reckless gamble that had cost them every cent they had to their name.

Later, Mrs. Jorgensen called Elizabeth back inside to help prepare supper. The meal passed much as lunch had, with ravenous men eating too quickly to allow for conversation. Afterward, Oscar instructed Lars to show Henry around the farm, to let him know how things were done on Jorgensen land.

When the men left, Mary Katherine took her daughters off to play while Elizabeth stayed behind to clean up the kitchen.

When she had finished the dishes, Mrs. Jorgensen said, "You've put in a good day's work. If this is how things are going to be, and not just a show for your first day, you'll work out fine here."

"Thank you," said Elizabeth.

Mrs. Jorgensen nodded, opened the kitchen door, and called for Annalise. "You have your own place to fix up," she said as her granddaughter came running. "Annalise will show you the way. I'll expect you here tomorrow morning, five o'clock sharp, to start breakfast."

"Five o'clock," Elizabeth repeated, hoping the cabin had an alarm clock.

"Wait. Before you go—" Mrs. Jorgensen disappeared around the corner and returned with a mop, broom, and a bucket full of clean rags, a scrub brush, and a box of soap powder. "You'll need these."

"Thank you, Mrs. Jorgensen. I'll bring them back tomorrow."

"There's no need. We have others."

Annalise chattered happily as she helped Elizabeth lug the two suitcases and the cleaning supplies a half mile east of the farmhouse to the cabin. "It's been here forever, even before my great-grandfather came to California from Norway," she said proudly as they climbed a low hill from which Elizabeth first caught sight of her new home. "No one's lived in it for ages, not since Nana was a little girl. Sometimes my sister and I play there, but not so much anymore."

"Why not?" asked Elizabeth, wincing as the suitcase banged into her shin.

"Margaret doesn't like spiders."

"Well," said Elizabeth uneasily, "one could hardly blame her. Are there . . . many?"

"Loads," said Annalise enthusiastically.

For an abandoned cabin, it didn't look too bad from the outside. It was a square structure, only one story high but twice as wide as it was tall, with what looked to be a sound roof and a shaded porch running the length of the front of the cabin. There were glass windows, and to Elizabeth's relief, both a chimney and the vent pipe for a cookstove. She had envisioned herself cooking outdoors over an open fire.

The old wooden boards creaked as they climbed the three stairs and crossed the porch. When the front door stuck, Annalise shoved it open and darted inside; Elizabeth followed, but not before sweeping a cobweb from the doorway. It took a moment for her eyes to adjust to the darkness, for the windows, coated with years of grime, let in only feeble trickles of the fading daylight. As Annalise ran from here to there, exclaiming over forgotten treasures, Elizabeth stood in the center of the room, slowly turning, taking the measure of her new home. The front room took up half of the cabin, with the right side set up as a kitchen and the left as a sitting room, where a rocking chair and a three-legged stool stood before the fireplace. An old braided rag rug lay on the floor, so filthy that in the dim light Elizabeth could not tell what color it was. Cinders and soot from the fireplace spilled out onto the hearth, while on the opposite wall, a thick layer of black grease covered the cookstove. Spiderwebs were everywhere, and a rustling in the corners suggested that field mice had made homes in the walls.

Elizabeth pressed a hand to her stomach and took a deep breath. There were cupboards, she told herself firmly. There was a sink with a pump, so she would not have to haul water from the well. The roof—she glanced up at the ceiling to be sure, and felt a wave of relief when she could glimpse neither sunlight nor water stains. The longest wall, facing the front entrance, had two doors hanging ajar. Elizabeth crossed the room and gingerly pushed upon the door on the left. It creaked open to reveal a room half the size of the front room, with a window, a bed, a narrow wardrobe, and a faded steamer trunk. The other room was the same size, but contained two smaller beds, their mattresses sagging in the middle.

Elizabeth leaned against the wall for support, then quickly pushed herself away from it and brushed the dust from her shoulder, resisting the urge to flee. What would Henry say when he saw the accommodations she had arranged for them? She never should have agreed to take the cabin without seeing it first. Had she learned nothing from Henry's mistake?

"Nana says I can stay to help, but I have to come home before dark," said Annalise, who had followed Elizabeth inside the second bedroom.

Elizabeth closed her eyes and took a deep breath. Perhaps she could ask to see the loft above the carriage house and choose between the two. Perhaps Mrs. Jorgensen would agree to allow the Nelsons to share the yellow guest room until they could fix up the cabin. But this would not do. They could not live here, not in this state.

"Elizabeth?"

Elizabeth jumped. "Yes, Annalise?"

"Don't you like it here?" Annalise's smooth brow furrowed in worry. "I know it's messy but I'll help you tidy it up. Nana says . . ."

"What does your nana say?" Elizabeth prompted gently when the girl did not continue.

"She says one day's work doesn't make you a farmer. She thinks you and your husband came out here to buy a house in Meadowbrook Hills or Oakwood Glen like all the other city people but you lost your money and so you had to find work."

"That's not true," said Elizabeth. "We never even heard of Meadowbrook Hills or Oakwood Glen until last night. Henry and I come from farming families. We came to the Arboles Valley for the land."

"I knew it. Mama said so, too. She says no city girl knows her way around a garden the way you do." Then Annalise's smile faded. "Nana says if you turn up your nose at the cabin, you don't have the mettle to last a week on the farm."

"She said that, did she?"

"I probably shouldn't have told you."

"It'll be our secret." First Mrs. Diegel, now Mrs. Jorgensen. Elizabeth was growing impatient with these people who expected the Nelsons to fail.

Henry would be making his way to the cabin soon. She could not let him see the place like this.

"All right," she said briskly. "Let's start with the other bedroom first. My husband will be tired and he might want to go straight to bed. I must have it ready for him."

Annalise nodded and ran off for the cleaning supplies they had left on the porch. She swept the room while Elizabeth wrestled the thin, musty mattress outside and beat it with the mop handle. Her skin crawled when she thought of how long it had been abandoned in the cabin, what sort of creatures might infest it, but it would have to do until their first payday. She hoped their first week's wages would cover the cost of a new mattress.

When the mattress was as clean as she could make it, she wiped down the bed frame, brought the mattress back inside, and set it in place. Annalise had finished sweeping the floor and had turned to clearing the spiderwebs from the corners and the window frame. The window stuck, but with Annalise's help, Elizabeth managed to shove it open. Soon an evening breeze began to clear away the stale air.

Elizabeth searched the wardrobe for bed linens, but found only a small parcel of mothballs, a sock that needed darning, and something that suspiciously resembled mouse droppings. She pried open the rusted clasp of the steamer trunk and discovered a worn, grayed bedsheet and two faded patchwork quilts. Elizabeth took them outside and shook them fiercely, relieved to see that the trunk had kept them relatively clean. She thought longingly of the crisp sheets and pillowcases in one of the trunks she had left at the Grand Union Hotel, gifts from Great-Aunt Lydia. Mrs. Diegel surely must be wondering why the Nelsons had not returned for their belongings. Elizabeth would find a way to retrieve them as soon as she could.

Annalise helped her make the bed with the better of the two quilts, but the sun was slipping behind the Santa Monica Mountains to the west, and soon the girl had to run off for home. Elizabeth finished the master bedroom, shut the door firmly on the other bedroom to hide the mess, and started in on the kitchen. The pump groaned and complained when she worked the handle, but a spurt of rusty water splashed into the sink, smelling of iron. She pumped until her arms ached, but at last, clear water gushed forth. By then Elizabeth was so thirsty that she threw caution aside and drank from the stream of water, praying that it was clean. She would have preferred to boil it first, but she had no fire, no pot.

She filled the bucket with soapy water, seized a rag, and scrubbed the stove, stripping off layers of grease and decades' worth of caked-on dust. Twice she had to empty and refill the bucket with fresh water. As the gold-specked white enamel began to shine through, words in her mind echoed the rhythm of her strokes: *We should have known it was too good to be true. We should have known.* She wished Henry were there to put his arms around her and assure her that everything would be all right, that somehow they would find their footing again.

By the time Henry came in, exhausted and smelling of sweat and soil, Elizabeth was filthy and sore, but the cookstove was clean, inside and out, and the rest of the kitchen was tolerable. She quickly put away her scrub brush and washed her hands at the pump as Henry looked around at the cabin, expressionless.

"You should have seen it before I cleaned up," she said, forcing a smile.

"You can't stay here."

"Yes, we can. I know it's not what we expected but it's a home. Once I've cleaned it properly, once we've spread our own things around, it will be as cozy and comfortable as we could ever want." Elizabeth took his hand and led him to the armchair, but she had to push him into it. When he sat, she unlaced and removed his boots. "Are you hungry?"

He glanced at the kitchen. "Do we have anything to eat?"

"I saved some biscuits from supper." She took the biscuits from her apron pocket, unfolded the napkin she had wrapped them in, and placed them on his lap. "I'm afraid we don't have any plates or cutlery. Or drinking glasses. Tomorrow I'll ask Mrs. Jorgensen if she has a few she could spare."

Henry raised a biscuit to his mouth, staring straight ahead at the wall, chewing and swallowing mechanically until he had eaten the last crumb. "I don't want you to go begging for their castoffs."

Elizabeth was so astonished she laughed. "It's not begging, Henry, just borrowing a few necessities to get us through until we can collect our own things from the hotel. Honestly. Would you rather eat with your fingers and drink straight from the pump?"

Elbows on his knees, Henry leaned forward and buried his head in his hands. He was silent so long Elizabeth worried that he might have fallen asleep. "You will write to your parents," he said at last, wearily, without looking up. "You'll write to them tonight and ask them to wire you the train fare home."

"What about you?"

"I'll stay behind and work until I've earned enough to repay my debt to your family."

"And earn your own fare home," Elizabeth finished for him.

Henry said nothing.

"I don't think that's a good plan at all," she declared. "We'll earn the train fare to Pennsylvania much faster if we both work. Besides, I wouldn't dream of going back to Harrisburg without you. What would people think?"

Henry straightened, his mouth set in a grim line. "I've made my decision. You're going back. This is not what I promised you when I asked you to marry me. This is not what you agreed to. I won't have you living like this."

"You can't force me to get on a train," Elizabeth retorted, her voice shaking with anger. "I am not going without you and that's final."

Henry hauled himself to his feet. "I'm too tired to argue." He paused, looking from one of the bedroom doors to the other. "Is there a bed in this shack or do we sleep on the floor?"

"The door on the left is our bedroom. Our suitcases are in the wardrobe."

"Is it too much to hope that other door leads to a bathroom?"

"There's an outhouse in back."

Henry made a noise of disgust, shook his head, and went outside. Heart pounding, Elizabeth worked the pump, filling the sink with wash water for him. When he returned, she handed him a clean rag to use as a towel. Wordlessly, he took it and scrubbed his face, neck, and hands clean while she turned down the bed. When he finished, he undressed and dropped into bed without looking around the room, and she took his place in the kitchen, emptying and refilling the sink, washing herself as thoroughly as she could. She longed for the claw-footed iron tub back home. If she were there now, she would fill it and submerge herself in the steaming water until the weariness and filth that had worked into her skin melted away.

The cabin had grown dark. Elizabeth felt her way into the bedroom, slipped on her nightgown, and climbed into bed beside her husband. Bedsprings complained; the mattress sagged and gave off a faint, stale odor.

She knew Henry was bone-tired, but she also knew he wasn't yet asleep. "You never promised me a life of ease," she said softly. "We expected to work hard here. Nothing's changed."

"Everything's changed," retorted Henry. "We came here to work as owners of the Rancho Triunfo. Making decisions, supervising the hired hands, planning for the future of our own land. Now we work as hard as we planned to for ourselves, but for someone else."

Elizabeth lay silently listening to the crickets chirping outside, trying not to hear the whispery scuttling within the walls. "We'll go back to Two Bears Farm," she said. "But I won't go without you."

"Yes, you will," Henry said. "I can't face my family—I can't face *your* family—until I've earned back everything I've lost."

"Everything? Not just the train fare—"

"Every last cent I lost to that cheating, thieving liar. I won't go home worse off than when I left."

"But that was your life savings. It will take years to earn back."

"I know," said Henry. "If you don't think you can wait, if one of your rich boyfriends—"

"Stop right there, Henry Nelson," snapped Elizabeth. "Don't say it. Don't even think it. I am your wife, and I am going to stay your wife—unless you cheat on me, in which case you'll be in worse shape than you are right now. So don't suggest otherwise ever again."

"All right," said Henry, surprised. "I thought it was only fair to offer you a way out. But you're still going home as soon as your parents can wire the money."

"I can't go home yet. I can't face my family, either."

"Why not? You don't have anything to be ashamed of. It wasn't your idea to buy the ranch."

Elizabeth thought quickly. "My hair. Can you imagine what my mother will do when she sees how I've bobbed my hair? The sight of it will take years off her life. You've known my mother long enough to know I'm right."

"Then I guess you could—"

"Don't say I can just stay with Aunt Eleanor and Uncle Fred at Elm Creek Manor. You know someone will squeal."

Henry sighed heavily. "All right. You can stay until your hair grows out enough. Then you're getting on a train and going home."

"Promise? Not until then?"

"Yes. Fine. I promise."

"Then I agree."

Elizabeth pulled the worn quilt over herself and sank into a sleep of pure exhaustion, knowing that she had bought herself only a few months at best. As relieved as she was to know the haven of Two Bears Farm and Elm Creek Manor awaited them and that she would only have to endure the ramshackle cabin for a little while, she refused to set one foot on an eastbound train without Henry at her side.

❦

1898

Rosa was born within a week of Isabel and Miguel's first anniversary. Carlos followed two years later. Money was tight, but Isabel was used to that. Miguel was so kind and good-natured that even the worst days, when the children were tired and cranky and she felt that it was all she could do to keep the house clean and get food on the table, she was happy.

But as the children grew, Miguel's wages stretched thinner and thinner over the costs of raising a family. Sometimes Isabel's father gave them money, but she did not tell Miguel, who would have been too proud to accept it. Sometimes they stayed up late talking about how to get ahead, how to save up enough money to set aside for the future, but they already lived as frugally as they could.

In the summer when Rosa turned eight, Miguel came home for supper and announced that he had taken a second job. Isabel was torn. She would be grateful for the extra money when it came time to buy school clothes for the children, but she remembered how her father had worked such long hours that he hardly came home except to eat and sleep. She did not want that for her family.

Miguel quickly assured her that this would be only a short-term job, three weeks or so, just long enough to earn something to put away for a rainy day. "As soon as the apricot harvest is over, I'll be back to my usual hours."

Isabel's breath caught in her throat. "You signed on to help with the apricot harvest? At the Jorgensen farm?"

She could not bear to call it El Rancho Triunfo anymore, even though her father still did. Every other Rodriguez did, but not Isabel. El Rancho Triunfo was gone. It has ceased to exist the day her family had been forced to leave the land.

"It's good money, Isabel."

"I don't care if it's good money. It's *their* money, and I want no part of it."

"Isabel—" Miguel spread his hands, half smiling, half pleading, as if he could not quite believe that she meant it. "Think of what we could do with those wages.

Isabel had thought of it. It would be so easy to tell him to take the job, take their money, and pretend she was not betraying her family, betraying every ancestor back to the great-great-grandfather whose courage and service to a king had earned him that land. But she hardened her heart against temptation and thought of her mother, on her deathbed, refusing the medicines that would have saved her life. Isabel had not understood her mother's choice then, but time had taught her well.

She took a deep breath and locked her gaze with Miguel's. "I will not have you going to them, hat in hand."

Her appeal to his pride failed. "It's a job, not charity. You're making our children pay for a feud that should have ended long ago."

"This is no simple grudge," snapped Isabel. "The Jorgensens cost my family our dignity and our livelihood. They cost my mother her life."

"Your father tells me the Jorgensens bought the ranch fairly," said Miguel. "Your family did not have to sell. The Jorgensens bought drought-stricken land at the best price they could get. They didn't know the rains would fall two months later any more than your family did. They took a chance and won."

"They took advantage of us when we were desperate. My father and grandfather only sold the land because they thought they could earn enough to buy it back someday, when the land value dropped lower."

She could not continue. Miguel already knew how the family had struggled for so long just to make ends meet. Saving enough money to buy back the ranch had been nothing but a wistful dream, an impossible promise they had made to themselves to ease their parting. Once they had sold the land, they had lost any chance of ever again calling El Rancho Triunfo their home.

Unlike the Jorgensens, the Rodriguezes had taken a chance and lost.

As Miguel watched her soberly, Isabel struggled to regain her composure. "I don't make demands of you, but in this matter, I must have my way. If you want to take on a second job, do so, but not this job. Not this job. Not for them. Not ever."

After a long moment, Miguel sighed. "I'll do as you ask. I'll find another job. But I want you to remember something, *querida*. Bitterness and hatred can kill you as surely as cancer does. Think of your mother and remember that."

Chapter Six

1925

Elizabeth dreamed she was on safari on the African savannah, armed only with a pair of sewing shears and a broom. She had lost sight of Henry. Calling out his name as she pushed her way through the long grasses, she stopped short at the sound of a low growl. Heart pounding, she whirled around but saw nothing. When the grass rustled on her left, she broke into a run. Suddenly a roar sounded in her ear, she felt hot, moist breath upon her neck—

She bolted awake, clutching the worn quilt and gasping. Beyond the filthy window, dawn had not yet broken and mists hung over the yard in an eerie calm. She shook Henry awake. "Did you hear that?" she said.

"Hear what?" he mumbled, rolling over onto his side.

"That roar. It sounded like a lion. It woke me up." Elizabeth took a deep breath to clear her head. "Are there lions in California?"

"No, sweetheart." Henry yawned and sat up. "You must have been dreaming."

"What about mountain lions? Maybe it was a mountain lion. Or a bobcat."

"It was a dream." Henry bent down to pick up his watch from the floor beside his shoes. "It's ten minutes after five. I'll have to hurry or I'll be late."

Elizabeth's visions of Africa fled and she flung back the covers with a moan of dismay. She washed and dressed as well as she could manage at the kitchen pump, the cold water shocking her awake. She and Henry hurried to the yellow farmhouse together but parted at the door with a quick kiss, Henry striding off to the barn, Elizabeth darting into the kitchen, where Mrs. Jorgensen and Mary Katherine had already begun breakfast.

"You're late," said Mrs. Jorgensen. "Didn't the rooster wake you?"

"Something woke me, but it was no rooster." Elizabeth snatched from its hook the apron Mrs. Jorgensen had lent her the previous day. "Are there mountain lions living in the hills?"

"I doubt you heard a mountain lion," said Mary Katherine cheerfully, setting the table. "That was probably Charlie."

"Who's Charlie?"

"Charlie is a fourteen-year-old African lion." Mrs. Jorgensen motioned for Elizabeth to take her place at the stove. "Fry these potato pancakes until they're golden brown, no more."

Dumbfounded, Elizabeth took the spatula. "An African lion is stalking the Arboles Valley?"

"Of course not," said Mary Katherine. "He's in a pen. Except when his trainer brings him into the ring for a performance."

"Oh," said Elizabeth, relieved. "You mean he's a circus lion."

"Not at all. Charlie's a movie star."

"Retired movie star," Mrs. Jorgensen corrected. "A few years ago, an animal trainer from Hollywood bought land in the Arboles Valley for a lion farm, where he could raise lions and other wild animals and train them to be in the pictures. I believe they have six lions now, as well as other big cats, some camels, and bears. George Hanneman and his family put on shows on the weekends. I've never gone, but it's become quite a popular tourist attraction. Until those housing developments came, Safari World was the only reason anyone from Los Angeles visited the Arboles Valley."

Her tone suggested that, unlike Mrs. Diegel, she did not approve of the new construction. "I've heard that the developments will bring greater prosperity to the valley," Elizabeth offered.

"I can't imagine where you heard that," scoffed Mrs. Jorgensen. "The only folks who will prosper from these developments are the developers. They name those rows and rows of identical houses after the things they tear down and dig up to build them. In a decade, we'll look just like every other valley between here and Los Angeles: acres of cement and stucco where green growing things once flourished. Meadowbrook Hills and Oakwood Glen, indeed."

Mary Katherine sighed. "Now, Mother Jorgensen—"

"Don't 'Mother Jorgensen' me. I know you have your heart set on more neighbors so you can widen your social circle, but you should not put your own interests above those of future generations."

Mary Katherine planted a fist on her hip. "Whatever are you talking about?"

"Water. There won't be enough for all of those newcomers."

"But they aren't farmers. They aren't dependent upon rain for their livelihoods. We've always had enough water before."

"Not in drought years," said Mrs. Jorgensen. "We've had enough for the family and livestock, true, but that's because we have one well for one hundred twenty acres. What if we had one well for each acre?"

Mary Katherine considered that, then shrugged and turned back to her work. "I don't think it will be as bad as you say."

"Maybe you're right, but if I had my choice, I'd rather have lions and panthers for neighbors."

Elizabeth wished she had not brought up the subject. She flipped the potato pancakes, which sizzled in the skillet and gave off an aroma that made her mouth water. "Are you ever afraid, with so many dangerous animals so near?"

"Charlie's loud voice is deceiving," said Mrs. Jorgensen. "Safari World is about four miles to the southwest."

"None of the animals has ever gotten loose," Mary Katherine reassured her. "Although there are rumors that a panther escaped years ago and now lives in the hills on the eastern edge of our farm. Whenever sheep or calves go missing, the rumors fly."

"Stirred up by the boys who were supposed to be watching the livestock, no doubt." Mrs. Jorgensen bustled between the oven and the table with platters of food as the men came in to eat. "It's more likely that the missing sheep and calves fell into the canyon when the boys weren't paying attention."

Mary Katherine touched Elizabeth on the arm in passing. "The shows at Safari World are lots of fun. The girls and I will take you someday, all right?"

Elizabeth agreed with a quick smile and carried the platter of steaming potato pancakes to the table as Oscar Jorgensen sat down. He and the men were more talkative than the previous day, planning the day's work as they ate. When they had nearly finished, Mrs. Jorgensen said that she had some letters to mail and wondered if Oscar could spare someone to take them to the post office.

"I'll let you know after lunch," Oscar promised his mother. "We'll see how the day goes."

"Lars could take your letters for you," remarked Mary Katherine.

"I'm sure Lars is too busy," said Mrs. Jorgensen.

Lars continued eating, apparently unconcerned. "I'm not too busy."

"Why shouldn't Lars go?" asked Oscar.

Mrs. Jorgensen looked at him as if surprised he would ask such a question. "He's your foreman. You need him here."

"This time of year, I need everyone."

Mrs. Jorgensen waved a hand dismissively. "You're right, of course. My letters can wait for another day, when I can take them myself."

"I'd be happy to take them for you, Mother," said Lars mildly.

"Well, you're not going alone," said Mrs. Jorgensen, a fine, sharp edge to her voice.

"I'll go," said Mary Katherine. "I could use an outing."

Her mother-in-law shook her head. "Not you. I can't spare you today."

"Can you spare her?" asked Lars, nodding to Elizabeth. "We could leave your letters at the post office and then go by the Grand Union to pick up the Nelsons' things. They stored most of their luggage with Mrs. Diegel."

Annalise looked up at Elizabeth in awe. "You stayed at the Grand Union Hotel?"

Elizabeth nodded, aware of everyone's eyes upon her.

"Was it pretty?" asked Annalise. "Daddy took me to lunch in the dining room on my last birthday but I've never been upstairs."

"It was lovely." Elizabeth felt a tug of longing for the clean, soft bed she had considered too narrow, the china pitcher and washbowl, the crisp, fresh sheets. What she wouldn't give for them now.

Mrs. Jorgensen gave her a speculative look, then nodded to Lars. "Very well. After lunch, if Oscar doesn't need you elsewhere, you and Elizabeth may go. Elizabeth, I hope you packed an alarm clock with your things. When I say be here at five o'clock sharp, I mean not a minute later."

Elizabeth pretended not to notice how Henry bristled at Mrs. Jorgensen's tone. "I do have an alarm clock, actually. It was a wedding present from my sister."

"Odd sort of wedding present," one of the hired hands said.

"Not from a concerned older sister," said Elizabeth, smiling. "This isn't the first time I've overslept."

Several of the men chuckled. Elizabeth glanced at Henry and was dismayed to see him frowning at Mrs. Jorgensen. Fortunately, the older woman's attention was still on her sons, and she did not notice the dark looks the newest hired hand shot her way.

After breakfast, Elizabeth and Annalise tidied the kitchen together. Annalise kept up a cheerful patter as they worked, telling Elizabeth about the farm, her many pets, and so many cousins and aunts and uncles that Elizabeth had no hope of keeping them straight.

"I can tell you have a close family," said Elizabeth when Annalise paused for breath. She thought wistfully of the family she had left behind in Pennsylvania. "Your grandmother likes to keep you near, doesn't she?"

"What do you mean?"

"She didn't even want your uncle Lars to leave the farm for a simple errand."

"Oh, no, it's not that." Annalise carefully swept the kitchen floor. "He goes on errands all the time. Nana just doesn't like him to go to the post office."

Elizabeth smothered a laugh. "Why not? What's wrong with the post office?" Then she remembered the curt postmaster. "Or doesn't your uncle Lars get along with Mr. Barclay?"

"No one really gets along with Mr. Barclay," Annalise pointed out. "I don't think that's it, but I don't know. I've never been to the Barclay farm, either."

"Never? But they have a girl right around your age."

"I know. She's in my class at school. I see her and her sisters there but Nana says I'm not allowed to play with them."

Elizabeth paused in wiping up a spill on the counter. "Did your grandmother give you a reason?"

"Maybe she thinks we'll get sick like the Barclay kids." Annalise opened the kitchen door to sweep the dirt outside. "Did you know that Mrs. Barclay had eight babies and four of them died? They start out okay but they all get sick. Well, not all of them. Marta, the girl my age, she's never gotten sick. Neither has her little sister, Lupita. But the rest of them all do sooner or later. Don't you think that's sad?"

"I can't imagine anything sadder," said Elizabeth. Her heart ached for the poor woman with haunted eyes she had met the day before, for the limp child exhausted from illness in her arms. To lose one child must bring such unimaginable pain, but to lose four, and then to watch as the other children succumbed—

At the sound of footsteps approaching, Elizabeth quickly resumed wiping down the counter. Mrs. Jorgensen entered, took the broom from her granddaughter, and sent her off to help her mother. She and Elizabeth finished cleaning the kitchen in silence, and despite her concern for the Barclay children, Elizabeth decided not to ask Mrs. Jorgensen about their tragic illnesses. Even if Mrs. Jorgensen had forbidden her grandchildren to play with the Barclay children out of concern for their own health, shunning them struck Elizabeth as so unfair, so cruel, that she doubted she could rely upon Mrs. Jorgensen for an accurate account of their circumstances.

After the kitchen was tidy once more, Mrs. Jorgensen instructed Elizabeth to clean the upstairs bedrooms. Elizabeth did as she was told, unsure whether to interpret her employer's silence in the kitchen to mean that she had overheard the conversation and disapproved, or if it was merely her customary reticence.

At least Mrs. Jorgensen hadn't scolded her—this time. Worry pricked Elizabeth when she remembered how Henry had glowered as Mrs. Jorgensen rebuked her for her tardiness. She knew he was likely to rush to her defense rather than allow Mrs. Jorgensen to reprimand her a second time, however deservedly—and get them both fired in the process. This was not Elm Creek Manor, where she was surrounded by loving aunts who doted upon her, who laughed off her mistakes and encouraged her to do better next time. It was not her parents' hotel, where she charmed the customers and her father thought she could do no wrong. She had never known how much her family had tolerated out of love for her. She had always felt so trapped in Harrisburg, bound by her mother's propriety and her father's expectations. Only from a distance did she see how much freedom she had truly enjoyed within the circle of her family's affection.

She worked alone upstairs until Mrs. Jorgensen called her to the kitchen to help prepare lunch. As the men came to the table, Elizabeth managed to pull Henry aside for a kiss, but he only shrugged and pulled away when she asked how his morning had gone. She pressed her lips together and busied herself with serving the corn fritters and ham so that no one would notice her disappointment. Henry was tired and hungry, and he had never been one to kiss her with other people watching, even in his best moods. Once he had eaten and rested, he would regret being so abrupt with her. When he apologized, she would forgive him—although he had better not let it become a habit.

When lunch ended, Lars reminded Oscar about their mother's letters, and the two brothers quickly concluded that Lars could be spared long enough to run the errands to the post office and the Grand Union Hotel.

"Mary Katherine and I are accustomed to working without Elizabeth, so she can be spared as well," said Mrs. Jorgensen as the men pushed back their chairs.

"I'm sorry, Mother," said Oscar. "I should have thought to ask you. I suppose Elizabeth doesn't have to go along."

"No, that's quite all right." Mrs. Jorgensen rose and began clearing the table. "Only Elizabeth or Henry would know if one of their bags was missing. We wouldn't want to make a second trip to pick up something that had been left behind."

Elizabeth tried to conceal her relief. Ever since breakfast she had been looking forward to a respite from the seemingly endless array of farm chores. She suspected occasions when she could escape from the drudgery of housework and see more of the Arboles Valley would be few and far between, and she meant to enjoy this one. She tried to catch Henry's eye so he could share in her pleasure, but he left the kitchen with the rest of the men without looking her way. Stung, Elizabeth vowed to speak to him as soon as they had a moment alone.

She helped Mary Katherine and the girls clean the kitchen—a mere few hours before they would make a mess of it again preparing supper—and met Lars outside the barn, where he waited with the wagon and horses. He helped her onto the wagon seat and chirruped to the horses.

"The car's too small," Lars said when they reached the main road.

"I beg your pardon?"

"I didn't think all of your stuff would fit in the car. That's why we're taking the wagon instead, though the car's more comfortable."

"I don't mind the wagon." In fact, today she rather preferred it. It was a beautiful afternoon, the sun warm and bright in a cloudless blue sky. She was in no hurry to return to sweeping floors and peeling potatoes.

"I guess not." There was a hint of amusement in his voice that suggested he knew what she was thinking. It occurred to her that she ought to thank him for choosing her to accompany him, although she suspected he would have preferred to go alone.

"You were right to warn us about John Barclay," she said. "I don't think he would have been as helpful if we had not approached him with the proper deference."

"He was helpful?"

Elizabeth smiled. "Not very. But it's not all his fault. There was very little he could do to help us. And . . . I think he might have been preoccupied with other things. His children."

"Well, that didn't take long," said Lars dryly. "I guess Mary Katherine told you."

"Annalise," said Elizabeth, hoping she would not get the young girl in trouble.

Lars shook his head, squinting in the sunlight. "It's a shame. Four little ones gone and no doctor can say why."

"Yes, of course, but I was referring to the two others who have fallen ill."

Lars gave her a sharp look. "What's that you say?"

"When Henry and I were there yesterday, two of the children seemed ill."

"Which two?"

His urgency took her by surprise. "I—I'm not sure of their names. Wait. Miguel. The youngest, the baby, his name was Miguel. The other was the middle girl. She sat on the steps, very weak, listless, while her sisters played."

Lars drew in a long breath. "Ana," he said, exhaling her name. "The middle girl's name is Ana. The eldest is Marta, and the youngest girl is Lupita. I knew Ana had gotten sick, but I didn't know about the baby."

"Annalise says she isn't allowed to play with the Barclay kids," said Elizabeth carefully, unwilling to seem critical of his mother. "Is Mrs. Jorgensen afraid she and Margaret might come down with the illness?"

"If she is, that's a mighty foolish fear," said Lars. "If it was catching, wouldn't Marta and Lupita catch it? Wouldn't Rosa and John?"

"I suppose so." Elizabeth hesitated. "No one knows what causes this disease?"

"Some folks say it's bad water on their place, too much alkali. Others say . . ." Lars shrugged. "Some blame one thing, some another. When folks don't have any facts, they imagine every kind of craziness."

"Have the children seen a doctor?"

"Only every doctor between Oxnard and Los Angeles. None of them can explain it. It always starts the same way. For the first year, the baby looks as healthy as any other. Then the illness takes hold and the child just wastes away. Sometimes it might take two years, sometimes four, but the end is always the same. Another child in the ground before the age of eight."

"Except for Marta and Lupita," said Elizabeth.

"Lupita is young yet," Lars reminded her. "But Marta—yes, it looks like Marta has been spared."

They drove along in silence the rest of the way to the Barclay farm. From a distance, Elizabeth spotted John Barclay plowing his fields. Marta and Lupita played in the shade of three live oaks near the house, but Rosa and the other two children were nowhere to be seen. Lars pulled the horses to a stop, jumped down from the wagon seat, and crossed the dusty yard to the front door. Rosa answered his knock, baby Miguel in her arms.

"I came to collect the mail," said Lars gruffly, his gaze fixed on Rosa's care-worn and exhausted face. "And my mother would like to mail these."

Rosa shifted the baby and took the letters. "I'll give them to John when he comes in from the fields. There's no mail for your family this time."

"I hear Miguel has taken ill."

Rosa nodded and looked away. Elizabeth thought she saw tears in her eyes.

"Rosa—" Lars reached out as if to touch her shoulder, but let his hand fall back to his side. "What do you need? What can I do?"

"There's nothing you can do."

"But you have no one to help you."

Rosa straightened and regarded him almost defiantly. "I have Marta. She is a great help to me."

"But she's just a girl. What about Carlos and Lupe?"

Rosa gave a bitter laugh. "My brother and his wife want nothing to do with us. You know that." She glanced past his shoulder. "John is coming. You'd better go."

When Lars did not budge, she disappeared inside the house and closed the door. John shouted to Lars as he approached, crossing the newly plowed field at a fast pace. Reluctantly, Lars left the house and met him halfway.

"What's your business here?" demanded John, panting.

"Just mailing some letters for my mother. I gave them to Rosa."

John eyed him, squinting, then turned his attention to Elizabeth. "I got a couple of letters here for an Elizabeth Nelson at Triumph Ranch. There's no such place, so I wasn't sure what to do with them."

Elizabeth felt color rise in her cheeks. "I'll take them, thank you."

John Barclay grinned, enjoying her embarrassment. "You might want to tell folks to address your mail correctly or it might get misdirected."

"Don't be a fool, Barclay," said Lars. "She's the only Elizabeth Nelson in the Arboles Valley."

John scowled and spat into the dirt. "I'll get your letters," he told Elizabeth, and sauntered off to the house. Lars climbed back onto the wagon seat and took up the reins while they waited. From inside the house came the sound of raised voices, John shouting while a child cried. Lars stiffened and wrapped the leather reins around his fist. Another few minutes passed before John returned and placed two envelopes in Elizabeth's hand. Her heart lifted when she saw the Pennsylvania postmarks and the return addresses, one from her parents in Harrisburg, the second from Elm Creek Manor.

She thanked John, but he waved her off and headed back to the fields. Lars started the wagon and turned down the road toward the western edge of the valley. When the Barclay farm was well behind them, Lars said, "Triumph Ranch?"

Elizabeth could not look at him. "It's hard to explain."

"You didn't get taken in by that Rancho Triunfo scam, did you? Your Henry seems too smart for that."

"Don't tell anyone, please," begged Elizabeth. "I don't know what Henry would do if Oscar or your mother found out. It's such an embarrassment to end up working as hired hands at the farm we thought we owned."

"Your secret's safe with me," Lars assured her. "But you're not the first to be swindled. You ought to swallow your pride and contact the police. Maybe they can help you get your money back."

"As far as we know, the man who cheated us is on the other side of the country."

"Maybe so, but it's worth a shot."

"What did the others do, the others who were cheated? Did they go to the police? Did they get their money back?"

"No. They mostly slunk off with their tails between their legs the moment they found out they'd been swindled. You and Henry are the first to stay more than a day afterward."

Elizabeth sighed softly, fingering the precious letters from home. What did that say about her and Henry, that they had stayed when the others had departed? Were the Nelsons more resilient or simply more foolish?

Before long they reached the row of shops and offices that made up the town proper nestled in the Santa Monica foothills, and soon the wagon was clattering along the cobblestone road leading to the Grand Union Hotel. Carlos stepped from the carriage house at the sound of their approach. He called out a greeting to Elizabeth, a question in his eyes. No doubt he wondered how things had gone at the Jorgensen farm after he had deposited the Nelsons there. Elizabeth returned his greeting with a smile to assure him all was well, but when Lars acknowledged the welcome, Carlos gave him only a wordless nod and quickly disappeared back into the carriage house.

Lars did not seem surprised by the curt welcome, so Elizabeth pretended not to notice it. As Lars helped her down from the wagon seat, it occurred to her that if John Barclay was the most unpopular man in town, Lars seemed to be a close second. She remembered Rosa's words, her despondent claim that Carlos and his wife wanted nothing to do with her. Elizabeth had seen for herself that Carlos had stayed in the yard instead of holding his sick nephew or comforting his sister. Perhaps Carlos, like Mrs. Jorgensen, feared contagion. If Lars's opinion that it was foolish to shun the Barclays was well known, that might account for the lack of friendliness between him and Carlos.

Lars waited with the horses while Elizabeth entered the hotel. She found Mrs. Diegel in the kitchen, which smelled of roasting chickens, cilantro, and orange. They expected a large crowd that evening, Mrs. Diegel said cheerfully, explaining her early start on preparing the meal. Both Mr. Milton and Mr. Donovan had parties of prospective homeowners spending the night at the hotel. Dinner promised to be lively, with both men and their clients gathered at the same table extolling the virtues of their own developments and pointing out the flaws in their competitor's.

"Will you stay for dinner?" Mrs. Diegel asked, wiping her hands on a dish towel. "I promise it will be entertaining."

"I wish I could, but I have to get back to work. I just came by to pick up our luggage."

"I suppose I don't have the space at the table tonight anyway." Mrs. Diegel led Elizabeth to the storage room. "It's none of my business, but I'm curious where you're staying tonight."

Elizabeth had been prepared for this. She forced a smile and said, "Our original plans fell through, but Henry and I were fortunate to find work on the Jorgensen farm. We have a quaint little cabin all to ourselves on their property."

"Not that ramshackle old place," said Mrs. Diegel, aghast. "That's not fit for human habitation. Oscar should have torn it down long ago."

"It has seen better days," Elizabeth admitted, "but we'll fix it up nicely."

"With what? Did you pack tools? Supplies? How will you furnish it? You can't possibly have beds and tables and chairs packed away in these trunks."

"There was some furniture in the cabin already. Whatever else we need can wait until payday."

"Oh, my heavens." Mrs. Diegel clasped a hand to her brow and shook her head. "I admire your fortitude, but you need to pause a minute and think. How far do you think your paycheck will stretch if you have to furnish an entire cabin, even one that small? That place doesn't even have indoor plumbing. Where do you bathe? How will you cook for yourselves?"

"So far we've eaten all our meals with the Jorgensens," said Elizabeth. "If we want to dine alone sometime, we do have a cookstove."

"Yes, but do you have any coal? Any pots and pans?"

"No," said Elizabeth. Triumph Ranch was supposed to come furnished. She and Henry had assumed that included kitchen implements, and if not, they had planned to buy what they needed after taking inventory. Now their inventory included three old beds with worn and soiled mattresses, a chair and a stool, and two worn and faded quilts, and they had neither the money nor the credit to buy what they lacked.

Mrs. Diegel gestured to the Nelsons' luggage. "And all this? The wedding trousseau, I assume. Finery rather than the practical things you really need."

Elizabeth nodded, although that was only partially correct. She and Henry needed the quilts, bed linens, and dishes as much as they needed cooking pots and coal. But the wedding gifts were more meaningful to her than the sum of the practical roles they performed. They were the comforts of home, tangible reminders of loved ones so far away, relics of a time when they had been full of confidence and hope and promise. Elizabeth needed to surround herself with these souvenirs of a different age or she feared she might forget how she had felt on the train west as Henry's bride. Worse yet, Henry might forget.

But Mrs. Diegel was right. How long could they get by washing up at the kitchen sink? How would Elizabeth cook for them on Sundays, their day off?

"I suppose I could sell some of our things," she said reluctantly. She dragged one of the trunks into the open. There was a faint, musical chime of china delicately clinking.

"Is that china?" asked Mrs. Diegel.

Elizabeth nodded, unfastened the lock, and opened the trunk. She reached within the folds of the quilt and withdrew a cup and saucer. "It's our Blue Willow china," she said steadily. "Twelve five-piece place settings and several serving dishes. It was a gift from my grandparents."

"You certainly expected to entertain in high style, didn't you?" said Mrs. Diegel, admiring the china. "Well. I don't think you'll find much of a market for fine china in the Arboles Valley, but perhaps . . ." She glanced over her shoulder into the kitchen, and her gaze lingered on her own china closet before she turned back to Elizabeth. "I'd be willing to trade you some more practical necessities for the china service. You can try to sell them elsewhere first if you like; I'm in no hurry."

But Elizabeth was, and she would have no idea where to begin trying to sell her things. "What would you be willing to offer?"

Mrs. Diegel wanted to inspect the entire service first, so Elizabeth carefully unpacked the plates and cups and casseroles and placed them on the table. Not a single piece had broken, and as Mrs. Diegel held up a dinner plate to the light to admire the design, she proposed a trade: a mattress—rarely used, as it had been her grown daughter's before she moved to San Francisco and not for hotel guests—two feather pillows, a simple pewter table service for four, and three kerosene lamps for all of the china. Elizabeth pointed out that the china was new, whereas Mrs. Diegel's things were not. Mrs. Diegel added two scuttles of coal and a large copper stockpot to the deal, and since Elizabeth doubted she would go any higher, she agreed.

"What else do you have in there?" asked Mrs. Diegel, eying the remaining trunks eagerly.

With a twinge of regret, Elizabeth opened the rest of the trunks. She traded away the silver plate for a set of used flatware, a teakettle, and five pieces of cast-iron cookware. A pair of elegant candlesticks went for sacks of sugar, coffee, and flour. Mrs. Diegel tried to talk her into parting with all of the bedsheets, but Elizabeth insisted upon keeping one set for her and Henry. One by one she parted with her beautiful things, acquiring the practical necessities of everyday life in return.

When the last trunk had been emptied, Mrs. Diegel seemed sorry to end their bargaining, but Elizabeth felt drained, bereft. While she repacked the trunks with the secondhand goods, Mrs. Diegel instructed the porter to take the mattress from the spare bedroom in the family wing of the hotel and load it into Lars's wagon. Humming merrily, Mrs. Diegel carefully arranged the Blue Willow pieces in her china closet. "You brought this all the way from Pennsylvania bouncing and jolting in trains and wagons, and not one broken teacup, not one single chipped plate," she marveled.

And now it seemed all for nothing. "I suppose the quilts protected them."

"Quilts? What quilts?"

Elizabeth gestured. "In the first trunk. You saw them when I took out the china."

"I saw muslin sheets, not quilts." Mrs. Diegel put away the last saucer and hurried over. "Well, bring them out. Let's have a look at them."

"My aunts wrapped the quilts in muslin sheets to keep them clean," Elizabeth explained as she withdrew the bundles from the trunk. She unfolded the wedding quilt and spread it upon her lap, pride a warm glow in her chest as Mrs. Diegel exclaimed in awe and delight over the Bergstrom women's handiwork. Great-Aunt Lucinda's homespun scrap Chimneys and Cornerstones quilt evoked a more subdued reaction than the elegant Double Wedding Ring, but Elizabeth was pleased and comforted by Mrs. Diegel's declaration that they were the two most beautiful and well-made quilts she had ever seen.

"The women of your family clearly take pride in their work," she said. As Elizabeth thanked her and folded the quilts, Mrs. Diegel added, "What will you take for them?"

Elizabeth let out a small laugh of surprise. "Sorry, nothing. I couldn't part with them."

"Surely there's something else you need."

"Not more than I need these quilts."

"I have a copper bathtub left over from before we had indoor plumbing. It's been in storage in the carriage house for years. Polish it up a bit and it will be as good as new."

Elizabeth hesitated, but shook her head. "I'm sorry, but no."

"Oh, come now," said Mrs. Diegel. "A young girl like yourself, a new bride no less, and you're willing to go without a good soak in the tub at the end of a long day?"

Elizabeth closed her eyes, the quilts a soft, comforting weight in her arms. She could almost feel the steam rise from the hot bath, feel the water enveloping her, bubbles tickling her toes. Then she opened her eyes. "I'm sorry. It's not enough."

"We'll see how you feel after a month without a proper bath. We'll see how your husband feels."

Elizabeth felt a lump in her throat. She shook her head and returned the folded quilts to the trunk.

"What are these two quilts compared to a hot bath?" persisted Mrs. Diegel. "You've seen my needlework. I could never make anything so lovely, but you could always make others to replace these."

"Not like these, I couldn't. Not with only a needle and thread."

"I have a sewing machine."

"Our cabin doesn't have electricity."

"This runs by a treadle."

Elizabeth paused, her hand on the latch of the trunk.

Mrs. Diegel leaned forward conspiratorially. "The bathtub, the treadle sewing machine with enough thread and fabric to get you started, and I'll throw in ten dollars. There's bound to be something else you need, something you aren't thinking of at the moment. Or maybe you'll want to buy something nice for your husband. What do you say?"

Elizabeth knew what answer she wanted to give, and she knew what the only sensible reply could be. A bathtub was not only a luxury for soaking her cares away. Henry would want it, too, perhaps more than the beautiful quilts. And how long, indeed, would he continue to find her beautiful if she had to make do with the pump at the kitchen sink? Already her nails had become ragged, the skin of her hands red and rough. Already she was not the lovely young bride he had married.

"Someday," said Elizabeth. "Someday, when our circumstances have improved, will you allow me to buy the quilts back from you?"

Mrs. Diegel considered. "I suppose that's reasonable, but I can't guarantee their condition. I intend to use them in the hotel guest rooms."

Pained by the admission, Elizabeth said, "But you will allow me to buy them back, at a fair price, when I am able?"

"Very well." Mrs. Diegel extended a hand. "It's a deal."

Elizabeth shook on it, her heart aching. It was not much of a deal. They had not agreed on a price, and the quilts might be well worn by the time she had saved up enough money to buy them back. But without that agreement, without the glimmer of hope that she might one day have the quilts restored to her, she never could have parted with them.

Outside, Lars and the porter finished loading the wagon as Elizabeth climbed back onto the seat. She knew she had done the right thing, the only sensible thing, given their circumstances, but she felt hollow inside from longing. For months she had watched as her mother, aunts, and grandmother labored over her bridal quilt, each leaving her unique imprint upon the cloth. For months she had dreamed of sleeping beneath it in the arms of her adoring husband. In her mind's eye she could still see Great-Aunt Lucinda explaining the symbolism of the Chimneys and Cornerstones quilt to little cousin Sylvia, how the quilt carried with it the love and the steadfastness of her family, a reminder that no matter how far she journeyed from them, she would always be welcomed home to a loving embrace. But now the beautiful quilts to which the Bergstrom women had contributed their finest handiwork would grace the beds of itinerant strangers, who might admire their beauty but would never suspect what they truly represented.

She blinked back tears and rested her hand upon the letters from home in her pocket. She could not cry over quilts and china when Henry had lost his life savings and his dream. The last thing he needed was the burden of his wife's childish grief. He would be proud of her when he discovered what she had acquired to make the cabin more comfortable. She would make it as cozy a home as the farmhouse of Triumph Ranch would have been.

Lars drove the wagon back to the Jorgensen farm in silence, sparing her questions about the unexpected change in their cargo. He bypassed the farmhouse and went straight to the cabin, where he helped her unload the wagon and carry things inside. They worked quickly, mindful of the chores awaiting them. Together they wrestled the old mattress out of the cabin and replaced it with the newer one. The trunks and smaller parcels they left in the middle of the front room for Elizabeth to sort out later. Lars set up the sewing machine inside in the front room between the window and the fireplace, but he hesitated at the sight of the old copper bathtub. "Where do you want this?" he asked.

"Let's put it in the second bedroom for now," said Elizabeth, pushing open the door. Her nose wrinkled at the stale, musty-sweet odor. She should have left the door open to allow the room to air out rather than vainly try to conceal the mess. "If we get that crate out of the way, we'll have enough space."

She crossed the room to the large wooden crate beneath the window, but Lars brushed past her and took hold of it first. "I can get it."

"It looks heavy," said Elizabeth, placing a hand on the lid. "Let me help."

"No need." Lars pushed himself between Elizabeth and the crate, jostling the lid aside a few inches, enough for Elizabeth to glimpse dozens and dozens of empty glass liquor bottles piled inside.

As the sticky-sweet odor wafted forth, Elizabeth stepped back, waving her hand in front of her face. "So that's what that smell was," she said. "It must be someone's pre-Prohibition stash."

"Some fool drank away a lot of years in this place," said Lars.

"It can't be anyone in your family, or you'd know," said Elizabeth. "Drinkers think they're keeping it a secret, they think they're fooling everyone just because they get up and go to work every day, but everybody knows. They're just afraid to say anything. As long as everyone pretends everything's fine, they can pretend he's different from that drunken bum on the street corner. The only real difference is that no one's afraid to tell the bum he's a drunk. As for the other kind—well, no one thanks the person who pops the bubble of the family's collective delusion, let me tell you."

Lars was staring at her.

"I'm not talking about Henry," she hastened to add. "My father. My father's the drinker of the family."

Lars regarded her with a mixture of curiosity and surprise. "Seems like every family's got one."

Elizabeth shrugged, feeling suddenly ashamed of her spiteful, disloyal words. "I suppose so. I—I don't want you to misunderstand. He's a good man. But—you just don't know what it's like, loving someone, wanting to believe in him, and knowing that sooner or later, he's going to let you down. That's one of the reasons I agreed to move so far from home. I just don't want to see him that way anymore."

"You didn't think you'd end up in a place like this or you wouldn't have come." Lars glanced around the room. "This cabin should be torn down, every last board and nail."

"Is that any way to talk about my lovely new home?" When Lars did not respond to her attempt at levity, she said, "You know our circumstances. You know we're lucky to have a roof over our heads."

"I know Mrs. Diegel is a shrewd businesswoman and you left that hotel a far cry more miserable than you walked in." Lars hefted the crate, ropes of muscles visible through his shirtsleeves. "You should have held out for more, both from her and my mother."

He hauled the crate from the room, glass clattering. Elizabeth sighed and rested a hand upon the copper bathtub, worn out from unloading the wagon, from disappointment and uncertainty. She had done the best she could. She did not know how to haggle over prices. At her father's hotel, he decided what to charge for a night's stay, for a meal, for any service a guest could imagine. He stuck a price tag on things and accepted that amount from the guest in cash or credit. Nothing in her life had prepared her for what she had faced today. Henry could do the work he had signed on for, but Elizabeth had no idea how to be a poor farmhand's wife.

She thought then of Mrs. Jorgensen, of the work Elizabeth needed to finish that day before she could return to the cabin and the tasks awaiting her there. She roused herself, left the letters from home on the chair in the front room, and joined Lars in the wagon, empty now except for the crate of bottles.

"I wonder what your brother will think when he sees those," said Elizabeth. "Will he suspect the farmhands?"

"By the look of them, those bottles have been empty for years," said Lars shortly. "I don't see what's to be gained by letting my brother know about them."

"Agreed," said Elizabeth. She saw no point in getting anyone in trouble. It was not as if she and Lars had discovered an illicit still, the farmhands gathered around filling flasks and hollow canes.

Mrs. Jorgensen put Elizabeth to work in the garden almost as soon as the wagon pulled up to the barn. Mary Katherine and her daughters were already there, and their cheerful company softened the ache in Elizabeth's heart. Before long they returned to the kitchen to help prepare supper. This time when the men came in, Henry took her aside, kissed her softly, and asked how her errand to the Grand Union Hotel had gone. She was torn between relief that he had not brushed her aside again and regret that he had chosen that particular question. "Mrs. Diegel was helpful," she began, but Oscar had sat down and was waiting to say grace, so she said in a quick whisper that she had much more to tell him when they had time.

She would rather show him, anyway. She hoped to leave as soon as she finished tidying the kitchen as she had the previous evening, but as if to make up for the time off she had been granted earlier that day, Mrs. Jorgensen kept her busy until dusk. When she was finally dismissed, she ran most of the way back to the cabin and raced to unpack the trunks before Henry arrived. She put their own fresh sheets on the almost-new mattress and tossed the larger of the two worn quilts over it, pausing for a moment to take in the unusual star design. She had never seen the pattern before, nor that of the second quilt, which she folded and draped over the foot of the bed. In the front room, she lit one of the hurricane lamps, stacked the pewter dishes in the cupboard, and put the teakettle on the stove. Twenty minutes later, her bustle of cleaning came to an abrupt halt as Henry came home. From the doorway, he took in the sight of their own trunks, open in the center of the front room and spilling forth unfamiliar contents. "More castoffs from the Jorgensens?" he asked tiredly as he shut the cabin door behind him.

"No, these belong to us," said Elizabeth, and explained how she and Mrs. Diegel had traded goods.

Henry stood in the center of the room, fixed in place by shock and anger. "You gave away your family's wedding gifts?"

"I traded them for other things we needed more." Elizabeth searched his face for some clue to explain his reaction. She had expected him to be proud of her pragmatic sacrifice. "I didn't think you cared about china or silver plate. I thought we'd be better off able to cook for ourselves and bathe. Was I wrong?"

"No." He dropped wearily into a chair and tugged off his boots. "Of course not. You were right."

"Then why are you so angry?"

"I'm not angry with you." He rose, went to the kitchen, and pumped water into the sink. He scrubbed his face and hands, drying himself on one of their last clean rags. "I'm just sorry. Sorry that it has come to this. Remember what I said to you on the train? You should always be surrounded by beauty. Look what I've done to you. I've taken you from your family to live in a hovel and work at someone else's beck and call."

"It's not that bad," said Elizabeth. "I'm not waiting hand and foot on a spoiled lady of leisure. Mrs. Jorgensen doesn't ask me to work any harder than she does herself."

She did not expect that to satisfy Henry but it was the truth. He left her standing in the kitchen and disappeared into the bedroom, but he almost immediately emerged, his expression twisted and pained. "That old quilt is still on the bed."

"I know. It's fairly clean, and the pattern is nice. Once I can give it a proper washing, it will be lovely."

"The other one's even worse. It's full of holes and the stuffing's falling out."

"I can mend the holes. It will still keep us warm if the star quilt isn't enough."

"Where's our wedding quilt? That one your mother and all your aunts made, the one with the rings and the flowers?"

Elizabeth did not reply.

"All you've talked about for months was how much you wanted to see that wedding quilt on our bed." A muscle in Henry's jaw tightened and relaxed. "Tomorrow you'll go back to the Grand Union Hotel and give back whatever you traded for it."

"I can't," said Elizabeth sharply. "As much as I want my quilts back, we need the bathtub more. And she gave me ten dollars cash. We're going to need that, Henry. Until we get back on our feet and find our way clear of this, we're going to need it."

Henry sighed and rubbed hard at his jaw as if working the pain and disappointment out of it. "There's only one way out of this, Elizabeth, and that's for you to go home to your parents."

"I won't accept that. We'll find a way, Henry. This is not the way things are always going to be. In less than a year, we'll have enough money saved for the train fare home. What's one year? We'll go back to Pennsylvania and work Two Bears Farm with your family the way we always thought we would. They'll be so happy to have us back. And—and I'll be glad, too. California is lovely, but really, we will be much better off back home, with our families."

The bleakness in his eyes told her he did not believe it. Without another word, he disappeared into the bedroom again. She heard clothing drop to the floor and bedsprings creak. For a moment she hoped he would call out to her to come join him, playfully asking her to help him test out the almost new mattress and the clean linen sheets she had wisely held back from Mrs. Diegel. But he said nothing, and all the wistful hope and expectation drained from her like fragrance from a pressed flower.

She stood there listening until the steady rhythm of his breathing told her he slept. She ought to join him. She needed her rest, too; she ought to save the kerosene. But instead she picked up the letters from home and sank into the rocking chair to read. Her mother's letter, written two days after their departure, was full of wistful encouragement, fond recollections of the wedding celebration, and reminders to send out thank-you notes for the lovely gifts she and Henry had received. Tears sprang into Elizabeth's eyes, but she laughed softly, imagining how she would phrase those notes: "Dear Great-Aunt Lydia, thank you so much for the soup tureen. I'm sure the prospective buyers of Oakwood Glen will appreciate the beauty it adds to the table of the Grand Union Hotel."

The second letter was from little cousin Sylvia, whose accusatory tone had survived the filter of Aunt Eleanor's transcription: "Dear Elizabeth, I hope you had a good trip. I hope you like California. I don't think you will like it as much as home, but I hope it is nice. I love you. I miss you. I hope you can come home soon to visit. Please bring me an orange from your tree when you come. Henry does not have to come. Love, Sylvia."

Aunt Eleanor had added a postscript: "Sylvia is happy for you in her own way. I'm sure you understand. We all miss you and hope it won't be long before you and Henry can visit. When you have a spare moment, Sylvia would love to hear from you. I hope ranch life isn't too busy to allow you time to write home, because we eagerly await news of your California adventure. I hope Triumph Ranch is everything you dreamed it would be. Love always, Aunt Eleanor."

Elizabeth returned the letters to their envelopes and closed her eyes. Aunt Eleanor had struck closer to the heart of the truth than she would ever know. Triumph Ranch was everything Elizabeth had dreamed, but it was no more than a dream, vanished now that she had awakened.

She did not have the heart to put that into a letter.

Soon Sylvia and the others would receive the letters Elizabeth had mailed the previous day, the last letters she had written in happy anticipation of reaching Triumph Ranch at last. Sylvia would expect more. Elizabeth's mother would expect more. Elizabeth could not put off responding forever. The family would worry and—she was struck by the sudden horror of realization—they might send someone to California to be sure she and Henry were safe. She could not lie to them—but how could she tell them the truth?

Her next letter home would have to wait until she knew how to write it.

When Elizabeth climbed into bed beside Henry, she tentatively snuggled into the crook of his arm. Instead of holding her close, he drew his arm free and rolled over onto his side, his back to her, never waking, or so she told herself. She lay on her back and looked up at the shadowed ceiling until she fell asleep.

❧

1904

As her children grew, Isabel resolved that they would have everything she had been denied as a young girl—an education, friends, a loving and happy home. Thanks to Miguel, they never lacked for the latter. He showered them with love and praise, and they returned his affection in equal measure. Their eyes shone when they knew they had pleased him; his pride in their achievements spurred them on to work hard at school and help their mother around the house, for which Isabel was grateful. Her children had what mattered most, she knew, but she also wanted them to have the same material things their friends had, and that cost money.

When the children were old enough, Isabel took a job as a housecleaner, starting with the few families who could afford one in the Arboles Valley and adding new clients as far away as Oxnard as one satisfied customer after another recommended her to friends. She arranged her schedule so she could see the children off to school before leaving for work and return home in time to greet them at the door after classes. In the summer, she worked mornings and traded babysitting with a friend from church who worked afternoons. The long, exhausting hours were worth it when she saw Carlos running across a grassy field in new, sturdy shoes, or Rosa laughing and playing in a new cotton dress and bright hair ribbons.

Isabel had no words to describe how she adored her children. Every night she prayed for God to watch over them; every week she lit a candle before a picture of the Blessed Mother, the Lady of Guadalupe, and prayed for her guidance and wisdom. She could not seek advice from her own mother, so she would turn to the Lord. It was all she could do. She had only a child's memory of how her mother had raised her, and her father's example was not one she wished to follow. Some days she did not know what to do or what to say so that her bright and lively children would grow into good and faithful adults. Some days she thought she ought to just stay out of the way rather than risk interfering with their intrinsic goodness. Some days she wanted to do nothing more than stand back and watch, basking in happiness as her children learned and grew.

But on other days, she longed to grasp hold of them and keep them close by her side, where she could keep a watchful eye over them. Rosa worried her more than Carlos—sweet, happy Carlos, so much like his father, forgiving and patient. Rosa was willful and intelligent, quick to anger, quick to laugh. She was also very beautiful, and becoming more so with each passing year. Her father joked that she would be a heartbreaker one day. Isabel did not doubt it. The question that troubled her most was whose heart would she shatter.

When Rosa was fourteen and Carlos twelve, they came home from school on a mid-February afternoon munching candy hearts and carrying paper sacks stuffed full of valentines. Rosa ran off straight to her room and shut her door. "Is she upset?" Isabel asked Carlos as he plunked his book bag on the kitchen table and reached for the plate of cookies.

"No," he said, disgusted. "She's just crazy."

"Carlos."

"It's true. She's acting like a dumb girl all because some boy gave her a flower."

"Don't call your sister dumb," Isabel said automatically, but her heart clenched. She left Carlos to his snack and rapped softly on her daughter's door. "Rosa?"

"What is it, Mami?" Rosa called from within.

Isabel opened the door. Rosa sat up in her bed and scrambled to hide something beneath her pillow. "Carlos said you were given a flower at school today."

Rosa shrugged dismissively. "Lots of girls got them. It's Valentine's Day."

Though she kept her eyes downcast, she could not hide her smile, or her glow.

"Let me see it," said Isabel sternly.

Frowning, Rosa reached beneath her pillow and handed her mother a long -stemmed pink carnation, identical to those she had seen for sale in the Arboles Grocery. Although slender pink-and-white ribbons were tied around the stem, no card or note was attached to reveal the identity of Rosa's admirer.

"Who gave this to you?"

"Someone left it in my valentine bag when I was away from my desk. There's no name."

"I can see there's no name. Who gave it to you?"

"I guess . . . it could have been any of the boys."

Isabel leveled a hard gaze at her daughter, recognizing the evasive words of a girl who did not want to confess the truth but was as yet unwilling to lie to her mother. Thank God she still had enough sense for that, enough respect. Isabel and Miguel could still nip this nonsense in the bud.

"I wonder what your father will think of your answer."

Rosa shrugged as if she were only mildly curious, but she bit her lower lip and glanced at the paper bag stuffed full of valentines. Isabel knew at once that the card for the flower was inside.

She resisted the urge to snatch up the bag and search through the valentines until she found the proof she needed. The Arboles School had only two classrooms, twenty-three students. It would not be difficult to figure out who had sent the flower. Carlos probably knew. Isabel knew and liked all the boys Rosa's age, but there were other children she did not know. It did not matter, however, whether she liked Rosa's unknown admirer. Rosa was too young to be accepting gifts and attention from boys.

She left Rosa alone to start her homework. Later, after the children had gone to bed, she told Miguel that she was astonished the teachers allowed tokens of affection to be exchanged in the classroom. "It's a valentine," said Miguel mildly. "At that age, a flower is a token of friendship, nothing more. It's no wonder the boys admire Rosa. She's a lovely girl, just like you were at her age."

"I was not as beautiful as Rosa," said Isabel, "but I was far more obedient. If I had come home with a flower from a boy, my parents would have been incensed."

"Maybe the boys knew this and that's why they didn't dare send you any flowers. Otherwise I'm sure they would have thrown bouquets at your feet, and not only on Valentine's Day."

Isabel was too troubled to be charmed by her husband's flattery. "We are talking about our daughter. Miguel, she's growing up too quickly. We've given her too much freedom." *I've given her too much freedom,* she thought. *I wanted her to have my share as well as her own.*

Miguel smiled and kissed her on the cheek. "You were just as beautiful as Rosa, but you're right, you were also more demure. Rosa is a good girl. Let her have her secret admirer. Nothing bad will come of it."

But Isabel brooded over this unknown boy who had turned her daughter secretive. As the days passed, Rosa had taken to smiling to herself at unexpected moments—while washing dishes, folding clothes. She gazed out windows dreamily when she was supposed to be studying.

Finally Isabel could bear it no longer. One evening as Rosa sat at the kitchen table with a half smile on her lips, staring at the fire instead of the schoolbook open before her, Isabel asked, "Did you ever find out who gave you the flower?"

Her question snatched Rosa from her reverie. "What, Mami?"

"The flower," said Isabel. "Who was it from?"

Rosa took a quick breath. "I don't know," she said. "Maybe it wasn't really for me. Whoever he is, maybe he put it in my bag by mistake. I sit next to Julia, you know. She's very pretty."

"I see," said Isabel. She gestured to Rosa's book. "Finish up. It's almost time for bed."

She knew Miguel would tell her not to worry, that Rosa was fourteen and a half now and many years away from wanting to carry on with boys. She was flattered by the admiration, nothing more. It was a harmless crush that would swiftly fade unless they made a fuss.

But Isabel knew differently. First her daughter had kept a secret from her, and then she had lied. Rosa knew who had given her the flower, but she did not want her mother to know.

Chapter Seven

1925

E lizabeth was grateful for the work that kept her too busy to write a letter home, work that filled up her hours and exhausted her so that she was too numb to feel fully the pain of her disappointment. For weeks she carried out the tasks Mrs. Jorgensen assigned her without complaint, as if she were watching someone else haul water and sweep floors and cook three meals a day for fourteen. As her hands grew calloused and shoulders strong, she observed the changes in herself with detached disbelief, as if a beloved character in a favorite book suddenly began saying and doing things that had never happened the other times she had read the story. This wasn't right, she thought as she went through her day, from the time she hurried to the yellow farmhouse before the sun had peeked over the eastern hills until she trudged back to the cabin as the last rays of light disappeared behind the Santa Monica Mountains to the west. Something had gone terribly wrong, but if she just went along and made do with her circumstances for a little while, eventually the error would be corrected and everything would return to its proper course.

After the shock wore off, she realized that she would have to make do for much longer than she had imagined when she had made Henry promise not to send her home without him. She found comfort in knowing that their exile couldn't last more than a year or two, and at the end of that time, Henry could resume his rightful place with his father and brothers at Two Bears Farm. From the Nelsons' house it was only a short, pleasant walk through the woods to Elm Creek Manor and all the familiar, beautiful places she had loved since childhood. Knowing what awaited her, Elizabeth resolved to endure any hardship, any humiliation, until their homecoming. She did not need Great-Aunt Lucinda's Chimneys and Cornerstones quilt to remind her of the welcoming fires on the hearth back home.

In the meantime, she resolved to make the best of things so that Henry would know she did not blame him for their circumstances. After all, she had wanted an adventure, and in the years to come, she would certainly be able to say she had found one.

As the weeks passed, the days took on a sameness, a pattern of daily chores and mealtimes that altered only in the work performed and the food prepared. Even that showed little variation. Sundays were not as restful as she had thought they would be when Mary Katherine had arranged for her to have the day off, for even though she could set aside the usual work of the week, she still had her own housekeeping to attend to, and Henry. On Sundays more than any other time of the week, she missed Elm Creek Manor, where all the women of the family pitched in and many hands made light work. Ruefully she told herself that she was fortunate that the cabin was so small, and that she had so little furniture to dust and linens to wash.

It was a small blessing, but fortunately not the only one Elizabeth was able to find. The Arboles Valley was truly as beautiful a place as she could have dreamed, with warm sunshine and balmy breezes that felt like a gentle benediction, a reassurance that all would be well in time. High, rolling foothills and low mountains sheltered the green and fertile land, in which it seemed any seed planted would flourish. The mornings were cool and misty, which Elizabeth supposed was a consequence of their nearness to the ocean. Sometimes she stood on the front porch of the cabin, looked toward the western mountains, and imagined waves crashing on the beach miles beyond them. Her heart stirred with the memory of happiness whenever she remembered how close the ocean was even though she could not see it, and how bracing the winds off the Pacific had been when she waded in the water for the first time. Sometimes she still felt the promise of prosperity in the air, although she did not speak of it to Henry, who seemed to have forgotten he had ever admired any part of the Arboles Valley.

Triumph Ranch was not quite as it had been described in the land agent's papers, and although this was the least of the deceptions played upon them, it still caught Elizabeth by surprise. The Jorgensen farm was not a cattle ranch at all, but a farm much like the Nelsons' back home, except that the Jorgensens grew barley and alfalfa instead of corn and wheat. Instead of herds of cattle, there were flocks of sheep, and a large, thriving apricot orchard on the southeastern portion of the property. Once Elizabeth remarked to Henry that she thought those particular crops and livestock suited his experience better than cattle would have done, but he merely returned a silent, bemused stare. She felt foolish and did not bother to explain that she had not meant to suggest that they were better off than if Triumph Ranch had been real. But perhaps, in the long run, they would be. They had been cheated and humiliated, but as a result, they would be going home to Pennsylvania. They were young enough to recover from a mistake even as great as this one, with the help of their families. In the years to come, they would look back with fond amusement upon their brief adventure in California and thank God they had returned to the people and land they so loved.

Elizabeth tried to say as much to Henry, but he cut her off abruptly whenever she said or did anything that smacked of optimism. Before long, she stopped trying, bewildered by his behavior. Would he prefer for her to mope and wail about how miserable she was, how homesick and lonely? She thought she was being a good wife by pointing out the bright side of things, especially the transitory nature of their predicament. He did not seem to hear her.

Elizabeth was grateful for Mary Katherine's company while she worked, even though she could never replace Henry as a confidant. Mary Katherine was friendly and kind, and if she complained too often about her mother-in -law, she did not seem to mind when Elizabeth did not join in. For her part, Mrs. Jorgensen remained as formidable a woman as she had first appeared, forthright and demanding, with no patience for jokes or teasing. Elizabeth quickly learned to treat her with respect and deference even if it meant biting her tongue rather than defend herself when Mrs. Jorgensen criticized the way she scalded a pan or ironed a shirt. Her patience for the sake of household harmony paid off, for the more Elizabeth proved herself to be a capable worker, the more Mrs. Jorgensen trusted her, rewarding her with more important, more interesting responsibilities.

Working so closely with the Jorgensen family, she learned a great deal about them in a short time. The farm had been in the family for three generations. Mrs. Jorgensen's grandfather, a Norwegian immigrant who had settled in Minnesota, bought the land after his physician diagnosed him with consumption and told him a milder climate would ease the suffering of his final years. The doctor's remedy succeeded so well that he lived another three decades in vigorous good health and might have continued to do so for many years to come if he had not been thrown from a horse and struck his head on a rock two weeks after his sixty-second birthday. But until his untimely death, he had lived so robustly and had touted the attributes of his new home so tirelessly that other Norwegian friends and relations had been encouraged to settle on nearby farms, creating a Norwegian colony within the Arboles Valley. United by kinship and a common language, they mostly kept to themselves. Only in the most recent generation had the old mistrust of strangers begun to fade.

Because the farm was so remote, the Nelsons had little opportunity to meet any of the neighbors, who often lived as much as a mile away. Elizabeth expected that would change in the years to come, but perhaps not before she and Henry returned to Pennsylvania. A frequent topic of dinner conversation was the sale—or rumors of upcoming sales—of nearby farmland to developers like Mr. Milton and Mr. Donovan. Oscar Jorgensen received a few offers from time to time, offers so good he wouldn't have believed them if he had not seen them in black and white with his own eyes. Developers encouraged him to sell the land, buy a cheaper farm in another part of southern California, and pocket a hefty profit, but Oscar refused. He would not sell the farm his father and grandfather had given their lives to cultivate so that their descendants would prosper. Sometimes over breakfast he eyed his two daughters as if wondering whether they would hold on, or if they would be the generation to sell out.

Strangely, or so Elizabeth thought, Lars never offered an opinion on whether the Jorgensen family should accept one of the offers for their farm. Elizabeth would have thought his opinion mattered, because surely the farm belonged to him as much as to Oscar, the younger of the two brothers. Mrs. Jorgensen, on the other hand, could not conceal her feelings on the subject, and it was readily apparent that she did not share Mrs. Diegel's opinion that these new housing developments would allow the valley to thrive and prosper. Elizabeth suspected she hated to see the farmland give way to streets and houses, because whenever someone mentioned Oakwood Glen or Meadowbrook Hills, her mouth pinched in a tight line and she drew in a sharp breath as if she expected to smell something foul. It reminded Elizabeth of the expression Grandmother Bergstrom assumed when little cousin Sylvia and her sister Claudia argued at the supper table. Elizabeth understood Mrs. Jorgensen's feelings; the folks at Elm Creek Manor would not like it if the Nelson family sold off their land and forty families built houses there, all closely packed together. Their rural seclusion would be gone forever, and the advantage of many new potential friends close by could not begin to compensate for that.

Although Elizabeth saw the other hired hands only in passing, she learned enough about them to know that Henry worked twice as hard as anyone except Oscar and Lars. He plunged himself into his work with a ferocity that worried Elizabeth, as if the unfinished tasks were an enemy he meant to wrestle into submission. At the close of day he was so exhausted that he fell asleep almost as soon as he drew the quilt over himself, leaving Elizabeth disappointed and lonely beside him, hungry for a kind word, a gentle caress. She missed those nights on the train when he could not bear to let her go.

At those times, alone in the dark with her husband by her side, she missed her family and Elm Creek Manor so much she did not think she would be able to bear it. She even found herself longing for her parents' apartment at the hotel in Harrisburg and her own familiar room, which she had shared with her sister until she was sixteen, when her sister married. Their home had always seemed cramped and stuffily formal compared with the gracious country elegance of Elm Creek Manor, but it was a palace compared with the miserable cabin. She wished she had not taken for granted the comforts of home—or the presence of her family.

But as remote as home and family were, Henry seemed more distant still. Elizabeth told herself that their honeymoon had spoiled her, and that it was unreasonable to expect Henry to be her constant companion when there was so much work to be done. Even if he were the owner of Triumph Ranch, he would not have been able to grant her that. And yet, she had expected things to be different between them. Sometimes she wished they were still on the train heading west, with everything before them.

On nights when sleep eluded her, Elizabeth wrapped herself in the older quilt and settled in the front room with her scrap basket and needle and thread. The unexpected turn their journey had taken had not lessened Elizabeth's desire to sew a patchwork album of her memories. To the scraps Mrs. Diegel had given her, Elizabeth had added a few squares cut from an old bedsheet, worn so thin from use that it was almost translucent. Worn cotton from the cabin contrasted sharply with the silk scarf from Venice Beach and the elegant chintz floral from the Grand Union Hotel, but she was determined to include them in her quilt, determined to try to make something useful and even beautiful from them. The fabric was good, sturdy, printed muslin, and use had only made it softer. The pink rosebuds were faded, but the blue background was the lovely shade of the California sky on a sunny afternoon. Those patches would always remind Elizabeth of her first night on Triumph Ranch, and whatever else befell her until she returned safely home, she did not believe her quilt would be complete without them. In the months to come she would do her best to collect more appealing scraps—something newer, or prettier, or fancier—but faded cotton was what she had and it would do for now.

Just as the fabrics she gathered for her quilt had changed, so too had the pattern altered in her mind's eye. She felt herself drawn toward a Postage Stamp design, a straightforward arrangement of two-inch squares in horizontal rows, soothing in its simplicity. Artistic as well as pragmatic factors made a Postage Stamp quilt the appropriate choice. Her fabric scraps were too small for large star points or sweeping arcs or background panels for appliqué, and the use of so many different prints and colors almost required her to use a simple design or the quilt would be so dizzyingly busy no one could possibly sleep well beneath it. A Postage Stamp quilt required only simple squares and straight seams, making it the perfect sewing project for dim light and late nights when she wanted her thoughts to drift, when repetitive tasks would help ease her into sleep. She also found a certain ironic poetry in the name, considering that the troubles had begun with a visit to the Arboles Valley post office, and the only way Elizabeth could speak to the people she loved most in the world was through the mail. But most of all, she found comfort in reducing the troubles of her day to simple shapes, to cutting and shaping the upheaval in her life into simple two-inch squares.

Perhaps as autumn approached she could gather scraps of cloth made from the wool of the sheep Henry tended. Better things were coming. They had to be.

❧

When the men finished sowing the barley fields, Oscar split the crew between tending the fields and caring for the sheep. Lars taught Henry how to tend the animals, what commands to call to the border collies to get them to round up the flock, how to spot potential hazards and avoid them. On those days Henry came home at night giving off the thick smell of sweat and sheep. When Elizabeth peeled off his clothes and ordered him into the hot bath she had waiting for him, he sank into the tub and closed his eyes without a word.

Elizabeth chewed the inside of her lip as she watched him from the doorway. She had hoped for at least a thank-you or a kiss on the cheek. Putting aside her hurt feelings, she rolled up her sleeves, knelt beside the tub, and picked up a washcloth and a bar of soap. "You're filthy," she told him as she washed his shoulders and neck, working the knots out of his muscles. "And you stink, too."

"Thanks," he said dryly, sinking deeper into the tub, eyes closed.

Encouraged by the brief glimpse of his old humor, she rinsed the washcloth, soaped it up again, and moved on to his chest. He rested his head against the rim of the tub and breathed out a barely audible moan. Emboldened, she worked her way lower, down the firm washboard of his waist to his hips, to his thighs—

Suddenly Henry shot upright, grasping the sides of the tub. "What are you doing?"

Startled, Elizabeth fell back onto her heels. "I'm sorry—I—I was only trying to help—"

He reached for a towel, bolted from the tub, and wrapped the towel around his waist, all without looking at her. "I'm going to bed."

Stung, Elizabeth watched him go. So this is it, she thought. This is married life. He had grown tired of her already.

They had spent their first few Sundays repairing the cabin and making it more comfortable. When there was nothing more toward that end they could do on their budget, Elizabeth resolved that they would enjoy their next day off. Whether they spent it relaxing on their own front porch or venturing out to explore the Arboles Valley, she didn't care as long as they passed the day together. If only they could spend some time enjoying each other's company instead of racing from one chore to the next, Henry would remember the hope and confidence that had brought them to California, and he would be affectionate again.

On Friday morning as they hurried to the Jorgensen home, Elizabeth proposed a picnic. "We could explore the Salto Canyon," she said. "I'll make us a lunch, and we can look for that waterfall Mary Katherine told us about."

"I can't," said Henry. "I have to work."

"But it's Sunday."

"The animals need to be tended on Sundays, too. Oscar offered to pay me extra if I'd take on the job, and you know I can't afford to turn away work." Henry spared her a glance. "But you should go. Ask Mary Katherine and the girls. They could show you the waterfall themselves and you wouldn't have to search for it."

"Maybe I'll do that." A spark of anger kindled within her. She didn't care about the waterfall. The search was part of the fun. She wanted to be with her husband. But if he didn't want her, she was not going to sit around the cabin every Sunday pining for him.

She gave him until lunchtime to reconsider, but when he seemed to have forgotten the invitation, she asked Mary Katherine if she and her daughters were free to go on a picnic Sunday afternoon. Mary Katherine suggested they go to Safari World instead. "It will be my treat," she added. "I haven't taken the girls in far too long."

Elizabeth agreed, curious to meet Charlie the movie-star lion, who woke her at least two mornings out of every seven with a threatening roar that made a shiver run down her spine each time it jolted her awake. When she announced her plans to Henry, it was with a hint of defiance. If he did not want her company, there were others who welcomed it. But without a hint of jealousy or regret, he told her to have a good time and that he would see her at home for supper.

On Sunday, long after Henry had left for work with nothing more for his bride than a quick kiss on the cheek, Elizabeth met Mary Katherine, Annalise, and Margaret at the Jorgensens' garage, where Mary Katherine was tolerantly accepting some last-minute instructions from Lars about how to handle the temperamental automobile. "I'm going to the post office tomorrow," he said to Elizabeth, "if you have any letters you'd like me to send."

Elizabeth thought of the letters to Sylvia and Aunt Eleanor she had struggled to write and could not bring herself to mail, full as they were of half-truths. "I have two I can finish tonight," she replied. "I'll bring them to breakfast tomorrow."

"You'll probably end up riding along to the post office," said Mary Katherine after she had turned east onto the main road. "Or running the errand on your own. Mother Jorgensen doesn't like Lars to go to the Barclays' alone. He and John don't get along. Do you know how to drive?"

"A little." Back in Harrisburg, Gerald had allowed her to take the wheel of his roadster, but only on a little-used stretch of road on the outskirts of town or on the broad, cobblestone circular drive in front of his parents' mansion.

She had not thought of Gerald since Christmas, since Henry's proposal. She wondered how he had reacted to the news of her marriage. Gerald probably would not have tired of her so soon, judging by how often he encouraged her to drive that roadster into the seclusion of the countryside. How she had enjoyed teasing him by pretending not to know why he wanted to drive so far from prying eyes, and then turning around and driving them back to the city without setting the parking brake even once.

Gerald had probably moved on to another girl by now, one of the Dumb Doras in fringed dresses who clung to his arm at the speaks, a girl who wouldn't mind if he pulled over the roadster for a nip from a silver flask and a petting party.

"If you've driven only a little," said Mary Katherine as she pulled over to the side of the road, "you need the practice more than I do."

Elizabeth put up a show of protest but gladly took the wheel when Mary Katherine insisted they trade seats. Mary Katherine coached her through the unfamiliar controls, and soon they were jolting down the dirt road, Annalise and Margaret shrieking with delight in the backseat. They turned south where a road cut through the Jorgensen farm, passing newly sown fields and hills dotted with grazing sheep. Her attention on driving, Elizabeth caught only a glimpse of the high, rocky bluffs that marked the eastern edge of the valley and Jorgensen land. Before long, the southern road linked up with the road she and Henry had taken in Lars's wagon little more than a month before.

"Turn right here," Mary Katherine instructed, almost too late for Elizabeth to make the turn. They headed west, away from the Norwegian Grade and toward the Grand Union Hotel. Elizabeth had a sudden vision of Mrs. Diegel setting the long redwood dining table with her Blue Willow wedding china and had to quickly make herself think of something else.

"Turn left, turn left," Mary Katherine shrieked as they crossed through an intersection with a dirt road. Elizabeth yanked hard on the steering wheel and made the turn with a foot or two to spare. "Sorry," Mary Katherine gasped, clutching her seat with one hand and her hat with the other. "I forget you don't know the way. I didn't mean to take us on such a wild ride."

"What do you mean?" said Elizabeth innocently. "I always drive like this."

She caught Mary Katherine's eye and they laughed.

"We're almost to Uncle Lars's farm," Annalise sang out.

Elizabeth threw Mary Katherine a questioning glance. "It used to be his farm," Mary Katherine quickly explained. "He sold it long ago, years before I married Oscar. Now it's—well, you'll see in a moment."

The car climbed to the top of a low rise, and as it rumbled downhill, Elizabeth saw rows and rows of newly dug foundations and houses spread out before them, some only half complete, sprouting up like a strange experimental crop between furrows of freshly paved, blacktop roads.

"Welcome to Meadowbrook Hills," announced Mary Katherine as they approached.

Construction workers raised wooden frames for one-story dwellings as men in suits and ladies in smart dresses and heels wandered from one plot to another guided by real estate agents in loosened neckties. Bulldozers and hammers created such a din that Annalise and Margaret covered their ears, and the real estate agents were clearly shouting to be heard by the customers on the tour. The well-dressed couples carried themselves with so much carefree self-assurance that Elizabeth understood at once why Mrs. Jorgensen had suspected the Nelsons intended to be among them. No one would mistake them for prospective residents of a fashionable new neighborhood now.

"All this was Jorgensen land once," said Mary Katherine. "Everything from Moorpark Road to that hill. In his will, Oscar's father divided the farm and left one half to each of his sons."

"And Lars sold his half to developers?" It made no sense. Why would he sell his own land only to become foreman of his brother's farm?

"Oh, no. Mother Jorgensen wouldn't let him in the house if he had. He sold to the Fraisers, but they went broke in the drought a few years ago. They sold the land to the developers." Mary Katherine shook her head and sighed. "Lars tried to buy it back, but the developers beat his offer. When Mother Jorgensen found out what the new owners intended to do with those lovely, fertile fields, she vowed that she would never forgive them. Of course, I suppose the Fraisers don't know how much Mother Jorgensen despises them, and if they did, they wouldn't care. They moved out of the valley as soon as the sale was final."

"It's a shame Lars couldn't buy back the farm after he changed his mind." Elizabeth felt a deep pang of sympathy for Lars, who despite his taciturn reserve seemed to be a decent, respectable man. "I suppose the price had gone up since he sold to the Fraisers."

"Oh, that money was long gone. He invested it poorly." Inclining her head slightly toward the backseat with a look of warning, Mary Katherine extended her thumb and pinkie and made a tippling gesture her daughters could not see. "Prohibition was the best possible thing in the world for some people."

"I see." Elizabeth suddenly remembered the crate of empty liquor bottles she had discovered in the cabin and how disparagingly Lars had spoken of the man who drank away so many years there. She never would have guessed he was describing himself. She wanted to ask how Lars had come to such a bad pass, but she doubted Mary Katherine would reveal much in front of her daughters.

"All this happened long before I met Oscar," Mary Katherine said. "By the time I came to the Arboles Valley, all that land belonged to the Fraisers."

Surprised, Elizabeth said, "I assumed you were born and raised here, like the Jorgensens."

"Doesn't Mother Jorgensen *wish,*" said Mary Katherine with a laugh. "I'm a Reilly, one of the Oxnard Reillys. My father made his fortune in sugar. Perhaps you've heard of the Reilly sugar beet? My father developed the variety himself. It has the highest yield of sugar of any sugar beet ever grown."

Mary Katherine regarded her so hopefully that Elizabeth hated to shake her head. "I'm sorry. I'm not familiar with the sugar industry."

Disappointed, Mary Katherine shrugged. "Well, you're new to this part of the country. Everyone from Oxnard to Los Angeles knows of the Reilly family, but of course that didn't matter to Oscar's mother. She nearly wept when he told her he intended to marry me. She wanted so badly for him to marry a local girl who knew the local ways. She's never quite forgiven me for being an outsider and stealing her son's affections." She shifted to face the backseat. "I don't think I need to tell you girls not to repeat that to anyone."

"No, Mama," said Annalise indignantly. Margaret shook her head emphatically.

"I probably shouldn't speak so freely in front of them," Mary Katherine remarked, turning back around to face front. "It's just so difficult sometimes with so few other ladies around to chat with. My friends told me I was crazy to move out here to the country, but I was head over heels for Oscar and wouldn't listen to reason. I still am, and I still don't." She laughed. "That's one reason why I'm so glad you came to the valley. It puts my heart at ease to have a friend so near."

Elizabeth smiled, pleased that Mary Katherine claimed her as a friend, but she could not help thinking of someone else who might have been grateful for Mary Katherine's company. "Rosa Barclay isn't far away."

"I suppose not, but Rosa isn't exactly someone a girl can drop in on for coffee and a chat, is she?"

"What do you mean?"

Mary Katherine shrugged as if the answer was so obvious, the only mystery was why anyone would pose the question. "The Barclays keep to themselves."

"Is that their choice?"

Mary Katherine gave her a speculative look. "Well, I don't know exactly. Why do you ask?"

"It seems strange to me that John Barclay would run the post office out of his house if he craved solitude."

Mary Katherine hesitated. "I never thought of that. I suppose . . . I suppose it's fair to say that their isolation isn't entirely of their own choosing. But don't judge us too harshly. We have good reason to leave them alone. John Barclay is so unpleasant even on his best days, and Rosa—well, it breaks your heart just to look in her eyes."

Elizabeth knew exactly what she meant.

"I don't think anyone means to be unkind, but it's hard not to be suspicious, and perhaps even fearful, when so much death and misfortune have beset that poor family." Mary Katherine clasped her hands together in her lap and gazed out the window at the construction site as they passed. "Some people say Rosa and John are doing something to bring on their children's illnesses—poison, or bad food, or even simple neglect. Others say it's God's will, and that He must be punishing Rosa or John for some terrible sin the rest of us can only imagine. I know that one of John's sisters died of a wasting illness as a young girl, so maybe it *is* a problem with their water, as some people think."

For someone who claimed to have few friends to chat with, Mary Katherine kept herself well informed regarding the opinions of her neighbors. "And what do you think?"

"I can't believe Rosa would ever harm her children," declared Mary Katherine. "She grieves every day for those lost babies. If anyone is to blame—and I'm not saying anyone is—I would look to John. If bitterness in a man's heart can poison a child, then he's the guilty party."

"Mr. Barclay poisoned his babies?" exclaimed Annalise in horror.

"Of course not! It's just an expression." Mary Katherine rolled her eyes at Elizabeth. "This is how rumors get started. Mark my words, the next time you go to the Arboles Grocery, someone will whisper in your ear that the sheriff found ten bottles of poison buried in the Barclays' barley field."

Elizabeth smiled and drove on.

Soon they left Meadowbrook Hills behind and reached the edge of the town, where Mary Katherine instructed Elizabeth to turn south. Accustomed to her guide's last-minute warnings, Elizabeth had slowed the car in anticipation as they approached the intersection and made the turn easily. In the backseat, the girls made noises of disappointment as they failed to be sent careening from one side of the leather seat to the other.

They drove south down Ventura Boulevard until they arrived at a long, low building with four-foot-tall letters spelling out HANNEMAN'S SAFARI WORLD on the peak of the roof, which had been covered in thatch to give it a rustic appearance. Automobiles filled the parking lot, and a line of families with young children and couples holding hands snaked along the sidewalk to the front gate. They joined the end of the line, and when they reached the entrance, Mary Katherine paid their admission and thrust a souvenir map into Elizabeth's hand. "In case we get separated," she said, as Margaret seized her hand and pulled her through the open gate.

Elizabeth, who was expecting either a circus or a zoo, found that Safari World seemed to be a combination of both. As the girls darted from the monkey house to the camel rides to the elephant pens, Mary Katherine tried valiantly to keep up with them while giving Elizabeth a running commentary on the sights around them and the history of the place. George Hanneman, she explained as she pursued her daughters, had worked as an animal trainer and occasional movie extra for Galaxy Pictures. If an elephant went on a rampage in a film, it was almost certain George Hanneman was the rajah he seemed to trample underfoot. If a lion tried to bite off the head of a British explorer in the wilds of Africa, George Hanneman was the man Tarzan rescued in the nick of time. When Galaxy Pictures decided to close its studio zoo, George, who had become fond of the lions in particular, decided to open his own animal farm to supply movie studios with well-trained animal actors as needed. Never one to overlook a business opportunity, after local boys began peering through knotholes in the fences to watch him train the lions, George decided to set up bleachers and charge admission. Within a year, he added monkeys, camels, panthers, tigers, and horses to the roster of performers and built a snack bar and gift shop on the compound. Circus troupes from all parts of the west came to Safari World for the winter, taking the train to Simi Valley and then parading over the grade and through the Arboles Valley, the smaller animals hauled along in cages on gaudily painted wagons, the elephants marching single file, each grasping the tail of the one before it with its trunk. The ground shook as they marched, frightening the residents of farms along the road with thoughts of earthquakes until they remembered it was circus season.

When a tall man in an elegant red coat and jodhpurs announced that the lion show was about to begin, Elizabeth and Mary Katherine grasped the hands of the younger girls and made their way through the crowd to the central stage. The bars separating the bleachers from the performance space seemed dangerously insubstantial to Elizabeth, especially when three lions suddenly bounded onstage guided by a slim, muscular man in a black shirt and slacks. At his command, the largest of the cats, an enormous male with a thick, shaggy mane, leapt onto a tall platform and let out a roar that made the crowd gasp. Margaret covered her ears and Elizabeth sank back into her seat, trembling.

"Charlie," said Mary Katherine breathlessly, her eyes on the lion. Elizabeth swallowed and nodded. She would have recognized that roar anywhere.

She watched, entranced, as George Hanneman put the lions through their paces. They jumped from platform to platform, awing the audience with their strength and agility. They reenacted scenes Elizabeth remembered from jungle movies she had seen years before. George Hanneman demonstrated how a lion attack would be staged and filmed, first explaining how he had trained Charlie to pounce upon him without hurting him, as he might in play. Even then, he warned, only a trainer who knew his cat exceptionally well should attempt such a stunt. In all the years he had known and cared for Charlie, he never allowed himself to forget that Charlie was not a pet, but a dangerous and potentially lethal wild carnivore.

The crowd shuddered and murmured in respectful fear, but Mary Katherine sighed and rested her chin on her palm. "The movies always lose a little magic once you know how it's done. I can't ever see an animal attack in a film now without seeing a trainer and a well-fed animal looking for the favorite toy hidden in his pocket."

Elizabeth did not agree. When George wrestled with Charlie, it looked every bit as dangerous as on film—and felt even more real with the musky animal scent and low snarls in the air, the scuffling of sharp claws in the dirt. She was so fearful for George's life that her stomach hurt.

When the lions' performance ended, she clapped until her palms stung. Some of the onlookers began to leave, but others remained in their seats to await the horse show. "May we stay?" asked Elizabeth when Annalise and Margaret took their mother's hands and began to drag her off to buy them peanuts and lemonade.

Mary Katherine hesitated, clearly surprised that Elizabeth wanted to stay. Like the Jorgensens, she should have had her fill of horses every day on the farm. But those were work horses, not show horses, and certainly not trained, performing horses. For Elizabeth, they called to mind Bergstrom Thoroughbreds and Elm Creek Manor, and even though she knew it was unlikely any of Safari World's horses had come from Uncle Fred and Aunt Eleanor's farm, she felt a sharp stab of longing to see them, just in case.

Mary Katherine must have read the longing on her face, for she suggested that she take the girls for their treats and meet up with Elizabeth after the show. After they left, Elizabeth waited for another ten minutes for the show to begin. When a woman in her midthirties rode into the ring on the back of the most beautiful horse Elizabeth had seen since leaving Pennsylvania, a shock of familiarity rippled through her. The gait, the coat, the speed—every feature identified the proud horse as a Bergstrom Thoroughbred.

Elizabeth could hardly tear her eyes from the horse throughout the twenty-minute performance, hungrily taking in the unexpected glimpse of home. An older gentleman who had taken Mary Katherine's seat misinterpreted her rapt attention. "She's quite a horsewoman, isn't she?" he remarked. "That's Caroline Hanneman. To look at her, you'd never suspect she didn't know anything about show biz until she married George."

Elizabeth looked away from the Bergstrom Thoroughbred long enough to reply. "She's not from Hollywood, like her husband?"

"Not at all. She was born and raised in the valley, on a farm right next to this one." He chuckled. "She tells a story about how she and George met. It so happened that George fed his lions at the same time every morning when it was milking time on her parents' farm. The lions' roars scared her cows so much that they kicked over their buckets of milk. One morning she got so fed up, she marched over here to give George Hanneman a piece of her mind. Two years later, they were married."

Elizabeth smiled. "I suppose there's a lesson there for all of us."

"That's for sure. The way George tells it, he had to marry her to get her to stop complaining."

Elizabeth managed to keep her smile in place as she returned her attention to the show. She would have preferred a lesson about how love could blossom from enmity, how affection could overcome anger. The last moral she wanted to hear was that marriage meant the end of a woman's right to speak her mind. She could not imagine any Bergstrom woman standing for that, or any Jorgensen woman, either. As for Caroline Hanneman, any woman who could handle a Bergstrom Thoroughbred with such confidence wouldn't back down to a mere husband.

Midway through the show, two men in denim and cowboy hats took over while Caroline disappeared backstage and emerged moments later in similar western attire. For the rest of the performance, the three demonstrated how horses were trained to fall down on command without injuring themselves, how to lie down as if wounded, how to rear back threateningly. "None of these learned behaviors hurt the horses," Caroline assured her listeners. "We would never allow our animals to appear on any set where they are not respected and properly cared for. That's the first thing we tell any producer who sets foot on this property."

Elizabeth instinctively sat up straighter and, with a glance around for anyone who looked out of place, fluffed the curls of her blond bob. A movie producer, here? It made sense, of course; it was far easier for producers to come to Safari World than for George Hanneman and his trainers to parade wild animals through the streets of Hollywood.

Perhaps Henry was wrong, and Elizabeth didn't live too far from Los Angeles for a career in the movies. He couldn't object if she would not have to travel far for a film role, especially if the job paid well.

The show ended and Elizabeth climbed down from the bleachers to join the flow of people leaving the arena. She consulted the map Mary Katherine had given her and made her way to the animal pens, where they had arranged to meet. On the way she passed a corral and a stable, where the two men from the show had removed their costumes—which meant that they had removed the cowboy trappings from their usual work clothes—and were tending to the horses. She paused to watch, wondering how on earth a Bergstrom-bred horse had ended up in Safari World, and with a Hollywood résumé that would make any would-be starlet envious.

As she lingered, she overheard the wranglers discussing a recent failed attempt to buy a horse. The prices local farmers charged amounted to robbery, the men griped, and that's if they had anything to sell. Safari World's wranglers did not have time to scout around the whole valley and beyond to find the animals they needed. Times were better, the taller of the two men said, when farmers brought the animals to them.

"I can find horses for you," said Elizabeth.

The two men looked up. The smaller man eyed her with a smirk. "What'd you say, girlie?"

"I can find the horses you need."

The taller man scratched at his beard. "Why would you want to do that?"

Why not? If Henry could take on extra work, so could she. "Because I know horses and I know where to find them, and you don't have the time to look. And because of the finder's fee you'll pay me in return."

The men exchanged a grin, amused. The shorter man said, "Listen, doll, why don't you send your husband over and we'll talk business with him?"

"Because my husband isn't here and your business is with me. I know horses better than he does, anyway. I was practically born and raised on a horse farm." That last bit was an exaggeration, but these men couldn't possibly know that. She indicated the horse the taller man was grooming. "I'll prove it. That impressive stallion is a Bergstrom Thoroughbred, bred at Elm Creek Manor in Pennsylvania. That brown horse with the black mane and the star on his forehead is a little more difficult to place, but I would guess that it was bred on the Compson farm in Maryland. Am I right?"

She held her breath while the men took this in. She knew of no other breeders by name besides her uncle and his strongest rival, but that might be enough to convince these two.

"Is she right?" the shorter man asked the other in an undertone, his smirk vanishing.

The taller man shrugged. "Beats me."

Elizabeth hid her relief with a smile. "Well, gentlemen?"

"All right," the taller man said grudgingly. "You find us horses, and we'll pay you ten cents for each one we buy."

"Twenty-five."

"Ten," the shorter man shot back. "And we ain't payin' an arm and a leg for the horses, neither, so talk the price down before dragging us out somewhere to buy a horse we haven't seen."

"You won't have to go anywhere," Elizabeth assured them. "I know a place that will send the horses to you—Bergstrom Thoroughbreds."

The taller man looked perplexed. "Didn't you just say they were in Pennsylvania?"

"We can't wait for horses to come all that way," the shorter man said irritably. "What do you think this is? We need them now."

"All right," said Elizabeth, taken aback. "I'll find some horses a little closer to home, but I can tell you right now they won't be as good as Bergstrom Thoroughbreds."

"They'll be good enough," the taller man said.

Elizabeth promised to bring them a list of horses and prices within the week. They responded by frowning and shaking their heads as they returned to their work, as if they did not expect to see her again and would forget their arrangement as soon as she left their sight.

She hurried off to meet Mary Katherine and the girls, her thoughts racing. When she had asked for the job, she assumed she would simply be the middleman between her uncle and Safari World. Now she would have to scout throughout the Arboles Valley and perhaps beyond, finding suitable horses where those two had already failed. She would need a car, and time to search. From the looks the men gave her, they expected her to fail—but that just made her more determined to succeed. All she had to do was find a horse or two that met their expectations, and perhaps then they would trust her judgment enough to consider Bergstrom Thoroughbreds for future purchases. The movie producers would surely recognize quality when they saw it, and perhaps one day, movie studios throughout Hollywood would insist upon Bergstrom Thoroughbreds for their pictures. It would benefit them, it would benefit Uncle Fred—and it would put some money in Elizabeth's pocket. If she happened to catch the eye of a movie producer at the same time, so much the better.

She must put the wages she earned from the Jorgensens toward Henry's lost savings and their train fare back to Pennsylvania. Anything she earned from additional work accomplished on her days off—time she would much rather spend enjoying Henry's company—was hers to do with as she pleased. It would please her very much to buy back her quilts from Mrs. Diegel.

She found Mary Katherine and her daughters by the monkey cages. The girls had saved some peanuts for Elizabeth, and Mary Katherine insisted upon treating her to a glass of lemonade as they strolled through the park.

Trailing after the girls as they bounded from one spectacle to another, Elizabeth asked Mary Katherine if it was true that movie producers occasionally came to Safari World.

"Not only to Safari World, but all over the Arboles Valley," Mary Katherine replied. "Think of any Western you've ever seen, and chances are it was filmed beneath the bluffs west of our farm."

"Is that so?"

"When Annalise was a baby, our pasture and sheep appeared in a movie about Nebraskan pioneers." Mary Katherine frowned comically. "You'd think that we could have asked for more for their wool after that, but you'd be wrong."

Elizabeth laughed, spirits rising. "It must have been exciting to watch a Western being filmed."

"It was a lot of standing around, mostly, or so it seemed to me. I couldn't see much of the action from the garden and the house. A movie called *Trouble at Rocky Ranch* was filmed out here more recently, but I saw even less of that."

"I saw that movie," said Elizabeth, as the familiarity of the bluffs east of the Jorgensen farm suddenly made perfect sense. "At the Egyptian Theater in Hollywood, the night before we came to the Arboles Valley."

"I bet you've seen the Arboles Valley in more movies than that. It's been the setting for more than just Westerns. How do you think Lake Sherwood got its name?"

Elizabeth had not known of any Lake Sherwood in the Arboles Valley, but she guessed. "Not *Robin Hood,* with Douglas Fairbanks?"

"The one and only. Once I saw him and Mary Pickford having lunch at the Grand Union Hotel. She was even more beautiful in person, and he was so handsome." Mary Katherine looked wistful. "Can you imagine such a glamorous life? Fame and fortune, the prettiest clothes, people to do all the cooking and cleaning and laundry for you, the chance to travel and see the world— and all because you know how to pose and recite some lines. It must be heavenly."

Privately, Elizabeth agreed, but she knew that for every Mary Pickford there were probably hundreds of chorus girls and thousands of aspirants whose faces never made it to the silver screen. But one producer had already told her she had star quality, so perhaps her chances were not so remote. If the Jorgensen sheep could land movie roles, surely she could.

When the girls grew tired, they drove home, Mary Katherine at the wheel so that Lars would not become incensed when he saw Elizabeth in the driver's seat. "Not that I've ever seen him terribly angry," said Mary Katherine with a grin. "He's as mild as an afternoon in May. He wasn't always like that, or so I've heard. He had a temper back in the day when he was drinking."

She spared a quick glance for the backseat, and was visibly relieved to find that the girls had fallen asleep. Since Mary Katherine was apparently the only Jorgensen who willingly divulged information about the family, Elizabeth decided to risk pressing her for more details. "I understand why Lars couldn't buy back the old farm," she said as they drove past Meadowbrook Hills, where construction continued at the same industrious pace, although the real estate agents and flocks of prospective residents had departed. "But why did he sell it in the first place?"

"Why does anyone sell a family farm?" Mary Katherine replied. "Maybe he was tired of the hardships and uncertainties of farming. We all know we could be only one drought away from going belly-up. Maybe he wanted to leave the Arboles Valley, strike out on his own, go into business in a larger city. Or put his earnings into the stock market and get rich without having to drag himself out of bed before dawn every day. Maybe the money sounded too good to pass up. How was he to know how much more the land would be worth in just a few short years?"

Elizabeth knew there had to be more. "But to do nothing with the money once he had it in hand, to just drink it all away, and then to return to farming anyway—"

"Once the money was gone, he probably had no other choice. And of course my Oscar would never turn his brother away. Lars was the true Prodigal Son."

Silently Elizabeth disagreed. The biblical father had welcomed back his wayward son with great joy and celebration and restored him fully to his birthright. He had not, as far as Elizabeth could recall, allowed him to come home only to serve his more dutiful brother.

When Henry returned to Two Bears Farm, his family would celebrate his homecoming even more than the Prodigal's so long ago, for Henry had never sold his birthright, nor squandered his inheritance. He had been deceived through no fault of his own, but he would earn back what he had lost. Although they might not return to Two Bears Farm for years, it was a great comfort to know that someday they would.

"It seems like such a waste," said Elizabeth. She was not sure if she meant Lars's rash behavior as a young man, or all the years since then he had spent atoning for his youthful mistakes.

Mary Katherine sighed. "I'm not sure what sorrows Lars was trying to drown back then, but in all the time I've known him, he's never shirked his duties and he's never fallen off the wagon—and we all know liquor isn't that hard to come by, Prohibition or no Prohibition. I think everyone would just as soon forget that he was ever anyone but the man he is today."

Elizabeth understood this as a gentle admonition to stop probing into Lars's past, and she reluctantly complied.

Back home in the cabin, she made supper and had it waiting on the table when Henry came in, smelling of sheep. She tried to amuse him by revealing that the sheep he tended were no ordinary barnyard animals but a flock of woolly movie stars. Henry seemed not to hear her as he hungrily cleaned his plate of fried potatoes, dried apples, and onions seasoned with the black pepper and caraway seed Mary Katherine had generously offered from her own pantry. Elizabeth kept up her cheerful patter even though inside she was seething with annoyance. If he were determined to avoid her on their one day off and then not even listen to how she had spent her afternoon away from him, she would not bother sharing her good news about her prospective business deal with the wranglers of Safari World. She would wait until she could fan a handful of greenbacks in Henry's face. That would make him pay attention.

After supper, he built a fire on the hearth to ward off the chill brought on by the ocean mists that cooled the late spring nights. She cleared the table and heated bathwater for him. While he bathed—alone, with the door closed—she searched her pocketbook and retrieved the business card that Grover Higgins of Golden Reel Productions had given her at the dance marathon in Venice Beach. If a movie producer didn't come to the Arboles Valley, she did have other options.

If only the cabin had a telephone. She could imagine Mrs. Jorgensen's response if Elizabeth asked to borrow hers to make a long-distance call to a movie producer.

She sat down on the bed, working out a plan. Mrs. Diegel had a phone. Lars seemed protective of the car, but twice already she had seen him reach out a hand to someone in need. If she explained why she needed the car, he might let her borrow it. As she drove around the valley in search of horses, she could stop by the Grand Union Hotel and call Grover Higgins. What Mrs. Diegel would expect in trade, Elizabeth could only guess. Perhaps a lien on any future quilts Elizabeth pieced on the treadle sewing machine.

Her gaze fell upon the worn scrap quilt she had found in the cabin. It had held up well to washing, but she had paid little attention to it since then except to feel grateful each night for the warmth it provided. It was wrinkled and faded, especially compared with the quilts she had given up, but now that she studied it more carefully, she could not help admiring the ingenious design. She had never seen a star pattern quite like it before, despite the hundreds of quilts she had witnessed the Bergstrom women make through the years. At first glance she had mistaken it for a traditional Blazing Star quilt, the blocks arranged in seven rows of five blocks each, but on closer inspection, she saw that smaller diamonds fanned out in a half star in the four corner squares of each block, giving the quilt the illusion of brilliance and fire. Such care must have gone into the making of each block for each divided star to fit the corner exactly so.

Elizabeth wondered who had made it. Mrs. Jorgensen's grandmother, perhaps, or could the quilt be even older than that? It seemed to be pieced of scraps of clothing, which always made it more difficult to date. Had the fading and wear to the fabric occurred before or after the pieces were sewn into a quilt? Perhaps the quilt had been made far away and brought to the Arboles Valley by a young bride trusting in her husband's decision to bring her out West, far from home and family, trusting that he would always cherish her and never give her reason to regret her decision.

Elizabeth rose and reached for the second quilt, neatly folded at the foot of the bed. She spread it out on top of the star quilt, marveling at how much her first dismissive glances had missed. Pieced of homespuns and wools, it was sturdy and warm, obviously intended for daily use rather than a best quilt brought out only on special occasions or for visitors, but for all that, it was as complex and well fashioned as any quilt to grace a bed at Elm Creek Manor. It was composed not of square blocks but of hexagons, each formed from twelve triangular wedges with a smaller hexagon appliquéd in the center where the points met. Elizabeth smiled, recognizing the familiar quilter's trick of covering a bulky seam or hiding a place where points did not match up as precisely as they should. Sewing the pieced hexagons together was much more challenging than simply stitching together rows of square blocks, but this unknown quilter had managed admirably. Even now, with some of the binding hanging from the edge and the cotton batting thin in patches, the quilt lay perfectly flat, with no puckering or bulging seams except for an overall patina of wrinkles created by the slight shrinkage of the wool in the wash.

Had the same unknown woman made both quilts? Though both were the work of accomplished quilters, the fabrics used and patterns chosen suggested they were not of the same era. And yet Elizabeth had found them folded together. Surely they had both belonged to the Jorgensen family. But why had they been left in the cabin? Why had such painstaking needlework not earned these quilts a place in the yellow farmhouse? They certainly would have endured better had they been sheltered behind sturdy walls rather than left to the drafts and damp of the cabin and the nibbles of inquisitive mice.

Her thoughts flew to the scraps she had brought from home and the pieces of fabric Mrs. Diegel had included in the sewing machine trade. While none of the fabrics was identical to those in the two quilts, some were a fairly close match. She ought to have enough to repair them.

Henry refused to return to Pennsylvania until he had earned back all he had lost. Well, Elizabeth had lost things, too, and she was just as determined to recover them. When they finally did go home to the Elm Creek Valley, it would be with her bridal quilt and the Chimneys and Cornerstones quilt tucked safely in their trunk with two newly restored antique quilts beside them. The Bergstrom women would marvel at her fortunate discovery and praise her for her skill when she described how she had restored the worn pieces and replaced the broken threads. Elizabeth's heart sank a little when she realized that she could never tell her mother and aunts the whole truth of how the quilts had come to her, not if she meant to spare Henry from shame.

She would tell them as much as she could. She had already written about the Jorgensens, so she would not be divulging too much to say that she believed the quilts had been made by one of the first women of their family to come to the Arboles Valley. She could say that she had stumbled over the quilts in an old, abandoned cabin on the ranch property without adding that she and Henry had made the ramshackle place their home. The Bergstrom women would be more interested in the quilts themselves, anyway—the remarkable patterns, the exceptional handiwork, the charming fabrics. They would not think to ask the questions she least wanted to answer.

The Bergstrom women need never know how she and Henry had lived while they were far from home, nor that Elizabeth had ever parted with the precious quilts they had so lovingly sewn for her.

ઝટ

1910

Isabel had dreamed of Rosa finishing school and going off to college to become something important, perhaps a teacher like her aunt, but when the time came, Rosa did not want to go. She loved the Arboles Valley, she told her parents passionately, and her soul would wither away to dust if she had to leave it.

Miguel accepted her dramatic declaration, but Isabel grieved, not only to watch her daughter throw away an opportunity her parents had never had, but to hear another lie pass her lips. It was indeed love that kept her in the Arboles Valley, but not love for the land.

Rosa, who had always excelled at math, obtained a job as a clerk and book-keeper at the Grand Union Hotel. For two years she balanced accounts and paid bills for Mrs. Diegel, the young widow who had returned to the Arbo-les Valley from Los Angeles to assume responsibility for the hotel when her father's health failed. For two years Rosa was, by all appearances, a good and obedient daughter. After working all day at the hotel, she returned home and helped her mother with the housework. She gave half of her earnings to her parents for household necessities and saved the rest, except for the little she spent on sensible clothes suitable for work. She went to Mass with her family every Sunday morning, helped her brother with his homework, and spent Saturday afternoons in the company of friends, young women from good families with whom Isabel could find no fault.

But there were also mornings when Isabel went to the kitchen to find Rosa already awake, breathless and bright-eyed, preparing breakfast for the family, overly solicitous of her mother—squeezing her a glass of orange juice, ask-ing if she had slept well. There were afternoons when Isabel passed through the Arboles Valley on her housecleaning route and crossed paths with the friend Rosa had said she planned to spend the day with—but Rosa was nowhere in sight. There were rumors passed along to Isabel by observant friends claiming that a young man stopped by the hotel on Rosa's lunch hour nearly every day, and that he and Rosa had been spotted in the citrus grove holding hands or in the Arboles Grocery buying food for a picnic. Isabel did not trust the rumors entirely because some described the young man as black-haired and others as blond, but she knew the tales must have sprouted from some seed of truth.

When Isabel shared her worries with her husband, Miguel spread his hands helplessly and said there was little they could do. It was disappointing to think that their daughter might be keeping a secret romance from them, but she was twenty years old, a woman grown, and it was hardly surprising that she had fallen in love. They had done their best to raise her properly, and they had to trust that she would use good judgment and not stray into anything that might ruin her reputation.

"With all the rumors flying about, she may have already ruined her reputation," retorted Isabel. "If she has such good judgment, why keep this romance secret? If she's in love with a decent young man, why hasn't she told us about him? If his intentions are good, why hasn't he asked to meet us?"

Miguel had no answer for her except to say that perhaps an introduction would come in time. He did not like to argue, and he could not believe that his beautiful daughter could do any wrong. Isabel reluctantly dropped the subject. Without Miguel's support, she could not bear to confront the daughter she adored with accusations that might have no merit. Perhaps Miguel was right. Perhaps Rosa was not sure how she felt about her admirer, and she was waiting until she knew her own heart before bringing the young man home.

Then one afternoon Miguel came home from work, beaming. He took Isabel aside and quietly told her that he believed he had discovered the identity of Rosa's young man. Earlier that day he had stopped by the feed store on an errand for his employer, and while he was making his purchases, a young man struck up a conversation with him. "He knew a lot about Rosa," Miguel said. "Things only someone who spoke with her often would know. Who her best friends are, what she thinks of her job, that your father's tamales were the best in the valley—"

"Everyone knows that," Isabel broke in. Her father's cooking had become the stuff of local legend. She always regretted not forcing him into the kitchen sooner.

"The point is," said Miguel, amused, "that since he felt confident enough to approach me in the feed store instead of ducking into another aisle, Rosa might intend to tell us about him soon. I almost invited him over for dinner, but I thought Rosa would never forgive me."

"But who is he?" demanded Isabel in a whisper, peering over her shoulder to be sure Rosa was not within earshot.

"John Barclay. You remember. Donald and Evelyn's son."

"But he's four years older than Rosa."

"And maybe that's why she hasn't told us about him."

Suddenly Rosa's secrecy made perfect sense. Isabel and Miguel certainly would not have approved of an eighteen-year-old man giving their fourteen-year-old daughter a Valentine's Day carnation so many years ago. But Rosa was twenty now, and no longer had any excuse not to reveal the truth to her parents. If John Barclay truly loved their daughter, why did he not insist upon it? Unless he wanted to, but had promised to abide by Rosa's wishes. Perhaps her secrecy had become a habit she had forgotten to break, even after the need for it had passed.

Isabel sighed. Apparently they would still have to wait and see. When Rosa was ready, she would tell them everything. In the meantime, Rosa's circumstances were not as bad as Isabel had feared. While her prolonged secrecy was insufferable, at least she had chosen well. John Barclay was Catholic, thank goodness, although he did not attend Mass as regularly as Isabel would have liked. He owned his own land, a small farm near the Salto Canyon that he had inherited upon his father's death and had run almost single-handedly ever since his mother moved to Oxnard to live with John's only living sibling, an elder sister. If John could at twenty-four run his own thriving farm, he surely was hardworking and industrious and would be a good provider. If Rosa married him, she would have land of her own, very near the old Rancho Triunfo, the land that should have been her inheritance.

Isabel waited for Rosa to confide in her, but the days passed as they always had, with the customary routine occasionally broken by those strange early mornings when Rosa was up before the sun rose, bustling about the kitchen with bright eyes and flushed cheeks. Then one night Isabel started from an unpleasant dream and went to the kitchen for a glass of water. On a sudden impulse, she quietly peeked into Rosa's bedroom and found the quilt turned back and the curtains swaying in the open window. Rosa was nowhere to be seen.

Her heart sinking, Isabel returned to bed and lay awake until morning. She left her room only after she heard someone opening cupboards and turning on a tap in the kitchen. There she found Rosa preparing breakfast, smiling to herself and humming. She looked up in surprise when her mother entered. "You're up early," she said, offering Isabel a cup of coffee.

Isabel took it with a murmur of thanks. She did not point out the obvious, that Rosa had risen even earlier, if she had slept at all.

Isabel brooded throughout the morning as she worked, scrubbing bathtubs with angry vigor. By midday she had resolved to confront Rosa with the truth. If she and John were in love and his intentions honorable, they had nothing to hide. If not, Isabel had a mother's duty to demand they break off their relationship without delay.

Between stops on her housecleaning route, Isabel went to the Grand Union Hotel, unwilling to wait until after supper to speak to her daughter, when her resolve might weaken beneath Miguel's constant reassurances and calls for patience. As she crossed the front porch, she passed one of the Jorgensen boys on his way out. He greeted her politely, but she pretended not to see him. If she had her way, she would never lay eyes on any Jorgensen. She caught a whiff of alcohol on his breath and she recoiled in disdain and disgust. Drinking at one o'clock in the afternoon on a weekday, when he ought to be working! He had inherited one-half of what had once been the Rancho Triunfo upon his father's death, and this was how he respected that legacy. She should have expected as much from that family, but the unfairness of fate wrenched at her. It was a disgrace, and she would not be surprised if that Jorgensen boy drank those precious acres away.

It was a pity the hotel had a bar. Isabel did not care for the sort of person it brought into her daughter's workplace.

Inside, she found Rosa at her desk in the small office off the lobby. She was just sitting down after finishing her lunch, but she jumped to her feet at the sight of Isabel. "Mother," she exclaimed, coming around the desk to kiss her on the cheek. Her hand upon Isabel's shoulder trembled. "What a surprise! Is everything all right?"

"No, in fact, something is very wrong." Isabel regarded her sternly, but her resolve melted when Rosa sank into her chair, blanching from alarm. "I didn't mean to worry you, but *mija,* I am very troubled by your secrecy. I know— your father and I know—that you are in love. We think we know why you've been hiding this from us, but the time has come for you to tell the truth."

Rosa clenched her hands in her lap, her dark, lovely eyes wide and apprehensive. "How long have you known?"

Since Rosa was fourteen. "We waited as long as we could, hoping you would tell us on your own."

"You aren't angry?"

"Because you have deceived us, yes, very. Because you have fallen in love, no. Never." Isabel managed a small smile. "You're a beautiful, loving young woman, Rosa. If you've found the love of a good man, we're happy for you. We want to share in your happiness."

"I—" Rosa hesitated. "I didn't think you would approve. And I love him, but—I'm still not sure. He's a good man, but—it's just so hard to know what to do. There are things about him I wish he would change. I pray for him to change. Can I really love him if I want him to be different?"

"Oh, Rosa." Isabel embraced her. "Why did you keep your troubles to yourself for so long? I'm your mother. You can always talk to me about anything. You know I will always love you."

"And I will always love you." Tears welled up in Rosa's eyes. "And I will always love him. I know I will. But that doesn't mean I should marry him."

Isabel was surprised—and proud—to hear Rosa express such wisdom in the midst of her uncertainty. Most young women her age would think only of the passion of first love and not of the hard, practical realities of building a strong, enduring marriage. "Has he asked you to marry him?"

Rosa nodded.

"He should not have done that without speaking to your father."

"You're right. I know that. But it's—well, you know how things are." Tentatively, Rosa added, "I'm surprised you're taking it so well yourself."

"It's your deception that troubles me, not your feelings for this man, or his for you."

Rosa's cheeks flushed. "It seemed best to keep it to ourselves."

"There's no need for secrecy any longer," Isabel assured her. "Invite John to join us for Sunday dinner. We need to get to know the man who wants to marry our daughter."

Rosa stared at her. "Invite . . . John?"

"Yes, and without delay. We must have this out in the open. I don't approve of how he has handled things so far, but your father and I are willing to give him a chance to redeem himself. This will help you, too. Concealing the truth from us has distracted you from deciding how you really feel about him."

When Rosa did not reply, Isabel said, "Either invite him to meet the family or promise never to see him again. Your father and I are willing to overlook how this matter began so we can see that it has a proper resolution. We will allow him to court you in a respectable manner, but this sneaking around and staying out all night must end."

Still Rosa stared at her. Finally she said, "I'll speak to John today."

"Good." Isabel embraced her daughter, but Rosa seemed dazed and shaken in her arms. "It will be all right in the end, whether you accept John's proposal or marry someone else. Take all the time you need. Don't let him rush you. If he truly loves you, he'll wait until you're ready to answer." She thought of the three years she had made Miguel wait, three years that seemed like only moments now. Their marriage had been blessed, and well worth the wait. She wished someday for her children to know such a rich blessing.

Wordlessly Rosa clung to her, tears in her eyes.

Chapter Eight

1925

After Henry went off to bed, Elizabeth tore up her unfinished letters home and started over, writing cheerful, breezy accounts of their arrival at Triumph Ranch, the Jorgensen family, and the work of the farm. "Although the ranch is not precisely as it was described to us," she wrote to Aunt Eleanor, "it is a lovely, thriving place, and I hope we will do well here." She described their discovery of sheep where they had expected cattle as a comical misunderstanding, and wrote in lavish detail of the beauty of the landscape. To Sylvia she wrote of befriending Mary Katherine and her daughters, and of their visit to Safari World, where she met Charlie the lion and discovered a Bergstrom Thoroughbred among the performing horses.

Then she sat awake in the front room with the homespuns-and-wool hexagon quilt spread upon her lap, unable to silence her nagging conscience long enough to drift off to sleep. Sylvia admired her, and Elizabeth had always tried to be worthy of her young cousin's trust. Nothing in her letter was, strictly speaking, a lie; she had written that she liked to walk among *the* apricot trees, not *her* apricot trees, and it was fair to call the sheep Henry's flock because he tended them. While Elizabeth's mother might chide her for lies of omission, no one could say that she had betrayed Sylvia's trust by lying outright—except when she referred to Triumph Ranch. No such place existed anymore, and to pretend she lived there crossed the line from evasiveness into outright dishonesty.

Elizabeth worked her needle in tiny stitches through a wool patch she was appliquéing over a small hole in the quilt top. The quilt's hexagonal pattern made her think of wagon wheels rambling over the Norwegian Grade into the Arboles Valley, or the sun rising over the bluffs east of the ranch. When she looked upon the quilt, she wondered about the woman who had made it, whether she pieced these unusual hexagons here or in a city back east, and whether she found happiness in the Arboles Valley or disappointment. What had she written to loved ones far away?

Exasperated with herself, Elizabeth set the quilt aside. She could not tell the truth for Henry's sake, and yet she could not bear to lie. She had to write something, or the folks back in Pennsylvania would fear the worst.

Her gaze fell upon the smoldering embers in the fireplace. Suddenly a way out of her predicament occurred to her, and although it did not completely silence her nagging conscience, it would have to do until she thought of something better or Henry changed his mind about divulging the truth. She drew her dressing gown tightly around herself and hurried outside into the starlit night, trying not to think about coyotes and rattlesnakes and the other nocturnal creatures Annalise had enthusiastically assured her lurked in the valley. She dug into a stack of discarded wood behind the cabin until she found a flat board about two feet long and a foot wide. She brushed off the dirt and took it inside.

Kneeling beside the fireplace, she searched the embers until she found a thick splinter of wood that was charred on one end but unburned and cool on the other. Using the blackened tip as a pencil, she wrote upon the board in clear, bold letters: TRIUMPH RANCH. She took her hand-lettered sign outside and propped it against the cabin wall on the porch near the front door.

"I hereby christen thee Triumph Ranch," she said softly, a lonely soloist backed by a choir of chirping insects. If she had a bottle of champagne, she would smash it against the porch steps. Better yet, she would trade it to Mrs. Diegel for eggs, coffee, and bacon for Henry's Sunday breakfast.

They were no better off, but at least a place named Triumph Ranch existed now. It was not only a dream, and when she wrote to her family of her new home, she would not be a liar.

She returned to bed and was at last able to sleep.

In the morning, when Henry returned from the outhouse, his face was grim. "Is that your idea of a joke?"

For a moment Elizabeth had no idea what he was talking about, and then she remembered the sign. "It's not a joke. When I write home, my family will expect me to talk about Triumph Ranch, my new home. I don't want to lie to them, and now I won't have to."

"You don't consider this a lie?"

The bitterness in his voice shook her. "It's the best I can do under the circumstances. Would you prefer that I tell them the whole story? Should I borrow a camera and send some snapshots?"

Henry muttered something she couldn't make out, but his meaning was perfectly clear. He strode off to the farmhouse so quickly that she could barely keep up with him. He did not kiss her good-bye at the back door or tell her he would see her at breakfast, as he had done every other morning since they had come to work for the Jorgensens.

She was upset and worried and angry, and she regretted ever trying to ease her conscience with a silly sign that she should have known would insult him. Mrs. Jorgensen looked at her sharply when she came into the kitchen, red-faced and breathless, but Elizabeth composed herself as best she could and got to work. She knew Mrs. Jorgensen wasn't fooled, but she was not the sort of woman to pry into someone else's business. When Henry came in for breakfast with the other men, he no longer seemed angry, but the kiss he gave her every morning on his way to the table, the kiss the others would have noted for its absence, was so swift she barely felt his lips brush her cheek.

After breakfast, Lars reminded Elizabeth of his intention to stop by the post office that afternoon and asked if she had any letters for him to send. As she took them from her pocket, Mrs. Jorgensen said, "Why don't you go with him? Mary Katherine tells me you can drive, so if you learn the way, on days when Lars is too busy you can run the errands for him."

Mary Katherine gave Elizabeth a meaningful look over her mother-in-law's shoulder while Elizabeth arranged to meet Lars in the garage after cleaning up the kitchen after lunch. She had not expected Mary Katherine's prediction that Mrs. Jorgensen would not allow Lars to go to the Barclay farm alone to come true. Did Lars really need a watchful eye more than Mary Katherine needed Elizabeth's help in the garden? If Lars's old temper really could resurface after years of dormancy, Elizabeth doubted her presence would do anything to prevent it.

She spent the morning doing the laundry, load after load of men's work shirts and denim overalls so filthy that she expected to look out at the barley field and discover that an entire layer of topsoil was missing. She much preferred to wash the ladies' cotton dresses and the girls' sweet pinafores, admiring them as she hung them on the line to dry in the fresh air that blew down from the Santa Monica Mountains from the west, but she would have gladly given up that pleasure if it meant never again having to wash a stranger's undergarments. She knew her distaste was prim and patrician, but she could not help it. As much as she liked the other hired hands, as much as she was learning to respect Oscar and his mother, handling their undergarments was too intimate, and in the case of some of the hired hands, too overpowering. On laundry day, she could always tell who had spent most of the week in the orchard and who had been herding sheep.

For hours, she and Mary Katherine and the girls went from washhouse to clothesline hauling water and heavy baskets of damp clothes. After several weeks of working for the Jorgensens, Elizabeth had grown accustomed to the labor, but even so, the muscles in her neck and shoulders ached long before Mrs. Jorgensen called her to the kitchen to help prepare lunch. Still, it could be worse and she counted her blessings, especially the Aerobell washing machine Oscar had purchased for Mary Katherine on their eighth anniversary. ("Mother Jorgensen called it a waste of money," marveled Mary Katherine as they filled the round copper tub with soiled clothes. "She wouldn't think so if *she* had to do the laundry for the family and eight farmhands.") Since the washhouse was not wired for electricity, Oscar had hooked up the machine to a kerosene generator, which gave off a deafening roar and made conversation in the washhouse difficult.

On that day, Elizabeth preferred not to chat, because for all her aspirations of stardom, she doubted she could act well enough to conceal her dismal mood. Also, Mary Katherine was still smarting from some disagreement with Mrs. Jorgensen the previous evening and was determined to draw Elizabeth into finding fault with her. While Elizabeth liked Mary Katherine and preferred her company to that of her demanding mother-in-law, she was far too clever to be caught saying anything against Mrs. Jorgensen that might be used against her later. Back in Harrisburg, her taste for gossip had been nearly unrivaled among her friends and she had never shied away from speaking her mind, but now she was a different person in a different world. Her position on the farm was far too uncertain to risk, no matter how good it might make her feel at that moment to top Mary Katherine's complaints with the mental list she had been keeping since her first day with the Jorgensens. How Mrs. Jorgensen swore there was only one proper way to slice a potato, for example, or how she made Elizabeth clean every last speck of dirt from the corners of a room by digging the sharpened end of a clothespin into the crevices where the baseboards met.

After washing the lunch dishes, Elizabeth hurried to the garage to meet Lars, grateful for the reprieve and worried that he might leave without her if she was late. Instead, she was the first to the car, and it was Lars who arrived a few moments after, coming not from the fields but from the house, his face and hands washed, his thinning blond hair neatly parted and combed. He crossed in front of the car and opened the driver's side door for her. "I best see how you can drive before I let you take her out on your own," he said.

She gladly climbed into the driver's seat, and before long they were on their way. As they rode along, Lars provided directions, which were helpful, and driving advice, which was not. When they reached the Barclay farm, Elizabeth set the parking brake and gave Lars a bright, inquisitive smile. "Well, what do you know?" she said. "We made it in one piece."

"I guess you can handle an automobile all right," he said reluctantly. "But maybe you should get more practice."

"I'm glad I've earned your trust," she said, smothering a laugh. He was not the first man to contrive some excuse to be in her company, and although Lars was at least fifteen years her senior, his interest was flattering. Henry had scarcely touched her since they had made the cabin their home. She had begun to believe that she was no longer pretty, that worry and hard work had robbed her of her beauty. She did not know whether to be relieved or upset by this sign that men still found her attractive. If Henry did not, it mattered very little what other men thought.

She decided to press her advantage. "Do we have time to swing by the Grand Union Hotel on our way home?"

"It's not on our way," he pointed out, "but we have time."

She smiled at him, but he looked away as Marta and Lupita came running up. "Hello, Mr. Jorgensen," Marta said shyly.

"Hello, Marta," Lars said gently, although he looked pained. "Where are your parents?"

"Papi's working and Mami's inside with Miguel and Ana."

"How are they?" asked Elizabeth.

Marta bit her lip and glanced at the house. "Miguel cried and cried and cried, but now he doesn't cry anymore. Ana didn't get out of bed today. Mami stays inside all the time."

"All the time?" echoed Lars.

Marta nodded. Grim, Lars drew in a deep breath, and Elizabeth followed his gaze as it traveled around the yard. The neatly planted flowers had turned dry and brown; a layer of windblown dirt covered the stone walkway that had been so carefully swept on Elizabeth's last visit.

Lars pulled a brown paper sack from his pocket and handed it to Lupita. "Share the candy with your big sister," he instructed. The girls beamed, thanked him, and ran off to enjoy the treat in the shade of the orange tree.

"Should we fetch the doctor?" asked Elizabeth as she trailed after Lars to the small, silent adobe house.

"No doctor around here can help them," Lars said, with a trace of anger, as if he was certain that other, more capable doctors elsewhere could, if only the children could get to them. He knocked on the door, and after a long moment, Rosa opened the door a crack and gazed out at him without speaking.

"How long has it been since you've been outside?" he asked gruffly.

"I don't know," she replied softly. "Days, perhaps."

"You're killing yourself, you know."

She blinked, surprised, as if that had not occurred to her. "Do you think I care?"

"Marta and Lupita will still need you after—after—"

"After my other two children die?"

"Come out into the sunshine," said Lars. "It's a beautiful day. Fresh air will do you good."

Rosa glanced over her shoulder into the darkened room. "And leave my babies alone in this house?"

"I'll stay with them," said Elizabeth quickly. "I love children. I've cared for my nieces and nephews from the time they were born. They'll be fine."

"They will not be fine," said Rosa without emotion.

Lars gently pushed the door open wider, and Rosa did not prevent it. "Come on outside. You don't have to go far. If anything happens, Elizabeth can yell for us and we'll come running."

Lars held out his hand. Rosa looked at it, then took a deep breath and nodded. She did not take his hand, but she did step through the doorway and tell Elizabeth where she could find the children.

Though the house was larger than the cabin, it was small enough that Elizabeth would have found them just as quickly on her own. Miguel slept in a cradle next to his parents' bed, while Ana tossed fitfully in a bed in the smallest of the bedrooms, which she likely shared with her sisters. Assured that they were fine for the moment, Elizabeth explored the house, listening for Rosa's return. From the bright quilts on the children's beds to the tidy kitchen and the front room decorated with religious illustrations, nothing hinted at the misery that had occurred—that *was* occurring—within those walls. It could have been any small adobe farmhouse in southern California.

Little more than ten minutes passed before Rosa and Lars returned. "The children?" Rosa asked breathlessly as she closed the door behind her.

"Sleeping," Elizabeth assured her. Rosa managed a small smile of thanks. It did seem to Elizabeth that the bleak worry in her eyes had eased somewhat. Elizabeth found herself wishing she could come every day to offer the overwhelmed mother a brief respite, a few minutes to catch her breath, to play in the sun with Marta and Lupita.

"We'll come back next week," Lars promised, as if he had been reading her thoughts.

For an instant Rosa looked pleased, but then her mouth creased in worry. "John won't like it."

"Then he shouldn't be postmaster," said Elizabeth, feigning ignorance. "I can't help it that my family expects me to write to them."

"Oh, your letters," said Rosa with a start. "I forgot. Several have come for you."

"We have an errand at the Grand Union Hotel," said Elizabeth, thinking of Rosa's brother, "if you have any messages you'd like us to deliver."

"No messages," said Rosa. "But perhaps you would take them their mail."

She disappeared into the kitchen and returned with two envelopes, which Elizabeth traded for the two she had brought along. Rosa also gave Lars several envelopes and a Sears Roebuck catalog tied into a bundle with twine for the Jorgensens, and a smaller bundle of letters for the hotel. They thanked her and left the house.

Outside, they spotted John Barclay approaching almost in a run. "What are you doing in my house?" he demanded, glaring at Lars.

"Picking up the mail," he replied.

"You don't need to go inside for that."

"I invited them in," said Rosa. "I needed time to sort the Jorgensens' mail and I saw no reason to keep them waiting on the doorstep."

John turned his glare upon Elizabeth. "Weren't you afraid you might catch something?" His eyes shifted to his wife. "But why should she? I haven't got-

ten sick, you haven't gotten sick, Marta and Lupita haven't. Why do you figure that is? Why the others, but not Marta and Lupita?"

"Some men would consider that a blessing," said Lars.

"Maybe, maybe not. Maybe he'd start to wonder how this 'blessing' came
to be. Maybe I'm getting wiser every day." John strode toward his wife, who
instinctively took a step back, her grip on the door tightening. "Maybe Rosa
knows. Want to explain why Lupita hasn't taken sick?"

"Have a care, John," warned Lars.

"Don't tell me how to speak to my wife," John shot back. "This is my family, my house, and don't you ever set foot inside it again."

Rosa said, "John, please—"

"You shut your mouth." John pushed Rosa ahead of him into the house
and slammed the door. Lars hesitated for a moment as if considering
whether to follow, but he turned away. After a moment, Elizabeth followed,
and her gaze fell upon Marta and Lupita, who had watched the whole scene
unfold from the shade of the orange tree.

"Take care of yourselves, girls," Lars said to them as he helped Elizabeth
into the passenger side of the car. Marta nodded, but Lupita just watched
them go, wide-eyed.

"What a cruel, spiteful man," Elizabeth said as Lars turned the car around
and drove back to the main road. "As if Rosa isn't suffering enough. Why
does he add to her burden with his ridiculous questions? It's almost as if he
believes she's responsible for her children's illness."

"He wouldn't be the only one," said Lars.

"That's just the speculation of gossipy, small-minded people who ought to
put their idle time to better use. You can't listen to that."

"I don't."

"There must be a doctor somewhere who can help the children."

"Not one around here, not one they can afford."

Elizabeth fell silent as they drove on to the Grand Union Hotel, wishing
she could do something to help Rosa. She thought of her own family's doctor back in Harrisburg and Dr. Malcolm Granger in the Elm Creek Valley,
who was reputed to be a brilliant physician. His care had seen Aunt Eleanor
through many struggles with her weak heart, and by all accounts he had
seen the entire valley through the influenza pandemic of 1918 almost single
-handedly, assisted only by volunteers and his aged father, a retired doctor.

She would write to Dr. Granger and seek his advice. Perhaps he could recommend a treatment or knew of a skilled doctor in southern California who would waive his fees for a family in need.

When they pulled up to the hotel, Carlos stepped out from the garage to see who had arrived. At the sight of Lars, his face turned to stone. He greeted Elizabeth stiffly, his watchful gaze fixed on Lars until he turned and disappeared back into the garage. Elizabeth glanced questioningly at Lars, but he ignored her curiosity and told her he would wait outside.

She found Mrs. Diegel behind the front desk in the lobby, writing in a ledger. "Well, hello there, Elizabeth," she said. "What can I do for you? Have you come to trade?"

"You know I don't have anything left to trade," said Elizabeth, without acrimony. She placed the bundle of letters on the desk. "Lars and I stopped by the post office and brought you your mail. I've also come to ask a favor."

Mrs. Diegel peered across the room and out the window, where Lars stood by the automobile. "The post office and then here," she remarked offhandedly. "One might almost think he was on the sauce again, the way he insists upon putting himself in the way of the two men in the valley who most despise him."

"You knew about his drinking?" said Elizabeth.

Mrs. Diegel paged through the envelopes. "Everyone knew about his drinking. It was hard to miss."

"Why would Carlos and John despise Lars?"

Mrs. Diegel looked up sharply. "You caught me gossiping. You should know better than to listen to an old woman rambling on wherever her mind wanders."

"Please tell me. Why would they hate him? He seems like a good man."

"He is, now. Perhaps he was then, too, in his way, despite the drinking, or Rosa never would have loved him."

"Rosa loved Lars?" exclaimed Elizabeth.

Exasperated, Mrs. Diegel held up her hands to quiet her. "Must you shout?"

"I'm sorry. I'm—just surprised." Astounded was more like it. "How do you know?"

"Rosa worked for me for a few years after high school, until she married. Lars and John both used to call on her here, to bring her flowers, take her to lunch, pass the time—you know how young men carry on. Rosa preferred Lars, or so it seemed to me, but she was fond of John, too, or she would have told him to leave her alone. She was straightforward like that back then."

"If Rosa loved Lars, then why did she marry a man like John Barclay?"

"I've often wondered that myself." Mrs. Diegel sighed, thoughtful. "I suppose because she couldn't marry Lars and she had to marry someone, or she thought she did. I've done just fine many years without a husband, but not all women believe it's possible."

"Why couldn't she marry Lars? Because of his drinking?"

"That was part of it. She hated his drinking and begged him to quit. If he showed up here drunk she sent him right back out that door. But more important, her parents wouldn't allow her to marry a Jorgensen. You're a newcomer, so you wouldn't know anything about their feud. The Jorgensen farm used to belong to the Rodriguez family. A distant ancestor was awarded the land grant back when the Spanish still owned most of California. When Rosa and Carlos's great-grandparents went bankrupt after a two-year drought, they sold the farm to Hannah Jorgensen's grandfather for pennies on the dollar. The Rodriguez family has never forgiven the Jorgensens for taking advantage of them when they were in desperate need, for profiting from their misfortune." Mrs. Diegel shrugged. "It happens all the time. It's just sensible business to buy as cheaply as you can."

"Not if it's unfair," said Elizabeth. "It's unethical to offer less than the land is worth if the person has no choice but to accept or starve."

Mrs. Diegel smiled at her fondly. "And that, my dear, is why you will never be a businesswoman. But the Rodriguezes agree with you, not me. Allow a Rodriguez girl to marry a Jorgensen boy? Absolutely unthinkable."

"Even after so many years?"

"Resentment has a long memory."

"That explains why Rosa couldn't marry Lars, but not why she settled for John."

"It probably didn't seem like settling at the time. He might not look like much to a girl your age today, but back then, he was considered one of the more handsome young men in the valley—and he owned his own farm. He was someone Rosa's family accepted, and he had always admired Rosa. John and Lars had vied for her affection since they were boys in school." A troubled frown briefly clouded Mrs. Diegel's expression. "Although Lars was the one Rosa truly loved, I believe she was still fond of John. They might have had a happy life, had tragedy not turned John so bitter."

Perhaps, but Rosa never could have imagined what would befall her in the years to come. She had chosen a path when she chose her husband, as all brides did. It had probably seemed as smooth and as sunny as any she could have walked along. But no young wife knows what sort of man her husband will become. She only knows what he is at the moment she marries him and trusts that he will not fail her, that his love will always be true, no matter what hardships they encounter.

"That's all in the past," said Mrs. Diegel. "Rosa married John and that was the end of it. You said you had a favor to ask me?"

Her question brought an abrupt end to Elizabeth's reverie. "Yes. I wanted to know if I could use your phone. I'll pay the charges, of course."

Mrs. Diegel's eyebrows rose. "Is the Jorgensens' phone out?"

"No, but I wanted some privacy."

"And you didn't want to ask Hannah's permission." Mrs. Diegel gestured toward her office, through an open doorway behind the desk. "Help yourself. Don't worry about the charges. You brought me my mail and spared Carlos a drive today. I suppose I owe you a favor in return."

Elizabeth thanked her, with misgivings. It had not occurred to her that by bringing Mrs. Diegel her mail, she would cost the isolated Rosa a visit from her brother. Even though the siblings were apparently estranged, Rosa probably would have been glad to see him, and perhaps the sight of his nieces and nephew would eventually soften his heart.

Suddenly Elizabeth was struck by a puzzling question: Why should Rosa and Carlos be estranged? Hadn't Rosa followed her family's wishes and married the man they approved of, even though she loved his rival more?

Elizabeth pondered this as she dialed the operator and read Grover Higgins's number off the business card, but she quickly set her curiosity aside when the operator connected her with the office of Golden Reel Productions. "Go ahead," a man barked into the phone before she had prepared herself.

"Mr. Higgins? Grover Higgins?"

"Speaking. Who's this?"

"I'm Elizabeth Nelson. We met at Venice Beach a couple of months ago. You gave me your card and encouraged me to call you if I was interested in appearing in one of your films."

"I did, did I? Venice Beach . . . Hold on, I think I remember. Are you that redhead?"

"No, I'm a blonde." Confidence wavering, Elizabeth added, "You said that girls only half as pretty as I am become stars in Hollywood every day."

He chuckled. "I say that to a lot of dolls. You're going to have to remind me."

"We met at a dance marathon," said Elizabeth. "At first you mistook me for the actress from *Thief of Baghdad*. You said you had several scripts on your desk that I would be ideal for."

"Say, I remember you now. You're that wholesome-looking girl from Ohio, the one with the pushy husband."

"Pennsylvania," said Elizabeth. "But otherwise, that's me."

"And now you've decided you want to be a star after all."

"Yes, please. I would. Is the offer still open?"

"Maybe it is and maybe it isn't. How's your husband feel about this?"

Elizabeth took a quick breath and instinctively glanced over her shoulder as if she expected to find Henry there, arms folded over his chest, glaring at her. "Like you said that day, I'm a girl who makes her own decisions."

"I'm glad to hear it. Well, when are you coming to Hollywood? I could set up a screen test. Not this week, maybe next week." She heard his chair creak and papers rustle. "We could have dinner, maybe go dancing. I can get us into the most exclusive speakeasies in Los Angeles. A looker like you would fit right in. Are you a drinking girl?"

"Not really. Actually, I was rather hoping that you might be coming my way. I live in the Arboles Valley now and I understand that—"

"You live where?"

"The Arboles Valley."

"Where the hell is that?"

"It's about forty-five miles north of Los Angeles. It's where Safari World—"

"Oh, right, right. George Hanneman's wild animal farm. Great fellow. You're really out in the sticks, aren't you?"

Elizabeth ignored that. "I thought that perhaps if you came out to Safari World, we could arrange to meet—"

"Hold on, sister. As much as I hate to turn down a meeting with a pretty blonde, I'm not producing anything that would take me out to Safari World any time soon. Besides, we always do our casting here in the office, not on location."

"I see, but if you—"

"If you want to be a star, you have to go where the action is. Why don't you ditch the stiff and come out to Hollywood?"

"Ditch the—"

"The husband. Lose the husband. He's holding you back, doll."

"I couldn't leave my husband," said Elizabeth. "I love him."

"That's too bad. If you ever change your mind—"

"It's not something I can change my mind about. You either love someone or you don't, and I do."

"If you say so, sister. You don't need to bite my head off. I'm not the one calling on the sly."

"Thanks anyway, Mr. Higgins. Good afternoon." Elizabeth hung up the phone. How dare he suggest she leave her husband? How dare he imply that she was so fickle that she would cast Henry aside and dash off to Hollywood on his word alone? Not that she would leave Henry even for an iron-clad contract and a guaranteed starring role as Rudolph Valentino's leading lady, but still. What did he take her for?

She could never work for Mr. Higgins, that much was obvious. Her only hope now was to meet a director through Safari World. Perhaps if she pleased Caroline Hanneman and the wranglers by finding them the perfect horses for their show, they would introduce her to some of their Hollywood friends. She would not count herself out yet.

Mrs. Diegel peered at her inquiringly as she stormed out of the office. "Bad news?"

"Not bad, exactly, just disappointing. It wasn't even worth the price of the call."

"Good thing you're not paying for it, then." Mrs. Diegel glanced toward the bar as a burst of laughter floated through the open doorway. "Such carrying on in the middle of the day when honest folk are working. Still, can't complain, as long as they keep buying her ginger ales. Goodness knows how she's doctoring it up. No one likes ginger ale that much."

Elizabeth was lost. "Who are you talking about?"

"A woman from back east who came up from Los Angeles last night." Mrs. Diegel shook her head in amused disapproval. "I didn't like the look of her at first. She's not the sort of young lady I usually welcome into my hotel. I thought she was searching for gentlemen callers of the paying kind, if you get my meaning. But she hasn't gone upstairs with a man on her arm, so I suppose she's harmless. It would be bad for business, you know. These days most of my guests are married men looking for lots in the new developments. Their wives would put a stop to any deal if they thought we encouraged licentious behavior in the Arboles Valley, and that's money out of my pocket."

"You mean you get a cut from the real estate agents?"

Mrs. Diegel winced as if she had said too much. "To steer customers their way, yes. Don't say anything. They each think I'm working for them alone, to praise their development and criticize their competitors.' I'm not doing any harm. All I do is figure out which way the customer is leaning and then prod them along in that direction."

"It's just business," Elizabeth finished for her, although something about it seemed vaguely improper.

"You're catching on." Mrs. Diegel shook her head at another roar of laughter. "Funny, she didn't seem especially witty to me, especially the way she kept going on about that Triumph Ranch, but she sure knows how to entertain."

Elizabeth's heart thumped. "What?"

"She didn't strike me as very witty. You know the type—scandalously short skirt, cigarette holder, bobbed hair—no offense to you, of course—but maybe not a lot going on upstairs."

"No, I mean—you said she was talking about a place called Triumph Ranch?"

"Oh, yes. She insists it's a prosperous cattle ranch here in the Arboles Valley. When I told her I had never heard of it, she looked at me as if I must not be very bright or I don't get out much. She has some nerve. I know the name of every ranch in this valley, and if I haven't heard of it, it isn't here." Mrs. Diegel frowned thoughtfully. "Carlos and Rosa's great-grandparents called their land El Rancho Triunfo before they sold to the Jorgensen family, but it hasn't been known by that name for decades. If that's what this girl is looking for, why didn't she simply ask for the Jorgensen farm?"

"Oh, no." Even through her surprise Elizabeth felt the prickling of conscience. She and Henry had only thought of themselves when they decided not to go to the authorities to report how they had been swindled. Why had it not occurred to them that the con man who had sold Triumph Ranch to the Nelsons and two others before them would stop there?

"What's wrong?" Mrs. Diegel asked.

"I think your new guest has been deceived by a con man," said Elizabeth, steeling herself. Someone had to tell this unfortunate woman the truth, and it would be better to hear it from a sympathetic fellow victim than John Barclay, who had been more concerned with the inconvenience to himself than the

Nelsons' misfortune when they tried to pick up the deed of trust at the land office.

Before Mrs. Diegel could press her for more details, Elizabeth entered the barroom.

There, sitting at the bar, surrounded by a cluster of admiring men, was a slender, fashionably dressed young woman wearing dark red lipstick and a cloche hat on her sleek black bob. She glanced toward the doorway and her face lit up in recognition.

"Hiya, kid," Mae called to her. "How's tricks?"

"Mae," Elizabeth managed to say. "What—you're—"

"Yeah, I'm happy to see you, too." Mae slipped gracefully from her bar stool and crossed the room. The men's eyes followed her swaying hips appreciatively. Elizabeth stood frozen just inside the doorway as Mae gave her air kisses on both cheeks. "Where have you been hiding? Not even the hotel keeper knows about this ranch of yours, and there can't be *that* many ranches for her to keep straight."

Elizabeth forced a shaky smile. "Things didn't turn out as we had planned. What—what are you doing here?"

"I came to visit you and that handsome husband of yours, of course." Mae linked her arm through Elizabeth's and steered her from the barroom. "I've been cooped up in this hotel long enough. Let's go to your place."

Mrs. Diegel watched them cross the lobby together, but with an innkeeper's practiced discretion, she pretended to find nothing unusual in the sight of a stylish flapper carrying on as if she were the stunned farm wife's dearest friend. Outside, at the sight of Mae, Lars's stoic mask slipped and he shot Elizabeth a look of astonishment.

"Why, Henry," Mae said with mock sternness when Elizabeth failed to introduce them. "Ranch life has not been kind to you."

"Mae, this is Lars Jorgensen," Elizabeth quickly said. "Lars, this is Mae. We met on the train coming west."

"Charmed, I'm sure." Mae gave Lars a winning smile and gracefully extended a hand.

Lars shook it somewhat awkwardly and helped her into the front seat of the car while Elizabeth climbed into the back. As they drove away from the hotel, Mae held up the burden of conversation, asking questions about the town with a curiosity that would have been charming in other circumstances, admiring the scenic beauty of the landscape, marveling at the loveliness of the weather. Elizabeth responded as well as she could, but all the while her thoughts were racing. This could not possibly be a simple social call. When they had parted with Mae in St. Louis, she had said she would return to New York. What was she doing in California, and in a place as remote as the Arboles Valley?

What would Henry say?

All too soon and not soon enough, the yellow farmhouse came into view. "This is quite a place you have here," said Mae admiringly.

"Thank you," said Lars, although Elizabeth knew the remark had been directed at her. Mae glanced at Lars, eyebrows arched in mild surprise, but she said nothing.

"Henry and I have our own place about a half mile south," said Elizabeth quickly. "Lars, I don't think Mae can make that walk in those shoes. Would you mind dropping us off there?"

Lars shrugged and agreed. When the cabin came into sight, Mae said nothing until the car came to a stop a few yards away. Then she laughed in astonishment. "This is the place?"

Elizabeth nodded. "This is home."

"And the cattle?" Mae asked. "They're hiding out back, I guess?"

"There are no cattle." Elizabeth could not bear to look Lars's way as she climbed out of the car, clutching the mail. "Come on. I'll take you inside."

"It's . . . cozy. A little rustic, but nice," said Mae consolingly as she picked her way across the dusty yard and up the front stairs. "I think I'll be staying at the hotel tonight, though."

Elizabeth showed Mae inside, leaving the letters on the mantel. "Please make yourself at home. There's bread in the pantry and you can get fresh water from the pump at the kitchen sink. I'm sorry I can't stay. I have to get back to work."

"Don't worry about me." Mae settled herself into the best of the chairs. "I'll just put my feet up and relax, you know, take in the fresh country air."

"I'll be back by seven," Elizabeth promised. "I'm sorry to be such a poor hostess. I'll bring you supper."

When Mae cheerfully waved off her apologies, Elizabeth gave her a quick smile and hurried outside to the car. "Don't ask," she told Lars as she climbed in and slammed the door.

"I wasn't going to," he replied.

They drove the short distance back to the garage in silence. Once there,

Elizabeth said, "Mae will need a ride back to the hotel this evening. May I borrow the car?"

"That's all right. I'll take her."

"That's kind of you, but I don't want to impose."

"It's no trouble."

Grateful, Elizabeth thanked him and hurried into the kitchen. Later, when Henry and the other men came inside for supper, Elizabeth took him aside for a moment. "We have company back at the cabin."

Henry blanched. "Who?"

"Mae. From the train."

Relief mingled with surprise in Henry's expression. "I thought you were going to say it was someone from home." Then surprise won out. "Mae? Here? What does she want?"

"I don't know."

"Is Peter with her?"

Elizabeth shook her head. "She hasn't spoken a word about him. I assume he's in prison."

"She's not coming up to the house for supper, is she?"

"I hadn't thought to invite her." How could she extend an invitation without seeking Mrs. Jorgensen's permission first? "I promised to bring her something to eat."

"Get back to the cabin as soon as you can and keep an eye on her. I'll try to find some excuse to come home early. The last thing we need is for her to rob us blind."

Elizabeth knew he was thinking of their carefully saved wages, hidden in a coffee can in the chimney. "If she wanted to rob someone, I think she would have chosen a more affluent victim."

"She and Peter aren't exactly pillars of the community. I don't think she'd pass up an opportunity to make a fast buck."

Elizabeth could not defend Mae, so she merely nodded and hurried to the kitchen to begin serving dinner. Mae had been kind to her on the train, but obviously she wanted something from the Nelsons or she would not have come. If she *had* intended to rob them, she had surely changed her mind when she discovered that they were not wealthy ranch owners after all.

Throughout the meal, Elizabeth waited for Lars to mention the unexpected guest he had escorted back from the Grand Union Hotel, but he said nothing. The longer she knew him, the more she realized that he knew how to keep a secret. Afterward, as she cleared the table, she wrapped two pieces of fried chicken and several biscuits in a clean cloth and hid them in the pantry. When Mrs. Jorgensen dismissed her for the evening, she quickly retrieved the bundle and raced back to the cabin.

There she discovered Mae had built a fire on the hearth and was sitting beside it in a rocking chair reading Elizabeth's mail. Not only the new letters she had left on the mantel, but all of the letters from home she kept tied with a ribbon in her trunk.

"What do you think you're doing?" Elizabeth exclaimed, crossing the room and snatching up the letters.

"Don't be sore," said Mae. "I got bored. There's not a lot of entertainment around here. Say, what kind of scam are you running on the folks back home?"

"It's not a scam." Elizabeth returned the letters to the trunk and fastened the latch firmly.

"They seem to believe you and Henry are big-time cattle ranchers. Come to think of it, that's what you told Peter and me. What happened?"

Elizabeth hated to admit the truth, but that was preferable to being thought of as a con artist. "We aren't scamming anyone. We're the ones who were cheated. It was all a lie. Henry gave his life savings for a handful of worthless papers. Now we work for the real owners of the property—but they don't know the truth about us, so please don't tell them."

"My lips are sealed." Mae shook her head in sympathy. "That's a tough break, honey. Any chance you'll find the guy and get your money back?"

"I doubt it." Elizabeth looked up as the door swung open and Henry entered, grim-faced. "Hi, sweetheart. You remember Mae."

"Of course." Henry went to the kitchen, pumped water into the sink, and briskly washed his face and hands. Elizabeth quickly offered him a towel. "What brings you to the Arboles Valley? I have to admit, you're the last person I expected to see here."

"You get right down to business. I like that." Mae crossed her ankles and folded her hands in her lap. "Why don't you pull up a chair and we'll talk?"

Henry left the damp towel on the kitchen counter and took a seat on Elizabeth's steamer trunk across from Mae. Elizabeth hesitated before following. When all were seated, Mae gave them a dim smile. "I think you know that Peter works for some tough characters."

"He's in prison now, though, isn't he?" Elizabeth asked. Somehow that seemed to offer some protection against whatever it was that Mae had come to tell them.

"Yes, but that doesn't let him off the hook," said Mae. "His bosses sent him to Los Angeles to solve a transportation problem bringing certain goods from the city to their clients in Oxnard and other places further north. If they manage to avoid getting hijacked or having their drivers run off with the merchandise, they have to dump the cargo when the Feds set up a roadblock. It's always one thing or another, and it's ruining business."

"Peter mentioned that," said Henry. "He asked for my help and I refused. I haven't changed my mind."

Mae held up a hand, a request for patience so she could continue. "Peter was also supposed to deliver a payment—a huge chunk of change—to the Los Angeles bosses. When the cops took Peter in St. Louis, they also took the money." Mae took a deep breath and clasped her hands tightly in her lap. "They expect me to pay them back, or work off Peter's debt."

"Why you?" exclaimed Elizabeth. "None of this is your fault."

"That's not how they look at it. They don't like losing money. They think— or at least they *say*—that Peter's too smart to allow himself to be taken in with that kind of cash on him. They think he must have left it on the train, and that I picked it up."

"Is that true?" asked Henry.

"No," retorted Mae. "What do you take me for, some Dumb Dora who'd steal from the Mob? If I did have the money, you'd better believe I'd hand it over rather than be in the spot I'm in now."

"What spot is that, exactly?" asked Elizabeth.

"Like I said, I have to pay them back. Either I give them the cash or I work it off by setting up the deal Peter wasn't able to arrange."

Henry's expression was stony. "And if you don't?"

Mae took in a shaky breath, but she met Henry's gaze steadily. "They'll kill me. Not only because I'll have proven that I'm not useful, but to get back at Peter for letting himself get caught with their cash on him."

"You should go to the police at once," said Elizabeth.

Mae made a strangling noise, incredulous. "You're a regular laugh riot, Liz. You should be on the radio. Me, go to the police with this story? I don't think it would wash."

"We can't help you," said Henry, rising abruptly from his chair. "I'm not about to get mixed up in criminal activities. Even if I were, take a look around. This is all we have now, and it's not even really ours. Peter would be the first to tell you to look somewhere else."

"No, he wouldn't. Are you kidding?" Mae rose and turned around in the center of the room, taking in the cabin. "This is even better than Triumph Ranch. This is perfect. What cop is going to suspect a farmhand and his wife living in a dilapidated old cabin in the middle of nowhere? Let me tell you, the people who work for Peter's bosses live it up. They don't rough it. No one would ever think to look here."

"And we're going to keep it that way." Henry strode across the room and opened the door. "I'm sorry you're in trouble, Mae, but I have to ask you to leave."

"But her life is in danger." Elizabeth rose and put her arm around Mae's shoulders. "They've threatened to kill her. We can't just send her away."

Henry hesitated before closing the door. "Can't you just disappear, Mae? Can't you change your name, start over in San Francisco or Seattle, someplace as far from New York as you can get?"

"You don't know these people. They'll look for me no matter where I go." Mae chewed on her lip then shrugged "If I lie low for a few years, dye my hair, keep my nose clean—I don't know. It might work. Except that I'm broke. Peter's bosses took every cent I had. I can't even pay for that tiny room in that hotel where Liz found me. If I get caught stowing away on a train to San Francisco, Peter's bosses will send someone to finish me off."

"You won't have to stow away." Henry went to the fireplace, reached up into the flue, and pulled out the coffee can, covered in soot. He lifted the lid and took out three rolls of bills bound with rubber bands. It was every dollar they had saved since coming to work for the Jorgensens.

Henry weighed the rolls in his palm for a moment, and then pressed them into Mae's hands. "Here. Take them." He let the coffee can fall to the floor with a thin clank. "Make a better life for yourself somewhere, and don't come back."

Mae fingered one of the rolls, and Elizabeth could tell she was rapidly calculating her windfall. "Are you sure you can spare it?"

Henry dropped tiredly into a chair. "Just take it and go before I change my mind."

Elizabeth quickly guided Mae to the door. "Come on." Without a word, Mae hurried along beside her across the sagging porch and down the steps. "Lars Jorgensen offered to drive you back to the hotel. Wait in the garage while I get him." How she would do that without provoking curiosity from the other Jorgensens, she had no idea.

When they were halfway to the yellow farmhouse, Mae said, "Thank you for this."

"You're welcome," said Elizabeth, because she could think of nothing else to say. She was proud of Henry for the sacrifice he had made to save Mae's life, and yet—all of their wages, gone. They were as poor as they had been on their first day in the Arboles Valley.

"I'll repay you someday."

"When you can," agreed Elizabeth, although she did not expect to hear from Mae ever again.

"Wait, Liz." Mae stopped short. "Even if I disappear, Peter's bosses are still going to want a place to stash their merchandise. If not Triumph Ranch, then somewhere else in the valley. Someone's going to get paid to help them. It might as well be you."

"You heard Henry. It won't be us. We can't help it if someone else goes into business with Peter's bosses, but we won't. How could you suggest we get tangled up with those people after what they've done to you?"

Mae shrugged, acknowledging her point. "Maybe there's another way. What's the name of the fellow who conned you?"

"J. T. Simmons, or at least that's what he called himself. But he's long gone. As far as we know, he's back east looking for his next victim."

"Peter has connections all along the East Coast. Maybe they can track this fellow down and get your money back."

"If he hasn't spent it already."

"It's worth a try." Mae grinned. "At least we can make him sorry he picked Henry for his mark."

"No, Mae." A vision of how Peter's friends might punish the con artist came unbidden to her mind. Sickened, she forced the thoughts away. "Please don't do anything rash. If Peter's contacts do find this Mr. Simmons, turn him in to the police."

"Liz, don't you know me by now?" Mae gave her a smile that was almost wistful. "Peter and me and his friends, we don't go to the cops. Cops aren't for people like us. They're for people like you."

Elizabeth muffled a sigh. Mae did not sound like a woman who intended to break all ties with her past and start a new life as a law-abiding citizen. "I don't want any man, however despicable, to be killed for any wrong done to me. Besides, you can't contact any of Peter's old friends. Someone will talk, and then Peter's bosses will know where to start searching for you."

Mae nodded, and Elizabeth could read in her expression her dawning awareness of all that her self-imposed exile would require to succeed.

They walked the rest of the way in silence. To Elizabeth's relief, Lars had anticipated their arrival and was waiting for them in the garage, sparing her a trip into the farmhouse, where Mrs. Jorgensen and Mary Katherine were sure to wonder why she had come. Mae squeezed her hand in farewell and gave a jaunty wave as the car pulled away. Then she was gone.

Elizabeth made her way carefully along the moonlit path back to the cabin, where she found Henry slumped wearily in his chair, staring at the dying embers in the fireplace. "I'll get more wood," she said, turning to go back outside.

Henry jumped up from his chair. "No, I'll do it." He paused as he passed her in the doorway, then reached out to brush a loose curl off her cheek. "Your hair is growing out."

She nodded, knowing what that meant.

"You would have been able to go home soon." His hand fell to his side. "Now it will be months."

"You did what you had to do," said Elizabeth firmly. "We couldn't send Mae back to those vicious men."

"How do we know she isn't on her way to them right now?" he countered. "She could use our money to pay off part of Peter's debt, then turn around and find someone else to help stash his bosses' contraband. Next thing you know, she'll be up to her neck in a sea of other problems."

"When someone desperately needs your help, you don't stand around and ponder what they'll do once you help them, or philosophize about whether they deserve your help. You simply help them."

Henry stared at her for a moment before choking out a bleak laugh. "You sound exactly like your aunt Eleanor. Without a doubt, you belong back in Pennsylvania with your family."

"*You* are my family," said Elizabeth. "I'm getting tired of repeating myself. I'm not going home without you."

Without a word, Henry touched her cheek gently with the back of his fingers, but his eyes told her he was resolute. Before she could seize hold of his hand, he stepped outside into the night. For one fearful moment, she forgot he was only going out back for more wood for the fire. For a moment, she forgot that he would return to her.

🌹

1912

John Barclay courted Rosa for two years. Once a month he came to Sunday dinner at the Diazes' home, and every other Saturday he took Rosa out on a date—a picnic, a dance at the church social hall, a day at Lake Sherwood with friends. John was courteous, polite, with a smoldering reserve that lingered long after the couples' secret was exposed. Isabel was glad that Rosa seemed to be taking her time to make up her mind about him, because she wasn't sure how she felt about him herself. John had a steeliness about him that made Isabel uncomfortable. He was so unlike her Miguel, warm and affectionate, that she wondered how Rosa had ever become fond of him. Perhaps he had hidden qualities, rich strains deep within, that only Rosa had discovered. In time, perhaps Isabel and Miguel would find them, too.

Isabel had hoped that allowing Rosa to see John openly would bring an end to her late-night disappearances, but in this, Rosa bitterly, bewilderingly failed her. Isabel begged her to stop running off at night, wept over her, threatened to tell her father, but it was little use. Rosa would mend her ways for a little while to appease her mother, but within a month or two, Isabel would wake in the night to find her daughter's bed empty.

"Why don't you just marry him?" she begged, meeting her daughter at the door one morning before dawn. Rosa was pale and frightened to have been caught in the act of returning home after staying out all night, but she was also resolute. Although she apologized for upsetting her mother, she would not promise to put an end to her illicit disappearances. Isabel knew then that nothing she said or did would prevent her daughter from following the path she had chosen, even if it led to her ruin.

She was at a loss to explain Rosa's behavior. She was twenty-two, old enough to be married with a home of her own. Why sneak off at night to be with the man she loved when she could become his wife and be by his side for the rest of her life? Nothing impeded Rosa except her inexplicable reluctance to give her consent. Isabel marked John's growing impatience and feared that he would tire of waiting, tire of Rosa herself. What would Rosa do if John decided not to wait anymore and found someone else, someone more willing to become his bride?

After so many years, if Rosa could not decide whether to marry John, perhaps that was a sign he was wrong for her. But there was nothing Isabel could do but hold her breath, pray for God's protection, and wait for Rosa to reach her own conclusions.

Carlos had finished school and, with a recommendation from his sister, had obtained a job as a handyman at the Grand Union Hotel. He had his father's friendly, cheerful disposition and had become an entertaining storyteller as well. As Isabel cooked in the kitchen or sewed in the evenings in her rocking chair, Carlos would have her alternately laughing and marveling over his tales of the people who came and went at the hotel. She hoped he embellished his stories liberally, because otherwise she was not sure she should allow her children to work there. A married, churchgoing businessman who met his sister-in-law in a private room every Monday at ten in the morning and checked out by noon. The card shark who passed through town in a whirlwind and left the wallets of some of the Arboles Valley's most prominent citizens lighter when the dust settled. Strange phone calls Mrs. Diegel received on the last Friday of every month, sending Rosa out of the office as soon as the operator rang so not a word would be overheard by anyone.

Most of his tales were so shocking or amusing or both that it passed unnoticed when Lars Jorgensen, the eldest of the two sons, began appearing more frequently in them. Lars frequently came to the hotel to drink at the bar; Isabel already knew this disgraceful fact about him and dismissed his presence at the hotel as she dismissed the whole Jorgensen family. Then Carlos mentioned that he had heard raised voices in the citrus garden once, and when he had gone to see what was wrong, he found Lars and John Barclay in a shoving match. Then one afternoon in July he came home from work remarking that the Jorgensens' apricot harvest must have gone well, because he had seen Lars carrying a basket of the fresh, ripe fruit into the hotel office. "Probably gave it to Mrs. Diegel to pay off his bar tab," he joked.

Not ten minutes later, Rosa walked in smiling and carrying a basket of apricots.

Isabel went cold, but she forced herself to remain calm. "Where did you get those?"

Rosa glanced at the basket in her hands. "Mrs. Diegel gave them to me."

She set the basket down on the counter, too quickly. "She didn't want them, so she gave them to me."

It was a lie. Mrs. Diegel never gave away anything unless she received something in return. And she would never give an employee an entire basket of fruit that could be put to better use as dessert for the guests of the hotel.

Suddenly all the lies and deception since Rosa was a girl of fourteen made perfect sense.

It was that Jorgensen boy Rosa loved, not John Barclay. Lars Jorgensen, who stank of alcohol and whose grandfather had stolen the Rancho Triunfo from her own dear *abuelo* and *abuelita*.

"You will never see him again," she said quietly.

Rosa looked back at her, eyes wide and startled. "Mami?"

"Marry John or don't marry him, but you will never see Lars Jorgensen again. If you promise me this, I will not tell your father. I am thinking of him as much as you. You would break his heart if he knew."

"He wouldn't care," Rosa choked out through her tears. "*You're* the only one who cares. Papi doesn't hate the Jorgensens; you do."

"They have destroyed our family!"

"They haven't! We're here, aren't we?"

"They stole our land. They killed my mother."

"They *bought* our land. Cancer killed your mother. If you were not such a bitter old woman with nothing but hatred in your soul, you would see that. Then Lars and I could be happy."

"Happy? With that drunk? If you think he would make you so happy, then why don't you tell your father about him? He'll be home soon. You tell him how you've been running out at night to meet with that Jorgensen boy and see how happy he is to hear the news. We'll see whose side he takes—the deceitful daughter's or the bitter old woman's. We'll see."

Sobbing, Rosa fled to her room, overturning the basket of apricots. The fruit tumbled to the floor. Isabel scrambled after it, but it was too late; the fruit was bruised and soiled.

She did not care, except for the mess. She would never feed her family anything that grew in Jorgensen soil. It was poison to her, just as she had told Miguel so many years before. Everything that grew on Jorgensen land was poison to her, to her family, to her children.

Chapter Nine

1925

With their savings exhausted, Elizabeth resolved to allow nothing to prevent her from searching for horses for Safari World on her next day off—assuming Lars would let her borrow his car. When Mary Katherine invited her to spend the next Sunday afternoon at Lake Sherwood with her and the girls, Elizabeth reluctantly made the excuse that she had letters to write and work to catch up on at home.

"You and that husband of yours," exclaimed Mary Katherine. "Honestly. You two are a perfect pair. All you enjoy is work, work, work."

"I didn't say I enjoyed it," Elizabeth said, smiling. But her amusement swiftly faded. Once, not very long ago, she had considered herself and Henry to be a perfect pair, too, if not for the reasons Mary Katherine stated. She was surprised anyone found them a perfect pair anymore. Elizabeth felt as if a chasm stretched between them, so wide and deep that it could not have existed without years of erosion and toil. But it was newly sprung up between them, and for that reason alone, Elizabeth clung to the hope that the distance was not unbridgeable.

If only she could figure out why Henry insisted upon standing alone on his side of the gulf, when all she wanted to do was stand beside him.

All week she tried to think of an excuse to borrow the car, but she could not. Finally, on Friday afternoon, she went to Lars and told him straight out that she had errands to run the next day. "Barclay doesn't open the post office on Saturdays," he told her.

"I'm not going to the post office."

He regarded her with barely concealed amusement. "Before I let you drive off in my car, I'd like to know where you might be taking it."

"Very well, if you insist, I have a business arrangement with Safari World and I need transportation to carry it out."

"Becoming a lion tamer, are you?"

"And give up my glamorous life here? Not likely. May I borrow the car? Yes or no?"

"No." Before she could protest, he added, "Oscar and my mother need it on Saturday, but I'll hitch up Bonnie to the wagon for you if that will do."

"In that case, I'd prefer to go on horseback."

Lars seemed surprised that she knew how to ride, but he agreed. On Saturday, when Mrs. Jorgensen allowed her a few hours off after lunch, he saddled up a horse for her, although she had assured him she could do it herself. She rode off along country roads, exploring the southern half of the valley and taking note of the horses she spotted in corrals and pastures along the way. She found many suitable animals, but none as swift or as beautiful as Bergstrom Thoroughbreds. When she came across an especially fine animal, she would stop and inquire at the farmhouse to see if it was for sale. Most often the owners were not interested in parting with their horses; other times they were, but set a price far higher than she suspected the wranglers would be willing to pay. Still, she wrote down the relevant information for the most likely purchases and by the time she had to return to the farmhouse to help prepare supper, she had a modest list of horses comparable to those she had seen performing at Safari World.

On Sunday, she did not bother to ask Henry if he wanted to spend the day together. She could not bear for him to refuse her again, and for a change, she actually preferred to be on her own. Lars had a horse saddled and ready for her, so she set out for the northern half of the valley. Since fewer farms were scattered over a wider area, and the Salto Canyon took up much of the land, she hoped to finish searching the valley by late afternoon, allowing her just enough time to ride out to Safari World and report her findings to the wranglers before the end of the day.

She added two prospective horses from the northeastern part of the valley to her list, wondering how the wranglers had missed them, since they were fine animals and the owner eager to sell. Then she headed west, where the road passed by a mesa that stretched as flat as a tabletop for acres before dropping abruptly at the canyon's edge.

In the distance, not far from a sudden descent so sharp that it looked as if a blade had cut into the earth, Elizabeth spotted a wagon and, nearby, two horses grazing. The wagon appeared empty, but in the golden-brown grasses between it and the canyon, several smaller figures moved. Curious, thinking that perhaps the wagon had thrown an axle and its passengers might be waiting for help, Elizabeth directed her horse off the road and across the mesa toward them. When she had closed the distance to a quarter mile, she recognized Rosa Barclay and her children.

Seated on the grass, Rosa looked up quickly when Elizabeth's horse whinnied a greeting. Just as quickly, Rosa turned her head away and tugged on the wide brim of her hat to partially conceal her face. Pretending she had not noticed the snub, Elizabeth called out, "Hello, Rosa. What brings you out this way?"

"I promised the children a picnic," said Rosa, stroking Miguel's dark, curly locks as he rested on her lap. Her voice was hesitant, but not chilly.

Encouraged, Elizabeth dismounted from her horse, who promptly lowered his neck and began grazing. "I think you found the perfect place for it." She smiled as she went to join Rosa, watching Marta and Lupita play. Ana sat just outside the circle of her sisters' play, laughing at their antics. She looked as if she had long ago accepted that she could not join in.

"The mesa offers the most beautiful view of the canyon and it is not too far from home." Softly, Rosa added, "It is just far enough away for me to feel as if I am somewhere else." Suddenly she smiled as if they shared a secret. "My husband believes my mother's spirit haunts the mesa. He does not wish to see her, so he avoids it."

Elizabeth tucked her skirt around her legs and sat down beside her. "Ana seems better today."

"Yes, she is out of bed for now," said Rosa. She hesitated before adding, "That is how the illness runs its course. They fall ill, then recover, then fall ill again, and recover, until one time they fall ill and do not recover."

"Perhaps . . . perhaps Ana and Miguel are not doomed to that fate. Don't lose hope."

"They're my children. I'll never stop praying for a miracle. Not while there is breath in my body."

Tentatively, Elizabeth said, "Forgive me for prying, but have you considered a doctor in a larger city, Los Angeles or San Francisco, perhaps?"

Rosa gazed down at her sleeping son. "We don't have the money to travel so far, or the money to pay for such a skilled doctor."

"Some doctors are willing to waive their fees in certain circumstances."

Rosa shook her heard. "Even so, I doubt my husband would be willing to travel so far. He will not leave the farm. He has no hired hands to look after our place."

How could any father, even John Barclay, not pursue any course that might save the lives of his children? "Why don't you at least write to some other doctors and tell them about your children's affliction? Maybe they've seen cases like this before. What if they could recommend a new treatment the doctors around here haven't considered? If a doctor could figure out why some of your children fall ill and some do not—"

Sharply, Rosa turned to look at her—and that was when Elizabeth saw her bruised face, her swollen, cut lip, which she had tried to conceal with the wide-brimmed hat. "Rosa," she gasped. "What happened to you?"

Rosa looked away and with her fingers tried to comb her dark brown hair over her bruised cheek. "It's nothing. I tripped on a stone and fell against the wagon."

"How many times?"

Rosa held perfectly still for a moment, but then her hand came to rest lightly upon Miguel's head. "I told you, it's nothing."

"It never ceases to amaze me how the wives of cruel men are always so clumsy."

"I know you're trying to be kind, but this is not your concern. You don't know how I have provoked him."

Elizabeth began to rise. "If you aren't going to defend yourself, perhaps your brother will."

"Elizabeth, no." Rosa seized her hand and pulled until Elizabeth had to sit back down or fall. "Don't get Carlos involved in this. He would do nothing to help me even if he knew."

Elizabeth immediately thought of Lars, but said nothing, suspecting that would only upset Rosa more. "Rosa, please. You can't stay with a man who beats you."

"He's my husband and the father of my children. Where else would I go?"

"You and the children can stay with me and my husband."

At that, Rosa smiled. "You're very gracious, but I don't think your husband would like to share that little cabin with five strangers."

"Henry would be the first to insist you stay as long as you like. We have plenty of room. Our cabin is more spacious than it seems from the outside."

Rosa shook her head, but she regarded Elizabeth kindly. "I have seen the inside of the cabin as well as the outside, and I know there isn't room for seven."

Surprised, Elizabeth said, "When did you ever visit the cabin?"

"Long ago. My great-grandparents built it. My mother was born there."

"I had no idea."

Rosa watched her daughters for a moment, and when she spoke again, her voice was far away. "It was a good home, once, before it fell into ruin. My mother lived there as a very young child with her parents and grandparents, after they sold the ranch and stayed on as hired hands. Her stories of her childhood there were full of happiness and longing, even though her family left when she was very young, even though our own home was just as happy and full of love as the cabin of her memories."

"If you grew up surrounded by love," said Elizabeth, "I don't know how you can settle for anything less now."

"I brought this fate upon myself," replied Rosa. "Every choice I ever made led me to this place. Please don't feel sorry for me. I have my children. I am not without love."

Elizabeth did not know what to say. Rosa had her children, but for how long, unless she could get them the medical care they so urgently needed? And why on earth would John Barclay stand in the way? She would not expect compassion from any man who beat his wife, but even so, how could anyone be so coldhearted toward his own children?

"If there is anything I can do for you," said Elizabeth, "if you ever need help or a place to go, my house is small, but the door is always open to you and your children."

Rosa smiled and reached out for her hand. "Thank you. You are very kind, kinder than I deserve, considering how my husband treated you in your misfortune. I can see why Lars thinks so highly of you."

"I don't consider any woman responsible for her husband's behavior." Elizabeth stood and brushed off her skirt, surprised to find herself warmed by Lars's approval. Suddenly she wondered how Rosa would know how Lars felt about her. When would he have told her? Elizabeth had accompanied him on every trip to the post office since she came to the Arboles Valley, and they had only left her sight that one time she had stayed in the adobe with Ana and Miguel. That must have been it, she supposed. She wondered what Lars would do if he could see Rosa now. He had loved her once, and he had treated her with compassion when no one else would. He would not stand by and let John hurt Rosa—but if Lars interfered, John might lash out at Rosa in revenge. If Rosa would not help herself, anyone else's actions might only make matters worse.

Reluctant to leave Rosa before convincing her to seek help, Elizabeth nonetheless mounted her horse and rode off, wishing she could do more for her. Rosa was in her thoughts as she rode through the rest of the valley, skipping only the Barclay farm in her search for suitable horses. By midafternoon she had compiled a list of more than a dozen possibilities, none new to the valley, which convinced her that the wranglers must have been lazy, disinterested, or tightfisted in their own efforts or they would have found the same horses she had.

On her way south toward Safari World, she decided to stop by the Grand Union Hotel to see if Mrs. Diegel knew of any farmers with horses to sell that she had overlooked. She found the innkeeper in the kitchen, discussing the supper menu with the cook. "You're too late to bid your friend good-bye," said Mrs. Diegel. "She checked out this morning."

Elizabeth waited for Mrs. Diegel to add that Mae had skipped out without paying her bill, and breathed a sigh of relief when she did not. "She's not really a friend," she felt compelled to explain. "I met her on the train and we parted ways in St. Louis. Her visit was . . . a surprise."

"She left a far sight happier than when she arrived, I'll say that much for her." Mrs. Diegel broke off to correct the kitchen maid's choice of serving platters, then took Elizabeth by the arm and led her to the parlor. Elizabeth had not intended to make a lengthy visit, so she explained her errand as they walked. Mrs. Diegel seemed surprised that Safari World had assigned her the task of finding performing horses, since usually Caroline Hanneman preferred to select them herself from a favorite horse breeder just north of Los Angeles. She scanned Elizabeth's list, said that she couldn't think of any other possibilities Elizabeth had missed, and commended her for striking out on her own in business.

"I'm just doing what's necessary," Elizabeth replied. "The sooner I earn enough money, the sooner I can buy back my quilts from you."

Mrs. Diegel's approving smile faded. "Well. As to that . . ." She gestured to an overstuffed armchair, but something in her tone fixed Elizabeth in place. "I'm still happy to sell you the Chimneys and Cornerstones quilt, but you'll have to contact the new owner if you wish to purchase the Double Wedding Ring."

Elizabeth felt faint. "New owner?"

"One of my guests fell in love with it and insisted upon buying it. She made such a generous offer I couldn't reasonably turn her down."

"Of course you could have," said Elizabeth. "We had an agreement. You said I could buy it back from you when I had saved enough money."

"I didn't promise to wait forever," said Mrs. Diegel. "If you recall, I told you I couldn't promise what condition the quilt would be in by the time you could afford it."

"Yes, but I expected it to be here. Worn or faded, perhaps, but still here. I never dreamed you'd sell my quilt to anyone else."

"Elizabeth, dear, you know I'm a businesswoman. My guest made an offer you couldn't possibly match, not without years of saving."

Elizabeth had intended to do exactly that, if necessary. "I didn't know our understanding had a time limit." She took a deep breath to calm the swirl of her emotions. "Would you at least be willing to give me the new owner's name, so I can look into buying it back from her?"

For the first time, Mrs. Diegel looked as if she regretted what she had done. "Certainly, but I doubt she'll sell. It may not be easy to reach her. She and her husband came to view lots in Meadowbrook Hills, but I overheard her tell her husband several times that she's reluctant to live so far from Los Angeles." Shaking her head, Mrs. Diegel led Elizabeth to the lobby, where she looked up the woman's name and address in the guest registry and wrote them down in a quick scrawl. Handing the slip of paper to Elizabeth, she added, "I sold her the quilt as one last goodwill gesture to entice her to buy, but she was adamant, and her husband seemed eager to please her. I doubt she'll return."

Elizabeth's heart sank as she imagined the precious quilt that the women of her family had sewn with such care and affection lost in the city far to the south. She never should have agreed to part with it, not for the world.

She was too upset to do more than close her hand around the paper and leave without another word for Mrs. Diegel. If she could have taken the Chimneys and Cornerstones quilt with her, she would have. She stormed into the stable, where Carlos had offered to care for her horse. "Are you all right?" he asked as she brushed past him and began to saddle the horse.

It galled her that he showed concern for her while ignoring his own sister, who was in much greater need. "If you want to help someone, help Rosa," she said shortly, tightening the girths.

She had caught him off guard, but he quickly recovered. "She made her bed, and now she has to lie in it."

"With a husband who beats her?"

He hesitated. "John Barclay is not a kind man, but he loves my sister. He would never lay a hand on her."

"Oh, really?" Elizabeth tugged on the horse's reins and led him from the stable. "Then I wonder who gave her that black eye and split her lip."

Carlos stopped her with a touch on her arm. "What do you mean?"

"I saw her myself, on the mesa, right before I came here." It occurred to her then that the children had not seemed disturbed by their mother's appearance, which implied that they had grown accustomed to seeing her in that condition. "At first she claimed that she had tripped and hit her head on the wagon. I told her to seek help, but she seemed to think she would search in vain. Now I'm inclined to believe her."

"You saw her on the mesa? Near the Salto Canyon?"

"Is there any other mesa in the Arboles Valley?" Elizabeth swung herself up into the saddle and touched the horse with her heels. As she left, she called over her shoulder, "My brother would never allow any man to hit me."

She rode off, but she had not gone far before she began to regret her words. She had not meant to goad Carlos into retaliating against John, which could make matters much worse for Rosa and the children. Rosa had refused Elizabeth's offers of help and would not thank her for her interference.

But she could not bear to stand aside and do nothing while the people of the Arboles Valley continued to ignore Rosa's suffering. Still, what could she do, especially if Rosa refused to leave her husband?

Deeply troubled, she continued south to Safari World, eager to complete her task and return home. Henry had grown so distant since they had come to this place. He had not kissed her or held her in his arms at night, and although her aunts had warned her that sometimes a husband's ardor faded, she had not expected that of Henry, and never so suddenly or so soon. She ached for him to love her as he had in the first days of their marriage, but if she could not have that, at least, perhaps, they could return to the friendship they had shared in the years before they married. She had been able to tell him anything then, and he had listened and offered his opinion—even when it starkly contradicted her own. If she could unburden herself to him now, perhaps he would help her figure out what to do. He had helped Mae, a woman he disapproved of and did not trust. Surely he would do even more for Rosa.

When she arrived at Safari World, she tied up the horse at the hitching post near the parking lot, more than three-quarters full. Over the roars of Charlie and his pride, she explained her errand to the woman at the ticket booth, who eyed her curiously for a moment before allowing her through the gate without paying admission. Elizabeth waited at the corral for the trainers to finish a performance, and waited some more rather than interrupt them as they cared for the horses afterward. Only then did she approach, striding confidently into the stable yard rather than calling out to the men over the fence as she had done before. If she expected them to see her as a woman of business, she had to play the part.

The men looked up as she approached. "Miss, all visitors have to stay on the other side of the fence," the taller man called out.

"I'm not a tourist. I'm here on business." She patted the flank of the horse whose reins the man held. "I'm sure you remember me. We spoke a week ago after the three o'clock performance."

The shorter man looked her over. "Yeah, I remember you. You don't forget a blonde with gams like yours. You ought to be in the movies."

Despite the rather crude appraisal of her figure, Elizabeth fervently hoped he would pass along his opinion to the very next movie producer to come to Safari World. "Then I'm sure you also remember our arrangement. You needed horses, and I agreed to find them for you."

"That's right," said the shorter man. "We said we'd pay you five cents each."

"Ten cents, and a bargain at that rate," replied Elizabeth, giving both men a winning smile and taking the list from her skirt pocket. "I've found fourteen horses whose owners are willing to part with them for a reasonable price, and although none of them are as fine as this Bergstrom Thoroughbred here, I'm sure you'll find them suitable."

The men exchanged a look of surprise as the taller reached for the list. "Fourteen?" he asked his companion. "How could we have missed fourteen? The valley's not that big."

Elizabeth shrugged modestly, but the men were busy scanning the list. "What happened to Cormier's mare?" the shorter man asked. "That there's a fine horse. Did she come up lame?"

"No, she's perfectly sound," said Elizabeth. "All of these horses are, or I wouldn't have put them on the list."

The shorter man glanced up at her, perplexed, but the taller shook his head and smacked the paper with the back of his hand. "Look at these prices. They're outrageous! We could almost buy two-year-old show horses for what they want to charge us."

"Well, of course." Elizabeth looked from one man to the other, uncertain. "Isn't that the idea?"

"You got it all wrong, girlie," the shorter man said. "We don't need performers. We need meat."

"Meat?"

"For the lions," the taller man said. "So unless you have a list of lame old nags we can get for a song, you're wasting our time."

Elizabeth pressed a hand to her throat. "You feed the horses to the lions?"

"Well, what do you think we feed them?" the shorter man retorted. "Apricots? Barley? Let them graze in the pasture?"

With a heavy sigh, the taller man removed his hat and scratched his head wearily. "Did you find the horses we need or not?"

"I'm afraid not."

He jerked his thumb toward the fence. "Then you need to get out of my corral."

Elizabeth nodded and hurried through the gate, pausing only long enough to latch it behind her. She had never felt more humiliated—or rather she had, but only once, when she and Henry tried to pick up the deed to Triumph Ranch. Two whole days of searching, wasted. Her chance to earn her own money, ruined. An opportunity to impress people who might introduce her to a movie producer, lost.

Henry had abandoned her, Mrs. Diegel had betrayed her, and her own ignorance had undone her. If she had any sense, she would give up hoping for a better life in this place, as Henry and Rosa had done.

In her only stroke of good luck that day, no one was in the stable when Elizabeth returned to the Jorgensen farm. She tended to the mare and the tack, and gave the mare extra feed to thank her for carrying her on such a long journey. She managed to avoid any of the family or their hired hands as she hurried home to the cabin. She quickly prepared a simple supper, which was on the table just as Henry came through the door. He washed, ate, and then stumbled wearily off to bed with barely a word.

Her thoughts were too troubled for sleep. Slipping quietly into the bedroom, she took the hexagonal quilt from the trunk at the foot of the bed and carried it to the fireside, where she had left her sewing basket. The summer nights were mild enough for only one quilt. Henry seemed to favor the one she called the Arboles Valley Star, although sometimes he kicked it off, restless in his sleep.

By Elizabeth's best guess, the Arboles Valley Star quilt was at least fifty years newer than the wool-and-homespun quilt she had named the Road to Triumph Ranch. The twelve wedges making up each large hexagon reminded her of the spokes of a wagon wheel, with the small solid hexagon appliquéd in the center as the hub. As she patched the holes and mended ripped seams, she thought of all the pioneer women who had come to the valley in wagons whose wheels rumbled over the rocky grade, women who had dreamed of the prosperity and happiness they were certain to find on those sun-drenched hills. Now trains sped the overland journey, machines made the work of farming easier, but the promise of prosperity remained as elusive as it had been in those bygone days.

If not for her quilts to work on in the evenings, she might not have endured her longing for Henry's company. She had never imagined married life would be so lonely. If she had known— She could not bring herself to say that she would not have married Henry if she had known, because she loved him despite everything, but she would have insisted they remain in Pennsylvania, among the women of her family. Often she recalled her father's pronouncement that there was no money in farming anymore, and that business was the place for a young man with ambition. At the time she had dismissed the notion, believing that her father was only trying to keep them close, and perhaps to justify his own decision to sacrifice his birthright to marry her mother. Now his words rang with truth. All around them, people were enjoying their newfound wealth; she saw it in the expensive automobiles and fashionable clothes of the men and women who toured the Arboles Valley on their way to view lots in Oakwood Glen and Meadowbrook Hills. Fortunes were won every day in business, as her father had said, but the boom times had not reached the farms.

Taking up her scissors, Elizabeth trimmed a small octagon from a scrap of blue-and-brown wool she had found among the fabrics Mrs. Diegel had traded to her. With careful stitches that would have made Aunt Eleanor proud, she appliquéd the shape to the center of one of the larger hexagons where the original patch had worn away to a frame a few threads wide. When she had first begun restoring the quilt, she had assumed the long-ago quiltmaker had used the appliqués to disguise a bulge in the seams where the six wedges met in the center, but while replacing some of the worn pieces, she discovered that the center points of the wedges met perfectly, with the bulk of the seams neatly trimmed away so the quilt top would lie flat. Why would any quilter disguise such an impressive display of her skills? Had she valued the artistry of her design more than the opportunity to show off her mastery of precise piecing? Perhaps she had taken such pride in her painstaking handiwork that it did not matter if anyone else knew it was there. Some of Elizabeth's aunts were like that. As for Elizabeth, she preferred to showcase her quilts' best features in hopes of distracting the viewer's eye away from the flaws that inevitably appeared despite her best efforts, scattered throughout her quilts like dandelions in a field.

Elizabeth sewed as thoughts of Henry, of Rosa, and of her failures that day tumbled through her mind. She worked her needle through scraps of wool until the windstorm of thoughts subsided. Only then did she put away her needle and thread, fold the quilt carefully, and tuck it away in the trunk they used as a table. Sleep eluded her so many nights that she knew it would not be long until she worked on the quilt again.

Back in Pennsylvania, a good night's sleep could cure her of most worries, but not so in the Arboles Valley, where her secrets were many and confidants few—and where a captive lion roaring with indignation woke her before daybreak. There was no time before hurrying off to the Jorgensen farmhouse in the morning to speak with Henry about Rosa, so Elizabeth's worries steadily grew as she helped Mrs. Jorgensen and Mary Katherine prepare breakfast. Elizabeth did not want to goad John Barclay into lashing out at Rosa again, but if she did nothing, she would become his silent accomplice, and she could not bear that.

Finally she decided not to wait until Henry found time for her but to speak to Mrs. Jorgensen instead. Despite her stern demeanor and strict management of the household—which Elizabeth would gladly have done without—she was a woman of great common sense, and even kindness. In the months they had worked side by side, Elizabeth had grown to respect her, though she doubted they would ever become close friends. Mrs. Jorgensen might keep her granddaughters away from the Barclay children out of fear of disease, but in this she was not unlike the others in the valley, and Elizabeth could forgive her that. Mrs. Jorgensen had agreed to take on the Nelsons as nothing more than would-be homeowners down on their luck. Elizabeth could not believe she would close her heart to Rosa if she knew what John had done.

The story spilled from her as they set the table for breakfast. Mrs. Jorgensen drew herself up, her mouth in a hard line, as Elizabeth described Rosa's bruises, her split lip, and how the children had played on as if nothing out of the ordinary had befallen their mother. At Elizabeth's mention of Carlos, Mrs. Jorgensen pressed, "What did he say when you told him you had found his sister on the mesa?"

"You found Rosa where?"

Elizabeth spun around to discover Lars standing behind her in the kitchen doorway, his face a thundercloud. For a moment she glimpsed the man he might have been in his younger years, the man who drank, the man who had frightened the love of his life into marriage with a man she thought safer.

"At the Salto Canyon," said Mrs. Jorgensen when Elizabeth did not speak. "On the mesa. You know the place."

Without a word, Lars stormed back outside. "Go with him," barked Mrs. Jorgensen, pushing Elizabeth toward the door.

Elizabeth snatched off her apron and pursued him, bumping into Oscar Jorgensen on the way out the door, brushing past Henry as she ran. She reached the garage only moments after Lars, but he ignored her pleas to wait and drove off in a cloud of gravel and dust.

Naturally Oscar and the other men couldn't help speculating over the source of Lars's fury. As she set platters of food on the table, Elizabeth overheard Mrs. Jorgensen briefly inform Oscar. Even her discreet words set in motion rounds of conjecture about what Lars intended to do to John Barclay, until Mrs. Jorgensen finally insisted that they not speak of the matter at the table, in a voice that strongly encouraged them not to speak of it elsewhere, either. The men fell into a subdued silence, and for the rest of the meal, Mrs. Jorgensen kept a watchful eye on the window.

The men returned to their work, with still no sign of Lars. As they cleared away the dishes and cleaned the kitchen, Mary Katherine questioned Elizabeth so precisely on her encounter with Rosa that revealing each new detail made Elizabeth feel as if she were gossiping rather than seeking help for a woman in trouble. "Why does everyone seem more concerned with where I found Rosa than with what John did to her?" Elizabeth exclaimed.

"The Salto Canyon takes its name from a Spanish word meaning 'the jumping-off place,'" said Mary Katherine. "It was called that because of the many people who fell to their deaths there, often by accident while crossing the mesa in darkness or heavy fog, but sometimes not. Rosa's mother took her own life in the exact spot where you say you found Rosa with the children."

Elizabeth felt a sudden swell of fear. "Do you think Rosa intends—"

"I don't know, but Lars—" Mary Katherine shook her head, pressing her lips together tightly. "I'm sure that's what he fears."

Filled with a sickening dread, Elizabeth imagined Rosa poised on the edge of the canyon, frozen in space for one dreadful moment before leaning forward to embrace the air and plunging to the rocks below. She pressed a trembling hand to her mouth and grasped the counter behind her for support. She never should have left Rosa alone on the mesa.

She worked through the morning anxiously awaiting Lars's return. It was nearly lunchtime when at last she heard the sound of the car pulling up to the garage. At once, she and Mary Katherine dropped their gardening tools and ran to meet him, passing Mrs. Jorgensen on the way. Lars took one look at their worried faces and answered their unspoken question. "She's all right," he said, dropping his gaze and heading out to meet the other men in the orchard.

"Lars." Mrs. Jorgensen caught him by the arm in passing. "What happened?"

"I found her at the house. She didn't want me to see her, but when I told her I wouldn't leave without making sure she was safe, she let me in. Barclay won't hurt her again, not if he values his life."

"Lars," Mrs. Jorgensen said, a faint tremor in her voice. "What did you do?"

Without a word, Lars patted his mother's hand before freeing himself from her grasp and continuing on his way.

"He didn't hurt John," said Mary Katherine, as if thinking aloud, as if trying to persuade herself. "John would have put up a fight, and Lars doesn't have a mark on him."

"Mrs. Jorgensen, I'm so sorry I brought this trouble on your family," said Elizabeth. "I came to you because I didn't know what else to do. I never meant for Lars to threaten John Barclay."

"We don't know if that's what he did," said Mrs. Jorgensen, resigned. "You did the right thing, Elizabeth. Rosa needed help, and you may be the only person in the Arboles Valley who is not too busy avoiding her to notice."

"Lars doesn't avoid her," corrected Mary Katherine, her eyes fixed on him as he strode off into the distance.

Mrs. Jorgensen gave her a quick, inscrutable glance before returning her gaze to her elder son. "It's tempting to turn away when a woman is mistreated by her husband, to call it a private family matter and hope it cures itself. That's the last thing we should do. If we don't stand together as women against such behavior, it will worsen and spread. If one man hits his wife and gets away with it, it will become more tolerable for other men to do the same. If one woman accepts a beating, other women will believe they should bear it as well."

"Rosa never should have married John," said Mary Katherine.

"Well, she did, and that's that," said Mrs. Jorgensen sharply. "We have work to do, so get back to it. That garden won't weed itself."

She strode off briskly to the house, the screen door slamming shut behind her. Elizabeth trailed after Mary Katherine back to the garden, wondering what Lars had done at the Barclay farm. How could he be so sure that John would not harm Rosa again? How could any of them be sure she was safe?

"You said that Rosa's mother took her own life," said Elizabeth after she and Mary Katherine had pulled weeds in silence for several minutes. "Do you know why?"

Mary Katherine stuck her trowel into the earth and sat back on her heels. "Why does anyone do such a dreadful thing? No one knows for certain—or if they do, they aren't telling. I suppose Rosa or Carlos might know, but who can ask them?" She shook her head and nimbly plucked a few spindly weeds from between the lush carrot tops. "Some people say Mrs. Diaz was never right in the mind after her first grandchild took sick and died, but I think it goes back even further than that, to the time when her parents sold the farm to Mother Jorgensen's grandparents. To go from owning the land to working it as hired hands for another family must have turned them bitter. I often wonder why they stayed instead of moving on, starting new somewhere else."

"Perhaps they loved the land too much to leave it," said Elizabeth. "Perhaps they thought one day they could earn back the farm they had lost, or if they couldn't do that, perhaps their children might."

"It could be something like that, I suppose. At any rate, when Rosa and Lars fell in love, Mother Jorgensen and Lars's father didn't object. Lars was still drinking then and I think they thought marriage would settle him down.

It was Rosa's parents who were absolutely dead set against it. Rosa might have disobeyed them if not for Lars's drinking. Oscar told me once that she had agreed to marry Lars on the condition that he get sober, and that he tried, and had nearly succeeded even before Prohibition."

"Then why on earth did she marry John?" asked Elizabeth.

"I don't know. Maybe Lars's sobriety didn't come soon enough, or maybe she didn't believe it would take. He sure fell off the wagon hard when Rosa married John. No one had seen that coming. When he finally learned of it, two days after the wedding, Lars got as drunk as a lord and nearly killed himself driving over to the Barclay farm to beg her to run off with him. She wouldn't even open the door, not that any sensible woman would have to a man in that condition. Oscar had to drag him away before John turned the shotgun on him. Lars was sick for weeks, but after that he never touched another drop of liquor. It was too late, though. He had already lost her."

When Mary Katherine's voice trailed off, Elizabeth could not bear to prompt her to continue. It was so unbearably sad for everyone involved, but why had Rosa married John instead of waiting for Lars, as she had promised? As for the tragic fate of Rosa's mother, surely she must have blamed herself for her daughter's grief, for the burdens of sorrow she was forced to bear. If she and her husband had not objected to Rosa's marriage to Lars, they could have lived out their lives in happiness, and the old resentments between the two families might have been forgiven.

❧

A few days later, when Lars announced that he would be going for the mail after lunch, his mother said sharply, "You were up at the Barclay farm for hours on Monday and you forgot to fetch the mail?"

"I guess it slipped my mind."

She turned to her younger son. "Don't you need him in the orchards today, so close to picking time?"

Oscar held his brother's gaze for a moment. "I've put Henry in charge of the orchards," he said shortly. "He can manage without Lars for a while."

Surprise lit Henry's expression, and Elizabeth immediately knew that this was the first he had heard of his promotion. Mrs. Jorgensen was clearly displeased, but she never undermined her son's authority in front of the hired hands, so she merely nodded. As soon as she could get Elizabeth alone, however, she instructed her to accompany Lars to the post office.

"Last time he drove off without me," Elizabeth pointed out, although she was more than willing to accept the errand. She was eager to see Rosa again, to see with her own eyes that she was all right.

"Be sure that he doesn't this time," said Mrs. Jorgensen. "Under no circumstances is my son to go to the Barclay farm alone."

This time, when Lars went to the garage after lunch, he discovered Elizabeth waiting for him in the car. He did not seem surprised to see her. "Don't you have work to do?"

She gave him her most disarming smile. "You know me. Always ready to shirk my duties."

He snorted, but took the driver's seat and started the car. If he did not openly object to her presence, he did not seem to welcome it, either. He drove along in studied silence, ignoring her, until they reached the end of the Barclays' driveway. "Thanks for speaking up for Rosa."

"Of course," said Elizabeth. "Anyone would have, if they had seen her."

"That's where you're wrong."

Elizabeth did not know what to say. The car rumbled to a stop just before the house. Marta and Lupita came running, their feet bare, their long, dark hair hanging loose and streaked with bronze from the sun. "Hi, Mr. Jorgensen," said Marta, reaching shyly for his hand.

"Hi, girls." He knelt down to hug them. "Where's your mother?"

"Inside," said Marta.

"Don't go in." Lupita took his other hand and tugged him toward the grass beneath the orange tree. "Play with us."

When he hesitated, Elizabeth smiled and waved him on. "Go ahead. I can get the mail."

With an uncertain smile, he let the girls lead him off to play. When Elizabeth knocked on the door, Rosa opened it quickly, as if she had been waiting. "I have some letters to mail," said Elizabeth, including hers in the pile from the Jorgensen family. "How are you?"

Rosa took the bundle. "Better, thank you." The bruises on her face had taken on a yellowish hue and a scab had formed on her split lip. As far as Elizabeth could tell, John had not added to her injuries. Whatever Lars had said or done, apparently it had stayed John's hand, for now.

Rosa disappeared into the kitchen and soon returned with a small bundle of mail for the Jorgensens and three letters for the Nelsons. "Thank you," said Elizabeth, tucking the Jorgensens' mail under her arm and leafing through her letters to read the return addresses—Aunt Eleanor, Elizabeth's parents, Henry's mother.

"I think you should know," said Rosa, "while I appreciate your concern, I would never take my own life, not while my children live and need me."

Startled by Rosa's directness, Elizabeth looked up from her letters and was even more surprised to discover Rosa smiling at her with something close to amusement. "And after that?" said Elizabeth, deciding to be equally direct. "What then?"

Rosa was silent for a moment. "I no longer believe all of my children are fated to die from this cursed illness. Some of them will be spared, and they will need me."

She spoke with so much certainty that Elizabeth believed her. "Children always need their mothers in some way, even after they are grown. I know I still depend upon my mother's advice—and my aunt's. That's why I write so many letters home."

Rosa's smile deepened, became more knowing. "You tell me this because you hope to convince me to wait until I am an old woman before I take my own life. I assure you, you—and Lars as well—you need not trouble yourselves."

"Then why were you there, in that place?"

"You mean where my mother died?"

Elizabeth nodded.

"Because I loved my mother deeply and I feel her presence most strongly there." Rosa glanced over her shoulder at the sound of Miguel murmuring in his sleep. "My mother often told me she considered the view of the canyon from the mesa to be the most beautiful place in the valley. She never would have despoiled it by committing such a terrible act there. I miss my mother very much, but I find consolation in knowing what happened to her must have been a terrible accident. She never would have taken her own life, I am sure of it."

Unwilling to dispel a belief that seemed to bring Rosa comfort, Elizabeth merely nodded.

"Would you like to see her photograph?" asked Rosa. "It was taken on her wedding day."

When Elizabeth agreed, Rosa took a brown leather album from a shelf beside the fireplace and turned to a page about halfway through the book. A young dark-haired woman, lovely but wearing only a hint of a smile, sat tall in a straight-backed wooden chair, her eyes fixed on the camera and bright with happiness. She wore a dark dress with a satin ribbon around the waist and a cascade of white lace around her neck and shoulders. Behind her stood a solemn, handsome man with a neatly trimmed mustache, broad-shouldered but only of medium height. His hand rested upon his bride's shoulder.

"You would not know it from this picture, but my father was a very cheerful man. He was almost always smiling." Rosa smiled herself, wistful, and turned a few more pages, flipping past newspaper articles, letters, and sketches pasted into the album. "Here is a picture you may enjoy more."

She held out the album, and Elizabeth gasped in recognition at a newer, sounder version of the cabin where she and Henry now lived. A little girl about four years old sat on the front porch steps wearing a lacy white dress, ankles together, hands clasped in her lap. On the grass to her left stood a couple in their midtwenties, but they were not the same couple from the wedding portrait. The man grasped the railing and had planted one foot on the bottom step; the woman stood with her hands straight at her sides. Behind them on the porch, an elderly man and woman sat on rocking chairs. The woman held a baby on her lap bundled in the quilt Elizabeth called the Road to Triumph Ranch.

"My grandparents, and my grandfather's parents," said Rosa, indicating the younger and older couples in turn. She pointed to the young girl on the porch steps. "My mother. She could not have been more than four years old when this portrait was made."

"Did your grandmother or great-grandmother make this quilt?" asked Elizabeth.

Shouts from outside interrupted Rosa's reply. She hurriedly set the album aside and ran for the door, Elizabeth close behind. In the shade of the orange trees, John had seized his daughters by the arms and was dragging them away from Lars, his face red with rage. "I told you to stay away from my family!"

"Settle down." Lars raised his palms in a gesture of calm, keeping pace with John as he wrestled the stumbling girls toward the house. "You're hurting the girls."

Rosa darted past Elizabeth and flung herself at her husband, fighting to tear his hands from her daughters. John shoved her hard with his shoulder and she fell to the ground. In an instant, Lars was beside her, helping her to her feet. Cursing, John shoved the girls ahead of him into the house and slammed the door.

When Lars began pursuit, Rosa seized him by the arm. "Don't," she begged. She placed her hands on his chest and refused to let him pass. "Stay away from him. He'll kill you."

Lars did not look as if he cared. "I won't let him hurt them."

"It's you he wants to hurt, not the girls. If you leave now—"

"Rosa, I've done everything you've ever asked of me but I won't—"

"Please, just go." Desperate, Rosa pushed him toward the car. "Go!"

She whirled around and ran back toward the adobe, but before she reached it, John tore open the door and stormed out, something hard and glinting in his grasp. Elizabeth cried out in alarm as he raised his hand to Lars, but suddenly he drew back his arm and flung the object at Lars's chest. Instinctively, Lars caught it. Clear liquid sloshed inside the glass bottle.

"I remember what you are even if she doesn't," John snarled. "Crawl back inside your bottle and leave us alone."

Rosa threw Lars one last, beseeching look as John clamped his hand around her arm and shoved her inside. Lars stood frozen in place, clutching the bottle in stunned disbelief. Elizabeth expected him to cast the liquor aside, but he turned the bottle over in his hands in a trembling caress, his eyes fixed on the closed door of Rosa's home.

"Lars, leave it." When he did not seem to hear her, Elizabeth hurried over and reached for the bottle. "Just leave it and let's go."

But Lars's grasp tightened on the bottle. "I can't just leave them. Not again."

"There's nothing you can do today." Elizabeth tried again to take the liquor from him. "We'll think of something. We'll come back. Leave the bottle and let's go."

Slowly Lars's gaze traveled from the adobe to the bottle. He stared hard at the label and took a step back, then tucked the bottle into his pocket.

Elizabeth wanted to snatch it from him and pour it out on the dusty ground, but Lars returned to the car so quickly she had to run to catch up with him. He started the engine barely before she had shut her door and drove off as if determined to put distance between himself and John before his anger overcame his better judgment. Suddenly he shifted in his seat, winced, then pulled the liquor bottle from his pocket and tossed it into the backseat.

"You should have thrown it from the car," said Elizabeth. "What good is that going to do you?"

Lars ignored her. When they reached the Jorgensen farm, she scrambled over the backseat for the bottle, but he grabbed it from her fingertips. He slipped it into his pocket as he strode off to the house.

She watched him go for a moment before collecting the mail she had scattered over the front seat, disappointed and afraid. It chilled her to think how precisely John Barclay had aimed his attack, stabbing at Lars's old wound, handing him the means with which he could destroy himself. Should Elizabeth tell Oscar his brother had a bottle on him? Should she warn Mrs. Jorgensen?

Mary Katherine had declared that her brother-in-law had lost so much because of his drinking that liquor had lost the power to tempt him anymore. How could she be so sure? Why keep the liquor if not to drink it?

How could Lars risk falling back into his old ways when Rosa needed him so desperately?

❧

Henry surprised Elizabeth by returning to the cabin early, before she had a chance to read the letters from home. "What's going on with Lars and the postmaster?" he asked, tugging off his boots.

She bent her head over the envelopes to conceal her disappointment. When the door had swung open, her first, foolish instinct was to think he had hurried home to see her, the way he had once hurried over to Elm Creek Manor as soon as his chores were done. Now he came home in a rush only to satisfy his curiosity, not because he couldn't bear another moment apart.

As she fixed him a cup of tea, she told him what she knew about Lars, John, and Rosa. Henry listened intently, prompting her with questions until the entire story had drained from her. Or at least, most of the story.

When she had finished, Henry disappeared outside and returned with firewood. With nightfall, the cool ocean mists had rolled in to blanket the valley. As Henry lit the fire, he said, "Why were you out riding that Sunday when you found Rosa on the mesa?"

After all that had happened, she had almost forgotten what had taken her past the mesa that day. "After everything I've told you, that's what you find most curious?"

"Don't evade the question. Why were you going for a ride by yourself?"

She leveled her gaze at him. "I've asked you many times to spend Sundays with me. I would have preferred to have your company that day, but as you've often said, you have to work."

"So why go alone?"

"It's better than staying here," she snapped, "shut inside the four walls of this cabin wondering what I did to displease my husband so much that he can't bear to spend a Sunday alone with me."

"That's not why I took on the extra work and you know it."

"Oh, yes, I know." She flung back the lid of the blue trunk, snatched up the Road to Triumph Ranch quilt, and sat down with her back to him. "You can't wait to earn enough money to put me on the fastest train east."

"What were you up to, Elizabeth?" He came around to face her and planted his hands on the arms of her chair, but she ignored him and threaded her needle with trembling fingers. "I know you weren't out sightseeing. What were you looking for—or whom?"

"Oh, for pity's sakes! Horses! I was looking for horses! Do you honestly believe I was riding around looking for some handsome farmer to cure me of my loneliness?"

He drew back as if she had struck him. "No. I thought you might be looking for Mae."

"Mae?" she echoed, incredulous. "Mae's long gone. Honestly, Henry."

He scrubbed a hand through his hair distractedly until it tumbled into his face. He looked suddenly like a hurt little boy. "Is it true that you're lonely?"

"Of course I am. How could I not be?"

"But we're together every day."

"You hardly speak to me. You never touch me. I feel farther apart from you than when I lived in Harrisburg and you lived at Elm Creek Manor."

"I never lived at Elm Creek Manor."

"You know what I mean. When I stayed at Elm Creek Manor, and you came to see me there."

"I know exactly what you mean." He lowered himself wearily into the other chair. "Why were you looking for horses?"

For a moment she considered refusing to tell him, to punish his silence with her own. Instead she told him about the deal she had struck at Safari World, her misguided search of the valley, her inevitable failure. She did not tell him that she had meant to put her earnings toward buying back her quilts from Mrs. Diegel, or that she had hoped to win over the wranglers so they might introduce her to their colleagues in the movie business. Henry would not approve of either venture.

"I should have known they didn't want prize horses when they dismissed my suggestion to buy Bergstrom Thoroughbreds," said Elizabeth. "That Bergstrom is the most beautiful horse in their stables. Why wouldn't they want another?"

"It's a good thing they didn't."

"Why not? Everyone stood to gain. My uncle would have made a good sale, Safari World would have acquired more of the finest horses anywhere, and I would have made a commission."

"I guess you didn't consider how those horses would have been delivered to their new owners."

Elizabeth did not understand his concern. "By train, of course."

"Yes, and your uncle Fred likely would have come with them. He never sells to any man he hasn't shaken hands with, and he never delivers horses to a new home sight unseen. Can you really imagine him putting his horses on a train in Pennsylvania and taking a chance they'll be well cared for on the trip west and that the new owners will be there to meet them in Los Angeles? Of course not. He'd accompany them every step of the way. And do you really think that after traveling all the way to Safari World, he wouldn't go the extra few miles to visit his niece?"

"I certainly hope he would."

"Do you? Do you really? Do you really want the folks back home to see how we live here?"

"I'm not ashamed of where we live," she retorted. "We've fixed up the cabin nicely considering our circumstances, and anyway, it's not forever. It's just until we can go home."

"We can't go home."

"Of course we can. We've had a setback, but we'll save up the money again, and then we'll go—but not until we can go together."

"You don't understand," said Henry, agitated. "We can't go home. There's nothing waiting for us back in Pennsylvania. Nothing."

Elizabeth stared as he bolted from his chair and began to pace the floor. "You're not making any sense. How can you say nothing's waiting for us? What about our families? What about Two Bears Farm? Your family will be overjoyed to have you back. You're the oldest son. Two Bears Farm is your rightful place."

"Not anymore it isn't." Henry halted and covered his eyes with his hand. "Elizabeth. How do you think I got the money to pay for Triumph Ranch?"

"You said . . ." She tried to remember exactly what he had told her. "You said it was your life savings."

"What is the life savings of a man who works the family farm?"

Then she understood.

At first she said nothing. Until she said the words aloud, she could pretend nothing had changed, that the haven of Two Bears Farm still awaited their homecoming. When the silence stretched on unbearably long, she murmured, "Your inheritance."

Henry nodded bleakly. "When I told my father I wanted to strike out on my own, he gave me my inheritance in cash. No part of Two Bears Farm belongs to me anymore. If I go back, it will be as Lars returned to the Jorgensen farm, as a hired hand working for my brothers."

"But—" Elizabeth's thoughts churned. "But when we told your parents about our plans to go to California, your father seemed as surprised as anyone."

"That was a show for my mother. I knew she would object to my leaving and I didn't want her to blame my father."

Elizabeth remembered how Mr. Nelson had studied the photographs of Triumph Ranch, how he had nodded approvingly and passed them on to his wife, how he had not voiced a single concern about his son's sudden announcement. At the time, she had assumed he trusted his son's judgment so implicitly that he had simply had no reason to believe Henry had not made a sound decision. Now she imagined the weeks of debate and argument and persuasion that must have preceded the purchase of the land. Henry would have worn his father down with the facts, with the logic of his plan, and his father would have given in out of love, because he could not bear to stand in the way of his son's dream.

"You see now why I can't go back," said Henry. "I can't face my father. I can't look him in the eye and tell him I lost everything he had given me. It wasn't my life savings I lost, but his."

Elizabeth could hardly bear to look at him, but she could not tear her gaze away. Before her eyes he had transformed into a man she did not know. "Why didn't you tell me?" In all the years she had known him, he had never lied to her. His integrity and truthfulness were the bedrock of her world. "You never intended to return to Pennsylvania, did you?"

"I can't. But you still can."

"How can you say that?" she cried. "How can I go without you? I love you."

"It's Elm Creek Manor you love," he shot back. "My family's farm was right next door, the closest you could come to owning the land you loved. Out of all the men who wanted to marry you, only I could offer you that."

Her heart cinched. At last she understood why he had bought Triumph Ranch, why he had not included her in his plans but made his decision before asking her to marry him. Unless he gave up Two Bears Farm, he would never know if she had married him for love or to be close to the land she longed for, the land that could never be hers. It had been a test, and she had passed, and yet he still doubted her.

She felt the blood rush into her head until it spun. He had lied to her. Like every other man she had known, he had created a world of lies and expected her to live in it without questioning the fragile threads of deception that bound it together. He was no different from her father. He had sold his birthright and would regret it for the rest of his days. He expected her to believe his words and not the evidence of her own senses. He desperately wanted her to pretend that the ground was not constantly shifting beneath their feet, because only then could he keep walking.

She sat with her fists knotted in the patched and faded quilt, angry, helpless, lost.

Then the truth whispered, gently but urgently. That was her father, not Henry. Henry had never pretended that what had befallen them was anything but the most brutal of disappointments. He had never blamed anyone but himself for the choices that had led them there. He had never asked her to pretend that everything was fine when their world was crumbling apart all around them.

As for his test of her love, she could not bring herself to fault him for that. If not for her flirting, her capricious teasing, her foolish attempts to make him jealous, he would never have questioned whether she loved him or only his land.

Henry broke the silence with words that threatened to strangle him. "You never should have married me. I thought if you went back, alone, you could start over. . . ."

His voice faltered and failed. Elizabeth set the Road to Triumph Ranch quilt aside and went to him.

"Henry." She touched his shoulder gently.

He trembled but did not pull away as she kissed his cheek, tracing the rough stubble of his beard with her lips. "I lied to you. I deceived you."

"I know. But it's going to be all right."

"All these weeks I've wanted to tell you the truth. I've taken you away from the home you love and given you nothing in return."

"That's not so." She pressed herself against him until Henry put his arms around her. "All I've ever wanted since I was fourteen was for you to love me. It wasn't Elm Creek Manor I wanted. It was you. It was always you. *You're* the home I love."

"Elizabeth—" Then he said nothing more, because he was kissing her. She tangled her fingers in his hair and returned his kisses fiercely, to make up for the long weeks when shame and secrets had kept them apart.

❧

1913

Isabel wrapped the warm tortillas in a towel and placed them in the basket on top of the layered tamales, still hot within their cornhusks. She smiled as she drew on her shawl, remembering her own pregnancies. After the queasiness of the first three months had passed, she had craved tortillas and tamales at all hours of the day and night. Isabel had never been able to equal her father's skill at making perfect tamales, but hers were still tasty and nourishing, just the thing to satisfy an expectant mother's appetite.

She did not know for certain whether Rosa's cravings mirrored her own, but they were alike in other ways, so Isabel took a chance that their tastes would be similar. If only she saw her daughter more frequently, she would know what aromas tempted her to eat her fill so her baby would grow strong, but Isabel had seen her daughter only infrequently since her marriage seven months before. The five miles separating the Barclay farm and Rosa's childhood home might as well have been one hundred. Isabel supposed Rosa's unexpected withdrawal from her mother was only natural. If it was not, Isabel would not know it. Her mother had died before she had even met Miguel. She had never been in Rosa's place, leaving behind a mother who missed her as she embarked on a new life as a married woman. With no similar experience of her own to consult, Isabel told herself Rosa was a young bride and wanted to devote herself to her new husband, rather than come to her mother's kitchen for a home-cooked meal and unsolicited advice. Once Rosa was settled and more confident about running her own household, she would visit more often, especially when she wanted help with the baby.

But what expectant mother, fiercely independent or not, would turn down tortillas and tamales, a Christmas delicacy in June? Isabel smiled to herself as she placed one last gift into her basket—a cradle quilt, pieced of the softest cottons she could find. As Isabel had sewn the Four-Patch blocks, she had imagined snuggling her tiny grandchild within its soft folds. In less than two months, God willing, she would. She prayed that Rosa would have an easy labor and a strong, healthy baby blessed with his mother's beauty and his grandfather's kindness and—Isabel searched for something of John's she hoped the child would inherit. His diligence. His cleverness. They had served John well and perhaps would do the same for her grandchild one day.

Isabel walked to the Barclay farm, enjoying the brilliant sunshine and clear skies of late June. The farmers were hard at work in their fields. Oranges, lemons, and apricots thrived in the orchards. Late summer and autumn would bring a bountiful harvest to the farmers of the Arboles Valley. Isabel, who would soon receive the richest blessing of all, did not envy any of them. She could almost wish even the Jorgensens well. By the end of summer, Rosa would surely be ready for an excursion. They could take the baby to the mesa and play with him on a blanket as they enjoyed the view of the canyon and marveled at his darling little feet, his sweet toothless smile, his strong and insistent grip when he curled his fist around their fingertips. Or perhaps the baby would be a little girl, with a tumble of dark curls and a sweet rosebud mouth. Isabel would tell her stories and when she was old enough, teach her to quilt and make tortillas and tamales the way her mother and grandmother had taught her.

At last her daughter's new home came into view, a snug adobe house on a hill with orange trees in the front yard. Acres of rye stretched to the hills lining the western edge of the Salto Canyon; John walked among the rows, inspecting the slender shafts that swayed in unison as the wind moved over them. Isabel broke into a smile, called out a greeting, and quickened her pace, careful not to jostle the basket.

John looked up and crossed the fields to the dirt road leading up to the house. He stood there and waited for her to come to him.

"How's Rosa?" Isabel asked, breathless from her five-mile walk.

He shrugged, removed his hat, and mopped his brow with his shirtsleeve. "Fine, I guess."

"Well, it won't be much longer now. I imagine you must be getting excited." Isabel was determined to be cheerful and pleasant to her son-in-law, although he did not make it easy. "Does Rosa say if she has a feeling whether the baby is a boy or a girl? Sometimes a mother knows."

John flicked his unsmiling gaze over her. "It's a girl."

Isabel had to laugh. "You sound very certain, but for the next two months, we can only guess." She indicated the basket. "I brought Rosa some things, some food and a gift for the baby. Is she resting?" As much as she longed to see her daughter and chat about their plans for the baby, if she had to, she would leave the basket in the kitchen rather than disturb Rosa's sleep.

John took the basket from her so unexpectedly that Isabel had no time to protest. "I'll see that she gets it."

"I don't want to interrupt your work." She reached for the basket, but to her astonishment, John held it out of reach. "Honestly, John, I'm happy to take it to her myself."

"She doesn't want any visitors."

"I'm not a visitor; I'm her mother."

"She doesn't want to see you."

Bewildered, at first Isabel could only stare at him. "I don't believe that," she said. "I came to help. I'll cook supper for the three of us and do some housekeeping so my daughter can rest. I know Rosa, and I know she'll try to keep the house in perfect order even though she should stay off her feet as much as she can in her condition."

"We don't need your help. My mother and sister came down from Oxnard to help out when the baby was born."

His flat statement staggered her. "What? The baby—"

"A girl. Born three weeks ago. Isabel calls her Marta."

"Three weeks ago! But—that's much too early. And you sent no word to us. Is she—is my granddaughter—"

"She's healthy. She's fine."

"And Rosa?"

His expression hardened. "She's fine, too. But she doesn't want to see you. If you come, I'm supposed to send you away."

Isabel felt tears gathering. "But why?"

"You know you two haven't always gotten along. Rosa needs peace and quiet. She doesn't need someone around always criticizing, always questioning what she does, who she marries."

Stung, Isabel said, "We didn't object to you. It was just so sudden. We didn't understand the reason for such haste."

"Haste? I courted Rosa for years. We were practically engaged for most of that time."

As his voice rose, Isabel suddenly wanted nothing more than to put the past behind them. "I've made many mistakes as a mother. I've done things I regret. But I have always loved my children and cared for them as best I knew how. Please don't keep me from seeing her. Please let me see my granddaughter."

"It's Rosa's choice, not mine," he said. "I'll tell her you came by."

Isabel walked home in a daze.

At home that night, Isabel wept in her husband's arms. "What did I do?" she asked over and over. "Why would Rosa turn me away?"

Miguel tried his best to console her, but Rosa's thoughtless cruelty distressed and bewildered him. "She'll change her mind," he said, patting Isabel on the shoulder. "It's new-mother nerves, that's all. When things settle down, she'll let us see the baby. You'll see."

Isabel desperately wanted to believe him.

She waited. Two months passed. She was in the Arboles Grocery picking out a chicken for Sunday dinner when from behind her, a voice she had ached to hear said, "Mami?"

She whirled around. "Rosa."

Rosa smiled at her, soft and wistful, yet guarded. Isabel rushed forward to embrace her and stopped short at the sight of the baby in her arms, nestled in a familiar quilt, the one she had made, the one she had left in the basket John had taken. "Oh, my darling." She began to weep for joy. "Oh, what a perfect angel."

Rosa beamed and passed baby Marta to Isabel. Isabel held her gently, soaking in every detail—her sweet baby scent, her long eyelashes, her tiny nails on tiny fingers. She was precious, and yet she was larger and more robust than Isabel had expected of a child born nearly two months early.

She closed her eyes and tried to shut out the sudden thoughts that crowded in. It did not matter. Nothing mattered except that she held her grandchild at last.

"Thank you for the quilt," said Rosa hesitantly. "And the tortillas and tamales. They were delicious."

Isabel held the baby close as if some small part of her feared Rosa would snatch her away. "I wanted to do so much more."

"I've missed you. I—I understand why you stayed away."

Did Rosa have any idea how Isabel had longed, every day, to rush to her door and pound upon it until someone let her in? "I stayed away because you asked me to. Otherwise I would have been there, every moment."

Rosa shook her head, bewildered. "I never asked you to stay away."

Isabel did not want to argue. All she wanted was to savor that moment, to rain kisses upon her granddaughter and be thankful that her daughter had apparently forgiven her for whatever offense Isabel had inadvertently committed. "Your husband passed along your message."

Rosa shook her head. "No. You must have misunderstood him. He wanted you to reconsider. He told me that you and Papi had disowned me when you heard about Marta, about when she was born. . . ."

Isabel stared at her daughter, at her perfectly healthy grandchild, and suddenly could no longer ignore the truth. "Marta was not born early."

Rosa flinched, and Isabel knew she had only at that moment realized her parents had not known her secret shame. She dropped her shopping basket and quickly took Marta back. "I have to go."

"Rosa—"

"Tell Papi I'm sorry."

Before Isabel could beg her to stay, Rosa fled from the store.

Sick at heart, Isabel went home and told Miguel what she had learned, that it was John Barclay who was keeping them apart. But that disturbing revelation was lost on Miguel, who heard only that his beloved, precious only daughter had been two months pregnant when she married. The daughter he had cherished had lied to them. She had disgraced herself and betrayed them all.

"What does it matter?" Isabel pleaded with him when he insisted that Rosa was dead to him, that Isabel must disown her as well. "They're married now. They have a beautiful child. Their sins are between them and God. If Rosa confesses to Him and atones for her sin, God will forgive her, and we must forgive her, too."

She said this for Miguel's sake. She wanted Rosa and Marta in her life. She would have forgiven her daughter even if God could not. But Miguel had believed in Rosa's perfection too long to recognize this flawed woman as the daughter he loved.

His heart had been shattered, and he could not endure a second betrayal. His wife and son must stand with him or he could not bear it. But even as Isabel promised to abandon her daughter to the fate she had willfully chosen, she resolved to break her promise as soon as she could. She could not forget John's sullen dishonesty that June afternoon when he turned her away.

She feared for her daughter.

Chapter Ten

1925

With freedom from upholding the pretense that they could return to Two Bears Farm came Henry's determination to make the cabin a suitable permanent home. He told Oscar he could work only half days on Sundays and instead spent his Sunday afternoons sealing cracks in the walls, repairing the sagging porch, and making the outhouse more tolerable. He spent his evenings in Elizabeth's company and his nights in her arms. It was in this way that Henry told her he would never again think of sending her back to Pennsylvania alone.

Elizabeth was so grateful to have her husband restored to her that the thought of Rosa's unhappiness became increasingly unbearable. She readily assented when Mrs. Jorgensen assigned her sole responsibility for the weekly mail run and other errands, thinking that this would allow her more opportunities to look in on the Barclay family. Yet Lars squandered no opportunity to express his feelings of betrayal. For a time he hardly spoke to her, although he always happened to be in the garage when she returned from the post office, and pressed her to report on what she had seen at the Barclay farm. John glared at her ever more mistrustfully, but he did not try to prevent her from seeing Rosa. Ana and Miguel continued their slow and inexorable decline into sickness. Marta and Lupita played together beneath the orange trees as they had always done, so that Elizabeth thought they were unaware of the turmoil in the family until she saw how they darted away at their father's approach. Once, when Elizabeth did not see John in the fields and knew he was not in the adobe, Marta confided that her parents had fought a few days before, after her father went to Oxnard one morning and came home with a new car.

Appalled that John could find money for a car when he had none to spare for a doctor for his children, Elizabeth concluded that his cruelty knew no limits. She kept a watchful eye out for any sign that he had resumed his violence toward his wife, but whenever she asked Rosa how she fared, Rosa forced a tight smile and said that every day with her children was a blessing. And yet she could not disguise her anger about the car. Whenever John left the fields early to go for a drive or raced up the gravel road to the house after an invented errand into town, her eyes narrowed and her mouth turned in disgust until Elizabeth thought she would rather endure another beating than the sight of that gleaming, elegant Chrysler roadster.

It seemed the entire Arboles Valley had an opinion about John Barclay's new car. Some of the men acknowledged that he was entitled to spend his money as he saw fit, but they were surprised he would put his money into something so impractical when his tractor and tiller were falling apart. A handful of foolish, ignorant women envied Rosa and considered befriending her so she might invite them for a ride, unaware that Rosa refused to set foot in the car. Most of the other women shared Mrs. Jorgensen's opinion that the roadster was a wasteful extravagance for a family with little money to spare.

Elizabeth agreed. "The only benefit of that car is that it takes John away from the farm for hours at a time," she declared upon returning from one trip to the post office to find Lars waiting for news. "These days he's more likely to be out tearing around the Arboles Valley than working in his fields."

Lars helped her gather up the mail from the passenger seat. "Is that so?"

"Even I can see that he's neglecting his crops. He'd much rather play with his new toy. I don't know how he expects to feed his family if he doesn't tend his farm. The post office can't possibly pay that much."

"Rosa will contrive something," said Lars, more confidently than Elizabeth thought the circumstances warranted. She was not surprised when later that evening, Henry told her that Lars had left the orchards early, telling no one where he was going and returning just in time for supper as tired and dirty as if he had worked the barley fields all day. Elizabeth assumed he had gone to help Rosa, but she worried about what John might do if he found Lars working his fields, caring for his family in his absence.

Henry told her not to worry. As the summer waned, he had worked every day side by side with Lars—except for those few hours Lars stole off alone—and Henry had seen nothing to suggest that Lars was doing anything more than helping a neighbor in need, or that he had resumed drinking. Elizabeth considered herself a reluctant expert on that subject and after watching Lars carefully for several weeks, she was forced to admit that her observations contradicted her instincts. She could not believe a drinking man would tuck a bottle into his pocket unless he intended to empty it later, but Lars had never once smelled of alcohol, nor did his hands shake, his words slur, or his eyes grow bloodshot. He had become neither more violent nor more charming. Without a doubt, he had become more secretive about his comings and goings, but she knew he had other reasons for that. Perhaps, contrary to all the wisdom on the subject she had gathered since childhood, he had been able to quit after that one bottle, after that first drink. Perhaps he was made of stronger stuff than her father and had thrown away the bottle untasted.

By mid-July, the apricot trees were heavy with fruit. Elizabeth admired the flourishing orchard with some alarm until Mary Katherine explained that Oscar always hired high school and college students on summer break to pick the fruit. Helping with the apricot harvest had become a summertime tradition for young people from miles around, who came to the Jorgensen farm to work, earn money for school, and socialize with friends.

On the first morning of the harvest, young men and women from throughout the Arboles Valley and from as far away as Oxnard descended upon the Jorgensen farm in droves. Elizabeth reveled in the festive atmosphere, looking on with pride as Henry organized the most recent arrivals into work teams. Even though he had never worked an apricot harvest before, Oscar trusted his judgment so much that he had placed Henry in charge of the seasonal workers. When Elizabeth reflected upon how well Henry had proven himself, and how he had come to be second only to Lars in authority on the farm, she could not help thinking of how he would have thrived as the owner of Triumph Ranch. As she watched her husband issuing instructions to the new employees, she allowed herself a moment of regret that they had not taken Mae up on her offer to use Peter's underworld contacts to track down the man who had swindled them. She quickly dismissed the notion. Justice would have to catch up with J. T. Simmons on its own. The Nelsons could not allow themselves to be drawn into any dealings with the sort of men Mae and Peter called friends.

Mary Katherine called Elizabeth over to help distribute buckets, hooks, and punch cards to the pickers while Oscar and Lars set up the cutting shed. Earlier, several yards from the first row of apricot trees, the hired hands had set tall, sturdy posts into holes that looked as if they had been dug years ago. The Jorgensen brothers made a roof by tying wooden trays about eight feet long and three feet wide to the top of the frame, then, in a similar fashion, they added a wall of trays along the southern side. By the look of it, Elizabeth guessed that the structure was meant only to provide shade, which was surely all the protection from the elements they needed. The clear, blue skies promised sunshine and warm breezes.

While the women worked in teams to arrange sawhorses in the cutting shed and place more of the long trays on top of them to make tables, the men dispersed into the orchard. They chose trees and set up their ladders, ten feet tall and broader at the base than the top. Using the hooks Mary Katherine and Elizabeth had given them, each picker attached a bucket to the top of his ladder and plucked all the ripe, sun-warmed fruit within reach. When a bucket was full, the picker climbed down the ladder and emptied it into a wooden box that Mary Katherine said could hold about forty pounds of plump apricots. When a box could hold no more, an empty box was stacked on top of it and filled in its turn. Up and down the ladders the pickers went, filling buckets and boxes, moving their ladders to find boughs still laden with fruit. They called out to one another as they worked, laughing and joking and grinning at the young women who watched.

The women did not have much time to stand idle and observe them. Not long after they finished setting up the makeshift tables in the cutting shed, Lars drove a flatbed wagon pulled by a team of horses through the rows of trees. Every few yards, the wagon halted and Henry and another regular hired hand jumped off to load the boxes into the back and to punch the pickers' cards to indicate how many boxes each had filled.

When Lars turned the wagon around, the women hurried back to their places in the cutting shed, four to a table. Mary Katherine waved Elizabeth over to her side, so Elizabeth joined her, unaware that she had committed a serious breach of etiquette. "What did I do?" she asked Mary Katherine as a few of the younger women let out cries of disappointment.

"You took the best place," remarked another woman at their table, who appeared to be in her early forties. "Newcomers are supposed to start out at the tables in the back and work their way closer to the orchard as they become more experienced."

"I'd be happy to move," said Elizabeth, reluctant to offend anyone who deserved the coveted spot.

"Don't be ridiculous," said Mary Katherine. "If I have to be on my feet all day, I ought to get a say in who stands next to me. Those girls pretend they want these places so they're closer to the truck, but the men unload the boxes and bring them to each table anyway, so what's the difference? They just want to have a better view of the pickers."

The last woman at their table, slightly younger than the first, shook her head. "Work slows down terribly when they do that. Me, I can cut apricots and admire a handsome young man without missing a beat."

The first woman grinned. "I'm going to tell your husband you said that."

"You go right ahead."

Henry interrupted the teasing by emptying a box of apricots onto their table. Working swiftly, the other three women took up their knives and began slicing fruit even as the apricots were still rolling down the tray. Elizabeth scrambled for an apricot, but the other women worked so rapidly that they had already finished stoning their second and third fruits while she fumbled with her knife for a secure grip.

"Here. Watch me," said Mary Katherine when she saw how Elizabeth struggled to slice the fruit cleanly with one swift stroke as the others did. She held the knife firmly in one hand and ran it around the fruit, separating the halves and removing the stone, which she tossed into a basket on the side of the table. Then she lay the halves split up in the center of the tray. "That's all there is to it."

Elizabeth nodded and tried again, and before long, the motions became more confident, smoother, though her pace still lagged well behind that of her companions. When they had cut all the apricots on their table, a hired hand named Marco brought them another box, which he stacked upon the empty box Henry had left beside their table. Elizabeth noticed that whenever the stack beside a table reached four empty boxes high, Marco collected the cutters' punch cards and added one mark to each. They were given credit for finishing the four boxes as a team, Elizabeth understood, since it was impossible for Marco to tell who at the table had cut which apricots.

Elizabeth realized that the complaints over her joining Mary Katherine's group had a second, more pragmatic bent. She quickened her pace, determined not to drag down her team and make Mary Katherine regret her decision.

When her table finished their first stack of four boxes, Marco put two punches each in the cards of the other two women. "What about Elizabeth?" asked Mary Katherine.

"I don't have a punch card," said Elizabeth. Since Henry and the other regular hired hands were receiving their usual pay for working on the farm, she had thought nothing of it. "Oscar didn't give me one."

"It must have been an oversight." Mary Katherine beckoned to Marco. "Give Elizabeth a punch card, please."

"I can't do that, ma'am," said Marco. "Your husband said only the harvest workers."

"That's nonsense. This is extra work on top of her regular duties, and she should receive extra pay."

Marco grimaced as if he wished he were somewhere else. "I guess you'll have to take it up with your husband, ma'am."

"I'll talk to him, all right," said Mary Katherine indignantly as Marco walked away.

"That's not necessary," said Elizabeth quickly. "It's not really extra work. I'd be working in the garden or cleaning the house if I weren't cutting apricots."

"You still have to help with the cooking," Mary Katherine countered. "This is extra work, and it's more taxing. I'm sure this is Mother Jorgensen's idea, not my husband's."

Unwilling to be drawn into a public discussion of Mrs. Jorgensen's faults, Elizabeth made no reply. On the opposite side of the table, the other two women pretended to be engrossed in their work, oblivious to the exchange.

When the entire surface of their table was covered with sliced apricots, they lifted the wooden tray and carried it from the shed to the truck, which would take the apricots to the sulfur house. Without pausing to rest, the other three women returned to the shed. Elizabeth hurried after them and helped place another long wooden tray on the sawhorses. In the few moments' wait before Marco brought them another box of apricots, Elizabeth flexed her wrists and fingers, worked the knots from her muscles, and ruefully realized she would probably be too sore to quilt that evening, and possibly for many evenings to come.

"Do we ever get a turn to pick the apricots?" she asked Mary Katherine, who smiled and told her she was lucky they didn't. The pickers had an even more difficult job, climbing up and down ladders and hauling forty-pound boxes of fruit in the hot sun. Just then, Lars pulled up in the wagon with another load of boxes. Elizabeth stifled a groan and picked up her knife.

All day long the pickers plucked sweet, ripe fruit from the trees for the women to cut, on and on, pausing only for lunch beneath the apricot trees. There the men and women mingled, friends greeted one another, laughing, talking, as if they were enjoying a picnic on a summer holiday. All too soon for Elizabeth they returned to work, chatting and gossiping about who had shared whose blanket in the shade and which young lady had brought what special treat in her lunch basket to share with which admirer. Since Elizabeth recognized few of the names that came up in conversation, she half listened to the talk while giving most of her attention to the task at hand. Although she had grown accustomed to the work, she still felt as if she had been thrown into the middle of an elaborate country dance in which everyone else knew the right places to spin and twirl and bow while all she could do was struggle to hear the caller over the band, doing the Charleston for all she was worth and hoping no one would notice.

By the third day, Elizabeth noted with some pride that no one who didn't know her would have been able to pick her out as the novice among the more accomplished cutters. While Oscar had not consented to grant her a punch card, the two beneficiaries of her labors must have felt either gratitude or pangs of conscience, for both brought Elizabeth gifts of food from their lunch baskets, delicacies like chicken pie and jars of preserves, which Elizabeth was clearly meant to take home rather than add to the picnic.

Elizabeth had assumed that the sulfur curing process was the last step in preserving the sliced apricots, but learned differently once the first trays were removed from the sulfur house. Local children joined the older harvest workers for the last task, carrying the large trays of cured apricots from the truck to a flat stretch of ground just south of the orchard. The trays were placed close together, with only enough space to walk single file between them, and left to dry in the sun for five or six days. During her infrequent breaks from cutting, Elizabeth enjoyed walking past the rows of plump, juicy cured apricots, breathing deeply of their sweet fragrance and admiring their bright orange hue. She admired the children, too, who were happy in their work but diligent, well aware of how essential they were to the success of the harvest. They reminded her of Henry and his siblings back at Two Bears

Farm and of the Bergstrom children at Elm Creek Manor. Their work had been play to them, and they had been proud to contribute to the success of the farm.

One morning, Elizabeth was surprised to discover Marta and Lupita among the children arranging trays in the sun. Lupita was still too little to hold her own among the older children, but Marta kept her younger sister close and praised her efforts. Marta's smile was brighter than Elizabeth had ever seen it. Lupita was so happy she sometimes could not resist jumping up and down instead of remembering to carry her edge of the tray.

When Elizabeth mentioned seeing the Barclay girls, Mary Katherine seemed even more surprised than Elizabeth had been. "They've never helped with the harvest before, not since the Rodriguezes left the farm," she said, adding with an impish grin, "Maybe they need the extra cash to pay for John's car."

At lunchtime, Elizabeth discovered the truth. As she spread out her blanket in the shade of the apricot trees and unpacked her basket, she looked up at the sound of laughter to find Rosa seated on a blanket in the sunshine several yards away. Miguel lay in her lap, smiling up at Marta, who tickled him under the chin with a leafy twig from an apricot tree while Lupita and Ana dug into their picnic basket. Marta and Lupita had spent so much time in the sun that their hair had turned from dark brown to rich bronze.

As Elizabeth watched, Lars emerged from the orchard and crossed the grassy clearing, hastily finger-combing his thinning blond hair before replacing his hat. Elizabeth expected him to continue toward the house, where Mrs. Jorgensen had lunch ready for the immediate family and a few of the farmhands who preferred their usual table to a picnic blanket, but instead he paused at Rosa's blanket. She smiled up at him, they exchanged a few words, and Lupita jumped up to tug on his hand. Lars settled down on their blanket and smiled as he thanked Rosa for the leg of fried chicken she handed him. He almost dropped it as Lupita scrambled onto his lap. Rosa laughed, and Lars smiled warmly back. They sat so close together that their shoulders nearly touched.

"I hope John Barclay doesn't show up."

Elizabeth started at Henry's voice, but quickly turned to smile at him as he sat down beside her on the blanket. "He wouldn't like it," Elizabeth acknowledged. "He's a jealous man. He must not know they're here. I can't believe he would stand for it."

Henry glanced at the couple for a moment before deliberately turning away. "Lars better be careful," he said, reaching into the basket. "She's a married woman. It doesn't look right."

Henry disliked gossip, and Elizabeth knew that would be his last word on the subject. Still, she could not help observing Lars, Rosa, and the children as they enjoyed their picnic—and worrying about what others would think. Gossip and rumor already swirled around Rosa because of her children's mysterious illness, and although Lars had become a respected member of the community, he did not have a spotless past. They seemed oblivious to anything but their own happiness, unaware of the curious glances of their neighbors. Elizabeth, who had considered herself an expert in the art of gossip once upon a time, could imagine all too well the nature of their speculations: Could anyone remember seeing either Rosa or Lars so content in anyone else's company? Weren't they being rather bold, for two people who had once been in love? Wasn't it interesting how well the children took to Lars, who was not exactly known for his playful temperament?

At that moment, as Marta threw back her head and laughed at something Lars had said, her long, sun-bronzed hair slipped free of the red ribbon that had held it away from her face. As Rosa retied it, Elizabeth was suddenly struck by the realization that Ana had spent nearly as much time in the sun as Marta and Lupita had that summer, watching them play, and yet her hair was still the same dark hue as her mother's. Miguel, too, had hair so dark brown it was almost black.

Unbidden, an image of John Barclay swam to the surface of Elizabeth's thoughts—shouting at Lars to stay away from his family, his blue eyes snapping with anger as he snatched his hat to mop his brow. His hair was nearly as dark as his wife's.

It could mean nothing, Elizabeth told herself, but she could not make herself believe it.

❧❧

As she had done every day of the apricot harvest, Elizabeth left the shed earlier than the other cutters so she could help Mrs. Jorgensen prepare a late supper for the family and finish other necessary tasks the work of the harvest had prevented Mrs. Jorgensen from completing. As she approached the yellow farmhouse, she spied an unfamiliar automobile parked near the carriage house. Three men, two in dark suits and one in a police officer's uniform, stood talking to Lars. They were too far away for Elizabeth to make out their words. Lars handed something wrapped in a handkerchief to one of the dark -suited men, they all shook hands, and the men climbed back into their automobile and drove away. Lars turned too suddenly for Elizabeth to pretend she had not been watching them. Annoyance clouded his face briefly, but he offered her a nod in greeting and strode back to the orchard without a word.

Elizabeth hurried on into the kitchen, where Mrs. Jorgensen set her to peeling a pile of carrots, freshly washed and glistening on the drainboard. What had Lars done to warrant a visit from the police? She could not believe he had committed any crime. It was not in his nature—unless he had begun drinking again, which was unbearable to contemplate. Had John Barclay, his only enemy, falsely accused him of something out of spite? Who were the other two men, and what had they taken from Lars?

Elizabeth took up her potato peeler and got to work. "Who were those men?" She knew Mrs. Jorgensen would have heard the unfamiliar car pull up to the carriage house.

"One is Tom Jeffries, the county sheriff," said Mrs. Jorgensen, quartering a chicken with a sharp cleaver. "The other two men aren't from around here. I don't know who they are. Why didn't you ask Lars?"

He had not given her a chance, but perhaps Mrs. Jorgensen knew that.

They worked in silence for several minutes. "May I ask you a question?" said Elizabeth, setting down her peeler.

Mrs. Jorgensen poured cooking oil into the frying pan and turned on the gas. "I suppose so."

"How many grandchildren do you have?"

For a moment, Mrs. Jorgensen froze, but she quickly resumed her work, and when she spoke, her voice was even. "What an odd sort of question. I think you know the answer."

"How many?"

Mrs. Jorgensen said nothing. The oil in the pan sizzled. She adjusted the gas and arranged chicken pieces in the pan with a pair of metal tongs, jerking her hand away as a spatter of oil touched skin. "Do you know anything about the language of flowers?" She quickly wiped the oil from the back of her wrist. "It's an old-fashioned belief that every flower has a symbolic meaning. Do you know what the apricot blossom is supposed to represent?"

Elizabeth shook her head, although Mrs. Jorgensen was not looking at her.

"Doubt. Perhaps in bygone days it meant doubt that a lover was true, but I think it could also act as a warning not to believe everything one sees, not to jump to conclusions based upon rumor and suspicion." Mrs. Jorgensen turned over the chicken pieces and set down the tongs. "The orchard was full of apricot blossoms in the spring. It was only a matter of time before they bore fruit. The soil may be rich, the rains ample and gentle, but if you sow mistrust, that is what you will harvest."

"John is dark-haired and Lars is fair," said Elizabeth. "Only two of Rosa's children have hair that lightens in the sun—Marta and Lupita. Rosa's children have been struck down by the same mysterious illness—all but two, Marta and Lupita. Mary Katherine once told me that one of John's sisters died in childhood after suffering an unknown sickness. Lars's siblings are healthy and strong."

At last Mrs. Jorgensen turned around. "I never took you for the sort to spread malicious rumors."

"I'm not," said Elizabeth. "I care about Rosa and her children. And Lars. I worry what John might do if he discovers he's been betrayed."

Mrs. Jorgensen gave a sharp laugh. "If *you* figured it out after knowing them for only a few short months, do you really believe John hasn't?"

Shocked into silence, Elizabeth could only stare at her. "Then why—"

"Why has John not accused Rosa of adultery? Why has he not cast her out?" Mrs. Jorgensen shook her head. "Only John knows that. I think he still loves her in his way—although love is perhaps the wrong word for it. He desires her. He covets her. He was willing to ignore what he did not want to see, because if he didn't, he would lose her."

"Lars and Rosa were lovers," said Elizabeth. It was not a question. "Rosa became pregnant with his child, but her parents had forbidden her to marry him. She was desperate to marry someone for the sake of her child and herself, and John was there—sober, a landowner, a man who claimed to love her."

"I don't know why liquor had such a hold on Lars," said Mrs. Jorgensen, an uncharacteristic ache in her voice. "My father was the same way. I'll never understand such men, not as long as I live. If only Lars had been able to stop drinking all those years ago, he and Rosa might have defied her parents and married. They might as well have. Rosa's obedience to her parents' demands gained her nothing. When Marta was born, two months earlier than expected but as perfect and healthy as only a full-term child could be, they knew Rosa had been pregnant when she married. The shame she had brought upon the family was so great they shunned her from that day forward."

"That's unfair," said Elizabeth. "What she did was wrong, but not unforgivable."

"Mr. and Mrs. Diaz were devout Catholics. Rosa had defied them, deceived them, and broken one of the strictest tenets of their religion. They believed she had committed a terrible sin. Worse yet, in their eyes, she was unrepentant. Her determination to conceal her sin was proof enough of that."

"But Marta was an innocent baby," Elizabeth protested. "Say what you will about how Rosa had disappointed her parents, how could the sight of their beautiful grandchild not move them to reconcile, regardless of the circumstances of her birth?"

The chicken began to smoke and spatter. With a start, Mrs. Jorgensen snatched the tongs and transferred the chicken from the frying pan to a serving platter. "I don't know that the Diazes ever saw Marta."

"What?"

"There was some talk around the valley that John had banned the Diazes from his property. Oscar heard it from their neighbor, a kindly soul who picked up their mail for years, until Rosa's father passed on, since they could no longer visit the post office."

"What did John have against Rosa's parents?" asked Elizabeth, bewildered. "They allowed him to marry Rosa, didn't they? And I myself have seen Carlos at the post office. He drove Henry and me there on our second day in the valley."

"Well, perhaps Carlos wasn't included in the ban. As for Rosa's parents, they believed John had relations with Rosa before their marriage, didn't they? From their point of view, he led their beloved daughter into sin. For all I know, it was their choice not to set foot on the Barclay farm, and John never banned them at all. I suppose that is a more plausible explanation."

Elizabeth did not agree. She could not believe the bright-eyed young bride gazing out warmly from the pages of Rosa's album could have transformed into a woman coldhearted enough to sever all ties with her only daughter. Rosa had spoken of her parents so lovingly, describing her father as a man who was always cheerful and laughing. She said she had grown up surrounded by love. If that was true, how could her mother and father have disowned her, even after she had broken their hearts?

"John must have suspected Marta was not his child," said Elizabeth.

"Suspected? I'm sure he knew it for an outright fact when she was born only seven months into their marriage. John Barclay is a man of many unadmirable qualities, but he is not stupid. He can count as well as the next man."

"Then he forgave Rosa. He forgave her, even when her parents did not."

"I don't know if he ever forgave her entirely. He certainly never forgave Lars. Accepting Marta as his own child was the price he had to pay to keep the woman he desired as his wife. He is a proud man, but I think he would have been content if Rosa had forgotten my son."

"But she didn't."

"For many years, I'm sure John was able to convince himself that she had. Everyone in the valley believed that Rosa chose sensibly when she married John instead of Lars, taking a sober man with a good living over a drunkard who had lost his farm. They have no reason to question her fidelity. If Rosa gave John reason, however, if he thought everyone knew she had betrayed him, exposed him to ridicule—then he would confront her. He would think he had no choice."

Mrs. Jorgensen's mouth was a grim line in the soft curves of her face, and Elizabeth knew they shared the same thought: Lupita's health, a blessing to be cherished by all who loved her, was to John nothing more than a sign that Rosa had betrayed him.

Mrs. Jorgensen gestured to the carrots. "Come. Let's finish. The others will be here soon."

Elizabeth picked up the peeler. "How long until John is forced to face the truth?"

"The other children took sick before the end of their fourth year," said Mrs. Jorgensen. "Lupita will be five in September."

For nearly a year, John Barclay had been watching his daughter, watching and waiting, torn between relief and rage. For nearly a year longer than should have been possible, Lupita had evaded the trap that had ensnared his other children. Lupita had thrived, her blossoming good health a mockery of John's willingness to overlook Rosa's sin and accept her as his wife. How much longer could he be expected to pretend, all for the sake of keeping an ungrateful wife who bore him only sickly children, who taunted him with the fruits of her infidelity?

But surely a man as suspicious as John Barclay would not have waited for Lupita's fifth year to doubt his wife's faithfulness. He must have been constantly vigilant all the years of their marriage, waiting for Rosa to betray him.

In the forge of suspicion and mistrust, any love he might have had for his wife had turned to jealous cruelty. It was little wonder the grieving, heartsick woman had turned to her steadfast first love for comfort and solace.

"You were wrong to say that John forgave Rosa when her parents did not." Mrs. Jorgensen broke off at the sound of approaching voices just outside the window. The men had come in for a supper that was not yet prepared for them. "Mrs. Diaz's heart softened at the end. A friend of mine spotted her lingering out of sight in the back of the church at Ana's christening, and I myself saw her leave flowers on the graves of her grandchildren. She even approached me at the Arboles Grocery once and asked after Lars. That was shortly before her death, only a year before Lupita was born. Mrs. Diaz's death was such a shock. I have always suspected that she took her own life out of shame and remorse for forbidding Rosa to marry Lars. She wanted to make amends, I'm sure of it. If she had only lived a little time longer—"

The kitchen door swung open and the men trooped in, tired but in good spirits. Oscar declared that he had never seen such a bountiful harvest. Henry kissed Elizabeth on his way to the table, but his grin faded at the sight of her troubled expression. She smiled and patted his arm to assure him he had no need to worry, that she would explain later, when they were alone.

She urgently wanted to ask him if he, too, thought it was unfathomable that a mother—especially one known as a devout Catholic—would take her own life when reconciliation with her estranged daughter seemed imminent.

❧

1917

Isabel watched the baptism from the vestibule of the church, shrouded in a dark shawl and veil. She crossed herself as the priest poured water over her newborn granddaughter's head, and again when he anointed her with oil. Her heart ached to see the emptiness in Rosa's eyes on a day that would have been joyous had it not come so soon after the death of her son.

As the ceremony ended, Isabel ducked into a shadowy alcove. Her disguise would not fool four-year-old Marta, who would surely call out a happy greeting and scamper down the aisle of the church to hug her grandmother the moment she spotted her. Hugs and kisses would have to wait until the next time Rosa could slip away from home and bring the children to meet Isabel on the mesa, a secluded spot with a breathtaking view of the canyon. Every week at the appointed time, Isabel went and waited, hoping Rosa would come. In recent months, the sudden illness and sudden death of Rosa's son and the last weeks of her pregnancy had kept her at home, and Isabel had walked home from the mesa discouraged and lonely. She resented her son-in-law for keeping her away from Rosa, but contrary to her heart's yearnings, she could not help blaming Rosa, as well. Why did Rosa not stand up to her husband? She had not learned such meek acceptance in her parents' house. Was it love that made Rosa so determined to please him?

Somehow Isabel could not believe it was so.

She watched, hidden in the alcove, as the family departed. John passed by first, escorting his mother, who beamed with proud satisfaction. She ought to be happy, that other grandmother, Isabel thought ungraciously. She possessed everything Isabel desired and because it came so easily to her, she could not have any sense of its true worth.

Marta trailed behind her, holding on to John's sister's hand, questioning her unhappily about something Isabel could not discern. Last of all came Rosa, carrying baby Ana. Isabel choked back a sob, longing to stretch out her arms to embrace her precious granddaughters. It was too painful to see them so close and not be able to speak to them, to hold them. She should not have come.

Suddenly, just as Rosa tugged a quilt over the baby's head and stepped from the warmth of the church into the cold November rain outside, a flash of white fell to the tile floor over her shoulder, like a dove descending.

Isabel waited until the door closed and the church grew still before stepping from her hiding place. She stooped over to pick up the fallen object, her fingers closing around soft satin. Ana's cap, trimmed in lace to match her baptismal gown. A gift from Rosa, an apology for all she had denied Isabel that day.

Years ago, Isabel would have been infuriated by the very idea that a baby's cap could compensate for the insult she had been forced to endure that morning, and so many other mornings since John had banished Isabel from his home. She never should have had to lurk in the back of the church at her granddaughter's baptism instead of sitting proudly in the first pew, as was a grandmother's right. But that was long ago. The years of waiting and hoping had drained her anger from her. Now all the spaces of her heart had room for was longing, and a fervent hope that someday John's resentment would abate and Isabel would no longer have to meet her daughter and grandchildren in secret.

She clutched the soft white satin cap and prayed.

Chapter Eleven

1925

After the apricot harvest, Elizabeth spent the summer evenings on the cabin's newly mended front porch, working on the quilts she had found in the old steamer trunk. Henry sat beside her, reading aloud from the newspaper or letters from home while she sewed. They sat together, talking quietly, content in each other's company, as the sun set behind the Santa Monica Mountains. Elizabeth imagined the fading daylight offering the valley below one last caress as it slipped behind the western hills, pulling a veil of darkness over the Norwegian Grade, then the Jorgensen farm, then the adobe where Rosa lived with her children, then Safari World, and last of all, the Grand Union Hotel. Then the sun disappeared behind the mountain range, and Elizabeth and Henry watched the stars appear, talking about the next day's work or reminiscing about summers in Pennsylvania—swimming in Elm Creek, riding the wooded trails that crisscrossed the valley, savoring the hint of autumn that came only at night, a gentle, wistful warning that summer could not endure forever.

Henry usually went to bed soon after the moon rose, and Elizabeth always joined him. If she could not sleep, she would leave the bed without disturbing her husband, light a lamp in the front room, and stay up to work on the quilts, mending torn seams, patching holes, replacing worn pieces with sturdy scraps, adding soft cotton batting to the places where the quilt had worn thin. When the top was whole and sound again, she restored the missing quilting stitches that had held top, batting, and lining together, following the tiny needle pricks left behind from the original threads. Some had broken over time; others Elizabeth had been forced to pick out in the act of mending. She followed her predecessor's patterns as closely as possible, even to the length of her stitches, so that her handiwork would blend in harmoniously with what had gone before.

She put her last stitch into the Road to Triumph Ranch quilt at the end of August, and when she finished, the hexagons no longer resembled wagon wheels that had broken and splintered on a hard road. They might roll on steadily for miles into the distance, even into an uncertain future.

Elizabeth washed the quilt, hung it to dry in a freshening breeze, and turned her attention to the Arboles Valley Star. On closer inspection, she became even more certain that it had rarely been used, or perhaps not at all. The binding around the edges, one of the first places signs of wear appeared on a quilt, had not rubbed to a threadbare thinness from use. She found no holes or tears aside from two places where a mouse had nibbled through the lining and removed some soft batting to make a nest elsewhere. What she had mistaken for stains was merely dust that came out in the first wash. The creases that she had attributed to the uneven shrinkage of the fabric and batting through many washings had disappeared during the months that the quilt had been draped over their bed instead of folded and crushed at the bottom of the steamer trunk. Curious, Elizabeth picked out a seam at the tip of one star and discovered that the fabric was the same shade from edge to edge. If the fabric had faded after the quilt was complete, the edges hidden within the seam would have been darker than the part in the center, which had been exposed to sunlight. The fading of the fabric must have occurred before the quiltmaker pieced her blocks, perhaps when the calico was still part of a favorite dress, worn by a child who played in the sunshine. As far as Elizabeth could tell, all of the damage to the quilt could have occurred while it was stored within the trunk.

Compared with the extensive restoration the older, homespun-and-wool quilt had required, repairing the Arboles Valley Star was a simple matter. Elizabeth replaced the missing batting and patched the holes. She replaced the stitches she had picked out to check for uneven fading of the fabric. Last of all, she studied an embroidered satin patch trimmed in lace appliquéd on the back of the quilt. Within the circle of rosebuds, the initials R.D. and L.J. were intertwined. There was no question in Elizabeth's mind whose names those letters represented, or who had made the quilt, or why.

She thought of her own floral Double Wedding Ring quilt, beautifully and lovingly made by the women of her family, and lost to her forever. She thought more wistfully of the Chimneys and Cornerstones quilt, sturdy and cheerful, delighting guests at the Grand Union Hotel. She could do without the quilts, as she certainly must learn to do, but what a comfort it would be to have them with her now, offering with their soft and gentle warmth the memory of love and the promise of happiness.

With one last, fond caress, she folded the quilts she had restored with such care, the quilts that were not truly hers. They had given her purpose and distraction in her loneliness, comfort and warmth in her need. Now it was time to pass them along to their rightful owner, whose need was so much greater.

❧

The next time Elizabeth made the mail run, on a cool, overcast day when the air tasted of the metallic tang of rain, she took the quilts with her, folded carefully and stacked on the backseat of Lars's car. When she arrived at the Barclay farm, no one was outside, neither in the fields nor beneath the orange trees, where she had grown accustomed to the sight of Marta and Lupita playing while Ana watched. A glance into the barn told her that John had gone off somewhere in the roadster. Suddenly anxious, she hurried to the adobe and knocked on the door, but her relief when Rosa answered was quickly tempered by concern. The haunted despair had returned to the mother's dark eyes, and her mouth was a tight knot of worry and pain.

Elizabeth's first thoughts were of the children. "What's wrong?"

"Nothing." Rosa quickly amended, "Nothing new. Nothing that has not been wrong for a very long time." She opened the door wider and beckoned Elizabeth inside. "Please come in while I get your letters."

Marta and Lupita played with dolls on the floor in the center of the room. They glanced up warily when she entered, but after recognizing her, they returned to their game. She did not see the other two children and assumed they were in bed. Days when they felt strong enough to get out of bed to play had become less frequent.

Rosa returned from the kitchen with a bundle of mail. Elizabeth took it, thanked her, and said, "I found something in the cabin that belongs to you."

While Rosa looked on, perplexed, Elizabeth took the mail to the car and returned with the quilts. She set the Arboles Valley Star quilt on the sofa and unfolded the Road to Triumph Ranch. Rosa's eyes widened as she reached out to take the bottom corners of the quilt, lifting them so the quilt unfurled between their hands. *"Dios mio,"* she breathed.

"It is your great-grandmother's, isn't it?" said Elizabeth. "I recognized it from the photograph you showed me."

"Without a doubt, it is hers." Rosa's gaze ran over the quilt as if she were drinking in the memories stitched into the cloth. "It is just as I remember it."

"Almost but not exactly," said Elizabeth apologetically. "It needed some mending. I matched the fabric as best as I could when I replaced worn pieces."

Rosa smiled. "Then it is even lovelier than I remember." She sat down in a rocking chair, draped the quilt across her lap, and ran her hand over it. "I remember my mother cuddling me in this quilt when I was a little girl no bigger than Lupita. My great-grandmother made it when she was a young bride-to-be in Texas. Her parents had arranged for her to marry my great-grandfather through a cousin who lived in Los Angeles. The first time she saw him was the day he came to San Antonio to bring her back to El Rancho Triunfo."

"Triumph Ranch," said Elizabeth.

"Yes, and for many years the name rang true. They raised barley and rye. One hundred head of cattle grazed where the sheep pasture and the apricot orchard stand today. But my family lost everything in a terrible drought, the worst ever to strike the Arboles Valley. Every farm in the valley suffered. Some families sold their land after the first summer without rain, but by the time my great-grandparents decided to put El Rancho Triunfo up for sale the following year, there were no buyers. My great-grandparents sold all the cattle to slaughterhouses rather than let them starve. They were thankful and relieved when Mrs. Jorgensen's grandfather bought the ranch and permitted them to remain on the land in exchange for their labor. The rains fell two months later. My great-grandparents never forgave themselves for not holding out a little while longer, for giving up too soon and accepting less than the land was truly worth."

"They never forgave the Jorgensens, either, or so I've heard."

"That is also true." Rosa glanced at the other quilt, almost forgotten on the sofa. Elizabeth unfolded it and held it up high by the corners so that only the bottom edge touched the floor. Rosa admired it politely, but she soon returned her gaze to her great-grandmother's quilt.

"I call this quilt the Arboles Valley Star," said Elizabeth, surprised by Rosa's reaction. She folded the quilt in half and draped it over the sofa. "I found it with your great-grandmother's. Don't you recognize it?"

"I've never seen it before," said Rosa. "I suppose I could look through the album and see if it appears in any of my family's photographs, but I've looked at them so many times. I think I would have recognized this quilt if it were in any of them. It seems too new for my great-grandmother's handiwork."

"I thought you had made it."

"Me?" Rosa shook her head. "Why would you think that?"

"Because of this."

Elizabeth turned the quilt over and showed Rosa the embroidered monogram on the square of lace-trimmed satin appliquéd to the back, the intertwined initials surrounded by a wreath of rosebuds. As if in a dream, Rosa touched the letters with her fingertips and pressed her other hand to her mouth. Her eyes widened in astonishment and, Elizabeth thought, confusion and anguish.

"What is it?" Elizabeth prompted her. "Do you remember the quilt now?"

"No." Rosa shook her head. "I've never seen this quilt, but I—I do know this embroidery. This is my mother's work. She made these stitches. And this satin and lace. It came from Ana's baptismal cap. But—why? And when?" Rosa swiftly turned the quilt over and studied the pieced stars, running her hands over the patches. Her long, slender fingers came to rest on a piece of ivory sateen. "This was from her wedding gown. I know it. And this—" She touched a triangle of pink floral calico. "This was from the dress Marta wore on her first day of school. But how did my mother come to have it? I don't understand." She threw Elizabeth a beseeching look. "Where did you find this quilt?"

"Both quilts were in an old steamer trunk in the cabin," said Elizabeth. "On the Jorgensen farm, where Henry and I live. Where your family once lived. I assumed your grandmother had forgotten the older quilt there when they moved out, but as for the newer—"

"Oh, no, no. They left nothing behind. The homespun-and-wool quilt was in my mother's home all my life. It never left her bed. But this star quilt . . ." Rosa looked from one quilt to the other in bewilderment. "My mother must have taken the quilts to the cabin and left them there. But I don't understand—" Suddenly Rosa grew very still. "She wanted me to have them. And she could not bring them to me here."

"Why not?"

"My husband would not allow my parents on his property, not even to visit their grandchildren. When I wanted to see my mother, we had to meet on the mesa. Once a week, when John went to pick up the mail from the train station, I would take the children to see her. You know the place."

"Rosa," said Elizabeth, gripped by a sudden fear. "The day your mother died—were you supposed to meet her on the mesa?"

"I was, but she didn't know that I could not come. A few days before, John had returned home with the mail and found me and the children gone. I—I had to tell him where we had been." A shadow of remembered pain crossed her features for a moment, and Elizabeth could imagine how she had been compelled to confess. "After that, he varied his schedule so I never knew when he would be gone or how soon he would return. I was never able to meet my mother again." She clutched her mother's quilt, her gaze far away. "I can't help but think of her waiting for me, waiting and waiting, every week without fail, hoping I would come. I cannot help but imagine her despair when I never appeared. Perhaps she thought she would never see her grandchildren again. Perhaps—perhaps I have been fooling myself all these years, telling myself her death was an accident."

Elizabeth's breath caught in her throat. "Perhaps you were."

Rosa looked up sharply and read the fear written on Elizabeth's face. "No. No. I know what you're thinking. I can't believe it."

But Elizabeth saw the doubt in her eyes. John had known that Rosa's mother waited for her daughter alone on the mesa on the days he traveled to the train station for the mail.

"Mami?" said Lupita fearfully.

With a start, Rosa turned to her daughters. "Marta, go and see if Miguel and Ana are still sleeping, would you, please?" she said. "Take Lupita with you."

Reluctantly, Marta did as she was told. She had barely left the room when outside, the roadster roared up the gravel road and braked hard. With preternatural calm, Rosa folded her mother's quilt, set it aside, and stood. She was on her feet when the door burst open and John stormed in.

"Where is he?" John's sharp gaze scanned the room, alighting on Elizabeth for a moment before moving on. "I know he's here."

"No one else is here," said Rosa. "Only Elizabeth."

John shoved Rosa aside and strode into the kitchen. Elizabeth heard the table overturn, glass shatter. John appeared in the doorway, his eyes ablaze with fury. "I saw his car."

"I drove it," said Elizabeth quickly. "I work for the Jorgensens."

"Did you come to help my dear wife plan the birthday party?" John addressed Elizabeth in a voice of acid. "Lupita turns five next week, did you know that?"

"I just came for the mail," said Elizabeth steadily.

John threw her a look of contempt and strode off toward the children's room in the back of the adobe. Rosa drew in a shaky breath at the sound of a child's cry and gripped the back of the rocking chair so hard her knuckles turned white. Elizabeth put her arm around Rosa's shoulders and was startled when Rosa flinched in pain. She knew at once that John had not stopped hitting his wife; he had only become more discreet about where he left bruises.

Without warning John returned. Rosa drew back but not quickly enough to evade his grasp. He seized her by the shoulders and shook her. "Where is he?"

"I don't know," Rosa choked out. "He's not here."

Elizabeth tried to put herself between John and Rosa, but he knocked her to the floor. Instinctively Elizabeth grabbed for the rocking chair as she fell, but her fingers slipped and her head struck the floor. Dazed, she tried to sit up, her head ringing with the sound of a fist striking flesh and Rosa crying out in pain. Then the door slammed, the roadster roared to life, and, but for Rosa's gasps as she fought for breath, silence.

"Are you all right?" said Elizabeth as she clutched the arm of the rocking chair and shakily pulled herself to her feet.

Rosa's face was a mess of tears and blood, but she nodded. "The children." She sped to the back of the adobe and returned moments later to report that they were unharmed. "John's going after Lars. I'm sure of it."

"You shouldn't be here when he returns," said Elizabeth. "Gather the children and come with me. You can stay in the cabin with me and Henry."

Rosa shook her head. "It's not safe. We'll have to pass John on the way."

"Then take a room at the Grand Union Hotel. Carlos will look after you."

"No," said Rosa, suddenly calm. "I know a better place. A place my husband fears."

The canyon. Elizabeth nodded. "Then take warm clothes and food. It looks like rain."

"I have to warn Lars. John keeps a pistol in the car."

"I'll warn Lars." Elizabeth hurried to the door, fully aware that John had a head start and a faster car. "Pack quickly. Take only what you need. John might double back at any time."

Rosa did not need the warning. Before the door closed behind her, Elizabeth heard Rosa call to Marta and Lupita to wake the other children.

❦

The overcast sky had turned steel gray, mottled with charcoal. As Elizabeth turned onto the main road back to the Jorgensen farm, a steady, cold drizzle began to fall, but she dared not slow the car. She tried to remember what work assignments Oscar had given the men at breakfast that morning. If Lars was alone in the garage, waiting impatiently for Elizabeth's return as he usually did after her trips to the post office, he would have no chance. John would come upon him and kill him before Lars realized he was there. If Lars was in the pasture looking after the sheep or working in the orchard, he might see the roadster coming and have time to hide—but he would not know that he needed to hide.

Suddenly Elizabeth remembered. Lars was delivering the dried apricots to the packing house in Camarillo that day and was not expected back until close to suppertime. At that moment, he was probably driving the horse and wagon over the Norwegian Grade. Her relief at the realization that John would not cut down Lars in the garage was short-lived. John might lie in wait until Lars returned—or harm someone else when the object of his rage failed to appear.

She gunned the engine and raced for home.

She arrived at the Jorgensen farm in a driving rain stirred by strong gusts of wind from the west. The roadster was parked close to the house at the end of two rivers of mud the tires had cut through the front garden. John stood a few yards from the front door, brandishing a pistol and shouting up at the second-floor windows. Someone inside had drawn the curtains.

John spun around at the sound of her approaching car and leveled the pistol at Elizabeth. She slammed on the brake and flung herself down upon the seat just as the shot rang out. "Send him out," she heard John yell. "Send him out now or her blood is on his hands."

Elizabeth crouched out of sight, threw the car into reverse, and spun around, driving back the way she had come. Only when she reached the main road out of range of his pistol did she dare risk a glance over the dashboard. John had pursued her partway down the road, but he had given up. He shouted something unintelligible at her before turning and striding back to the house.

Her hands shook so badly she almost could not shut off the engine. Her thoughts raced. Mrs. Jorgensen was likely inside with Mary Katherine and the girls, but where were the men? Where was Henry? Surely Mrs. Jorgensen had called the police, but they were miles away, too far to help them now. All she could do was pray that they arrived in time to stop John before he killed someone—and if that failed, that Rosa would have enough time to get away with the children.

She would have to make sure Rosa had enough time.

Swallowing hard, she sat up, started the engine, and set the car in motion, creeping forward until she reached the driveway's narrowest point, thanking God for the downpour that drowned out the sound of the automobile. Slowly, so that she would not attract the attention of the madman shouting at the yellow farmhouse, she turned the wheel and maneuvered the car until it blocked access to the road. She shut down the engine again and crouched low in her seat, her gaze fixed on John, listening for sirens that did not come.

She almost screamed when the car door opened. "Slide over," a man's voice said in her ear.

It was Henry. Tears of relief filled her eyes as she flung her arms around him. "Where were you? Are you all right? Has he hurt anyone?"

"Not yet." Henry returned her embrace, but then gently freed himself. "Darling, I've got to get closer."

"What do you mean? What are you going to do?"

"I'm going to drive around back and get the women and girls out through the kitchen door. Oscar and Marco are waiting around the corner of the house to jump John if necessary."

"But he's armed."

"And sooner or later he's going to realize the Jorgensen women aren't, and he's going to break down the door and hurt someone." He kissed her quickly. "You've got to get out of the car."

"Henry—"

He kissed her again, a long, hard, almost painful kiss, then half led, half carried her from the car. "Stay in the ditch," he ordered as he slammed the door behind him and started the engine. "Keep your head down, no matter what."

She screamed his name and ran after the car until her foot slipped in the mud and she came down hard on her ankle. Pain shot up her right leg and she staggered to a halt, watching as Henry sped toward John. At the sound of the automobile, John turned and fired. The car swerved, struck a rock, and flipped over on its side. Cursing, soaked with rain, John approached the car, weapon leveled at the driver's door. Suddenly the door swung open and Henry dragged himself free of the wreckage. As John took aim, Henry ran at him, low and fast. A shot rang out as Henry tackled John and brought him to the ground.

"Henry!" Elizabeth screamed.

Limping, she ran toward the two still figures lying in the mud. From behind the house sprinted Oscar and Marco, one of the hired hands. Oscar fell to his knees beside Henry and rolled him onto his back; Marco pinned John to the muddy ground and kicked the gun away.

From behind the thunder came the scream of sirens.

1920

Isabel wanted to place the quilts in her daughter's arms, to see Rosa's face light up with happiness when she discovered how Isabel's heart had changed, but she did not know when Rosa would come again to the mesa. Isabel's message was too urgent to wait. She must insure that Rosa received the quilts soon, even if she would not see her mother again for a very long time.

Isabel rode on horseback to the Jorgensen farm, the quilts folded into a pack on the saddle behind her. No one would notice one lone woman among the throng of workers who had come for the apricot harvest.

She rode past the yellow farmhouse and over the hill to the cabin she had once called home. Many years had passed since she had last played on that front porch with her grandmother and baby sister, since she had last climbed the orange trees and picked the ripe, sweet fruit. Rosa had visited much more recently—of this, Isabel was certain. Where else could the young lovers have met? What better place than this, where Rosa knew her parents would never come?

Isabel dismounted and went inside, allowing herself only a moment's regret over the state of the home her mother and grandmother had once kept with such pride. She carried the quilts into the bedroom she and her parents had once shared. There she spotted a crate pushed against the window, more than large enough to accommodate the quilts. She removed the lid and discovered Lars's liquor stash. Disappointed, she replaced the lid. After all Lars had lost because of liquor, he should have smashed these bottles on the hard, dusty earth. When Lars drained the last of those bottles, would he then become the man her daughter needed? Could he ever be the man her daughter needed if the only reason he stopped drinking was because he had nothing left to drink?

Lars had so much left to prove before he would be worthy of her precious girl, her rose, but Isabel knew now she had been wrong not to allow him that chance. She only hoped it was not too late.

She went into her grandparents' old bedroom, where she found a dusty steamer trunk at the foot of a rusty bedstead with a sagging mattress, added to the room after her family's departure. Unbidden, images of her daughter embracing Lars upon the bed came to her, but she quickly closed her mind to such thoughts.

Inside the trunk she discovered an old blue-and-white checkered table-cloth and a candlewick bedspread, with ample room left over for the two quilts. She placed them gently inside and closed the lid. Either Rosa would discover them herself someday, or Lars would find them, recognize the initials Isabel had embroidered, and take them to Rosa.

Rosa would understand what the quilts meant, what Isabel could not say aloud.

Isabel could never tell her daughter to forsake her sacred wedding vows. Rosa had married a cruel man, the wrong man, but that made her promises before God no less binding. But when Rosa saw the quilt, the wedding quilt pieced from precious fabrics, she would know that Isabel would forgive her if she corrected a mistake made long ago, a mistake she never would have made if she had not feared losing her mother's love.

Isabel left the cabin, but hesitated on the porch and returned to her old bedroom. One by one she took the liquor bottles from the crate and emptied them out the window. Someone had to prod Lars down the road to sobriety. Rosa waited at the end of it, but she could not wait forever.

Isabel returned to her horse and set off on the road to the mesa. Today might be the day Rosa came. She would make excuses for John, but Isabel would not pretend to believe them anymore for the sake of her daughter's pride. Didn't Rosa know that every scathing word John spoke to her burned Isabel's ears as well? Didn't she know that every blow that fell upon Rosa left bruises on her mother's heart?

She waited at the edge of the canyon, breathing in the scent of wildflowers.

Someday Rosa would come again, bringing the children, and Isabel would be waiting for them. She would not forsake her daughter a second time. Let weeks or months or years pass, Isabel would come to the mesa, undaunted, patient, awaiting the day her daughter would return to her.

Over the sound of the creek rushing through the canyon, Isabel heard a horse approaching. For a moment she was filled with joy and light, but the prayer of thanksgiving died on her lips at the sight of John Barclay crossing the mesa at a determined trot. His face was grim, his eyes dark with anger.

So. He knew where they met. Isabel had guessed as much the first day Rosa failed to appear.

She rose, brushed the grasses from her skirt, and faced him without fear. He would tell her Rosa was not coming, that she would never come. He would lie and say it was Rosa's choice. He would call Isabel a fool, a pathetic old woman, for clinging so desperately to futile hopes.

As John approached, Isabel prepared herself for what was to come. Let him say what he would. She would ignore his poison words. Her love for her daughter was stronger than his hate.

She had failed Rosa once, but never again.

Chapter Twelve

1925

Lars returned home a few hours after the police took John Barclay into custody. Elizabeth, riding with Henry to the hospital in the back of the makeshift ambulance, saw none of this. Only later, after the surgeon removed the bullet from Henry's shoulder and he had recovered enough for her to bring him home, did she learn that, upon hearing what had happened, Lars set the car upright and drove off toward the Barclay farm. The deputies searching the adobe for clues confirmed that Lars had spoken with them briefly, but left after determining Rosa and her children were not there.

That was the last time Lars Jorgensen was seen in the Arboles Valley.

Henry was still unconscious, recovering from surgery at the Oxnard General Hospital, when an investigator from the county came to take Elizabeth's statement. She told them about John's violent outburst and Rosa's plan to seek shelter in the canyon.

The investigator looked up sharply from his notepad. "The Salto Canyon?"

He seemed so apprehensive that Elizabeth quickly assured him that Rosa knew the canyon well—so well that Elizabeth assumed she must have known of a cave or other shelter from the rain, or she would not have kept the children outside overnight. Rosa was probably awaiting word that it was safe to come out from hiding. "Lars Jorgensen should go," she said. "Rosa trusts him."

The investigator nodded and jotted some notes. He did not tell her that Lars was missing. He also did not mention that the Salto Creek had overflowed its banks that day, or that a flash flood had swept through the canyon with a force strong enough to uproot trees and tear boulders from the canyon walls. He didn't want to upset her.

When the investigator finished with Elizabeth, he radioed the county sheriff. Two deputies found John Barclay's team and wagon on the mesa where Elizabeth had told them to look. Later that week, a child's rag doll was pulled from the mud two miles downstream of the canyon's edge where Isabel Rodriguez Diaz had fallen to her death. Rosa and her four children were presumed drowned. Their bodies were never recovered.

In the course of searching the Barclay farm for evidence to explain John's assault on the Jorgensen home, the police discovered two large crates buried in straw in the hayloft. Inside were a stash of small arms, a valise full of cash, and more than fifty gallons of contraband liquor in bottles that matched the one Lars Jorgensen had turned in to the Feds during the apricot harvest. They had been tracking Mob activity in southern California for years, but until Lars's tip, they had lacked proof that the Mob had enlisted the services of local farmers in their illegal liquor and weapons activities. Thanks to Lars, they were on the track of some highly placed figures in organized crime, and hoped soon to be able to put some of them away for good.

Privately, the Feds agreed that they didn't blame Lars for disappearing. He'd have to be a fool not to lie low for the rest of his life, now that he had made himself an enemy of the Mob. For all they knew, the Mob had already found him, and his bones were bleaching in the Mojave Desert.

John served two years in prison on federal racketeering charges. Carlos looked after his farm while he was away, although no one thought it was out of love for his brother-in-law. Carlos refused to believe that his sister, nieces, and nephew had drowned. Someday they would return and he would not allow their home to fall to ruin in the meantime. The post office moved to a small building next to the Arboles Grocery. Since no one else wanted the job, Carlos took over as postmaster.

Three weeks after John was released from prison, a hiker discovered his body at the bottom of Salto Canyon. The coroner concluded that he had jumped to his death. Rumors sped through the Arboles Valley like a brushfire in summer. Some people thought he had killed himself out of grief for the loss of his wife and children. Others noted that with his postmaster job gone and his ties to organized crime severed, John had realized he would actually have to work for a living again, and he just couldn't take it. A few people whispered that he had not intended to take his own life but that he had fallen to his death after fleeing in terror from the ghost of Isabel Rodriguez

Diaz. Older women in the valley, the friends of Isabel's youth, knew such a thing was impossible but found a certain satisfaction in the tale.

The years passed. Carlos maintained the adobe and the outbuildings out of respect for his sister's memory, but he allowed the native grasses and scrub to take over the fields. No farmer could ride past the old Barclay place without shaking his head and thinking that it was a shame to let so many fertile acres go to waste. Developers, eyeing the land hungrily, felt the same way. When Carlos would not accept any price for the farm, saying that it was not his to sell, they became determined to work around him. They cornered every government official with any possible influence over land issues and insisted the government should sell that abandoned farm near the canyon. It was a race pitting one developer against another to find someone in authority who would agree the city, state, or county owned the land and could make a deal. But the developers' efforts proved futile. There was no mortgage on the land, so the developers could not anticipate a bank foreclosure. The property taxes were being paid regularly, so the government had no reason to interfere. If the developers wanted the land so badly, they should take the matter up with John and Rosa Barclay's heirs.

The developers gave up in frustration. They had already approached Carlos and had been turned away. But they could wait. He obviously was not much of a farmer. He would change his mind someday when he finally realized his sister wasn't coming back. Every man came upon hard times sooner or later, and someday he would be glad to have money in the bank.

♒

1933

Elizabeth sat at the kitchen table in the cabin, counting out bills and change. At last she had enough money saved to buy back the Chimneys and Cornerstones quilt from Mrs. Diegel, but now that she did, she could not help thinking of other, more sensible uses for the money. There would be doctor bills when the baby came. Little Thomas outgrew clothes almost as quickly as she could sew them. Eleanor would need new shoes and school supplies in the fall. It seemed frivolous to spend so much on a quilt she did not truly need. She had pieced other quilts for the family, quilts that equaled the Chimneys and Cornerstones in beauty and warmth. As much as she longed for her quilt, she had managed to do without it for eight years. She could wait a few years more.

She sighed softly, bound the roll of bills with a rubber band, and returned the money to the coffee can. To think she had once teased Henry for refusing to put his money in a bank. His mistrust had spared them from losing everything after the stock market crashed and the banks failed. The Jorgensens had lost thousands, but the Nelsons had not lost a dime.

Henry looked up from his seat on the floor in front of the fireplace, where he and Thomas were engrossed in a game involving toy fire trucks and a wooden elephant. "Don't tell me you've changed your mind."

"I can't justify the expense," she said. "As soon as I spend this money, a better use for it will appear. It always does."

He couldn't deny it. They both knew how many times through the years one emergency or another had forced them to nearly deplete their savings. Slowly they would build it up again, just in time for the next crisis. They managed to stay afloat, and in those troubled times they were grateful for that much, but they could never quite get ahead. Henry assured Elizabeth that better times were coming, and Elizabeth wanted to believe him, but she feared better times would not come soon enough. Not for them, and not for the migrant families who had abandoned Dust Bowl farms for the promise of work in the Arboles Valley. Almost daily, Oscar Jorgensen had to turn a carload of hungry, exhausted people away with nothing more than dried apricots to eat and milk for the children. Even during the apricot harvest, there were more workers than jobs on the farm.

"Go ahead and ransom your quilt," said Henry. "You've waited long enough. Consider it an early birthday present."

Elizabeth smiled, but said, "After all these years, it might be worn to tatters."

"You can mend it."

"Yes, but the money will still be gone. Times are hard. We don't know how much longer the Jorgensens will be able to keep you on." They had already been forced to let Elizabeth go, but except for the loss of wages and Mary Katherine's daily company, she did not mind. She was content to tend her own garden, keep her own house, and care for her children.

Henry grinned. "Oscar would never fire me and you know it."

Of course she knew it. Henry had taken over Lars's responsibilities upon his disappearance nearly eight years before. Elizabeth could not imagine how the Jorgensens would manage without Henry. His job was as secure as any job could be.

"If the quilt is worn out," she said, "maybe I can talk Mrs. Diegel into setting a lower price."

"That's the spirit." Henry came to her and kissed her on both cheeks. "So beautiful and yet so shrewd."

The next afternoon, Annalise agreed to babysit the children while Elizabeth went into town. First she stopped by the post office to send a letter to her parents and collect the mail. Cousin Sylvia had sent her a postcard from the World's Fair in Chicago, where she had apparently spent most of her time at the Sears exhibition hall admiring the winners of a national quilt contest. She and her sister had collaborated on an entry, but they had been eliminated at the regional level, not a bad showing for two teenage girls. "My mother would have loved this show," Sylvia had written. "If she were still with us, and if she had entered one of her quilts, she would have won first place."

Sylvia's wistful note decided the matter for Elizabeth. Her beloved aunt Eleanor was gone. So was Grandma Bergstrom. The quilts the Bergstrom women made were becoming increasingly rare and precious with each passing year. Extravagance or not, she wanted her quilt back.

"Carlos," she asked, "do you have any advice for someone on her way to haggle with Mrs. Diegel over the price of a used quilt?"

"Remind her that the quilt has lost value since you sold it to her, new," Carlos said dryly. He had resigned as the handyman of the Grand Union Hotel to become the full-time postmaster after the post office expanded to accommodate the growing population of the Arboles Valley. "Mention the limited market for used quilts. She catered to those developer types for so many years, that's language she'll understand." He hesitated, struggling with conflicting loyalties. "I don't think you'll have much trouble getting her to lower her price. She . . . could use the money."

Elizabeth thanked him and continued on to the Grand Union Hotel. She had not visited in several years, not since Henry treated her to supper in the dining room to celebrate their fifth anniversary. She had heard that the hotel had fallen on hard times after Mrs. Diegel's favorite developers went bankrupt after the stock market crash, but she was still startled to find peeling paint on the eaves and weeds overtaking the once meticulously kept front garden. Inside, the lobby was as neat and tidy as ever, the bar even more crowded with imbibers than in more prosperous days. Elizabeth could guess how Mrs. Diegel had managed to eke out a living after overnight guests became scarce. She only hoped that for her sake, Mrs. Diegel kept her own still and had not become involved with what might euphemistically be described as an outside supplier. Elizabeth knew all too well what happened to people who became tangled up with that lot.

She found Mrs. Diegel in the kitchen stirring a pot of chicken stew. The cook was nowhere to be seen, but a girl a few years older than Annalise stood at the sideboard peeling apples for pie. Mrs. Diegel greeted Elizabeth like an old friend and offered her a glass of lemonade. Elizabeth gladly accepted and pulled up a stool so they could talk while Mrs. Diegel worked.

"Did you hear the big news?" Mrs. Diegel asked before Elizabeth could bring up the quilt. "Hoot Gibson is coming to the Arboles Valley to shoot a new picture. It's called *Raging Gulch*. They're going to film most of the out-door scenes on the mesa and in the Salto Canyon."

"Is that so?"

Mrs. Diegel's sharp gaze did not miss a thing. "Now, I know you lost a friend in that canyon, but you can't hold that against Hoot Gibson. The can-yon is a great setting for a movie. It might even bring more tourists back to the valley."

"I suppose you're right."

"That's not the best part. They've decided to use the Grand Union for many of the indoor scenes. Lucky for me, they chose this place based upon some old photographs George Hanneman has hanging on the wall in his office at Safari World. If they had gone to the trouble to see it for themselves, they might have chosen the Conejo Lodge instead." She shook her head and frowned. "I have to spruce this place up before the production crew arrives next month, but where I'm going to find the money to buy paint or hire a painter, I have no idea."

Elizabeth smiled. "I have an idea how you could make some extra cash."

They haggled over the price for a time, but eventually Mrs. Diegel admit-ted that she needed new paint more than an old quilt, and she accepted Elizabeth's fair offer. Elizabeth waited in the lobby while the innkeeper went to fetch the quilt, climbing the stairs slowly and grasping the smooth oak banister for support. Until that moment, Elizabeth had not realized how much Mrs. Diegel had aged in the past few years, her shoulders stooped as if weighed down by worry. It saddened Elizabeth to know that not even the crafty and indomitable Mrs. Diegel could evade the hard times that had struck them all.

Before long, Mrs. Diegel returned downstairs with the quilt, which was in better condition than Elizabeth had hoped. The colors had faded somewhat, the binding was worn, but Elizabeth found no stains, no holes or tears. Not that it would have mattered. She was so glad to hold her quilt again after so many years that half the batting could have been hanging out of popped seams and she would not have regretted her purchase.

She bade Mrs. Diegel good-bye and was nearly at the door when the older woman called her back. "I recall you once had a hankering to be in the pictures," Mrs. Diegel said. "When the producers contacted me about shooting at the Grand Union, they mentioned that they would be looking for local folks to fill in the scene. I don't expect you would have any lines, but it might be good for a laugh, and a small paycheck, and who knows what else? You might impress the director and be on your way to bigger and better things."

Once, that news would have thrilled her. Once, Elizabeth would have seized any chance for even the smallest, nonspeaking role in any film. But Mrs. Diegel was not the only one who had aged beyond her years since the Depression had begun. Elizabeth knew she was no longer the lovely, bright-eyed girl who had come to the Arboles Valley with her new husband and the boundless hopes and expectations of youth. If she were to enter that dance hall at Venice Beach today, a farmhand's wife in a homemade calico dress, she knew no movie director would think to give her his card—even if she weren't seven months pregnant with her third child. By the time Hoot Gibson came to the valley, directors and producers in tow, Elizabeth would have a new baby in her arms and too much to do to consider reviving her old dreams of stardom.

"Thanks for letting me know," she told Mrs. Diegel, knowing she would not audition for a part. She was content with the role she had already won. Her children were joyful and healthy. She loved and was beloved. She had a home and friends. She needed nothing else.

Elizabeth drove back to the Jorgensen farm to return Oscar's car—a 1926 Model T Ford he had bought to replace the one that had vanished along with Lars—and to collect Eleanor and Thomas from Annalise. As she pulled up to the garage, she spotted an unfamiliar car parked near the house. Curious, she glanced in through the kitchen window as she went around back to search for the children, but she saw no one. Either the guest was with Oscar in the barley fields or Mrs. Jorgensen was entertaining in the front parlor.

She found the children in the garden with Annalise, helping her pull weeds. The young woman was infinitely patient with them, willingly pointing out over and over again the difference between carrot tops and weeds. Thomas looked up first and toddled over to Elizabeth with a fistful of grass, dirt still clinging to the roots. "Look," he crowed. "Weeds!"

Elizabeth awkwardly stooped to pick him up, keeping his fat little legs clear of her belly. "What a good little farmer you're turning out to be," she praised him. To Annalise, she said, "How were they?"

"Perfect little angels, as always."

Eleanor beamed at her. She admired the older girl and drank up her praise. The same words from any other source never seemed to satisfy her in quite the same way.

Elizabeth indicated the yellow farmhouse with a nod. "Who's visiting?"

"I don't know." Annalise rose and brushed dirt from her shins. She wore dungarees instead of skirts, in keeping with the recent fashion among young women her age in the valley, much to her grandmother's chagrin. "He can't be from around here or I'd know him."

Elizabeth wasn't convinced. So many housing developments had sprung up around them that no one knew everyone who lived in the Arboles Valley anymore.

"The man came to see Daddy," Eleanor piped up.

Elizabeth smiled at her sweet, golden-haired girl. "Why would you say that, darling?"

"It's true," said Annalise. "Nana sent Margaret running to fetch him from the orchard a few minutes after the man arrived."

A tremor of uneasiness stirred within Elizabeth. "What sort of business would anyone have with Henry?"

Annalise shrugged. "I could watch the kids while you go find out."

Elizabeth nodded, handed Thomas to her, and strode back to the house as quickly as her ample belly would allow. Although she no longer worked for the Jorgensens, she had been nearly part of the family so long that she entered through the kitchen door without knocking, as they would have expected her to do. She found Mrs. Jorgensen, Oscar, Henry, and another man seated in the formal parlor with teacups and cookies close at hand.

They all looked up when she appeared in the doorway. The men rose and Mrs. Jorgensen beckoned her inside. "Come, Elizabeth," she said. "Sit down. This gentlemen has some interesting news for you."

Her heart leaped into her throat even as she noted that Mrs. Jorgensen had said *interesting,* not *unfortunate,* and that Henry's expression was a mix of surprise and doubt, but not alarm. She took a deep breath and sat down as Mrs. Jorgensen introduced the visitor as Horace Tomilson from the law firm of Tomilson, Hanks, and Dunbar of San Francisco.

"You're a long way from home," said Elizabeth nervously. Mrs. Jorgensen pressed a cup of tea into her hands.

"Only a commission of a sensitive nature would have induced me to travel so far," he admitted. "My clients, Mr. and Mrs. Nils Ottesen of Sonoma County, own a parcel of land not far from here. I believe they bought the land intending to farm it, but the vineyard on their property up north has thrived, so they have decided to remain there. They would like to put the land up for sale, and they thought you and your husband might be prospective buyers."

Elizabeth regarded him in disbelief. How would a vintner from hundreds of miles away know anything about her and Henry? They must have her confused with some other Nelsons, a much wealthier Nelson family with ties to the real estate business. "What land?" she asked, stalling for time. "How much?"

"He's talking about the Barclay farm," said Henry.

"Five dollars an acre," added Mr. Tomilson.

Elizabeth looked around the circle of faces. "This must be some kind of a joke."

"That's what I thought," said Henry, who had good reason to be suspicious. "Five dollars an acre is practically giving it away. Developers have been salivating over that land for years. These Ottesens could make a small fortune off that land."

"If it's theirs to sell," said Elizabeth.

"I assure you, it's all very legal." Mr. Tomilson opened his briefcase and showed them a host of documents with official seals and stamps indicating that the parcel of land formerly known as the Barclay farm belonged free and clear to the Ottesens. He presented a notarized copy of the title as well as several receipts indicating that the Ottesens had paid the property taxes on the farm for the past four years.

But Elizabeth had been taken in by such documents before. She set her cup of tea aside and began to rise. "Thank you for coming," she said tightly. "But my husband and I never heard of Nils Ottesen and we know better than to buy land that isn't really for sale."

"Mrs. Ottesen thought you might say that," he replied. "She asked me to make sure you saw this."

He took a page from the sheaf of documents and placed it in her hands. Elizabeth read it over and found it to be a bill of sale transferring the Barclay farm from Mr. and Mrs. John Barclay to Mr. and Mrs. Nils Ottesen for a modest sum of one hundred dollars.

"You'll see this land has a history of selling for less than what it is worth," remarked Mr. Tomilson.

What interested Elizabeth more was the date stamped on the document. She wondered if Mr. Tomilson realized that John Barclay had signed and dated the bill of sale in Sonoma County at the same time he was also imprisoned in the Ventura County jail.

She looked to Henry. He gave her an almost imperceptible nod, which told her he realized it, even if the lawyer did not.

Mr. Tomilson peered at her over the rims of his glasses. "I'm surprised that you don't remember the Ottesens. She told me that you had once done her a great kindness, helped her in her most desperate hour, when all others had turned their backs upon her. She wants this land to belong to you, even if it means suffering a financial loss herself. I advised her against this, of course, but she insisted. She's quite a remarkable woman."

"I think I remember her," said Elizabeth. "Tell me, what does she look like?"

"Oh, she's quite lovely. Slender, tall, long dark hair—some Spanish blood, perhaps."

"And her husband?" Mrs. Jorgensen broke in. "What about him?"

Mr. Tomilson shrugged, smiling. "Well, he's rather tall and thin and sunburned. Losing his hair. I'm sure he's a fine man, but not the sort that I would have thought capable of plucking such a lovely Spanish rose. Forgive me—I'm not being forward, I'm merely quoting him. I've overheard him call his wife his Spanish rose. Perhaps that's his secret. Romantic words?"

"Yes, he's quite a poet," said Oscar dryly, adding, "or so it seems."

Elizabeth calculated quickly. One hundred acres at five dollars an acre was five hundred dollars, or 480 more than she and Henry had left after ransoming the quilt. "Please give Mrs. Ottesen our thanks," said Elizabeth. "As much as we appreciate their generous offer, I'm afraid we can't afford it."

"In that case, I'm authorized to hire you and your husband to run the Ottesens' farm in their absence."

Elizabeth stared at him. "What?" said Henry.

"They're willing to offer very generous terms. In exchange for farming the land, maintaining the property, and paying the property taxes, the Ottesens will give you a modest salary and let you keep any profits you earn from whatever crops you decide to raise."

"This can't be real," murmured Elizabeth.

"There are a couple of conditions," said Mr. Tomilson, taking a page from his briefcase. "The first is that you send the Ottesens a quarterly payment of twenty-five dollars, which will be put toward the five-hundred-dollar purchase price. All payments will be made through my office. In five years, the title will be transferred over to you."

"What's the second condition?" asked Henry.

Mr. Tomilson frowned at the page as if he considered the request rather odd and was almost too embarrassed to mention it. "They want you to rename the farm 'Triumph Ranch.' "

Elizabeth laughed aloud.

"Legally, once the title is in your name, you can call the farm anything you like," Mr. Tomilson hastened to add. "Surely you can live with an unusual name for a few short years."

"No, no. The name is perfect." Elizabeth reached out her hand to Henry. "What do you think, sweetheart? How does 'Triumph Ranch' sound to you?"

"It sounds perfect." Elizabeth knew he meant too perfect. "What's the catch?"

Mr. Tomilson began gathering up his papers. "There is no catch, simply an offer and your decision, which I await. Eagerly."

"What happens to the farm if we decline?" asked Elizabeth. "I imagine the same offer would be made to her brother."

Mr. Tomilson regarded her curiously. "Whose brother?"

"Mrs. Ottesen's, of course."

"Mrs. Ottesen has no brothers or sisters." He glanced at his notes. "She does have six children, however. Six healthy children who are seen once a year by a skilled physician whether they need to or not. She wanted me to make sure you knew that."

"Six?" said Mrs. Jorgensen in wonder. "My heavens."

Henry had not forgotten Elizabeth's question. "What happens to the land if we don't take their offer?"

"In that case, I have been authorized to put it up for auction between three respected land developers."

"You'll find no such creature," said Mrs. Jorgensen sharply. "I can't believe that—what was his name now? That this Nils Ottesen intends for that beautiful, arable land to become a housing development." She looked from Elizabeth to Henry, rapping a finger upon the table for emphasis so hard she made the teapot rattle. "He's obviously trying to force your hand, and I say—let him!"

Oscar shifted in his seat. "Don't I get any say in this matter?"

"No, son, you don't," said Mrs. Jorgensen. "You're Henry's employer, not his father."

"Even so," said Henry, "I value your opinion."

Elizabeth waited to hear what he would say. Oscar Jorgensen knew the valley better than anyone. He knew about the probability of devastating drought, crop failure, and plunging prices for food that made it barely more profitable to farm than to let the land grow fallow. But he also loved the land, felt the rhythm of the seasons in his blood, and would always respect those who could do the same.

"I say, take the offer before they change their minds," Oscar declared. "You'll never get land in the Arboles Valley at that price ever again."

Henry grinned. "I thought you were going to try to talk me out of leaving because you need me too much."

"I considered that, but I figured you wouldn't listen."

Henry stood, took Elizabeth's hands in his, and pulled her to her feet. "Darling—"

"You don't have to talk me into it," she said. "Yes. A hundred times yes. Once for each acre."

❧

The matter was settled quickly. Within a month, the Nelsons moved from the cabin to the adobe home on Triumph Ranch. Eleanor and Thomas played in the shade of the orange trees as Rosa's children had before them. Since it was too late for spring planting, Henry agreed to work for the Jorgensens through the apricot harvest. In the meantime, he planned for the next season.

As she awaited the birth of her baby, Elizabeth sorted through the belongings the Barclays had been forced to leave so abruptly. The furniture was well made and in good condition, far sturdier and more comfortable than what she and Henry had grown accustomed to in the cabin. The kitchen was fully furnished with all the dishes, pots, pans, and tools a farm wife could ever need. Many items of a more personal nature had been abandoned, too, and Elizabeth could not touch them without thinking of Rosa's desperate flight to the canyon. How had she decided what to take and what to leave? What in that last moment had become most precious to her?

She bid a last farewell to her absent friend as she put away Rosa's belongings to make room for her own. Some things she packed up to give to Carlos, whom she felt would be glad for mementos of his sister, nieces, and nephews. Other things—toys, dolls, clothing—she saved for her own children. She was sure Rosa would have given them freely, generously, just as she had the land and the home.

But what she searched for most was the photograph album and the portraits Rosa had shown her of the first quilters of Triumph Ranch. She longed to hold her children on her lap and show them the women who had lived in their old cabin, just as she now told them about the children who had once lived in their adobe.

She never found the album. Nor did she find the quilts the women had made, stitching their hopes and prayers into the fabric, the patterns of their unspoken regrets and unanswered questions like fingerprints upon the cloth. Elizabeth knew the quilts had once comforted frightened children hiding in a canyon, and that they now graced a loving home on a vineyard where a happy family rejoiced in everyday moments—fresh strawberries for breakfast, a hair ribbon, a game of tag, a bedtime story.

Elizabeth knew the quilters of Triumph Ranch, past and present, rejoiced in their happiness.

FICTION CHIAVERINI
Chiaverini, Jennifer.
An Elm Creek quilts collection :
R2001052915 PALMETTO

ODC

Atlanta-Fulton Public Library